W9-AFY-075

Kings Full of Aces

Other Books by Rex Stout

Novels

HOW LIKE A GOD · GOLDEN REMEDY · SEED ON THE WIND
O CARELESS LOVE! · MR. CINDERELLA · FOREST FIRE
THE PRESIDENT VANISHES

Nero Wolfe Mysteries

FER-DE-LANCE · THE LEAGUE OF FRIGHTENED MEN
THE RUBBER BAND · THE RED BOX · SOME BURIED CAESAR
OVER MY DEAD BODY · BLACK ORCHIDS
WHERE THERE'S A WILL · NOT QUITE DEAD ENOUGH
TOO MANY COOKS · THE SILENT SPEAKER
TOO MANY WOMEN · AND BE A VILLAIN
TROUBLE IN TRIPLICATE · THE SECOND CONFESSION
THREE DOORS TO DEATH · IN THE BEST FAMILIES
CURTAINS FOR THREE · MURDER BY THE BOOK
TRIPLE JEOPARDY · PRISONER'S BASE · THE GOLDEN SPIDERS
THREE MEN OUT · THE BLACK MOUNTAIN
FULL HOUSE: A NERO WOLFE OMNIBUS · BEFORE MIDNIGHT
THREE WITNESSES · MIGHT AS WELL BE DEAD
THREE FOR THE CHAIR · IF DEATH EVER SLEPT
AND FOUR TO GO · ALL ACES: A NERO WOLFE OMNIBUS
CHAMPAGNE FOR ONE · PLOT IT YOURSELF
THREE AT WOLFE'S DOOR · TOO MANY CLIENTS
FIVE OF A KIND: THE THIRD NERO WOLFE OMNIBUS
HOMICIDE TRINITY: A NERO WOLFE THREESOME
THE FINAL DEDUCTION · GAMBIT · THE MOTHER HUNT
TRIO FOR BLUNT INSTRUMENTS · A RIGHT TO DIE
THE DOORBELL RANG
ROYAL FLUSH: THE FOURTH NERO WOLFE OMNIBUS
DEATH OF A DOXY · THE FATHER HUNT

Tecumseh Fox Mysteries

DOUBLE FOR DEATH · THE BROKEN VASE · BAD FOR BUSINESS

Mysteries

THE HAND IN THE GLOVE · MOUNTAIN CAT
ALPHABET HICKS · RED THREADS

Kings Full of Aces

A NERO WOLFE OMNIBUS

Rex Stout

NEW YORK / THE VIKING PRESS

Published in 1969 by The Viking Press, Inc.
625 Madison Avenue, New York, N.Y. 10022

Published in Canada by
The Macmillan Company of Canada Limited

Library of Congress catalog card number: 67-20290
Printed in the U.S.A.

Acknowledgment is made to the *American Magazine*, in which three short novels in this volume originally appeared: "The Cop-Killer," "The Squirt and the Monkey" as "See No Evil," and "Home to Roost" as "Nero Wolfe and the Communist Killer."

Contents

Too Many Cooks

FOREWORD

I used as few French and miscellaneous fancy words as possible in writing up this stunt of Nero Wolfe's, but I couldn't keep them out altogether, on account of the kind of people involved. I am not responsible for the spelling, so don't write me about mistakes. Wolfe refused to help me out on it, and I had to go to the Heinemann School of Languages and pay a professor thirty bucks to go over it and fix it up. In most cases, during these events, when anyone said anything which for me was only a noise, I have either let it lay—when it wasn't vital—or managed somehow to get the rough idea in the American language.

Archie Goodwin

1

Walking up and down the platform alongside the train in the Pennsylvania Station, having wiped the sweat from my brow, I lit a cigarette with the feeling that after it had calmed my nerves a little I would be prepared to submit bids for a contract to move the Pyramid of Cheops from Egypt to the top of the Empire State Building with my bare hands, in a swimsuit, after what I had just gone through. But as I was drawing in the third puff I was stopped by a tapping on a window I was passing, and, leaning to peer through the glass, I was confronted by a desperate glare from Nero Wolfe, from his seat in the bedroom which we had engaged in one of the new-style Pullmans, where I had at last got him deposited intact.

He shouted at me through the closed window, "Archie! Confound you! Get in here! They're going to start the train! You have the tickets!"

I yelled back at him, "You said it was too close to smoke in there. It's only 9:32. I've decided not to go. Pleasant dreams."

I sauntered on. Tickets, my eye. It wasn't tickets that bothered him; he was frantic with fear because he was alone on the train and it might begin to move. He hated things that moved and was fond of arguing that nine times out of ten the places that people were on their way to were no improvement whatever on those they were coming from. But, by gum, I had got him to the station twenty minutes ahead of time, notwithstanding such items as three bags and two suitcases and two overcoats for a four days' absence in the month of April, Fritz Brenner standing on the stoop with tears in his eyes as we left the house, Theodore Horstmann running out, after we had got Wolfe packed in the sedan, to ask a few dozen more questions about the orchids, and even tough little Saul Panzer, after dumping us at the station, choking off a tremolo as he told Wolfe good-by. You might have thought we were bound for the stratosphere to shine up the moon and pick wild stars.

At that, just as I flipped my butt through the crack between the train and the platform, I could have picked a star right there—or at least touched one. She passed by close enough for me to get a faint whiff of something that might have come from a perfume bottle but seemed only natural under the circumstances, and while her facial effect might have been technicolor, it too gave you the impression that it was intended that way from the outset and needed no alterations. The one glance I got was enough to show that she was no factory job but handmade throughout. Attached to the arm of a tall, bulky man in a brown cape and a brown floppy cloth hat, she unhooked herself to precede him and follow the porter into the car back of ours. I muttered to myself, "My heart was all I had and now that's gone—I should have put my bloody blinders on," shrugged with assumed indifference, and entered the vestibule as they began the all aboard.

In our room, Wolfe was on the wide seat by the window, holding himself braced with both hands; but in spite of that they fooled him on the timing, and when the jerk came he lurched forward and back again. From the corners of my eyes I saw the fury all over him, decided it was better to ignore realities, got a magazine from my bag, and perched on the undersized chair in the corner.

Still holding on with both hands, he shouted at me, "We are due at Kanawha Spa at 11:25 tomorrow morning! Fourteen hours! This car is shifted to another train at Pittsburgh! In case of delay we would have to wait for an afternoon train! Should anything happen to our engine—"

I put in coldly, "I am not deaf, sir. And while you can beef as much as you want to, because it's your own breath if you want to waste it, I do object to your implying either in word or tone that I am in any way responsible for your misery. I made this speech up last night, knowing I would need it. This is your idea, this trip. You wanted to come—at least, you wanted to be at Kanawha Spa. Six months ago you told Vukčić that you would go there on April sixth. Now you regret it. So do I. As far as our engine is concerned, they use only the newest and best on these crack trains, and not even a child—"

We had emerged from under the river and were gathering speed as we clattered through the Jersey yards. Wolfe shouted, "An engine has two thousand three hundred and nine moving parts!"

I put down the magazine and grinned at him, thinking I might as well. He had enginephobia and there was no sense in letting him brood, because it would only make it worse for both of us. His mind had to be switched to something else. But before I could choose a pleasant subject to open up on, an interruption came which showed that while he may have been frantic with fear when I was smoking a cigarette on the platform, he had not been demoralized. There was a rap on the door, and it opened to admit a porter with a glass and three bottles of beer on a tray. He pulled out a trick stand for the glass and one bottle, which he opened, put the other two bottles in a rack with an opener, accepted currency from me in payment, and departed. As the train lurched around a curve Wolfe scowled with rage; then, as it took the straightaway again, he hoisted the glass and swallowed once, twice, five times, and set it down empty. He licked his lips for the foam, then wiped them with his handkerchief, and observed with no sign at all of hysterics, "Excellent. I must remember to tell Fritz my first was precisely at temperature."

"You could wire him from Philadelphia."

"Thank you. I am being tortured and you know it. Would you mind earning your salary, Mr. Goodwin, by getting a book from my bag? *Inside Europe* by John Gunther."

I got the bag and fished it out.

By the time the second interruption came, half an hour later, we were rolling smooth and swift through the night in middle Jersey, the three beer bottles were empty, Wolfe was frowning at his book but actually reading, as I could tell by the pages he turned, and I had waded nearly to the end of an article on "Collation of Evidence" in the *Journal of Criminology*. I hadn't got much from it because I was in no condition to worry about collating evidence, on account of my mind being taken up with the problem of getting Nero Wolfe undressed. At home, of course, he did it himself, and equally, of course, I wasn't under contract as a valet—being merely secretary, bodyguard, office manager, assistant detective, and goat—but the fact remained that in two hours it would be midnight, and there he was with his pants on, and someone was going to have to figure out a way of getting them off without upsetting the train. Not that he was clumsy, but he had had practically no practice at balancing himself while on a moving vehicle, and to pull pants from under him as he lay was out of the question, since he weighed something between 250 and a ton. He had never, so far as I knew, been on a scale, so it was anybody's guess. I was guessing high that night, on account of the problem I was confronted with, and was just ready to settle on 310 as a basis for calculations when there was a knock on the door and I yelled come in.

It was Marko Vukčić. I had known he would be on our train, through a telephone conversation between him and Wolfe a week before, but the last time I had seen him was when he had dined with us at Wolfe's house early in March—a monthly occurrence. He was one of the only two men whom Wolfe called by their first names, apart from employees. He closed the door behind him and stood there, not fat but huge, like a lion upright on its hind legs, with no hat covering his dense tangle of hair.

Wolfe shouted at him, "Marko! Haven't you got a seat or a bed somewhere? Why the devil are you galloping around in the bowels of this monster?"

Vukčić showed magnificent white teeth in a grin. "Nero, you damn old hermit! I am not a turtle in aspic, like you. Anyhow, you are really on the train—what a triumph! I have found you, and also a colleague, in the next car back, whom I had not seen for five years. I have been talking with him and suggested he should meet you. He would be glad to have you come to his compartment."

Wolfe compressed his lips. "That, I presume, is funny. I am not an acrobat. I shall not stand up until this thing is stopped and the engine unhooked."

"Then how—" Vukčić laughed and glanced at the pile of luggage. "But you seem to be provided with equipment. I did not really expect you to move. So instead I'll bring him to you. If I may. That really is what I came to ask."

"Now?"

"This moment."

Wolfe shook his head. "I beg off, Marko. Look at me. I am in no condition for courtesy or conversation."

"Just briefly then, for a greeting. I have suggested it."

"No. I think not. Do you realize that if this thing suddenly stopped, for some obstacle or some demoniac whim, we should all of us continue straight ahead at eighty miles an hour? Is that a situation for social niceties?" He compressed his lips again and then moved them to pronounce firmly, "Tomorrow."

Vukčić, probably almost as accustomed as Wolfe to having his own way, tried to insist, but it didn't get him anywhere. He tried to kid him out of it, but that didn't work either. I yawned. Finally Vukčić gave it up with a shrug. "Tomorrow then. If we meet no obstacle and are still alive. I'll tell Berin you have gone to bed—"

"Berin?" Wolfe sat up and even relaxed his grip on the arm of his seat. "Not Jerome Berin?"

"Certainly. He is one of the fifteen."

"Bring him." Wolfe half closed his eyes. "By all means. I want to see him. Why the devil didn't you say it was Berin?"

Vukčić waved a hand and departed. In three minutes he was back, holding the door open for his colleague to enter—only it appeared to be two colleagues. The most important one, from my point of view, entered first. She had removed her wrap but her hat was still on, and the odor, faint and fascinating, was the same as when she had passed me on the station platform. I had a chance now to observe that she was as young as love's dream, and her eyes looked dark purple in that light, and her lips told you that she was a natural but reserved smiler. Wolfe gave her a swift, astonished glance, then transferred his attention to the tall, bulky man behind her, whom I recognized even without the brown cape and the floppy cloth hat.

Vukčić had edged around. "Mr. Nero Wolfe. Mr. Goodwin. Mr. Jerome Berin. His daughter, Miss Constanza Berin."

After a bow I let them amplify the acknowledgments while I steered the seating in the desired direction. It ended with the three big guys on the seats and love's dream on the undersized chair with me on a suitcase beside it. Then I realized that was bad staging and shifted across with my back to the wall so I could see it better. She had favored me with one friendly innocent smile and then let me be. From the corners of my eyes I saw Wolfe wince as Vukčić got a cigar going and Jerome Berin filled up a big old black pipe and lit it behind clouds. Since I had learned this was her father, I had nothing but friendly feelings for him. He had black hair with a good deal of gray in it, a trimmed beard with even more gray, and deep eyes, bright and black.

He was telling Wolfe, "No, this is my first visit to America. Already I see the nature of her genius. No drafts on this train at all! None! And a motion as smooth as the sail of a gull! Marvelous!"

Wolfe shuddered, but Berin didn't see it. He went on. But he had given me a scare, with his "first visit to America." I leaned forward and muttered at the dream-star, "Can you talk English?"

She smiled at me. "Oh, yes. Very much. We lived in London three years. My father was at the Tarleton."

"Okay." I nodded and settled back for a better focus. I was reflecting, It only goes to show how wise I was not to go into harness with any of the temptations I have been confronted with previously. If I had, I would be gnashing my teeth now. So the thing to do is to hold everything until my teeth are too old to be gnashed. But there was no law against looking.

Her father was saying, "I understand from Vukčić that you are to be Servan's guest. Then the last evening will be yours. This is the first time an American has had that honor. In 1932, in Paris, when Armand Fleury was still alive and was our dean, it was the premier of France who addressed us. In 1927 it was Ferid Khaldah, who was not then a professional. Vukčić tells me you are an *agent de sûreté*. Really?" He surveyed Wolfe's area.

Wolfe nodded. "But not precisely. I am not a policeman; I am a private detective. I entrap criminals and find evidence to imprison them or kill them, for hire."

"Marvelous! Such dirty work."

Wolfe lifted his shoulders half an inch for a shrug, but the train jiggled him out of it. He directed a frown, not at Berin, but at the train. "Perhaps. Each of us finds an activity he can tolerate. The manufacturer of baby carriages, caught himself in the system's web and with no monopoly of greed, entraps his workers in the toils of his necessity. Dolichocephalic patriots and brachycephalic patriots kill each other, and the brains of both rot before their statues can get erected. A garabageman collects table refuse, while a senator collects evidence of the corruption of highly placed men—might one not prefer the garbage as less unsavory? Only the table scavenger gets less pay; that is the real point. I do not soil myself cheaply. I charge high fees."

Berin passed it. He chuckled. "But you are not going to discuss table refuse for us, are you?"

"No. Mr. Servan has invited me to speak on, as he stated the subject, 'Contributions Américaines à la Haute Cuisine.' "

"Bah!" Berin snorted. "There are none."

Wolfe raised his brows. "None, sir?"

"None. I am told there is good family cooking in America. I haven't sampled it. I have heard of the New England boiled dinner and corn pone and clam chowder and milk gravy. This is for the multitude and certainly not to be scorned if good. But it is not for masters." He snorted again. "Those things are to *la haute cuisine* what sentimental love songs are to Beethoven and Wagner."

"Indeed." Wolfe wiggled a finger at him. "Have you eaten terrapin stewed with butter and chicken broth and sherry?"

"No."

"Have you eaten a planked porterhouse steak, two inches thick, surrendering hot red juice under the knife, garnished with American parsley and slices of fresh lime, encompassed with mashed potatoes which melt on the tongue, and escorted by thick slices of fresh mushrooms faintly underdone?"

"No."

"Or the Creole Tripe of New Orleans? Or Boone County Missouri Ham, baked with vinegar, molasses, Worcestershire, sweet cider, and herbs? Or Chicken Marengo? Or Chicken in Curdled Egg Sauce, with raisins, onions, almonds, sherry, and Mexican sausage? Or Tennessee Opossum? Or Lobster Newburgh? Or Philadelphia Snapper Soup? But I see you haven't." Wolfe pointed a finger at him. "The gastronome's heaven is France, granted. But he would do well, on his way there, to make a detour hereabouts. I have eaten Tripe à la mode de Caen at Pharamond's in Paris. It is superb, but no more so than Creole Tripe, which is less apt to stop the gullet without an excess of wine. I have eaten bouillabaisse at Marseilles, its cradle and its temple, in my youth, when I was easier to move, and it is mere belly-fodder, ballast for a stevedore, compared with its namesake at New Orleans. If no red snapper is available—"

I thought for a second Berin was spitting at him but saw it was only a vocal traffic jam caused by indignation. I left it to them and leaned to Constanza again. "I understand your father is a good cook."

The purple eyes came to me, the brows faintly up. She gurgled. "He is *chef de cuisine* at the Corridona at San Remo. Didn't you know that?"

I nodded. "Yeah, I've seen a list of the Fifteen. Yesterday, in the magazine section of the *Times*. I was just opening up. Do you do any cooking yourself?"

"No. I hate it. Except I make good coffee." She looked down as far as my tie—I had on a dark brown polka-dot four-in-hand with a pin-stripe tan shirt—and up again. "I didn't hear your name when Mr. Vukčić said it. Are you a detective too?"

"The name is Archie Goodwin. Archibald means sacred and good, but in spite of that my name is not Archibald. I've never heard a French girl say Archie. Try it once."

"I'm not French." She frowned. Her skin was so smooth that the frown was like a ripple on a new tennis ball. "I'm Catalána. I'm sure I could say Archie. Archiearchiearchie. Good?"

"Wonderful."

"Are you a detective?"

"Certainly." I got out my wallet and fingered in it and pulled out a fishing license I had got in Maine the summer before. "Look. See my name on that?"

She read at it. "Ang—ling?" She looked doubtful and handed it back. "And that Maine? I suppose that is your *arrondissement?*"

"No. I haven't got any. We have two kinds of detectives in America, might and main. I'm the main kind. That means that I do very little of the hard work, like watering the horses and shooting prisoners and greasing the chutes. Mostly all I do is think, as for instance when they want someone to think what to do next. Mr. Wolfe there is the might kind. You see how big and strong he is. He can run like a deer."

"But what are the horses for?"

I explained patiently. "There is a law in this country against killing a man unless you have a horse on him. When two or more men are throwing dice for the drinks, you will often hear one of them say, 'horse on you' or 'horse on me.' You can't kill a man unless you say that before he does. Another thing you'll hear a man say, if he finds out something is only a hoax, he'll call it a mare's nest, because it's full of mares and no horses. Still another trouble is a horse's feathers. In case it has feathers—"

"What is a mare?"

I cleared my throat. "The opposite of a horse. As you know, everything must have its opposite. There can't be a right without a left, or a top without a bottom, or a best without a worst. In the same way there can't be a mare without a horse or a horse without a mare. If you were to take, say, ten million horses—"

I was stopped, indirectly, by Wolfe. I had been too interested in my chat with the Catalána girl to hear the others' talk; what interrupted me was Vukčić rearing himself up and inviting Miss Berin to accompany him to the club car. It appeared that Wolfe had expressed a desire for a confidential session with her father, and I put the eye on him, wondering what kind of a charade he was arranging. One of his fingers was tapping gently on his knee, so I knew it was a serious project. When Constanza got up I did too.

I bowed. "If I may?" To Wolfe: "You can send the porter to the club car if you need me. I haven't finished explaining to Miss Berin about mares."

"Mares?" Wolfe looked at me suspiciously. "There is no information she can possibly need about mares which Marko can't supply. We shall—I am hoping—we shall need your notebook. Sit down."

So Vukčić carried her off. I took the undersized chair again, feeling like issuing an ultimatum for an eight-hour day, but knowing that a moving train was the last place in the world for it. Vukčić was sure to disillusion her about the horse lesson and might even put a crimp in my style for good.

Berin had filled his pipe again. Wolfe was saying, in his casual tone that meant look out for an attack in force, "I wanted, for one thing, to tell you of an experience I had twenty-five years ago. I trust it won't bore you."

Berin grunted.

Wolfe went on. "It was before the war, in Figueras."

Berin removed his pipe. "Ha! So?"

"Yes. I was only a youngster but, even so, I was in Spain on a confidential mission for the Austrian government. The track of a man led me to Figueras, and at ten o'clock one evening, having missed my dinner, I entered a little inn at a corner of the plaza and requested food.

The woman said there was not much and brought me wine of the house, bread, and a dish of sausages."

Wolfe leaned forward. "Sir, Lucullus never tasted sausage like that. Nor Brillat-Savarin. Nor did Vatel or Escoffier ever make any. I asked the woman where she got it. She said her son made it. I begged for the privilege of meeting him. She said he was not at home. I asked for the recipe. She said no one knew it but her son. I asked his name. She said Jerome Berin. I ate three more dishes of it and made an appointment to meet the son at the inn the next morning. An hour later my quarry made a dash for Port-Vendres, where he took a boat for Algiers, and I had to follow him. The chase took me eventually to Cairo, and other duties prevented me from visiting Spain again before the war started." Wolfe leaned back and sighed. "I can still close my eyes and taste that sausage."

Berin nodded, but he was frowning. "A pretty story, Mr. Wolfe. A real tribute, and thank you. But of course Saucisse Minuit—"

"It was not called Saucisse Minuit then; it was merely sausage of the house in a little inn in a little Spanish town. That is my point, my effort to impress you: in my youth, without a veteran palate, under trying circumstances, in an obscure setting, I recognized that sausage as high art. I remember well: the first one I ate, I suspected, and feared that it was only an accidental blending of ingredients carelessly mixed; but the others were the same, and all those in the subsequent three dishes. It was genius. My palate hailed it in that place. I am not one of those who drive from Nice or Monte Carlo to the Corridona at San Remo for lunch because Jerome Berin is famous and Saucisse Minuit is his masterpiece. I did not have to wait for fame to perceive greatness; if I took that drive it would be not to smirk but to eat."

Berin was still frowning. He grunted. "I cook other things besides sausages."

"Of course. You are a master." Wolfe wiggled a finger at him. "I seem to have somehow displeased you. I must have been clumsy, because this was supposed to be a preamble to a request. I won't discuss your consistent refusal, for twenty years, to disclose the recipe for that sausage; a chef de cuisine has himself to think of as well as humanity. I am acquainted with the efforts that have been made to imitate it—all failures. I can—"

"Failures?" Berin snorted. "Insults! Crimes!"

"To be sure. I agree. I can see that it is reasonable of you to wish to prevent the atrocities that would be perpetrated in ten thousand restaurant kitchens all over the world if you were to publish that recipe. There are a few great cooks, a sprinkling of good ones, and a pestiferous host of bad ones. I have in my home a good one, Mr. Fritz Brenner. He is not inspired, but he is competent and discriminating. He is discreet, and I am too. I beseech you—this is the request I have been leading up to—I beseech you, tell me the recipe for Saucisse Minuit."

"God above!" Berin nearly dropped his pipe. He gripped it and stared. Then he laughed. He threw up his hands and waved them around, and shook all over, and laughed as if he never expected to hear a joke again and would use it all up on this one. Finally he stopped and stared in scorn. "To *you?*" he wanted to know. It was a nasty tone. Especially was it nasty coming from Constanza's father.

Wolfe said quietly, "Yes, sir. To me. I would not abuse the confidence. I would impart it to no one. It would be served to no one except Mr. Goodwin and myself. I do not want it for display, I want it to eat. I have—"

"God above! Astounding. You really think—"

"No, I don't think. I merely ask. You would, of course, want to investigate me; I would pay the expense of that. I have never violated my word. In addition to the expense, I would pay three thousand dollars. I recently collected a sizable fee."

"Ha! I have been offered five hundred thousand francs."

"For commercial purposes. This is for my guaranteed private use. It will be made under my own roof, and the ingredients bought by Mr. Goodwin, whom I warrant immune to corruption. I have a confession to make. Four times, from 1928 to 1930, when you were at the Tarleton, a man in London went there, ordered Saucisse Minuit, took away some in his pocket, and sent it to me. I tried analysis—my own, a food expert's, a chef's, a chemist's. The results were utterly unsatisfactory. Apparently it is a combination of ingredients and method. I have—"

Berin demanded with a snarl, "Was it Laszio?"

"Laszio?"

"Phillip Laszio." He said it as if it were a curse. "You said you had an analysis by a chef—"

"Oh. Not Laszio. I don't know him. I have confessed that attempt to show you that I was zealous enough to try to surprise your secret, but I shall keep inviolate an engagement not to betray it. I confess again: I agreed to this outrageous journey only partly because of the honor of the invitation. Chiefly my purpose was to meet you. I have only so long to live—so many books to read, so many ironies to contemplate, so many meals to eat." He sighed, half closed his eyes, and opened them again. "Five thousand dollars. I detest haggling."

"No." Berin was rough. "Did Vukčić know of this? Was it for this he brought me—"

"Sir! If you please. I have spoken of confidence. This enterprise has been mentioned to no one. I began by beseeching you. I do so again. Will you oblige me?"

"No."

"Under no conditions?"

"No."

Wolfe sighed clear to his belly. He shook his head. "I am an ass. I should never have tried this on the train. I am not myself." He reached for the button on the casing. "Would you like some beer?"

"No." Berin snorted. "I am wrong, I mean yes. I would like beer."

"Good." Wolfe leaned back and closed his eyes. Berin got his pipe lit again. The train bumped over a switch and swayed on a curve, and Wolfe's hand groped for the arm of his seat and grasped it. The porter came and received the order, and soon afterward was back again with glasses and bottles, and served, and again I coughed up some jack. I sat and made pictures of sausages on a blank page of my expense book as the beer went down.

Wolfe said, "Thank you, sir, for accepting my beer. There is no reason why we should not be amicable. I seem to have put the wrong foot forward with you. Even before I made my request, while I was relating a tale which could have been only flattering to you, you had a hostile eye. You growled at me. What was my misstep?"

Berin smacked his lips as he put down his empty glass, and his hand descended in an involuntary movement for the corner of an apron that wasn't there. He reached for a handkerchief and used it, leaned forward and tapped a finger on Wolfe's knee, and told him with emphasis, "You live in the wrong country."

Wolfe lifted his brows. "Yes? Wait till you taste Terrapin Maryland, or even, if I may say so, Oyster Pie Nero Wolfe, prepared by Fritz Brenner. In comparison with American oysters, those of Europe are mere blobs of coppery protoplasm."

"I don't speak of oysters. You live in the country which permits the presence of Phillip Laszio."

"Indeed. I don't know him."

"But he makes slop at the Hotel Churchill in your own city of New York! You must know that."

"I know of him, certainly, since he is one of your number—"

"My number? Pah!" Berin's hands, in a wide swift sweep, tossed Phillip Laszio through the window. "Not of my number!"

"Your pardon." Wolfe inclined his head. "But he is one of Les

Quinze Maîtres, and you are one. Do you suggest that he is unworthy?"

Berin tapped Wolfe's knee again. I grinned as I saw Wolfe, who didn't like being touched, concealing his squirm for the sake of sausages. Berin said slowly through his teeth, "Laszio is worthy of being cut into small pieces and fed to pigs! But no, that would render the hams inedible. Merely cut into pieces." He pointed to a hole in the ground. "And buried. I tell you, I have known Laszio many years. He is maybe a Turk? No one knows. No one knows his name. He stole the secret of Rognons aux Montagnes in 1920 from my friend Zelota of Tarragona and claimed the creation. Zelota will kill him; he has said so. He has stolen many other things. He was elected one of Les Quinze Maîtres in 1927 in spite of my violent protest. His young wife—have you seen her? She is Dina, the daughter of Domenico Rossi of the Empire Café in London; I have had her many times on this knee!" He slapped the knee. "As you no doubt know, your friend Vukčić married her, and Laszio stole her from Vukčić. Vukčić will kill him undoubtedly, only he waits too long!" Berin shook both fists. "He is a dog, a snake, he crawls in slime! You know Leon Blanc, our beloved Leon, once great? You know he is now stagnant in an affair of no reputation called the Willow Club in a town by the name of Boston? You know that for years your Hotel Churchill in New York was distinguished by his presence as *chef de cuisine*? You know that Laszio stole that position from him—by insinuation, by lies, by chicanery, stole it? Dear old Leon will kill him! Positively. Justice demands it."

Wolfe murmured, "Thrice dead, Laszio. Do other deaths await him?"

Berin sank back and quietly growled, "They do. I will kill him myself."

"Indeed. He stole from you too?"

"He has stolen from everyone. God apparently created him to steal, let God defend him." Berin sat up. "I arrived in New York, Saturday, on the *Rex*. That evening I went with my daughter to dine at the Churchill, driven by an irresistible hatred. We went to a salon which Laszio calls the Resort Room—I don't know where he stole that idea. The waiters wear the liveries of the world-famous resorts, each one different: Shepheard's of Cairo, Les Figuiers of Juan-les-Pins, the Continental of Biarritz, the Del Monte of your California, the Kanawha Spa where this train carries us—many of them, dozens—everything is big here. We sat at a table, and what did I see? A waiter—a waiter carrying Laszio slop—in the livery of my own Corridona! Imagine it! I would have rushed to him and demanded that he take it off, I would have torn it from him with these hands"—he shook them violently at

Wolfe's face—"but my daughter held me. She said I must not disgrace her. But my own disgrace? No matter, that?"

Wolfe shook his head, visibly in sympathy, and reached to pour beer.

Berin went on. "Luckily his table was far from us, and I turned my back on it. But wait. Hear this. I looked at the menu. Fourth of the entrées, what did I see? What?"

"Not, I hope, Saucisse Minuit."

"Yes! I did! Printed fourth of the entrées! Of course I had been informed of it before. I knew that Laszio had for years been serving minced leather spiced with God knows what and calling it Saucisse Minuit—but to see it printed there, as on my own menu! The whole room, the tables and chairs, all those liveries, danced before my eyes. Had Laszio appeared at that moment I would have killed him with these hands. But he did not. I ordered two portions of it from the waiter—my voice trembled as I pronounced it. It was served on porcelain—bah!—and looked like—I shall not say what. This time I gave my daughter no chance to protest. I took the services, one in each hand, arose from my chair, and with calm deliberation turned my wrists and deposited the vile mess in the middle of the carpet! Naturally there was comment. My waiter came running. I took my daughter's arm and departed. We were intercepted by a *chef des garçons*. I silenced him! I told him in a sufficient tone, 'I am Jerome Berin of the Corridona at San Remo! Bring Phillip Laszio here and show him what I have done, but keep me from his throat!' I said little more; it was not necessary. I took my daughter to Rusterman's and met Vukčić, and he soothed me with a plate of his goulash and a bottle of Château Latour. The '29."

Wolfe nodded. "It would soothe a tiger."

"It did. I slept well. But the next morning, yesterday, do you know what happened? A man came to me at my hotel with a message from Phillip Laszio inviting me to lunch. Can you credit such effrontery? But wait, that was not all. The man who brought the message was Alberto Malfi."

"Indeed. Should I know him?"

"Not now. Now he is not Alberto, but Albert, Albert Malfi, once a Corsican fruit slicer whom I discovered in a café in Ajaccio. I took him to Paris—I was then at the Provençal—trained and taught him, and made a good entrée man of him. He is now Laszio's first assistant at the Churchill. Laszio stole him from me in London in 1930—stole my best pupil and laughed at me! And now the brazen frog sends him to me with an invitation to lunch. Alberto appears before me in a morning coat, bows, and, as if nothing had ever happened, delivers such a message in perfect English!"

"I take it you didn't go."

"Pah! Would I eat poison? I kicked Alberto out of the room." Berin shuddered. "I shall never forget, once in 1926, when I was ill and could not work, I came that close"—he held thumb and forefinger half an inch apart—"to giving Alberto the recipe for Saucisse Minuit. God above! If I had! He would be making it now for Laszio's menu. Horrible!"

Wolfe agreed. He had finished another bottle, and he now started on a suave speech of sympathy and understanding. It gave me a distinct pain. He might have seen it was wasted effort, that there wasn't a chance of his getting what he wanted; and it made me indignant to see him belittling himself trying to horn a favor out of that wild-eyed sausage cook. Besides, the train had made me so sleepy I couldn't keep my eyes open. I stood up.

Wolfe looked at me. "Yes, Archie?"

I said in a determined voice, "Club car," opened the door, and beat it.

It was after eleven o'clock, and half the chairs in the club car were empty. Two of the wholesome young fellows who pose for the glossy hair ads were there drinking highballs, and there was a scattering of the bald heads and streaked grays who had been calling porters George for thirty years. Vukčić and Miss Berin were seated with empty glasses in front of them, neither looking animated or entranced. Next to her on the other side was a square-jawed, blue-eyed athlete in a quiet gray suit who would obviously be a self-made man in another ten years. I stopped in front of my friends and dropped a greeting on them. They replied. The blue-eyed athlete looked up from his book and made preparations to raise himself to give me a seat.

But Vukčić was up first. "Take mine, Goodwin. I'm sure Miss Berin won't mind the shift. I was up most of last night."

He said good night and was off. I deposited myself and flagged the steward when he stuck his nose out. It appeared that Miss Berin had fallen in love with American ginger ale, and I requested a glass of milk. Our needs were supplied and we sipped.

She turned the purple eyes on me. They looked darker than ever, and I saw that that question would not be settled until I met them in daylight. She said, with throat in her voice, "You really are a detective, aren't you? Mr. Vukčić has been telling me. He dines every month at Mr. Wolfe's house, and you live there. He says you are very brave and have saved Mr. Wolfe's life three times." She shook her head and let the eyes scold me. "But you shouldn't have told me that about watering the horses. You might have known I would ask about it and find out."

I said firmly, "Vukčić has only been in this country eight years and knows very little about the detective business."

"Oh, no!" She gurgled. "I'm not young enough to be such a big fool as that. I've been out of school three years."

"All right." I waved a hand. "Forget the horses. What kind of a school do girls go to over there?"

"A convent school. I did. At Toulouse."

"You don't look like any nun I ever saw."

She finished a sip of ginger ale and then laughed. "I'm not anything at all like a nun. I'm not a bit religious. I'm very worldly. Mother Cecilia used to tell us girls that a life of service to others was the purest and sweetest, but I thought about it, and it seemed to me that the best way would be to enjoy life for a long while, until you got fat or sick or had a big family, and then begin on service to others. Don't you think so?"

I shook my head doubtfully. "I don't know, I'm pretty strong on service. But of course you shouldn't overdo it. You've been enjoying life so far?"

She nodded. "Sometimes. My mother died when I was young, and my father has a great many rules for me. I saw how American girls acted when they came to San Remo, and I thought I would act the same way, but I found out I didn't know how, and anyway father heard about it when I sailed Lord Gerley's boat around the cape without a chaperon."

"Was Gerley along?"

"Yes, he was along, but he didn't do any of the work. He went to sleep and fell overboard, and I had to tack three times to get him. Do you like Englishmen?"

I lifted a brow. "Well, I suppose I could like an Englishman if the circumstances were exactly right. For instance, if it was on a desert island, and I had had nothing to eat for three days and he had just caught a rabbit—or, in case there were no rabbits, a wild boar or a walrus. Do you like Americans?"

"I don't know." She laughed. "I have only met a few since I grew up, at San Remo and around there, and it seemed to me they talked funny and tried to act superior. I mean the men. I liked one I knew in London once, a rich one with a bad stomach who stayed at the Tarleton, and my father had special things prepared for him, and when he left he gave me nice presents. I think lots of them I have seen since I got to New York are very good-looking. I saw one at the hotel yesterday who was *quite* handsome. He had a nose something like yours, but his hair was lighter. I can't really tell whether I like people until I know them pretty well . . ."

She went on, but I was busy making a complicated discovery. When she had stopped to sip ginger ale my eyes had wandered away from her face to take in accessories, and as she had crossed her knees like American girls, without undue fuss as to her skirt, the view upward from a well-shaped foot and a custom-built ankle was as satisfactory as any I had ever seen. So far, so good; but the trouble was that I became aware that the blue-eyed athlete on the other side of her had one eye focused straight past the edge of his book, and its goal was obviously the same interesting object that I was studying, and my inner reaction to that fact was unsociable and alarming. Instead of being pleased at having a fellow man share a delightful experience with me, I became conscious of an almost uncontrollable impulse to do two things at once: glare at the athlete and tell her to put her skirt down!

I pulled myself together inwardly and considered it logically: there was only one theory by which I could possibly justify my resentment at his looking at that leg and my desire to make him stop, and that was that the leg belonged to me. Obviously, therefore, I was either beginning to feel that the leg was my property, or I was rapidly developing an intention to acquire it. The first was nonsense; it was *not* my property. The second was dangerous, since, considering the situation as a whole, there was only one practical and ethical method of acquiring it.

She was still talking. I gulped down the rest of the milk, which was not my habit, waited for an opening, and then turned to her without taking the risk of another dive into the dark purple eyes.

"Absolutely," I said. "It takes a long time to know people. How are you going to tell about anyone until you know them? Take love at first sight, for instance, it's ridiculous. That's not love, it's just an acute desire to get acquainted. I remember the first time I met my wife, out on Long Island. I hit her with my roadster. She wasn't hurt much, but I lifted her in and drove her home. It wasn't until after she sued me for twenty thousand dollars' damages that I fell in what you might call love with her. Then the inevitable happened, and the children began to come, Clarence and Merton and Isabel and Melinda and Patricia and—"

"I thought Mr. Vukčić said you weren't married."

I waved a hand. "I'm not intimate with Vukčić. He and I have never discussed family matters. Did you know that in Japan it is bad form to mention your wife to another man or to ask him how his is? It would be the same as if you told him he was getting bald or asked him if he could still reach down to pull his socks on."

"Then you *are* married."

"I sure am. *Very* happily."

"What are the names of the rest of the children?"

"Well, I guess I told you the most important ones. The others are just tots."

I chattered on, and she chattered back, in the changed atmosphere, with me feeling like a man just dragged back from the edge of a perilous cliff, but with sadness in it too. Pretty soon something happened. I wouldn't argue about it—I am perfectly willing to admit the possibility that it was an accident, but all I can do is describe it as I saw it. As she sat talking to me, her right arm was extended along the arm of her chair on the side next to the blue-eyed athlete, and in that hand was her half-full glass of ginger ale. I didn't see the glass begin to tip, but it must have been gradual and unobtrusive, and I'll swear she was looking at me. When I did see it, it was too late; the liquid had already begun to trickle onto the athlete's quiet gray trousers. I interrupted her and reached across to grab the glass. She turned and saw it and let out a gasp. The athlete turned red and went for his handkerchief. As I say, I wouldn't argue about it, only it was quite a coincidence that four minutes after she found out that one man was married she began spilling ginger ale on another one.

"Oh, I hope—does it stain? *Si gauche!* I am *so* sorry! I wasn't thinking. I wasn't looking—"

The athlete said, "Quite all right, really—really—rite all kight—it doodn't stain . . ."

More of the same. I enjoyed it. But he was quick on the recovery, for in a minute he quit talking Chinese, collected himself, and spoke to me in his native tongue. "No damage at all, sir, you see there isn't. Really. Permit me, my name is Tolman—Barry Tolman, prosecuting attorney of Marlin County, West Virginia."

So he was a trouble-vulture and a politician. But in spite of the fact that most of my contacts with prosecuting attorneys had not been such as to induce me to keep their photographs on my dresser, I saw no point in being churlish. I described my handle to him and presented him to Constanza, and offered to buy a drink as compensation for us spilling one on him.

For myself, another milk, which would finish my bedtime quota. When it came I sat and sipped it and restrained myself from butting in on the progress of the new friendship that was developing on my right, except for occasional grunts to show that I wasn't sulking.

By the time my glass was half empty Mr. Barry Tolman was saying, "I heard you—forgive me, but I couldn't help hearing—I heard you mention San Remo. I've never been there. I was at Nice and Monte Carlo back in 1931, and someone, I forget who, told me I should see San Remo because it was more beautiful than any other place on the Riviera, but I didn't go. Now I—well, I can well believe it."

"Oh, you should have gone!" There was throat in her voice again, and it made me happy to hear it. "The hills and the vineyards and the sea!"

"Yes, of course. I'm very fond of scenery. Aren't you, Mr. Goodwin? Fond of—" There was a concussion of the air and a sudden obliterating roar as we thundered past a train on the adjoining track. It ended. "Fond of scenery?"

"You bet." I nodded and sipped.

Constanza said, "I'm so sorry it's night. I could be looking out and seeing America. Is it rocky—I mean, is it the Rocky Mountains?"

Tolman didn't laugh. I didn't bother to glance to see if he was looking at the purple eyes; I knew that must be it. He told her no, the Rocky Mountains were fifteen hundred miles away, but that it was nice country we were going through. He said he had been to Europe three times, but that on the whole there was nothing there, except of course the historical things, that could compare with the United States. Right where he lived, in West Virginia, there were mountains that he would be willing to put alongside Switzerland and let anyone take his pick. He had never seen anything anywhere as beautiful as his native valley, especially the spot in it where they had built Kanawha Spa, the famous resort. That was in his county.

Constanza exclaimed, "But that's where I'm going! Of course it is! Kanawha Spa!"

"I—I hoped so." His cheeks showed red. "I mean, three of these Pullmans are Kanawha Spa cars, and I thought it likely—I thought it possible I might have a chance of meeting you, though of course I'm not in the social life there."

"And then we meet on the train. Of course I won't be there very long. But since you think it's nicer than Europe I can hardly wait to see it, but I warn you I love San Remo and the sea. I suppose on your trips to Europe you take your wife and children along?"

"Oh, now!" He was groggy. "Now, really! Do I look old enough to have a wife and children?"

I thought, You darned nut, cover up that chin! My milk was finished. I stood up.

"If you folks will excuse me, I'll go and make sure my boss hasn't fallen off the train. I'll come back soon, Miss Berin, and take you to your father. You can't be expected to learn the knack of acting like the American girls the first day out."

Neither of them broke into tears to see me go.

In the first car ahead I met Jerome Berin striding down the passage. He stopped, and of course I had to.

He roared, "My daughter? Vukčić left her!"

"She's perfectly all right." I thumbed to the rear. "She's back in the club car talking with a friend of mine I introduced to her. Is Mr. Wolfe okay?"

"Okay? I don't know. I just left him."

He brushed past me, and I went on.

Wolfe was alone in the room, still on the seat, the picture of despair, gripping with his hands, his eyes wide open. I stood and surveyed him. I said, "See America first. Come and play with us in vacationland! Not a draft on the train and sailing like a gull."

He said, "Shut up."

He couldn't sit there all night. The time had come when it must be done. I rang the bell for the porter to do the bed. Then I went up to him —but no. I remember in an old novel I picked up somewhere it described a lovely young maiden going into her bedroom at night and putting her lovely fingers on the top button of her dress, and then it said, "But now we must leave her. There are some intimacies which you and I, dear reader, must not venture to violate; some girlish secrets which we must not betray to the vulgar gaze. Night has drawn its protecting veil; let us draw ours!"

Okay by me.

2

I said, "I wouldn't have thought this was a job for a house dick, watching for a kid to throw stones. Especially a ritzy house dick like you."

Gershom Odell spit through his teeth at a big fern ten feet away from where we sat on a patch of grass. "It isn't. But I told you. These birds pay from fifteen to fifty bucks a day to stay at this caravansary and to write letters on Kanawha Spa stationery, and they don't like to have niggers throwing stones at them when they go horseback riding. I didn't say a kid, I said a nigger. They suspect it was one that got fired from the garage about a month ago."

The warm sun was on me through a hole in the trees, and I yawned. I asked, to show I wasn't bored, "You say it happened about here?"

He pointed. "Over yonder, from the other side of the path. It was old Crisler that got it both times, you know, the fountain pen Crisler, his daughter married Ambassador Willetts."

There were sounds from down the way. Soon the hoofbeats were plainer, and in a minute a couple of genteel but good-looking horses came down the path from around a curve and trotted by, close enough so that I could have tripped them with a fishing pole. On one of them was a dashing chap in a loud-checked jacket, and on the other a dame plenty old and fat enough to start on service to others any time the spirit moved her.

Odell said, "That was Mrs. James Frank Osborn, the Baltimore Osborn, ships and steel, and Dale Chatwin, a good bridge player on the make. See him worry his horse? He can't ride worth a damn."

"Yeah? I didn't notice. You sure are right there on the social list."

"Got to be, on this job." He spit at the fern again, scratched the back of his head, and plucked a blade of grass and stuck it in his mouth. "I guess nine out of ten that come to this joint, I know 'em without being told. Of course sometimes there's strangers. For instance, take your crowd. Who the hell are they? I understand they're a bunch of good cooks that the chef invited. Looks funny to me. Since when was Kanawha Spa a domestic science school?"

I shook my head. "Not my crowd, mister."

"You're with 'em."

"I'm with Nero Wolfe."

"He's with 'em."

I grinned. "Not this minute he ain't. He's in Suite 60, on the bed, fast asleep. I think I'll have to chloroform him Thursday to get him on the train home." I stretched in the sun. "At that, there's worse things than cooks."

"I suppose so," he admitted. "Where do they all come from, anyway?"

I pulled a paper from my pocket—a page I had clipped from the magazine section of the *Times*—and unfolded it and glanced at the list again before passing it across to him:

LES QUINZE MAÎTRES

Jerome Berin, the Corridona, San Remo.
Leon Blanc, the Willow Club, Boston.
Ramsey Keith, Hotel Hastings, Calcutta.
Phillip Laszio, Hotel Churchill, New York.
Domenico Rossi, Empire Café, London.
Pierre Mondor, Mondor's, Paris.
Marko Vukčić, Rusterman's Restaurant, New York.
Sergei Vallenko, Château Montcalm, Quebec.
Lawrence Coyne, The Rattan, San Francisco.
Louis Servan, Kanawha Spa, West Virginia.
Ferid Khaldah, Café de l'Europe, Istanbul.
Henri Tassone, Shepheard's Hotel, Cairo.

DECEASED:

Armand Fleury, Fleury's, Paris.
Pasquale Donofrio, the Eldorado, Madrid.
Jacques Baleine, Emerald Hotel, Dublin.

Odell took a look at the extent of the article, made no offer to read it, and then went over the names and addresses with his head moving slowly back and forth. He grunted. "Some bunch of names. You might think it was a Notre Dame football team. How'd they get all the press? What does that mean at the top, less quinzy something?"

"Oh, that's French." I pronounced it adequately. "It means 'The Fifteen Masters.' These babies are famous. One of them cooks sausages that people fight duels over. You ought to see him and tell him you're a detective and ask him to give you the recipe; he'd be glad to. They meet every five years on the home grounds of the oldest one of their number; that's why they came to Kanawha Spa. Each one is allowed to bring one guest—it's all there in the article. Nero Wolfe is Servan's guest, and Vukčić invited me so I could be with Wolfe. Wolfe's the guest of honor. Only ten of 'em are here. The last three died since 1932, and Khaldah and Tassone couldn't come. They'll do a lot of cooking and eating and drinking, and tell each other a lot of lies, and elect three new members, and listen to Nero Wolfe make a speech—and, oh yeah, one of 'em's going to get killed."

"That'll be fun." Odell spit through his teeth again. "Which one?"

"Phillip Laszio, Hotel Churchill, New York. The article says his salary is sixty thousand berries per annum."

"Which may be. Who's going to kill him?"

"They're going to take turns. If you want tickets for the series, I'd be glad to get you a couple of ringsides, and here's a tip, you'd better tell the desk to collect for his room in advance, because you know how long it takes—well, God bless my eyes! All with a few spoonfuls of ginger ale!"

A horseman and horsewoman had cantered by on the path, looking sideways at each other, laughing, their teeth showing and their faces flushed. As their dust drifted toward us I asked Odell, "Who's that happy pair?"

He grunted. "Barry Tolman, prosecuting attorney of this county. Going to be president someday, ask him. The girl came with your crowd, didn't she? Incidentally, she's easy on the eyes. What was the crack about ginger ale?"

"Oh, nothing." I waved a hand. "Just an old quotation from Chaucer. It wouldn't do any good to throw stones at them—they wouldn't notice anything less than an avalanche. By the way, what is this stone-throwing gag?"

"No gag. Just part of the day's work."

"You call this work? I'm a detective. In the first place, do you suppose anyone is going to start a bombardment with you and me sitting here in plain sight? And this bridle path winds around here for six miles, and why couldn't he pick another spot? Second, you told me that an employee that got fired from the garage is suspected of doing it to annoy the management, but in that case was it just a coincidence that he picked fountain-pen Crisler for a target both times? It's a phony. You didn't show me the bottom. Not that it's any of my business, but just for fun I thought I'd demonstrate that I'm only dumb on Sundays and holidays."

He looked at me with one eye, then with both, and then he grinned at me. "You seem to be a good guy."

I said warmly, "I am."

He was still grinning. "Honest to God, it's too good not to tell you. You would enjoy it better if you knew Crisler. But it wasn't only him. Another trouble was that I never got any time to myself around here. Sixteen hours a day! That's the way it works out. I've only got one assistant, and you ought to see him, he's somebody's nephew. I had to be on duty from sunrise to bedtime. Then there was Crisler—just a damn bile factory. He had it in for me because I caught his chauffeur swiping grease down at the garage, and boy, when he was mean he was mean. The nigger that helped me catch the chauffeur, Crisler had him fired. He was after my scalp too. I made my plans and they worked."

Odell pointed. "See that ledge up there? No, over yonder, the other side of those firs. That's where I was when I threw stones at him. I hit him both times."

"I see. Hurt him much?"

"Not enough. His shoulder was pretty sore. I had fixed up a good alibi in case of suspicions. Crisler checked out. That was one advantage. Another is that almost whenever I want to I can say I'm going out for the stone thrower, and come to the woods for an hour or two and be alone and spit and look at things. Sometimes I let them see me from the bridle path, and they think they're being protected and that's jake."

"Pretty good idea. But it'll play out. Sooner or later you'll either have to catch him or give it up. Or else throw some more stones."

He grinned. "Maybe you think it wasn't a good shot the time I got him in the shoulder! See how far away that ledge is? I don't know whether I'll try it again or not, but if I do, I know damn well who I'll pick. I'll point her out to you." He glanced at his wrist. "Jumping Jesus, nearly five o'clock. I've got to get back."

He scrambled up and started off headlong, and as I was in no hurry I let him go and moseyed idly along behind. As I had already discovered, wherever you went around Kanawha Spa, you were taking a walk in the garden. I don't know who kept the woods swept and dusted off the trees for what must have been close to a thousand acres, but it was certainly model housekeeping. In the neighborhood of the main hotel, and the pavilions scattered around, and the building where the hot springs were, it was mostly lawns and shrubs and flowers, with three classy fountains thirty yards from the main entrance. The things they called pavilions, which had been named after the counties of West Virginia, were nothing to sneeze at themselves in the matter of size, with their own kitchens and so forth, and I gathered that the idea was that they offered more privacy at an appropriate price. Two of them,

Pocahontas and Upshur, only a hundred yards apart and connected by a couple of paths through trees and shrubs, had been turned over to the Fifteen Masters—or rather, ten—and our Suite 60, Wolfe's and mine, was in Upshur.

I strolled along, carefree. There was lots of junk to look at if you happened to be interested in it—big clusters of pink flowers everywhere on bushes which Odell had said was mountain laurel, and a brook zipping along with little bridges across it here and there, and some kind of wild trees in bloom, and birds and evergreens and so on. That sort of stuff is all right, I've got nothing against it, and of course out in the country like that something might as well be growing or what would you do with all the space, but I must admit it's a poor place to look for excitement. Compare it, for instance, with Times Square or Yankee Stadium.

Closer to the center of things, in the section where the pavilions were, and especially around the main building and the springs, there was more life—plenty of folks, such as they were, coming and going in cars or on horseback and sometimes even walking. Most of those walking were Negroes in the Kanawha Spa uniform, black breeches and bright green jackets with big black buttons. Off on a side path you might catch one of them grinning, but out in the open they looked as if they were nearly overcome by something they couldn't tell you, like bank tellers.

It was a little after five when I got to the entrance of Upshur Pavilion and went in. Suite 60 was in the rear of the right wing. I opened its door with care and tiptoed across the hall so as not to wake the baby, but, opening another door with even more care, I found that Wolfe's room was empty. The three windows I had left partly open were closed, the hollow in the center of the bed left no doubt as to who had been on it, and the blanket I had spread over him was hanging at the foot.

I glanced in the hall again; his hat was gone. I went to the bathroom and turned on the faucet and began soaping my hands. I was good and sore. For ten years I had been accustomed to being as sure of finding Nero Wolfe where I had left him, as if he had been the Statue of Liberty, unless his house had burned down, and it was upsetting, not to mention humiliating, to find him flitting around like a hummingbird for a chance to lick the boots of a sausage cook.

After splashing around a little and changing my shirt, I was tempted to wander over to the hotel and look-to-see around, but I knew Fritz and Theodore would murder me if I didn't bring him back in one piece, so instead I left by the side entrance and followed the path to Pocahontas Pavilion.

Pocahontas was much more ambitious than Upshur, with four good-sized public rooms located centrally on the ground floor, and suites in the wings and the upper story. I heard noises before I got inside and, entering, found that the masters were having a good time. I had met the whole gang at lunch, which had been cooked at the pavilion and served there, with five different ones contributing a dish, and I admit it hadn't been hard to get down—which, since Fritz Brenner's cooking under Nero Wolfe's supervision had been my steady diet for ten years, would be a tribute for anyone.

I let a greenjacket open the door for me, trusted my hat to another one in the hall, and began the search for my lost hummingbird. In the parlor on the right, which had dark wooden things with colored rugs and stuff around everywhere—Pocahontas was all Indian as to furnishings—three couples were dancing to a radio. A medium brunette about my age, medium also as to size, with a high white brow and long sleepy eyes, was fastened onto Sergei Vallenko, a blond Russian ox around fifty with a scar under one ear. She was Dina Laszio, daughter of Domenico Rossi, onetime wife of Marko Vukčić, and stolen from him, according to Jerome Berin, by Phillip Laszio. A short middle-aged woman built like a duck, with little black eyes and fuzz on her upper lip, was Marie Mondor, and the popeyed chap with a round face, maybe her age and as plump as she, was her husband, Pierre Mondor. She couldn't speak English, and I saw no reason why she should. The third couple consisted of Ramsey Keith, a little sawed-off Scotsman at least sixty, with a face like a sunset preserved in alcohol, and a short and slender black-eyed affair who might have been anything under thirty-five to my limited experience, because she was Chinese. To my surprise, when I had met her at lunch, she had looked dainty and mysterious, just like the geisha propaganda pictures. I believe geishas are Japanese, but it's all the same. Anyway, she was Lio Coyne, the fourth wife of Lawrence Coyne; and hurrah for Lawrence, since he was all of three score and ten and as white as a snowbank.

I tried the parlor on the left, a smaller one. The pickings there were scanty. Lawrence Coyne was on a divan at the far end, fast asleep, and Leon Blanc, dear old Leon, was standing in front of a mirror, apparently trying to decide if he needed a shave. I ambled on through to the dining room. It was big and somewhat cluttered. Besides the long table and a slew of chairs, there were two serving tables and a cabinet full of paraphernalia, and a couple of huge screens with pictures of Pocahontas saving John Smith's life and other things. There were four doors: the one I had come in by, a double one to the large parlor, a double glass one to a side terrace, and one out to the pantry and the kitchen.

There were also, as I entered, people. Marko Vukčić was on a chair by the long table, with a cigar in his mouth, shaking his head at a telegram he was reading. Jerome Berin was standing with a wineglass in his hand, talking to a dignified old bird with a gray mustache and a wrinkled face—that was Louis Servan, dean of the Fifteen Masters and their host at Kanawha Spa. Nero Wolfe was on a chair too small for him over by the glass door to the terrace, which stood open, leaning back uncomfortably so that his half-open eyes could take in the face of the man standing looking down at him. It was Phillip Laszio—chunky, not much gray in his hair, with clever eyes and a smooth skin and slick all over.

Alongside Wolfe's chair was a little stand with a glass and a couple of beer bottles, and at his other elbow, almost sitting on his knee, with a plate of something in her hand, was Lisette Putti. Lisette was as cute as they come and had already made friends, in spite of a question of irregularity regarding her status. She was the guest of Ramsey Keith, who, coming all the way from Calcutta, had introduced her as his niece. Vukčić had told me that Marie Mondor's sputterings after lunch had been to the effect that Lisette was a *coquine* and Keith had picked her up in Marseilles, but after all, Vukčić said, it was physically possible for a man named Keith to have a niece named Putti, and even if it was a case of mistaken identity, it was Keith who was paying the bills. Which sounded like a loose statement, but it was none of my affair.

As I approached, Laszio finished some remark to Wolfe and Lisette began spouting to him in French, something about the stuff she had on the plate, which looked like fat brown crackers. But just then there was a yell from the direction of the kitchen, and we all turned to see the swinging door open and Domenico Rossi come leaping through with a steaming dish in one hand and a long-handled spoon in the other.

"It curdled!" he shrieked. He rushed across to us and thrust the dish at Laszio. "Look at that dirty mud! What did I tell you? By God, look! You owe me a hundred francs! A devil of a son-in-law you are, and twice as old as I am anyhow, and ignorant of the very first essentials!"

Laszio quietly shrugged. "Did you warm the milk?"

"Me? Do I look like an egg-freezer?"

"Then perhaps the eggs were old."

"Louis!" Rossi whirled and pointed the spoon at Servan. "Do you hear that? He says you have old eggs!"

Servan chuckled. "But if you did it the way he said to, and it curdled, you have won a hundred francs. Where is the objection to that?"

"But everything wasted! Look—mud!" Rossi puffed. "These damn modern ideas! Vinegar is vinegar!"

Laszio said quietly, "I'll pay. Tomorrow I'll show you how." He turned abruptly and went to the door to the large parlor and opened it, and the sound of the radio came through.

Rossi trotted around the table with the dish of mud to show it to Servan and Berin. Vukčić stuffed his telegram in his pocket and went over to look at it. Lisette became aware of my presence and poked the plate at me and said something. I grinned at her and replied, "Jack Spratt could eat no fat, his wife could—"

"Archie." Wolfe opened his eyes. "Miss Putti says that those wafers were made by the two hands of Mr. Keith, who brought the ingredients from India."

"Did you try them?"

"Yes."

"Are they any good?"

"No."

"Then will you kindly tell her that I never eat between meals?"

I wandered over to the parlor door and stood beside Phillip Laszio, looking at the three couples dancing—only it was apparent that he was seeing only one. Mamma and Papa Mondor were panting but game, Ramsey Keith and the geisha were funny to look at but obviously not concerned with that aspect of the matter, and Dina Laszio and Vallenko apparently hadn't changed holds since my previous view. However, they soon did. Something was happening beside me. Laszio said nothing and made no gesture that I saw, but he must have achieved some sort of communication, for the two stopped abruptly, and Dina murmured something to her partner and then alone crossed the floor to her husband. I sidestepped a couple of paces to give them room, but they weren't paying any attention to me.

She asked him, "Would you like to dance, dear?"

"You know I wouldn't. You weren't dancing."

"But what—" She laughed. "They call it dancing, don't they?"

"They may. But you weren't dancing." He smiled—that is, technically; it looked more like a smile to end smiles.

Vallenko came up. He stopped close to them, looked from his face to hers and back again, and all at once burst out laughing. "Ah, Laszio!" He slapped him on the back, not gently. "Ah, my friend!" He bowed to Dina. "Thank you, madame." He strode off.

She said to her husband, "Phillip dear, if you don't want me to dance with your colleagues you might have said so. I don't find it so great a pleasure . . ."

It didn't seem likely that they would need me to help out, so I went back out to the dining room and sat down. For half an hour I sat there and watched the zoo. Lawrence Coyne came in from the small parlor, rubbing his eyes and trying to comb his white whiskers with his fingers. He looked around and called "Lio!" in a roar that shook the windows, and his Chinese wife came trotting from the other room, got him in a chair, and perched on his knee. Leon Blanc entered, immediately got into an argument with Berin and Rossi, and suddenly disappeared with them into the kitchen. It was nearly six o'clock when Constanza blew in. She had changed from her riding things. She looked around and offered a few greetings, which nobody paid much attention to, then saw Vukčić and me and came over to us and asked where her father was. I told her, in the kitchen, fighting about lemon juice. In the daylight the dark purple eyes were all and more than I had feared.

I observed, "I saw you and the horses a couple of hours ago. Will you have a glass of ginger ale?"

"No, thanks." She smiled as to an indulgent uncle. "It was very nice of you to tell my father that Mr. Tolman is your friend."

"Don't mention it. I could see you were young and helpless, and thought I might as well lend a hand. Are things beginning to shape up?"

"Shape up?"

"It doesn't matter." I waved a hand. "As long as you're happy."

"Certainly I'm happy. I *love* America. I believe I'll have some ginger ale after all. No, don't move, I'll get it." She moved around the table toward a button.

I don't believe Vukčić, right next to me, heard any of it, because he had his eyes on his former wife as she sat with Laszio and Servan talking to Wolfe. I had noticed that tendency in him during lunch. I had also noticed that Leon Blanc unobtrusively avoided Laszio and had not once spoken to him who, according to Berin, had stolen Blanc's job at the Hotel Churchill. Berin himself was inclined to find opportunities for glaring at Laszio at close quarters, also without speaking. There was undoubtedly a little atmosphere around, what with Mamma Mondor's sniffs at Lisette Putti and a general air of comradely jealousy and arguments about lettuce and vinegar and the thumbs-down clique on Laszio —and last, but not least, the sultry mist that seemed to float around Dina Laszio. I have always had a belief that the swamp-woman—the kind who could move her eyelids slowly three times and you're stuck in a marsh and might as well give up—is never any better than a come-on for suckers; but I could see that if Dina Laszio once got you alone and she had her mind on her work and it was raining outdoors, it would take more than a sense of humor to laugh it off. She was way beyond the stage of spilling ginger ale on lawyers.

I watched the show and waited for Wolfe to display signs of motion. A little after six he made it to his feet, and I followed him onto the terrace and along the path to Upshur. Considering the terrible hardships of the train, he was navigating fine. In Suite 60 there had been a chambermaid around, for the bed was smoothed out again and the blanket folded up and put away. I went to my room and a little later rejoined Wolfe in his. He was by the window, in a chair which was almost big enough for him, leaning back with his eyes closed and a furrow in his brow, with his fingers meeting at the center of his paunch. It was a pathetic sight. No Fritz, no atlas to look at, no orchids to tend to, no bottle caps to count! I was sorry that the dinner was to be informal, since three or four of the masters were cooking it, because the job of getting into dinner clothes would have made him so mad that it would have taken his mind off of other things and really been a relief to him. As I stood and surveyed him he heaved a long, deep, shuddering sigh, and to keep the tears from coming to my eyes I spoke.

"I understand Berin is going to make Saucisse Minuit for lunch tomorrow. Huh?"

No score. I said, "How would you like to go back in an airplane? They have a landing field right here. Special service, on call, sixty bucks to New York, less than four hours."

Nothing doing. I said, "They had a train wreck over in Ohio last night. Freight. Over a hundred pigs killed."

He opened his eyes and started to sit up, but his hand slipped on the arm of the foreign chair and he slid back again. He declared, "You are dismissed from your job, to take effect upon our arrival at my house in New York. I *think* you are. It can be discussed after we get home."

That was more like it. I grinned at him. "That will suit me fine. I'm thinking of getting married anyhow. The little Berin girl. What do you think of her?"

"Pfui."

"Go on and phooey. I suppose you think living with you for ten years has destroyed all my sentiment. I suppose you think I am no longer subject—"

"Pfui."

"Very well. But last night in the club car it came to me. I don't suppose you realize what a pippin she is, because you seem to be immune. And of course I haven't spoken to her yet, because I couldn't very well ask her to marry a—well, a detective. But I think if I can get into some other line of work and prove that I can make myself worthy of her—"

"Archie." He was sitting up now, and his tone was a menacing murmur. "You are lying. Look at me."

I gave him as good a gaze as I could manage and I thought I had him. But then I saw his lids begin to droop and I knew it was all off. So the best I could do was grin at him.

"Confound you." But he sounded relieved at that. "Do you realize what marriage means? Ninety per cent of men over thirty are married, and look at them! Do you realize that if you had a wife she would insist on cooking for you? Do you know that all women believe that the function of food begins when it reaches the stomach? Have you any idea that a woman can ever—what's that?"

The knocking on the outer door of the suite had sounded twice, the first time faintly, and I had ignored it because I didn't want to interrupt him. Now I went out and through the inner hall and opened up. Whereupon I, who am seldom surprised, was close to astonished. There stood Dina Laszio.

Her eyes looked longer than ever but not quite so sleepy. She asked in a low voice, "May I come in? I wish to see Mr. Wolfe."

I stood back, she went past, and I shut the door, I indicated Wolfe's room. "In there, please"—and she preceded me.

The only perceptible expression on Wolfe's face as he became aware of her was recognition. He inclined his head. "I am honored, madam. Forgive me for not rising. I permit myself that discourtesy. That chair around, Archie?"

She was nervous. She looked around. "May I see you alone, Mr. Wolfe?"

"I'm afraid not. Mr. Goodwin is my confidential assistant."

"But I—" She stayed on her feet. "It is hard to tell even you."

"Well, madam. If it is too hard—" Wolfe let it hang in the air.

She swallowed, looked at me again, and took a step toward him. "But it would be harder—I must tell someone. I have heard much of you, of course—in the old days, from Marko—and I must tell someone, and there is no one but you to tell. Somebody is trying to poison my husband."

"Indeed." Wolfe's eyes narrowed faintly. "Be seated, please. It's easier to talk sitting down, don't you think, Mrs. Laszio?"

3

The swamp-woman lowered it into the chair I had placed. Needless to say, I leaned against the bedpost, not as nonchalant as I looked. It sounded as if this might possibly be something that would help to pass the time and justify my foresight in chucking my pistol and a couple of notebooks into my bag when I had packed.

She said, "Of course I know you are an old friend of Marko's. You probably think I wronged him when I . . . left him. But I count on your sense of justice . . . your humanity."

"Weak supports, madam." Wolfe was brusque. "Few of us have enough wisdom for justice or enough leisure for humanity. Why do you mention Marko? Do you suggest that he is poisoning Mr. Laszio?"

"Oh, no!" Her hand fluttered from her lap and came to rest on the arm of her chair. "Only I am sorry if you are prejudiced against my husband and me, for I have decided that I must tell someone, and there is no one but you to tell."

"Have you informed your husband that he is being poisoned?"

She shook her head, with a little twist on her lips. "He informed me. Today. You know, of course, that for luncheon several of them prepared dishes, and Phillip did the salad, and he had announced that he was going to make Meadowbrook dressing, which he originated. They all know that he mixes the sugar and lemon juice and sour cream an hour ahead of time, and that he always tastes in spoonfuls. He had the things ready, all together on a corner table in the kitchen, lemons, bowl of cream, sugar shaker. At noon he started to mix. From habit he shook sugar onto the palm of his hand and put his tongue to it, and it seemed gritty and weak. He shook some onto a pan of water, and little particles stayed on top, and when he stirred it some still stayed. He put sherry in a glass and stirred some of into that, and only a small portion of it would dissolve. If he had mixed the dressing and tasted a spoonful or two, as he always does, it would have killed him. The sugar was mostly arsenic."

Wolfe grunted. "Or flour."

"My husband said arsenic. There was no taste of flour."

Wolfe shrugged. "Easily determined, with a little hydrochloric acid and a piece of copper wire. You do not appear to have the sugar shaker with you. Where is it?"

"I suppose, in the kitchen."

Wolfe's eyes opened wide. "Being used for our dinner, madam? You spoke of humanity—"

"No. Phillip emptied it down the sink and had it refilled by one of the Negroes. It was sugar that time."

"Indeed." Wolfe settled, and his eyes were again half shut. "Remarkable. Though he was sure it was arsenic, he didn't turn it over to Servan? Or report it to anyone but you? Or preserve it as evidence? Remarkable."

"My husband is a remarkable man." A ray of the setting sun came through the window to her face, and she moved a little. "He told me that he didn't want to make things difficult for his friend Louis Servan. He forbade me to mention it. He is a strong man and he is very contemptuous. That is his nature. He thinks he is too strong and competent and shrewd to be injured by anyone." She leaned forward and put out a hand, palm up. "I come to you, Mr. Wolfe. I am afraid."

"What do you want me to do? Find out who put the arsenic in the sugar shaker?"

"Yes." Then she shook her head. "No. I suppose you couldn't, and even if you did, the arsenic is gone. I want to protect my husband."

"My dear madam." Wolfe grunted. "If anyone not a moron has determined to kill your husband, he will be killed. Nothing is simpler than to kill a man; the difficulties arise in attempting to avoid the consequences. I'm afraid I have nothing to suggest to you. It is doubly difficult to save a man's life against his will. Do you think you know who poisoned the sugar?"

"No. Surely there is something—"

"Does your husband think he knows?"

"No. Surely you can—"

"Marko? I can ask Marko if he did it?"

"No! Not Marko! You promised me you wouldn't mention—"

"I promised nothing of the sort. Nothing whatever. I am sorry, Mrs. Laszio, if I seem rude, but the fact is that I hate to be taken for an idiot. If you think your husband may be poisoned, what you need is a food taster, and that is not my profession. If you fear bodily violence for him, the best thing is a bodyguard, and I am not that either. Before he gets into an automobile, every bolt and nut and connection must be thoroughly tested. When he walks the street, windows and tops of buildings must be guarded, and passers-by kept at a distance. Should he attend the theater—"

The swamp-woman got up. "You make a joke of it. I'm sorry."

"It was you who started the joke—"

But she wasn't staying for it. I moved to open the door, but she had the knob before I got to it, and since she felt that way about it I let her go on and do the outside one too. I saw that it was closed behind her and then returned to Wolfe's room and put on a fake frown for him, which was wasted, because he had his eyes shut.

I told his big round face, "That's a fine way to treat a lady client who comes to you with a nice, straight, open-and-shut proposition like that. All we would have had to do would be go down to the river where the sewer empties and swim around until we tasted arsenic—"

"Arsenic has no taste."

"Okay." I sat down. "Is she fixing up to poison him herself and preparing a line of negative presumptions in advance? Or is she on the level and just poking around trying to protect her man? Or is Laszio making up tales to show her how cute he is? You should have seen him looking at her when she was dancing with Vallenko. I suppose you've observed Vukčić lamping her with the expression of a moth in a cage surrounded by klieg lights. Or was someone really gump enough to endanger all our lives by putting arsenic in the sugar shaker? Incidentally, it'll be dinnertime in ten minutes, and if you intend to comb your hair and tuck your shirt in—did you know that you can have one of these greenjackets for a valet for an extra five bucks per diem? I swear to God I think I'll try it for half a day. I'd be a different person if I took proper care of myself."

I stopped to yawn. Insufficient sleep and outdoor sunshine had got me.

Wolfe was silent. But presently he spoke. "Archie. Have you heard of the arrangement for this evening?"

"No. Anything special?"

"Yes. It seems to have come about through a wager between Mr. Servan and Mr. Keith. After the digestion of dinner there is to be a test. The cook will roast squabs, and Mr. Laszio, who volunteered for the function, will make a quantity of Sauce Printemps. That sauce contains nine seasonings, besides salt: cayenne, celery, shallots, chives, chervil, tarragon, peppercorn, thyme, and parsley. Nine dishes of it will be prepared, and each will lack one of the seasonings, a different one. The squabs and sauce dishes will be arrayed in the dining room, and Mr. Laszio will preside. The gathering will be in the parlor, and each will go to the dining room, singly to prevent discussion, taste the sauces on bits of squab, and record which dish lacks chives, which peppercorn, and so on. I believe Mr. Servan has wagered on an average of eighty per cent correct."

"Well." I yawned again. "I can pick the one that lacks squab."

"You will not be included. Only the members of Les Quinze Maîtres and myself. It will be an instructive and interesting experiment. The chief difficulty will be with chives and shallots, but I believe I can distinguish. I shall drink little wine with dinner, and of course no sweet. But the possibility occurred to me of a connection between this affair and Mrs. Laszio's strange report. Mr. Laszio is to make the sauce. You know I am not given to trepidation, but I came here to meet able men, not to see one or more of them murdered."

"You came here to learn how to make sausage. But forget it; I guess that's out. But how could there be a connection? It's Laszio that's going to get killed, isn't it? The tasters are safe. Maybe you'd better go last. If you get sick out here in the jungle I will have a nice time."

He shut his eyes. Soon he opened them again. "I don't like stories about arsenic in food. What time is it?"

He was too darned lazy to reach in his pocket so I told him, and he sighed and began preparations for getting himself upright.

The dinner at Pocahontas Pavilion that evening was elegant as to provender but a little confused in other respects. The soup, by Louis Servan, looked like any consommé, but it wasn't just any. He had spread himself, and it was nice to see his dignified old face get red with pleasure as they passed remarks to him. The fish, by Leon Blanc, was little six-inch brook trout, four to a customer, with a light brown sauce with capers in it, and a tang that didn't seem to come from lemon or any vinegar I had ever heard of. I couldn't place it, and Blanc just grinned at them when they demanded the combination, saying he hadn't named it yet. All of them, except Lisette Putti and me, ate the trout head and bones and all, even Constanza Berin, who was on my right. She watched me picking away and smiled at me and said I would never make a gourmet, and I told her not eating fishes' faces was a matter of sentiment with me on account of my pet goldfish. Watching her crunch those trout heads and bones with her pretty teeth, I was glad I had put the kibosh on my attack of leg-jealousy.

The entrée, by Pierre Mondor, was of such a nature that I imitated some of the others and had two helpings. It appeared to be a famous creation of his, well known to the others, and Constanza told me that her father made it very well and that the main ingredients were beef marrow, cracker crumbs, white wine, and chicken breast. In the middle of my second portion I caught Wolfe's eye across the table and winked at him, but he ignored me and hung on to solemn bliss. As far as he was concerned, we were in church and St. Peter was speaking. It was during the consumption of the entrée that Mondor and his plump wife, without any warning, burst into a screaming argument, which ended with his bouncing up and racing for the kitchen and her hot on his tail. I learned afterward that she had heard him ask Lisette Putti if she liked the entrée. She must have been abnormally moral for a Frenchwoman.

The roast was young duck à la Mr. Richards, by Marko Vukčić. This was one of Wolfe's favorites, and I was well acquainted with the Fritz Brenner-Nero Wolfe version of it, and by the time it arrived I was so nearly filled that I was in no condition to judge, but the other men took a healthy gulp of Burgundy for a capital letter to start the new paragraph, and waded in as if they had been waiting for some such little snack to take the edge off their appetites. I noticed that the best the women could do was peck, particularly Lio, Lawrence Coyne's Chinese wife, and Dina Laszio. I also noticed that the greenjacket waiters were aware that they were looking on at a gastronomical World's Series, though they were trying not to show it. Before it was over those birds disposed of nine ducks. It looked to me as if Vukčić was overdoing it a little on the various brands of wine, and maybe that was why he was so quick on the trigger when Phillip Laszio began making remarks about duck stuffings which he regarded as superior to Mr. Richards' and proceeded from that to comments on the comparative discrimination of the clientele of the Hotel Churchill and Rusterman's Restaurant. I had come as Vukčić's guest, and anyway I liked him, and it was embarrassing to me when he hit Laszio square in the eye with a hunk of bread. The others seemed to resent it chiefly as an interruption, and Servan, next to Laszio, soothed him, and Vukčić glared at their remonstrances and drank more Burgundy, and a greenjacket retrieved the bread from the floor, and they went back to the duck.

The salad, by Domenico Rossi, was attended by something of an uproar. In the first place, Phillip Laszio left for the kitchen while it was being served, and Rossi had feelings about that and continued to express them after Servan had explained that Laszio must attend to the preparation of the Sauce Printemps for the test that had been arranged. Rossi didn't stop his remarks about sons-in-law twice his age. Then he noticed that Pierre Mondor wasn't pretending to eat and wanted to know if perchance he had discovered things crawling on the lettuce. Mondor replied, friendly but firm, that the juices necessary to impart a flavor to salads, especially vinegar, were notoriously bad companions for wine, and that he wished to finish his Burgundy.

Rossi said darkly, "There is no vinegar. I am not a barbarian."

"I have not tasted it. I smell salad juice, that is why I pushed it away."

"I tell you there is no vinegar! That salad is mostly by the good God, as He made things! Mustard sprouts, cress sprouts, lettuce! Onion juice with salt! Bread crusts rubbed with garlic! In Italy we eat it from bowls, with Chianti, and we thank God for it!"

Mondor shrugged. "In France we do not. France, as you well know, my dear Rossi, is supreme in these things. In what language—"

"Ha!" Rossi was on his hind legs. "Supreme because we taught you! Because in the sixteenth century you came and ate our food and copied us! Can you read? Do you know the history of gastronomy? Any history at all? Do you know that of all the good things in France, of which there are a certain number, the original is found in Italy? Do you know . . ."

I suppose that's how the war will start. On that occasion it petered out. They kept Mondor from firing up and got Rossi started on his own salad, and we had peace.

Coffee was served in the two parlors: two, because Lawrence Coyne got stretched out on the divan in the small one again, and Keith and Leon Blanc sat by him and talked. I'm always more comfortable on my feet after a meal, and I wandered around. Back in the large parlor, Wolfe and Vukčić and Berin and Mondor were in a group in a corner, discussing the duck. Mamma Mondor came waddling in from the hall with a bag of knitting and got settled under a light. Lio Coyne was in a big chair with her feet tucked under her, listening to Vallenko tell her stories. Lisette Putti was filling Servan's coffee cup, and Rossi stood frowning at an Indian blanket thrown over a couch, as if he suspected it was made in France.

I couldn't see Dina Laszio anywhere and wondered idly whether she was off somewhere mixing poison or had merely gone to her room, which was in the left wing of Pocahontas, for some bicarbonate. Or maybe out in the kitchen helping her husband? I moseyed out there. In the dining room, as I went through, they were getting ready for the sauce test, with the chairs moved back to the walls, and the big screens in front of the serving tables, and a fresh cloth on the long table. I sidestepped a couple of greenjackets and proceeded. Dina wasn't in the kitchen. Half a dozen men in white aprons paid no attention to me, since in the past twelve hours they had got accustomed to the place being cluttered up with foreign matter. Laszio, also in an apron, was at the big range, stirring and peering into a pan, with a helper at each elbow waiting for commands. The place smelled sort of unnecessary on account of what I still had in me, and I went out again and down the pantry hall and back to the parlor. Liqueurs were being passed, and I snared myself a stem of cognac and sought a seat and surveyed the scene.

It occurred to me that I hadn't noticed Constanza around. In a little while she came in, from the hall, ran her eyes over the room, and came and sat down beside me and crossed her knees flagrantly. I saw signs on her face and leaned toward her to make sure.

"You've been crying."

She nodded. "Of course I have! There's a dance at the hotel, and Mr. Tolman asked me to go and my father won't let me! Even though we're in America! I've been in my room crying." She hitched her knee up a little. "Father doesn't like me to sit like this, that's why I'm doing it."

I grunted. "Leg-jealousy. Parental type."

"What?"

"Nothing. You might as well make yourself comfortable, he isn't looking at you. Can I get you some cognac?"

We whiled away a pleasant hour, punctuated by various movements and activities outside our little world. Dina Laszio came in from the hall, got herself a liqueur, stopped for a few words with Mamma Mondor, and then moved on to the little stool in front of the radio. She sipped the liqueur and monkeyed with the dials but got nothing on it. In a minute or two Vukčić came striding across the room, pulled a chair up beside the stool, and sat down. Her smile at him, as he spoke to her, was very good, and I wondered if he was in any condition to see how good it was. Coyne and Keith and Blanc came in from the small parlor. Around ten o'clock we had a visitor—nothing less than Mr. Clay Ashley, the manager of Kanawha Spa. He was fifty, black-haired with no gray, polished inside and out, and had come to make a speech. He wanted us to know that Kanawha Spa felt itself deeply honored by this visit from the most distinguished living representatives of one of the greatest of the arts. He hoped we would enjoy and so forth. Servan indicated Nero Wolfe, the guest of honor, as the appropriate source of the reply, and for once Wolfe had to get up out of his chair without intending to go anywhere. He offered a few remarks, and thanks to Mr. Ashley, saying nothing about train rides and sausages, and Mr. Ashley went, after being presented to those he hadn't met.

It was then time for another little speech, this time by Louis Servan. He said everything was in readiness for the test and explained how it would be. On the dining table would be nine dishes of Sauce Printemps on warmers, each lacking one of the nine seasonings; also, a server of squabs and plates and other utensils. Each taster would slice his own bits of squab; it was not permitted to taste any sauce without squab. Water would be there to wash the palate. Only one taste from each dish was allowed. In front of each dish would be a number on a card, from 1 to 9. Each taster would be provided with a slip of paper on which the nine seasonings were listed, and after each seasoning he would write the number of the dish in which that was lacking. Laszio, who had prepared the sauce, would be in the dining room to preside. Those who had tasted were not to converse with those who had not tasted until all were finished. To avoid confusion the tasting would be done in this order—Servan read it from a slip:

Mondor
Coyne
Keith
Blanc
Servan
Berin
Vukčić
Vallenko
Rossi
Wolfe

Right away there was a little hitch. When the slips were passed out and came to Leon Blanc, he shook his head. He told Servan apologetically but firmly, "No, Louis, I'm sorry. I have tried not to let my opinion of Phillip Laszio make discomfort for any of you, but under no circumstances will I eat anything prepared by him. He is—all of you know—but I'd better not say."

He turned on his heel and beat it from the room to the hall. The only thing that ruptured the silence was a long low growl from Jerome Berin, who had already accepted his slip.

Ramsey Keith said, "Too bad for him. Dear old Leon. We all know—but what the devil! Are you first, Pierre? I hope to God you miss all of 'em! Is everything ready in there, Louis?"

Mamma Mondor came trotting up to face her husband, holding her knitting against her tummy, and squeaked something at him in French. I asked Constanza what it was, and she said she told him that if he made one mistake on such a simple thing there would be no forgiveness either by God or by her. Mondor patted her on the shoulder impatiently and reassuringly and trotted for the door to the dining room, which he closed behind him. In ten minutes, maybe fifteen, the door opened again and he reappeared.

Keith, who had made the bet with Servan which had started it, approached Mondor and demanded, "Well?"

Mondor was frowning gravely. "We have been instructed not to discuss. I can say, I warned Laszio against an excess of salt and he ignored it. Even so, it will be utterly astounding if I have made a mistake."

Keith turned and roared across the room, "Lisette, my dearest niece! Give all of them cordials! Insist upon it! Seduce them!"

Servan, smiling, called to Coyne, "You next, Lawrence!"

The old snowbank went. I could see it would be a long-drawn-out affair. Constanza had been called across to her father. I wondered what it would be like to dance with a swamp-woman and went to where Dina Laszio still sat on the radio stool with Vukčić beside her, but got turned down. She gave me an indifferent glance from the long sleepy eyes and said she had a headache. That made me stubborn, and I looked around for another partner, but it didn't look promising. Coyne's Chinese wife, Lio, wasn't there, though I hadn't noticed her leave the room. Lisette had taken Keith's command literally and was on a selling tour with a tray of cordials. I didn't care to tackle Mamma Mondor for fear Pierre would get jealous. As for Constanza—well, I thought of all the children at home, and then I considered her, with her eyes close to me and my arm around her and that faint fragrance which made it seem absolutely necessary to get closer so you could smell it better, and I decided it wouldn't be fair to my friend Tolman. I cast another disapproving glance at Vukčić as he sat glued to the chair alongside Dina Laszio, and went over and copped the big chair where Lio Coyne had been.

I'm pretty sure I didn't go to sleep, because I was conscious of the murmur of the voices all the time, but there's no question that my eyes were closed for a spell, and I was so comfortable otherwise that it annoyed me that I couldn't keep from worrying about how those guys could swallow the squabs and sauces less than three hours after the flock of ducks had gone down. It was the blare of the radio starting that woke me—I mean, made me open my eyes. Dina Laszio was on her feet, leaning over twisting the dial, and Vukčić was standing waiting for her. She straightened up and melted into him and off they went. In a minute Keith and Lisette Putti were also dancing, and then Louis Servan with Constanza. I looked around. Jerome Berin wasn't there, so apparently they had got down to him on the tasting list. I covered a yawn and stretched without putting my arms out, and arose and moseyed over to the corner where Nero Wolfe was talking with Pierre Mondor and Lawrence Coyne. There was an extra chair and I took it.

Pretty soon Berin entered from the dining room and crossed the room to our corner. I saw Servan, without interrupting his dancing, make a sign to Vukčić that he was next, and Vukčić nodded back but showed no inclination to break his clinch with Dina. Berin was scowling.

Coyne asked him, "How about it, Jerome? We've both been in. Number 3 is shallots. No?"

Mondor protested, "Mr. Wolfe hasn't tried it yet. He goes last."

Berin growled. "I don't remember the numbers. Louis has my slip. God above, it was an effort I tell you, with that dog of a Laszio standing there smirking at me." He shook himself. "I ignored him. I didn't speak to him."

They talked. I listened with only one ear because of a play I was enjoying out front. Servan had highballed Vukčić twice more to remind him it was his turn to taste, without any result. I could see Dina smile into Vukčić's face, and I noticed Mamma Mondor was also seeing it and was losing interest in her knitting. Finally Servan parted from Constanza, bowed to her, and approached the other couple. He was too polite and dignified to grab, so he just got in their way and they had to stop. They untwined.

Servan said, "Please. It is best to keep the order of the list. If you don't mind."

Apparently Vukčić was no longer lit, and anyway he wouldn't have been rude to Servan. With a toss of his head he shook his hair-tangle back and laughed. "But I think I won't do it. I think I shall join the revolt of Leon Blanc." He had to speak loud on account of the radio.

"My dear Vukčić." Servan was mild. "We are civilized people, are we not? We are not children."

Vukčić shrugged. Then he turned to his dancing partner. "Shall I do it, Dina?" Her eyes were up to him, and her lips moved but in too low a voice for me to catch it. He shrugged again and turned and headed for the dining-room door and opened it and went in, with her watching his back. She went back to the stool by the radio, and Servan resumed with Constanza. Pretty soon, at eleven-thirty, there was a program change and the radio began telling about chewing gum, and Dina switched it off.

She asked, "Shall I try another station?"

Apparently they had had enough, so she left it dead. In our corner, Wolfe was leaning back with his eyes shut and Coyne was telling Berin about San Francisco Bay when his Chinese wife entered from the hall, looked around and saw us and trotted over, and stuck her right forefinger into Coyne's face and told him to kiss it because she had got it caught in a door and it hurt.

He kissed it. "But I thought you were outside looking at the night."

"I was. But the door caught me. Look! It hurts."

He kissed the finger again. "My poor little blossom!" More kisses. "My flower of Asia! Now we're talking—run away and let us alone."

She went off, pouting.

Vukčić entered from the dining room and came straight across to Dina Laszio. Servan told Vallenko he was next.

Vukčić turned to Servan. "Here's my slip. I tasted each dish once. That's the rule, eh? Laszio isn't there."

Servan's brows went up. "Not there? Where is he?"

Vukčić shrugged. "I didn't look for him. Perhaps in the kitchen."

Servan called to Keith, "Ramsey! Phillip has left his post! Only Vallenko and Rossi and Mr. Wolfe are left. What about it?"

Keith said he would trust them if Servan would, and Vallenko went in. In due time he was back, and it was Rossi's turn. Rossi hadn't been in a scrap for over three hours, and I pricked my ears in expectation of hearing through the closed door some hot remarks about sons-in-law, in case Laszio had got back on the job, but there was so much jabber in the parlor that I wouldn't have heard it anyway. When Rossi returned he announced to the gathering that no one but a fool would put as much salt as that in Sauce Printemps, but no one paid any attention to him. Nero Wolfe, last but not least, pried himself loose from his chair and, as the guest of honor, was conducted to the door by Louis Servan. I was darned glad that at last I could see bedtime peeping over the horizon.

In ten minutes the door opened and Wolfe reappeared. He stood on the threshold and spoke. "Mr. Servan! Since I am the last, would you mind if I try an experiment with Mr. Goodwin?"

Servan said no, and Wolfe beckoned to me. I was already on my feet, because I knew something was up. There are various kinds of experiments that Wolfe might try with me as the subject, but none of them would be gastronomical. I crossed the parlor and followed him into the dining room, and he shut the door. I looked at the table. There were the nine dishes, with numbered cards in front of them, and a big electric server, covered, and a pitcher of water and glasses, and plates and forks and miscellany.

I grinned at Wolfe. "Glad to help you out. Which one did you get stuck on?"

He moved around the table. "Come here." He went on, to the right, to the edge of the big Pocahontas screen standing there, and I followed him. Behind the screen he stopped and pointed at the floor. "Look at that confounded mess."

I stepped back a step, absolutely surprised. I had discounted all the loose talk about killing on account of its being Italians, and whatever I might have thought about the swamp-woman's little story, at least it hadn't prepared me for blood. But there was the blood, though there wasn't much of it, because the knife was still sticking in the left middle of Phillip Laszio's back, with only the hilt showing. He was on his face, with his legs straight out, so that you might have thought he was asleep if it hadn't been for the knife. I moved across and bent over and twisted the head enough to get a good look at one eye. Then I got up and looked at Wolfe.

He said bitterly, "A pleasant holiday. I tell you, Archie—but no matter. Is he dead?"

"Dead as a sausage."

"I see. Archie. We have never been guilty of obstructing justice. That's the legal term, let them have it. But this is not our affair. And at least for the present—what do you remember about our trip down here?"

"I think I remember we came on a train. That's about as far as I could go."

He nodded. "Call Mr. Servan."

4

At three o'clock in the morning I sat in the small parlor of Pocahontas Pavilion. Across a table from me sat my friend Barry Tolman, and standing back of him was a big-jawed, squint-eyed ruffian in a blue serge suit, with a stiff white collar, red tie, and pink shirt. His name and occupation had not been kept a secret: Sam Pettigrew, sheriff of Marlin County. There were a couple of nondescripts, one with a stenographer's notebook at the end of the table, and a West Virginia state cop was on a chair tilted against the wall. The door to the dining room stood open and there was still a faint smell of photographers' flashlight bombs, and a murmur of voices came through from sleuths doing fingerprints and similar chores.

The blue-eyed athlete was trying not to sound irritated. "I know all that, Ashley. You may be the manager of Kanawha Spa, but I'm the prosecuting attorney of this county, and what do you want me to do, pretend he fell on the damn knife by accident? I resent your insinuation that I'm making a grab for the limelight—"

"All right, Barry. Forget it." Clay Ashley, standing beside me, slowly shook his head. "Of all the rotten breaks! I know you can't suppress it, of course, but for God's sake, get it over with and get 'em out of here. All right, I know you will as soon as you can. Excuse me if I said things. I'm going to try to get some sleep. Have them call me if I can do anything."

He beat it. Someone came from the dining room to ask Pettigrew a question, and Tolman shook himself and rubbed his bloodshot eyes with his fingers. Then he looked at me. "I sent for you again, Mr. Goodwin, to ask if you have thought of anything to add to what you told me before."

I shook my head. "I gave you the crop."

"You haven't remembered anything at all that happened, in the parlor or anywhere else, any peculiar conduct, any significant conversation?"

I said no.

"Anything during the day, for instance?"

"Nope. Day or night."

"When Wolfe called you secretly into the dining room and showed you Laszio's body behind the screen, what did he say to you?"

"He didn't call me secretly. Everybody heard him."

"Well, he called you alone. Why?"

I lifted the shoulders and let them drop. "You'll have to ask him."

"What did he say?"

"I've already told you. He asked me to see if Laszio was dead, and I saw he was, and he asked me to call Servan."

"Was that all he said?"

"I think he remarked something about its being a pleasant holiday. Sometimes he's sarcastic."

"He seems also to be cold-blooded. Was there any special reason for his being cold-blooded about Laszio?"

I put my foot down a little harder on the brake. Wolfe would never forgive me if by some thoughtless but relevant remark I got this buzzard really down on us. I knew why Wolfe had bothered to get me in the dining room alone and inquire about my memory before broadcasting the news: it had occurred to him that in a murder case a material witness may be required to furnish bond not to leave the state without permission, or to return to testify at the trial, and it was contrary to his idea of the good life to do either one. It wasn't easy to maintain outward respect for a guy who had been boob enough to fall for that ginger-ale act in the club car, but while I had nothing at all against West Virginia I wasn't much more anxious to stay there or return there than Wolfe was.

I said, "Certainly not. He had never met Laszio before."

"Had anything happened during the day to make him—er, indifferent to Laszio's welfare?"

"Not that I know of."

"And had you or he knowledge of a previous attempt on Laszio's life?"

"You'll have to ask him. Me, no."

My friend Tolman forsook friendship for duty. He put an elbow on the table and pointed a finger at me and said in a nasty tone, "You're lying." I also noticed that the squint-eyed sheriff had a scowl on him not to be sneezed at, and the atmosphere of the whole room was unhealthy.

I put my brows up. "Me lying?"

"Yes, you. What did Mrs. Laszio tell you and Wolfe when she called at your suite yesterday afternoon?"

I hope I didn't gulp visibly. I know my brain gulped, but only once. No matter how he had found out, or how much, there was but one thing to do. I said, "She told us that her husband told her that he found arsenic in the sugar shaker and dumped it in the sink, and she wanted Wolfe to protect her husband. She also said that her husband had instructed her not to mention it to anyone."

"What else?"

"That's all."

"And you just told me that you had no knowledge of a previous attempt on Laszio's life. Didn't you?"

"I did."

"Well?" He stayed nasty.

I grinned at him. "Look, Mr. Tolman. I don't want to try to get smart with you, even if I knew how. But consider a few things. In the first place—without any offense, you're just a young fellow in your first term as a prosecutor—Nero Wolfe has solved more tough ones than you've even heard about. You know that, you know his reputation. Even if either of us knew anything that would give you a trail, which we don't, it wouldn't pay you to waste time trying to squeeze juice out of us without our consent, because we're old hands. I'm not bragging, I'm just stating facts. For instance, about my knowing about an attempt to kill Laszio, I repeat I didn't. All I knew was that Mrs. Laszio told us that her husband told her that he found something in the sugar shaker besides sugar. How could he have been sure it was arsenic? Laszio wasn't poisoned, he was stabbed. In my experience—"

"I'm not interested in your experience." Still nasty. "I asked you if you remember anything that might have any significance regarding this murder. Do you?"

"I've told you what Mrs. Laszio told us—"

"So has she. Pass that for the moment. Anything else?"

"No."

"You're sure?"

"Yes."

Tolman told the state cop, "Bring Odell in."

It came to me. So that was it. A fine bunch of friends I had made since entering the dear old Panhandle State—which nickname I had learned from my pal Gershom Odell, house dick of Kanawha Spa. My brain was gulping again, and this time I wasn't sure whether it would get it down or not. The process was interrupted by the entry of my pal, ushered in by the cop. I turned a stare on him which he did not meet. He came and stood near me at the table, so close I could have smacked him one without getting up.

Tolman said, "Odell, what was it this man told you yesterday afternoon?"

The house dick didn't look at me. He sounded gruff. "He told me Phillip Laszio was going to be killed by somebody, and when I asked him who was going to do it he said they were going to take turns."

"What else?"

"That's all he said."

Tolman turned to me, but I beat the gun. I gave Odell a dig in the ribs that made him jump. "Oh, that's it!" I laughed. "I remember now, when we were out by the bridle path throwing stones, and you pointed out that ledge to me and told me—sure! Apparently you didn't tell Mr. Tolman *everything* we said, since he thinks—did you tell him how I was talking about those foreign-type cooks, and how they're so jealous of each other they're apt to begin killing each other off any time, and how Laszio was the highest paid of the bunch, sixty thousand bucks a year, so they would be sure to pick on him first, and how they would take turns killing him first and then begin on the next one? And then I remember you began telling me about the ledge and how it happened you could leave the hotel at that time of day—" I turned to Tolman. "That's all that was, just a couple of guys talking to pass the time. You're welcome to any significance you can find in it. If I told you what Odell told me about that ledge—" I laughed and poked my pal in the ribs again.

Tolman was frowning but not at me. "What about it, Odell? That's not the way you told it. What about it?"

I had to hand it to Odell for a good poker face, at that. He was the picture of a Supreme Court Justice pretending that he had no personal interest in the matter. Still he didn't glance at me, but he looked Tolman quietly in the eye. "I guess my tongue kinda ran away with me. I guess it was about like he says, just shootin' off. But of course I remembered the name, Phillip Laszio, and any detective would jump at a chance to have a hot one on a murder."

The squint-eyed ruffian spoke, in a thin mild drawl that startled me. "You sound pretty inaccurate to me, Odell. Maybe you ought to do less guessin'?"

Tolman demanded, "Did he or did he not tell you Laszio was going to be killed?"

"Well, the way he just said it, yes. I mean about them all being jealous foreign types and Laszio getting sixty thousand—I'm sure he said that. I guess that's all there was to it."

"What about it, Goodwin? Why did you pick on Laszio?"

I showed a palm. "I didn't pick on him. I happened to mention him because I knew he was the tops—in salary, anyhow. I had just read an article—want to see it?"

The sheriff drawled, "We're wastin' time. Get the hell out of here, Odell."

My pal, without favoring me with a glance, turned and made for the door.

Tolman called to the cop, "Bring Wolfe in."

I sat tight. Except for the little snags that had threatened to trip me up, I was enjoying myself. I was wondering what Inspector Cramer of the New York Homicide Squad would say if he could see Nero Wolfe letting himself be called in for a grilling by small-town snoops at half-past three in the morning because he didn't want to offend a prosecuting attorney! He hadn't been up as late as that since the night Clara Fox slept in his house in my pajamas. Then I thought I might as well offer what help I could and got up and brought a big armchair from the other end of the room and put it in position near the table.

The cop returned with my boss. Tolman asked the cop who was left out there, and the cop said, "That Vookshish or whatever it is, and Berin and his daughter. They tried to shoo her off to bed, but she wouldn't go. She keeps making passes to come in here."

Tolman was chewing his lip, and I kept one sardonic eye on him while I used the other one to watch Nero Wolfe getting himself into the chair I had placed. Finally Tolman said, "Send them to their rooms. We might as well knock off until morning. All right, Pettigrew?"

"Sure. Bank it up and sleep on it." He squinted at the cop. "Tell Plank to wait out there until we see what arrangements he's made. This is no time of night for anyone to be taking a walk."

The cop departed. Tolman rubbed his eyes, then, chewing at his lip again, leaned back and looked at Wolfe. Wolfe seemed placid enough, but I saw his forefinger tapping on the arm of his chair and knew what a fire was raging inside of him. He offered as a bit of information, "It's nearly four o'clock, Mr. Tolman."

"Thanks." Tolman sounded peevish. "We won't keep you long. I sent for you again because one or two things have come up." I observed that he and the sheriff both had me in the corners of their eyes, and I'd have sworn they were putting over a fast one and trying to catch me passing some kind of a sign to Wolfe. I let myself look sleepy, which wasn't hard.

Wolfe said, "More than one or two, I imagine. For instance, I suppose Mrs. Laszio has repeated to you the story she told me yesterday afternoon. Hasn't she?"

"What story was that?"

"Come now, Mr. Tolman." Wolfe stopped tapping with the finger and wiggled it at him. "Don't be circuitous with me. She was in here with you over half an hour. She must have told you that story. I figured she would. That was why I didn't mention it; it seemed preferable that you should get it fresh from her."

"What do you mean, you figured she would?"

"Only an assumption." Wolfe was mild and inoffensive. "After all, she is a participant in this tragedy, while I am merely a bystander—"

"Participant?" Tolman was frowning. "Do you mean she had a hand in it? You didn't say that before."

"Nor do I say it now. I merely mean, it was her husband who was murdered, and she seems to have had, if not premonition, at least apprehension. You know more about it than I do, since you have questioned her. She informed you, I presume, that her husband told her that at noon yesterday, in the kitchen of this place, he found arsenic in a sugar shaker which was intended for him; and that without her husband's knowledge or consent she came to ask my assistance in guarding him from injury and I refused it."

"Why did you refuse it?"

"Because of my incompetence for the task. As I told her, I am not a food taster or a bodyguard." Wolfe stirred a little; he was boiling. "May I offer advice, Mr. Tolman? Don't waste your energy on me. I haven't the faintest idea who killed Mr. Laszio, or why. It may be that you have heard of me; I don't know. If so, you have perhaps got the impression that when I am engaged on a case I am capable of sinuosities, though you wouldn't think it to look at me. But I am not engaged on this case, I haven't the slightest interest in it, I know nothing whatever about it, and you are as apt to receive pertinent information from the man in the moon as you are from me. My connection with it is threefold. First, I happened to be here; that is merely my personal misfortune. Second, I discovered Mr. Laszio's body; as I told you, I was curious as to whether he was childishly keeping secret surveillance over the table, and I looked behind the screen. Third, Mrs. Laszio told me someone was trying to poison her husband and asked me to prevent it. You have that fact; if there is a place for that piece in your puzzle, fit it in. You have, gentlemen, my sympathy and my best wishes."

Tolman, who after all wasn't much more than a kid, twisted his head to get a look at the sheriff, who was slowly scratching his cheek with his middle finger.

Pettigrew looked back at him and finally turned to Wolfe. "Look, mister, you've got us wrong I think. We're not aiming to make you any trouble or any inconvenience. We don't regard you as one of that bunch that if they knew anything they wouldn't tell us if they could help it. But you say maybe we've heard of you. That's right. We've heard of you. After all, you was around with this bunch all day talking with 'em. You know? I don't know what Tolman here thinks, but it's my opinion it wouldn't hurt any to tell you what we've found out and get your slant on it. Since you say you've got no interest in it that might conflict. All right, Barry?"

Wolfe said, "You'd be wasting your time. I'm not a wizard. When I get results, I get them by hard work, and this isn't my case and I'm not working on it."

I covered a grin. Tolman put in, "The sooner this thing is cleaned up, the better for everybody. You realize that. If the sheriff—"

Wolfe said brusquely, "Very well. Tomorrow."

"It's already tomorrow. God knows how late you'll sleep in the morning, but I won't. There's one thing in particular I want to ask you. You told me that the only one of these people you know at all well is Vukčić. Mrs. Laszio told me about her being married to Vukčić and getting divorced from him some years ago to marry Laszio. Could you tell me how Vukčić has been feeling about that?"

"No. Mrs. Laszio seems to have been quite informative."

"Well, it was her husband that got killed. Why? Have you got anything against her? That's the second dig you've taken at her."

"Certainly I have something against her. I don't like women asking me to protect their husbands. It is beneath the dignity of a man to rely, either for safety or salvation, on the interference of a woman. Pfui."

Of course Wolfe wasn't in love. I hoped Tolman realized that.

He said, "I asked you that question, obviously, because Vukčić was one of the two who had the best opportunity to kill him. Most of them are apparently out of it, by your own testimony among others." He glanced at one of the papers on the table. "The ones who were in the parlor all the time, according to present information, are Mrs. Laszio, Mrs. Mondor, Lisette Putti, and Goodwin. Servan says that when he went to the dining room to taste those sauces Laszio was there alive and nothing wrong, and at that time Mondor, Coyne, and Keith had already been in, and it is agreed that none of them left the parlor again. They too are apparently out of it. The next two were Berin and Vukčić. Berin says that when he left the dining room Laszio was still there and still nothing wrong, and Vukčić says that when he entered, some eight or ten minutes later on account of a delay, Laszio was gone and he saw nothing of him and noticed nothing wrong. The three who went last, Vallenko and Rossi and you, are also apparently out of it, but not as conclusively as the others, since it is quite possible that Laszio had merely stepped out to the terrace or gone to the toilet, and returned after Vukčić left the dining room. According to the cooks, he had not appeared in the kitchen, so he had not gone there."

Tolman glanced at the paper again. "That makes two probabilities, Berin and Vukčić, and three possibilities, Vallenko and Rossi and you. Besides that, there are three other possibilities. Someone could easily have entered the dining room from the terrace at any time; the glass doors were closed and the shades drawn, but they were not locked. And there were three people who could have done that: Leon Blanc, who refused to take part on account of animosity toward Laszio and was absent; Mrs. Coyne, who was outdoors alone for nearly an hour, including the interval between Berin's visit to the dining room and that of Vukčić; and Miss Berin. Blanc claims he went to his room and didn't leave it, and the hall attendants didn't see him go out, but there is a door to the little side terrace at the end of the left-wing corridor which he could have used without observation. Mrs. Coyne says she was on the paths and lawns throughout her absence, was not on the dining-room terrace, and re-entered by the main entrance and went straight to the parlor. As for Miss Berin, she returned to the parlor, from her room, before the tasting of the sauces began and did not again leave; I mentioned her absence only to have the record complete."

I thought to myself, You cold-blooded hound! She was in her room crying for you, that was her absence, and you make it just part of a list!

"You were there, Mr. Wolfe. That covers it, doesn't it?"

Wolfe grunted.

Tolman resumed. "As for motive, with some of them there was enough. With Vukčić, the fact that Laszio had taken his wife. And immediately preceding Vukčić's trip to the dining room he had been talking with Mrs. Laszio and gazing at her and dancing with her—"

Wolfe said sharply, "A woman told you that."

"By God," the sheriff drawled, "you seem to resent the few little things we have found out. I thought you said you weren't interested."

"Vukčić is my friend. I'm interested in him. I'm not interested in this murder, with which he had no connection."

"Maybe not." Tolman looked pleased—I suppose because he had got a rise out of Nero Wolfe. "Anyway, my talk with Mrs. Mondor was my first chance to make official use of my French. Next there is Berin. I got this not from Mrs. Mondor but from him. He declares that Laszio should have been killed long before now, that he himself would have liked to do it, and that if he has any opportunity to protect the murderer he will do so."

Wolfe murmured, "Berin talks."

"I'll say he does. So does that little Frenchman Leon Blanc, but not the same style. He admits that he hated Laszio because he cheated him out of his job at the Hotel Churchill some years ago, but he says he wouldn't murder anybody for anything. He says that it does not even please him that Laszio is dead, because death does not heal, it amputates. Those were his words. He's soft-spoken and he certainly doesn't seem aggressive enough to stab a man through the heart, but he's no fool and possibly he's smooth.

"There's the two probabilities and one possibility with motives. Of the four other possibilities, I guess you didn't do it. If Rossi or Vallenko had any feelings that might have gone as far as murder, I haven't learned it yet. As for Mrs. Coyne, she never saw Laszio before, and I can't discover that she has spoken to him once. So until further notice we have Berin and Vukčić and Blanc. Any of them could have done it, and I think one of them did. What do you think?"

Wolfe shook his head. "Thank heaven, it isn't my problem, and I don't have to think."

Pettigrew put in, in his mild drawl, "Do you suppose there's any chance you suspect your friend Vukčić did it and so you'd rather not think about it?"

"Chance? Certainly. Remote. If Vukčić did it, I hope with all my heart he left no rope for you to hang him by. And as for information regarding it, I have none, and if I had I wouldn't reveal it."

Tolman nodded. "That's frank but not very helpful. I don't have to point out to you that if you're interested in your friend Vukčić and think he didn't do it, the quickest way to clear him is to find out who did. You were right there on the spot; you saw everyone and heard everything that was said. It seems to me that under those circumstances a man of your reputation and ability should find it possible to offer some help. If you don't it's bound to put more suspicion on your friend Vukčić, isn't it?"

"I don't know. Your suspicions are your affair; I can't regulate them. Confound it, it's four o'clock in the morning." Wolfe sighed. Then he compressed his lips. He sat that way and finally muttered, "Very well, I'll help for ten minutes. Tell me about the routine, the knife, fingerprints, anything found—"

"Nothing. There were two knives on the table for slicing the squab, and it was one of them. You saw for yourself there was not the slightest sign of a struggle. Nothing anywhere. No prints that seem to mean anything; those on the knife handle were all smudged. The levers on the door to the terrace are rough wrought iron. Men are still in there working it over, but that angle looks hopeless."

Wolfe grunted. "You've omitted possibilities. The cooks and waiters?"

"They've all been questioned by the sheriff, who knows how to deal with them. None of them went to the dining room, and they didn't see or hear anything. Laszio had told them he would ring if anything was wanted."

"Someone could have gone from the large parlor to the small one and from there entered the dining room and killed him. You should establish beyond doubt the presence of everyone in the large parlor, especially during the interim between Berin's leaving the dining room and Vukčić's entering it, which, as you say, was some eight or ten minutes."

"I have done so. Of course, I covered everybody pretty fast."

"Then cover them again. Another possibility: someone could have been concealed behind either of the screens and struck from there when the opportunity offered."

"Yeah? Who?"

"I'm sure I couldn't say." Wolfe frowned. "I may as well tell you, Mr. Tolman, I am extremely skeptical regarding your two chief suspects, Mr. Berin and Mr. Vukčić. That is putting it with restraint. As for Mr. Blanc, I am without an opinion; as you have pointed out, he could unquestionably have left his room, made an exit at the end of the left-wing corridor, circled the building, entered by the dining-room terrace, achieved his purpose, and returned the way he had come. In that case, might he not have been seen by Mrs. Coyne, who was outdoors at the time, looking at the night?"

Tolman shook his head. "She says not. She was at the front and the side both. She saw no one but a uniformed attendant and stopped him and asked him what the sound of a whippoorwill was. We've found him—one of the boys from the spring on his way to Mingo Pavilion."

"So. As for Berin and Vukčić, if I were you I would pigeonhole them for the present. Or at least—I offer a suggestion—get the slips, the tasting reports, from Mr. Servan—"

"I have them."

"Good. Compare them with the correct list, which you also got from Mr. Servan no doubt—"

"He didn't have it. It was in Laszio's pocket."

"Very well. Compare each list with it, and see how nearly each taster was correct."

Sheriff Pettigrew snorted. Tolman asked dryly, "You call that being helpful, do you?"

"I do. I am already. By the way"—Wolfe straightened a little—"if you have the correct list there, the one you took from Laszio's pocket, do you mind if I look at it a moment?"

Tolman, with his brows up, shuffled through the papers before him, extracted one, handed it to me, and I passed it to Wolfe. Wolfe looked at it with his forehead wrinkled and exclaimed, "Good God!" He looked at it again and turned to me, shaking the paper in his hand. "Archie. Coyne was right. Number 3 was shallots."

Tolman asked sarcastically, "Comedy relief? Much obliged for *that* help."

I grinned at him. "Comedy, hell, he won't sleep for a week. He guessed wrong."

Wolfe reproved me. "It was not a guess. It was a deliberate conclusion, and it was wrong." He handed me the paper. "Pardon me, Mr. Tolman, I've had a blow. Actually. I wouldn't expect you to appreciate it. As I was saying, I am already more than skeptical regarding Berin and Vukčić. I have known Mr. Vukčić all my life. I can conceive of his stabbing a man, under hypothetical conditions, but I am sure that if he did you wouldn't find the knife in the man's back. I don't know Mr. Berin well, but I saw him at close range and heard him speak less than a minute after he left the dining room last night, and I would stake something that he wasn't fresh from the commission of a cowardly murder. He had but a moment before sunk a knife in Mr. Laszio's back, and I detected no residue of that experience in his posture, his hands, his eyes, his voice? I don't believe it."

"And about comparing these lists—"

"I'm coming to that. I take it that Mr. Servan has described the nature of that test to you—each sauce lacking one or another of the seasonings. We were permitted but one taste from each dish—only one. Have you any conception of the delicacy and sensitivity required? It took the highest degree of concentration and receptivity of stimuli. To detect a single false note in one of the wood winds in a symphonic passage by a full orchestra would be the same. So, compare those lists. If you find that Berin and Vukčić were substantially correct—say, seven or eight out of nine—they are eliminated. Even six. No man about to kill another, or just having done so, could possibly control his nervous system sufficiently to perform such a feat. I assure you this is not comedy."

Tolman nodded. "All right, I'll compare them."

"It would be instructive to do so now."

"I'll attend to it. Any other suggestions?"

"No." Wolfe got his hands on the chair arms, pulled his feet back, braced, and arose. "The ten minutes are up." He did his little bow. "I offer you again, gentlemen, my sympathy and best wishes."

The sheriff said, "I understand you're sleepin' in Upshur. Of course you realize you're free to go anywhere you want to around the grounds here."

"Thank you, sir." Wolfe sounded bitter. "Come, Archie."

Not to crowd the path, I let him precede me among the greenery back to Upshur Pavilion. We didn't go through darkness but through the twilight of dawn, and there were so many birds singing you couldn't help noticing it. In the main hall of the pavilion the lights were turned on, and a couple of state cops were sitting there. Wolfe passed them without a glance.

I went to his room with him to make sure that everything was jake. The bed had been turned down, and the colored rugs and things made it bright and pleasant, and the room was big and classy enough to make it worth at least half of the twenty bucks a day they charged for it, but Wolfe frowned around as if it had been a pigpen.

I inquired, "Can I help on the disrobing?"

"No."

"Shall I bring a pitcher of water from the bathroom?"

"I can walk. Good night."

"Good night, boss." I went.

His voice halted me at the door. "Archie. This Mr. Laszio seems to have had unpleasant characteristics. Do you suppose there is any chance he deliberately made that list incorrect, to disconcert his colleagues—and me?"

"Huh-uh. Not the faintest. Professional ethics, you know. Of course I'm sorry you got so many wrong—"

"Two! Shallots and chives! Leave me! Get out!"

He sure was one happy detective that night.

5

At two o'clock the next day, Wednesday, I was feeling pretty screwy and dissatisfied with life, but in one way completely at home. Getting to bed too late, or having my sleep disturbed unduly, poisons my system, and I had had both to contend with. Having neglected to hang up a notice, a damn-fool greenjacket had got me to the door of our suite at nine o'clock to ask if we wanted baths drawn or any other little service, and I had told him to return at sundown. At ten-thirty the phone woke me; my friend Barry Tolman wanted to speak to Wolfe. I explained that Wolfe's first exposure to the light of day would have to be on his own initiative, and I told the operator no more calls until further notice. In spite of that, an hour later the phone rang again and kept on ringing. It was Tolman, and he just had to speak to Wolfe. I told him absolutely nothing doing, without a search and seizure warrant, until Wolfe had announced himself as conscious. But that time I was roused enough to become aware of other necessities besides sleep, so I bathed and shaved and dressed and phoned Room Service for some breakfast, since I couldn't go and get it under the circumstances. I had finished the third cup of coffee when I heard Wolfe yelling for me. He was certainly getting demoralized. At home in New York I hadn't heard him yell more than three times in ten years.

He gave me his breakfast order, which I phoned, and then issued the instructions which made me feel at home. It was his intention to confine his social contacts for that afternoon exclusively to me. Business and professional contacts were out. The door was to be kept locked, and any caller, unless it should happen to be Marko Vukčić, was to be told that Wolfe was immersed in something, no matter what. Telephone calls were to be handled by me, since he knew nothing that I didn't know. (This jarred my aplomb, since it was the first time he had ever admitted it.) Should I feel the need of more fresh air than was obtainable through open windows, which was idiotic but probable, the DO NOT DISTURB card was to be hung on the door and the key kept in my pocket.

I phoned for whatever morning papers were available, and when they came passed a couple to Wolfe and made myself comfortable on a couch with the remainder. Those from New York and Pittsburgh and Washington, being early train editions, had no mention of the Laszio murder, but there were big headlines and a short piece in the *Charleston Journal,* which had only sixty miles to come.

But before the day was out Wolfe's arrangements for peaceful privacy got shot full of holes. The first and least important of the upsets came before he had finished with the newspapers when, around two o'clock, there were sounds at the outer door and I went and opened it a discreet twelve inches to find myself confronted by two gentlemen who did not look local and whom I had never seen before. One was shorter than me and somewhat older, dark-skinned, wiry and compact, in a neat gray herringbone with padded shoulders and cut-in waist; the other, medium both in age and size, wore his hairline well above his temples and had small gray eyes that looked as if nobody would ever have to irritate him again because he was already irritated for good. But he spoke and listened politely as he asked me if this was Mr. Nero Wolfe's suite and I informed him it was. He announced that he was Mr. Liggett and the padded specimen was Mr. Malfi, and he would like to see Wolfe. I explained that Wolfe was immersed, and he looked impatient and dug an envelope from his pocket and handed it to me. I apologized for shutting them in the hall before I did so, and returned to the pigpen.

"Two male strangers, vanilla and caramel. To see you."

Wolfe's eyes didn't leave his newspaper. "If either of them was Mr. Vukčić, I presume you would have recognized him."

"Not Vukčić, no, but you didn't prohibit letters, and he handed me one."

"Read it."

I took it from the envelope, saw that it was on engraved stationery, and wired it for sound:

New York
April 7, 1937

Dear Mr. Wolfe:

This will introduce my friend Mr. Raymond Liggett, manager and part owner of the Hotel Churchill. He wants to ask your advice or assistance, and has requested this note from me.

I hope you're enjoying yourself down there. Don't eat too much, and don't forget to come back to make life in New York pleasanter for us.

Yours

BURKE WILLIAMSON

Wolfe grunted. "You said April seventh? That's today."

"Yeah, they must have flown. Formerly a figure of speech, now listed under common carriers. Do we let them in?"

"Confound it." Wolfe let the paper down. "Courtesy is one's own affair, but decency is a debt to life. You remember that Mr. Williamson was kind enough to let us use the grounds of his estate for the ambush and robbery of Miss Anna Fiore." He sighed. "Show them in."

I went and got them, pronounced names around, and placed chairs. Wolfe greeted them, made his customary statement regarding his tendency to stay seated, and then glanced a second time at the padded one.

"Did I catch your name, sir? Malfi? Perhaps Albert Malfi?"

The wiry one's black eyes darted at him. "That's right. I don't know how you know the Albert."

Wolfe nodded. "Formerly Alberto. I met Mr. Berin on the train coming down here, and he told me about you. He says you are an excellent entrée man, and it is always a pleasure to meet an artist and a sound workman."

Liggett put in, "Oh, you were with Berin on the train?"

"I was." Wolfe grimaced. "We shared that ordeal. Mr. Williamson says you wish to ask me something."

"Yes. Of course you know why we came. This—Laszio. It's terrible. You were right there, weren't you? You found the body."

"I did. You wasted no time, Mr. Liggett."

"I know damn well I didn't. I usually turn in late and get up late, but this morning Malfi had me on the telephone before eight o'clock. Reporters had been after me earlier but of course didn't get through. The city editions had the story. I knew Williamson was a friend of yours and sent to him for that note and hired a plane from Newark. Malfi insisted on coming along, and I'm afraid one of your jobs will be to watch him as soon as they find out who did it." Liggett showed a thin smile. "He's a Corsican, and while Laszio wasn't any relation of his, he's got pretty devoted to him. Haven't you, Malfi?"

The padded one nodded emphatically. "I have. Phillip Laszio was a mean man and a great man. He was not mean to me." He spread both palms at Wolfe. "But of course Mr. Liggett is only joking. The world thinks all Corsicans stab people. That is a wrong idea and a bad one."

"But you wanted to ask me something, Mr. Liggett?" Wolfe sounded impatient. "You said one of my jobs. I have no jobs."

"I'm hoping you will have. First, to find out who killed Laszio. Judging from the account in the papers, it looks as if it will be too tough for a West Virginia sheriff. It seems likely that whoever did it was able to use finesse for purposes other than tasting the seasonings in Sauce Printemps. I can't say I was devoted to Laszio in the sense that Malfi here was, but after all he was the chef of my hotel, and I understand he had no family except his wife, and I thought—it's an obligation. It was a damned cowardly murder, a stab in the back. He ought to be caught, and I suspect it will take you to do it. That's what I came for. Knowing your—er, peculiarities, I took the precaution of getting that note from Williamson."

"It's too bad." Wolfe sighed. "I mean too bad you came. You could have telephoned from New York."

"I asked Williamson what he thought about that, and he said if I really wanted your services I'd better come and get them."

"Indeed. I don't know why Mr. Williamson should assume difficulties. My services are on the market. Of course, in this particular instance they are unfortunately not available. That's why I say it's too bad you came."

"Why not available?"

"Because of the conditions."

"Conditions?" The irritation in Liggett's eyes became more intense. "I've made no conditions."

"Not you. Space. Geography. Should I undertake to discover Mr. Laszio's murderer, I would see it through. That might take a day, a week, with bad luck a fortnight. I intend to board a train for New York tomorrow night." Wolfe winced.

"Williamson warned me." Liggett compressed his lips. "But good Lord, man! It's your business! It's your—"

"I beg you, sir. Don't. I won't listen. If I offend by being curt, very well. Anyone has the privilege of offending who is willing to bear the odium. I will consider no engagement that might detain me in this parasitic outpost beyond tomorrow night. You said 'jobs.' Is there anything else you wish to discuss?"

"There was." Liggett looked as if he would prefer to continue the discussion with shrapnel or a machine gun. He sat and stared at Wolfe a while, then finally shrugged it off. He said, "The fact is, the main job is something quite different. The main thing I came down here for. Laszio is dead, and the way he died was terrible, and as a man I have, I hope, the proper feelings about it, but in addition to being a man

I'm a business man, and the Hotel Churchill is left without a *chef de cuisine*. You know the Churchill's world-wide reputation, and it has to be maintained. I want to get Jerome Berin."

Wolfe's brows went up. "I don't blame you."

"Of course you don't. There are a few others as good as Berin, but they're out. Mondor wouldn't leave his Paris restaurant. Servan and Tassone are too old. I wouldn't mind having Leon Blanc back, but he is also too old. Vukčić is tied up at Rusterman's, and so on. I happen to know that Berin has received five offers from this country, two of them from New York, in the past two years, and has turned them all down. I'd like to have him. In fact, he's the only one that I consider both available and desirable. If I can't get him, Malfi can put a blue ribbon on his cap." He turned to his companion. "Is that in accord with our agreement, Albert? When you got that offer from Chicago a year ago I told you that if you would stick, and the position of *chef de cuisine* at the Churchill should become vacant, I would first try to get Berin, and if I couldn't, you could have it. Right?"

Malfi nodded. "That was the understanding."

Wolfe murmured, "This is all very interesting. But you were speaking of a job—"

"Yes. I want you to approach Berin for me. He's one of the best seven chefs in the world, but he's hard to handle. Last Saturday he deliberately spilled two plates of sausage in the middle of the carpet in my Resort Room. Williamson says you have remarkable ability as a negotiator, and you are the guest of honor here and Berin will listen to you with respect, and I believe unquestionably you can swing him. I would offer him forty thousand, but I tell you frankly I am willing to go to sixty, and your commission—"

Wolfe was showing him a palm. "Please, Mr. Liggett. It's no go. Absolutely out of the question."

"You mean you won't do it?"

"I mean I wouldn't undertake to persuade Mr. Berin to do anything whatever. I would as soon try to persuade a giraffe. I could elaborate, but I can't see that I owe you that."

"You won't even attempt it?"

"I will not. The truth is, you have come to me at the most inauspicious moment in the past twenty years, and with proposals much more likely to vex me than to interest me. I don't care a hang who your new chef will be, and while I always like to make money, that can wait until I am back in my office. There are others here better qualified to approach Mr. Berin for you than I am—Mr. Servan or Mr. Coyne, for instance, old friends of his."

"They're chefs themselves. I don't want that. You're the man to do it for me."

He was a persistent cuss, but it didn't get him anywhere. When he tried to insist, Wolfe merely got curter, as he naturally would, and finally Liggett realized he was calling the wrong dog and gave it up. He popped up out of his chair, snapped at Malfi to come along, and without any ceremony showed Wolfe his back. Malfi trotted behind, and I followed them to the hall to see that the door was locked after them.

When I got back to the room Wolfe was already behind his paper again. I felt muscle-bound and not inclined to settle down, so I said to him, "You know, werowance, that's not a bad idea—"

A word he didn't know invariably got him. The paper went down to the level of his nose. "What the devil is that? Did you make it up?"

"I did not. I got it from a piece in the *Charleston Journal*. 'Werowance' is a term that was used for an Indian chief in Virginia and Maryland. I'm going to call you 'werowance' instead of 'boss' as long as we're in this part of the country. As I was saying, werowance, it might be a good idea to start an employment bureau for chefs and waiters, maybe later branch out into domestic help generally. You are aware, I suppose, that you have just turned down a darned good offer for a case. That Liggett has really got it in quantities. I suspect he may be half bright too; for instance, do you imagine he might have come to see you in order to let Alberto know indirectly that if he tried sticking something into Berin in order to make Berin ineligible for the Churchill job, it would have deplorable consequences? Which opens up a train of thought that might solve the unemployment question. If a job becomes vacant and you want it, first you kill all the other candidates and then—?"

The paper was up again, so I knew I had made myself sufficiently obnoxious. I said, "I'm going out and wade in the brook, and maybe go to the hotel and ruin a few girls. See you later."

I got my hat, hung up the DO NOT DISTURB, and wandered out, noting that there was a greenjacket at the door of the main hall but no cop. Apparently vigilance was relaxed. I turned my nose to the hotel, just to see what there was to see, and it wasn't long before I regretted that, for if I hadn't gone to the hotel first I would have got to see the whole show that my friend Tolman was putting on, instead of arriving barely in time for the final curtain. As it was, I found various sights around the hotel entrance and lobby that served for mild diversion, including an intelligent-looking horse stepping on a fat dowager's foot so hard they had to carry her away, and it was around 3:30 when I decided to make an excursion to Pocahontas Pavilion and thank Vukčić, my host, for the good time I was having.

In a secluded part of the path a guy with his necktie over his shoulder and needing a shave jumped out from behind a bush and grabbed my elbow, talking as he came. "Hey, you're Archie Goodwin, aren't you, Nero Wolfe's man? Listen, brother—"

I shook him off and told him, "Damn it, quit scaring people. I'll hold a press conference tomorrow morning in my study. I don't know a thing, and if I did and told you I'd get killed by my werowance. Do you know what a werowance is?"

He told me to go to hell and started looking for another bush.

The tableau at Pocahontas Pavilion was in two sections when I got there. The first section, not counting the pair of troopers standing outside the entrance, was in the main hall. The greenjacket who opened the door for me was looking popeyed in another direction as he pulled it open. The door to the large parlor was closed. Standing with her back against the right wall, with her arms folded tight against her and her chin up, and her dark purple eyes flashing at the guys who hemmed her in, was Constanza Berin. The hemmers were two state cops in uniform and a hefty bird in cits with a badge on his vest, and while they weren't actually touching her at the moment I entered, it looked as though they probably had been. She didn't appear to see me. A glance showed me that the door to the small parlor was open, and a voice was coming through. As I started for it one of the cops called a sharp command to me, but it seemed likely he was too occupied to interfere in person, so I ignored it and went on.

There were cops in the small parlor too, and the squint-eyed sheriff, and Tolman. Between two of the cops stood Jerome Berin, with handcuffs on his wrists. I was surprised that under the circumstances Berin wasn't breaking furniture or even skulls, but all he was doing was glaring and breathing.

Tolman was telling him, ". . . we appreciate that you're a foreign visitor and a stranger here, and we'll show you every consideration. In this country a man charged with murder can't get bail. Your friends will of course arrange for counsel for you. I have not only told you that anything you say may be used against you, I have advised you to say nothing until you have consulted with counsel. Go on, boys. Take him by the back path to the sheriff's car."

But they didn't get started right then. Yells and other sounds came suddenly from the main hall, and Constanza Berin came through the door like a tornado with the cops behind. One in the parlor tried to grab her as she went by, but he might as well have tried to stop the great blizzard. I thought she was going right on over the table to get at Tolman, but she stopped there and turned, with her eyes blazing at the cops, and then wheeled to Tolman and yelled at him, "You fool! You pig of a fool! He's my father! Would he kill a man in the back?" She pounded the table with fists. "Let him go! Let him go, you fool!"

A cop made a pass at her arm. Berin growled and took a step, and the two held him. Tolman looked as if the one thing he could use to advantage would be a trapdoor. Constanza had jerked away from the cop, and Berin said something to her, low and quiet, in Italian. She walked to him, three steps, and he went to lift a hand and couldn't on account of the bracelets, and then stooped and kissed her on top of the head. She turned and stood still for ten seconds, giving Tolman a look which I couldn't see, but which probably made a trapdoor all the more desirable, and then turned again and walked out of the room.

Tolman couldn't speak. At least he didn't. Sheriff Pettigrew shook himself and said, "Come on, boys, I'll go along."

I shoved off without waiting for their exit. Constanza wasn't in the main hall. I halted there for an instant, thinking I might explore the large parlor in search of persons who might add to my information, and then decided that I had better first deposit what I had. So I went on out and hot-footed it back to Upshur.

Wolfe had finished with the papers and piled them neatly on the dresser, and was in the big chair, not quite big enough for him, with a book. He didn't look up as I went in, which meant that for the time being my existence was strictly my own affair. I adopted the suggestion and parked myself on the couch with a newspaper, which I opened up and looked at but didn't read.

In about five minutes, after Wolfe had turned two pages, I said, "By the way, it's a darned good thing you didn't take that job for Liggett. I mean the last one he offered. If you had, you would now be up a stump. As it stands now, you'd have a sweet time persuading Berin to be chef even for a soda fountain."

Neither he nor the book moved, but he did speak. "I presume Mr. Malfi has stabbed Mr. Berin. Good."

"No. He hasn't and he won't, because he can't get at him. Berin is wearing gyves on his way to jail. My friend Tolman has made a pinch. Justice has lit her torch."

"Pfui. If you must pester me with fairy tales, cultivate some imagination."

I said patiently, "Mr. Tolman has arrested Mr. Berin for the murder of Mr. Laszio and removed him to custody without bail. I saw it with these eyes."

The book went down. "Archie. If this is flummery—"

"No, sir. Straight."

"He has charged Berin?"

"Yes, sir."

"In the name of God, why? The man's a fool."

"That's what Miss Berin said. She said 'pig of a fool.'"

The book had remained suspended in the air; now it was lowered to rest on the expanse of thigh. In a few moments it was lifted again and opened for a page to get turned down, and was then deposited on a little stand beside the chair. Wolfe leaned back and shut his eyes and his fingers met at the front of his belly; and I saw his lips push out, then in again . . . then out, then in. . . . It startled me, and I wondered what all the excitement was about.

After a while he said without opening his eyes, "You understand, Archie, that I would hesitate to undertake anything which might conceivably delay our return to New York."

"It could be called hesitating. There's stronger words."

"Yes. On the other hand, I should be as great a fool as Mr. Tolman were I to ignore such an opportunity as this. It looks as if the only way to take advantage of it is to learn who killed Mr. Laszio. The question is, can we do it in thirty-one hours? Twenty-eight really, since at the dinner tomorrow evening I am to deliver my talk on American contributions to *la haute cuisine.* Can we do it in twenty-eight hours?"

"Sure we can." I waved a hand. "Gosh, with me to do the planning and you to handle the details—"

"Yes. Of course they may have abandoned the idea of that dinner, but I should think not, since only once in five years—well, the first step—"

"Excuse me." I had dropped the paper to the floor and straightened up, with a warm feeling that here was going to be a chance to get my circulation started. "Why not get in touch with Liggett and accept his offer? Since we're going to do it anyway, we might as well annex a fee along with it."

"No. If I engage with him and am not finished by tomorrow evening —no. Freedom is too precious collateral for any fee. We shall proceed. The first step is obvious. Bring Mr. Tolman here at once."

That was like him. Someday he would tell me to go get the Senate and the House of Representatives. I said, "Tolman's sore at you because you wouldn't come to the phone this morning. Also, he thinks he has his man and is no longer interested. Also, I don't believe—"

"Archie. You said you will do the planning. Please go for Mr. Tolman and plan how to persuade him on the way."

I went for my hat.

6

I jogged smartly back along the path to Pocahontas, thinking I might catch Tolman before he got away, with my brain going faster than my feet, trying to invent a swift one for him, but I was too late. The greenjacket at the door so advised me, saying that Tolman had got in his car on the driveway and headed west. I about-faced and broke into a gallop. If there had been a stop at the hotel, as seemed probable, I might head him off there. I was panting a little by the time I entered the lobby and began darting glances around through the palms and pillars and greenjackets and customers in everything from riding togs to what resembled the last safeguard of Gypsy Rose Lee.

I was about to advance to the desk to make an inquiry when I heard a grim voice at my elbow. "Hello, cockroach."

I wheeled and narrowed my eyes at it. "Hello, rat. Not even rat. Something I don't know the name of, because it lives underground and eats the roots of weeds."

Gershom Odell shook his head. "Not me. Wrong number. What you said about Laszio getting croaked, I had already told the night clerk just as conversation, and of course they faced me with it after it happened, and what could I do? But your shooting off your face about throwing stones—didn't you have brains enough to know you would make that damn sheriff suspicious?"

"I haven't got any brains, I'm a detective. The sheriff's busy elsewhere anyhow." I waved a hand. "Forget it. I want to see Tolman. Is he around here?"

Odell nodded. "He's in the manager's office with Ashley. Also a few other people, including a man from New York named Liggett. Which reminds me, I want to see you. You think you're so damn smart I'd like to lay you flat and sit on you, but I'll have to let that go because I want you to do me a favor."

"Let it go anyway. Sit not lest you be sat on."

"Okay. What I wanted to ask you about, I'm fed up with the sticks.

It's a good job here in a way, but in other ways it's pretty crummy. Today when Raymond Liggett landed here in a plane, the first person he asked for was Nero Wolfe, and he hoofed it right over to Upshur without going to his room or even stopping to say hello to Ashley. So I figured Wolfe must stand pretty high with him, and it occurred to me that about the best berth in this country for a house detective is the Hotel Churchill." Odell's eyes gleamed. "Boy, would that be a spot for a good honest man like me! So while Liggett's here, if you could tell Wolfe about me and he could tell Liggett and arrange for me to meet him without the bunch here getting wise in case I don't land it . . ."

I was thinking, Sure as the devil we're turning into an employment agency. I hate to disappoint people, and therefore I kidded Odell along, without actually misrepresenting the condition of Wolfe's intimacy with Raymond Liggett, and keeping one eye on the closed door which was the entrance to the manager's office. I told him that I was glad to see that he wasn't satisfied to stay in a rut and had real ambition and so forth, and it was a very nice chat, but I knocked off abruptly when I saw the closed door open and my friend Barry Tolman emerge alone. Giving Odell a friendly clap on the shoulder with enough muscle in it to give him an idea how easy I would be to sit on, I left him and followed my prey among the pillars and palms, and at a likely spot near the main entrance pounced on him.

His blue eyes looked worried and his whole face untidy. He recognized me. "Oh. What do you want? I'm in a hurry."

I said, "So am I. I'm not going to apologize about Wolfe not coming to the phone this morning, because if you know anything about Nero Wolfe you know he's eccentric and try and change him. I happened to see you going by just now, and I met you on the train Monday night and liked your face because you looked like a straight-shooter, and a little while ago I saw you pinching Berin for murder—I suppose you didn't notice me but I was there—and I went back to the suite and told Wolfe about it, and I think you ought to know what he did when I told him. He pinched his nose."

"Well?" Tolman was frowning. "As long as he didn't pinch mine—what about it?"

"Nothing, except that if you knew Wolfe as I do—I have never yet seen him pinch his nose except when he was sure that some fellow being was making a complete jackass of himself. Do as you please. You're young and so you've got most of your bad mistakes ahead of you yet. I just had a friendly impulse, seeing you go by, and I *think* I can persuade Wolfe to have a talk with you if you want to come over to the suite with me right now. Anyhow, I'm willing to try it." I moved back a step. "Suit yourself, since you're in a hurry."

He kept the frown on. But I was pleased to see that he didn't waste time in fiddle-faddle. He frowned into my frank eyes a few seconds, then said abruptly, "Come on," and headed for the exit. I trotted behind, glowing like a Boy Scout.

When we got to Upshur I had to continue the play, but I didn't feel like leaving him loose in the public hall, so I took him to the suite and put him in my room and shut the door on him. Then I went across to Wolfe's room, shutting that door too, and sat down on the couch and grinned at the fat son-of-a-gun.

"Well?" he demanded. "Couldn't you find him?"

"Of course I could find him. I've got him." I thumbed to indicate where. "I had to come in first to try to persuade you to grant him an audience. It ought to take about five minutes. It's even possible he'll sneak into the foyer to listen at the door." I raised my voice. "What about justice? What about society? What about the right of every man . . ."

Wolfe had to listen because there was no way out. I laid it on good and thick. When I thought enough time had elapsed I closed the valve, went to my room and gave Tolman the high sign with a look of triumph, and ushered him in. He looked so preoccupied with worry that for a second I thought he was going to miss the chair when he sat down.

He plunged into it. "I understand that you think I'm pulling a boner."

Wolfe shook his head. "Not my phrase, Mr. Tolman. I can't very well have an intelligent opinion until I know the facts that moved you. Offhand, I fear you've been precipitate."

"I don't think so." Tolman had his chin stuck out. "I talked with people in Charleston on the phone, and they agreed with me. Not that I'm passing the buck; the responsibility is mine. Incidentally, I'm supposed to be in Charleston at six o'clock for a conference, and it's sixty miles. I'm not bullheaded about it. I'll turn Berin loose like that"—he snapped his fingers—"if I'm shown cause. If you've any information I haven't got I'd have been damned thankful to get it when I phoned you this morning, and I'd be thankful now. Not to mention the duty of a citizen—"

"I have no information that would prove Mr. Berin innocent." Wolfe's tone was mild. "It was Mr. Goodwin's ebullience that brought you here. I gave you my opinion last night. It might help if I knew what you based your decision on, short of what you value as secret. You understand I have no client. I am representing no one."

"I have no secrets. But I have enough to hold Berin and indict him and I think convict him. As for opportunity, you know about that. He threatened Laszio's life indiscriminately, in the hearing of half-a-dozen people. I suppose he figured that it would be calculated that a murderer would not go around advertising it in advance, but I think he overplayed it. This morning I questioned everybody again, especially Berin and Vukčić, and I counted Vukčić out. I got various pieces of information. But I admit that the most convincing fact of all came through a suggestion from you. I compared those lists with the one we found in Laszio's pocket. No one except Berin got more than two wrong."

He got papers from his pocket and selected one. "The lists of five of them, among them Vukčić, agreed exactly with the correct list. Four of them, including you, made two mistakes each, and the same ones." He returned the papers to his pocket and leaned forward at Wolfe. "Berin had just two right. Seven wrong."

In the silence Wolfe's eyes went nearly closed. At length he murmured, "Preposterous. Nonsense."

"Precisely!" Tolman nodded with emphasis. "It is incredible that in a test on which the other nine averaged over ninety per cent correct, Berin should score twenty-two per cent. It is absolutely conclusive of one of two things: either he was so upset by a murder he had just committed or was about to commit that he couldn't distinguish the tastes, or he was so busy with the murder that he didn't have time to taste at all and merely filled out his list haphazardly. I regard it as conclusive, and I think a jury will. And I want to say that I am mighty grateful to you for the suggestion you made. I freely admit it was damned clever and it was you who thought of it."

"Thank you. Did you inform Mr. Berin of this and request an explanation?"

"Yes. He professed amazement. He couldn't explain it."

"You said 'absolutely conclusive.' That's far too strong. There are other alternatives. Berin's list may be forged."

"It's the one he himself handed to Servan, and it bears his signature. It hadn't been out of Servan's possession when he gave the lists to me. Would you suspect Servan?"

"I suspect no one. The dishes or cards might have been tampered with."

"Not the cards. Berin says they were in consecutive order when he tasted, as they were throughout. As for the dishes, who did it, and who put them back in place again after Berin left?"

After another silence Wolfe murmured again, obstinately, "It remains preposterous."

"Sure it does." Tolman leaned forward, further than before. "Look here, Wolfe. I'm a prosecuting attorney and all that, and I've got a career to make, and I know what it means to have a success in a sensational case like this, but you're wrong if you think it gave me any pleasure to make a quick grab for Berin as a victim. It didn't. I—" He stopped. He tried it again. "I—well, it didn't. For certain reasons, it was the hardest thing I've ever done in my life. But let me ask you a question. I want to make it a tight question. Granted these premises as proven facts: one, that Berin made seven mistakes on the list he filled out and signed; two, that when he tasted the dishes they and the cards were in the same condition and order as when the others did; three, that nothing can be discovered to cast doubt on those facts; four, that you have taken the oath of office as prosecuting attorney—would you have Berin arrested for murder and try to convict him?"

"I would resign."

Tolman threw up both hands. "Why?"

"Because I saw Mr. Berin's face and heard him speak less than a minute after he left the dining room last night."

"Maybe you did, but I didn't. If our positions were reversed, would you accept my word and judgment as to the evidence of Berin's face and voice?"

"No."

"Or anyone's?"

"No."

"Have you any information that will explain, or help to explain, the seven errors on Berin's list?"

"No."

"Have you any information in addition to what you have given me that would tend to prove him innocent?"

"No."

"All right." Tolman sat back. He looked at me resentfully and accusingly, which struck me as unfair, and then let his eyes go back to Wolfe. His jaw was working in a nervous side-to-side movement, and after a while he seemed to become suddenly aware of that and clamped it tight. Then he loosened it again. "Candidly, I was hoping you would have. From what Goodwin said, I thought maybe you did. You said if you were in my place you'd resign. But what the devil good . . ."

I didn't get to hear the rest of it, on account of another rupture to

Wolfe's plans for an afternoon of peaceful privacy. The knock on the outer door was loud and prolonged. I went to the foyer and opened up, half expecting to see the two visitors from New York again, in view of the recent developments, but instead it was a trio of a different nature: Louis Servan, Vukčić, and Constanza Berin.

Vukčić was brusque. "We want to see Mr. Wolfe."

I told them to come in. "If you wouldn't mind waiting in here?" I indicated my room. "He's engaged at the moment with Mr. Barry Tolman."

Constanza backed up, and bumped the wall of the foyer. "Oh!" Her expression would have been justified if I had told her that I had my pockets full of toads and snakes and poisonous lizards. She made a dive for the knob of the outer door. Vukčić grabbed her arm, and I said, "Now, hold it. Can Mr. Wolfe help it if an attractive young fellow insists on coming to cry on his shoulder? Here, this way, all of you."

The door to Wolfe's room opened and Tolman appeared. It was a little dim in the foyer, and it took him a second to call the roll. When he saw her, what aplomb he had called it a day. He stared at her and turned a muddy white, and his mouth opened three times for words which got delayed en route. It didn't seem that she got any satisfaction out of the state he was in, for apparently she didn't see him; she looked at me and said that she supposed they could see Mr. Wolfe now, and Vukčić took her elbow, and Tolman sidestepped in a daze to let them by. I stayed behind to let Tolman out, which I did after he had exchanged a couple of words with Servan.

The new influx appeared neither to cheer Wolfe nor enrage him. He received Miss Berin without enthusiasm but with a little extra courtesy, and apologized to Vukčić and Servan for having stayed away all day from the gathering at Pocahontas Pavilion. Servan assured him politely that under the unhappy circumstances no apology was required, and Vukčić sat down and ran all his fingers through his dense tangle of hair and growled something about the rotten luck for the meeting of the Fifteen Masters. Wolfe inquired if the scheduled activities would be abandoned, and Servan shook his head. No, Servan said, they would continue with affairs although his heart was broken. He had for years been looking forward to the time when, as *doyen* of Les Quinze Maîtres, he would have the great honor of entertaining them as his guests; it was to have been the climax of his career, fitting and sweet in his old age; and what had happened was an incredible disaster. Nevertheless they would proceed; he would that evening, as dean and host, deliver his paper on "Les Mystêres du Goût," on the preparation of which he had spent two years; at noon the next day they would elect new members—now, alas, four—to replace those deceased; and Thursday evening they would hear Mr. Wolfe's discourse on "Contributions Américaines à la Haute Cuisine." What a calamity, what a destruction of friendly confraternity!

Wolfe said, "But such melancholy, Mr. Servan, is the worst possible frame of mind for digestion. Since placidity is out of the question, wouldn't active hostility be better? Hostility for the person responsible?"

Servan's brows went up. "You mean for Berin?"

"Good heavens, no. I said the person responsible. I don't think Berin did it."

"Oh!" It was a cry from Constanza. From the way she jerked up in her chair and the look she threw at Wolfe, I was expecting her to hop over and kiss him, or at least spill ginger ale on him, but she just sat and looked.

Vukčić growled, "They seem to think they have proof. About those seven mistakes on his list of the sauces. How the devil could that be?"

"I have no idea. Why, Marko, do you think Berin did it?"

"No. I don't think." Vukčić ran his fingers through his hair again. "It's a hell of a thing. For a while they suspected me; they thought because I had been dancing with Dina my blood was warm. It was warm!" He sounded defiant. "You wouldn't understand that, Nero. With a woman like that. She has a fire in her that warmed me once, and it could again, no doubt of that; if it came near and I felt it and let my head go, I could throw myself in it." He shrugged and suddenly got savage. "But to stab that dog in the back—I would not have done him that honor! Pull his nose well, is all one does with that sort of fellow!

"But look here, Nero." Vukčić tossed his head around. "I brought Miss Berin and Mr. Servan around to see you. I suggested it. If we had found that you thought Berin guilty, I don't know what could have been said, but luckily you don't. It has been discussed over there among most of us, and the majority have agreed to contribute to a purse for Berin's defense—since he is here in a country strange to him—and certainly I told them that the best way to defend him is to enlist you—"

"But, please," Servan broke in earnestly, "please, Mr. Wolfe, understand that we deplore the necessity we can't avoid—you are our guest, my guest, and I know it is unforgivable that under the circumstances we should dare to ask you—"

"But the fact is," Vukčić took it up, "that they were quite generous in their contributions to the purse, after I explained your habits in the matter of fees—"

Constanza had edged to the front of her chair and now put in an oar. "The eleven thousand francs I promised, it will take a while to get them because they're in the bank in Nice—"

"Confound it." Wolfe had to make it almost a shout. He wiggled a finger at Servan. "Apparently, sir, Marko has informed you of my rapacity. He was correct. I need lots of money, and ordinarily my clients get soaked. But he could have told you that I am also an incurable romantic. To me the relationship of host and guest is sacred. The guest is a jewel resting on the cushion of hospitality. The host is king, in his parlor and his kitchen, and should not condescend to a lesser role. So we won't discuss—"

"Damn all the words!" Vukčić gestured impatiently. "What do you mean, Nero? You won't do anything about Berin?"

"No. I mean we won't discuss purses and fees. Certainly I shall do something about Berin—I had already decided to before you came—but I won't take money from my hosts for it. And there is no time to lose, and I want to be alone here to consider the matter. But since you are here—" His eyes moved to Constanza. "Miss Berin. You seem to be convinced that your father didn't kill Mr. Laszio. Why?"

Her eyes widened at him. "Why? You're convinced too. You said so. My father wouldn't."

"Never mind about me. Speaking to the law, which is what we're dealing with, what evidence have you? Any?"

"Why, only—it's absurd! Anyone—"

"I see. You haven't any. Have you any notion or any evidence as to who did kill Laszio?"

"No! And I don't care! Only anyone would know—"

"Please, Miss Berin. I warn you, we have a difficult task and little time for it. I suggest that on leaving here you go to your room, compose your emotions, and in your mind thoroughly recapitulate—go back over—all you have seen and heard, everything, since your arrival at Kanawha Spa. Do it thoroughly. Write down anything that appears to have the faintest significance. Remember this is a job, and the only one you can perform that offers any chance of helping your father."

He moved his eyes again. "Mr. Servan. First, the same questions as Miss Berin. Proof of Berin's innocence or surmise or evidence of another's guilt. Have you any?"

Servan slowly shook his head.

"That's too bad. I must warn you, sir, that it will probably develop that the only way of clearing Berin is to find where the guilt belongs and fasten it there. We can't clear everybody; after all, Laszio's dead. If you know of anything that would throw suspicion elsewhere and withhold it, you can't pretend to be helping Berin."

The dean of the masters shook his head again. "I know of nothing that would implicate anybody."

"Very well. About Berin's list of the sauces. He handed it to you himself?"

"Yes, immediately on leaving the dining room."

"It bore his signature?"

"Yes. I looked at each one before putting it in my pocket, to be sure they could be identified."

"How sure are you that no one had a chance to change Berin's list after he handed it to you, before you gave it to Mr. Tolman?"

"Positive. Absolutely. The lists were in my inside breast pocket every moment. Of course, I showed them to no one."

Wolfe regarded him a little, sighed, and turned to Vukčić. "You, Marko. What do you know?"

"I don't know a damned thing."

"Did you ask Mrs. Laszio to dance with you?"

"I—what's that got to do with it?"

Wolfe eyed him and murmured, "Now, Marko. At the moment I haven't the faintest idea how I shall discover what must be discovered, and I must be permitted any question short of insult. Did you ask Mrs. Laszio to dance or did she ask you?"

Vukčić wrinkled his forehead and sat. Finally he growled, "I think she suggested it. I might have if she didn't."

"Did you ask her to turn on the radio?"

"No."

"Then the radio and the dancing at that particular moment were her ideas?"

"Damn it." Vukčić was scowling at his old friend. "I swear I don't see, Nero—"

"Of course you don't. Neither do I. But sometimes it's astonishing how the end of a tangled knot gets buried. It is said that two sure ways to lose a friend are to lend him money and to question the purity of a woman's gesture to him. I wouldn't lose your friendship. It is quite likely that Mrs. Laszio found the desire to dance with you irresistible. No, Marko, please; I mean no flippancy. And now, if you don't mind, Miss Berin? Mr. Servan? I must consider this business."

They got up. Servan tried, delicately, to mention the purse again, but Wolfe brushed it aside. Constanza went over and took Wolfe's hand and looked at him with an expression that may or may not have been pure but certainly had appeal in it. Vukčić hadn't quite erased his scowl but joined the others in their thanks and seemed to mean it. I went to the foyer with them to open the door.

Returning, I sat and watched Wolfe consider. He was leaning back in his favorite position, though by no means as comfortably as in his own chair at home, with his eyes closed. He might have been asleep but for the faint movement of his lips. I did a little considering on my own hook, but I admit mine was limited. It looked to me like Berin, but I was willing to let in either Vukčić or Blanc in case they insisted. As far as I could see, everyone else was absolutely out. Of course there was still the possibility that Laszio had been absent from the dining room only temporarily, during Vukčić's session with the dishes, and had later returned and Vallenko or Rossi had mistaken him for a pincushion before or after tasting, but I couldn't see any juice in that. I had been in the large parlor the entire evening, and I tried to remember whether I had at any time noticed anyone enter the small parlor—or, rather, whether I would have been able to swear that no one had. I thought I would. After over half an hour of overworking my brain, it still looked to me like Berin, and I thought it just as well Wolfe had turned down two offers of a fee, since it didn't seem very probable he was going to earn one.

I saw Wolfe stir. He opened his mouth but not his eyes.

"Archie. Those two colored men on duty in the main foyer of Pocahontas Pavilion last evening. Find out where they are."

I went to the phone in my room, deciding that the quickest way was to get hold of my friend Odell and let him do it. In less than ten minutes I was back again with the report.

"They went on at Pocahontas again at six o'clock. The same two. It is now 6:07. Their names—"

"No, thanks. I don't need the names." Wolfe pulled himself up and looked at me. "We have an enemy who has sealed himself in. He fancies himself impregnable, and he well may be—no door, no gate, no window in his walls—or hers. Possibly hers. But there is one little crack, and we'll have to see if we can pry it open." He sighed. "Amazing what a wall that is; that one crack is all I see. If that fails us—" He shrugged. Then he said bitterly, "As you know, we are dressing for dinner this evening. I would like to get to the pavilion as quickly as possible. What the tongue has promised the body must submit to."

He began operations for leaving his chair.

7

It was still twenty minutes short of seven o'clock when we got to Pocahontas. Wolfe had done pretty well with the black and white, considering that Fritz Brenner was nearly a thousand miles away, and I could have hired out as a window dummy.

Naturally I had some curiosity about Wolfe's interest in the greenjackets, but it didn't get satisfied. In the main hall, after we had been relieved of our hats, he motioned me on into the parlor, and he stayed behind. I noted that Odell's information was correct; the two men were the same that had been on duty the evening before.

It was more than an hour until dinnertime, and there was no one in the large parlor except Mamma Mondor, knitting and sipping sherry, and Vallenko and Keith, with Lisette Putti between them, chewing the rag on a divan. I said hello and strolled over and tried to ask Mamma Mondor what was the French word for knitting, but she seemed dumb at signs and began to get excited, and it looked as if it might end in a fight, so I shoved off.

Wolfe entered from the hall, and I saw by the look in his eye that he hadn't lost the crack he had mentioned. He offered greetings around, made a couple of inquiries, and was informed that Louis Servan was in the kitchen, overlooking the preparations for dinner. Then he came up to me and in a low tone outlined briefly an urgent errand. I thought he had a nerve to wait until I had my glad rags on to ask me to work up a sweat, particularly since no fee was involved, but I went for my hat without stopping to grumble.

I cut across the lawn to get to the main path and headed for the hotel. On the way I decided to use Odell again instead of trying to develop new contacts, and luckily I ran across him in the corridor by the elevators without having to make inquiries. He looked at me, pleased and expectant.

"Did you tell Wolfe? Has he seen Liggett?"

"Nope, not yet. Give us time, can't you? Don't you worry, old boy.

Right now I need some things in a hurry. I need a good ink pad, preferably a new one, and fifty or sixty sheets of smooth white paper, preferably glazed, and a magnifying glass."

"Jumping Jesus!" He stared at me. "Who you working for, J. Edgar Hoover?"

"No. It's all right, we're having a party. Maybe Liggett will be there. Step on it, huh?"

He told me to wait there and disappeared around the corner. In five minutes he was back with all three items. As I took them he told me, "I'll have to put the pad and paper on the bill. The glass is a personal loan—don't forget and skip with it."

I told him okay, thanked him, and beat it. On the way back I took the path which would carry me past Upshur, and I made a stop there and sought Suite 60. I got a can of talcum powder from my bathroom and stuck it in my pocket, and my pen and a notebook, then found the copy of the *Journal of Criminology* I had brought along and thumbed through it to some plates illustrating new classifications of fingerprints. I cut one of the pages out of the magazine with my knife, rolled it up in the paper Odell had given me, and trotted out again and across to Pocahontas. All the time I was trying to guess at the nature of the crack Wolfe thought he was going to pry open with that array of materials.

I got no light on that point from Wolfe. He had apparently been busy, for though I hadn't been gone more than fifteen minutes I found him established in the biggest chair in the small parlor, alongside the same table behind which Tolman had been barricaded against the onslaught of Constanza Berin. Across the table from him, looking skeptical but resigned, was Sergei Vallenko.

Wolfe finished a sentence to Vallenko and then turned to me. "You have everything, Archie? Good. The pad and paper here on the table, please. I've explained to Mr. Servan that if I undertake this inquiry I shall have to ask a few questions of everyone and take fingerprint samples. He has sent Mr. Vallenko to us first. All ten prints, please."

That was a hot one—Nero Wolfe collecting fingerprints, especially after the cops had smeared all over the dining room and it had been reopened to the public! I knew darned well it was phony but hadn't guessed his charade yet, so once again I had to follow his taillight without knowing the road. I got Vallenko's specimens, on two sheets, and labeled them, and Wolfe dismissed him with thanks.

I demanded, when we were alone, "What has this identification bureau—"

"Not now, Archie. Sprinkle powder on Mr. Vallenko's prints."

I stared at him. "In the name of God, why? You don't put powder—"

"It will look more professional and mysterious. Do it. Give me the page from the magazine. Good. Satisfactory. We'll use only the upper half; cut it off and keep it in your pocket. Put the magnifying glass on the table—ah, Mme. Mondor? *Asseyes-vous, s'il vous plaît.*"

She had her knitting along. He asked her some questions of which I never bothered him for a translation, and then turned her over to my department and I put her on record. I never felt sillier in my life than dusting that talcum powder on those fresh clear specimens. Our third customer was Lisette Putti, and she was followed by Keith, Blanc, Rossi, Mondor. Wolfe asked a few questions of all of them, but knowing his voice and manner as well as I did, it sounded to me as if his part of it was as phony as mine. And it certainly didn't sound as if he was prying any crack open.

Then Lawrence Coyne's Chinese wife came in. She was dressed for dinner in red silk, with a sprig of mountain laurel in her black hair, and with her slim figure and little face and narrow eyes she looked like an ad for a Round-the-World cruise. At once I got a hint that it was she we were laying for, for Wolfe told me sharply to take my notebook, which he hadn't done for any of the others, but all he did was ask her the same line of questions and explain about the prints before I took them. However, there appeared to be more to come. As I gave her my handkerchief, already ruined, to wipe the tips of her fingers on, Wolfe settled back.

He murmured, "By the way, Mrs. Coyne, Mr. Tolman tells me that while you were outdoors last evening you saw no one but one of the attendants on one of the paths. You asked him about a bird you heard and he told you it was a whippoorwill. You had never heard a whippoorwill before?"

She had displayed no animation and didn't now. "No, there aren't any in California."

"So I understand. I believe you went outdoors before the tasting of the sauces began and returned to the parlor shortly after Mr. Vukčić entered the dining room. Isn't that right?"

"I went out before they began. I don't know who was in the dining room when I came back."

"I do. Mr. Vukčić." Wolfe's voice was so soft and unconcerned that I knew she was in for something. "Also, you told Mr. Tolman that you were outdoors all the time you were gone. Is that correct?"

She nodded. "Yes."

"When you left the parlor, after dinner, didn't you go to your room before you went outdoors?"

"No, it wasn't cold and I didn't need a wrap."

"All right. I'm just asking. While you were outdoors, though, perhaps you entered the left-wing corridor by way of the little terrace and went to your room that way?"

"No." She sounded dull and calm. "I was outdoors all the time."

"You didn't go to your room at all?"

"No."

"Nor anywhere else?"

"Just outdoors. My husband will tell you, I like to go outdoors at night."

Wolfe grimaced. "And when you re-entered, you came straight through the main hall to the large parlor?"

"Yes, you were there. I saw you there with my husband."

"So you did. And now, Mrs. Coyne, I must admit you have me a little puzzled. Perhaps you can straighten it out. In view of what you have just told me, which agrees with your account to Mr. Tolman, what door was it that you hurt your finger in?"

She deadpanned him good. There wasn't a flicker. Maybe her eyes got a little narrower, but I couldn't see it. But she wasn't good enough to avoid stalling. After about ten seconds of the stony-facing she said, "Oh, you mean my finger." She glanced down at it and up again. "I asked my husband to kiss it."

Wolfe nodded. "I heard you. What door did you hurt it in?"

She was ready. "The big door at the entrance. You know how hard it is to push, and when it closed—"

He broke in sharply, "No, Mrs. Coyne, that won't do. The doorman and the hallman have been questioned and their statements taken. They remember your leaving and re-entering—in fact, they were questioned about it Tuesday night by Mr. Tolman. And they are both completely certain that the doorman opened the door for you and closed it behind you, and there was no caught finger. Nor could it have been the door from the hall to the parlor, for I saw you come through that myself. What door was it?"

She was wearing the deadpan permanently. She said calmly, "The doorman is telling a lie because he was careless and let me get hurt."

"I don't think so."

"I know it. He is lying." Quickly and silently, she was on her feet. "I must tell my husband."

She was off, moving fast. Wolfe snapped, "Archie." I skipped around and got in front of her, on her line to the door. She didn't try dodging, just stopped and looked up at my face. Wolfe said, "Come back and sit down. I can see that you are a person of decision, but so am I. Mr. Goodwin could hold you with one hand. You may scream and people will come, but they will go again and we'll be where we are now. Sit down, please."

She did so and told him, "I have nothing to scream about. I merely wanted to tell my husband—"

"That the doorman lied. But he didn't. However, there's no need to torment you unnecessarily. Archie, give me the photograph of those fingerprints on the dining-room door."

I thought to myself, darn you, someday you're going to push the button for my wits when they're off on vacation, and then you'll learn to let me in on things ahead of time. But of course there was only one answer to this one. I reached in my pocket for the plate of reproductions I had cut from the magazine page and handed it to him. Then, being on at last, I pushed across the specimens I had just taken from Lio Coyne's fingers. Wolfe took the magnifying glass and began to compare. He took his time, holding the two next to each other, looking closely through the glass back and forth, with satisfied nods at the proper intervals.

Finally he said, "Three quite similar. They would probably do. But the left index finger is absolutely identical and it's exceptionally clear. Here, Archie, see what you think."

I took the prints and the glass and put on a performance. The prints from the magazine happened to be from some blunt-fingered mechanic, and I don't believe I ever saw any two sets more unlike. I did a good job of it with the comparison, even counting out loud, and handed them back to Wolfe.

"Yes, sir." I was emphatic. "They're certainly the same. Anyone could see it."

Wolfe told Mrs. Coyne gently, almost tenderly, "You see, madam. I must explain. Of course everyone knows about fingerprints, but some of the newer methods of procuring them are not widely known. Mr. Goodwin here is an expert. He went over the doors from the dining room to the terrace, among other places, and brought out prints which the local police had been unable to discover, and made photographs of them. So, as you see, modern methods of searching for evidence are sometimes fertile. They have given us conclusive proof that it was the door from the terrace to the dining room in which you caught your finger Tuesday evening. I had suspected it before, but there's no need to go into that. I am not asking you to explain anything. Your explanation, naturally, will have to be given to the police, after I have turned this evidence over to them, together with an account of your false statement that it was the main entrance door in which you caught your finger. And by the way, I should warn you to expect little courtesy from the police. After all, you didn't tell Mr. Tolman the truth, and they won't like that. It would have been more sensible if you had admitted frankly, when he asked about your excursion to see the night, that you had entered the dining room from the terrace."

She was as good at the wooden-face act as anyone I could remember. You would have sworn that if her mind was working at all it was on nothing more important than where she could have lost one of her chopsticks. At last she said, "I didn't enter the dining room."

Wolfe shrugged. "Tell the police that. After your lie to Mr. Tolman, and your lies to us here, which are on record in Mr. Goodwin's notebook, and your attempt to accuse the doorman, and, above all, these fingerprints—"

She stretched a hand out. "Give them to me. I'd like to see them."

"The police may show them to you—if they choose. Forgive me, Mrs. Coyne, but this photograph is important evidence, and I'd like to be sure of turning it over to the authorities intact."

She stirred a little, but there was no change on her face. After another silence she said, "I did go into the left-wing corridor. By the little terrace. I went to my room and hurt my finger in the bathroom door. Then when Mr. Laszio was found murdered I was frightened and thought I wouldn't say I had been inside at all."

Wolfe nodded and murmured, "You might try that. Try it, by all means, if you think it's worth it. You realize, of course, that that would leave your fingerprints on the dining-room door to be explained. Anyhow you're in a pickle; you'll have to do the best you can." He turned abruptly to me and got snappy. "Archie, go to the booth in the foyer and phone the police at the hotel. Tell them to come at once."

I arose without excessive haste. I was prepared to stall with a little business with my notebook and pen, but it wasn't necessary. Her face showed signs of life. She blinked up at me and put out a hand at me, and then blinked at Wolfe and extended both her cute little hands in his direction.

"Mr. Wolfe," she pleaded. "Please! I did no harm. I did nothing! Please, not the police!"

"No harm, madam?" Wolfe was stern. "To the authorities investigating a murder you tell lies, and to me also, and you call that no harm? Archie, go on."

"No!" She was on her feet. "I tell you I did nothing!"

"You entered the dining room within minutes, perhaps seconds, of the moment that Laszio was murdered. Did you kill him?"

"No! I did nothing! I didn't enter the dining room!"

"Your hand was on that door. What did you do?"

She stood with her eyes on him, and I stood with a foot poised, aching to call the cops I don't think. She ended the tableau by sitting down and telling Wolfe quietly, "I must tell you, mustn't I?"

"Either me or the police."

"But if I tell you, you tell the police anyway."

"Perhaps. Perhaps not. It depends. In any event, you'll have to tell the truth sooner or later."

"I suppose so." Her hands were on the lap of her red dress with the fingers closely twined. "You see, I'm afraid. The police don't like the Chinese, and I am a Chinese woman, but that isn't it. I'm afraid of the man I saw in the dining room, because he must have killed Mr. Laszio."

Wolfe asked softly, "Who was it?"

"I don't know. But if I told about him, and he knew that I had seen him and had told—anyway, I am telling now. You see, Mr. Wolfe, I was born in San Francisco and educated there, but I am Chinese, and we are never treated like Americans. Never. But anyway, what I told Mr. Tolman was the truth. I was outdoors all the time. I like outdoors at night. I was on the grass among the trees and shrubs, and I heard the whippoorwill, and I went across the driveway where the fountain is. Then I came back, to the side—not the left wing, the other side—and I could see dimly through the window curtains into the parlor, but I couldn't see into the dining room because the shades were drawn on the glass doors. I thought it would be amusing to watch the men tasting those dishes, which seemed very silly to me, so I went to the terrace to find a slit I could see through, but the shades were so tight there wasn't any. Then I heard a noise as if something had fallen over in the dining room. I couldn't hear just what it was like, because the sound of the radio was coming through the open window of the parlor. I stood there I don't know how long, but no other sound came, and I thought that if one of the men had got mad and threw the dishes on the floor that would be amusing, and I decided to open the door a crack and see, and I didn't think I'd be heard on account of the radio. So I opened it just a little. I didn't get it open enough even to see the table, because there was a man standing there by the corner of the screen, with his side turned to me. He had one finger pressed against his lips—you know, the way you do when you're hushing somebody. Then I saw who he was looking at. The door leading to the pantry hall was open, just a few inches, and the face of one of the Negroes was there, looking at the man by the screen. The man by the screen started to turn toward me, and I went to close the door in a hurry and my foot slipped and I grabbed with my other hand to keep from falling, and the door shut on my finger. I thought it would be silly to get caught peeking in the dining room, so I ran back among the bushes and stood there a few minutes, and then I went to the main entrance—and you saw me enter the parlor."

Wolfe demanded, "Who was the man by the screen?"

She shook her head. "I don't know."

"Now, Mrs. Coyne, don't start that again. You saw the man's face."

"I only saw the side of his face. Of course that was enough to tell he was a Negro."

Wolfe blinked. I blinked twice. Wolfe demanded, "A Negro? Do you mean one of the employees here?"

"Yes. In livery. Like the waiters."

"Was it one of the waiters at this pavilion?"

"No, I'm sure it wasn't. He was blacker than them and—I'm sure it wasn't. It wasn't anyone I could recognize."

" 'Blacker than them and' what? What were you going to say?"

"That it wouldn't have been one of the waiters here because he came outdoors and went away. I told you I ran back among the bushes. I had only been there a few seconds when the dining-room door opened and he came out and went around the path toward the rear. Of course I couldn't see very well from behind the bushes, but I supposed it was him."

"Could you see his livery?"

"Yes, a little, when he opened the door and had the light behind him. Then it was dark."

"Was he running?"

"No. Walking."

Wolfe frowned. "The one looking from the door to the pantry hall—was he in livery or was it one of the cooks?"

"I don't know. The door was only open a crack, and I saw mostly his eyes. I couldn't recognize him either."

"Did you see Mr. Laszio?"

"No."

"No one else?"

"No. That's all I saw, just as I've told you. Everything. Then, later, when Mr. Servan told us that Mr. Laszio had been killed, then I knew what it was I had heard. I had heard Mr. Laszio fall, and I had seen the man that killed him. I knew that. I knew it must be that. But I was afraid to tell about it when they asked me questions about going outdoors, and anyway—" Her two little hands went up in a gesture to her bosom and fell to her lap again. "Of course I was sorry when they arrested Mr. Berin, because I knew it was wrong. I was going to wait until I got back home, to San Francisco, and tell my husband about it, and if he said to I was going to write it all down and send it here."

"And in the meantime?" Wolfe shrugged. "Have you told anyone anything about it?"

"Nothing."

"Then don't." Wolfe sat up. "As a matter of fact, Mrs. Coyne, while you have acted selfishly, I confess you have acted wisely. But for the accident that you asked your husband to kiss your finger in my hearing, your secret was safe and therefore you were too. The murderer of Mr. Laszio probably knows that he was seen through that door but not by whom, since you opened it only a few inches and outdoors it was dark. Should he learn that it was you who saw him, even San Francisco might not be far enough away for you. It is in the highest degree advisable to do nothing that will permit him to learn it or cause him to suspect it. Tell no one. Should anyone show curiosity as to why you were kept so long in here while the other interviews were short, and ask you about it, tell him—or her—that you have a racial repugnance to having your fingerprints taken, and it required all my patience to overcome it. Similarly, I undertake that for the present the police will not question you or even approach you, for that might arouse suspicion. And by the way—"

"You won't tell the police?"

"I didn't say I wouldn't. You must trust my discretion. I was about to ask, has anyone questioned you particularly—except the police and me—regarding your visit to the night? Any of the guests here?"

"No."

"You're quite sure? Not even a casual question?"

"No, I don't remember." Her brow was puckered above the narrow eyes. "Of course my husband—"

A tapping on the door interrupted her. Wolfe nodded at me, and I went and opened it. It was Louis Servan. I let him in.

He advanced and told Wolfe apologetically, "I don't like to disturb you, but the dinner—it's five minutes past eight."

"Ah!" Wolfe made it to his feet in less than par. "I have been looking forward to this for six months. Thank you, Mrs. Coyne. Archie, will you take Mrs. Coyne? Could I have a few words with you, Mr. Servan? I'll make it as brief as possible."

8

The dinner of the dean of the Fifteen Masters that evening, which by custom was given on the second day of their gathering once in every five years, was ample and elaborate as to fleshpots but a little spotty as an occasion of festivity. The chatter during the hors d'œuvres was nervous and jerky, and when Domenico Rossi made some loud remark in French three or four of them began to laugh and then suddenly stopped, and in the silence they all looked at one another.

To my surprise, Constanza Berin was there, but not adjoining me as on the evening before. She was on the other side, between Louis Servan, who was at the end, and a funny little duck with an uncontrolled mustache who was new to me. Leon Blanc, on my right, told me he was the French Ambassador. There were several other extra guests, among them my friend Odell's prospective employer, Raymond Liggett of the Hotel Churchill, Clay Ashley, the manager of Kanawha Spa, and Albert Malfi. Malfi's black eyes kept darting up and down the table, and on meeting the eyes of a master he delivered a flashing smile. Leon Blanc pointed a fork at him and told me, "See that fellow Malfi? He wants votes for tomorrow morning as one of Les Quinze Maîtres. Bah! He has no creation, no imagination! Berin trained him, that's all!" He waved the fork in contemptuous dismissal and then used it to scoop a mouthful of shad roe mousse.

The swamp-woman, now a swamp-widow, was absent, but everyone else—except Berin, of course—was there. Apparently Rossi hadn't been much impressed by the murder of his son-in-law; he was still ready for a scrap and full of personal and national comments. Mondor paid no attention to him. Vukčić was gloomy and ate like ten minutes for lunch. Ramsey Keith was close to pie-eyed, and about every five minutes he had a spell of giggles that might have been all right coming from his niece.

During the entrée Leon Blanc told me, "That little Berin girl is a good one. You see her hold herself? Louis put her between him and the Ambassador as a gesture to Berin. She justifies him; she represents her father bravely." Blanc sighed. "You heard what I told Mr. Wolfe in there when he questioned me. This was to be expected of Phillip Laszio, to let his sins catch up with him on this occasion. Infamy was in his blood. If he were alive I could kill him now—only I don't kill. I am a chef, but I couldn't be a butcher." He swallowed a mouthful of stewed rabbit and sighed again. "Look at Louis. This is a great affair for him, and this civet de lapin is in fact perfection, except for a slight excess of bouquet garni, possibly because the rabbits were young and tender-flavored. Louis deserved gaiety for this dinner and this salute to his cuisine, and look at us!" He went at the rabbit again.

The peak of the evening for me came with the serving of coffee and liqueurs, when Louis Servan arose to deliver his talk, which he had worked on for two years, on "the mysteries of taste." I was warm and full inside, sipping a cognac which made me shut my eyes as it trickled into my throat—and I'm not a gourmet—so as not to leave any extra openings for the vapor to escape by, and I was prepared to be quietly entertained, maybe even instructed up to a point. Then he began: *"Mesdames et messieurs, mes confrères des Quinze Maîtres, Il y a plus que cent ans un homme fameux, Brillat-Savarin le grand . . ."*

He went on from there. I was stuck. If I had known beforehand of the dean's intentions as to language I would have negotiated some sort of arrangement, but I couldn't simply get up and beat it. Anyway, the cognac bottle was two-thirds full, and the fundamental problem was to keep my eyes open, so I settled back to watch his gestures and mouth work. I guess it was a good talk. There were signs of appreciation throughout the hour and a half it lasted, nods and smiles and brows lifted, and applause here and there, and once in a while Rossi cried "Bravo!" And when Ramsey Keith got a fit of giggles Servan stopped and waited politely until Lisette Putti got him shushed. Once it got embarrassing, at least for me, when at the end of a sentence Servan was silent, and looked slowly around the table and couldn't go on, and two big tears left his eyes and rolled down his cheeks. There were murmurs, and Leon Blanc beside me blew his nose, and I cleared my throat a couple of times and reached for the cognac. When it was over they all left their places and gathered around him and shook hands, and a couple of them kissed him.

They drifted into the parlor in groups. I looked around for Constanza Berin, but apparently she had used up all her bravery for one evening, for she had disappeared. I turned to a hand on my arm and a voice.

"Pardon me, you are Mr. Goodwin? Mr. Rossi told me your name. I saw you this afternoon with Mr. Wolfe."

I acknowledged everything. It was Albert Malfi, the entrée man with no imagination. He made a remark or two about the dinner and Servan's speech and then went on, "I understand that Mr. Wolfe has changed his mind. He has been persuaded to investigate the—that is, the murder. I suppose that was because Mr. Berin was arrested?"

"No, I don't think so. It's just because he's a guest. A guest is a jewel resting on the cushion of hospitality."

"No doubt. Of course." The Corsican's eyes darted around and back to me. "There is something I think I should tell Mr. Wolfe."

"There he is." I nodded at where Wolfe was chinning with a trio of the masters. "Go tell him."

"But I don't like to interrupt him. He is the guest of honor of Les Quinze Maîtres." Malfi sounded awed. "I just thought I would ask you—perhaps I could see him in the morning? It may not be important. Today we were talking with Mrs. Laszio, Mr. Liggett and I, and I was telling her about it—"

"Yeah?" I eyed him. "You a friend of Mrs. Laszio's?"

"Not a friend. A woman like her doesn't have friends, only slaves. I know her of course. I was telling about this Zelota, and she and Mr. Liggett thought Mr. Wolfe should know. That was before Berin was arrested, when it was thought someone might have entered the dining room from the terrace and killed Laszio. But if Mr. Wolfe is interested to clear Berin, certainly he should know." Malfi smiled at me. "You frown, Mr. Goodwin? You think if Berin is not cleared that would suit my ambition, and why am I so unselfish? I am not unselfish. It would be the greatest thing in my life if I could become *chef de cuisine* of the Hotel Churchill. But Jerome Berin saw my talent in the little inn at Ajaccio and took me into the world, and guided me with his genius, and I would not pay for my glory with his misfortune. Besides, I know him; he would not have killed Laszio that way, from behind. So I think I should tell Mr. Wolfe about Zelota. Mrs. Laszio and Mr. Liggett think the same. Mr. Liggett says it would do no good to tell the police, because they are satisfied with Berin."

I meditated on him. I was trying to remember where I had heard the name Zelota, and all at once it came to me. I said, "Uh-huh. You mean Zelota of Tarragona. Laszio stole something from him in 1920."

Malfi looked surprised. "You know of Zelota?"

"Oh, a little. A few things. What's he been up to? Or would you rather wait and tell Wolfe about it in the morning?"

"Not necessarily. Zelota is in New York."

"Well, he's got lots of company." I grinned. "Being in New York is no crime. It's full of people who didn't kill Laszio. Now if he was in Kanawha Spa, that might be different."

"But maybe he is."

"He can't be in two places at once. Even a jury wouldn't believe that."

"But he might have come here. I don't know what you know about Zelota, but he hated Laszio more than—" Malfi shrugged. "He hated him bitterly. Berin often spoke to me about it. And about a month ago Zelota turned up in New York. He came and asked me for a job. I didn't give him one, because there is nothing left of him but a wreck, drink has ruined him, and because I remembered what Berin had told me about him and I thought perhaps he wanted a job at the Churchill only for a chance to get at Laszio. I heard later that Vukčić gave him a job on soup at Rusterman's, and he only lasted a week." He shrugged again. "That's all. I told Mrs. Laszio and Mr. Liggett about it, and they said I should tell Mr. Wolfe. I don't know anything more about Zelota."

"Well, much obliged. I'll tell Wolfe. Will you still be here in the morning?"

He said yes, and his eyes began to dart around again and he shoved off, apparently to electioneer. I strolled around a while, finding opportunities for a few morsels of harmless eavesdropping, and then I saw Wolfe's finger crooked at me and went to him. He announced that it was time to leave.

Which suited me. I was ready for the hay. I went to the hall and got our hats and waited with them, yawning, while Wolfe completed his good nights. He joined me and we started out, but he stopped on the threshold and told me, "By the way, Archie, give these men a dollar each. Appreciation for good memories."

I shelled out to the two greenjackets, from the expense roll.

In our own Suite 60, over at Upshur, having switched on the lights and closed a window so the breeze wouldn't chill his delicate skin while undressing, I stood in the middle of his room and stretched and enjoyed a real yawn.

"It's a funny thing about me. If I once get to bed really late, like last night at four o'clock, I'm not really myself again until I catch up. I was afraid you were going to hang around over there and chew the rag. As it is, it's going on for midnight—"

I stopped because his actions looked suspicious. He wasn't even unbuttoning his vest. Instead, he was getting himself arranged in the big chair in a manner which indicated that he expected to be there a while.

I demanded, "Are you going to start your brain going at this time of night? Haven't you done enough for one evening?"

"Yes." He sounded grim. "But there is more to do. I arranged with Mr. Servan for the cooks and waiters of Pocahontas Pavilion to call on us as soon as they have finished. They will be here in a quarter of an hour."

"Well, for God's sake!" I sat down. "Since when have we been on the night shift?"

"Since we found Mr. Laszio with a knife in him." He sounded grimmer. "We have but little time. Not enough, perhaps, in view of Mrs. Coyne's story."

"And those blackbirds coming in a flock? At least a dozen."

"If by blackbirds you mean men with dark skin, yes."

"I mean Africans." I stood up again. "Listen, boss. You've lost your sense of direction, honest you have. Africans or blackbirds or whatever you like, they can't be handled this way. They don't intend to tell anything or they would have told that squint-eyed sheriff when he questioned them. Are you expecting me to use a carpetbeater on the whole bunch? The only thing is to get Tolman and the sheriff here first thing in the morning to hear Mrs. Coyne's tale, and let them go on from there."

Wolfe grunted. "They arrive at eight o'clock. They hear her story and they believe it or they don't—after all, she is Chinese. They question her at length, and even if they believe her they do not immediately release Berin, for her story doesn't explain the errors on his list. At noon they begin with the Negroes, singly. God knows what they do or how much time they take, but the chances are that Thursday midnight, when our train leaves for New York, they will not have finished with the Negroes, and they may have discovered nothing."

"They're more apt to than you are. I'm warning you, you'll see. These Negroes can take it, they're used to it. Do you believe Mrs. Coyne's tale?"

"Certainly, it was obvious."

"Would you mind telling me how you knew she had hurt her finger in the dining-room door?"

"I didn't. I knew she had told Tolman that she had gone directly outside, had stayed outside, and had returned directly to the parlor; and I knew that she had hurt her finger in a door. When she told me she had caught her finger in the main entrance door, which I knew to be untrue, I knew she was concealing something, and I proceeded to make use of the evidence we had prepared."

"*I* had prepared." I sat down. "Someday you'll try to bluff the trees out of their leaves. Would you mind telling me now what motive one of these fellows had for bumping off Laszio?"

"I suppose he was hired." Wolfe grimaced. "I don't like murderers, though I make my living through them. But I particularly dislike murderers who buy the death they seek. One who kills at least keeps the blood on his own hands. One who pays for killing—pfui. That is worse than repugnant, it is dishonorable. I presume the colored man was hired. Naturally, that's an annoying complication for us."

"Not so terrible." I waved a hand. "They'll be here pretty soon. I'll arrange them for you in a row. Then you'll give them a little talk on citizenship and the Ten Commandments, and explain how illegal it is to croak a guy for money even if you get paid in advance, and then you'll ask whoever stabbed Laszio to raise his hand and his hand will shoot up, and then all you'll have to do is ask who paid him and how much—"

"That will do, Archie." He sighed. "It's amazing how patiently and with what forbearance I have tolerated—but there they are. Let them in."

That was an instance when Wolfe himself jumped to an unwarranted conclusion, which was a crime he often accused me of. For when I made it through the foyer and opened the door to the hall, it wasn't Africans I found waiting there but Dina Laszio. I stared at her a second, adjusting myself to the surprise.

She put her long sleepy eyes on me and said, "I'm sorry to disturb you so late, but may I see Mr. Wolfe?"

I told her to wait and returned to the inner chamber.

"Not men with dark skin but a woman. Mrs. Phillip Laszio wants to see you."

"What? Her?"

"Yes, sir. In a dark cloak and no hat."

Wolfe grimaced. "Confound that woman. Bring her in here."

9

I sat and watched and listened and felt cynical. Wolfe rubbed his cheek with the tip of his forefinger, slowly and rhythmically, which meant he was irritated but attentive. Dina Laszio was on a chair facing him, with her cloak thrown back, her smooth neck showing above a plain black dress with no collar, her body at ease, her eyes dark in shadow.

Wolfe said, "No apology is needed, madam. Just tell me about it. I'm expecting callers and am pressed for time."

"It's about Marko," she said.

"Indeed. What about Marko?"

"You're so brusque." She smiled a little, and the smile clung to the corners of her mouth. "You should know that you can't expect a woman to be direct like that. We don't take the road, we wind around. You know that. Only I wonder how much you know about women like me."

"I couldn't say. Are you a special kind?"

She nodded. "I think I am. Yes, I know I am. Not because I want to be or try to be, but–" She made a little gesture. "It has made my life exciting but not very comfortable. It will end–I don't know how it will end. Right now I am worried about Marko, because he thinks you suspect him of killing my husband."

Wolfe stopped rubbing his cheek. He told her, "Nonsense."

"No, it isn't. He thinks that."

"Why? Did you tell him so?"

"No. And I resent–" She stopped herself. She leaned forward, her head a little on one side, her lips not quite meeting, and looked at him. I watched her with pleasure. I suppose she was telling the truth when she said she didn't try to be a special kind of woman, but she didn't have to try. There was something in her–not only in her face, it came right out through her clothes–that gave you an instinctive impulse to start in that direction. I kept on being cynical, but it was easy to appreciate that there might be a time when cynicism wouldn't be enough.

She asked with a soft breath, "Mr. Wolfe, why do you always jab at me? What have you got against me? Yesterday, when I told you what Phillip told me about the arsenic, and now when I tell you about Marko . . ." She leaned back. "Marko told me once, long ago, that you don't like women."

Wolfe shook his head. "I can only say, nonsense again. I couldn't rise to that impudence. Not like women? They are astounding and successful animals. For reasons of convenience, I merely preserve an appearance of immunity which I developed some years ago under the pressure of necessity. I confess to a specific animus toward you. Marko Vukčić is my friend; you were his wife and you deserted him. I don't like you."

"So long ago!" She fluttered a hand. Then she shrugged. "Anyway, I am here now in Marko's behalf."

"You mean he sent you?"

"No. But I came for him. It is known, of course, that you have engaged to free Berin of the charge of killing my husband. How can you do that except by accusing Marko? Berin says Phillip was in the dining room, alive, when he left. Marko says Phillip was not there when he entered. So if not Berin, it must have been Marko. And then, you asked Marko today if he asked me to dance or suggested that I turn on the radio. There could be only one reason why you asked him that: because you suspected that he wanted the radio going so that no noise would be heard from the dining room when he—if anything happened in there."

"So Marko told you that I asked about the radio?"

"Yes." She smiled faintly. "He thought I should know. You see, he has forgiven what you will not forgive . . ."

I missed the rest of that on account of a knock on the door. I went to the foyer, closing the door of Wolfe's room behind me, and opened up. The sight in the hall gave me a shock, even though I had been warned. It looked like half of Harlem. Four or five were greenjackets who a couple of hours back had been serving the dean's dinner to us, and the others, the cooks and helpers, were in their own clothes. The light brown, middle-aged one in front with the bottom of one ear chopped off was the headwaiter in charge at Pocahontas, and I felt friendly to him because it was he who had left the cognac bottle smack in front of me at the table. I told them to come on in and stepped aside not to get trampled, and directed them through to my room and followed them in.

"You'll have to wait in here, boys. Mr. Wolfe has a visitor. Sit on something. Sit on the bed—it's mine and it looks like I won't be using it anyway. If you go to sleep, snore a couple of good ones for me."

I left them there and went back to see how Wolfe was getting along with the woman he didn't like. Neither of them bothered with a glance at me as I sat down.

She was saying, ". . . but I know nothing about it beyond what I told you yesterday. Certainly I know there are other possibilities besides Berin and Marko. As you say, someone could have entered the dining room from the terrace. That's what you're thinking of, isn't it?"

"It's a possibility. But go back a little, Mrs. Laszio. Do you mean to say that Marko Vukčić told you of my asking him about the radio and expressed the fear that I suspected him of having the radio turned on to give him an opportunity for killing your husband?"

"Well—" She hesitated. "Not exactly like that. Marko would not express a fear. But the way he told me about it—that was obviously in his mind. So I've come to you to find out if you do suspect him."

"You've come to defend him? Or to make sure that my clumsiness hasn't missed *that* inference from the timeliness of the radio?"

"Neither." She smiled at him. "You can't make me angry, Mr. Wolfe. Why, do you make other inferences? Many of them?"

Wolfe shook his head impatiently. "You can't do that, madam. Give it up. I mean your affected insouciance. I don't mind fencing when there's time for it, but it's midnight and there are men in that other room waiting to see me. Please let me finish. Let me clear away some fog. I have admitted an animus toward you. I knew Marko Vukčić both before and after he married you. I saw the change in him. Then why was I not grateful when you suddenly selected a new field for your activities? Because you left debris behind you. It is not decent to induce the cocaine habit in a man, but it is monstrous to do so and then suddenly withdraw his supply of the drug. Nature plainly intends that a man should nourish a woman, and a woman a man, physically and spiritually, but there is no nourishment in you for anybody; the vapor that comes from you, from your eyes, your lips, your soft skin, your contours, your movements, is not beneficent but malignant. I'll grant you everything: you were alive, with your instincts and appetites, and you saw Marko and wanted him. You enveloped him with your miasma—you made that the only air he wanted to breathe—and then by caprice, without warning, you deprived him of it and left him gasping."

She didn't bat an eyelash. "But I told you I was a special kind—"

"Permit me. I haven't finished. I am seizing an opportunity to articulate a grudge. I was wrong to say caprice; it was cold calculation. You went to Laszio, a man twice your age, because it was a step up, not emotionally but materially. Probably you had also found that Marko had too much character for you. The devil only knows why you went no higher than Laszio, in so broad a field as New York, who after all, from your standpoint, was only a salaried chef. But of course you were young, in your twenties—how old are you now?"

She smiled at him.

He shrugged. "I suppose, too, it was a matter of intelligence. You can't have much. Essentially, in fact, you are a lunatic, if a lunatic is an individual dangerously maladjusted to the natural and healthy environment of its species—since the human equipment includes, for instance, a capacity for personal affection and a willingness to strangle selfish and predatory impulse with the rope of social decency. That's why I say you're a lunatic." He sat up and wiggled a finger at her. "Now look here. I haven't time for fencing. I do not suspect Marko of killing your husband, though I admit it is possible he did it. I have considered all the plausible inferences from the coincidence of the radio, am still considering them, and have reached no conclusion. What else do you want to know?"

"All that you said"—her hand fluttered and rested again on the arm of her chair—"did Marko tell you all that about me?"

"Marko hasn't mentioned your name for five years. What else do you want to know?"

She stirred. I saw her breast go up and down, but there was no sound of the soft sigh. "It wouldn't do any good, since I'm a lunatic. But I thought I would ask you if Malfi had told you about Zelota."

"No. What about him? Who is he?"

I horned in. "He told me." Their eyes moved to me, and I went on, "I hadn't had a chance to report it. Malfi told me in the parlor after dinner that Laszio stole something a long time ago from a guy named Zelota, and Zelota had sworn to kill him, and about a month ago he showed up in New York and went to Malfi to ask for a job. Malfi wouldn't give him one, but Vukčić did, at Rusterman's, and Zelota only lasted a week and then disappeared. Malfi said he told Liggett and Mrs. Laszio about it, and they thought he ought to tell you."

"Thanks. Anything else, madam?"

She sat and looked at him. Her lids were so low that I couldn't see what her eyes were like, and I doubted if he could. Then without saying anything she pulled a hot one. She got up, taking her time, leaving her cloak there on the back of the chair, and stepped over to Wolfe and put her hand on his shoulder and patted it. He moved and twisted his big neck to look up at her, but she stepped away again with a smile at the corners of her mouth and reached for the cloak. I hopped across to hold it for her, thinking I might as well get a pat too, but apparently she didn't believe in spoiling the help. She told Wolfe good night, neither sweet nor sour, just good night, and started off. I went to the foyer to let her out.

I returned and grinned down at Wolfe. "Well, how do you feel? Was she marking you for slaughter? Or putting a curse on you? Or is that how she starts the miasma going?" I peered at the shoulder she had patted. "About this Zelota business, I was going to tell you when she interrupted us. You noticed that Malfi said she told him to tell you about it. It seems that Malfi and Liggett were with her during the afternoon to offer consolation."

Wolfe nodded. "But, as you see, she is inconsolable. Bring those men in."

10

It looked hopeless to me. I would have made it at least ten to one that Wolfe's unlimited conceit was going to cost us most of a night's sleep with nothing to chalk up against it. It struck me as plain silly, and I might have gone so far as to say that his tackling that array of Africans in a body showed a dangerous maladjustment to the natural and healthy environment of a detective. Picture it: Lio Coyne had caught a glimpse of a greenjacket she couldn't recognize standing by the end of the screen with his finger on his lips, and another Negro's face—chiefly his eyes, and she couldn't recognize him either—peeking through a crack in the door that led to the pantry hall and on to the kitchen. That was our crop of facts. And the fellows had already told the sheriff that they had seen and heard nothing. Fat chance. There might have been a slim one if they had been taken singly, but in a bunch like that, not for my money.

The chair problem was solved by letting them sit on the floor. Fourteen altogether. Wolfe, using his man-to-man tone, apologized for that. Then he wanted to know their names and made sure that he got everyone; that used up ten minutes. I was curious to see how he would start the ball rolling, but there were other preliminaries to attend to; he asked what they would like to drink. They mumbled that they didn't want anything, but he said nonsense, we would probably be there most of the night, which seemed to startle them and caused some murmuring. It ended by my being sent to the phone to order an assortment of beer, bourbon, ginger ale, charged water, glasses, lemons, mint, and ice. An expenditure like that meant that Wolfe was in dead earnest.

When I rejoined the gathering he was telling a plump little man, not a greenjacket, with a ravine in his chin, "I'm glad of this opportunity to express my admiration, Mr. Crabtree. Mr. Servan tells me that the shad roe mousse was handled entirely by you. Any chef would have been proud of it. I noticed that Mr. Mondor asked for more. In Europe they don't have shad roe."

The man nodded solemnly, with reserve. They were all using plenty of reserve, not to mention constraint, suspicion, and reticence. Most of them weren't looking at Wolfe or at much of anything else.

Wolfe sat facing them, running his eyes over them. Finally he sighed and began. "You know, gentlemen, I have had very little experience in dealing with black men. That may strike you as a tactless remark, but it really isn't. It is certainly true that you can't deal with all men alike. It is popularly supposed that in this part of the country whites adopt a well-defined attitude in dealing with the blacks, and blacks do the same in dealing with whites. That is no doubt true up to a point, but it is subject to enormous variation, as your own experience will show you. For instance, say you wish to ask a favor here at Kanawha Spa, and you approach either Mr. Ashley, the manager, or Mr. Servan. Ashley is bourgeois, irritable, conventional, and rather pompous. Servan is gentle, generous, sentimental, and an artist—and also Latin. Your approach to Mr. Ashley would be quite different from your approach to Mr. Servan.

"But even more fundamental than the individual differences are the racial and national and tribal differences. That's what I mean when I say I've had limited experience in dealing with black men. I mean black Americans. Many years ago I handled some affairs with dark-skinned people in Egypt and Arabia and Algiers, but of course that has nothing to do with you. You gentlemen are Americans, much more completely Americans than I am, for I wasn't born here. This is your native country. It was you and your brothers, black and white, who let me come here to live, and I hope you'll let me say, without getting maudlin, that I'm grateful to you for it."

Somebody mumbled something. Wolfe disregarded it and went on. "I asked Mr. Servan to have you come over here tonight because I want to ask you some questions and find out something. That's the only thing I'm interested in: the information I want to get. I'll be frank with you; if I thought I could get it by bullying you and threatening you, I wouldn't hesitate a moment. I wouldn't use physical violence even if I could, because one of my romantic ideas is that physical violence is beneath the dignity of a man, and that whatever you get by physical aggression costs more than it is worth. But I confess that if I thought threats or tricks would serve my purpose with you, I wouldn't hesitate to use them. I'm convinced they wouldn't, having meditated on this situation, and that's why I'm in a hole. I have been told by white Americans that the only way to get anything out of black Americans is by threats, tricks, or violence. In the first place, I doubt if it's true; and even if it is true generally, I'm sure it isn't in this case. I know of no threats that would be effective, I can't think up a trick that would work, and I can't use violence."

Wolfe put his hands at them, palms up. "I need the information. What are we going to do?"

Someone snickered, and others glanced at him—a tall skinny one squatting against the wall, with high cheekbones, dark brown. The man whom Wolfe had complimented on the shad roe mousse glared around like a sergeant at talking in the ranks. The one that sat stillest was the one with the flattest nose, a young one, big and muscular, a greenjacket that I had noticed at the pavilion because he never opened his mouth to reply to anything.

The headwaiter with the chopped-off ear said in a low silky tone, "You just ask us and we tell you. That's what Mr. Servan said we was to do."

Wolfe nodded at him. "I admit that seems the obvious way, Mr. Moulton, and the simplest. But I fear we would find ourselves confronted by difficulties."

"Yes, sir. What is the nature of the difficulties?"

A gruff voice boomed, "You just ask us and we tell you anything."

Wolfe aimed his eyes at the source of it. "I hope you will. Would you permit a personal remark? That is a surprising voice to come from a man named Hyacinth Brown. No one would expect it. As for the difficulties—Archie, there's the refreshment. Perhaps some of you would help Mr. Goodwin?"

That took another ten minutes, or maybe more. Four or five of them came along, under the headwaiter's direction, and we carried the supplies in and got them arranged on a table against the wall. Wolfe was provided with beer. I had forgot to include milk in the order, so I made out with a bourbon highball. The muscular kid with the flat nose, whose name was Paul Whipple, took plain ginger ale, but all the rest accepted stimulation. Getting the drinks around, and back to their places on the floor, they loosened up a little for a few observations, but fell dead silent when Wolfe put down his empty glass and started off again.

"About the difficulties, perhaps the best way is to illustrate them. You know of course that what we are concerned with is the murder of Mr. Laszio. I am aware that you have told the sheriff that you know nothing about it, but I want some details from you, and besides, you may have recollected some incident which slipped your minds at the time you talked with the sheriff. I'll begin with you, Mr. Moulton. You were in the kitchen Tuesday evening?"

"Yes, sir. All evening. There was to be the œufs au cheval served after they got through with those sauces."

"I know. We missed that. Did you help arrange the table with the sauces?"

"Yes, sir." The headwaiter was smooth and suave. "Three of us helped Mr. Laszio. I personally took in the sauces on the serving wagon. After everything was arranged he rang for me only once, to remove the ice from the water. Except for that, I was in the kitchen all the time. All of us were."

"In the kitchen, or the pantry hall?"

"The kitchen. There was nothing to go to the pantry for. Some of the cooks were working on the œufs au cheval, and the boys were cleaning up, and some of us were eating what was left of the duck and other things. Mr. Servan told us we could."

"Indeed. That was superlative duck."

"Yes, sir. All of these gentlemen can cook like nobody's business. They sure can cook."

"They are the world's best. They are the greatest living masters of the subtlest and kindliest of the arts." Wolfe sighed, opened beer, poured, watched the foam to the top, and then demanded abruptly, "So you saw and heard nothing of the murder?"

"No, sir."

"The last you saw of Mr. Laszio was when you went in to take the ice from the water?"

"Yes, sir."

"I understand there were two knives for slicing the squabs—one of stainless steel with a silver handle, the other a kitchen carver. Were they both on the table when you took the ice from the water?"

The greenjacket hesitated only a second. "Yes, sir, I think they were. I glanced around the table to see that everything was all right, because I felt responsible, and I would have noticed if one of the knives had been gone. I even looked at the marks on the dishes—the sauces."

"You mean the numbered cards?"

"No, sir, I mean the marks. We had put numbers on the dishes with chalk so they wouldn't get mixed up in the kitchen or while I was taking them in."

"I didn't see them."

"No, sir, you wouldn't, because the numbers were small, below the rim on the far side from you. When I put the dishes by the numbered cards I turned them so the chalk numbers were at the back, facing Mr. Laszio."

"And the chalk numbers were in the proper order when you took the ice from the water?"

"Yes, sir."

"Was someone tasting the sauces when you were in there?"

"Yes, sir, Mr. Keith."

"Mr. Laszio was there alive?"

"Yes, sir, he was plenty alive. He bawled me out for putting in too much ice. He said it froze the palate."

"So it does. Not to mention the stomach. When you were in there, I don't suppose you happened to look behind either of those screens."

"No, sir. We had shoved the screens back when we cleaned up after dinner."

"And after, you didn't enter the dining room again until after Mr. Laszio's body was discovered?"

"No, sir, I didn't."

"Nor look into the dining room?"

"No, sir."

"You're sure of that?"

"Sure I'm sure. I guess I'd remember my movements."

"I suppose you would." Wolfe frowned, fingered at his glass of beer, and raised it to his mouth and gulped. The headwaiter, self-possessed, took a sip of his highball, but I noticed that his eyes didn't leave Wolfe.

Wolfe put his glass down. "Thank you, Mr. Moulton." He put his eyes on the one on Moulton's left, a medium-sized one with gray showing in his kinky hair and wrinkles on his face. "Now Mr. Grant. You're a cook?"

"Yes, sir." His tone was husky, and he cleared his throat and repeated, "Yes, sir. I work on fowl and game over at the hotel, but here I'm helping Crabby. All of us best ones, Mr. Servan sent us over here, to make an *im*pression."

"Who is Crabby?"

"He means me." It was the plump little man with a ravine in his chin, the sergeant.

"Ah, Mr. Crabtree. Then you helped with the shad roe mousse?"

Mr. Grant said, "Yes, sir. Crabby just su*per*vised. I done the work."

"Indeed. My respects to you. On Tuesday evening you were in the kitchen?"

"Yes, sir. I can make it short and sweet, mister. I was in the kitchen, I didn't leave the kitchen, and in the kitchen I *re*mained. Maybe that covers it."

"It seems to. You didn't go to the dining room or the pantry hall?"

"No, sir. I just said about *re*maining *in* the kitchen."

"So you did. No offense, Mr. Grant. I merely want to make sure." Wolfe's eyes moved on. "Mr. Whipple. I know you, of course. You are an alert and efficient waiter. You anticipated my wants at dinner. You seem young to have developed such competence. How old are you?"

The muscular kid with the flat nose looked straight at Wolfe and said, "I'm twenty-one."

Moulton, the headwaiter, gave him an eye and told him, "Say 'sir.'" Then he turned to Wolfe. "Paul's a college boy."

"I see. What college, Mr. Whipple?"

"Howard University. Sir."

Wolfe wiggled a finger. "If you feel rebellious about the 'sir,' dispense with it. Enforced courtesy is worse than none. You are at college for culture?"

"I'm interested in anthropology."

"Indeed. I have met Franz Boas and have his books autographed. You were, I remember, present on Tuesday evening. You waited on me at dinner."

"Yes, sir. I helped in the dining room after dinner, cleaning up and arranging for that demonstration with the sauces."

"Your tone suggests disapproval."

"Yes, sir. If you ask me, it's frivolous and childish for mature men to waste their time and talent, and other people's time—"

"Shut up, Paul." It was Moulton.

Wolfe said, "You're young, Mr. Whipple. Besides, each of us has his special set of values, and if you expect me to respect yours, you must respect mine. Also, I remind you that Paul Lawrence Dunbar said, 'The best thing a 'possum ever does is fill an empty belly.'"

The college boy looked at him in surprise. "Do you know Dunbar?"

"Certainly. I am not a barbarian. But to return to Tuesday evening, after you finished helping in the dining room did you go to the kitchen?"

"Yes, sir."

"And left there—"

"Not at all. Not until we got word of what had happened."

"You were in the kitchen all the time?"

"Yes, sir."

"Thank you." Wolfe's eyes moved again. "Mr. Daggett . . ."

He went on and got more of the same. I finished my highball and tilted my chair back against the wall and closed my eyes. The voices, the questions and answers, were just noises in my ears. I didn't get the idea, and it didn't sound to me as if there was any. Of course Wolfe's declaration that he wouldn't try any tricks because he didn't know any was the same as a giraffe saying it couldn't reach up for a bite on account of its short neck. But it seemed to me that if he thought that monotonous ring-around-the-rosy was a good trick, the sooner he got out of the mountain air of West Virginia and back to sea level, the better. On the questions and answers went; he didn't skimp anybody and he kept getting personal; he even discovered that Hyacinth Brown's wife had gone off and left him three little ones to take care of. Once in a while I opened my eyes to see how far around he had got and then closed them again. My wristwatch said a quarter to two when I heard, through the open window, a rooster crowing away off.

I let my chair come down when I heard my name. "Archie. Beer please."

I was a little slow on the pickup, and Moulton got to his feet and beat me to it. I sat down again. Wolfe invited the others to replenish, and a lot of them did. Then, after he had emptied a glass and wiped his lips, he settled back and ran his eyes over the gang, slowly around and back, until he had them all waiting for him.

He said in a new crisp tone, "Gentlemen, I said I would illustrate the difficulty I spoke of. It now confronts us. It was suggested that I ask for the information I want. I did so. You have all heard everything that was said. I wonder how many of you know that one of you told me a direct and deliberate lie."

Perfect silence. Wolfe let it gather for five seconds and then went on. "Doubtless you share the common knowledge that on Tuesday evening some eight or ten minutes elapsed from the moment that Mr. Berin left the dining room until the moment that Mr. Vukčić entered it, and that Mr. Berin says that when he left Mr. Laszio was there alive, and Mr. Vukčić says that when he entered Mr. Laszio was not there at all. Of course Mr. Vukčić didn't look behind the screen. During that interval of eight or ten minutes someone opened the door from the terrace to the dining room and looked in and saw two colored men. One, in livery, was standing beside the screen with his finger to his lips; the other had opened the door, a few inches, which led to the pantry hall, and was peering through, looking directly at the man by the screen. I have no idea who the man by the screen was. The one peering through the pantry-hall door was one of you who are now sitting before me. That's the one who has lied to me."

Another silence. It was broken by a loud snicker, again from the tall skinny one who was still squatting against the wall. This time he followed it with a snort. "You tell 'em, boss!" Half-a-dozen heads jerked at him, and Crabtree said in disgust, "Boney, you damn drunken fool!" and then apologized to Wolfe, "He's a no good clown, that young man.

Yes, sir. About what you say, we're all sorry you've got to feel that one of us told you a lie. You've got hold of some bad information."

"No. I must contradict you. My information is good."

Moulton inquired in his silky musical voice, "Might I ask who looked in the door and saw all that?"

"No. I've told you what was seen, and I know it was seen." Wolfe's eyes swept the faces. "Dismiss the idea, all of you, of impeaching my information. Those of you who have no knowledge of that scene in the dining room are out of this anyway. Those who know of it know also that my information comes from an eyewitness. Otherwise how would I know, for instance, that the man by the screen had his finger to his lips? No, gentlemen, the situation is simple: I know that at least one of you lied, and he knows that I know it. I wonder if there isn't a chance of ending so simple a situation in a simple manner and have it done with? Let's try. Mr. Moulton, was it you who looked through that door —the door from the dining room to the pantry hall and saw the man by the screen with his finger to his lips?"

The headwaiter with the chopped-off ear slowly shook his head. "No, sir."

"Mr. Grant, was it you?"

"No, *sir.*"

"Mr. Whipple, was it you?"

"No, sir."

He went on around and piled up fourteen negatives out of fourteen chances. Still batting a thousand. When he had completed that record he poured a glass of beer and sat and frowned at the foam. Nobody spoke and nobody moved. Finally, without drinking the beer, Wolfe leaned back and sighed patiently. He resumed in a murmur.

"I was afraid we would be here most of the night. I told you so. I also told you that I wasn't going to use threats, and I don't intend to. But by your unanimous denial you've turned a simple situation into a complicated one, and it has to be explained to you.

"First, let's say that you persist in the denial. In that case, the only thing I can do is inform the authorities and let them interview the person who looked into the dining room from the terrace. They will be convinced, as I am, of the correctness of the information, and they will start on you gentlemen with that knowledge in their possession. They will be certain that one of you saw the man by the screen. I don't pretend to know what they'll do to you, or how long you'll hold out, but that's what the situation will be, and I shall be out of it."

Wolfe sighed again and surveyed the faces. "Now, whoever you are, let's say that you abandon your denial and tell me the truth—what will happen? Similarly, you will sooner or later have to deal with the local authorities, but under quite different circumstances. I am talking now to one of you—you know which one, I don't. It doesn't seem to me that any harm will be done if I tell Mr. Tolman and the sheriff that you and your colleagues came to see me at my request, and that you volunteered the information about what you saw in the dining room. There will be no reason why the person who first gave me the information should enter into it at all, if you tell the truth—though you may be sure that I am prepared to produce that person if necessary. Of course, they won't like it that you withheld so important a fact Tuesday night, but I think I can arrange beforehand that they'll be lenient about that. I shall make it a point to do so. None of the rest of you need be concerned in it at all.

"Now"—Wolfe looked around at them again—"here comes the hard part. Whoever you are, I can understand your denial and sympathize with it. You looked through the door, doubtless on account of a noise you had heard, and saw a man of your race standing by the screen, and some forty minutes later, when you learned what had happened, you knew that man had murdered Laszio—or at the least, strongly suspected it. You not only knew that the murderer was a black man, you probably recognized him, since he wore the Kanawha Spa livery and was therefore a fellow employee, and he directly faced you as you looked through the door. And that presents another complication. If he is a man who is close to you and has a place in your heart, I presume you'll hold to your denial in spite of anything I may say and the sheriff may do. In that event, your colleagues here will share a lot of discomfort with you, but that can't be helped.

"But if he is not personally close to you, if you have refused to expose him only because he is a fellow man—or, more particularly, because he is of your color—I'd like to make some remarks. First, the fellow man. That's nonsense. It was realized centuries ago that it is impossible for a man to protect himself against murder, because it's extremely easy to kill a man, so it was agreed that men should protect each other. But if I help protect you, you must help protect me, whether you like me or not. If you don't do your part, you're out of the agreement, you're an outlaw.

"But this murderer was a black man, and you're black too. I confess that makes it ticklish. The agreements of human society embrace not only protection against murder, but thousands of other things, and it is certainly true that in America—not to mention other continents—the whites have excluded the blacks from some of the benefits of those agreements. It is said that the exclusion has sometimes even extended to murder—that in parts of this country a white man may kill a black one, if not with impunity, at least with a good chance of escaping the penalty which the agreement imposes. That's bad. It's deplorable, and I don't blame black men for resenting it. But you are confronted with a fact, not a theory, and how do you propose to change it?

"I am talking to you who saw that man by the screen. If you shield him because he is dear to you, or for any valid personal reason, I have nothing to say, because I don't like futile talk, and you'll have to fight it out with the sheriff. But if you shield him because he is your color, there is a great deal to say. You are rendering your race a serious disservice. You are helping to perpetuate and aggravate the very exclusions which you justly resent. The ideal human agreement is one in which distinctions of race and color and religion are totally disregarded. Anyone helping to preserve those distinctions is postponing that ideal; and you are certainly helping to preserve them. If in a question of murder you permit your action to be influenced by the complexion of the man who committed it, no matter whether you yourself are white or pink or black—"

"You're wrong!"

It was a sharp explosion from the mouth of the muscular kid with the flat nose, the college boy. Some of them jumped, I was startled, and everybody looked at him.

Wolfe said, "I think I can justify my position, Mr. Whipple. If you'll let me complete—"

"I don't mean your position. You can have your logic. I mean your facts. One of them."

Wolfe lifted his brows. "Which one?"

"The complexion of the murderer." The college boy was looking him straight in the eye. "He wasn't a black man. I saw him. He was a white man."

11

Right away I got another shock. It was another explosion—this time something crashing to the floor. It took our attention away from the college boy, until we saw it was Boney, the tall skinny one by the wall, who had been lulled to sleep by Wolfe's oration and, partly awakened by the electricity of Whipple's announcement, had jerked himself off balance and toppled over. He started to grumble, and Crabtree glared him out of it. There was a general stir.

Wolfe asked softly, "You saw the man by the screen, Mr. Whipple?"

"Yes."

"When?"

"When he was standing by the screen. It was I who opened the door and looked through."

"Indeed. And you say he was white?"

"No." Whipple's gaze was steadfast at Wolfe; he hadn't turned at the sound of Boney's crash. "I didn't say he was white, I said he was a white man. When I saw him he was black, because he had blacked himself up."

"How do you know that?"

"Because I saw him. Do you think I can't tell burnt cork from the real thing? I'm a black man myself. But that wasn't all. As you said, he was holding his finger against his lips, and his hand was different. It wouldn't have taken a black man to see that. He had on tight black gloves."

"Why did you go to the pantry hall and look through the door?"

"I heard a noise in the dining room. Grant wanted some paprika for the œufs au cheval, and the can was empty, and I went to the cupboard in the hall for a fresh can. That was how I happened to hear the noise. They were making a lot of racket in the kitchen and didn't hear it in there. I was up on the ladder steps looking for the paprika, and after I found it and got down I opened the door a crack to see what the noise had been."

"Did you enter the dining room?"

"No."

Wolfe slowly wiggled a finger. "May I suggest, Mr. Whipple, that the truth is usually good, and lies are sometimes excellent, but a mixture of the two is an abomination?"

"I'm telling the truth and nothing else."

"You didn't before. Since the murderer wasn't a colored man, why not?"

"Because I've learned not to mix up in the affairs of the superior race. If it had been a colored man I would have told. Colored men have got to stop disgracing their color and leave that to white men. You see how good your logic was."

"But, my dear sir, that doesn't impugn my logic, it merely shows that you agree with me. We must discuss it some time. Then you withheld this fact because you considered it white men's business and none of yours, and you knew if you divulged it you'd be making trouble for yourself."

"Plenty of trouble. You're a northerner—"

"I'm a man, or try to be. You're studying me; you're an anthropologist. You expect to be a scientist. Give me a considered answer: how sure are you that it was a white man?"

Whipple considered. In a moment he said, "Not sure at all. Burnt cork would look like that on a light brown skin or even a rather dark one, and of course anyone can wear black gloves. But I'm sure about the burnt cork or something similar, and I'm sure about the gloves, and I don't see why a colored man should be painting the lily. Therefore I took it for granted he was a white man, but of course I'm not sure."

"It seems a safe deduction. What was he doing when you saw him?"

"Standing at the end of the screen, turning around. He must have seen me by accident; he couldn't have heard me. That door is noiseless, and I only opened it two or three inches, and there was quite a lot of sound from the radio in the parlor, though the door was closed."

"He was wearing the Kanawha Spa livery?"

"Yes."

"What about his hair?"

"He had a livery cap on. I couldn't see the back of his head."

"Describe him, height, weight."

"He was medium. I would guess five feet eight or nine, and a hundred and fifty-five or sixty. I didn't inspect him much. I saw at once that he was blacked up, and when he put his finger to his lips I thought he was one of the guests doing a stunt, probably a practical joke, and I supposed the noise I had heard was him jolting the screen or something.

I let the door come shut and came away. As I did that, he was starting to turn."

"Toward the table?"

"I would say, toward the door to the terrace."

Wolfe pursed his lips. Then he opened them. "You thought it was a guest playing a joke. If you had tried to decide who it was, which guest would you have picked?"

"I don't know."

"Come, Mr. Whipple, I'm merely trying for general characteristics. Longheaded or round?"

"You asked me to name him. I couldn't name that man. I couldn't identify him. He was blacked up and his cap was pulled low. I think he had light-colored eyes. His face was neither round nor long but medium. I only saw him one second."

"What about your feeling? Would you say that you had a feeling that you had ever seen him before?"

The college boy shook his head. "The only feeling I had was that I didn't want to interfere in a white man's joke. And afterward, that I didn't want to interfere in a white man's murder."

The foam on Wolfe's glass of beer was all gone. Wolfe picked it up, frowned at it, and carried it to his mouth and gulped five times, and set it down empty.

"Well." He put his eyes on Whipple again. "You must forgive me, sir, if I remind you that this story has been extracted from you against your will. I hope you haven't blacked it up—or whitewashed it. When you returned to the kitchen, did you tell anyone what you had seen?"

"No, sir."

"The unusual circumstance of a stranger in the dining room, in Kanawha Spa livery, blacked up with black gloves—you didn't think that worth mentioning?"

"No, sir."

"You damn fool, Paul." It was Crabtree, and he sounded irritated. "You think we ain't as much man as you are?" He turned to Wolfe. "This boy is awful conceited. He's got a good heart hid from people's eyesight, but his head's fixin' to bust. He's going to pack all the burden. No, sir. He came back to the kitchen and told us right off, just the same as he's told it here. We all heard it, passing it around. And for something more special about that, you might ask Moulton there."

The headwaiter with the chopped-off ear jerked around at him. "You talking, Crabby?"

The little man met his stare. "You heard me. Paul spilled it, didn't he? I didn't see anybody put you away on a shelf to save up for the Lord."

Moulton grunted. He stared at Crabtree some more seconds, then shrugged and turned to Wolfe, and was again smooth and suave. "What he's referring to. I was about to tell you when Paul got through. I saw that man too."

"The man by the screen?"

"Yes, sir."

"How was that?"

"It was because I thought Paul was taking too long to find the paprika, and I went to the pantry hall after him. When I got there he was just turning away from the door, and he motioned to the dining room with his thumb and said somebody was in there. I didn't know what he meant; of course I knew Mr. Laszio was there, and I pushed the door a little to take a look. The man's back was toward me. He was walking toward the door to the terrace, so I couldn't see his face, but I saw his black gloves, and of course I saw the livery he had on. I let the door come shut and asked Paul who it was, and he said he didn't know, he thought it was one of the guests blacked up. I sent Paul to the kitchen with the paprika and opened the door another crack and looked through, but the man wasn't in sight, so I opened the door wider, thinking to ask Mr. Laszio if he wanted anything. He wasn't by the table. I went on through, and he wasn't anywhere. That looked funny, because I knew how the tasting was supposed to be done, but I can't say I was much surprised."

"Why not?"

"Well, sir, you'll allow me to say that these guests have acted very individual from the beginning."

"Yes, I'll allow that."

"Yes, sir. So I just supposed Mr. Laszio had gone to the parlor or somewhere."

"Did you look behind the screen?"

"No, sir. I didn't see any call for a posse."

"There was no one in the room?"

"No, sir. No one in sight."

"What did you do, return to the kitchen?"

"Yes, sir. I didn't figure—"

"You ain't shut yet." It was the plump little chef, warningly. "Mr. Wolfe here is a kindhearted man and he might as well get it and let him have it. We all remember it exactly like you told us about it."

"Oh, you do, Crabby?"

"We do, you know."

Moulton shrugged and turned back to Wolfe. "What he's referring to, I was about to tell you. Before I went back to the kitchen I took a look at the table because I was responsible."

"The table with the sauces?"

"Yes, sir."

"Was one of the knives gone?"

"I don't know that. I think I would have noticed, but maybe I wouldn't, because I didn't lift the cover from the squabs, and one of them might have been under that. But I did notice something wrong. Somebody had monkeyed with the sauces. They were all changed around."

I let out a whistle before I thought. Wolfe sent me a sharp glance and then returned his eyes to Moulton and murmured, "Ah! How did you know?"

"I knew by the marks, the numbers chalked on the dishes. When I took them to the table I put the dish with the chalk mark 1 in front of the card numbered 1, and the 2 in front of the 2, and so on. They weren't that way when I looked. They had been shifted around."

"How many of them?"

"All but two. Numbers 8 and 9 were all right, but the rest had all been moved."

"You can swear to that, Mr. Moulton?"

"I guess it looks like I'm going to have to swear to it."

"And can you?"

"I can, yes, sir."

"How would it be if at the same time you were asked to swear that, having noticed that the dishes had been moved, you replaced them in their proper positions?"

"Yes, sir. That's what I did. I suppose that's what will get me fired. It was none of my business to be correcting things, I knew it wasn't. But if Mr. Servan will listen to me, it was him I did it for. I didn't want him to lose his bet. I knew he had bet with Mr. Keith that the tasters would be eighty per cent correct, and when I saw the dishes had been shifted I thought someone was framing him, so I shifted them back. Then I got out of there in a hurry."

"I don't suppose you remember just how they had been changed—where, for instance, number 1 had been moved to?"

"No, sir. I couldn't say that."

"No matter." Wolfe sighed. "I thank you, Mr. Moulton, and you, Mr. Whipple. It is late. I'm afraid we won't get much sleep, for we'll have to deal with Mr. Tolman and the sheriff as early as possible. I suppose you live on the grounds here?"

They told him yes.

"Good. I'll be sending for you. I don't think you'll lose your job, Mr. Moulton. I remember my commitment regarding beforehand arrangements with the authorities and I'll live up to it. I thank all of you gentlemen for your patience. I suppose your hats are in Mr. Goodwin's room?"

They helped me get the bottles and glasses cleared out and stacked in the foyer, and with that expert assistance it didn't take long. The college boy didn't help us because he hung back for a word with Wolfe. The hats and caps finally got distributed, and I opened the foyer door and they filed out. Hyacinth Brown had Boney by the arm, and Boney was still muttering when I shut the door.

In Wolfe's room the light of dawn was at the window, even through the thick shrubbery just outside. It was my second dawn in a row, and I was beginning to feel that I might as well join the Milkmen's Union and be done with it. My eyes felt as if someone had painted household cement on my lids and let it dry. Wolfe had his open and was still in his chair.

I said, "Congratulations. All you need is wings to be an owl. Shall I leave a call for twelve noon? That would leave you eight hours till dinnertime, and you'd still be ahead of schedule."

He made a face. "Where have they got Mr. Berin in jail?"

"I suppose at Quinby, the county seat."

"How far away is it?"

"Oh, around twenty miles."

"Does Mr. Tolman live there?"

"I don't know. His office must be there, since he's the prosecuting attorney."

"Please find out, and get him on the phone. We want him and the sheriff here at eight o'clock. Tell him—no—when you get him, let me talk to him."

"Now?"

"Now."

I spread out my hands. "It's 4:30 a.m. Let the man—"

"Archie. Please. You tried to instruct me how to handle colored men. Will you try it with white men too?"

I went for the phone.

12

Pettigrew, the squint-eyed sheriff, shook his head and drawled, "Thank you just the same. I got stuck in the mud and had to flounder around and I'd get that chair all dirty. I'm a pretty good stander anyhow."

My friend Barry Tolman didn't look any too neat himself, but he wasn't muddy and so he hadn't hesitated about taking a seat. It was 8:10 Thursday morning. I felt like the last nickel in a crap game, because like a darned fool I had undraped myself a little after 5 a.m. and got under the covers, leaving a call for 7:30, and hauling myself out again after only two hours had put me off key for good. Wolfe was having breakfast in the big chair, with a folding table pulled up to him, in a yellow dressing gown, with his face shaved and his hair combed. He possessed five yellow dressing gowns, and we had brought along the light woolen one with brown lapels and a brown girdle. He had on a necktie too.

Tolman said, "As I told you on the phone, I'm supposed to be in court at 9:30. If necessary, my assistant can get a postponement, but I'd like to make it if possible. Can't you rush it?"

Wolfe was sipping at his cocoa for erosion on the bite of roll he had taken. When that was disposed of he said, "It depends a good deal on you, sir. It was impossible for me to go to Quinby, as I said, for reasons that will appear. I'll do all I can to hurry it. I haven't been to bed—"

"You said you have information—"

"I have. But the circumstances require a preamble. I take it that you arrested Mr. Berin only because you were convinced he was guilty. You don't especially fancy him as a victim. If strong doubt were cast on his guilt—"

"Certainly." Tolman was impatient. "I told you—"

"So you did. Now let's suppose something. Suppose that a lawyer has been retained to represent Mr. Berin, and I have been engaged to discover evidence in Berin's defense. Suppose, further, that I have discovered such evidence, of a weight that would lead inevitably to his acquittal when you put him on trial, and it is felt that it would be imprudent to disclose that evidence to you, the enemy, for the present. Suppose you demand that I produce that evidence now. It's true, isn't it, that you couldn't legally enforce that demand? That such evidence is our property until the time we see fit to make use of it—provided you don't discover it independently for yourselves?"

Tolman was frowning. "That's true, of course. But damn it, I've told you that if the evidence against Berin can be explained—"

"I know. I offer, here and now, an explanation that will clear him, but I offer it on conditions."

"What are they?"

Wolfe sipped cocoa and wiped his lips. "They're not onerous. First, that if the explanation casts strong doubt on Berin's guilt, he is to be released immediately."

"Who will decide how strong the doubt is?"

"You."

"All right, I agree. The court is sitting, and it can be done in five minutes."

"Good. Second, you are to tell Mr. Berin that I discovered the evidence which set him free, I am solely responsible for it, and God only knows what would have happened to him if I hadn't done it."

Tolman, still frowning, opened his mouth, but the sheriff put in, "Now wait, Barry. Hold your horses." He squinted down at Wolfe. "If you've really got this evidence it must be around somewhere. I suppose we're pretty slow out here in West Virginia—"

"Mr. Pettigrew. Please. I'm not talking about the public credit. I'm not interested in it. Tell the newspapermen whatever you want to. But Mr. Berin is to know, unequivocally, that I did it, and Mr. Tolman is to tell him so."

Tolman asked, "Well, Sam?"

The sheriff shrugged. "I don't give a damn."

"All right," Tolman told Wolfe. "I agree to that."

"Good." Wolfe set the cocoa cup down. "Third, it is understood that I am leaving for New York at 12:40 tonight, and under no circumstances—short of a suspicion that I killed Mr. Laszio myself or was an accomplice—am I to be detained."

Pettigrew said good-humoredly, "You go to hell."

"No, not hell." Wolfe sighed. "New York."

Tolman protested, "But what if this evidence makes you a material and essential witness?"

"It doesn't—you must take my word for that. I'm preparing to take yours for several things. I give you my word that within thirty minutes you'll know everything of significance that I know regarding that business in the dining room. I want it agreed that I won't be kept here beyond my train time merely because it is felt I might prove useful. Anyway, I assure you that under those circumstances I wouldn't be useful at all. I would be an insufferable nuisance. Well, sir?"

Tolman hesitated and finally nodded. "Qualified as you put it, I agree."

If there is a way a canary bird sighs when you let it out of a cage, Wolfe sighed like that. "Now, sir. The fourth and last condition is a little vaguer than the others, but I think it can be defined. The evidence that I am going to give you was brought to me by two men. I led up to its disclosure by methods which seemed likely to be effective, and they were so. You will resent it that these gentlemen didn't give you these facts when they had an opportunity, and I can't help that. I can't stop your feelings, but I can ask you to restrain them, and I have promised to do so. I want your assurance that the gentlemen will not be bullied, badgered, or abused, or be deprived of their freedom, in any way persecuted. This is predicated on the assumption that they are merely witnesses and have no share whatever in the guilt of the murder."

The sheriff said, "Hell, mister, we don't abuse people."

"Bullied, badgered, abused, deprived of freedom, persecuted, all excluded. Of course you'll question them as much as you please."

Tolman shook his head. "They'll be material witnesses. They might leave the state. In fact, they will. You're going to, tonight."

"You can put them under bond to remain."

"Until the trial."

Wolfe wiggled a finger. "Not Mr. Berin's trial."

"I don't mean Berin—if this evidence is as good as you say it is. But you can be damn sure there's going to *be* a trial."

"I sincerely hope so." Wolfe was breaking off a piece of roll and buttering it. "What about it, sir? Since you want to get to court. I'm not asking much, merely a decent restraint with my witnesses. Otherwise you'll have to try to dig them out for yourself, and in the meantime the longer you hold Mr. Berin the more foolish you'll look in the end."

"Very well." The blue-eyed athlete nodded. "I agree."

"To the condition as I have stated it?"

"Yes."

"Then the preamble is finished. Archie, bring them in."

I smothered a yawn as I lifted myself up and went to my room to get them. They had been in there overlooking progress while I had dressed —Wolfe, having had a telephone plugged in in his own chamber, had done his own assembling for the morning meeting during my nap.

They had reported in livery. Paul Whipple looked wide-awake and defiant, and Moulton, the headwaiter, sleepy and nervous. I told them the stage was set, and let them precede me.

Wolfe told me to push chairs around, and Moulton jumped to help me. Tolman was staring. Pettigrew exclaimed, "Well, I'll be damned! It's a couple of niggers! Hey, you, take that chair!" He turned to Wolfe with a grievance. "Now listen, I questioned all these boys, and, by God, if they—"

Wolfe snapped, "These are my witnesses. Mr. Tolman wants to get to court. I said you'd resent it, didn't I? Go ahead, but keep it to yourself." He turned to the college boy. "Mr. Whipple, I think we'll have your story first. Tell these gentlemen what you told me last night."

Pettigrew had stepped forward with a mean eye. "We don't 'mister' niggers here in West Virginia, and we don't need anybody coming down here to tell us—"

"Shut up, Sam!" Tolman was snappy too. "We're wasting time. Your name's Whipple? What do you do?"

"Yes, sir." The boy spoke evenly. "I'm a waiter. Mr. Servan put me on duty at Pocahontas Pavilion Tuesday noon."

"What have you got to say?"

The upshot of it was that Tolman couldn't have got to court on time, for it was after nine-thirty when he left Kanawha Spa. It took only a quarter of an hour to get all the details of the two stories, but they went on from there, or rather, back and around. Tolman did a pretty good job of questioning, but Pettigrew was too mad to be of much account. He kept making observations about how educated Whipple thought he was, and how he knew what kind of lessons it was that Whipple really needed. Tolman kept pushing the sheriff off and doing some real cross-examining, and twice or thrice I saw Wolfe, who was finishing his breakfast at leisure, give a little nod as an acknowledgment of Tolman's neat job.

Whipple kept himself even-toned right through, but I could see him holding himself in when the sheriff made observations about his education and the kind of lessons he needed. Moulton started off jerky and nervous, but he smoothed off as he went along, and his only job was to stick to his facts in reply to Tolman's questions, since Pettigrew was concentrating on Whipple.

Finally Tolman's string petered out. He raised his brows at Wolfe, glanced at the sheriff, and looked back again at Moulton with a considering frown.

Pettigrew demanded, "Where did you boys leave your caps? We'll have to take you down to Quinby with us."

Wolfe was crisp right away. "Oh, no. Remember the agreement. They stay here on their jobs. I've spoken with Mr. Servan about that."

"I don't give a damn if you've spoken with Ashley himself. They go to jail till they get bond."

Wolfe's eyes moved. "Mr. Tolman?"

"Well, it was agreed they could be put under bond."

"But that was when you supposed that they were persons who were likely to leave your jurisdiction. These men have jobs here. Why should they leave? Mr. Moulton has a wife and children. Mr. Whipple is a university man." He looked at the sheriff. "Your assumption that you know how to deal with colored men and I don't is impertinent nonsense. Tuesday night, as an officer of the law engaged in the investigation of a crime, at which you are supposed to be expert, you questioned these men and failed to learn anything. You didn't even have your suspicions aroused. Last night I had a talk with them and uncovered vital information regarding that crime. Surely you have enough intelligence to see how utterly discredited you are. Do you want your whole confounded county to know about it? Pfui." He turned to the two greenjackets. "You men get out of here and go to your stations and get to work. You understand, of course, that Mr. Tolman will need your evidence and you will hold yourselves subject to his proper demands. If he requires bond, any lawyer can arrange it. Well, go on!"

Paul Whipple was already on his way to the door. Moulton hesitated only an instant, glancing at Tolman, and then followed. I got up and moseyed out to see that the outside door was shut behind them.

When I got back Pettigrew was in the middle of some remarks, using whatever words happened to come handy, regarding the tribal customs and personal habits of aborigines. Tolman was back on his shoulders with his hands thrust in his pockets, surveying Wolfe, and Wolfe was daintily collecting crumbs and depositing them on the fruit plate. Neither was paying any attention to the sheriff, and eventually he fizzed out.

Wolfe looked up. "Well, sir?"

Tolman nodded. "Yep, I guess you win. It looks like they're telling the truth. They can make up fancy ones when they feel like it, but this doesn't sound like their kind." His blue eyes narrowed a little. "Of course, there's something else to consider. I understand you've been appealed to, to get Berin clear, and also I've heard that you were offered a good commission to get Berin for the job that Laszio had. I learned that from Clay Ashley, who had it from his friend Liggett of the

Hotel Churchill. Naturally that raises the question as to how far you yourself might go in discovering evidence that would free Berin."

"You put it delicately." The corners of Wolfe's lips went up a little. "You mean manufacturing evidence. I assure you I'm not that stupid or that desperate, to bribe strangers to tell intricate lies. Besides, I would have had to bribe not two men, but fourteen. Those stories were uncovered in this room last night, in the presence of all the cooks and waiters on duty at Pocahontas Pavilion. You may question them all. No, sir, those stories are bona fide." He upturned a palm. "But you know that; you put them to a good test. And now, since you are anxious to return to Quinby in time for your appearance in court—"

"Yeah, I know." Tolman didn't move. "This is a sweet mess now, this murder. If those boys are telling it straight, and I guess they are, do you realize what it means? Among other things, it means that all of that bunch are out of it, except that fellow Blanc who says he was in his room. And he's a stranger here, and how the devil could he have got hold of a Kanawha Spa uniform? If you eliminate him, all you've got left is the wide world."

Wolfe murmured, "Yes, it's a pretty problem. Thank goodness it isn't mine. But as to our agreement, I've performed my part, haven't I? Have I cast strong doubt on Mr. Berin's guilt?"

The sheriff snorted. Tolman said shortly, "Yes. The fact that those sauce dishes were shifted around—certainly. But damn it, who shifted them?"

"I couldn't say. Perhaps the murderer, or possibly Mr. Laszio himself, to make a fool of Berin." Wolfe shrugged. "Quite a job for you. You will set Berin free this morning?"

"What else can I do? I can't hold him now."

"Good. Then if you don't mind, since you're in a hurry, and I haven't been to bed—"

"Yeah." Tolman stayed put. He sat with his hands still in his pockets, his legs stretched out, the toes of his shoes making little circles in the air. "A hell of a mess," he declared after a silence. "Except for Blanc, there's nowhere to begin. That boy's description might be almost anyone. Of course, it's possible that it was a black that did it and used black gloves and burnt cork to throw us off, but what black around here could have any reason for wanting to kill Laszio?" He was silent again. Finally he abruptly sat up. "Look here. I'm not sorry you got Berin out of it, whether you made it into a mess or not. And I'll meet the conditions I agreed to, including no interference with your leaving here tonight. But since you're turning over evidence, what else have you got? I admit you're good, and you've made a monkey out of me on this Berin business—not to mention the sheriff here. Maybe you can come across with some more of the same. What more have you found out?"

"Nothing whatever."

"Have you any idea who it was the boys saw in the dining room?"

"None."

"Do you think that Frenchman did it? Blanc?"

"I don't know. I doubt it."

"The Chinese woman who was outdoors—do you think she was mixed up in it?"

"No."

"Do you think the radio being turned on at that particular time had anything to do with it?"

"Certainly. It drowned the noise of Laszio's fall, and his outcry, if he made one."

"But was it turned on purposely for that?"

"I don't know."

Tolman frowned. "When I had Berin, or thought I had, I decided that the radio was a coincidence or a circumstance that he took advantage of. Now that's open again." He leaned forward at Wolfe. "I want you to do something for me. I don't pass for a fool, but I admit I'm a little shy on experience, and you're not only an old hand, you're recognized as one of the best there is. I'm not too proud to yell for help if I need it. It looks like the next step is a good session with Blanc, and I'd like to have you in on it. Better still, handle it yourself and let me sit and listen. Will you do that?"

"No, sir."

Tolman was taken aback. "You won't?"

"No. I won't even discuss it. Confound it, I came down here for a holiday." Wolfe made a face. "Monday night, on the train, I got no sleep. Tuesday night it was you who kept me up until four o'clock. Last night my engagement to clear Mr. Berin prevented my going to bed at all. This evening I am supposed to deliver an important address to a group of eminent men on their own subject. I need the refreshment of sleep, and there is my bed. As for your interview with Mr. Blanc, I remind you that you agreed to free Mr. Berin immediately upon presentation of my evidence."

He looked and sounded very final. The sheriff started to growl something, but I was called away by a knock on the door. I went to the foyer, telling myself that if it was anyone who was likely to postpone the refreshment of sleep any longer, I would lay him out with a healthy sock on the button and just leave him there.

Which might have done for Vukčić, big as he was, but I wouldn't strike a woman merely because I was sleepy, and he was accompanied by Constanza Berin. I flung the door the rest of the way, and she crossed the threshold. Vukčić began a verbal request, but she wasn't bothering with amenities, she was going right ahead.

I reached for her and missed her. "Hey, wait a minute! We have company. Your friend Barry Tolman is in there."

She wheeled on me. "Who?"

"You heard me. Tolman."

She wheeled again and opened the door to Wolfe's room and breezed on through. Vukčić looked at me and shrugged and followed her, and I went along, thinking that if I needed a broom and dustpan I could get them later.

Tolman had jumped to his feet at sight of her. For two seconds he was white, then a nice pink, and then he started for her. "Miss Berin! Thank God—"

An icy blast hit him and stopped him in his tracks with his mouth open. It wasn't vocal; her look didn't need any accompaniment. With him frozen, she turned a different look, practically as devastating, on Nero Wolfe.

"And you said you would help us! You said you would make them free my father!" Nothing but a superworm could deserve such scorn as that. "And it was you who suggested that about his list, about the sauces! I suppose you thought no one would know—"

"My dear Miss Berin—"

"Now everybody knows! It was you who brought the evidence against him! *That* evidence! And you pretending to Mr. Servan and Mr. Vukčić and me—"

I got Wolfe's look and saw his lips moving at me, though I couldn't hear him. I stepped across and gripped her arm and turned her. "Listen, give somebody a chance—"

She was pulling, but I held on. Wolfe said sharply, "She's hysterical. Take her out of here."

I felt her arm relax and turned her loose, and she moved to face Wolfe again.

She told him quietly, "I'm not hysterical."

"Of course you are. All women are. Their moments of calm are merely recuperative periods between outbursts. I want to tell you something. Will you listen?"

She stood and looked at him.

He nodded. "Thank you. I make this explanation because I don't want unfriendliness from your father. I made the suggestion that the lists be compared with the correct list, not dreaming that it would result in implicating your father—in fact, thinking that it would help to clear him. Unfortunately it happened differently, and it became necessary to undo the mischief I had unwittingly caused. The only way to do that was to discover other evidence which would establish his innocence. I have done so. Your father will be released within an hour."

Constanza stared at him and went nearly as white as Tolman had on seeing her, and then her blood came back as his had done. She stammered, "But—but—I don't believe it. I've just been over to that place and they wouldn't even let me see him—"

"You won't have to go again. He will rejoin you here this morning. I undertook with you and Mr. Servan and Mr. Vukčić to clear your father of this ridiculous charge, and I have done that. The evidence had been given to Mr. Tolman. Don't you understand what I'm saying?"

Apparently she was beginning to, and it was causing drastic internal adjustments. Her eyes were drawing together, diagonal creases were appearing from the corners of her nose to the corners of her mouth, her cheeks were slowly puffing up, and her chin began to move. She was going to cry, and it looked as if it might be a good one. For half a minute, evidently, she thought she was going to be able to stave it off, then all of a sudden she realized that she wasn't. She turned and ran for the door. She got it open and disappeared. That galvanized Tolman. Without stopping for farewells he jumped for the door she had left open, and he was gone too.

Vukčić and I looked at each other. Wolfe sighed.

The sheriff made a move. "Admitting you're smart," he drawled at Wolfe, "and all that, if I was Barry Tolman you wouldn't take the midnight or any other train out of here until certain details had been attended to."

Wolfe nodded and murmured, "Good day, sir."

He went—and banged the foyer door so hard behind him that I jumped. I sat down and observed, "My nerves are like fishing worms on hooks." Vukčić sat down too.

Wolfe looked at him and inquired, "Well, Marko? I suppose we might as well say good morning. Is that what you came for?"

"No." Vukčić ran his fingers through his hair. "It fell to me, more or less, to stand by Berin's daughter, and when she wanted to drive to Quinby—that's the town where the jail is—it was up to me to take her. Then they wouldn't let her see him. If I had known you had already found evidence to clear him—" He shook himself. "By the way, what's the evidence? If it isn't a secret."

"I don't know whether it's a secret or not. It doesn't belong to me any more. I've handed it over to the authorities, and I suppose they should be permitted to decide about divulging it. I can tell you one thing that's no secret: I didn't get to bed last night."

"Not at all?"

"No."

Vukčić grunted. "You don't look done up." He ran his fingers through his hair again. "Listen, Nero, I'd like to ask you something. Dina came to see you last night, didn't she?"

"Yes."

"What did she have to say? That is, if it's proper to tell me."

"You can judge of the propriety. She told me that she is a special kind of woman and that she thought that you thought that I suspected you of killing Laszio." Wolfe grimaced. "And she patted me on the shoulder."

Vukčić said angrily, "She's a damned fool."

"I suppose so. But a very dangerous fool. Of course, a hole in the ice offers peril only to those who go skating. This is none of my business, Marko, but you brought it up."

"I know I did. What the devil made her think that I thought you suspected me of murdering Laszio?"

"Didn't you tell her so?"

"No. Did she say I did?"

Wolfe shook his head. "She wasn't on the road, she was winding around. She did say, however, that you told her of my questions about the radio and the dancing."

Vukčić nodded gloomily and was silent. At length he shook himself. "Yes, I had a talk with her. Two talks. There's no doubt about her being dangerous. She gets—you must realize that she was my wife for five years. Again yesterday I had her close to me, I had her in my arms. It isn't her tricks—I'm on to all her tricks—it's the mere fact of what she is. You wouldn't see that, Nero, or feel it. It wouldn't have any effect on you, because you've put yourself behind a barricade. As you say, a hole in the ice is dangerous only to those who go skating. But damn it, what does life consist of if you're afraid to take—"

"Marko!" Wolfe sounded peevish. "I've often told you that's your worst habit. When you argue with yourself, do it inside your head. Don't pretend it's me you're persuading and shout platitudes at me. You know very well what life consists of—it consists of the humanities, and among them is a decent and intelligent control of the appetites which we share with dogs. A man doesn't wolf a carcass or howl on a hillside from dark to dawn; he eats well-cooked food, when he can get it, in judicious quantities; and he suits his ardor to his wise convenience."

Vukčić was standing up. He frowned and growled down at his old friend. "So I'm howling, am I?"

"You are and you know it."

"Well, I'm sorry. I'm damned sorry."

He turned on his heel and strode from the room.

I got up and went to the window to retrieve a curtain that had been whipped out by the draft from the opened door. In the thick shrubbery just outside a bird was singing, and I startled it. Then I went and planted myself in front of Wolfe. He had his eyes closed, and as I gazed at him his massive form went up with the leverage of a deep sigh and down again.

I yawned and said, "Anyhow, thank the Lord they all make a quick exit. It's moving along for ten o'clock, and you need sleep, not to mention me."

He opened his eyes. "Archie. I have affection for Marko Vukčić. I hunted dragonflies with him in the mountains. Do you realize that that fool is going to let that fool make a fool of him again?"

I yawned. "Listen to you. If I did a sentence like that you'd send me from the room. You're in bad shape. I tell you, we both need sleep. Did you mean it when you told Tolman that as far as this murder is concerned you're not playing any more?"

"Certainly. Mr. Berin is cleared. We are no longer interested. We leave here tonight."

"Okay. Then, for God's sake, let's go to bed."

He closed his eyes and sighed again. It appeared that he wanted to sit and worry about Vukčić a while, and I couldn't help him any with that, so I turned and started out, intending not only to display the DO NOT DISTURB but also to leave positive instructions with the greenjacket in the main hall. But just as I had my hand on the knob his voice stopped me.

"Archie. You've had more sleep than I have. I was about to say, we haven't gone over that speech since we got here. I intended to rehearse it at least twice. Do you know which bag it's in? Get it, please."

If we had been in New York I would have quit the job.

13

At ten o'clock I sat on a chair by the open window and yawned, with my eyes on the typescript, my own handiwork. We had worked through it to page nine.

Wolfe, facing me, was sitting up in bed with four cushions at his back, displaying half an acre of yellow silk pajamas. On the bedstand beside him were two empty beer bottles and an empty glass. He appeared to be frowning intently at my socks as he went on, "'. . . but the indescribable flavor of the finest of Georgia hams, the quality which places them, in my opinion, definitely above the best to be found in Europe, is not due to the post-mortem treatment of the flesh at all. Expert knowledge and tender care in the curing are indeed essential, but these are to be found in Czestochowa and Westphalia more frequently even than in Georgia. Poles and Westphalians have the pigs, the scholarship, and the skill. What they do not have is peanuts.'"

He stopped to blow his nose. I shifted position. He resumed. "'A pig whose diet is fifty to seventy per cent peanuts grows a ham of incredibly sweet and delicate succulence, which, well cured, well kept and well cooked, will take precedence over any other ham the world affords. I offer this as an illustration of one of the sources of the American contributions I am discussing, and as another proof that American offerings to the roll of honor of fine food are by no means confined to those items which were found here already ripe on the tree, with nothing required but the plucking. Red Indians were eating turkeys and potatoes before white men came, but they were not eating peanut-fed pigs. Those unforgettable hams are not gifts of nature; they are the product of the inventor's enterprise, the experimenter's persistence, and the connoisseur's discrimination. Similar results have been achieved by the feeding of blueberries to young chickens, beginning usually—'"

"Hold it. Not 'chickens,' 'poultry.'"

"Chickens are poultry."

"You told me to stop you."

"But not to argue with me."

"You started the argument, I didn't."

He showed me a palm. "Let's go on. '. . . beginning usually at the age of one week. The flavor of a four-month-old cockerel, trained to eat large quantities of blueberries from infancy, and cooked with mushrooms, tarragon, and white wine—or, if you would add another American touch, made into a chicken and corn pudding, with onion, parsley, and eggs—is not only distinctive, it is unique, and it is assuredly *haute cuisine*. This is even a better illustration of my thesis than the ham, for Europeans could not have fed peanuts to pigs, since they had no peanuts. But they did have chickens'—'chickens,' Archie?"

" 'Poultry.' "

"No matter. '. . . they did have chickens and blueberries, and for centuries no one thought of having the one assimilate the other and bless us with the result. Another demonstration of the inventiveness—' "

"Hey, wait! You left out a whole paragraph. 'You will say perhaps—' "

"Very well. Do you think you might sit still? You keep that chair creaking. 'You will say, perhaps, that all this does not belong in a discussion of cookery, but on consideration I believe you will agree that it does. Vatel had his own farm and gave his personal attention to its husbandry. Escoffier refused fowl from a certain district, however plump and well grown, on account of minerals in the drinking water available for them there. Brillat-Savarin paid many tributes . . .' "

I was on my feet. Seated, I had twitches in my arms and legs and I couldn't sit still. With the script in my hand, I moved across the table and got hold of the carafe and poured myself a glass of water and drank it. Wolfe went on, droning it out. I decided not to sit down again and stood in the middle of the floor, flexing and unflexing the muscles of my legs to make the twitching stop.

I don't know what it was that alarmed me. I couldn't have seen anything, because my eyes were on the script, and the open window was at my left, at least a dozen feet away, at right angles to my line of vision. I don't think I heard anything. But something made me jerk my head around, and even then all I saw was a movement in the shrubbery outside the window, and I have no idea what made me throw the script. But I threw it, straight at the window. At the same moment a gun went off, good and loud. Simultaneously smoke and the smell of powder came in at the window, the script fluttered and dropped to the floor, and I heard Wolfe's voice behind me.

"Look here, Archie."

I looked and saw the blood running down the side of his face. For a second I stood dead in my tracks. I wanted to jump through the window and catch the son-of-a—the sharpshooter, and give him personal treatment. And Wolfe wasn't dead, he was still sitting up. But the blood looked plenteous. I jumped to the side of the bed.

He had his lips compressed tight, but he opened them to demand, "Where is it? Is it my skull?" He shuddered. "Brains?"

"Hell, no." I was looking, and I was so relieved my voice cracked. "Where would brains come from? Take your hand away and hold still. Wait till I get a towel." I raced to the bathroom and back and wrapped one towel around his neck and sopped with the other one. "I don't think it touched the cheekbone at all. It just went through skin and meat. Do you feel faint?"

"No. Bring me my shaving mirror."

"You wait till I—"

"Bring the mirror!"

"For God's sake, hold that towel there." I hopped to the bathroom again for the mirror and handed it to him and then went to the phone. A girl's voice said good morning sweetly.

"Yeah. Swell morning. Has this joint got a doctor? No, wait, I don't want to speak to him. Send him over here right away—a man's been shot in Suite 60, Upshur Pavilion. I said shot, and step on it, and send the doctor, and that Odell the house detective, and a state cop if there's one around loose, and a bottle of brandy. Got it? Good for you, you're a wonder."

I went back to Wolfe, and whenever I want to treat myself to a laugh all I have to do is remember how he looked on that occasion. With one hand he was keeping the towel from unwinding from his neck, and with the other he was holding up the mirror, into which he was glaring with unutterable indignation and disgust. I saw he was holding his lips tight so blood wouldn't get in his mouth, and I went and got some of his handkerchiefs and did some more sopping.

He moved his left shoulder up and down a little. "Some blood ran down my neck." He moved his jaw up and down and from side to side. "I don't feel anything when I do that." He put the mirror down on the bed. "Can't you stop the confounded bleeding? Look out, don't press so hard! What's that there on the floor?"

"It's your speech. I think there's a bullet hole through it, but it's all right. You've got to get stretched out and turned over on your side. Now, damn it, don't argue—here, wait till I get rid of these cushions."

I got him horizontal, with his head raised on a couple of pillows, and went to the bathroom for a towel soaked in cold water and came back and poulticed him. He had his eyes shut. I had just got back to him with another cold towel when there was a loud knock on the door.

The doctor, a bald-headed little squirt with spectacles, had a bag in his hand and a nurse with him. As I was ushering them in somebody else came trotting down the hall, and I let him in too when I saw it was Clay Ashley, the Kanawha Spa manager. He was sputtering at me, "Who did it how did it happen where is he who is it—" I told him to save it up and followed the doctor and nurse inside.

The bald-headed doc was no slouch, at that. The nurse pulled up a chair for the bag and opened it, and I shoved a table over by the bed, while the doc bent over Wolfe without asking me anything. Wolfe started to turn over but was commanded to lie still.

Wolfe protested, "Confound it, I have to see your face."

"What for? To see if I'm compos mentis? I'm all right. Hold still."

Clay Ashley's voice sounded at my elbow. "What the devil is it? You say he was shot? What happened?"

The doctor spoke without turning, with authority. "Quiet in here, until I see what we've got."

There was another loud knock on the door. I went out to it, and Ashley followed me. It was my friend Odell and a pair of state cops, and behind them the greenjacket from the main hall.

Ashley told the greenjacket, "Get out of here, and keep your mouth shut."

"I just wanted to tell you, sir, I heard a shot, and two of the guests want to know—"

"Tell them you know nothing about it. Tell them it was a backfire. Understand?"

"Yes, sir."

I took the quartet to my room. I ignored Ashley, because I had heard Wolfe say he was bourgeois, and spoke to the cops.

"Nero Wolfe was sitting up in bed, rehearsing a speech he is to deliver tonight, and I was standing four yards from the open window looking at the script to prompt him. Something outside caught my attention, I don't know whether a sound or a movement, and I looked at the window, and all I consciously saw was a branch of the shrubbery moving, and I threw the script at the window. At the same time a gun went off, outside, and Wolfe called to me, and I saw his cheek was bleeding and went to him and took a look. Then I phoned the hotel and got busy mopping blood until the doctor came, which was just before you did."

One of the cops had a notebook out. "What's your name?"

"Archie Goodwin."

He wrote it down. "Did you see anyone in the shrubbery?"

"No. If you'll permit a suggestion, it's been less than ten minutes since the shot was fired. I've told you all I know. If you let the questions wait and get busy out there, you might pick up a hot trail."

"I want to see Wolfe."

"To ask him if I shot him? Well, I didn't. I even know who did. It was the man that stabbed Laszio in Pocahontas Pavilion Tuesday night. I don't know his name, but it was that guy. Would you like to grab that murderer, you two? Get out there on the trail before it cools off."

"How do you know it was the one that killed Laszio?"

"Because Wolfe started digging too close to his hole and he didn't like it. There's plenty of people that would like to see Nero Wolfe dead, but not in this neighborhood."

"Is Wolfe conscious?"

"Certainly. That way, through the foyer."

"Come on, Bill."

They tramped ahead, and Ashley and I followed, with Odell behind us.

In Wolfe's room the nurse had the table half covered with bandages and things, and an electric sterilizer had been plugged into an outlet. Wolfe, on his right side, had his back to us, and the doctor was bending over him with busy fingers.

"What about it, doc?"

"Who"—the doctor's head twisted at us—"oh, it's you fellows. Only a flesh wound in the upper cheek. I'll have to sew it."

Wolfe's voice demanded, "Who is that?"

"Quit talking. State police."

"Archie? Where are you, Archie?"

"Right here, boss." I stepped up. "The cops want to know if I shot you."

"They would. Idiots. Get them out of here. Get everybody out but you and the doctor. I'm in no condition for company."

The cop spoke up. "We want to ask you, Mr. Wolfe—"

"I have nothing to tell you, except that somebody shot at me through the window. Hasn't Mr. Goodwin told you that? Do you think *you* can catch him? Try it."

Clay Ashley said indignantly, "That's no attitude to take, Wolfe. All this damned mess comes from my permitting a gathering of people who are not of my clientele. Far from it. It seems to me—"

"I know who that is." Wolfe's head started to move, and the doctor held it firm. "That's Mr. Ashley. His clientele! Pfui. Put him out too. Put them all out. Do you hear me, Archie?"

The doctor said decisively, "That's enough. When he talks it starts bleeding."

I told the cops, "Come on, shove off. He's far enough away now so that you're in no danger." To Ashley, "You too. Give your clientele my love. Scat."

Odell had stayed over by the door and so was the first one out. Ashley and the cops were close behind. I followed them, on through the foyer, and into the public hall. There I stopped one of the cops and kept him by fastening onto a corner of his tunic, and his brother, seeing him stay, stayed with him while Ashley and Odell went on ahead. Ashley was tramping along in a fury, and Odell was trotting in the rear.

"Listen," I told the cop, "you didn't like my first suggestion to get jumping, I'll try another. This individual that stabbed Laszio and took a shot at Wolfe seems to be pretty active. He might even take it into his head to try some more target practice on the same range. It's a nice April day, and Wolfe wouldn't want the windows closed and the curtains drawn, and damned if I'm going to sit in there all day and watch the shrubbery. We came into your state alive, and we'd like to go out the same way at 12:40 tonight. How would it be if you stationed a guard where he could keep an eye on those windows and the shrubbery from behind? There's a nice seat not far away, by the brook."

"Much obliged." He sounded sarcastic. "Maybe you'd like to have the colonel come down from Charleston so you can give him instructions."

I waved a hand. "I'm upset. I've had no sleep, and my boss got shot and darned near had his brains spilled. I'm surprised I've been as polite as I have. It *would* be nice to know that those windows are being watched. Will you do it?"

"Yes. I'll phone in a report and get a couple of men." He eyed me. "You didn't see any more than you told me. Huh?"

I told him no, and he turned and took his brother with him.

In Wolfe's room the ministrations were proceeding. I stood at the foot of the bed and watched for a few minutes, then, turning, my eye fell on the script still lying on the floor, and I picked the script up and examined it. Sure enough, the bullet had gone right through it and had torn loose one of the metal fasteners that held the sheets together. I smoothed it out and tossed it on the bureau and resumed my post at the foot of the bed.

The doctor was a little slow but he was good and thorough. He had started the sewing, and Wolfe, who lay with his eyes closed, informed me in a murmur that he had declined the offer of a local anesthetic. His hand on the coverlet was clenched into a fist, and each time the needle went through the flesh he grunted. After a few stitches he asked, "Does my grunting hamper you?" The doctor told him no, and then the grunts got louder. When the sewing was done and the bandaging started, the doctor told me, as he worked, that the wound was superficial but would be somewhat painful and the patient should have rest and freedom from disturbance. He was dressing it so that it needn't be touched again until we got to New York. The patient insisted that he intended to deliver a speech that evening and wouldn't be persuaded out of it, and in case such excessive muscular action started a hemorrhage the doctor must be called. It was desirable for the patient to stay in bed until dinnertime.

He finished. The nurse helped him gather up paraphernalia and debris, including bloody towels. She offered to help Wolfe change the soiled pajama top for a fresh one, but he refused. I got out the expense roll, but the doctor said it would be put on the bill, and then he walked around to the other side of the bed to get a front view of Wolfe's face and give him some parting admonitions.

I accompanied them as far as the main hall to tell the greenjacket there that no visitors of any description would be desired in Suite 60. Back in Wolfe's room, the patient was still lying on his right side with his eyes closed.

I went to the phone. "Hello, operator? Listen. The doctor says Mr. Wolfe must have rest and quiet. Will you please announce to the switchboard that this phone is not to ring? I don't care who—"

"Archie. Cancel that."

I told the mouthpiece, "Wait a minute. Yes, sir?"

Wolfe hadn't moved, but he spoke again. "Cancel that order about the phone."

"But you—"

"Cancel it."

I told the operator to return to the status quo ante, hung up, and approached the patient. "Excuse me. I wouldn't butt in on your personal affairs for anything. If you want that phone bell jangling—"

"I don't want it." He opened his eyes. "But we can't do anything if we're incommunicado. Did you say the bullet went through my speech? Let me see it, please."

His tone was such that I got the script from the bureau and handed it to him without demur. Frowning, he fingered it, and as he saw the extent of the damage the frown deepened. He handed it back. "I suppose you can decipher it. What did you throw it for?"

"Because I had it in my hand. If it hadn't deflected the bullet you might have got it for good—or it might have missed you entirely, I admit that. Depending on how good a shot he is."

"I suppose so. That man's a dolt. I had washed my hands of it. He stood an excellent chance of avoiding exposure, and now he's done for. We'll get him."

"Oh. We will?"

"Certainly. I have plenty of forbearance, God knows, but I'm not a complacent target for firearms. While I was being bandaged I considered probabilities, and we have little time to act. Hand me that mirror. I suppose I'm a spectacle."

"You're pretty well decorated." I passed the mirror to him, and he studied his reflection with his lips compressed. "About getting this bird, I'm for it, but from the way you look and what the doctor said—"

"It can't be helped. Close the windows and draw the shades."

"It'll be gloomy. I told the cop to put a guard outside—"

"Do as I say, please. I don't trust guards. Besides, I would be constantly glancing at the window, and I don't want my mental processes interrupted. No, clear to the bottom, there'll be plenty of light. That's better. The others too. Good. Now bring me underwear, a clean shirt, the dressing gown from the closet—"

"You've got to stay in bed."

"Nonsense. There's more blood in the head lying down than sitting up. If people come here I can't very well make myself presentable, with the gibbosity of this confounded bandage, but at least I needn't give offense to decency. Get the underwear."

I collected garments while he manipulated his mass, first to a sitting position on the edge of the bed, and then onto his feet, using grunts for punctuation. He frowned in distaste at the bloody pajama top when he got it off, and I brought towels, wet and dry. As the operation progressed he instructed me as to details of the program.

"All we can do is try our luck on the possibilities until we find a fact that will allow only one interpretation. I detest alternatives, and at present that is all we have. Do you know how to black a man up with burnt cork? Well, you can try. Get some corks—I suppose we can use matches—and get a Kanawha Spa livery, medium size, including cap. But, first of all, New York on the telephone. No, not those socks, black ones, I may not feel like changing again before dinner. We'll have to find time to finish that speech. I presume you know the numbers of Saul Panzer and Inspector Cramer. But if we should get our fact from there, it would be undesirable to run the risk of that blackguard learning we had asked for it. We must prevent that . . ."

14

My friend Odell stood beside a lobby pillar with an enormous leaf of a palm spread over his head, looking at me with a doubtful glint in his eye that I didn't deserve.

I said, "Nor am I trying to negotiate a hot date, nor am I engaged in snooping. I've told you straight, I merely want to make sure that a private phone call is private. It's not suspicion, it's just precaution. As for your having to consult the manager, what the hell kind of a house dick are you if you haven't even got the run of your own corral? You come along and stay with me, and if I start anything you don't like you can throw stones at me. Which reminds me, this Kanawha Spa seems to be pretty hard on guests. If you don't get hit with a rock you get plugged with a bullet. Huh?"

Without erasing the doubt, he made to move. "Okay. The next time I tell a man a joke it'll be the one about Pat and Mike. Come on, Rollo."

He led me through the lobby, down past the elevators, and along a ways to a narrow side corridor. It had doors with frosted glass panels, and he opened one on the right side and motioned me in. It was a small room, and all its furniture consisted of a switchboard running its entire length, perhaps fifteen feet, six maidens in a row with their backs to us, and the straight-backed chairs which the maidens inhabited. Odell went to the one at the end and conversed a moment, and then thumbed me over to the third in the line. From the back her neck looked a little scrawny, but when she turned to us she had smooth white skin and promising blue eyes.

Odell said something to her, and she nodded, and I told her, "I've just thought up a new way to make a phone call. Mr. Wolfe in Suite 60, Upshur Pavilion, wants to put in a call to New York and I'm going to stay and watch you do it."

"Suite 60? That's the man that was shot."

"Yep."

"And it was you that told me I'm a wonder."

"Yep. In a way I came to check up. If you'll just get—"

"Excuse me." She turned and talked and listened and monkeyed with some plugs. When she was through I said, "Get New York, Liberty 2-3306, and put it on Suite 60."

She grinned. "Personally conducted phone calls, huh?"

"Right. I haven't had so much fun in ages."

She got busy. I became aware of activity at my elbow and saw that Odell had got out a notebook and pencil and was writing something down. I craned the neck for a glimpse of his scrawl and then told him pleasantly, "I like a man that knows his job the way you do. To save you the trouble of listening for the next one, it's going to be Spring 7-3100. New York Police Headquarters."

"Much obliged. What's he doing, yelling for help because he got a little scratch on the face?"

I made a fitting reply with my mind elsewhere, because I was watching operations. The board was an old style, and it was easy to tell if she was listening in. Her hands were all over the place, pushing and dropping plugs, and it was only five minutes or so before I heard her say, "Mr. Wolfe? Ready with New York. Go ahead, please." She flashed me a grin. "Who was I supposed to tell about it? Mr. Odell here?"

I grinned back. "Don't you bother your little head about it. Be good, dear child—"

"And let who will wear diamonds. I know. Have you heard the one —excuse me."

Odell stayed with me till the end. He had a long wait, for Wolfe's talk with Saul Panzer lasted a good quarter of an hour, and the second one, with Inspector Cramer—provided he got Cramer—almost as long. When it was finished and the plugs had been pulled, I thought it was only sociable to ask the maiden whether she preferred oblong diamonds or round ones, and she replied that she would much rather have a copy of the Bible because most of hers were getting worn out, she read them so much. I made a feint to pat her on the head and she ducked, and Odell plucked me by the sleeve.

I left him in the lobby with thanks and an assurance that I hadn't forgotten his aspirations to the Hotel Churchill, regarding which Mr. Wolfe would sound out Mr. Liggett at the first opportunity.

A minute later I had an opportunity myself but was too busy to take advantage of it. Going away from the main entrance in the direction of my next errand took me past the mounting block, and there was a bunch of horses around, some mounted and some not, with green-jacket grooms. I like the look of horses at a distance of ten feet or more, and I slowed down as I went by. It was there I saw Liggett, with the right clothes on, which I suppose he had borrowed, dismounting from a big bay. Another reason I slowed down was because I thought I might see another guest get stepped on, but it didn't happen so. Not that I have anything against guests as guests; it's only my natural feeling about people who pay twenty bucks a day for a room to sleep in, and they always look either too damn sleek or as if they had been born with a bellyache. I know if I was a horse . . .

But I had errands. Wolfe had already been alone in that room for over half an hour, and although I had left strict orders with the greenjacket to admit no one to Suite 60 under any pretext, and the door was locked, I didn't care much for the setup. So I got along to Pocahontas Pavilion in quick time. I met Lisette Putti and Vallenko, with tennis rackets, near the entrance, and Mamma Mondor was on the veranda, knitting. On the driveway a state cop and a plug-ugly in cits sat in a car smoking cigarettes. Inside, both parlors were empty, but there was plenty going on in the kitchen—cooks and helpers, greenjackets, masters, darting around, looking concentrated. Apparently another free-for-all lunch was in preparation, not to mention the dinner for that evening, which was to illustrate the subject of Wolfe's speech by consisting of dishes that had originated in America. That, of course, was to be concocted under the direction of Louis Servan, and he was there in white cap and apron, moving around, feeling, looking, smelling, tasting, and instructing. I allowed myself a grin at the sight of Albert Malfi, the Corsican fruit slicer, also capped and aproned, trotting at Servan's heels, before I went across to accost the dean, just missing a collision with Domenico Rossi as he bounced away from a range.

Servan's dignified old face clouded over when he saw me. "Ah, Mr. Goodwin! I've just heard of that terrible—to Mr. Wolfe. Mr. Ashley phoned from the hotel. That a guest of mine, our guest of honor—terrible! I'll call on him as soon as I can manage to leave here. It's not serious? He can be with us?"

I reassured him, and two or three others trotted up, and I accepted their sympathy for my boss and told them it would be just as well not to pay any calls for a few hours. Then I told Servan I hated to interrupt a busy man but needed a few words with him, and he went with me to the small parlor. After some conversation he called in Moulton, the headwaiter with a piece out of his ear, and gave him instructions.

When Moulton had departed, Servan hesitated before he said, "I wanted to see Mr. Wolfe anyway. Mr. Ashley tells me that he got a startling story from two of my waiters. I can understand their reluctance, but I can't have—my friend Laszio murdered here in my own dining room." He passed his hand wearily across his forehead. "This should have been such a happiness. I'm over seventy years old, Mr. Goodwin, and this is the worst thing that has ever happened to me—

and I must get back to the kitchen—Crabtree's a good man, but he's flighty and I don't trust him with all that commotion in there."

"Forget it." I patted his arm. "I mean, forget the murder. Let Nero Wolfe do the worrying, I always do. Did you elect your four new members this morning?"

"Yes. Why?"

"I was just curious about Malfi. Did he get in?"

"Malfi? In Les Quinze Maîtres? Good heavens, no!"

"Okay. I was just curious. You go on back to the kitchen and enjoy yourself. I'll give Wolfe your message about lunch."

He nodded and pattered away. I had then been gone from Upshur more than an hour, and I hotfooted it back by the shortest path.

Going in after the outdoor sunshine, Wolfe's room seemed somber, but the maid had been in and the bed was made and everything tidy. He had the big chair turned to face the windows and sat there with his speech in his hand, frowning at the last page. I had sung out from the foyer to let him know all was well and now approached to take a look at the bandage. It seemed in order, and there was no sign of any fresh bleeding.

I reported, "Everything's set. Servan turned the details over to Moulton. They all send their best regards and wish you were along. Servan's going to send a couple of trays of lunch over to us. It's a grand day outdoors—too bad you're cooped up like this. Our client has taken advantage of it by going horseback riding."

"We have no client."

"I was referring to Mr. Liggett. I still think that since he offered to pay for a job of detective work you might as well give him that pleasure. Not to mention hiring Berin for him. Did you get Saul and Cramer?"

"Weren't you at the switchboard?"

"Yes, but I didn't know who you got."

"I got them. That alternative is being cared for." He sighed. "This thing hurts. What are they cooking for lunch?"

"Lord, I don't know. Five or six of them are messing around. Certainly it hurts, and you won't collect a damn cent for it." I sat down and rested my head against the back of the chair because I was tired of holding it up. "Not only that, it seems to have made you more contrary even than usual, it and the loss of sleep. I know you sneer at what you call routine, but I've seen you get results from it now and then, and no matter how much of a genius you are, it wouldn't do any harm to find out what various people were doing at a quarter past ten this morning. For instance, if you found that Leon Blanc was in the kitchen making soup, he couldn't very well have been out there in the shrubbery shooting at you. I'm just explaining how it's done."

"Thank you."

"Thank me, and go on being contrary, huh?"

"I'm not contrary, merely intelligent. I've often told you, a search for negative evidence is a desperate last resort when no positive evidence can be found. Collecting and checking alibis is dreary and usually futile drudgery. No. Get your positive evidence, and if you find it confronted by an alibi, and if your evidence is any good, break the alibi. Anyhow, I'm not interested in the man who shot me. The man I want is the one who stabbed Laszio."

I stared. "What's this, a riddle? You yourself said it was the same one."

"Certainly. But since it was his murdering Laszio that led to his shooting me, obviously it's the murder we must prove. Unless we can prove he killed Laszio, how can we give him a motive for trying to kill me? And if you can't demonstrate a motive, what the devil does it matter where he was at a quarter past ten? The only thing that will do us any good is direct evidence that he committed the murder."

"Oh, well." I waved a hand feebly. "If that's all. Naturally you've got *that.*"

"I have. It is being tested."

"I'll call. What evidence and who?"

He started to shake his head, then winced and stopped. "It is being tested. I don't pretend that the evidence is conclusive, far from it. We must await the test. It is so little conclusive that I have arranged for this performance with Mr. Blanc because we are pressed for time and no alternative can be ignored. And, after all, it is quite possible—though I shouldn't think he would have a gun—there's someone at the door."

The performance with Blanc was elaborate but a complete washout. Its only advantage was that it kept me occupied and awake until lunchtime. I wasn't surprised at the result, and I don't think Wolfe was either. He was just being thorough and not neglecting anything.

The first arrivals were Moulton and Paul Whipple, and they had the props with them. I took them in to Wolfe for an explanation of the project and then deposited them in my room and shut the door on them. A few minutes later Leon Blanc came.

The chef and the gastronome had quite a chat. Blanc was of course distressed at Wolfe's injury and said so at length. Then they got on to the business. Blanc had come, he said, at Servan's request and would answer any questions Mr. Wolfe might care to ask. That was an order for anybody, but Blanc filled it pretty well, including the pointed and insistent queries regarding the extent of his acquaintanceship with Mrs. Laszio. Blanc stuck to it that he had known her rather well when she had been Mrs. Vukčić and he had been *chef de cuisine* at the Churchill, but that in the past five years, since he had gone to Boston, he had seen her only two or three times, and they had never been at all intimate. Then Wolfe got on to Tuesday night and the period Blanc had spent in his room at Pocahontas Pavilion, while the others were tasting Sauce Printemps and someone was stabbing Laszio. I heard most of it from a distance because I was in the bathroom, with the door open a crack, experimenting with the burnt cork on the back of my hand. Servan had sent an alcohol burner and enough corks for a minstrel show.

Blanc balked a little when Wolfe got to the suggestion of the masquerade test, but not very strenuously, and I opened the bathroom door and invited him in. We had a picnic. With him stripped to his underwear, I first rubbed in a layer of cold cream and then started with the cork. I suppose I didn't do it like an expert, since I wasn't one, but, by gosh, I got him black. The ears and the edge of the hair were a problem, and he claimed I got some in his eye, but it was only because he blinked too hard. Then he put on the suit of livery, including the cap, and it wasn't a bad job at all, except that Moulton hadn't been able to dig up any black gloves, and we had to use dark brown ones.

I took him in to Wolfe for approval, then telephoned Pocahontas Pavilion and got Mrs. Coyne and told her we were ready.

In five minutes she was there. I stepped into the corridor to give her a brief explanation of the program, explaining that she wasn't to open her mouth if she wanted to help Wolfe keep her out of it, and then, admitting her to the foyer and leaving her there, I went back in to pose Blanc. He had got pretty well irritated before I had finished with him in the bathroom, but now Wolfe had him all soothed down again. I stood him over beyond the foot of the bed, at what looked like the right distance, pulled his cap lower, had him put his finger to his lips, and told him to hold it. Then I went to the door to the foyer and opened it six inches.

After ten seconds I told Blanc that would do for that pose and went to the foyer and took Lio Coyne out to the corridor again.

"Well?"

She shook her head. "No. It wasn't that man."

"How do you know it wasn't?"

"His ears are too big. It wasn't him."

"Could you swear to that in a court?"

"But you"—her eyes got narrower—"you said I wouldn't—"

"All right, you won't. But how sure are you?"

"I'm very sure. This man is more slender too."

"Okay. Much obliged. Mr. Wolfe may want to speak to you later on."

The others said the same thing. I posed Blanc twice more, once facing the door for Paul Whipple, and the second time with his back to it for Moulton. Whipple said he would be willing to swear that the man he had seen by the screen in the dining room was not the one he had seen in Wolfe's room, and Moulton said he couldn't swear to it because he had only seen the man's back, but he thought it wasn't the same man. I sent them back to Pocahontas.

Then I had to help Blanc clean up. Getting it off was twice as hard as putting it on, and I don't know if he ever did get his ears clean again. Considering that he wasn't a murderer at all, he was pretty nice about it. What with Wolfe's blood and Blanc's burnt cork, I certainly raised cain with Kanawha Spa towels that day.

Blanc stood and told Wolfe, "I have submitted to all this because Louis Servan requested it. I know murderers are supposed to be punished. If I were one, I would expect to be. This is a frightful experience for all of us, Mr. Wolfe, frightful. I didn't kill Phillip Laszio, but if it were possible for me to bring him to life again by lifting a finger, do you know what I'd do? I would do this." He thrust both hands into his pockets as far as they would go and kept them there.

He turned to go, but his departure was postponed a few minutes longer by a new arrival. The change in program had of course made it necessary to tell the greenjacket in the hall that the embargo on visitors was lifted, and now came the first of a string that kept knocking at the door intermittently all afternoon.

This one was my friend Barry Tolman.

"How's Mr. Wolfe?"

"Battered and belligerent. Go on in."

He entered, opened his mouth at Wolfe, and then saw who was standing there.

"Oh. You here, Mr. Blanc?"

"Yes. At Mr. Servan's request—"

Wolfe put in, "We've been doing an experiment. I don't believe you'll need to waste time with Mr. Blanc. What about it, Archie? Did Mr. Blanc kill Laszio?"

I shook my head. "No, sir. Three outs and the side's retired."

Tolman looked at me, at Wolfe, at Blanc. "Is that so. Anyhow, I may want to see you later. You'll be at Pocahontas?"

Blanc told him yes, not very amiably, expressed a hope that Wolfe would feel better by dinnertime, and went. When I got back from escorting him to the door, Tolman had sat down and had his head cocked on one side for a look at Wolfe's bandage, and Wolfe was saying, ". . . not to me, no, sir. The doctor called it superficial. But I assure you it is highly dangerous to the man who did it. And look here." He displayed the mangled script of the speech. "The bullet did that before it struck me. Mr. Goodwin saved my life by tossing my speech at the window. So he says. I am willing to grant it. Where is Mr. Berin?"

"Here. At Pocahontas with—with his daughter. I brought him myself, just now. They phoned me at Quinby about your being shot. Do you think it was the one that stabbed Laszio who did it?"

"Who else?"

"But why was he after you? You were through with it."

"He didn't know that." Wolfe stirred in his chair, winced, and added bitterly, "I'm not through with it now."

"That suits me. I don't say I'm glad you got shot—and you started on Blanc? What made you decide it wasn't him?"

Wolfe started to explain, but another interruption took me away. This time it was the lunch trays, and Louis Servan had certainly put on the dog. There were three enormous trays and three waiters, and a fourth greenjacket as an outrider for opening doors and clearing traffic. I was hungry, and the smells that came from under the covered services made me more so. The outrider, who was Moulton himself, after a bow and an announcement to Wolfe, unfolded serving stands for the trays and advanced to the table with a cloth in his hand.

Wolfe told Tolman, "Excuse me, please." With a healthy grunt he lifted himself from his chair and made his way across to the serving stands. Moulton joined him and hovered deferentially. Wolfe lifted one of the covers, bent his head, gazed, and sniffed. Then he looked at Moulton. "Piroshki?"

"Yes, sir. By Mr. Vallenko."

"Yes. I know." He lifted other covers, bent, and smelled, with careful nods to himself. He straightened up again. "Artichokes barigoule?"

"I think, sir, he called them 'drigante.' Mr. Mondor. Something like that."

"No matter. Leave it all here, please. We'll serve ourselves, if you don't mind."

"But Mr. Servan told me—"

"I prefer it that way. Leave it here on the trays."

"I'll leave a man—"

"No. Please. I'm having a conversation. Out, all of you."

They went. It appeared that if I was going to get anything to eat I'd have to work for it, so I called on the muscles for another effort. As

Wolfe returned to his chair I asked, "How do we do it? Boarding-house style à la scoop shovel?"

He waited until he got deposited before he answered. But he sighed first. "No. Telephone the hotel for a luncheon menu."

I stared at him. "Maybe you're delirious?"

"Archie." He sounded savage. "You may guess the humor I'm in. That piroshki is by Vallenko, and the artichokes are by Mondor. But how the devil do I know who was in that kitchen or what happened there? These trays were intended for us, and probably everyone knew it. For me. I am still hoping to go home tonight. Phone the hotel, and get those trays out of here so I can't smell them. Put them in your room and leave them there."

Tolman said, "But, my God, man—if you really think—we can have that stuff analyzed—"

"I don't want to analyze it, I want to eat it. And I can't. I'm not going to. There probably is nothing at all wrong with it, and look at me, terrorized, intimidated, by that blackguard! What good would it do to analyze it? I tell you, sir—Archie?"

It was the door again. The smell from those covered dishes had me in almost as bad a state as Wolfe, and I was hoping it might be a food inspector from the Board of Health to certify them unadulterated, but it was only the greenjacket from the hall. He had a telegram addressed to Nero Wolfe.

I went back in with it, tore the envelope open, and handed it to him. He pulled it out and read it.

He murmured, "Indeed." At the sound of the new tone in his voice I gave him a sharp glance. He handed the telegram back to me, unfolded. "Read it to Mr. Tolman."

I did so:

NERO WOLFE KANAWHA SPA W VA
NOT MENTIONED ANY PAPER STOP CRAMER COOPERATING
STOP PROCEEDING STOP WILL PHONE FROM DESTINATION
PANZER

Wolfe said softly, "That's better. Much better. We might almost eat that piroshki now, but there's a chance—no. Phone the hotel, Archie. And, Mr. Tolman, I believe there will be an opportunity for you also to cooperate."

15

Jerome Berin shook both his fists so that his chair trembled under him. "God above! Such a dirty dog! Such a—" He stopped himself abruptly and demanded, "You say it was not Blanc? Not Vukčić? Not my old friend Zelota?"

Wolfe murmured, "None of them, I think."

"Then I repeat, a dirty dog!" Berin leaned forward and tapped Wolfe on the knee. "I tell you frankly, it did not take a dog to kill Laszio. Anyone might have done that, anyone at all, merely as an incident in the disposal of garbage. *En passant*. True, it is bad to stab a man in the back, but when one is in a hurry the niceties must sometimes be overlooked. No, only for killing Laszio, even in that manner, I would not say a dog. But to shoot at you through a window—you, the guest of honor of Les Quinze Maîtres! Only because you had interested yourself in the cause of justice! Because you had undertaken to establish my innocence! Because you had the good sense to know that I could not possibly have made seven mistakes of those nine sauces! And let me tell you—will you credit it when I tell you what they gave me to eat in that place, in that jail in that place?"

He went on to tell, and it sounded awful. He had come, with his daughter, to express his appreciation of Wolfe's efforts in his behalf. It was nearly four o'clock, and there was sunlight in the room, for Tolman had arranged for a double guard on the windows, the other side of the shrubbery, and the shades were up and the windows open. The lunch from the hotel may not have been piroshki by Vallenko, but it had been adequate for my purposes, and Wolfe had been able to get it down in spite of the difficulty he had chewing.

I had completely abandoned the idea of a little nap; there wasn't a chance. Tolman had stayed nearly until the end of lunch, and after that was finished Rossi and Mondor and Coyne had dropped in to offer commiseration for Wolfe's wound, and they had been followed by others. Even Louis Servan had made it for a few minutes, though I didn't understand how he had been able to get away from the kitchen. Also, around three o'clock, there had been a phone call from New York, which Wolfe took himself. His end of it consisted mostly of grunts, and all I knew about it when he got through was that he had been talking with Inspector Cramer. But I knew he hadn't got any bad news, for afterward he sat and rubbed the side of his nose and looked self-satisfied.

Constanza Berin sat for twenty minutes on the edge of her chair trying to get a word in, and when her father called an intermission to get his pipe lit she finally succeeded.

"Mr. Wolfe, I—I was terrible this morning."

He moved his eyes at her. "You were indeed, Miss Berin. I have often noticed that the more beautiful a woman is, especially a young one, the more liable she is to permit herself unreasonable fits. It's something that you acknowledge it. Tell me, when you feel it coming on like that, is there nothing you can do to stop it? Have you ever tried?"

She laughed at him. "But it isn't fits. I don't have fits. I was scared and mad because they had put my father in jail for murder, and I knew he hadn't done it, and they seemed to think they had proof against him, and then I was told that it was you who had found the proof. How was I going to be reasonable about that? And in a strange country I had never been in before. America is an awful country."

"There are those who would disagree with you."

"I suppose so. I suppose it isn't so much the country. Maybe it's the people who live here—oh, excuse me, I don't mean you, or Mr. Goodwin. I'm sure you are very amiable, and of course Mr. Goodwin is, with a wife and so many children—"

"Indeed." Wolfe shot me a withering glance. "How are the children, Archie? Well, I hope?"

"Fine, thanks." I waved a hand. "Doggone the little shavers, I sure do miss 'em, away from home like this. I can hardly wait to get back."

Berin took his pipe from his mouth to nod at me. "The little ones are nice. Now my daughter here"—he shrugged—"she is nice, naturally, but, God above, she drives me mad!" He leaned to tap Wolfe's knee with the stem of the pipe. "Speaking of getting back, is it true what I am told, that these dogs can keep us here on and on until they permit us to go? Merely because that Laszio got a knife in his back? My daughter and I were to leave tonight for New York, and then to Canada. I am out of jail but I am not free. Is that it?"

"I'm afraid that's it. Were you intending to take the midnight train to New York?"

"I was. And now they tell me no one leaves this place until they learn who killed that dog! If we wait on that for that imbecile Tolman, and that other one, that one who squints—" He replaced his pipe and puffed until he had clouds.

"But we needn't wait on them." Wolfe sighed. "Thank God. I think, sir, it would be wise to have your bags packed, and if you have reservations on that train, keep them. Fortunately you did not have to wait for Mr. Tolman to discover the truth about those sauces. If you had—"

"I might not have left at all. I know that. I might have got this." Berin used the edge of his hand for a cleaver to slice off his head. "Certainly I would still be in that jail, and within three days I would have starved. We Cataláns can take death when it comes, but, God above, a man that can swallow that food is not a man, he is not even a beast! I know what I owe you, and I called for blessings on you with every bite of my lunch. I discussed it with Servan. I told him how greatly I am indebted to you, and that I do no man the honor of remaining in debt to him. I told Servan I must pay you—he is our host here, and a man of delicacy. He said you would not take pay. He said it had been offered, and you had scorned it. I understand and respect your feeling, since you are our guest of honor—"

Another knock on the door made me leave Wolfe simmering in the juice of the stew he had made. I had always known that someday he would talk too much for his own good, and as I went to the foyer I was wearing a grin—I admit malicious—and reflecting on how it probably felt at the moment to be a jewel on the cushion of hospitality.

The new arrival was only Vukčić, but he served as well as another bullet through the window would have done to make a break in the conversation and take it away from vulgar things like payments for services rendered. Vukčić was in a mood. He acted embarrassed, gloomy, nervous, and abstracted. A few minutes after he arrived the Berins left, and then he stood in front of Wolfe with his arms folded, frowning down, and told him that in spite of Wolfe's impertinence that morning on the subject of howling on a hillside, it was a duty of old friendship to call personally to offer sympathy and regrets for an injury suffered.

Wolfe snapped, "I was shot over six hours ago. I might have died by now."

"Oh, come, Nero. Surely not. They said it was only your cheek, and I can see for myself—"

"I lost a quart of blood. Archie, did you say a quart?"

I hadn't said anything, but I'm always loyal. "Yes, sir. At least that. Closer to two. Of course I couldn't stop to measure it, but it came out like a river, like Niagara Falls, like—"

"That will do. Thank you."

Vukčić still stood frowning down. His tangle of hair was tumbling for his eyes, but he didn't unfold his arms to comb it back with his fingers. He growled, "I'm sorry. It was a close call. If he had killed you—" A pause. "Look here, Nero. Who was it?"

"I don't know. Not with certainty—yet."

"Are you finding out?"

"Yes."

"Was it the murderer of Laszio?"

"Yes. Confound it, I like to move my head when I talk, and I can't." Wolfe put the tips of his fingers gingerly to the bandage, felt it, and let his hand drop again. "I'll tell you something, Marko. This mist that has arisen between your eyes and mine—we can't ignore it and it is futile to discuss it. All I can say is, it will shortly be dispelled."

"The devil it will. How?"

"By the course of history. By Atropos, and me as her agent. At any rate, I am counting on that. In the meantime there is nothing we can say to each other. You are drugged again—there, I didn't mean to say that. You see, we can't talk. I would offend you, and you would bore me insufferably. *Au revoir*, Marko."

"Good God, I don't deny I'm drugged."

"I know it. You know what you're doing, and you do it anyway. Thank you for coming."

Vukčić did then unfold his arms to comb his hair. He ran his fingers through it three times, slowly, and then without saying anything turned and walked out.

Wolfe sat a long while with his eyes closed. Then he sighed deeply and asked me to take the script of the speech for a final rehearsal.

The only interruptions that time were some phone calls, from Tolman and Clay Ashley and Louis Servan. It was six o'clock before we had another caller, and when I opened the door and saw it was Raymond Liggett of the Hotel Churchill, I put on a welcoming grin because right away I smelled a fee, and among all the other irritations I was being subjected to was my dislike of seeing Wolfe exercising his brain, blowing money on long-distance calls and drinks for fourteen men, losing two nights' sleep, and getting shot, with maybe a permanent scar, all for nothing relating to the bank account. As a side issue, there was also the question of a job for my friend Odell. Not that I owed him anything, but in the detective business around New York you never know in which spot it may become desirable to be greeted by a friendly face. To have the house dick of the Churchill, or even one on his staff, a protégé of mine, might come in handy any time.

Sure enough, it appeared that a fee was in prospect. The first thing Liggett said, after he had got seated and expressed the proper sentiments regarding Wolfe's facial casualty, was that one of the objects of his call was to ask if Wolfe would be willing to reconsider the matter of approaching Berin about the job of chef de cuisine at the Hotel Churchill.

Wolfe murmured, "I'm surprised that you still want him—a man who has been accused of murder. The publicity?"

Leggett dismissed that with a gesture. "Why not? People don't eat publicity, they eat food. And you know what Berin's prestige is. Frankly, I'm more interested in his prestige than in his food. I have an excellent kitchen staff, from top to bottom."

"People do eat prestige then." Wolfe gently patted his tummy. "I don't believe I'd care for it."

Liggett smiled his thin smile. His gray eyes looked about as irritated as they had Wednesday morning, not less, and they couldn't more. He shrugged. "Well, they seem to like it. About Berin. I know that yesterday morning you said you wouldn't do it, but you also said you wouldn't investigate Laszio's murder, and I understand you've reconsidered that. Ashley tells me you've done something quite remarkable. I didn't gather just what."

Wolfe inclined his head an eighth of an inch. "Thank you."

"That's what Ashley said. Besides, it was what you discovered, whatever that was, that caused Berin's release. Berin knows that, and therefore you are in a particularly advantageous position to make a suggestion to him—or even a request. I explained to you yesterday why I'm especially anxious to get him. I can add to that, confidentially—"

"I don't want confidences, Mr. Liggett."

Liggett impatiently brushed that aside. "It's not much of a secret. A competitor has been after Berin for two years. Branting of the Alexander. I happen to know that Berin has an appointment with Branting in New York tomorrow afternoon. That's the main reason I rushed down here. I have to get at him before he sees Branting."

"And soon after your arrival he was taken to jail. That was unfortunate. But he's out now and is this minute probably at Pocahontas Pavilion. He left here two hours ago. Why the deuce don't you go and see him?"

"I told you yesterday. Because I don't think I can swing him." Liggett leaned forward. "Look here. The situation as it stands now is ideal. You got him out of jail, and he's impulsive and emotional, and he's feeling grateful to you. You can do it in one talk with him. One trouble is that I don't know what Branting has offered him, or is going to offer him, but whatever it is, I'll top it. I told you yesterday that I'd like to have him for forty thousand but would go to sixty if I had to. Now the time's short and I think I might even make it seventy. You can offer him fifty at the start—"

"I haven't agreed to offer him anything."

"But I'm telling you. You can offer him fifty thousand dollars a year. That's a lot more than he's getting at San Remo, but he may have a percentage there. Anyway, New York is something else. And if you land him I'll pay you ten thousand dollars cash."

Wolfe lifted his brows. "You want him, don't you?"

"I've got to have him. My directors have discussed this—after all, Laszio was getting along in years—and I must get him. Of course I don't own the Churchill, though I have a good block of stock. You still have time to start the ball rolling before dinner. I wanted to see you earlier this afternoon, when they brought Berin back, but on account of your accident—"

"Not an accident. Chance is without intention." Wolfe touched his bandage. "This was intended, or rather, worse."

"That's true. Of course. Will you see Berin now?"

"No."

"Tonight?"

"No."

Liggett jerked up. "But damn it, are you crazy? A chance to make ten thousand dollars"—he snapped his fingers—"just like that! Why not?"

"It's not my business, hiring chefs. I'm a detective. I stick to my profession."

"I'm not asking you to make a business of it. All it means probably, under the circumstances, is one good talk with him. You can tell him he will be executive chef, with complete control and no interference from the hotel administration, and nothing to report but results. Our cost distribution is handled—"

Wolfe was wiggling a finger. "Mr. Liggett. Please. This is a waste of time. I shall not approach Mr. Berin on behalf of the Hotel Churchill."

Silence. I covered a yawn. I was surprised that Liggett wasn't bouncing up with exasperation, since his tendencies seemed to run in that direction, but all he did was sit still, not a muscle moving, and look at Wolfe. Wolfe, likewise motionless, returned the gaze with half-shut eyes.

The silence lasted all of a minute. Finally Liggett said, in a level tone with no exasperation at all, "I'll give you twenty thousand cash to get Berin for me."

"It doesn't tempt me, Mr. Liggett."

"I'll—I'll make it thirty thousand. I can give it to you in currency tomorrow morning."

Wolfe stirred a little, without unfocusing his eyes. "No. It wouldn't be worth it to you. Mr. Berin is a master chef, but not the only one alive. See here. This childish pretense is ridiculous. You were ill advised to come to me like this. You are probably a man of some natural sense, and with only your own interests to consult, and left to your own counsel and devices, I am sure you would never have done such a thing. You were sent here, Mr. Liggett. I know that. It was a mistake that might have been expected, considering who did it. Pfui. You must, I suppose, go back and report your failure, but if you are moved to consult further it would be vastly better to consult only yourself."

"I don't know what you're talking about. I'm making you a straight proposal."

Wolfe shrugged. "If I am incoherent, that ends communication. Report failure, then, to yourself."

"I'm not reporting failure to anyone." Liggett's eyes were hard and so was his tone. "I came to you only because it seemed practical. To save annoyance. I can do—whatever I want done—without you."

"Then by all means do it."

"But I would still like to save annoyance. I'll pay you fifty thousand dollars."

Wolfe slowly, barely perceptibly, shook his head. "You'll have to report failure, Mr. Liggett. If it is true, as the cynic said, that every man has his price, you couldn't hand me mine in currency."

The phone rang. When a man turns cold and still I like to keep my eye on him just in case, so I sidled around beyond Liggett's chair without turning my back on him. The first voice I heard in the receiver sounded like the blue-eyed belle, and she said she had a New York call. Then I heard gruff tones demanding Nero Wolfe and was informed that Inspector Cramer wanted him. I turned. "For you, sir. Mr. Purdy."

With a grunt he labored to lift it from the chair. He stood and looked down at our caller. "This is a confidential affair, Mr. Liggett. And since our business is concluded—if you don't mind?"

Liggett took it as it was given. Without a word, without either haste or hesitation, he arose and departed. I strolled behind him to the foyer, and when he was out and the door closed I turned the key.

Wolfe's conversation with Cramer lasted more than ten minutes, and this time, as I sat and listened, I got something out of it besides grunts, but not enough to make a good picture. It seemed to me that he had distrusted my powers of dissimulation as far as was necessary, so when he hung up I was all set to put in a requisition for light and lucidity, but he had barely got back in his chair when the phone rang again. This time she told me it was a call from Charleston, and after some clicking and crackling I heard a voice in my ears that was as familiar as the Ventura Skin Preserver theme song.

"Hello, Mr. Wolfe?"

"No, you little shrimp, this is the Supreme Court speaking."

"Oh, Archie! How goes it?"

"Marvelous. Having a fine rest. Hold it, here's Mr. Wolfe." I handed him the receiver. "Saul Panzer from Charleston."

That was another ten-minute talk, and it afforded me a few more hints and scraps of the alternative that Wolfe had apparently settled on, though it still seemed fairly incredible in spots. When it was finished Wolfe ambled back to his seat again, leaned back with careful caution, and got his fingers joined at the dome of his rotunda.

He demanded, "What time is it?"

I glanced at my wrist. "Quarter to seven."

He grunted. "Only a little over an hour till dinner. Don't let me forget to have that speech in my pocket when we go over there. Can you remember a few things without putting them down?"

"Sure. Any quantity."

"They are all important. First, I must talk with Mr. Tolman—I suppose he is at the hotel as arranged. Then I must telephone Mr. Servan—that may be difficult. I believe it is not customary to have guests the last evening. In this case the tradition must be violated. While I am telephoning, you will lay out everything we shall need, pack the bags, and arrange for their delivery at the train. We may be pressed for time around midnight. Also send to the hotel for our bill and pay it. Did I hear you say you have your pistol along? Good. I trust it won't be needed but carry it. And confound it, send for a barber. I can't shave myself. Then get Mr. Tolman and start on the bags. I'll discuss the evening program while we're dressing."

16

The tradition was violated, and I overheard a few grumbles about it in the big parlor before the door to the dining room was thrown open and Louis Servan appeared on the threshold to invite us in. Chiefly, though, as they sipped sherry or vermouth in scattered groups, the grumbles were on another subject: the decree that had been issued that none of them was to leave the jurisdiction of West Virginia until permission had been given by the authorities. Domenico Rossi orated about it, making it plenty loud enough to be heard by Barry Tolman, who stood by the radio, looking worried but handsome. Ramsey Keith bellowed his opinion of the outrage; while Jerome Berin said, God above, it was barbarous, but they would be fools to let it interfere with digestion. Albert Malfi, looking a little subdued but with darts still in his eyes, seemed to have decided that courting Mamma Mondor was a sensible first step in his campaign for election in 1942. Raymond Liggett sat on the couch, conversing quietly with Marko Vukčić. My friend Tolman got it right in the neck, or rather he didn't get it at all, when Constanza Berin came in and he went up to her, looking determined, and spoke. She failed to see or hear him so completely that for a second I thought he wasn't there at all, I had just imagined it.

A couple of minutes before we started for the dining room Dina Laszio entered. The noise died down. Rossi, her father, hurried over to her, and not far behind him was Vukčić; then several others went up to pay their respects to the widow. She resembled a grieving widow about as much as I resemble a whirling dervish, but of course it can't be expected that every time a woman packs for a little trip with her husband she will take weeds along in case he happens to get bumped off. And I couldn't very well disapprove of her showing up at the feast, since I knew that Nero Wolfe had requested Servan to see her personally and insist on it.

At the table I was next to Constanza again, which was tolerable. Wolfe was at Servan's right. Vukčić was on the other side of Dina Laszio, down a ways. Liggett and Malfi were directly across from me, next to each other. Berin was across from Wolfe, on Servan's left, which seemed to me quite an honor for a guy just out of jail, and next to him was Clay Ashley, not making much of a success of attempts to appear affable. The others were here and there, with the meager supply of ladies spotted at intervals. On each plate, when we sat down, was an engraved menu:

LES QUINZE MAÎTRES

Kanawha Spa, West Virginia
Thursday, April 8th, 1937

AMERICAN DINNER

Oysters Baked in the Shell
Terrapin Maryland   Beaten Biscuits
Pan-Broiled Young Turkey
Rice Croquettes with Quince Jelly
Lima Beans in Cream   Sally Lunn
Avocado Todhunter
Pineapple Sherbet   Sponge Cake
Wisconsin Dairy Cheese   Black Coffee

As the waiters, supervised by Moulton, smoothly brought and took, Louis Servan surveyed the scene with solemn and anxious dignity. The first course should have helped to allay the anxiety, for the oysters were so plump and savory, not to mention aromatic, that it seemed likely they had been hand-fed on peanuts and blueberries. They were served with ceremony and a dash of pomp. As the waiters finished distributing the enormous tins, each holding a dozen oysters, they stood back in a line against one of the screens—the one which forty-eight hours previously had concealed the body of Phillip Laszio—and the door to the pantry hall opened to admit a brown-skinned cook in immaculate white cap and apron. He came forward a few paces, looking embarrassed enough to back right out again, but Servan stood up and beckoned to him and then turned to the table and announced to the gathering, "I wish to present to you Mr. Hyacinth Brown, the fish chef of Kanawha Spa. The baked oysters we are about to eat is his. You will judge whether it is worthy of the honor of being served to Les Quinze Maîtres. Mr. Brown wishes me to tell you that he appreciates that honor. Isn't that so, Brown?"

"Yes, sir. You said it."

There was a ripple of applause. Brown looked more embarrassed than ever, bowed, and turned and went. The masters lifted forks and waded in, and the rest of us followed suit. There were grunts and murmurs of appreciation. Rossi called something across the length of the table. Pierre Mondor stated with quiet authority, "Superb. Extreme oven?" Servan nodded gravely, and the forks played on.

With the terrapin the performance was repeated, this time the introduction being accorded to Crabtree; and when the course was finished there was a near riot of enthusiasm, and it was demanded that Crabtree reappear. Most of them got up to shake his hand, and he wasn't embarrassed at all, though he was certainly pleased. Two of them came in with the turkey. One was Grant, with wrinkled face and gray kinky hair, and the other was a tall black man that I didn't know, since he hadn't been at the party Wednesday night. I never tasted better turkey, but the other servings had been generous and my capacity limited me to one portion. Those guys eating were like a woman packing a trunk—it's not a question of capacity but of how much she has to put in. Not to mention the claret they washed it down with. They were getting merrier as they went along, and even old Servan was sending happy smiles around.

Unquestionably it was first-class fodder. I went slow on the wine. My head was fuzzy anyhow, and if I was going to be called on to save Wolfe's life again I might need what wits I had left.

There was nothing strained about the atmosphere—it was just a nice party with everyone well filled and the smell of good coffee and brandy in front of us—when finally, a little after ten o'clock, Wolfe arose to start his speech. He looked more like the plaintiff in a suit for damages than an after-dinner speaker, and he was certainly aware of it, but it didn't seem to bother him. We all got our chairs moved around to face him more comfortably and got settled into silence. He began in an easy informal tone.

"Mr. Servan, ladies, masters, fellow guests, I feel a little silly. Under different circumstances it might be both instructive and amusing for you, at least some of you, to listen to a discussion of American contributions to *la haute cuisine,* and it might be desirable to use what persuasiveness I can command to convince you that those contributions are neither negligible nor meager. But when I accepted an invitation to offer you such a discussion, which greatly pleased and flattered me, I didn't realize how unnecessary it would be at the moment scheduled for its delivery. It is delightful to talk about food, but infinitely more delightful to eat it, and we have eaten. A man once declared to me that one of the keenest pleasures in life was to chose his eyes and dream of beautiful women, and when I suggested that it would be still more agreeable to open his eyes and look at them, he said not at all, for the ones he dreamed about were *all* beautiful, far more beautiful than any his eye ever encountered. Similarly, it might be argued that if I am eloquent the food I talk to you about may be better than the food you have eaten; but even that specious excuse is denied me. I can describe, and pay tribute to, some superlative American dishes, but I can't surpass the oysters and terrapin and turkey which were so recently there" —he indicated the table—"and are now here." With a gentle palm he delicately patted the appropriate spot.

They applauded. Mondor cried, *"Bien dit!"* Servan beamed.

Properly speaking, he hadn't started the speech yet, for that wasn't in it. Now he started. For the first ten minutes or so I was uneasy. There was nothing in the world I would have enjoyed more than watching Nero Wolfe wallowing in discomfiture, but not in the presence of outsiders. When that happy time came, which it never had yet, I wanted it to be a special command performance for Archie Goodwin and no one else around. And I was uneasy because it seemed quite possible that the hardships on the train and loss of sleep and getting shot at might have upset him so that he would forget the darned speech, but after the first ten minutes I saw there was nothing to worry about. He was sailing along. I took another sip of brandy and relaxed.

By the time he was half through I began to worry about something else. I glanced at my wrist. It was getting late. Charleston was only sixty miles away, and Tolman had said it was a good road and could easily be made in an hour and a half. Knowing how complicated the program was, it was my opinion that there wasn't much chance of getting away that night anyhow, but it would have ruined the setup entirely if anything had happened to Saul. So my second big relief came when the greenjacket from the hall entered softly from the parlor, as he had been instructed, and gave me the high sign. I sidled out of my chair with as little disturbance as possible and tiptoed out.

There in the small parlor sat a little guy with a big nose, in need of a shave, with an old brown cap hanging on his knee. He stood up and stuck out his hand, and I took it with a grin.

"Hello, darling. I never would have thought that the time would come when you would look handsome to me. Turn around—how do you look behind?"

Saul Panzer demanded, "How's Mr. Wolfe?"

"Swell. He's in there making a speech I taught him."

"You sure he's all right?"

"Why not? Oh, you mean his casualty." I waved a hand. "A mere nothing. He thinks he's a hero. I wish to God they'd shoot me next time so he'd stop bragging. Have you got anything?"

Saul nodded. "I've got everything."

"Is there anything you need to explain to Wolfe before he springs it?"

"I don't think so. I've got everything he asked for. The whole Charleston police force jumped into it."

"Yeah, I know. My friend Mr. Tolman arranged that. I've got another friend named Odell that throws stones at people—remind me to tell you about it sometime. This is a jolly place. Then you wait here till you're called. I'd better go back in. Have you had anything to eat?"

He said his inside was attended to, and I left him.

Back in the dining room again, I resumed my seat beside Constanza, and when Wolfe paused at the end of a paragraph I took my handkerchief from my breast pocket, passed it across my lips, and put it back again. He gave me a fleeting glance to acknowledge the signal. He had reached the part about the introduction of filé powder to the New Orleans market by the Choctaw Indians on Bayou Lacombe, so I knew he had got to page fourteen. It looked as though he was putting it over in good style. Even Domenico Rossi looked absorbed, in spite of the fact that in one place Wolfe specifically stated that in the three most important centers of American contributions to fine cooking—Louisiana, South Carolina, and New England—there had been no Italian influence whatever.

He reached the end. Even though I knew his program, and knew the time was short, I had supposed he would at least pause there, and perhaps give Louis Servan a chance to make a few remarks of appreciation, but he didn't even stop long enough for them to realize that the speech was finished. He looked around—a brief glance at the rectangle of faces—and went right on.

"I hope I won't bore you if I continue, but on another subject. I count on your forbearance, for what I have to say is as much in your interest as in my own. I have finished my remarks on cooking. Now I'm going to talk to you about murder, the murder of Phillip Laszio."

There were stirs and murmurs. Lisette Putti squeaked. Louis Servan put up a hand. "If you please. I would like to say, Mr. Wolfe does this by arrangement. It is distressing to end thus the dinner of Les Quinze Maîtres, but it appears—unavoidable. We do not even—however, there is no help—"

Ramsey Keith, glancing at Tolman, Malfi, Liggett, Ashley, growled inhospitably, "So that's the reason these people—"

"Yes, that's the reason." Wolfe was brisk. "I beg you, all of you, don't blame me for intruding a painful subject into an occasion of festivity. The intruder was the man who killed Laszio, and thereby worked disaster on a joyous gathering, cast the gloom of suspicion over a group of eminent men, and ruined my holiday as well as yours. So not only do I have a special reason for rancor for that man"—he put the tip of a finger to his bandage—"but we all have a general one. Besides, before dinner I heard several of you complaining of the fact that you will all be detained here until the authorities release you. But you know that's a natural consequence of the misfortune that overtook you. The authorities can't be expected to let you disperse to the four corners of the earth as long as they have reason to suspect that one of you is a murderer. That's why I say I count on your forbearance. You can't leave here until the guilty man is discovered. So that's what I intend to do here and now. I'm going to expose the murderer and demonstrate his guilt before we leave this room."

Lisette Putti squeaked again and then covered her mouth with her palm. There were no murmurs. A few glanced around, but most of them kept their eyes on Wolfe.

He went on. "First, I think I'd better tell you what was done here—in this room—Tuesday evening, and then we can proceed to the question of who did it. There was nothing untoward until Mondor, Coyne, Keith, and Servan had all been here and tasted the sauces. The instant Servan left, Laszio reached across the table and changed the position of the dishes, all but two. Doubtless he would have shifted those also if the door had not begun to open for the entrance of Berin. It was a childish and malicious trick intended to discredit Berin, and possibly Vukčić too. It may be that Laszio intended to replace the dishes when Berin left, but he didn't, because he was killed before he got a chance to.

"While Berin was in here the radio in the parlor was turned on. That was a prearranged signal for a man who was waiting for it out in the shrubbery. He was close enough to the parlor window—"

"Wait a minute!" The cry wasn't loud or explosive; it was quite composed. But everyone was startled into turning to Dina Laszio, who had uttered it. There was as little turmoil in her manner as in her voice, though maybe her eyes were a little longer and sleepier even than usual. They were directed at Wolfe. "Do we interrupt you when you tell lies?"

"I think not, madam—granting your premise. If each of my statements is met with a challenge we'll never get anywhere. Why don't you wait till I'm through? By that time, if I have lied, you can bankrupt me with a suit for slander."

"I turned on the radio. Everyone knows that. You said it was a prearranged signal—"

"So I did. I beg you, let's don't turn this into a squabble. I'm discussing murder and making serious charges. Let me finish, let me expose myself, then rebut me if you can; and either I shall be discredited and disgraced, or someone here will be—do you hang in West Virginia, Mr. Tolman?"

Tolman, his eyes riveted on Wolfe's face, nodded.

"Then someone will die at the end of a rope. As I was saying, the man concealed in the shubbery out there"—he pointed to the door leading to the terrace—"was close enough to the open parlor window so that when the radio warned him he could observe the return of Berin to the parlor. Instantly he proceeded to the terrace and entered this room by that door. Laszio, here alone by the table, was surprised at the entrance of a liveried servant, for the man wore Kanawha Spa livery and had a black face. The man approached the table and made himself known, for Laszio knew him well. 'See,' the man said with a smile, 'don't you know me, I am Mr. White'—we may call him that for the present, for he was in fact a white man—'I am Mr. White, masquerading, ha ha, and we'll play a joke on these fellows. It will be quite amusing, ha ha, Laszio old chap. You go behind that screen and I'll stay here by the table . . .'

"I confess that no one except Laszio heard those words, or any others. The words actually spoken may have been quite different, but whatever they were, the upshot was that Laszio went behind the screen, and Mr. White, having procured a knife from the table, followed him there and stabbed him to the heart, from behind. It was certainly done with finesse and dispatch, since there was no struggle and no outcry loud enough to be heard in the pantry hall. Mr. White left the knife where he had put it, seeing that it had done its work, and emerged from behind the screen. As he did so a glance showed him that the door to the pantry hall—that door—was open a few inches and a man, a colored man, was peering at him through the crack. Either he had already decided what to do in case of such an emergency, or he showed great presence of mind, for he merely stood still at the end of the screen, looking straight at the eyes peering at him, and placed his finger to his lips. A simple and superb gesture. He may or may not have known—probably he didn't—that at the same moment the door leading to the terrace, behind him, had also opened, and a woman was looking through at him. But his masquerade worked both ways. The colored man knew he was a fake, a white man blacked up, took him for one of the guests playing a joke, and so was not moved to inquire or interfere. The woman supposed he was a servant and let it go at that. Before he left this room Mr. White was seen by still another man—the headwaiter, Moulton here—but by the time Moulton looked through the door Mr. White was on his way out and his back was turned, so Moulton didn't see his face.

"We might as well record names as we go along. The man who first peered through the door was Paul Whipple, one of our waiters here—who, by the way, is studying anthropology at Howard University. The one who saw Mr. White going out was Moulton. The woman who looked through the terrace door was Mrs. Lawrence Coyne."

Coyne jerked around to look, startled, at his wife. She put up her chin at Wolfe. "But you promised me—"

"I promised you nothing. I'm sorry, Mrs. Coyne, but it's much better not to leave out anything. I don't think—"

Coyne sputtered indignantly, "I've heard nothing—nothing—"

"Please." Wolfe put up a hand. "I assure you, sir, you and your wife have no cause for worry. Indeed, we should all be grateful to her. If she hadn't hurt her finger in the door and asked you to kiss it in my hearing, it's quite probable that Mr. Berin would have got the noose instead of the man who earned it. But I needn't go into that.

"That's what happened here Tuesday night. I'll clear up a point now about the radio. It might be thought, since it was turned on, as a prearranged signal, while Berin was in here tasting the sauces, that it was timed at that moment so as to throw suspicion on Berin, but not so. There was probably no intention to have suspicion aimed at any specific person, but if there was, that person was Marko Vukčić. The arrangement was that the radio should be turned on a few minutes prior to the visit of Vukčić to the dining room, no matter who was tasting the sauces at that moment. It was chance that made it Berin, and chance also that Laszio had shifted the sauces around to trick Berin. And the chance trap for Berin was actually sprung, innocently, by Moulton, who came to the table and changed the dishes back again before Vukčić entered. I haven't told you about that. But the point I am making is that the radio signal was given a few minutes prior to the scheduled entrance of Vukčić to the dining room, because Vukčić was the one man here whom Mrs. Laszio could confidently expect to detain in the parlor, delaying his visit to the dining room, and giving Mr. White the necessary time alone with Laszio to accomplish his purpose. As we all know, she insured the delay by putting herself into Vukčić's arms for dancing, and staying there."

"Lies! You know it's lies—"

"Dina! Shut up!"

It was Domenico Rossi, glaring at his daughter. Vukčić, with his jaw set, was gazing at her. Others sent glances at her and looked away again.

"But he tells lies—"

"I say shut up!" Rossi was much quieter, and more impressive, than when he was picking a scrap. "If he tells lies, let him tell all of them."

"Thank you, sir." Wolfe inclined his head half an inch. "I think now we had better decide who Mr. White is. You will notice that the fearful risks he took in this room Tuesday night were more apparent than real. Up to the moment he sank the knife into Laszio's back he was taking no risk at all; he was merely an innocent masquerader. And if afterward he was seen—well, he *was* seen, and what if he was, since he was blacked up? The persons who saw him here Tuesday night have all seen him since, with the blacking and livery gone, and none has suspected him. He depended for safety on his certainty that he would never be suspected at all. He had several bases for that certainty, but the chief one was that on Tuesday evening he wasn't in Kanawha Spa; he was in New York."

Berin burst out, "God above! If he wasn't here—"

"I mean he wasn't supposed to be here. It is always assumed that a man is where probability places him, unless suspicion is aroused that he is somewhere else, and Mr. White figured that such a suspicion was an impossibility. But he was too confident and too careless. He permitted his own tongue to create the suspicion in a conversation with me.

"As you all know, I've had wide experience in affairs of this kind. It's my business. I told Mr. Tolman on Tuesday night that I was sure Berin hadn't done it, but I withheld my best reason for that assurance, because it wasn't my case and I don't like to involve people where I have no concern. That reason was this: I was convinced that Mrs. Laszio had signaled to the murderer by turning on the radio. Other details connected with that might be attributed to chance, but it would take great credulity to believe that her hanging onto Vukčić in that dance, delaying his trip to the dining room while her husband was being killed, was also coincidence. Especially when, as I did, one saw her doing it. She made a bad mistake there. Ordinary intelligence might have caused her to reflect that I was present and that therefore more subtlety was called for.

"When Berin was arrested I did become interested, as you know, but when I had got him released I was again unconcerned with the affair. Whereupon another idiotic mistake was made, almost unbelievable. Mr. White thought I was discovering too much, and without even taking the trouble to learn that I had withdrawn, he sneaked through the shrubbery outside my window and shot me. I think I know how he approached Upshur Pavilion. My assistant, Mr. Goodwin, an hour or so later, saw him dismounting from a horse at the hotel. The bridle path runs within fifty yards of the rear of Upshur. He could easily have left the path, tied his horse, advanced through the shrubbery to my window, and after the shot got back to the horse again and off on the path without being seen. At all events, he made that mistake, and by it, instead of removing me, he encountered me. My concern revived.

"I assumed, as I say, that the murderer was in league with Mrs. Laszio. I dismissed the idea that it was solely her project and he had been hired by her, for that would have rendered the masquerade meaningless; besides, it was hard to believe that a hired murderer, a stranger to Laszio, could have entered this room, got a knife from the table, enticed Laszio behind the screen, and killed him, without an outcry or any struggle. And just as yesterday, when Berin was arrested and I undertook to find evidence to free him, I had one slender thread to start with, Mrs. Coyne's appeal to her husband to kiss her finger because she had caught it in a door, so today, when I undertook to catch the murderer, I had another thread just as slender. It was this. Yesterday about two o'clock Mr. Malfi and Mr. Liggett arrived at Kanawha Spa after a nonstop airplane flight from New York. They came directly to my room at Upshur Pavilion before talking with anyone but servants and had a conversation with me. During the conversation Liggett said—I think this is verbatim—'It seems likely that whoever did it was able to use finesse for purposes other than tasting the seasonings in Sauce Printemps.' Do you remember that, sir?"

"For God's sake." Liggett snorted. "You damn fool, are you trying to drag me into it?"

"I'm afraid I am. You may enter your action for slander along with Mrs. Laszio. Do you remember saying that?"

"No. Neither do you."

Wolfe shrugged. "It's unimportant now. It was vital in its function as my thread. Anyway, it seemed suitable for inquiry. It seemed unlikely that such a detail as the name of the sauce we were tasting had been included in the first brief reports of the murder wired to New York. I telephoned there, to an employee of mine, and to Inspector Cramer of the police. My requests to Mr. Cramer were somewhat inclusive: for instance, I asked him to check on all passengers of airplanes, scheduled or specially chartered, from all airports, leaving New York on Tuesday, which had stopped no matter where in this part of the country in time for a passenger to have arrived at Kanawha Spa by nine o'clock Tuesday evening. I made it nine o'clock because when we went to the parlor after dinner Tuesday, Mrs. Laszio immediately disappeared and was not seen again for an hour; and if there was anything to my theory at all, it seemed likely that that absence was for a rendezvous with her collaborator. I also asked Mr. Cramer to investigate Mrs. Laszio's life in New York, her friends and associates—now, madam, please, you'll get a chance—for suspicion was at that point by no means confined to Liggett. There was even one of you here not entirely clear, and I want to express publicly to Mr. Blanc my thanks for his tolerance and good nature in assisting with the experiment that eliminated him. No doubt he thought it ridiculous.

"At one o'clock this afternoon I received a telegram telling me that Sauce Printemps had not been mentioned in the account in any New York paper Tuesday morning. Since Liggett had left in the airplane before ten o'clock, had come nonstop, and had talked with no one before seeing me, how had he known it was Sauce Printemps? Probably he *had* talked with someone. He had talked with Mrs. Laszio around nine-thirty Tuesday evening, somewhere on the grounds around this building, making the arrangements that resulted in Laszio's murder."

I wasn't any too well pleased, because I couldn't see Liggett's hands; he was across from me and the table hid them. Nor his eyes either, because they were on Wolfe. All I could see was the corner of his thin smile on the side of his mouth that was toward me, and the cord on the side of his neck as he held his jaw clamped. From where he sat he couldn't see Dina Laszio, but I could, and she had her lower lip caught by her teeth. And at that, that was the only outward sign that she wasn't quite as nonchalant as she had been when she patted Wolfe's shoulder.

Wolfe went on. "At three o'clock I had a phone call from Inspector Cramer. Among other things, he told me that Saul Panzer, my employee, had left on an airplane for Charleston in accordance with my instructions. Then—I might as well mention this—around six o'clock another silly mistake was made. To do Mr. Liggett justice, I doubt if it was his own idea. I suspect it was Mrs. Laszio who thought of it and persuaded him to try it. He came to my room and offered me fifty thousand dollars cash to ask Mr. Berin to take the job of *chef de cuisine* at the Hotel Churchill."

Lisette Putti squeaked again. Jerome Berin exploded, "That robbers' den! That stinking hole! Me? Rather would I fry eggs on my fingernails—"

"Just so. I declined the offer. Liggett was foolish to make it, for I am not too self-confident to welcome the encouragement of confession from the enemy, and his offer of that preposterous sum was of course confession of guilt. He will deny that; he will probably even deny he made the offer; no matter. I received other and more important encouragement: another phone call from Inspector Cramer. Time is short, and I won't bore you with all the details, but among them was the information that he had uncovered rumors of a mutual interest, going back two years, between Liggett and Mrs. Laszio. Also, he had checked another point I had inquired about. Coming here on the train Monday night, Mr. Berin told me of a visit he had made last Saturday to the Resort Room of the Hotel Churchill, where the waiters were dressed in the liveries of famous resorts, among them that of Kanawha Spa. Inspector Cramer's men discovered that about a year ago Mr. Liggett had had a duplicate of the Kanawha Spa livery made for himself and had worn it at a fancy dress ball. No doubt it was the fact that he already owned that livery which suggested the technique he adopted for his project. So, as you see, I was getting a good sketch for my picture: Liggett had known of the Sauce Printemps before he had any right to; he was on terms with Mrs. Laszio; and he had a Kanawha Spa livery in his wardrobe. There were other items—for instance, he had left his hotel Tuesday noon, ostensibly to play golf, but had not appeared at either of the clubs where he habitually plays; but we shall have to do some skipping. Mr. Tolman can collect these things after Liggett is arrested. Now we'd better get on to Saul Panzer—I haven't mentioned that he telephoned me from Charleston immediately after the call from Inspector Cramer. Will you bring him, please, from the small parlor?"

Moulton trotted out.

Liggett said in an even tone, "The cleverest lie you've told is about my trying to bribe you. And the most dangerous lie, because there's some truth in it. I did go to your room to ask you to approach Berin for me. And I suppose your man is primed to back up the lie that I offered fifty thousand—"

"Please, Mr. Liggett." Wolfe put up a palm at him. "I wouldn't talk extempore if I were you. You'd better think it over carefully before you—ah, hello, Saul. It's good to see you."

"Yes, sir. Same to you." Saul Panzer came and stood beside my chair. He had on his old gray suit with the pants never pressed, and the old brown cap in his hand. After one look at Wolfe, his sharp eyes darted around the rectangle of faces, and I knew that each of those phizzes had in that moment been registered in a portrait gallery where it would stay forever in place.

Wolfe said, "Speak to Mr. Liggett."

"Yes, sir." Saul's eyes fastened on the target instantly. "How do you do, Mr. Liggett."

Liggett didn't turn. "Bah. It's a damned farce."

Wolfe shrugged. "We haven't much time, Saul. Confine yourself to the essentials. Did Mr. Liggett play golf Tuesday afternoon?"

"No, sir." Saul was husky and he cleared his throat. "On Tuesday at 1:55 p.m. he boarded a plane of Interstate Airways at the Newark Airport. I was on the same plane today, with the same hostess, and showed her Liggett's picture. He left the plane at Charleston when it stopped there at 6:18—and so did I, today. About half past six he appeared at Little's Garage on Marlin Street and hired a car, a 1936 Studebaker, leaving a deposit of two hundred dollars in twenty-dollar bills. I drove the same car here this evening; it's out in front now. I inquired at a few places on the way, but I couldn't find where he stopped on the way back to wash the black off his face—I had to hurry because you told me to get here before eleven o'clock. He showed up again at Little's Garage about a quarter after one Tuesday night and had to pay ten dollars for a fender he had dented. He walked away from the garage and on Laurel Street took a taxi, license C3428, driver Al Bissell, to the Charleston airport. There he took the night express of Interstate Airways, which landed him at Newark at 5:34 Wednesday morning. From there I don't know, but he went to New York, because he was in his apartment a few minutes before eight, when a telephone call was put through to him from Albert Malfi. At half past eight he phoned Newark to charter a plane to take him and Malfi to Kanawha Spa, and at 9:52—"

"That's enough, Saul. By then his movements were overt. You say you drove here this evening in the same car that Liggett hired Tuesday?"

"Yes, sir."

"Well. That's rubbing it in. And you had pictures of Liggett with you to show all those people—the hostess, the garage man, the taxi driver—"

"Yes, sir. He was white when he left the garage."

"No doubt he stopped for alterations on the way. It isn't as difficult as you might think; we blacked a man in my room this afternoon. Cleaning it off is harder. I don't suppose remnants of it were noticed by the man at the garage or the taxi driver?"

"No, sir. I tried that."

"Yes. You would. Of course they wouldn't examine his ears. You didn't mention luggage."

"He had a medium-sized suitcase, dark tan cowhide, with brass fastenings and no straps."

"At all appearances?"

"Yes, sir. Coming and going both."

"Good. Satisfactory. I think that will do. Take that chair over by the wall."

Wolfe surveyed the faces, and though he had kept their attention with his speech on cookery, he was keeping it better now. You could have heard a pin swishing through the air before it lit. He said, "Now we're getting somewhere. You understand why I said that such details as Liggett's mention of Sauce Printemps are no longer of much importance. It is obvious that he treated so fatal a crime as murder with incredible levity, but we should remember two things: first, that he supposed that his absence would never be questioned, and second, he was actually not sentient. He was drugged. He had drunk of the cup which Mrs. Laszio had filled for him. As far as Liggett is concerned, we seem to be done. There appears to be nothing left but for Mr. Tolman to arrest him, prepare the case, try him, and convict him. Have you any remarks on that, Mr. Liggett? I wouldn't advise any."

"I'm not saying anything"—Liggett's voice was as good as ever—"except that if Tolman swallows this and acts on it the way you've framed it, he'll be damn near as sorry as you're going to be." Liggett's chin went up a little. "I know you, Wolfe. I've heard about you. God knows why you've picked on me for this, but I'm going to know before I get through with you."

Wolfe gravely inclined his head. "Your only possible attitude. Of course. But I'm through with you, sir. I turn you over. Your biggest mistake was shooting at me when I had become merely a bystander. Look here." He reached in his pocket and pulled out the script and unfolded it. "That's where your bullet went, right through my speech, before it struck me. Mr. Tolman, do you have women on murder juries in your state?"

"No. Men only."

"Indeed." Wolfe directed his gaze at Mrs. Laszio; he hadn't looked at her since beginning on Liggett. "That's a piece of luck for you, madam. It'll be a job to persuade twelve men to pronounce your doom." Back to Tolman: "Are you prepared to charge Liggett with the murder of Laszio?"

Tolman's voice was clear. "I am."

"Well, sir? You didn't hesitate with Mr. Berin."

Tolman got up. He had only four paces to walk. He put his hand on Liggett's shoulder and said in a loud tone, "I arrest you, Raymond Liggett. A formal charge of murder will be laid tomorrow morning." He turned and spoke sharply to Moulton. "The sheriff is out front. Tell him to come in."

Liggett twisted his head around to get Tolman's eye. "This will ruin you, young man."

Wolfe, stopping Moulton with a gesture, appealed to Tolman. "Let the sheriff wait a little. If you don't mind? I don't like him." He put his eyes at Mrs. Laszio again. "Besides, madam, we still have you to consider. As far as Liggett is concerned, well, you see—" He moved a hand to indicate Tolman standing at Liggett's shoulder. "Now about you. You're not arrested yet. Have you got anything to say?"

The swamp-woman looked sick. I suppose she was good enough at make-up so that ordinarily only an expert would have noticed the extent of it, but it wasn't calculated to handle emergencies like this. Her face was spotty. Her lower lip didn't match the upper, on account of having been chewed on. Her shoulders were humped up and her chest pulled in. She said in a thin tone, not her rich swampy voice at all, "I didn't—only—only what I said, it's lies. Lies!"

"Do you mean what I've said about Liggett is lies? And what Saul Panzer has said? I warn you, madam, things that can be proven are not lies. You say lies. What?"

"It's all lies about me."

"And about Liggett?"

"I—I don't know."

"Indeed. But about you. You did turn on the radio, didn't you?"

She nodded without speaking.

Wolfe snapped, "Didn't you?"

"Yes."

"And whether by accident or design, you did detain Vukčić and dance with him while your husband was being murdered?"

"Yes."

"And Tuesday evening after dinner you were absent from the gathering here nearly an hour?"

"Yes."

"And since your husband is dead—if it were not for the unfortunate circumstance that Liggett will soon be dead too, you would expect to marry him, wouldn't you?"

"I—" Her mouth twisted. "No! You can't say—no!"

"Please, Mrs. Laszio. Keep your nerve. You need it." Wolfe's tone suddenly got gentle. "I don't want to bully you. I am perfectly aware that as regards you the facts permit of two vastly different constructions. One something like this: You and Mr. Liggett wanted each other—at least he wanted you, and you wanted his name and position and wealth. But your husband was the sort of man who hangs on to his possessions, and that made it difficult. The time finally arrived when the desire was so great, and the obstacle so stubborn, that you and Liggett decided on a desperate course. It appeared that the meeting of Les Quinze Maîtres offered a good opportunity for the removal of your husband, for there would be three persons present who hated him—plenty of targets for suspicion. So Liggett came to Charleston by airplane and on here by car, and met you somewhere outside, as previously arranged, at half past nine Tuesday evening. It was only then that the arrangements were perfected in detail, for Liggett could not previously have known about the wager between Servan and Keith and the test of Sauce Printemps that was being prepared to decide it. Liggett posted himself in the shrubbery. You returned to the parlor, and turned on the radio at the proper time, and delayed Vukčić by dancing with him in order to give Liggett the opportunity to enter the dining room and kill your husband. Confound it, madam, don't stare at me like that. As I say, that is one possible interpretation of your actions."

"But it's wrong. It's lies! I didn't—"

"Permit me. Don't deny too much. I confess there may be lies in it, for there's another possible construction. But understand this, and consider it well." Wolfe aimed a finger at her and pointed his tone. "It is going to be proven that Liggett came here, and was told by someone about the test of the sauces, and that he knew precisely the moment when he could safely enter this room to kill Laszio without danger of interruption; that he *knew* that Vukčić would not enter to disturb him before the deed was done. Otherwise his proceeding as he did was senseless. That's why I say don't deny too much. If you try to maintain that you didn't meet Liggett outdoors, that you made no arrangement with him, that your turning on the radio when you did was coincidence, that your keeping Vukčić from the dining room during those fatal minutes was also coincidence—then I fear for you. Even a jury of twelve men, and even looking at you on the stand—I'm afraid they wouldn't swallow it. I believe, to put it brutally, I believe you would be convicted of murder.

"But I haven't said you're a murderer." Wolfe's tone was almost soothing. "Since the crime was committed you have unquestionably, at least by silence, tried to shield Liggett, but a woman's heart being what it is—" He shrugged. "No jury would convict you for that. And no jury would convict you at all, you wouldn't even be in jeopardy, if it could be shown that the arrangement you entered into with Liggett on Tuesday evening, when you met him outdoors there, was on your part an innocent one. Merely as a hypothesis, let's say, for example, that you understood that Liggett was engaged in nothing more harmful than a practical joke. No matter what; I couldn't guess at the details even as a hypothesis, for I'm not a practical joker. But the joke required that he have a few minutes alone with Laszio before the entrance of Vukčić. That of course would explain everything—your turning on the radio, your detaining Vukčić, everything you did—without involving you in guilt. You understand, Mrs. Laszio, I'm not suggesting this as a retreat for you. I am only saying that while you can't deny what happened, you may possibly have an explanation for it that will save you. In that case, it would be quixotic to try to save Liggett too. You can't do it. And if there is such an explanation, I wouldn't wait too long—until it's too late—"

It was too much for Liggett. Slowly his head turned, irresistibly, as if gripped in enormous pliers, square around until he faced Dina Laszio.

She didn't look at him. She was chewing at her lip again, and her eyes were on Wolfe, fixed and fascinated. You could almost see her chewing her brain too. That lasted a full half a minute, and then, by God, she smiled. It was a funny one, but it was a smile; and then I saw that her eyes had shifted to Liggett and the smile was supposed to be one of polite apology. She said in a low tone but without anything shaky in it, "I'm sorry, Ray. Oh, I'm sorry, but—" She faltered. Liggett's eyes were boring at her.

She moved her gaze to Wolfe and said firmly, "You're right. Of course you're right and I can't help it. When I met him outdoors after dinner as we had arranged—"

"Dina! Dina, for God's sake—"

Tolman, the blue-eyed athlete, jerked Liggett back in his chair. The swamp-woman went on. "He had told me what he was going to do, and I believed him. I thought it was all a joke. Then afterward he told me that Phillip had attacked him, had struck at him—"

Wolfe said sharply, "You know what you're doing, madam? You're helping to send a man to his death."

"I know. I can't help it! How can I go on lying for him? He killed my husband. When I met him out there and he told me what he had planned—"

"You tricky bastard!" Liggett broke training completely. He jerked from Tolman's grasp, plunged across Mondor's legs, knocked Blanc and his chair to the floor, trying to get at Wolfe. I was on my way, but by the time I got there Berin had stopped him, with both arms around him, and Liggett was kicking and yelling like a lunatic.

Dina Laszio, of course, had stopped trying to talk, with all the noise and confusion. She sat quietly looking on with her long sleepy eyes.

17

Jerome Berin said positively, "She'll stick to it. She'll do whatever will push danger farthest from her, and that will be it."

The train was sailing like a gull across New Jersey on a sunny Friday morning, somewhere east of Philadelphia. In sixty minutes we would be tunneling under the Hudson. I was propped against the wall of the Pullman bedroom again, Constanza was on the chair, and Wolfe and Berin were on the window seats with beer between them. Wolfe looked pretty seedy, since of course he wouldn't have tried to shave on the train even if there had been no bandage, but he knew that in an hour the thing would stop moving, and the dawn of hope was on his face.

Berin asked, "Don't you think so?"

Wolfe shrugged. "I don't know and I don't care. The point was to nail Liggett down by establishing his presence at Kanawha Spa on Tuesday evening, and Mrs. Laszio was the only one who could do that for us. As you say, she is undoubtedly just as guilty as Liggett, maybe more, depending on your standard. I rather think Mr. Tolman will try her for murder. He took her last night as a material witness, and he may keep her that way to clinch his case against Liggett—or he may charge her as an accomplice. I doubt if it matters much. Whatever he does, he won't convict her. She's a special kind of woman, she told me so herself. Even if Liggett is bitter enough against her to confess everything in order to involve her in his doom, to persuade any dozen men that the best thing to do with that woman is to kill her would be quite a feat. I question whether Mr. Tolman is up to it."

Berin, filling his pipe, frowned at it. Wolfe upped his beer glass with one hand as he clung to the arm of the seat with the other.

Constanza smiled at me. "I try not to hear them. Talking about killing people." She shivered delicately.

I grunted. "You seem to be doing a lot of smiling. Under the circumstances."

She lifted brows above the dark purple eyes. "What circumstances?"

I just waved a hand. Berin had got his pipe lit and was talking again. "Well, it turned my stomach. Poor Rossi, did you notice him?

Poor devil. When Dina Rossi was a little girl I had her many times on this knee, and she was quiet and very sly but a nice girl. Of course, all murderers were once little children, which seems astonishing." He puffed until the little room was nicely filled with smoke. "By the way, did you know that Vukčić made this train?"

"No."

Berin nodded. "He came leaping on at the last minute—I saw him—like a lion with fleas after him. I haven't seen him around this morning, though I've been back and forth. No doubt your man told you that I stopped here at your room around eight o'clock."

Wolfe grimaced. "I wasn't dressed."

"So he told me. So I came back. I wasn't comfortable. I never am comfortable when I'm in debt, and I've got to find out what I owe you and pay it. There at Kanawha Spa you were a guest and didn't want to talk about it, but now you can. You got me out of a bad hole and maybe you even saved my life, and you did it at the request of my daughter for your professional help. That makes it a debt and I want to pay it, only I understand your fees are pretty steep. How much do you charge for a day's work?"

"How much do you?"

"What?" Berin stared. "God above, I don't work by the day. I am an artist, not a potato peeler."

"Neither am I." Wolfe wiggled a finger. "Look here, sir. Let's admit it as a postulate that I saved your life. If I did, I am willing to let it go as a gesture of amity and goodwill and take no payment for it. Will you accept that gesture?"

"No. I'm in debt to you. My daughter appealed to you. It is not to be expected that I, Jerome Berin, would accept such a favor."

"Well"—Wolfe sighed—"if you won't take it in friendship, you won't. In that case, the only thing I can do is render you a bill. That's simple. If any valuation at all is to be placed on the professional services I rendered it must be a high one, for the services were exceptional. So, since you insist on paying—you owe me the recipe for Saucisse Minuit."

"What!" Berin glared at him. "Pah! Ridiculous!"

"How ridiculous? You ask what you owe. I tell you."

Berin sputtered. "Outrageous, damn it!" He waved his pipe until sparks and ashes flew. "That recipe is priceless! And you ask it—God above, I've refused half a million francs! And you have the impudence, the insolence—"

"If you please." Wolfe snapped. "Let's don't row about it. You put a price on your recipe. That's your privilege. I put a price on my services. That's mine. You have refused half a million francs. If you were to send me a check for half a million dollars I would tear it up—or for any sum whatever. I saved your life or I rescued you from a minor annoyance, call it what you please. You ask me what you owe me, and I tell you, you owe me that recipe, and I will accept nothing else. You pay it or you don't, suit yourself. It would be an indescribable pleasure to be able to eat Saucisse Minuit at my own table—at least twice a month, I should think—but it would be quite a satisfaction, of another sort, to be able to remind myself—much oftener than twice a month—that Jerome Berin owes me a debt which he refuses to pay."

"Bah!" Berin snorted. "Trickery!"

"Not at all. I attempt no coercion. I won't sue you. I'll merely regret that I employed my talents, lost a lot of sleep, and allowed myself to get shot at, without either acquiring credit for a friendly and generous act or receiving the payment due me. I suppose I should remind you that I offered a guarantee to disclose the recipe to no one. The sausage will be prepared only in my house and served only at my table. I would like to reserve the right to serve it to guests, and of course to Mr. Goodwin, who lives with me and eats what I eat."

Berin, staring at him, muttered, "Your cook."

"He won't know it. I spend quite a little time in the kitchen myself."

Berin continued to stare in silence. Finally he growled, "It can't be written down. It never has been."

"I won't write it down. I have a facility for memorizing."

Berin got his pipe to his mouth without looking at it and puffed. Then he stared some more. At length he heaved a shuddering sigh and looked around at Constanza and me. He said gruffly, "I can't tell it with these people in here."

"One of them is your daughter."

"Damn it, I know my daughter when I see her. They'll have to get out."

I got up and put up my brows at Constanza. "Well?" The train lurched and Wolfe grabbed for the other arm of the seat. It would have been a shame to get wrecked then.

Constanza arose, reached down to pat her father on the head, and passed through the door as I held it open.

I supposed that was the fitting end to our holiday, since Wolfe was getting that recipe, but there was one more unexpected diversion to come. Since there was still an hour to go I invited Constanza to the club car for a drink, and she swayed and staggered behind me through three cars to that destination. There were only eight or ten customers in the club car, mostly hidden behind morning papers, and plenty of seats. She specified ginger ale, which reminded me of old times, and I ordered a highball to celebrate Wolfe's collection of his fee. We had only taken a couple of sips when I became aware that a fellow passenger across the aisle had arisen, put down his paper, walked up to us, and was standing in front of Constanza, looking down at her.

He said, "You can't do this to me, you *can't!* I don't deserve it and you can't do it." He sounded urgent. "You ought to see—you ought to realize—"

Constanza said to me, chattering prettily, "I didn't suppose my father would *ever* tell that recipe to *any*one. Once in San Remo I heard him tell an Englishman, some very important person—"

The intruder moved enough inches to be standing between us and rudely interrupted her. "Hello, Goodwin. I want to ask you—"

"Hello, Tolman." I grinned up at him. "What's the idea? You with two brand-new prisoners in your jail, and here you are running around—"

"I had to get to New York. For evidence. It was too important—look here. I want to ask you if Miss Berin has any right to treat me like this. Your unbiased opinion. She won't speak to me. She won't look at me. Didn't I have to do what I did? Was there anything else I could do?"

"Certainly. You could have resigned. But then of course you'd have been out of a job, and God knows when you'd have been able to marry. It was really a problem, I see that. But I wouldn't worry. Only a little while ago I wondered why Miss Berin was doing so much smiling, there didn't seem to be any special reason for it, but now I understand. She was smiling because she knew you were on the train."

"Mr. Goodwin! That isn't true!"

"But if she won't even speak to me—"

I waved a hand. "She'll speak to you all right. You just don't know how to go about it. Her own method is as good a one as I've seen recently. Watch me now, and next time you can do it yourself."

I tipped my highball glass and spilled about a jigger on her skirt where it was round over her knee.

She ejaculated and jerked. Tolman ejaculated and bent over and reached for his handkerchief. I arose and reassured them, "It's rite all kight, it doodn't stain." Then I went over and picked up his morning paper and sat down where he had been.

Recipes from the Fifteenth Annual Meeting
of
LES QUINZE MAÎTRES

As all his admirers know, Nero Wolfe has long been taunting and teasing his readers with suggestions of the exotic dishes that tickle his palate. At last he has been willing to reveal the secrets of a few of his favorites, carefully selected from the inventions of Les Quinze Maîtres. Here are recipes for dishes as hearty and robust as the crimes which he undertakes to solve; and rules for delicacies as ephemeral as the orchids he tends with such meticulous care. Here is regal fare, proudly and happily gathered together where each recipe can be readily found and easily followed.

IMPORTANT

I BEG you not to entrust these dishes to your cook unless she is an artist. Cook them yourself, and only for an occasion that is worthy of them.

They are items for an epicure, but are neither finicky nor pretentious; you and your guests will find them as satisfying to the appetite as they are pleasing to the palate. None is beyond your abilities if you have the necessary respect for the art of fine cooking—and are willing to spend the time and care which an excellent dish deserves and must have.

Good Appetite!

NERO WOLFE

RECIPES

Those followed by an asterisk are new creations which have been tried and found worthy, and have not been published; with two asterisks, they may be considered exceptional; those unmarked are traditional items of the common culture.

Terrapin Stewed in Butter
Planked Porterhouse Steak
Boone County Missouri Ham
Creole Tripe
Chicken Marengo
Chicken in Curdled Egg Sauce
Tennessee Opossum
Philadelphia Snapper Soup
Lobster Newburgh
Bouillabaisse of New Orleans
Saucisse Minuit**
Oyster Pie Nero Wolfe**
Rognons aux Montagnes*
Sauce Printemps**
Brook Trout with Brown Butter and Capers*
Pierre Mondor Entrée: Quenelles Bonne Femme**
Roast Duck Mr. Richards**
Shad Roe Mousse Pocahontas**
Civet de Lapin*
Œufs au Cheval*
Piroshki Vallenko**
Artichauts Drigantes*
Oysters Baked in the Shell**
Terrapin Maryland
Beaten Biscuits
Pan-Broiled Young Turkey
Sally Lunn
Rice Croquettes with Quince Jelly*

Lima Beans in Cream
Avocado Todhunter**
Pineapple Sherbet
Sponge Cake

Terrapin Stewed in Butter

2 cups terrapin meat
2 hard-cooked eggs
3 tbsps. butter
½ cup chicken broth
½ cup good sherry
salt and cayenne

Heat the sherry and broth in a saucepan and add the hard-cooked eggs, which have been run through a ricer. Add the terrapin meat and, as the mixture simmers, drop in small quantities of the butter until all is used. Season with salt and cayenne to taste and serve at once with triangles of buttered toast.

Planked Porterhouse Steak

Procure a porterhouse steak 2 inches thick, of fine-grained texture, bright red in color, and well marbled with fat. Trim off excess fat and wipe with a clean cloth. Heat a wire broiler, grease it with some of the fat, and broil the steak over a hot fire for 3 minutes on each side.

Take a well-seasoned oak plank which has never been washed, but which has been kept scrupulously clean by being scraped with a dull knife and wiped with good olive oil. Lay the steak on the plank, surround with a border of fluffy mashed potatoes, and put in a hot oven (450° F.) for 14 minutes. Five minutes before the end, brush the potatoes over with a little melted butter and salt and pepper the steak. Take from the oven, paint with soft butter, sprinkle with finely chopped parsley, dot with slices of fresh lime, and serve at once.

Boone County Missouri Ham

12 lb. Missouri ham
cloves
1 cup vinegar
1 cup black molasses
2 tsps. Worcestershire sauce
1 cup cider
½ tsp. thyme

Scrub the ham thoroughly and soak it for 24 hours in cold water. Remove the skin with a thin sharp knife, taking off as little of the fat as possible. Stick cloves ½ inch apart all over the fat side. Place in a turkey roaster with 1 quart of cold water, the vinegar, molasses, Worcestershire sauce, cider, and thyme. Cover the roaster and bake in a moderate oven (350° F.) for 2 hours. Lower the heat to 300° F. and continue cooking for another 2½ hours, basting frequently during the entire time of cooking. Remove the cover and bake 30 minutes longer uncovered. Take from the oven and allow to cool with the cover on.

Creole Tripe

3 cups fresh honeycomb tripe
2 pig's feet
1 whole carrot
1 whole stalk celery
1 whole clove garlic
1 tbsp. chopped parsley
1 onion
3 whole cloves
1 bay leaf
1 sprig thyme
¼ lb. salt pork
1 wineglass cognac
salt and pepper
cayenne
flour

Cover the tripe with salted water, bring to the boiling point, drain, cover with fresh boiling salted water, and cook for 15 minutes. Drain.

Line an earthenware pot with slices of the salt pork. Fill with the tripe in layers, alternating with the vegetables and herbs, seasoning with salt and cayenne. Lay the pig's feet, which have been cut in two, lengthwise, on top of all, season with salt and pepper, and place a slice of the salt pork on top. Pour the cognac over and put on a close-fitting lid, sealing it on with flour paste. Cook in a moderate oven (350° F.) for 5 hours. Unseal, remove celery, carrot, and garlic, and serve very hot in the cooking pot.

Chicken Marengo

1 large frying-age chicken
1 tbsp. olive oil
2 tbsps. butter
6 small white onions
1½ cups chicken broth
1 clove garlic
½ cup dry white wine
2 tsps. chopped parsley
1 tsp. chopped tarragon
2 egg yolks
1 tbsp. flour
8 pitted olives
salt and pepper

Clean and disjoint the chicken carefully, cutting the breast into 4 pieces. Heat the oil and butter in a heavy iron pot and fry the chicken to a golden brown. Carefully peel the small onions and parboil them for 18 minutes in salted water. Drain. Bring the broth to a boil and pour it over the chicken, add the onions, clove of garlic with unbroken skin, parsley, tarragon, wine, and salt and pepper to taste. Simmer gently 12 minutes. Beat the egg yolks with the flour and add a little cold broth, and pour into the boiling sauce. Let thicken on the fire for 90 seconds, stirring constantly. Add the olives and remove the clove of garlic. Pile the chicken on a hot platter, pour the sauce over, and serve at once.

Chicken in Curdled Egg Sauce

1 small fowl
2 tbsps. butter
2 tbsps. chopped onion
1 Mexican sausage
½ cup chopped almonds
¼ cup raisins
¼ cofsp. cinnamon
¼ cofsp. cloves
2 tsps. chopped parsley
juice of a lemon
rind of a lemon
½ cup sherry
4 egg yolks
1 tbsp. flour
salt and chili pepper
bunch of soup vegetables
cayenne

Clean the chicken carefully, disjoint as for frying, cover with three pints of cold water, add salt, pepper, and the bunch of soup vegetables. Cover well and cook slowly until the chicken is tender. Remove the soup vegetables and keep the chicken hot in the broth while preparing the following sauce.

Heat the butter in a saucepan and add the onion and sausage. As the onion begins to brown, add the almonds, which have been rolled fine as well as chopped, the raisins, parsley, cinnamon, and cloves. Cook for 2 minutes and pour in 3 cups of the broth in which the chicken was cooked, the lemon rind, salt, and cayenne, and let simmer for 5 minutes. Beat the egg yolks with the flour and the sherry and pour into the boiling broth, stirring constantly. Let thicken for a minute or two and add the lemon juice. Arrange the pieces of chicken in the middle of a platter and pour the sauce over after removing the lemon rind.

Tennessee Opossum

an opossum
4 tbsps. butter
half an onion
¾ cup breadcrumbs
1 tsp. chopped parsley
a little beef broth
1 tsp. Worcestershire sauce
salt and pepper

Skin and clean the opossum and rub inside and out with salt and pepper. Melt 3 tbsps. butter in a frying pan and in it brown the onion chopped fine and the chopped liver of the opossum. When well browned, add the breadcrumbs, parsley, salt, pepper, and enough beef broth to moisten. Stuff the body of the opossum with this mixture and sew up with a cotton string. Put in a baking pan with 2 tbsps. water and roast in a hot oven (450° F.) for 15 minutes. Lower the heat to 350° F. and continue cooking until it is tender and a rich brown. Baste frequently with this mixture: ½ cup water, 1 tbsp. butter, 1 tsp. Worcestershire sauce, and salt and pepper. Serve hot at once.

Philadelphia Snapper Soup

meat of a snapper turtle
1 large knuckle of veal
¼ lb. chicken fat
1 carrot
2 onions
1 stalk celery
1 pinch thyme
1 pinch marjoram
1 bay leaf
2 whole cloves
3 qts. chicken broth
3 chopped tomatoes
2 hard-cooked eggs
3 slices lemon
2 cups good sherry
½ cup flour
salt and pepper
Tabasco

Put the veal knuckle, cut into several pieces, into a baking pan with the chicken fat, sliced carrot, onions, and celery. When the fat is beginning to brown, add the flour and continue cooking until a light brown. Add the herbs and spices and turn all into the soup pot with the broth. Add the tomatoes and let simmer gently for 4 hours. Strain and add the snapper meat cut into small pieces, having first cooked it for 5 minutes in sherry, the lemon slices, and a dash of Tabasco. Remove the lemon slices, season with salt and Tabasco, add the chopped hard-cooked egg and more sherry to taste.

Lobster Newburgh

2 cups boiled lobster meat
½ pt. cream
2 tbsps. butter
3 egg yolks
1 wineglass sherry
salt and cayenne

Melt the butter in a saucepan or chafing dish and add to it the cream. Let boil gently for 30 seconds and add lobster meat cut into good-sized pieces. When the cream has again reached the boil, add the well-beaten egg yolks, to which has been added the sherry. Season to taste with salt and cayenne and let thicken for a minute or two, stirring constantly. Serve with a dish of hot buttered toast.

Bouillabaisse of New Orleans

2 lbs. red snapper
2 doz. small lake shrimp
½ green pepper, chopped fine
1 clove garlic, chopped fine
2 tbsps. chopped onion
2 cups beef broth
¾ cup dry white wine
3 tbsps. olive oil
1 pinch Spanish saffron
1 pinch thyme
flour
butter
slices of French bread
salt and pepper

Heat the olive oil in a soup pot and add the onion, garlic, and green pepper. Cook 2 minutes over a low fire, add broth, wine, and thyme, and continue cooking for 15 minutes. Remove bones and skin from the red snapper, cut it in 5 or 6 pieces, roll each piece in flour seasoned with salt and pepper, and drop into the boiling sauce. Prepare the shrimp likewise. Cook gently for 15 minutes. With the crust cut from the slices of French bread, fry them in butter, drain on brown paper, and lay on a hot platter. Add Spanish saffron to fish mixture and salt and pepper to taste. Let boil up once and serve on the pieces of toast.

Saucisse Minuit

(The recent death of Mr. Jerome Berin, killed by a Fascist bomb in Barcelona, where he had gone to fight for the Loyalists and the freedom of the Spanish people, a week after the wedding of his daughter to Mr. Barry Tolman, releases Mr. Nero Wolfe from his vow of secrecy and permits disclosure of this recipe. No proportions are given. Mr. Berin told Mr. Wolfe that they should vary with the climate, the season, the temperaments involved, the dishes to be eaten before and after, and the wine to be served. Mr. Berin's usual preference was an inexpensive Spanish wine, the Rioja of the Marqués de Murrieta, bottled on the estate at Ygay.)

pork
goose
pheasant
bacon
goose fat
brandy
red wine
beef broth
breadcrumbs
pig's intestines
pistachio nuts
onions
garlic
thyme
rosemary
ginger
nutmeg
cloves
salt
black pepper

Chop up some onions and a clove of garlic and brown them lightly in a generous quantity of goose fat. Pour in enough brandy to cover the onions, and twice as much good red wine as brandy, and as much strong beef broth as wine. Add a pinch of thyme and one of rosemary, the slightest dusting of ginger and nutmeg, and a mere threat of cloves. Let simmer gently for 10 minutes and add enough sifted breadcrumbs to make a soft, runny mush. Cook gently for 5 minutes. Add chopped boiled bacon, coarsely chopped roast fresh pork, twice as much coarsely cut up roast goose as pork, and as much coarsely cut up roast pheasant as goose. Season with salt and a generous quantity of freshly ground black pepper, add a few roasted pistachio nuts, and let simmer to the consistency of fresh sausage meat.

Get it perfectly cold.

Wash and scald the pig's intestines thoroughly. Fill with the cold stuffing, tying at intervals to form sausages. Broil on a slow fire, having pricked the skins to prevent bursting.

Oyster Pie Nero Wolfe

3 doz. oysters
3 thin slices Smithfield ham
3 cups strained oyster liquor
1 tbsp. chopped celery
2 tsps. chopped chervil
1 tsp. chopped parsley
3 tbsps. butter
2 shallots
3 tbsps. flour
1 tsp. soy sauce
salt and pepper
puff paste
milk

Melt the butter in a saucepan, add the finely chopped shallots, and as soon as they are tender, but before they begin to brown, add the flour. When well blended, pour in the oyster liquor, add the herbs chopped as fine as possible, the soy sauce, and salt and pepper, and let simmer 5 minutes. Lay the oysters and the ham, cut in small pieces, in a large deep baking dish, cover with a top of puff paste, brush over with milk, and bake 5 minutes in a hot oven (450° F.). Then lower heat twice at 5-minute intervals until 350° F. is reached. Continue baking until crust is a delicate brown and well risen. Serve at once.

Rognons aux Montagnes

8 lamb kidneys
3 tbsps. butter
2 shallots
1 clove garlic
1 carrot
2 tbsps. flour
1 cup broth
½ cup red wine
1 small bouquet parsley
1 small piece celery
1 pinch thyme
salt and pepper

Split the kidneys lengthwise and remove all fibers and skin. Soak in cold water for 1 hour, changing the water several times. Heat the butter in a saucepan, add chopped shallots, garlic, and sliced carrot, and let brown slightly. Add flour, let brown more, and pour in broth and wine. Add remaining seasonings and, when boiling, put in the halved kidneys, which have been drained. Cook until kidneys are tender. Place the kidneys on a small hot dish and strain the sauce over them. Garnish with triangles of toast fried in butter and serve at once.

Sauce Printemps

(Best for quail, squab, young grouse, young pheasant)

3 tbsps. butter
2 oz. diced bacon
2 chopped shallots
12 sliced mushrooms
½ glass brandy
½ pint good claret
½ pint strong chicken broth
1 tbsp. chopped parsley
1 tbsp. chopped chervil
1 tsp. chopped celery
½ tsp. chopped chives
a few tarragon leaves
a pinch of thyme
a few grains of cayenne
a few crushed peppercorns
salt
vinegar

Fry the butter and bacon in an earthenware saucepan, together with the shallots and mushrooms. When the whole is a rich brown, pour on the brandy, set fire to it, and as the blaze dies down add the claret and chicken broth. Add the parsley, chervil, celery, chives, tarragon, thyme, cayenne, peppercorns, and salt, tasting with the salt. Let simmer 15 minutes very gently, strain, and cook another 4 minutes. During these 4 minutes, thicken, first with a lump of butter, and then with the blood from the birds, which has been carefully saved in a bowl, and to which a few drops of vinegar have been added to prevent congealing.

Brook Trout with Brown Butter and Capers

fresh brook trout 6 to 7 inches long
salt and pepper
butter
flour
lemon juice
tarragon
Tabasco
capers

Clean the trout, leaving heads and tails on. Sprinkle with salt and pepper and roll lightly in flour. Heat butter in a frying pan, lay in the trout, being careful not to crowd them, and sauté to a golden brown, turning frequently. Arrange in a row on a hot platter.

The sauce: Allow 1 tbsp. lemon juice to ½ cup butter. Heat butter in a saucepan to a light brown. Flavor the lemon juice with tarragon leaves and strain them out. Add the lemon juice to the butter, salt and Tabasco to taste, and a few capers, and let boil up once. Pour over the trout and serve.

Pierre Mondor Entrée: Quenelles Bonne Femme

⅔ cup raw breast of chicken (ground)
4 tbsps. sifted cracker crumbs

4 tbsps. beef marrow	white wine
¾ tsp. chopped parsley	white pepper
3 tbsps. butter	2 eggs
¾ cup chicken jelly	salt and paprika
heavy sweet cream	1 shallot
2 tbsps. sour cream	6 mushrooms
2 egg whites	flour

The quenelles: Press the ground chicken through a sieve and add, gradually, the egg whites, ½ tsp. salt, a dusting of white pepper, and enough heavy sweet cream to make the right consistency to mold into ovals with the aid of two teaspoons. Drop carefully into gently boiling white wine and water mixed in equal parts and cook until firm. Take out with a draining spoon and lay gently on a hot shallow baking dish.

The marrow balls: Work the marrow until creamy. Add parsley, eggs, cracker crumbs, paprika, and a very few grains of salt, and drop into the same boiling mixture used for the quenelles. Drain and arrange on the baking dish alternately with the quenelles.

The sauce: Melt 3 tbsps. butter in a saucepan, add 1 chopped shallot and 6 sliced mushrooms, and before they begin to brown add 2 tbsps. flour. Pour in ½ cup dry white wine and ¾ cup of the strongest possible chicken jelly. Simmer 5 minutes, add 2 tbsps. thick sour cream, and cook long enough for perfect blending.

Pour the sauce over the quenelles and marrow and brown in a very hot oven or under a grill flame.

Roast Duck Mr. Richards

Remove giblets and liver from the duck, chop with shallots and 2 sprigs of parsley, season with salt and a few grains of cayenne, and put back in the duck, which has been well cleaned, singed, and rubbed with salt and pepper. Truss carefully and lay in a baking pan in a very hot oven (500° F.) for 15 minutes; reduce heat to 400° and continue cooking until done, basting with chicken broth which has been seasoned with tarragon, parsley, and fresh thyme, and from which the herbs have been strained. There should be about half a cupful of this basting and of the juices of the duck in the roasting pan when the duck is done. Arrange the duck on a hot platter, silver if you have it, pour a little warmed cognac over it, and set fire to it. As the flames die down, pour over it all that remains of the pan juices and carve at once.

Shad Roe Mousse Pocahontas

1 lb. halibut	1 carrot
2 shad roes	1 stalk celery
3 egg whites	1 small bouquet parsley
butter	3 egg yolks
1¾ cups heavy cream	1 tsp. flour
1 cup dry white wine	½ tsp. lemon juice
black peppercorns	salt
1 onion	white pepper

Remove all shin and bones from the halibut and save them. Put the halibut through the meatgrinder and then force it through a fine sieve. Mix in gradually the unbeaten whites of eggs and then, also gradually, ¾ cup cream. Season with salt and white pepper and leave in the icebox for 20 minutes. Sauté the roes in a generous amount of butter, remove the skin, and sprinkle with salt and pepper. Pull one of the roes apart with a silver fork into quite small pieces and fold it into the fish mixture. Butter a ring mold well and fill it with the mixture. Set it in a pan of hot water, cover the mold with Patapar paper, and bake in a good oven 20 minutes. Turn onto a hot platter and fill the inside of the ring with the following sauce, which must be ready when the ring is:

Put skin and bones of halibut into a saucepan with 2 cups water and 1 cup dry white wine, adding onion and carrot cut in pieces, celery, parsley, salt, and whole black peppercorns. Beat egg yolks, flour, and ½ cup cream together, and pour onto them 1½ cups of the strained court bouillon. Put in a double boiler and add the remaining ½ cup cream and the second shad roe broken into medium-sized fragments. If tasting suggests it, season with salt and pepper. Allow sauce to thicken, stirring constantly. Remove from the fire, add lemon juice, and fill the ring with it.

Civet de Lapin

1 wild rabbit
1 thick rasher of bacon, diced
3 tbsps. butter
2 shallots
¼ clove garlic, mashed
1 tsp. finely chopped parsley
4 small white onions
¾ cup red wine
1 cup broth
1 bouquet garni
1 bay leaf
1 sprig thyme
6 mushrooms, peeled and sliced
salt and pepper
flour
vinegar

Heat the butter in a heavy pot and add the diced bacon. Clean, skin, and disjoint the rabbit, saving the blood; rub the pieces with salt and pepper, dust with flour, and brown in the butter. When a good brown, pour on broth and wine and add the bouquet garni, chopped shallots, mashed garlic, thyme, bay leaf, and salt and pepper if taste suggests. Cover closely and simmer gently for 90 minutes. Parboil the onions 10 minutes, drain, and add them and the mushrooms to the cooking rabbit. Let simmer for another 30 minutes. Remove the bouquet garni and thicken the sauce with the blood of the rabbit to which has been added a few drops of vinegar to keep it from coagulating. Add the chopped parsley and serve at once very hot.

Œufs au Cheval

Fry circular slices of bread in butter until a delicate brown. Drain on brown paper. Spread each round with pâte de foie gras and on top carefully slip an egg which has been gently fried in butter and seasoned with salt and pepper. Sprinkle with freshly grated Parmesan cheese and a dash of paprika, moisten with a little melted butter, and leave under the broiler until a tempting brown.

Piroshki Vallenko

1 cup cold minced veal
2 chicken livers
2 tbsps. butter
1 tsp. chopped onion
6 mushrooms, peeled and sliced
⅓ cup broth
1 hard-cooked egg
1 tsp. flour
salt and pepper
puff paste
some parsley
a little milk

Heat the butter in a saucepan, add the mushrooms and chopped onion, and just before they begin to brown add the flour. Pour in the broth, add parsley, minced veal, chicken livers cut in small pieces, chopped egg, and salt and pepper. Let simmer until all the broth is absorbed.

Roll the paste to about ⅛ inch thickness and cut it in rounds the size of a saucer. Put a spoonful of the meat on each round, fold the paste to a semicircle, and press down and seal the edge with a fork. Brush over with milk, and bake in moderate oven (375° F.) until a good brown and well risen.

Artichauts Drigantes

Boil French artichokes (as many as needed) in salted water for 25 minutes. Drain, remove leaves and the burr, and lay in a flat baking dish. Sauté slices of tomato ½ inch thick in butter to a nice brown, season them with salt and pepper, and lay a slice on each artichoke heart. Cover with a thin cream sauce, sprinkle generously with grated Parmesan cheese, moisten with melted butter, and brown in a hot oven (450° F.).

Oysters Baked in the Shell

8 oysters to a portion

freezing salt	lemon juice
bacon	butter
chives	Tabasco
parsley	Worcestershire sauce
chervil	horseradish
thyme	salt and pepper

Fill layer-cake tins with freezing salt and put in a hot oven until the salt is thoroughly heated. Half-sink 8 oysters on the half shell in the salt of each tin and season them with salt and pepper. Run through a meat grinder some bacon, with a little chives, parsley, and chervil, and a very little fresh thyme, and then pound until the mixture becomes a paste. Dot the paste over the oysters and place in a very hot oven (500° F.) until the oysters curl up at the edges. Serve in the tins in which baked, with a little bowl of sauce at each place.

The sauce: Melt some butter in a double boiler and season with lemon juice, Tabasco, a very little Worchestershire sauce, salt, and a dash of horseradish. Each oyster is dipped into the sauce as eaten.

Terrapin Maryland

Use the eggs, liver, and all the meat portions of the terrapin except the white meat, which is tough and tasteless. To each terrapin, allow ¼ lb. of the best butter and 1 cup fine sherry. Cut the meat in medium-sized pieces. Melt the butter in a chafing dish, add the terrapin and sherry, and cook until tender. Add salt and pepper to taste, and more sherry if necessary.

Beaten Biscuits

1 quart flour
1 tsp. salt
1 tsp. sugar
1 tbsp. lard
1 tbsp. butter
milk

Sift the dry ingredients together, rub in the shortening, and add enough milk to make a stiff dough. Knead thoroughly. Place on a firm block or table and beat with a mallet for 30 minutes, keeping the dough in a round mass and turning in with the palm of the hand after each blow. When the dough is perfectly smooth, roll out to ½ inch thickness, cut with small biscuit cutter, prick with a fork, and bake in a fairly slow oven (275° F.) until a light brown.

Pan-Broiled Young Turkey

Procure a well-fed turkey ten weeks old. Clean it and split it and wipe it off with a damp cloth. Massage with butter, salt, and pepper, place in a hot well-greased broiler, and cook over live coals, finishing one side before starting the other, to a good brown. Take out of the broiler and lay in a roasting pan; dot with butter and pour over ¾ cup boiling water. Finish cooking in a moderately hot oven (375° F.) until done, basting several times. Just before serving, pour into the pan ¼ cup boiling water and 2 tbsps. butter; let boil up quickly once or twice and serve on a hot platter with the sauce poured over.

Sally Lunn

1 cup milk
¾ yeast cake
3 tbsps. butter
4 tbsps. sugar
1 tsp. salt
2 eggs
flour

Bring the milk to the boiling point, add butter, and pour into a china bowl. Sift in enough flour to make a soft dough and add yeast dissolved in a little warm milk. Beat eggs until very light, add sugar and salt, and beat again. Combine with the dough and sift in enough more flour to make the dough fairly stiff. Knead on a bread board and put back in the bowl to rise in a warm place. Let rise until double its bulk. Again turn onto bread board and knead. Put small pieces of the dough in buttered muffin pans, bake in a good oven (425° F.), and serve as soon as done.

Rice Croquettes with Quince Jelly

½ cup rice	salt
½ cup boiling water	quince jelly
1 cup scalded milk	breadcrumbs
2 egg yolks	parsley
1½ tbsps. butter	

Wash the rice well in several waters. Put in a double boiler with the boiling water and ½ tsp. salt and steam until all the water is absorbed. Pour in the milk and cook until the rice is soft. Remove from fire, add the butter and the slightly beaten egg yolks. Mix well, spread in a shallow pan, and leave in icebox until perfectly cold. Take a small square of jelly, form the rice mixture into a small cylinder around it, crumb fry in deep fat, and drain on brown paper. Serve as soon as cooked, on a hot platter, surrounded by fried parsley.

Lima Beans in Cream

Put fresh tender lima beans in a saucepan and pour onto them enough boiling water to cover. Add 1 tbsp. butter for each pint of lima beans and salt to taste. Cook for 6 minutes well covered, then remove cover, raise heat, and finish cooking quickly until water is absorbed. Pour in a little rich cream, let boil up once or twice, and serve.

Avocado Todhunter

4 avocados
2 cups watercress leaves
1 tsp. lemon juice
1 tsp. orange juice
1 tsp. lime juice
1 tsp. grapefruit juice
1 tsp. pineapple juice

Halve the avocados and remove the seeds; do not peel them. Pinch or cut off the watercress leaves singly, keeping no stems, and distribute them into the avocados, which should be fairly well filled. After straining the fruit juices through muslin, put 1 tsp. of each into a small atomizer, with 1 tsp. shredded ice, and shake until the ice is melted. Spray the watercress leaves thoroughly just before the avocados are to be eaten. Serve on nests of nasturtium leaves.

Pineapple Sherbet

Use a large handsome pineapple with plenty of foliage. Cut off the top to form a lid and scoop out the inside of the fruit. Make a strong lemonade, using 1 orange to 2 lemons. Grate or grind the pineapple pulp and add it to the lemonade, and after letting it stand for 30 minutes, strain through a sieve. Freeze until firm, then fill the scooped-out pineapple with the sherbet, piling it high, and perching the foliage on top.

Sponge Cake

6 egg whites
5 egg yolks
1 cup sugar, sifted twice
1 tbsp. lemon juice
grated rind of half a lemon
1 cup flour, sifted 3 times
¼ tsp. salt

Beat whites until stiff but not dry and beat in half of the sugar. Separately, beat yolks until thick and lemon-colored, add the lemon juice and grated rind, and beat again. Beat in the remaining sugar and continue beating until smooth. Combine the two mixtures. Fold in the flour to which has been added the salt. Pour into an ungreased cake pan (the type with a funnel in the middle) and cut through several times to break the large air bubbles. Bake in a slow oven (325° F.) for 1 hour. Turn the pan upside down on a cake cooler and let stand until cold. Loosen with spatula and let the cake drop out of the pan by its own weight.

Plot It Yourself

1

I divide the books Nero Wolfe reads into four grades: A, B, C, and D. If, when he comes down to the office from the plant rooms at six o'clock, he picks up his current book and opens to his place before he rings for beer, and if his place was marked with a thin strip of gold, five inches long and an inch wide, which was presented to him some years ago by a grateful client, the book is an A. If he picks up the book before he rings, but his place was marked with a piece of paper, it is a B. If he rings and then picks up the book, and he had dog-eared a page to mark his place, it is a C. If he waits until Fritz has brought the beer and he has poured to pick up the book, and his place was dog-eared, it's a D. I haven't kept score, but I would say that of the two hundred or so books he reads in a year not more than five or six get an A.

At six o'clock that Monday afternoon in May I was at my desk, checking the itemization of expenses that was to accompany the bill going to the Spooner Corporation for a job we had just finished, when the sound came of his elevator jolting to a stop and his footsteps in the hall. He entered, crossed to the oversized made-to-order chair behind his desk, sat, picked up *Why the Gods Laugh,* by Philip Harvey, opened to the page marked with the strip of gold, read a paragraph, and reached to the button at the edge of his desk without taking his eyes from the page. As he did so, the phone rang.

I got it. "Nero Wolfe's residence, Archie Goodwin speaking." Up to six o'clock I say "Nero Wolfe's office." After six I say "residence."

A tired baritone said, "I'd like to speak to Mr. Wolfe. This is Philip Harvey."

"He'll want to know what about. If you please?"

"I'll tell him. I'm a writer. I'm acting on behalf of the National Association of Authors and Dramatists."

"Did you write a book called *Why the Gods Laugh?*"

"I did."

"Hold the wire." I covered the transmitter and turned. "If that book has any weak spots here's your chance. The guy who wrote it wants to speak to you."

He looked up. "Philip Harvey?"

"Right."

"What does he want?"

"He says he'll tell you. Probably to ask you what page you're on."

He closed the book on a finger to keep his place and took his phone. "Yes, Mr. Harvey?"

"Is this Nero Wolfe?"

"Yes."

"You may possibly have heard my name."

"Yes."

"I want to make an appointment to consult you. I am chairman of the Joint Committee on Plagiarism of the National Association of Authors and Dramatists and the Book Publishers of America. How about tomorrow morning?"

"I know nothing about plagiarism, Mr. Harvey."

"We'll tell you about it. We have a problem we want you to handle. There'll be six or seven of us, members of the committee. How about tomorrow morning?"

"I'm not a lawyer. I'm a detective."

"I know you are. How about ten o'clock?"

Of course that wouldn't do, since it would take more than an author, even of a book that rated an A, to break into Wolfe's two morning hours with the orchids, from nine to eleven. Harvey finally settled for a quarter past eleven. When we hung up I asked Wolfe if I should check, and he nodded and went back to his book. I rang Lon Cohen at the *Gazette* and learned that the National Association of Authors and Dramatists was it. All the dramatists anyone had ever heard of were members, and most of the authors, the chief exceptions being some scattered specimens who hadn't decided if they cared to associate with the human race—or had decided that they didn't. The Book Publishers of America was also it, a national organization of all the major firms and many of the minor ones. I passed the information along to Wolfe, but I wasn't sure he listened. He was reading.

That evening around midnight, when I got home after taking a friend to a show, *A Barrel of Love*, by Mortimer Oshin, Wolfe had just finished his book and was making room for it on one of the shelves over by the big globe. As I tried the door of the safe I spoke.

"Why not leave it on your desk?"

He grunted. "Mr. Harvey's self-esteem needs no sop. If he were not so skillful a writer he would be insufferable. Why curry him?"

Before I went up two flights to my room I looked up "curry" in the dictionary. Check. I won't live long enough to see the day when Wolfe curries anybody, including me.

2

At 11:20 the next morning, Tuesday, Wolfe, seated at his desk, sent his eyes from left to right and back again, rested them on Philip Harvey, and inquired, "You're the spokesman, Mr. Harvey?"

Since Harvey had made the appointment and was chairman of the committee, I had put him in the red leather chair near the end of Wolfe's desk. He was a middle-aged shorty with a round face, round shoulders, and a round belly. The other five were in an arc on yellow chairs that I had had ready for them. Their names, supplied by Harvey, were in my notebook. The one nearest me, the big blond guy in a brown suit with tan stripes, was Gerald Knapp, president of Knapp and Bowen. The one next to him, the wiry-looking bantam with big ears and slick black hair, was Reuben Imhof of the Victory Press. The female about my age who might have been easy to look at if her nose would stop twitching was Amy Wynn. I had seen a couple of reviews of her novel, *Knock at My Door*, but it wasn't on Wolfe's shelves. The tall gray-haired one with a long bony face was Thomas Dexter of Title House. The one at the far end of the arc, with thick lips and deep-set dark eyes, slouching in his chair with his left ankle on his right knee, was Mortimer Oshin. He had written the play, *A Barrel of Love*, which I had seen last evening. He had lit three cigarettes in eight minutes, and with two of the matches he had missed the ashtray on a stand at his elbow and they had landed on the rug.

Philip Harvey cleared his throat. "You'll need all the details," he said, "but first I'll outline it. You said you know nothing about plagiarism, but I assume you know what it is. Of course a charge of plagiarism against a book or a play is dealt with by the author and publisher, or the playwright and producer, but a situation has developed that needs something more than defending individual cases. That's why the NAAD and the BPA have set up this joint committee. I may say that we, the NAAD, appreciate the cooperation of the BPA. In a plagiarism suit it's the author that gets stuck, not the publisher. In all book contracts the author agrees to indemnify the publisher for any liabilities, losses, damages, expenses—"

Reuben Imhof cut in. "Now wait a minute. What is agreed and what actually happens are two different things. Actually, in a majority of cases, the publisher suffers—"

"The suffering publisher!" Amy Wynn cried, her nose twitching. Mortimer Oshin had a comment too, and four of them were speaking at once. I didn't try to sort it out for my notebook.

Wolfe raised his voice. "If you please! You started it, Mr. Harvey. If the interests of author and publisher are in conflict, why a joint committee?"

"Oh, they're not always in conflict." Harvey was smiling, not apologetically. "The interests of slave and master often jibe; they do in this situation. I merely mentioned *en passant* that the author gets stuck. We deeply appreciate the cooperation of the BPA. It's damned generous of them."

"You were going to outline the situation."

"Yes. In the past four years there have been five major charges of plagiarism." Harvey took papers from his pocket, unfolded them, and glanced at the top sheet. "In February nineteen fifty-five, McMurray and Company published *The Color of Passion*, a novel by Ellen Sturdevant. By the middle of April it was at the top of the fiction best-seller list. In June the publishers recieved a letter from a woman named Alice Porter, claiming that the novel's plot and characters, and all important details of the plot development, with only the setting and names changed, had been stolen from a story written by her, never published, entitled 'There Is Only Love.' She said she had sent the story, twenty-four typewritten pages, to Ellen Sturdevant in November nineteen fifty-two, with a note asking for suggestions for its improvement. It had never been acknowledged or returned. Ellen Sturdevant denied that she had ever seen any such story. One day in August, when she was at her summer home in Vermont, a local woman in her employ came to her with something she said she had found in a bureau drawer. It was twenty-four typewritten sheets, and the top one was headed, 'There Is Only Love, by Alice Porter.' Its plot and characters and many details were the same as those of Ellen Sturdevant's novel, though in much shorter form. The woman, named Billings, admitted that she had been persuaded by Alice Porter to search the house for the typescript—persuaded by the offer of a hundred dollars if she found it. But, having found it, she had a pang of conscience and brought it to her employer. Mrs. Sturdevant has told me that her first impulse was to burn it, but on second thought she realized that that wouldn't do, since Mrs. Billings couldn't be expected to perjure herself on a witness stand, and she phoned her attorney in New York."

Harvey upturned a palm. "That's the meat of it. I may say that I am convinced, and so is everyone who knows her, that Ellen Sturdevant had never seen that typescript before. It was a plant. The case never went to trial. It was settled out of court. Mrs. Sturdevant paid Alice Porter eighty-five thousand dollars."

Wolfe grunted. "There's nothing I could do about it now."

"We know you can't. We don't expect you to. But that's only the beginning." Harvey looked at the second sheet of paper. "In January nineteen fifty-six, Title House published *Hold Fast to All I Give You,* a novel by Richard Echols. Will you tell him about it, Mr. Dexter? Briefly?"

Thomas Dexter passed a hand over his gray hair. "I'll make it as brief as I can," he said. "It's a long story. The publication date was January nineteenth. Within a month we were shipping five thousand a week. By the end of April nine thousand a week. On May sixth we got a letter from a man named Simon Jacobs. It stated that in February nineteen fifty-four he had sent the manuscript of a novelette he had written, entitled 'What's Mine Is Yours,' to the literary agency of Norris and Baum. Norris and Baum had been Echols' agent for years. Jacobs enclosed a photostat of a letter he had received from Norris and Baum, dated March twenty-sixth, nineteen fifty-four, returning the manuscript and saying that they couldn't take on any new clients. The letter mentioned the title of the manuscript, 'What's Mine Is Yours.' It was bona fide; there was a copy of it in Norris and Baum's files; but no one there could remember anything about it. More than two years had passed, and they get a great many unsolicited manuscripts."

Dexter took a breath. "Jacobs claimed that the plot of his novelette was original and unique, also the characters, and that the plot and characters of *Hold Fast to All I Give You,* Echols' novel, were obviously a steal. He said he would be glad to let us inspect his manuscript—that's how he put it—and would give us a copy if we wanted one. His presumption was that someone at Norris and Baum had either told Echols about it or had let him read it. Everyone at Norris and Baum denied it, and so did Echols, and we at Title House believe them. Utterly. But a plagiarism suit is a tricky thing. There is something about the idea of a successful author stealing his material from an unsuccessful author that seems to appeal to ordinary people, and juries are made up of ordinary people. It dragged along for nearly a year. The final decision was left to Echols and his attorney, but we at Title House approved of it. They decided not to risk a trial. Jacobs was paid ninety thousand dollars for a general release. Though we were not obligated by contract, Title House contributed one-fourth of it, twenty-two thousand, five hundred."

"It should have been half," Harvey said, not arguing, just stating a fact.

Wolfe asked, "Did you get a copy of Jacobs' manuscript?"

Dexter nodded. "Certainly. It supported his claim. The plot and characters were practically identical."

"Indeed. Again, Mr. Harvey, it seems to be too late."

"We're getting hotter," Harvey said. "Wait till you hear the rest of it. Next: In November nineteen fifty-six, Nahm and Son published *Sacred or Profane,* a novel by Marjorie Lippin. Like all of her previous books, it had a big sale; the first printing was forty thousand." He consulted his papers. "On March twenty-first, nineteen fifty-seven, Marjorie Lippin died of a heart attack. On April ninth Nahm and Son received a letter from a woman named Jane Ogilvy. Her claim was almost identical with the one Alice Porter had made on *The Color of Passion*—that in June nineteen fifty-five she had sent the manuscript of a twenty-page story, entitled 'On Earth but Not in Heaven,' to Marjorie Lippin, with a letter asking for her opinion of it, that it had never been acknowledged or returned, and that the plot and characters of *Sacred or Profane* had been taken from it. Since Mrs. Lippin was dead she couldn't answer the charge, and on April fourteenth, only five days after Nahm and Son got the letter, the executor of Mrs. Lippin's estate, an officer of a bank, found the manuscript of the story, as described by Jane Ogilvy, in a trunk in the attic of Mrs. Lippin's home. He considered it his duty to produce it, and he did so. With Mrs. Lippin dead, a successful challenge of the claim seemed hopeless, but her heirs, her son and daughter, were too stubborn to see it, and they wanted to clear her name of the stain. They even had her body exhumed for an autopsy, but it confirmed her death from a natural cause, a heart attack. The case finally went to trial last October, and a jury awarded Jane Ogilvy one hundred and thirty-five thousand dollars. It was paid by the estate. Nahm and Son didn't see fit to contribute."

"Why the hell should they?" Gerald Knapp demanded.

Harvey smiled at him. "The NAAD appreciates your cooperation, Mr. Knapp. I'm merely giving the record."

Dexter told Knapp, "Oh, skip it. It's common knowledge that Phil Harvey has an ulcer. That's why the gods laugh."

Harvey transferred the smile from Knapp and Bowen to Title House. "Many thanks for the plug, Mr. Dexter. At all bookstores—maybe." He returned to Wolfe. "The next one wasn't a novel; it was a play—*A Barrel of Love,* by Mortimer Oshin. You tell it, Mr. Oshin."

The dramatist squashed a cigarette in the tray, his fifth or sixth—I had lost count. "Very painful, this is," he said. He was a tenor. "Nauseous. We opened on Broadway February twenty-fifth last year, and when I say we had a smash hit I'm merely giving the record like Mr. Harvey. Around the middle of May the producer, Al Friend, got a letter from a man named Kenneth Rennert. The mixture as before. It said he had sent me an outline for a play in August nineteen fifty-six, entitled 'A Bushel of Love,' with a letter asking me to collaborate with him on writing it. He demanded a million dollars, which was a compliment. Friend turned the letter over to me, and my lawyer answered it, telling Rennert he was a liar, which he already knew. But my lawyer knew about the three cases you have just heard described, and he had me take precautions. He and I made a thorough search of my apartment on Sixty-fifth Street, every inch of it, and also my house in the country at Silvermine, Connecticut, and I made arrangements that would have made it tough for anybody trying to plant something at either place."

Oshin lit a cigarette and missed the ashtray with the match. "That was wasted effort. As you may know, a playwright must have an agent. I had had one named Jack Sandler that I couldn't get along with, and a month after *A Barrel of Love* opened I had quit him and got another one. One weekend in July, Sandler phoned me in the country and said he had found something in his office and would drive over from his place near Danbury to show it to me. He did. It was a typewritten six-page outline of a play in three acts by Kenneth Rennert, entitled 'A Bushel of Love.' Sandler said it had been found by his secretary when she was cleaning out an old file."

He ditched the cigarette. "As I said, nauseous. Sandler said he would burn it in my presence if I said the word, but I wouldn't trust the bastard. He said he and his secretary would sign affidavits that they had never seen the outline before and it must have been sneaked into the file by somebody, but what the hell, I was somebody. I took it to my lawyer, and he had a talk with Sandler, whom he knew pretty well, and the secretary. He didn't think that either of them had a hand in the plant, and I agreed with him. But also he didn't think we could count on Sandler not to get word to Rennert that the outline had been found, and I agreed with that too. And that's what the bastard did, because in September Rennert brought an action for damages, and he wouldn't have done that if he hadn't known he could get evidence about the outline. A million dollars. My lawyer has entered a countersuit, and I paid a detective agency six thousand dollars in three months trying to get support for it, with no luck. My lawyer thinks we'll have to settle."

"I dislike covering ground that has already been trampled," Wolfe said. "You omitted a detail. The outline resembled your play?"

"It didn't resemble it, it *was* my play, without the dialogue."

Wolfe's eyes went to Harvey. "That makes four. You said five?"

Harvey nodded. "The last one is fresher, but one member of the cast is the same as in the first one. Alice Porter. The woman who got eighty-five thousand dollars out of Ellen Sturdevant. She's coming back for more."

"Indeed."

"Yes. Three months ago the Victory Press published *Knock at My Door*, a novel by Amy Wynn. Amy?"

Amy Wynn's nose twitched. "I'm not very good . . ." She stopped and turned to Imhof, at her left. "You tell it, Reuben."

Imhof gave her shoulder a little pat. "You're plenty good, Amy," he assured her. He focused on Wolfe. "This one is fresh all right. We published Miss Wynn's book on February fourth, and we ordered the sixth printing, twenty thousand, yesterday. That will make the total a hundred and thirty thousand. Ten days ago we received a letter signed Alice Porter, dated May seventh, saying that *Knock at My Door* was taken from an unpublished story she wrote three years ago, with the title 'Opportunity Knocks.' That she sent the story to Amy Wynn in June of nineteen fifty-seven, with a letter asking for comment and criticism, and it has never been acknowledged or returned. According to pattern. Of course we showed the letter to Miss Wynn. She assured us that she had never received any such story or letter, and we accepted her assurance without reservation. Not having a lawyer or an agent, she asked us what she should do. We told her to make sure without delay that no such manuscript was concealed in her home, or any other premises where she could be supposed to have put it, such as the home of a close relative, and to take all possible steps to guard against an attempt to plant the manuscript. Our attorney wrote a brief letter to Alice Porter, rejecting her claim, and upon investigation he learned that she is the Alice Porter who made the claim against Ellen Sturdevant in nineteen fifty-five. I telephoned the executive secretary of the National Association of Authors and Dramatists to suggest that it might be desirable to make Miss Wynn a member of the Joint Committee on Plagiarism, which had been formed only a month previously, and that was done the next day. I was myself already a member. That's how it stands. No further communication has been received from Alice Porter."

Wolfe's eyes moved. "You have taken the steps suggested, Miss Wynn?"

"Of course." She wasn't bad-looking when her nose stayed put. "Mr. Imhof had his secretary help me look. We didn't find it—anything."

"Where do you live?"

"I have a little apartment in the Village—Arbor Street."

"Does anyone live with you?"

"No." She flushed a little, which made her almost pretty. "I have never married."

"How long have you lived there?"

"A little more than a year. I moved there in March last year—fourteen months."

"Where had you lived?"

"On Perry Street. I shared an apartment with two other girls."

"How long had you lived there?"

"About three years." Her nose twitched. "I don't quite see how that matters."

"It might. You were living there in June nineteen fifty-seven, when Alice Porter claims she sent you the story. That would be a suitable place for the story to be found. Did you and Mr. Imhof's secretary search that apartment?"

"No." Her eyes had widened. "Of course. Good heavens! Of course! I'll do it right away."

"But you can't guard against the future." Wolfe wiggled a finger. "I offer a suggestion. Arrange immediately to have that apartment and the one you now occupy searched throughout by two reliable persons, preferably a man and a woman, who have no connection with you or the Victory Press. You should not be present. Tell them that they must be so thorough that when they are through they must be prepared to testify under oath that no such manuscript was on the premises—unless, of course, they find it. If you don't know how to go about getting someone for the job, Mr. Imhof will, or his attorney—or I could. Will you do that?"

She looked at Imhof. He spoke. "It certainly should be done. Obviously. I should have thought of it myself. Will you get the man and woman?"

"If desired, yes. They should also search any other premises with which Miss Wynn has had close association. You have no agent, Miss Wynn?"

"No."

"Have you ever had one?"

"No." Again the little flush. "*Knock at My Door* is my first novel—my first published one. Before that I had only had a few stories in magazines, and no agent would take me—at least no good one. This has been a big shock, Mr. Wolfe—my first book such a big success, and you can imagine I was up riding the clouds, and then all of a sudden this—this awful business."

Wolfe nodded. "No doubt. Do you own a motor car?"

"Yes. I bought one last month."

"It must be searched. What else? Do you have a locker at a tennis court?"

"No. Nothing like that."

"Do you frequently spend the night away from your home? Fairly frequently?"

I expected that to bring a bigger and better flush, but apparently her mind was purer than mine. She shook her head. "Almost never. I'm not a very social creature, Mr. Wolfe. I guess I really have no intimate friends. My only close relatives, my father and mother, live in Montana, and I haven't been there for ten years. You said they should search any premises with which I have had close association, but there aren't any."

Wolfe's head turned. "As I told you on the phone, Mr. Harvey, I know nothing about plagiarism, but I would have supposed that it concerned an infringement of copyright. All five of these claims were based on material that had not been published and so were not protected by copyright. Why were the claims not merely ignored?"

"They couldn't be," Harvey said. "It's not that simple. I'm not a lawyer, and if you want it in legal terms you can get it from the NAAD counsel, but there's a property right, I believe they call it, in these things even if they haven't been copyrighted. It was in a court trial before a judge that a jury awarded Jane Ogilvy a hundred and thirty-five thousand dollars. Do you want me to get our counsel on the phone?"

"That can wait. First I need to know what you want to hire me to do. The first three cases are history, and apparently the fourth, Mr. Oshin's, soon will be. Do you want me to investigate on behalf of Miss Wynn?"

"No. I should say, yes and no. This committee was set up six weeks ago, before the claim on Miss Wynn was made. It had been authorized at a meeting of the NAAD council in March. It seemed fairly obvious to us what had happened. Alice Porter's putting the squeeze on Ellen Sturdevant, and getting away with it, had started a ball rolling. Her method was copied exactly by Simon Jacobs with Richard Echols, except for one detail, the way he established the priority of his manuscript and the assumption of Echols' access to it; and he changed that one detail because he actually had sent a novelette to that literary agency, Norris and Baum, and had it returned. He merely took advantage of something that had happened two years back. Of course the manuscript which was the basis of his claim—the one he allowed Title House and Echols to inspect—was not the one he had sent to Norris and Baum in nineteen fifty-four. He had written it after Echols' novel had been published and gave it the same title as the one he had sent to Norris and Baum—'What's Mine Is Yours.'"

Wolfe grunted. "You may omit the obvious. You are assuming, I take it, that that was the procedure in all five cases: plagiarism upside down. The manuscript supporting the claim was written after the book was published or the play produced and had achieved success."

"Certainly," Harvey agreed. "That was the pattern. The third one, Jane Ogilvy, followed it exactly, the only difference being that she had a stroke of luck. Whatever plan she had for discovery of the manuscript in Marjorie Lippin's home, she didn't have to use it, for Mrs. Lippin conveniently died. Again, with Kenneth Rennert, the only difference was the way the manuscript was found."

He stopped to cover his mouth with his palm, and a noise came, too feeble to be called a belch. "Sausage for breakfast," he said, for the record. "I shouldn't. That's how it stood when this committee had its first meeting. At the NAAD council meeting a prominent novelist had said that he had a new book scheduled for early fall and he hoped to God it would be a flop, and nobody laughed. At the first meeting of this committee Gerald Knapp, president of Knapp and Bowen— How did you put it, Mr. Knapp?"

Knapp passed his tongue over his lips. "I said that it hasn't hit us yet, but we have three novels on the best-seller list, and we hate to open our mail."

"So that's the situation," Harvey told Wolfe. "And now Alice Porter is repeating. Something has to be done. It has to be stopped. About a dozen lawyers have been consulted, authors' and publishers' lawyers, and none of them has an idea that is worth a damn. Except one maybe—the one who suggested that we put it up to you. Can you stop it?"

Wolfe shook his head. "You don't mean that, Mr. Harvey."

"I don't mean what?"

"That question. If you expect me to say no, you wouldn't have come. If you expect me to say yes, you must think me a swaggerer, and again you wouldn't have come. I certainly wouldn't undertake to make it impossible for anyone ever again to extort money from an author by the stratagem you have described."

"We wouldn't expect you to."

"Then what would you expect?"

"We would expect you to do something about this situation that would make us pay your bill not only because we had to but also because we felt that you had earned it and we had got our money's worth."

Wolfe nodded. "That's more like it. That was phrased as might be expected from the author of *Why the Gods Laugh*, which I have just read. I had been thinking that you write better than you talk, but you put that well because you had been challenged. Do you want to hire me on those terms?"

Harvey looked at Gerald Knapp, and then at Dexter. They looked at each other. Reuben Imhof asked Wolfe, "Could you give us some idea of how you would go about it and what your fee would be?"

"No, sir," Wolfe told him.

"What the hell," Mortimer Oshin said, squashing a cigarette, "he couldn't guarantee anything anyway, could he?"

"I would vote for proceeding on those terms," Gerald Knapp said, "providing it is understood that we can terminate the arrangement at any time."

"That sounds like a clause in a book contract," Harvey said. "Will you accept it, Mr. Wolfe?"

"Certainly."

"Then you're in favor, Mr. Knapp?"

"Yes. It was our attorney who suggested coming to Nero Wolfe."

"Miss Wynn?"

"Yes, if the others are. That was a good idea, having my apartment searched, and the one on Perry Street."

"Mr. Oshin?"

"Sure."

"Mr. Dexter?"

"With the understanding that we can terminate at will, yes."

"Mr. Imhof?"

Imhof had his head cocked. "I'm willing to go along, but I'd like to mention a couple of points. Mr. Wolfe says he can't give us any idea of how he'll go about it, and naturally we can't expect him to pull a rabbit out of a hat here and now, but, as he said himself, the first three cases are history and the fourth one soon will be. But Miss Wynn's isn't. It's hot. The claim has just been made, and it was made by Alice Porter, the woman who started it. So I think he should concentrate on that. My second point is this, if he does concentrate on Alice Porter, and if he gets her, if he makes her withdraw the claim, I think Miss Wynn might feel that it would be fair and proper for her to pay part of Mr. Wolfe's fee. Don't you think so, Amy?"

"Why—yes." Her nose twitched. "Of course."

"It might also," Harvey put in, "be fair and proper for the Victory Press to pay part. Don't you think so?"

"We will." Imhof grinned at him. "We'll contribute to the BPA's share. We might even kick in a little extra." He went to Wolfe. "How about concentrating on Alice Porter?"

"I may do that, sir. Upon consideration." Wolfe focused on the chairman. "Who is my client? Not this committee."

"Well . . ." Harvey looked at Gerald Knapp. Knapp smiled and spoke. "The arrangement, Mr. Wolfe, is that the Book Publishers of America and the National Association of Authors and Dramatists will each pay half of any expenses incurred by this committee. They are your clients. You will report to Mr. Harvey, the committee chairman, as their agent. I trust that is satisfactory?"

"Yes. This may be a laborious and costly operation, and I must ask for an advance against expenses. Say five thousand dollars?"

Knapp looked at Harvey. Harvey said, "All right. You'll get it."

"Very well." Wolfe straightened up, took a deep breath, and let it out. It looked as if he were going to have to dig in and do a little work, and it takes a lot of oxygen to face a prospect as dismal as that. "Naturally," he said, "I must have all records and documents pertaining to all of the cases, or copies of them. Everything. Including, for instance, the reports from the detective agency hired by Mr. Oshin. I can form no plan until I am fully informed, but it may help to get answers to a few questions now. Mr. Harvey. Has any effort been made to discover a connection among Alice Porter, Simon Jacobs, Jane Ogilvy, and Kenneth Rennert, or between any two of them?"

Harvey nodded. "Sure, that's been tried. By the lawyer representing Marjorie Lippin's heirs, her son and daughter, and by the detective agency Oshin hired. They didn't find any."

"Where are the four manuscripts on which the claims were based? Not copies, the manuscripts themselves. Are they available?"

"We have two of them, Alice Porter's 'There Is Only Love' and Simon Jacobs' 'What's Mine Is Yours.' Jane Ogilvy's 'On Earth but Not in Heaven' was an exhibit in evidence at the trial, and after she won the case it was returned to her. We have a copy of it—a copy, not a facsimile. Kenneth Rennert's play outline, 'A Bushel of Love,' is in the possession of Oshin's attorney, and he won't give us a copy of it. Of course we—"

Mortimer Oshin postponed striking a match to mutter, "He won't even let me have a copy."

Harvey finished, "Of course we know nothing about Alice Porter's 'Opportunity Knocks,' the basis of her claim against Amy Wynn. I have a suspicion that you'll find it when you search the apartment Miss Wynn lived in on Perry Street. If you do, then what?"

"I have no idea." Wolfe made a face. "Confound it, you have merely shown me the skeleton, and I am not a wizard. I must know what has been done and what has been overlooked, in each case. What of the paper and typing of the manuscripts? Did they offer no grounds for a challenge? What of the records and backgrounds of the claimants? Did Jane Ogilvy testify at the trial, and was she cross-examined competently? How did Alice Porter's manuscript get into Ellen Sturdevant's bureau drawer? How did Jane Ogilvy's manuscript get into the trunk in Marjorie Lippin's attic? How did Kenneth Rennert's play outline get into the file of Mr. Oshin's former agent? Was any sort of answer found, even a conjectural one, to any of those questions?"

He spread his hands. "And there is the question, what about your assumption that all of the claims were fraudulent? I can't swallow it with my eyes shut. I can accept it as a working hypothesis, but I can't dismiss the possibility that one or more of the supposed victims is a thief and a liar. 'Most writers steal a good thing when they can' is doubtless an—"

"Blah!" Mortimer Oshin exploded.

Wolfe's brows went up. "That was in quotation marks, Mr. Oshin. It was said, or written, more than a century ago by Barry Cornwall, the English poet and dramatist. He wrote *Mirandola*, a tragedy performed at Covent Garden with Macready and Kemble. It is doubtless an exaggeration, but it is not blah. If there had been then in England a National Association of Authors and Dramatists, Barry Cornwall would have been a member. So that question must remain open along with the others."

His eyes moved. "Miss Wynn. The search of the apartments should not be delayed. Will you arrange it, or shall I?"

Amy Wynn looked at Imhof. He told her, "Let him do it." She told Wolfe, "You do it."

"Very well. You will get permission from your former fellow tenants at Perry Street, and you will admit the searchers to your present apartment and then absent yourself. Archie, get Saul Panzer and Miss Bonner."

I turned to the phone and dialed.

3

Thirty-four hours later, at eleven o'clock Wednesday evening, Wolfe straightened up in his chair and spoke. "Archie."

My fingers, on the typewriter keys, stopped. "Yes, sir?"

"Another question has been answered."

"Good. Which one?"

"About the candor of the victims. Their bona fides is established. They were swindled. Look here."

I got up and crossed to his desk. To get there I had to detour around a table that had been brought from the front room to hold about half a ton of paper. There were correspondence folders, newspaper clippings, photographs, mimeographed reports, transcripts of telephone conversations, photostats, books, tear sheets, lists of names and addresses, affidavits, and miscellaneous items. With time out only for meals and sleep and his two daily sessions in the plant rooms on the roof, Wolfe had spent the thirty-four hours working through it, and so had I. We had both read all of it except the four books—*The Color of Passion,* by Ellen Sturdevant, *Hold Fast to All I Give You,* by Richard Echols, *Sacred or Profane,* by Marjorie Lippin, and *Knock at My Door,* by Amy Wynn. There was no point in wading through them, since it was acknowledged that their plots and characters and action were the same as those in the stories on which the claims had been based.

What I was typing, when he interrupted me, was a statement to be signed by Saul Panzer and Dol Bonner, who had come late that afternoon to report. Tuesday afternoon and evening they had spent seven hours at the apartment on Perry Street, and six hours Wednesday at Amy Wynn's current apartment on Arbor Street. They were prepared to swear on a stack of best-sellers that in neither place was there a manuscript of a story by Alice Porter entitled "Opportunity Knocks." At Perry Street there had been no manuscript at all, by anybody. At Arbor Street there had been a drawerful of them—two novels, twenty-eight stories, and nine articles—all by Amy Wynn and all showing signs of the wear and tear that comes from a series of trips through the mails. Saul had made a list of the titles and number of pages, but I had decided it wasn't necessary to include it in the statement. I had dialed Philip Harvey's number to report to the chairman, but there was no answer, so I had called Reuben Imhof at Victory Press. He was glad to get the good news and said he would tell Amy Wynn.

Having detoured around the table with its load of paper, I stood at the end of Wolfe's desk. Ranged before him were three of the items of the collection: the manuscripts of Alice Porter's "There Is Only Love," and Simon Jacobs' "What's Mine Is Yours," and the copy of Jane Ogilvy's "On Earth but Not in Heaven." In his hand were some sheets from his scratch pad. His elbow was on the chair arm with his forearm perpendicular. It takes energy to hold a forearm straight up, and he only does it when he is especially pleased with himself.

"I'm looking," I said. "What is it? Fingerprints?"

"Better than fingerprints. These three stories were all written by the same person."

"Yeah? Not on the same typewriter. I compared them with a glass."

"So did I." He rattled the sheets. "Better than a typewriter. A typewriter can change hands." He glanced at the top sheet. "In Alice Porter's story a character avers something six times. In Simon Jacobs' story, eight times. In Jane Ogilvy's story, seven times. You know, of course, that nearly every writer of dialogue has his pet substitute, or substitutes, for 'say.' Wanting a variation for 'he said' or 'she said,' they have him declare, state, blurt, spout, cry, pronounce, avow, murmur, mutter, snap—there are dozens of them; and they tend to repeat the same one. Would you accept it as coincidence that this man and these two women have the same favorite, 'aver'?"

"Maybe with salt. I heard you say once that it is not inconceivable that the fall in temperature when the sun moves south is merely a coincidence."

"Pfui. That was conversation. This is work. There are other similarities, equally remarkable, in these stories. Two of them are verbal." He looked at the second sheet. "Alice Porter has this: 'Not for nothing would he abandon the only person he had ever loved.' And this: 'She might lose her self-respect, but not for nothing.' Simon Jacobs has this: 'And must he forfeit his honor too? Not for nothing.' And this: 'Not for nothing had she suffered tortures that no woman could be expected to survive.' Jane Ogilvy has a man say in reply to a question, 'Not for nothing, my dear, not for nothing.'"

I scratched my cheek. "Well. Not for nothing did you read the stories."

He went to the third sheet. "Another verbal one. Alice Porter has this: 'Barely had she touched him when he felt his heart pounding.' And this: 'Night had barely fallen by the time she reached the door and got out her key.' And this: 'Was there still a chance? Barely a chance?' Simon Jacobs used 'barely' four times, in similar constructions, and Jane Ogilvy three times."

"I'm sold," I averred. "Coincidence is out."

"But there are two others. One is punctuation. They are all fond of semicolons and use them where most people would prefer a comma or a dash. The other is more subtle but to me the most conclusive. A clever man might successfully disguise every element of his style but one—the paragraphing. Diction and syntax may be determined and controlled by rational processes in full consciousness, but paragraphing—the decision whether to take short hops or long ones, whether to hop in the middle of a thought or action or finish it first—that comes from instinct, from the depths of personality. I will concede the possibility that the verbal similarities, and even the punctuation, could be coincidence, though it is highly improbable; but not the paragraphing. These three stories were paragraphed by the same person."

"Plot it yourself," I said.

"What?"

"Nothing. The title of a piece I happened to read in the *Times Book Review* just popped up. It was about the idea that a novelist should just create his characters and let them go ahead and develop the action and the plot. This guy was dead against it. He claimed you should plot it yourself. I was thinking that a detective working on a case can't plot it himself. It has already been plotted. Look at this. This is now a totally different animal. One thing: with all those similarities, why hasn't anyone noticed it?"

"Probably because no one has ever had the three manuscripts together and compared them. Until that committee was formed they were in different hands."

I returned to my desk and sat. "Okay. Congratulations. So I'll have to rearrange my mind. I suppose you already have."

"No. I hadn't even arranged it."

I glanced up at the clock. "Quarter past eleven. Harvey might be home. Do you want to swagger?"

"No. I'm tired. I want to sleep. There's no hurry." He pushed his chair back and got to his feet.

Sometimes he self-propels his seventh of a ton up one flight of stairs to his room, but that night he used the elevator. When he had gone I took the three stories to my desk and spent half an hour studying paragraphing, and though Lily Rowan told me once that I am about as subtle as a sledge hammer—at a moment when her diction was not determined and controlled by rational processes in full consciousness—I saw what Wolfe meant. I put the stories in the safe and then considered the problem of the table-load of paper. The statuses and functions of the inhabitants of that old brownstone on West 35th Street are clearly understood. Wolfe is the owner and the commandant. Fritz Brenner is the chef and housekeeper and is responsible for the condition of the castle with the exception of the plant rooms, the office, and my bedroom. Theodore Horstmann is the orchid-tender, with no responsibilities or business on the lower floors. He eats in the kitchen with Fritz. I eat in the dining room with Wolfe, except when we are not speaking; then I join Fritz and Theodore in the kitchen, or get invited somewhere, or take a friend to a restaurant, or go to Bert's diner around the corner on Tenth Avenue and eat beans. My status and function are whatever a given situation calls for, and the question who decides what it calls for is what occasionally creates an atmosphere in which Wolfe and I are not speaking. The next sentence is to be, "But the table-load of paper, being in the office, was clearly up to me," and I have to decide whether to put it here or start a new paragraph with it. You see how subtle it is. Paragraph it yourself.

I stood surveying the stacks of paper. Scattered through them were assorted items of information about the four claimants. Assuming that one of them had written the stories, which was the most likely candidate? I ran over them in my mind.

Alice Porter. In her middle thirties, unmarried. No physical description, but a photograph. Fleshy, say 150 pounds. Round face, small nose, eyes too close together. In 1955 had lived at Collander House on West 82nd Street, a hive-home for girls and women who couldn't afford anything fancy. Was now living near Carmel, sixty miles north of New York, in a cottage which she had presumably bought with some of the loot she had pried out of Ellen Sturdevant. Between 1949 and 1955 had had fourteen stories for children published in magazines, and one children's book, *The Moth That Ate Peanuts,* published by Best and Green in 1954, not a success. Joined the National Association of Authors and Dramatists in 1951, was dropped for nonpayment of dues in 1954, rejoined in 1956.

Simon Jacobs. Description and photograph. Sixty-two years old, thin and scrawny, hair like Mark Twain's (that item from Title House's lawyer), stuttered. Married in 1948, therefore at the age of fifty-one.

In 1956 was living with his wife and three children in a tenement on West 21st Street, and was still there. Overseas with AEF in First World War, wounded twice. Wrote hundreds of stories for the pulps between 1922 and 1940, using four pen names. Was with the OWI in the Second World War, writing radio scripts in German and Polish. After the war wrote stories again, but didn't sell so many, eight or ten a year at three cents a word. In 1947 had a book published by the Owl Press, *Barrage at Dawn,* of which 35,000 copies were sold, and got married in 1948 and took an apartment in Brooklyn Heights. No more books published. Fewer stories sold. In 1954 moved to the tenement on West 21st Street. Member of the NAAD since 1931, dues always paid promptly, even during the war when he didn't have to.

Jane Ogilvy. Descriptions from three sources and several photographs. Late twenties or early thirties, depending on the source. Nice little figure, pretty little face, dreamy-eyed. In 1957 was living with her parents in their house in Riverdale, and still was. Went to Europe alone immediately after she collected from Marjorie Lippin's estate, but only stayed a month. Her father was in wholesale hardware, high financial rating. She had testified in court that she had had seventeen poems published in magazines, and had read three of them on the witness stand at the request of her attorney. No stories or books published. Member of the NAAD since 1955; was behind a year on her dues.

Kenneth Rennert. I could supply several pages on him, from the reports of the detective agency hired by Mortimer Oshin. Thirty-four years old, single. Looked younger. Virile (not my word, the detective's), muscular, handsome. Piercing brown eyes and so on. Living in a nice big room with bath and kitchenette on East 37th Street; the detective had combed it twice. Had mother and sisters in Ottumwa, Iowa; father dead. Graduated from Princeton in 1950. Got a job with a brokerage house, Orcutt and Company, was discharged in 1954 for cause, exact cause not ascertained, but it was something about diddling customers. No public charges. Began writing for television. So far as could be learned had sold only nine scripts in four years, but no other known source of income. Has borrowed money right and left; probably owes thirty or forty grand. Never a member of the NAAD; not eligible. Has never submitted a play to an agent or producer.

There they were. My guess, just to sleep on, was Alice Porter. She had worked it first, back in 1955, and was now repeating. She had written a book entitled *The Moth That Ate Peanuts,* which showed that she would stop at nothing. Her eyes were too close together. My suggestion in the morning, if Wolfe asked for one, as he usually did just to be polite, would be to connect her up with Simon Jacobs in 1956, Jane Ogilvy in 1957, and possibly Kenneth Rennert in 1958. If she had written the stories and they had used them, there had certainly been contacts. Oshin's detective agency and the lawyer for Marjorie Lippin's estate hadn't found any, but whether something is found or not depends on who is looking for it.

Making room on the shelves of one of the cabinets, I lugged the stuff from the table to it, seven trips, locked the cabinet, returned the table to the front room, and went up to bed.

4

I never made that suggestion because I slept it off. I had a better one. At 8:15 Thursday morning I descended two flights, entered the kitchen, exchanged good mornings with Fritz, picked up my ten-ounce glass of orange juice, took that first sour-sweet sip, which is always the first hint that the fog is going to lift, and inquired, "No omelet?"

Fritz shut the refrigerator door. "You well know, Archie, what it means when the eggs are not broken."

"Sure, but I'm hungry."

It meant that when Fritz had taken Wolfe's breakfast tray up to his room he had been told that I was wanted, and he would not break eggs until he heard me coming down again. I will not gulp orange juice, so after a second sip I took it along—up a flight, left to the door standing open at the end of the hall, and in. Wolfe, barefooted, a yellow mountain in his pajamas, was in his next-to-favorite chair at the table by a window, spooning raspberry jam onto a griddle cake. I returned his greeting and went on, "Copies of *The Moth That Ate Peanuts* and *Barrage at Dawn* are probably available at the publishers', but it might take days to dig up the magazines with Jane Ogilvy's poems. Also will the books be enough for Alice Porter and Simon Jacobs, or will you want some stories too?"

He grunted. "No special sagacity was required."

"No, sir. I'm not swaggering. It's just that I'm hungry and wanted to save time."

"You have. First the books. No stories may be needed. Jane Ogilvy's poems would almost certainly be worthless; I have read three of them. A writer of gimcrack verse chooses words only to scan and rhyme, and there is no paragraphing."

I sipped orange juice. "If they want to know why we want the books, do I explain?"

"No. Evade." He forked a bite of cake and jam.

"What if Harvey calls?"

"We have nothing to report. Possibly later. I want those books."

"Anything else?"

"No." He lifted the fork and opened his mouth.

When I got back to the kitchen Fritz had broken the eggs and was stirring. I sat at the table by the wall, propped the morning *Times* on the rack, and sipped orange juice. Fritz asked, "A good case?"

For him a good case is one which will not interfere with meals, will not last long enough to make Wolfe cranky, and will probably produce a nice fat fee. "So-so," I told him. "All we have to do is read a couple of books. Maybe."

He put the skillet on. "That Miss Bonner is helping?"

I grinned at him. He regards every woman who enters the house as a potential threat to his kitchen, not to mention the rest of his precinct, and he was particularly suspicious of Dol Bonner, Dol being short for Theodolinda, the only female owner and operator of a detective agency in New York. "No," I said, "she came yesterday on a personal matter. Mr. Wolfe keeps phoning her to ask her to dinner, and she wants me to get him to stop annoying her."

He pointed the spoon at me. "Archie, if I could lie with your aplomb I would be an ambassador. You know women. You know quite well that one with eyes the color of that Miss Bonner and eyelashes of that length, her own, is a dangerous animal."

By nine o'clock the morning fog had gone entirely, thanks to the apricot omelet, griddle cakes with bacon and honey, and two cups of coffee, and I went to the office and dialed Philip Harvey's number. From his reaction you might have thought it was not yet dawn. After smoothing him down and promising never to call him again earlier than noon, short of a real emergency, I told him what I wanted—the names of people at Best and Green and the Owl Press who could be expected to cooperate. He said he knew no one at either place, told me to call the executive secretary of NAAD, and hung up. A hell of a chairman. When I got the executive secretary she wanted to know what kind of cooperation I was going to ask for. I told her, and she wanted to know why Nero Wolfe wanted the books. I said that no good detective ever tells anybody why he wants something, and if I gave her a reason it would be a phony, and I finally wore her down and got a couple of names.

Mr. Arnold Green of Best and Green was extremely suspicious. He didn't come right out with it, but I gathered that he suspected that the Joint Committee on Plagiarism was a conspiracy, abetted by some of his competitors, to twist the nose of Best and Green by getting something on an author whose book they had published five years ago; and anyway, *The Moth That Ate Peanuts* was a flop and had been remaindered, and the only copies they had left, maybe four or five, were in the morgue. And more anyway, what did that book have to do with the investigation Nero Wolfe was making? When he had simmered down a little I said I fully appreciated his point of view, and I would tell Mr. Knapp and Mr. Dexter and Mr. Imhof that for some reason, probably a good one, he refused to send Mr. Wolfe a copy of the book, and he said I had misunderstood, that he wasn't refusing, that there might possibly be a copy somewhere around the office. If so he would send it down by messenger, and if not he would send someone to the morgue for one.

Mr. W. R. Pratt of the Owl Press was strictly business. When I said that Nero Wolfe had been hired to make an investigation by the Joint Committee on Plag—he cut in to say he knew that and what did I want; and when I said that Mr. Wolfe wanted a copy of *Barrage at Dawn* as soon as possible and would be obliged if he would kindly—he cut in again to say that if I would give the address to his secretary she would send it at once by messenger. He asked no questions, but his secretary did. Her first words were, "Whom do we bill?" That outfit was right on its toes.

Barrage at Dawn arrived first, which didn't surprise me, with an invoice enclosed which included an item of $1.50 for messenger service. Wolfe had come down from the plant rooms and was looking through the morning's mail. When I handed him the book he made a face at it and dropped it on his desk, but in a couple of minutes he picked it up, frowned at the cover, and opened it. He was well into it when *The Moth That Ate Peanuts* arrived, and since, as I said, my function is whatever an occasion calls for, I tackled that one, looking for "aver" or "not for nothing" or something like "Barely had the moth swallowed the ten-thousandth peanut when it got a stomach-ache." Also, of course, semicolons and paragraphing. I was more than halfway through when Wolfe asked for it, and I got up and handed it to him and took *Barrage at Dawn.*

A little after one, with lunchtime approaching, Wolfe shut *The Moth That Ate Peanuts,* tossed it onto his desk, and growled, "Pfui. Neither one. Confound it."

I closed *Barrage at Dawn* and put it down. "I can see," I said, "that you might cross Simon Jacobs off, but Alice Porter's is a children's book. You wouldn't expect a moth to aver, even if it was a peanut addict. I would hate to give up Alice Porter. She started it and she's repeating."

He glared at me. "No. She didn't write those stories."

"If you say so. Why glare at me? I didn't write them. Is this final or are you just sore because he or she was smart enough to wear gloves?"

"It's final. No one is that smart. Those two are eliminated."

"Then that leaves Jane Ogilvy and Kenneth Rennert."

"Jane Ogilvy is highly unlikely. The woman who wrote those three pseudo-poems and used the terms and locutions that appear in her testimony at the trial is almost certainly incapable of writing those three stories, including the one that she claimed she had written. Kenneth Rennert is of course a possibility, the only one left of the quartet. But his claim is based on a play outline, not a story, and we don't have it. It might even be that his was an independent operation. Could we get copies of the television scripts he has written?"

"I don't know. Shall I find out?"

"Yes, but there is no urgency. According to that report, they were dramatic in form and so contained nothing but dialogue, and would tell us next to nothing. I would like your opinion. Our job now is to find a person, man or woman: the person who in nineteen fifty-five read *The Color of Passion,* by Ellen Sturdevant, wrote a story with the title 'There Is Only Love,' incorporating its characters and plot and action, persuaded Alice Porter to use it as the basis for a claim of plagiarism, putting her name on it, the bait being presumably a share of the proceeds, and at an opportune moment somehow entered the summer home of Ellen Sturdevant and concealed the manuscript in a bureau drawer; who repeated the performance a year later with *Hold Fast to All I Give You,* by Richard Echols, using another accomplice, Simon Jacobs, changing only the method of establishing the existence and priority of the manuscript, suggested by the convenient circumstance that Jacobs had once sent a story to Echols' agent and had it returned; who in nineteen fifty-seven again repeated the performance with *Sacred or Profane,* by Marjorie Lippin, using still another accomplice, Jane Ogilvy, following the same pattern, with the advantage of another convenient circumstance, the death of Marjorie Lippin. I would like your opinion. Is Kenneth Rennert that person?"

I shook my head. "I don't know him well enough."

"You have read that report."

"Yeah." I considered. "Offhand I would vote no. One will get you ten that he isn't. From the general impression I got of him. Especially I doubt if he would monkey around with accomplices. A specific point: There is no evidence that he had any connection with writing or writers until he took a shot at television in nineteen fifty-five, so how did he get on to Alice Porter and Jacobs and Jane Ogilvy? Another one: If he used them on the first three, splitting the take with them, because he didn't want to do it himself, why did he do it himself for the fourth and then go back to Alice Porter for the fifth?"

Wolfe nodded. "I agree. We are caught in our own noose. By discovering that those three stories were written by the same person we thought we had simplified the problem. It now appears that we have complicated it. If those four were merely cat's-paws, where is the monkey? He is presumably a United States citizen. There are a hundred and seventy million of them."

"It's not that bad," I averred. "He's probably in the metropolitan area. Fifteen million. Not counting children, illiterates, millionaires, people in jail—"

Fritz had appeared at the door. "Lunch is ready, sir."

"I have no appetite," Wolfe growled.

It was off a little. He only ate four Creole fritters with cheese sauce instead of the usual five.

5

So he pulled a mutiny, the first one in three years. His mutinies are not like other people's. Other people mutiny against the Army or Navy or some other authority, but he mutinies against himself. It was his house and his office, and he had taken the job, but now he turned his back on it. His discovery that the three stories had all been written by one person, which I admit was fairly neat, had backfired on him, and he quit. Of course business is never mentioned at the table, but from his mood I knew he was smoldering, so when we returned to the office after lunch I asked politely whether there would be instructions then or later.

"Now," he said. "You will see, at your convenience and theirs, Miss Porter, Miss Ogilvy, Mr. Jacobs, and Mr. Rennert. In whatever order you prefer. Make their acquaintance."

I stayed polite. "It will be a pleasure to meet them. What are we to talk about?"

"Whatever occurs to you. I have never known you to be short of words."

"How about bringing them, one at a time, to make *your* acquaintance?"

"No."

"I see." I stood and looked down at him. That annoys him because he has to tilt his head to look up. "It must be wonderful to be a genius. Like that singer, Doria Ricco, whenever anything goes wrong she just walks out. Then she has a press conference. Shall I set one up for six o'clock? You could tell them that a great artist like you can't be expected to take a setback which any ordinary detective would only—"

"You will please keep your remarks to yourself."

So it was a mutiny, not just a passing peeve. If he had merely barked at me "Shut up!" as he does two or three times a week, I would have known he would snap out of it in an hour or so and go to work, but that was bad. It would take time, no telling how much. And he left his chair, crossed to the bookshelves, took a volume of Shakespeare from the set, returned to his seat, leaned back, and opened the book. Bowing out not only from the case, but from the country and the century. I went. Leaving the room and the house, I walked to Ninth Avenue and flagged a taxi and told the driver 632 West 21st Street.

That building was a tenement not only as defined in the New York Tenement House Act, but also as what people usually mean when they say "tenement." It was a dump. Having decided in the taxi how to start a conversation with Simon Jacobs, I found his name in the row, next to the top, and pressed the button. When the click sounded I pushed the door open, entered, and went to the stairs and started up, smelling garlic. The smell of garlic in Spanish sauce as Fritz makes it is a come-on, but in a tenement hall where it has been seeping into the plaster for fifty years it's a pinch-nose. The best way is to pull in a long deep breath of it immediately and then your insides know it's hopeless.

Three flights up a woman was standing at an open door near the front of the hall, with a boy, nine or ten, at her elbow. As I approached, the boy said, "Oh, it's not Tommy," and disappeared. I asked the woman, "Mrs. Jacobs?"

She nodded. She was a surprise. Simon Jacobs, now sixty-two, had been fifty-one when he had married in 1948, but she was no crone. There wasn't a wrinkle showing, and there was no sign of gray in her soft brown hair. When I told her my name and I would like to speak with her husband, and she said he didn't like to be disturbed when he was working and would I please tell her what I wanted, and I said I wasn't selling anything, it was a business matter and might be to his advantage, she turned and went, leaving the door open. After a long moment he appeared, a good likeness to the photograph—thin and scrawny, with enough wrinkles for two, and, as Title House's lawyer had said, hair like Mark Twain's.

"Well, sir?" A thin high voice would have fitted him, but his was deep and full.

"My name's Goodwin, Mr. Jacobs."

"So my wife said."

"I'm on the staff of a magazine with national circulation. I won't name it until I find out if you're interested in an idea we are considering. May I come in?"

"That depends. I'm right in the middle of a story. I don't want to be rude, but what's the idea?"

"Well—we thought we might ask you to do an article for us. About how it feels to have a story you have written stolen by another author and turned into a best-seller. We thought 'Plot It Yourself' might be a good title for it. I'd like to tell you how we think it might be handled, and we can discuss—"

He shut the door in my face. You may think I'm not much of a detective, that an experienced snoop should have had sense enough to have it blocked with his foot, but in the first place it was totally unexpected, and in the second place you don't block a door unless you're on the offensive. So I merely put my thumb to my nose and wiggled my fingers, turned, and made for the stairs. When I got to the sidewalk I took a long, deep breath to let my insides know they could relax. Then I walked to Tenth Avenue, stopped a taxi, and told the driver 37th and Lexington.

That building, between Lexington and Third, was a house of a different color. It may have been nearly as old as the 21st Street tenement, but it had used make-up. Its brick front was painted silver-gray with bright blue trim, the doorframe was aluminum, and there were evergreens in boxes. There were eight names on the panel in the vestibule, two tenants to a floor, with a grill to talk through and a receiver on a hook. I pushed the button opposite Rennert and put the receiver to my ear, and in a moment had a crackle and then a voice.

"Who is it?"

"You don't know me. My name's Goodwin. Nothing to sell. I may want to buy something."

"Bill Goodwin?"

"No. Archie Goodwin."

"Archie? Not by any chance Nero Wolfe's Archie Goodwin?"

"In person."

"Well, well! I often wonder what detectives buy one-half so precious as the goods they sell. Come on up and tell me! Top floor."

I hung up and turned, and when the buzz sounded opened the door and entered. More aluminum, framing the self-service elevator. I stepped in and pushed the "4" button and was lifted. When it stopped and the door opened he was there in the little hall, shirt sleeves rolled up and no tie, virile, muscular, handsome, looking younger than thirty-four. I took his offered hand and returned his manly grip and was ushered through a door and was in the nice big room. It was even nicer and bigger than the report had led me to expect. He had me take a nice big chair and asked, "Scotch, rye, bourbon, gin?"

I declined with thanks, and he sat on a nice big couch which probably doubled as a bed. "This is a pleasure," he said, "unless you want my fingerprints to compare them with the ones you found on the dagger that was sticking in the back of the corpse. I swear I didn't do it. I always stab people in front. I like that suit. Matthew Jonas?"

I told him no, Peter Darrell. "Fingerprints wouldn't help," I said. "There were none on the dagger. It was one of those old Arabian antiques with a fancy handle. What I told you was straight. I may want to buy something—or rather, a client of Nero Wolfe's may. He's a guy with money who wants more. He gets ideas. He has the idea that he might like to buy your claim against Mortimer Oshin and Al Friend for stealing your play outline, 'A Bushel of Love,' and turning it into *A Barrel of Love*. He might pay ten thousand cash for an assignment of the claim and your affidavit supporting it, and another ten thousand if and when Oshin and Friend pay up. Of course he would expect you to testify without a subpoena if it goes to trial."

"Well, well." He stretched a leg on the couch. "Who is this fairy godfather?"

"A client of Mr. Wolfe's. We handled a problem for him once, not this kind. If we agree on a deal you'll meet him. The ten thousand is ready in bills."

"What if they never pay up?"

"That's his risk. He would be out ten grand."

"Nuts. They'll pay. They'll pay ten times ten. At least."

"Possibly," I conceded. "Some day. If it goes to trial, there'll be lawyers' fees and other expenses."

"Well." He put his other leg up. "Tell him I might be interested. I'm willing to meet him and discuss it with him."

I shook my head. "I'm here to discuss it. The reason he got Mr. Wolfe to handle it, there are a couple of little details to arrange. For one, he would like to have some evidence in his possession that that's not the only dramatic plot you ever hatched. That should be easy. I suppose you have copies of some of your television scripts."

"Sure. All of them."

"Fine. That would settle that. The other one, if it gets to court, it would help a lot to have some backing for your testimony that you wrote the outline with your name on it that was found in Jack Sandler's office files, and the best backing would be to produce the typewriter that you wrote it on. Our client would want it. Of course he would pay you for it."

"That would be sweet of him."

"He's not sweet. Between you and me, I don't like him."

"Neither do I. He stole my play." His legs swung around and he was on his feet. "All right, Hawkshaw. Beat it."

I stayed put. "Now listen, Mr. Rennert. I can understand how you—"

"I said beat it." He took a step. "Do you want help?"

I arose and took two steps, and was facing him at arm's length. "Would you like to try?"

I was hoping he would. Wolfe's mutiny had put me in a humor that would have made it a pleasure to take a swing at somebody, and this character was the right size and build to make it not only a pleasure but good exercise. He didn't oblige me. His eyes stayed with mine, but he backed up a foot.

"I don't want to get blood on the rug," he said.

I turned and went. As I was opening the door he called to my back, "Tell Mortimer Oshin this is like one of his lousy plots!" The elevator was still there, and I stepped in and pushed the button.

On the sidewalk I looked at my wrist: 4:05. Carmel was only a ninety-minute drive, and it would be good for my nerves, but I would phone first. What was Alice Porter's number? I stood at the curb and closed my eyes and concentrated, and dug it out of the cell that had filed it. Around the corner on Lexington Avenue I found a booth, dialed, counted fourteen rings, and hung up. No answer. I settled for a shorter drive. I hoofed it crosstown to Tenth Avenue and a block south to the garage, got the Heron sedan, which was Wolfe's by purchase but mine by mandate, and headed for the West Side Highway.

It was now twenty to one in my book, or maybe thirty to one, that Kenneth Rennert was not it. Whoever had planned and handled that campaign, writing the stories and picking the accomplices and taking advantage of the different circumstances for planting the manuscripts, was no fumbler, but Rennert was. Having suspected, or decided, that Mortimer Oshin was Wolfe's client and I was trying to slip one over, which had not required any strain on the brain, if he had been half smart he would have played me along instead of bouncing me. He was just one of the chorus, not the star. I had filed him away by the time I left the Henry Hudson Parkway at Exit Eleven.

Riverdale, whose streets were planned by someone who couldn't stand the idea of a straight line, is a jungle for a stranger, but I had a good map and only had to turn around twice on my way to 78 Haddon Place. Rolling to the curb in front, I gave it a look. There was too much bigger stuff, everything from tulip beds up to full-grown trees, to leave much room for lawns, but what grass there was would have been fine for putting practice. The house was stone up to your chin and then dark brown wood with the boards running up and down instead of horizontal. Very classy. I got out and started up the walk.

Hearing music as I neared the entrance, I stopped and cocked an ear. Not from inside; from the left. I took to the grass, rounded a corner of the house, passed a row of windows, turned another corner, and stepped onto a flagged terrace. The music, coming from a portable radio on a chair, had an audience of one: Jane Ogilvy. She was stretched out on a mat, on her back, with none of her skin covered except minimum areas at the two vital spots. Her eyes were closed. The deduction I had made from the photographs, in which she had been dressed, that she had a nice little figure, was confirmed. She even had good knees.

I was deciding whether to retreat around the corner and make another approach with sound effects, or stay put and cough, when her eyes suddenly opened and her head turned. She squinted at me five seconds and spoke. "I knew someone had come. The felt presence though not perceived. You're real, I suppose?"

It was strange. It wasn't like a hunch; it was more as if I had asked a question and she had answered it. When Wolfe had eliminated her because of her testimony at the trial and the three poems she had read, I had had my doubts, but those few words from her settled it. If Rennert was now thirty to one, she was a thousand to one.

"Don't speak," she said, "even if you're real. There's nothing you could say that would be worthy of the moment when I felt you here. You may think I heard you, but I didn't. My ears were filled with the music, all of me was, when I felt you. If it were the Eve of Saint Agnes—but it isn't, and I am not supperless, and I'm not in bed. . . . But what if your name were Porphyro? Is it—no, don't speak! Are you going to come closer?"

I agreed with her absolutely. There was nothing I could say that would be worthy of the occasion. Besides, my name wasn't Porphyro. But I didn't want to turn and go with no response at all, so I reached to the trellis beside me and picked a red rose, pressed it to my lips, and tossed it to her. Then I went.

At a phone booth in a drugstore a few blocks away I dialed Alice Porter's number in Carmel, and again there was no answer. That left me with nowhere to go and nothing to do. Of course Wolfe's idea in telling me to go and make the acquaintance of the quartet had been simply to get rid of me, since he knew that if I stuck around I would ride him; and even if I didn't ride him I would look at him. So I dialed another number, got an answer, made a suggestion about ways of passing the time for the next eight or nine hours, and had it accepted. Then I dialed the number I knew best and told Fritz I wouldn't be home for dinner. It was well after midnight when I mounted the stoop of the old brownstone on West 35th Street and used my key. There was no note for me on my desk. I left one in the kitchen for Fritz, telling him not to expect me for breakfast until ten o'clock. I can always use eight hours' sleep, and if Wolfe snapped out of it during the night he knew where to find me.

When I went down to breakfast Friday morning I had a packed bag with me, and at a quarter to eleven I took my second cup of coffee to the office, to my desk, and buzzed the plant rooms on the house phone. Wolfe's voice came. "Yes?"

"Good morning." I was cheerful. "You may remember that I have accepted an invitation for the weekend."

"Yes."

"Should I call it off?"

"No."

"Then I have a suggestion. I saw three of them yesterday, Jacobs and Rennert and Miss Ogilvy, but not Alice Porter. She didn't answer her phone. As you know, Miss Rowan's place, where I'm going, is near Katonah, and it's less than half an hour from there to Carmel. Miss Rowan expects me at six o'clock. If I leave now I can go to Carmel first and have the afternoon for making the acquaintance of Miss Porter."

"Is there anything in the mail that requires attention?"

"No. Nothing that can't wait."

"Then go."

"Right. I'll be back late Sunday evening. Do you want a report on the three I saw before I go?"

"No. If you had anything exigent to report you would have said so."

"Sure. Miss Rowan's phone number is on your desk. I'll give her your regards. Don't overdo."

He hung up. The big fat bum. I wrote the phone number on his memo pad, went to the kitchen to tell Fritz good-by, got my bag, and was gone.

There is always traffic on the West Side Highway, twenty-four hours a day, but it thinned out beyond the city limits, and north of Hawthorne Circle I had long stretches to myself. After leaving Route 22 at Croton Falls and meandering through patches of woods and along shores of reservoirs for a few miles, I stopped for an hour at the Green Fence, known to me, where a woman with a double chin fries chicken the way my Aunt Margie did out in Ohio. Fritz does not fry chicken. At two o'clock I was rolling again, with only a couple of miles to go.

There was no point in phoning, since I was there anyway, but I almost had to, to find out where her cottage was. The cop on Main Street had never heard of Alice Porter. The man in the drugstore had, he had put up prescriptions for her, but didn't know where she lived.

The man at the filling station thought her place was out toward Kent Cliffs but wasn't sure. He advised me to consult Jimmy Murphy, who ran a taxi. Jimmy rattled it off: a mile and a half west on Route 301, right on a blacktop for a mile, right on dirt for half a mile, mailbox on the right.

It checked. The half a mile of dirt was uphill, winding, narrow, and stony. The mailbox was at the mouth of a lane, even narrower, through a gap in a stone fence, no gate. I turned in and eased my way along the ruts to where the lane ended in front of a little house painted blue, one story. There was no car in sight. As I climbed out and shut the door a little bi-colored mutt trotted up and started to growl, but his curiosity to see what I smelled like close up was too much for him, and the growl petered out. I reached down and scratched the back of his neck, and we were pals. He went with me to help knock on the door, and when, after knocking got no response, I tried the knob and found it was locked, he was as disappointed as I was.

With my years of training as a detective, I reached a conclusion. Dogs have to be fed. There was no other house in sight, no nearby neighbor to pinch-feed for Alice Porter. Therefore she would return. A top-drawer detective, say Nero Wolfe, could have found out exactly when she would return by looking at the dog's teeth and feeling its belly, but I'm not in that class. I looked over the grounds—four young trees and half a dozen shrubs scattered here and there—and then moseyed around to the back. There was a neat little vegetable garden, no weeds, and I pulled some radishes and ate them. Then I went to the car and got a book from my bag, I forget what, but it wasn't *The Moth That Ate Peanuts,* sat on one of two garden chairs in the shade of the house, and read. The mutt curled up at my feet and shut his eyes.

She came at 5:28. A '58 Ford station wagon came bumping along the ruts and stopped back of the Heron, and she scrambled out and headed for me. The mutt went bounding to meet her, and she halted to give him a pat. I shut my book and stood up.

"You looking for me?" she asked.

"I am if you're Miss Alice Porter," I said.

She knew who I was. It's easy to make a mistake on a thing like that, I had made plenty in my time, but it was in her eyes that she had recognized me or I had better quit the detective business and take up truck-driving or window-washing. That was nothing startling; it happened now and then. My picture hadn't been in the papers as often as President Eisenhower's, but it had once made the front page of the *Gazette.*

"That's my name," she said.

From her photograph I had guessed 150, but she had put on ten pounds. Her round face was bigger and her nose smaller, and her eyes were closer together. There was sweat on her brow.

"Mine's Archie Goodwin," I said. "I work for Nero Wolfe, the private detective. Could you give me maybe ten minutes?"

"I can if you'll wait till I put some stuff in the refrigerator. While I'm doing that you might get your car around back of mine. Take it easy on the grass."

I did so. The grass was nothing like that at 78 Haddon Place, but no doubt she would see to that after she collected from Amy Wynn. I moved the Heron forward a car length, cramped the wheels and backed, and swung around past the Ford and back into the ruts. She had got an armload of bags from the Ford, declining my offer to help, and entered the house. I returned to the chair, and soon she came out and took the other one.

"I've been thinking," she said. "If you're Archie Goodwin and Nero Wolfe sent you clear out here, it's not hard to guess what for. Or I should say who for. I might as well come right out with it. The Victory Press has hired him, or Amy Wynn has, to try to find something wrong about my claim for damages. If that's what it is you've wasted a lot of gas. I'm not going to talk about it, not a word. I may not be very bright, but I'm not exactly a fool. Unless you came to make an offer. I'll listen to that."

I shook my head. "That's not a very good guess, Miss Porter. It's about your claim against Amy Wynn, that much is okay, but she hasn't hired Mr. Wolfe and neither has the Victory Press. I'm here on behalf of a New York newspaper that's looking for a scoop. Nothing has been published about your claim, so I don't know how the paper got onto it, but you know how that is, word gets around. What the paper is after, it wants to publish your story, 'Opportunity Knocks,' on which you base your claim, with an introductory statement by you. It wants to know how much you will take for what it calls first serial rights, and it's not breaking any confidence to tell you that you can go pretty high. The reason they got Nero Wolfe to handle it instead of coming to you direct is that they want him to check on certain details. You understand that; it's sort of tricky."

"There's nothing tricky about my claim."

"I didn't say there is. But there would be a risk of a libel suit against the paper, whether there is ground for it or not. Of course before the paper makes a definite commitment it would want to see the story. Mr.

Wolfe thought you might have a carbon copy and would let me take it. Have you got one?"

Her eyes met mine. They had been slanting off, first in one direction and then another, but now they came to me straight. "You're pretty good," she said.

"Thanks." I grinned at her. "I like to think so, but of course I'm biased. Good how?"

"Good with your tongue. I'll have to think it over. I'll do that. I'll think it over. Right now, as I said, I'm not going to talk about it. Not a word." She arose.

"But that was when you thought Mr. Wolfe had been hired by the Victory Press or Amy Wynn."

"I don't care who hired him, I'm not talking. You'll have to excuse me. I've got things to do." She headed for the door of the house. The mutt glanced at me and then at her, decided she was the best bet, and trotted after her. I went and got in the car and started the engine. On the stretch of blacktop a man with a bunch of wild columbine in his hand was following a herd of forty-seven cows (actual count; a detective is supposed to observe) who all had the same idea, that they would rather get hit by a Heron sedan than get milked, and it took me five minutes to get through.

Saturday afternoon at Lily Rowan's place, or it may have been Sunday afternoon, when half a dozen of us were loafing in the sun by the swimming pool, I told them about the incident on the terrace at Riverdale, leaving out the name and address and why I was there, and asked if they thought she was batty. The three women voted no and the two men yes, and of course that proved something but I still haven't decided what.

At midnight Sunday, full of air and with a sunburned nose, I dropped my bag in the hall of the old brownstone, went to the office, and found a note on my desk:

AG:

Mr. Harvey phoned Saturday morning. He will come with his committee Monday at 11:15.

NW

6

This time there were seven instead of six. In addition to the three from the BPA—Gerald Knapp, Thomas Dexter, and Reuben Imhof—and the three from NAAD—Amy Wynn, Mortimer Oshin, and Philip Harvey—there was a middle-aged woman named Cora Ballard whose spine stayed as stiff as a poker both standing and sitting. Harvey had explained that she was not a committee member but was there ex officio. She was the executive secretary of the NAAD. Harvey had seen to it that she was seated next to him, at his left. I had noted glances directed at her by Dexter and Knapp which led me to suspect that in a national poll to choose the Secretary of the Year the book publishers' vote would not go to Cora Ballard, and her return glances indicated that she most certainly wouldn't want it to. She had a stenographer's notebook on her lap and a pencil in her hand.

Philip Harvey, in the red leather chair, was yawning, probably because he had had to get up and out before noon for the second time in a week. Gerald Knapp was explaining that he had been willing to cancel two appointments in order to be present because he agreed with Mr. Imhof that the charge now made by Alice Porter against Amy Wynn and the Victory Press made it imperative that immediate and vigorous action be taken, and he agreed with Mr. Harvey that they should see Mr. Wolfe in a body to learn what progress had been made. Wolfe, his lips pressed tight, sat and scowled at him.

"That is," Knapp finished, "if there has been any progress. Has there?"

"No," Wolfe said. "To the contrary. There has been regress."

They all stared. Cora Ballard said, "Really." Mortimer Oshin demanded, "How the hell could there be?"

Wolfe took a breath. "I'll explain briefly, and if you would like me to return the five thousand dollars you have advanced you have only to say so. I told you last Tuesday that this may be a laborious and costly operation; it now appears that it may take more labor than I am prepared to give, and cost more than you are prepared to pay. You were assuming that Alice Porter's success in hoodwinking Ellen Sturdevant had led others to imitate her, but you were wrong. Alice Porter was merely a tool, and so were Simon Jacobs, Jane Ogilvy, and Kenneth Rennert."

Cora Ballard looked up from her notebook. "Did you say 'tool'?"

"I did. Two steps brought me to that conclusion. The first resulted from my examination of the stories used by the three first-named as the bases of their claims. They were all written by the same person. The internal evidence—diction, syntax, paragraphing—is ineluctable. You are professional word-and-language people; study those stories and you'll all agree with me."

"I'm not a writer," Cora Ballard said. "I just work for writers."

"Not *for*," Harvey corrected her. "You work *with* writers and *on* writers." To Wolfe: "This is important, if true. I want to compare those stories."

"It's not only important," Knapp declared, "it's remarkable. It seems to me you *have* made progress."

"So it seemed to me," Wolfe said, "until I took the next step. All that remained, it seemed, was to learn which of the three had written the stories; then it would be simple. I procured a book written by Alice Porter, and one written by Simon Jacobs, and studied them, and I reread the testimony Jane Ogilvy had given on the witness stand, including the three poems she had recited. I shall not expound; I merely state that I am convinced that none of them wrote the stories."

"But damn it," Imhof objected, "somebody did! And now Alice Porter is repeating."

"By God," Oshin exclaimed, squashing a cigarette, "Rennert! Kenneth Rennert!"

Wolfe shook his head. "I doubt it. The reasons for my doubt are not conclusive, but they are cogent." He upturned a palm. "So. When you left here six days ago I thought I had four culprits to expose. When I had read the stories I thought I had just one and he could be easily identified; the others were only tools. That was progress. Now there is still just one, but who and where is he? The only approach to him, the only hope of finding him, is through the contacts he must have made with his tools. That kind of investigation does not fit my talents, and it will probably be prolonged and expensive. It will demand an exhaustive and meticulous inquiry into the movements and associations of those three people—four, with Kenneth Rennert included. That is regress."

"Do you mean you're quitting?" Dexter asked.

"I mean that it no longer seems to be my kind of job. To do it properly and with expedition at least a dozen competent operatives will be needed, with competent supervision. That will cost six hundred dollars a day or more, plus expenses, seven days a week. I would not supervise such an operation. But I should finish my report. As I told Mr. Harvey on the phone on Saturday, I sent Mr. Goodwin to call on those four people, and he has seen them. Archie?"

I had tossed my notebook over my shoulder onto my desk. It looked as if we weren't even going to send a bill for expenses, and in that case I was out $3.80 for the fried chicken I had bought at the Green Fence. "Do you want it all?" I asked.

"Not I. They. Miss Ballard is taking notes. If it isn't too extensive."

"It isn't. Two minutes with Simon Jacobs, seven with Kenneth Rennert, one with Jane Ogilvy, and eight with Alice Porter."

"Then verbatim."

I obliged. Since I had developed that faculty to a point where I could give Wolfe a full and accurate account of a two-hour conversation with three or four people, this little chore was nothing. As I went along I noticed that Mortimer Oshin was lighting no cigarettes, and I was taking it as a compliment until I realized that, being a dramatist, he was sizing up the dialogue. When I finished he reacted first.

"That Jane Ogilvy speech," he said. "Of course you've dressed it up. Damn good."

"No dressing," I told him. "When I report I merely report."

"And you think Kenneth Rennert is not the—the instigator?" Gerald Knapp asked.

"Right. For the reasons given."

"It seems to me," Philip Harvey said, "that this doesn't alter the situation any. As Mr. Wolfe described it." His head moved to take them in. "So now what?"

They held a committee meeting. What made it a meeting was that when more than three of them talked at once Harvey yelled that he couldn't hear anybody. After a quarter of an hour the consensus seemed to be that they were in a pickle, and I was thinking that if I were chairman I would ask for a motion to that effect.

Thomas Dexter raised his voice. "I would like to suggest," he suggested, "that we take twenty-four hours to consider the matter as it now stands, and meet again tomorrow. It is possible that Mr. Wolfe—"

"Wait a minute," Oshin cut in. He had a cigarette going. "I've got an idea." He stretched his neck to see around Gerald Knapp, to look at me. "A question for you, Mr. Goodwin. Which one of those four people needs money most?"

"That depends on what you mean by 'money,'" I told him. "A ten-spot or a grand or half a million?"

"Something in between. Here's my idea, and I like it. We make one of them an offer. Nero Wolfe makes it for us. Say ten thousand dollars. What the hell, I'd be willing to kick in that much myself. My lawyer thinks I may have to pay Rennert between fifty and a hundred thousand, and if this works Rennert will be done. And you're in the same position, Miss Wynn, with Alice Porter. She's going to nick you—"

"Not the same," Reuben Imhof objected. "There's no evidence. Alice Porter has claimed that Miss Wynn plagiarized a story she wrote, but the story hasn't been produced."

"It will be. Miss Wynn, wouldn't you be willing to pay ten thousand dollars to have Alice Porter stopped? Stopped for good?"

Amy Wynn looked at Imhof. He patted her on the shoulder. "Stopped how?" he asked Oshin. "What's your idea?"

"Very simple. Brilliant but simple. We offer him, or her, twenty thousand dollars to spill it. Who wrote the story he based his claim on, how the manuscript was planted—everything. With evidence to back it up; that should be easy. We also offer to guarantee that he won't be prosecuted and he won't be asked to return his share of the loot. You've seen all four of them, Mr. Goodwin. Which one would you pick?"

"Simon Jacobs," I said.

"Why him?"

"Very simple. Not even brilliant. Rennert is going to collect a lot more than twenty grand from you, or thinks he is. The same goes for Alice Porter; she has just made her claim on Amy Wynn. As for Jane Ogilvy, God only knows. She testified in court that she wrote that story, 'On Earth but Not in Heaven,' because she was suffocating under the blanket of her father's bounty and her mother's devotion and sought another market for her soul, end of quotation. I suppose meaning that she wanted to get hold of some cash, and presumably this operator knew that and obliged her. When she got it she kicked loose and went to Europe, but in a month she came back to the blanket. She might grab at the twenty grand, or she might spurn it. Just talking about her I use words like 'spurn.'"

"Then that leaves Jacobs."

"Right. He probably used up his share of the take long ago. He's having a hard time placing his stories. He's living in a dump with his wife and children. I don't know if he's in debt, but he probably is, and he's not the kind of guy who would enjoy being in debt. He might open the bag for twenty grand if he had a tight guarantee that he wouldn't be prosecuted and he wouldn't be expected to repay what he got from Richard Echols more than two years ago. He hasn't got it any more. Of course the guarantee would have to come from Echols."

Oshin went to Thomas Dexter. "How about it, Mr. Dexter? You know Echols; you published his book. Of course I've met him, but I don't know him. Will he go along?"

The publisher passed his hand over his gray hair. "That's hard to say. I will say this, if Mr. Echols agrees to such an arrangement we at Title House will have no objection. We will concur, provided that Jacobs' affidavit—I presume it would be in the form of an affidavit—makes it clear that his charge of plagiarism was false. Provided it removes from Title House the stigma of having published a book that was—uh—a fraud. We would engage to make no demand for the return of our contribution to the payment made to Jacobs, or any part of it."

"That's fine. But what about Echols?"

"I couldn't say. He is a reasonable and sensible man in many respects. I think it quite possible that he would—uh—acquiesce, if properly approached."

"What do you think, Cora?" Philip Harvey asked. "You know him better than anyone here."

Cora Ballard pursed her lips. "Sure," she said, "I know Dick. I helped him with his first book contract twenty years ago, before he had an agent. The publisher wanted thirty per cent of the movie rights and twenty per cent of the first serial, and that was ridiculous. Dick's a little peculiar in some ways, but he likes to do the right thing and he's very generous. I'll ask him about this if you want me to, and see what he says. Actually, what he'll do, he'll go straight to Paul Norris, his agent, and ask him what he thinks. Of course I know Paul, and it might be better to take it up with him first. I could see him this afternoon."

"That's the kind of an executive secretary to have," Gerald Knapp said. "No wonder you authors always get the best of it."

Chairman Harvey snorted. "Comic relief. Always welcome. Speaking for myself, if I were Dick Echols I wouldn't hesitate. Unfortunately I'm not in his class and never will be. I've had six books published, and my last one, *Why the Gods Laugh,* is in its ninth thousand, which is a record for me." He looked around. "What about Mr. Oshin's idea? Do we like it?"

"I do," Oshin said. "Ten thousand dollars' worth, and I think Miss Wynn should match it."

Amy Wynn looked at Reuben Imhof. "We'll discuss it," he told her, and turned to the chairman. "It certainly won't do any harm for Miss Ballard to sound out Mr. Echols and his agent. If they agree to cooperate, then we can decide whether to go ahead."

"In my opinion," Gerald Knapp said, "we should decide that now. I fully approve of Mr. Oshin's suggestion and move that we adopt it. If Mr. Echols consents it shouldn't be necessary to have another meeting. Mr. Wolfe could proceed at once to have the necessary papers drawn and make the offer to Simon Jacobs."

"Second the motion," Oshin said.

"Further discussion?" Harvey asked. "If not, all in favor raise your hands. It seems to be unanimous. Miss Wynn, when can you let me know whether you will match Mr. Oshin's ten thousand? Today?"

"Oh, yes," she assured him. "Certainly by five o'clock."

"Good. If I'm not at home call Miss Ballard at the NAAD. Now, Mr. Wolfe, I hope this has changed your mind. I hope you'll agree that we're making some progress, and of course you and Mr. Goodwin made it possible. Have you any comment?"

"Yes," Wolfe said. "I am a detective, not a conveyor of bait. However, since Mr. Goodwin named Mr. Jacobs as the prospective receiver, he and I have a responsibility. If the preparations are satisfactory, we will act."

7

At twenty minutes past four that afternoon Amy Wynn told me, not on the phone, in person, that she would match Oshin's ten grand.

The development started shortly after three o'clock with a phone call from Reuben Imhof. Wolfe and I were in the office, having lunched together in the dining room in a slightly improved atmosphere. He was at his desk dictating letters, and I was at mine taking them, when the phone rang and I answered it.

"Nero Wolfe's office, Archie Goodwin speaking."

"This is Reuben Imhof. I understand that Wolfe never leaves his house on business."

"Correct. He doesn't."

"All right, you, then. Come up here quick. My office, Victory Press."

"I'm pretty busy. Say in an hour?"

"No. Now. Nothing I can tell you on the phone. *Now!*"

"Okay. Coming. Keep your shirt on." I hung up and told Wolfe, "Imhof. Something is biting him, he wouldn't say what, and he wants me quick. Our responsibility?"

Wolfe grunted. "Confound these interruptions." We were in the middle of a letter to Lewis Hewitt, describing the results of a cross of *C. gaskelliana alba* with *C. mossiae wageneri*. "Very well. Go."

I did so. At that time of day taxis are apt to crawl slightly faster on Eighth Avenue than on Tenth, so I headed east. We finally made it to 52nd and Sixth Avenue, and when we turned right and I saw that the whole block was choked I paid the hackie and quit him. The Victory Press address, on Madison in the Fifties, was one of the new concrete and glass boxes, with a green marble lobby and four banks of elevators. As I entered the suite on the thirty-second floor I half expected to find the place in an uproar, from the way Imhof had sounded on the phone, but all was serene. The two people on chairs in the reception room, one of them with a bulging briefcase on his lap, merely looked patient, and the bright-eyed receptionist at the desk merely lifted her brows as I approached. However, when I told her my name she said Mr. Imhof was expecting me and used the phone, and in a moment an attractive young woman entered through an arch and asked me to follow her, please; and being, as I have said, a trained observer, naturally I noticed that she had restless hips.

Reuben Imhof's room was an ideal setting for discussing the terms of a book contract with a member of the NAAD. Surely an author wouldn't be fussy about little things with a man who had a desk like that, and such fine comfortable chairs, and four windows on two sides, and genuine oil paintings on the walls, and real old Persian rugs. Having taken that in with a quick glance around, I crossed to the desk. Imhof, behind it, kept his seat and his hands. From his look he was in no mood to shake hands with William Shakespeare or Mark Twain if one of them had suddenly entered. He didn't greet me at all. Instead, he spoke to the young woman who had ushered me in. "Don't go, Judith. Sit down. Look at this, Goodwin."

I didn't hop. It may be true that, as a friend once told me, I have no more social grace than a conceited tiger, but Amy Wynn, being a member of the committee, was one-sixth of our client and not to be ignored. So before looking at the object Imhof had on his desk I turned to the chair where Amy Wynn was sitting and told her good afternoon. She nodded, just barely. Then I looked at the object.

It was some sheets of paper, 8½ by 11. The one on top was headed "Opportunity Knocks," and below that, "by Alice Porter." In the upper right-hand corner was a date, June 3, 1957. The text that followed was double-spaced. I lifted the edges to the last sheet: twenty-seven pages. There were no creases from folding.

"By God," Imhof said.

"I doubt it," I said. "I doubt if He had a hand in it. Probably not by Alice Porter, either. Where was it?"

"In a cabinet in the filing room down the hall. In a folder marked 'Amy Wynn.'"

"Who found it?"

"Miss Frey, my secretary." He aimed a thumb at the attractive young woman. "Miss Judith Frey."

"When?"

"About ten minutes before I phoned you. Miss Wynn was here with me. We were discussing the contents of a letter I wrote her last week, and I sent for Miss Frey and asked her to bring the carbon. She brought the whole folder, because, she said, of something that was in it. The 'something' was that. She says it wasn't in the folder last Wednesday, five days ago, the last time she had occasion to go to it. I want to ask you something. Do you remember that this morning Mortimer Oshin said Miss Wynn was in the same position with Alice Porter as he was with Kenneth Rennert, and I said it wasn't the same because the story hadn't been produced, and he said, 'It will be'? Not 'It may be,' 'It will be.' Remember that?"

"Nuts." I moved a chair around and sat. "People say things. How much have you handled it?"

"Not much. I glanced through it. So did Miss Wynn."

"It probably doesn't matter. Whoever put it there has probably heard of fingerprints. Who has access to that room?"

"Everybody here."

"How many?"

"In this department, executive and editorial, thirty-two. Altogether, more than a hundred, but people in other departments never go to that room."

"But they could?"

"Yes."

"Is there always somebody in that room? Someone stationed there?"

"No one is stationed there, but people are always going and coming."

"Then an outsider could just walk in?"

"I suppose he could." Imhof leaned forward. "Look, Goodwin. I got you here immediately. This is hot. Nero Wolfe is supposed to be the best there is, or you and he together are. We want you to get this sonofabitch, and get him quick. Miss Wynn wants you to, and so do I."

"Him or her."

"Okay. But quick. By God!" He hit the desk with his fist. "Planting it here in this office! What are you going to do? What do you want me to do?"

I crossed my legs. "It's a little complicated. Mr. Wolfe already has a client, the Joint Committee on Plagiarism, of which you and Miss Wynn are members. There could be a conflict of interest. For instance, considering this case alone, independently, possibly the best course would be to forget that this thing was found. Burn it or let me stash it. But the committee wouldn't like that because it may be helpful in stopping this plagiarism racket for good, which is what they want. How many people know this thing has been found?"

"Three. Miss Wynn, Miss Frey, and I. And you. Four."

"How long has Miss Frey been with you?"

"About a year."

"Then you don't know her very well."

"I know her well enough. She was recommended by my former secretary when she left to get married."

I looked at Judith Frey and back at Imhof. "There are two obvious questions about her. One, did she put that thing in the folder herself? Two, granting that she didn't, could she be trusted to forget that she found it if you asked her to? If not, it would be very risky—"

"I didn't, Mr. Goodwin." Miss Frey had a clear, strong voice. "I can see why you ask that, but I didn't. And if my employer asked me to do anything I couldn't be trusted to do, I would quit."

"Good for you." I returned to Imhof. "But actually I'm just talking. Even if you decide you can trust Miss Frey to keep her mouth shut and burn that thing, what about me? I have seen it. I will of course report to Mr. Wolfe, and he will act in the interest of his client, the committee, and you may find—"

"We're not going to burn it," Amy Wynn blurted. Her nose was twitching. Her eyes were red. Her hands, in her lap, were fists. She went on, "I never saw that thing before, and nobody can prove I did! I hate this! I *hate* it!"

I moved to her. "Naturally you do, Miss Wynn. And after all, you're the one that will get soaked if Alice Porter gets away with it. Would you like to know what I would advise you to do?"

"I certainly would."

"This is just off the cuff. After I report to Mr. Wolfe he may change it. First, let me take that manuscript. I'll try it for fingerprints, but that's probably hopeless. Mr. Wolfe will compare it with the others. Second, say nothing about it to anyone. You have no lawyer?"

"No."

"Okay. Third, don't communicate with Alice Porter. If you get a letter from her, don't answer it. If she calls you on the phone, hang up. Fourth, let Mr. Wolfe handle this as a part of what he has already been hired for. He can't question everyone who works here himself, or anyhow he won't, but he has a couple of good men who will do it for him—provided Mr. Imhof will cooperate."

"Cooperate hell," Imhof said. "I'm in this as much as she is. Are you through?"

"No." I stayed with Amy Wynn. "Fifth and last, I think there's at least an even chance that Mortimer Oshin's idea will work. From the look on Simon Jacobs' face when I asked him if he would do an article on how it felt to have his story stolen, I think he's hating himself. I think he did it because he was hard up and had a family and had to have cash, and he wishes he hadn't and would be glad to get it off his chest, and if he can spit it out without fear of going to jail, and get paid besides, I think he will. That's only what I think, but I saw his face. If I'm right this whole thing will be cracked wide open. And the bait ought to be as juicy as possible, and twenty thousand is twice as juicy as ten. So fifth, I strongly advise you to tell me now that we can make it twenty."

Her nose twitched. "You mean I agree to pay ten thousand dollars."

"Right. Provided Richard Echols does his part."

She looked at Imhof. "Should I?"

Imhof spoke to me. "That's what we were discussing earlier. We hadn't decided. I was inclined to be against it. But now, by God, I'm for it. I'm for it so much that I'll commit Victory Press right now to pay half of it. Five thousand. And five thousand from you, Amy?"

"Yes," she said. "Thank you, Reuben."

"Don't thank me. Thank the bastard that planted that thing here in my office. Do you want it in writing?"

"No." I stood up. "I'll go and see if Mr. Wolfe approves the advice I gave you. You'll be hearing from him. I need some sheets of glossy paper and a stamp pad. For sets of prints of you three so I can eliminate them. And some large envelopes."

That took some time, getting three sets of legible prints with an ordinary stamp pad, and it was nearly five o'clock when I got away, with Imhof doing me the honor of escorting me to the elevator. I decided to walk it. It would take only a few minutes more than a creeping taxi, and my legs needed stretching. After mounting the stoop and letting myself in, I stepped to the end of the hall to stick my head in the kitchen and let Fritz know I was back, and then went to the office, put the envelopes on my desk, and got brushes and powder and other items from a drawer of a cabinet. I couldn't qualify as a fingerprint expert in a courtroom, but for private purposes I will do.

When Wolfe came down from the plant rooms at six o'clock he started for his desk, saw the clutter on mine, stopped, and demanded, "What have you got there?"

I swiveled. "Very interesting. I've done the first nine pages of this manuscript, 'Opportunity Knocks,' by Alice Porter, and there's no sign of a print, let alone an identifiable one, except Amy Wynn's and Miss Frey's and Imhof's. That justifies the assumption that it was either carefully wiped or was only handled with gloves on. In that case—"

"Where did you get it?" He was at my elbow, surveying the clutter.

I told him, including the dialogue. When I got to where Imhof had said there were thirty-two people in the executive and editorial departments of Victory Press, he went to his desk and sat. At the end I said, "If you want to make any changes in the advice I gave her, I have her home phone number. As I told her, it was off the cuff and subject to your approval."

He grunted. "Satisfactory. You realize, of course, that this may be merely an added complication, not an advance."

"Sure. Some person unknown somehow got a key to that office and sneaked in after hours and put it in Amy Wynn's folder. As before, possibly, in Ellen Sturdevant's bureau drawer and Marjorie Lippin's trunk. The only difference is that this is hot—as Imhof said."

"It's recent," he conceded. "Give me the nine pages you have finished with."

I took them to him and returned to my desk and started on page ten. Fritz, responding to a summons, brought beer, and Wolfe opened the bottle and poured. Page ten had nothing. Page eleven had only two useless smudges, one on the front and one on the back, near a corner. Page twelve had a fair right thumb and a poor right index finger of Reuben Imhof. I was on page thirteen when Wolfe's voice came. "Give me the rest of it."

"I've only done three more pages. I want—"

"I want all of it. I'll take care."

I took it to him, taking care, and then went to the kitchen to see how Fritz was getting on with the braised duckling stuffed with crabmeat, because I didn't want to sit and watch Wolfe smearing up the last fifteen pages. It isn't that he doesn't believe in fingerprints; it's just that they are only routine and therefore a genius can't be expected to bother about them. However, by going to the kitchen I merely transferred from one genius to another. When I offered to spread the paste on the cheesecloth which was to be wrapped around the ducklings, Fritz gave me exactly the kind of look Wolfe has given me on various and numerous occasions. I was perched on a stool, making pointed comments to Fritz about the superiority of teamwork, when there was a bellow from the office.

"Archie!"

I went. Wolfe was leaning back with his palms on the chair arms. "Yes, sir?"

"This *is* a complication. It was written by Alice Porter."

"Sure. It says so at the top."

"Don't be flippant. You fully expected, and so did I, to find that it had been written by the same person as the other three. It wasn't. Pfui!"

"Well, well, as Kenneth Rennert would say. Of course you're sure?"

"Certainly."

"And also sure that Alice Porter did write it?"

"Yes."

I went to my chair and sat. "Then she decided to do one on her own, that's all. Obviously. That doesn't help any, but it doesn't hinder either. Does it?"

"It may. It makes it extremely likely that the one we're after, the one we must find and expose, had no hand in this, and therefore we should waste no time or effort on it. Miss Wynn is not our client, and neither is Mr. Imhof. They are merely members of that committee. Of immediate concern is the fact that they were under a misapprehension when they agreed to contribute ten thousand dollars to the bait for Simon Jacobs. They assumed that this is another operation by the same person, and it isn't. We must tell them so, and when we do they will probably decline to make the contribution."

"Yeah." I scratched my nose. I scratched my cheek. "Yeah. So they will. You work too hard. You read too much. I don't suppose you could forget you read the damn thing? Just forget it for twenty-four hours, say?"

"No, and neither could you. You'll have to phone them at once. Is it out of the question to offer Simon Jacobs as little as ten thousand?"

I shook my head. "No, not out of the question. I'd start at ten anyhow, but I'd like it better if I knew I could boost it. He might even take five. I could start at five."

"Very well. Call Miss Wynn. I'll speak with her."

I swiveled, but as I reached for the phone it rang. It was Philip Harvey. He asked for Wolfe, and Wolfe took his receiver. I stayed on.

"Yes, Mr. Harvey? This is Nero Wolfe."

"I have good news, Mr. Wolfe. Thanks to Cora Ballard. She has it all fixed with Richard Echols. She saw Paul Norris, his agent, and she saw him, and I've just had a talk with Echols, and it's all set. Dexter's lawyer will draw the necessary papers in the morning, one for Echols to sign and one for Title House, and they'll be ready by noon. I've spoken with Mortimer Oshin, and he wants to know whether you want the ten thousand in cash or a certified check."

"Cash would be better, I think."

"All right, I'll tell him. What about Amy Wynn? Is she coming across?"

"It's uncertain. There has been a development. The manuscript of the story on which Alice Porter bases her claim was found this afternoon in a file in the office of the Victory Press."

"*No!* I'll be damned! In Imhof's office? Wonderful! Marvelous! Then of course she will. She'll have to."

"She may. There are complexities, now unresolved, which I'll report on later. In any case, it will probably be best to give Jacobs only half of the agreed amount now, and the other half later, contingent on his satisfactory cooperation. If Miss Wynn won't supply it, someone will. Your committee will see to that."

"I suppose so. I can't promise it."

"I don't ask you to. I will engage to put it up to Mr. Knapp, Mr. Dexter, and Mr. Imhof. They couldn't possibly wriggle out of it."

"Ha! You don't know how publishers can wriggle. They're experts. They're champions."

"That will make it all the more satisfying to pin them. Satisfying both to you and to me—if it proves to be necessary. Ten thousand may be enough. I will be responsible for any commitments I make."

Wolfe hung up and turned to me. "Get Miss Wynn."

8

At half past five the next day, Tuesday, I entered the vestibule of the tenement at 632 West 21st Street and pressed the button by Simon Jacobs' name. In my breast pocket were two documents, one signed by Richard Echols and the other signed by Thomas Dexter for Title House. Both were notarized. In my side pocket was a neat little package containing five thousand dollars in twenties, fifties, and Cs. Another five thousand was distributed among other pockets, not in packages.

I could have been there two hours earlier but for the fact that no hurricane had hit town. Nothing less than a hurricane would make Wolfe cancel his afternoon session in the plant rooms, from four to six, and it had been decided that instead of trying to hook Jacobs myself I was to bring him to 35th Street and watch Wolfe do it, chiefly because it would be desirable to have a witness. I was not to be visible; I would be stationed in the alcove at the end of the hall with my notebook, at the hole in the wall, concealed by a trick picture on the office side, through which I could both see and hear. I had the documents and money with me because it might take more than words to get Jacobs to come.

There had been no snags. Shortly after twelve Cora Ballard, the executive secretary of NAAD, had come in person with the documents. She had brought them instead of sending them because she wanted to brief us on Simon Jacobs, whom she had known for nearly thirty years, ever since he had joined NAAD in 1931. He had always been a little odd, but she had always regarded him as honest and honorable, so much so that when he had accused Richard Echols of plagiarism she had had a faint suspicion that there might be something to it, but had abandoned it when she tried to get in touch with him and he wouldn't talk. He was proud and touchy and he loved his wife and kids, and her advice was not to threaten him or try to get tough with him but just show him the money and the documents and put it on a basis of common sense. All of which might have been very helpful if it hadn't been for the fact that he had already been dead about fourteen hours.

No, no snags. It couldn't be called a snag that Amy Wynn and Reuben Imhof had withdrawn their offer to sweeten the pot, since that had been expected. While Wolfe and I were at lunch a messenger had arrived with the ten thousand dollars' worth of lettuce from Mortimer Oshin.

So at five-thirty I pressed the button in the vestibule, the click came, and I opened the door and entered. I was ready for the garlic and took a deep breath as I headed for the stairs. My opening line was on my tongue. Three flights up I turned to the front, and there, at the open door where Mrs. Jacobs and the boy had awaited me on my previous visit, I was again awaited, but not by them. In the dim light I took two steps before I recognized him, then stopped. We spoke simultaneously, and spoke the same words.

"Not *you,*" we said.

I knew. As Jane Ogilvy would have put it, a fact felt though not perceived. The presence there of Sergeant Purley Stebbins of Homicide West might have meant any one of a dozen things—one of the kids had been killed by a hit-and-run driver, or Jacobs had killed his wife, or one of them was merely being questioned about some other death by violence—but I knew. It had to be. That was why I said, "Not *you.*"

"I've been here five minutes," Purley said. "Just five minutes, and here *you* come. Jumping Jesus!"

"I've been here five seconds," I said, "and here *you* are. I came to see a man named Simon Jacobs on business. Please tell him I'm here."

"What kind of business?"

"A private kind."

His jaw worked. "Look, Goodwin." He has been known to call me Archie, but in different circumstances. "I come here on a job. If I'm somewhere on a job and someone asks me who is the last person on God's earth I would want to show up, I would name you. What I'd like, I'd like to tell you to go somewhere and scratch your ass with your elbow. A man's body is found. He was murdered. We get him identified. I go to where he lived to ask some questions, and I no sooner get started than the bell rings and I go to the door, and it's you, and you say you came to see him on business. When you come to see a corpse on business, I know what to expect. I'm asking you, what kind of business?"

"I told you. Private and personal."

"When did you learn Jacobs had been killed? And how? He was identified only an hour ago."

"Just now. From you." I had joined him at the door. "Let's take a short cut, Sergeant. The long way would be for you to bark at me a while, getting upset because I won't unload, and then you would take me to Homicide West, only a short walk, which you have no right to do, so *I* would get upset, and then Inspector Cramer would go to see Mr. Wolfe, and so on. The short way would be for me to phone Mr. Wolfe and get his permission to tell you why I came to see Jacobs, which he would probably give because there's no reason why he shouldn't and it may be connected with his death. You know damn well that without his permission I tell you nothing."

"You admit it's connected."

"Nuts. You're not the DA and we're not in court. Of course Mr. Wolfe will want some details—when and how he was killed, and by whom, if you know."

Purley opened his mouth and shut it again. When I have facts he needs, he would like to force them out by jumping up and down on my belly, but for that I would have to be lying on my back.

"With me listening," he said.

"Sure, why not?"

"Okay. The body was found at two o'clock this afternoon behind a bush in Van Cortlandt Park. It had been dragged across the grass from the edge of the road, so it was probably taken there in a car. There was one stab wound in the chest with a broad blade. No weapon found. The ME says between nine o'clock and midnight. Probably nothing taken. Eighteen dollars in his wallet. You can call Wolfe on the phone in here."

"Any leads?"

"No."

"When or where he went last night, or who with?"

"No. I was asking his wife when you came. She says she doesn't know. The phone's in his room, where he worked. Where he wrote. He wrote stories."

"I know he did. What time did he go out?"

"Around eight o'clock. If he had an appointment he made it on the phone and she didn't know anything about it. So she says. I just got started with her. I brought her here from the morgue after she identified the body. She says he told her he was going to see somebody and might be late, and that was all. If Wolfe wants to know what he had in his stomach he'll have to wait until—"

"Don't be flippant. Where's the phone?"

We went inside and he shut the door and led the way down the narrow hall to a door on the left. It was a small room with one window, a table with a typewriter, shelves with books and magazines, and a row of drawers. There were two chairs, and on one of them was Mrs. Jacobs. I said she wasn't a crone when I saw her five days before, but she was now. I wouldn't have known her. As we entered her eyes came to us. She focused on me, staring, and blurted, "It was you!"

"What?" Purley asked her. "Do you know this man?"

"I've seen him." She was on her feet. "He was here last week. His name's Goodwin. My husband saw him just for a minute, and after he left Simon told me if he ever came again to shut the door on him." She was trembling all over. "I knew from the way—"

"Take it easy, Mrs. Jacobs." Purley had her arm. "I know this Goodwin. I'll handle him, don't worry. You can tell me about it later." He was easing her out. "You go and lie down a while. Drink something. Drink some hot tea. . . ."

He got her to the hall. In a moment he returned, shut the door, and turned. "So you've been here before."

"Sure. With Mr. Wolfe's permission I'll confess everything."

"There's the phone."

I sat at the table and dialed, and after five rings had Fritz, who always answers when Wolfe is up with the orchids. I told him to buzz the plant rooms, and after a wait Wolfe's voice came. "Yes?"

"I have to report another complication. I'm in Simon Jacobs' apartment, the room he wrote stories in. Sergeant Stebbins is with me. He is investigating the murder of Simon Jacobs, whose body was found at two o'clock this afternoon behind a bush in Van Cortlandt Park. Stabbed. Between nine and twelve last night. Body taken there in a car. No leads. No anything."

"Confound it!"

"Yes, sir. Stebbins was here when I arrived, and naturally he is curious. Are there any details I should save?"

Silence. Ten seconds, then: "No. There's nothing worth saving."

"Right. Tell Fritz to save some of that shashlik for me. I'll be home when I get there." I hung up and told Purley, "He says there's nothing worth saving. Shall I just tell it or would you rather grill me?"

"Try telling it," he said, and got the chair the widow had vacated, sat, and got out his notebook.

9

Thomas Dexter of Title House squared his shoulders and set his long, bony jaw. "I don't care how you look at it, Mr. Harvey," he said, "I know how *I* look at it. I'm not condemning Mr. Wolfe or the members of this committee, or even myself, but I have a feeling of guilt. I regard myself as guilty of incitation to murder. Unwittingly, yes, but what are wits for? I should have considered the possible consequences of signing that agreement not to prosecute Simon Jacobs."

It was noon the next day, Wednesday. If you are fed up with committee meetings, so was Wolfe and so was I, but that's one disadvantage of having a committee for a client. And it was no longer merely a Joint Committee on Plagiarism. Within two hours after I had supplied the details to Stebbins they had all been visited by city employees. Knapp had been interrupted in the middle of a bridge game. Oshin had been found at dinner at Sardi's. Imhof and Amy Wynn had been called from a conference with three other executives of Victory Press. Dexter and Harvey and Cora Ballard had received the callers at home. Harvey had elicited these details from them so Wolfe would realize the gravity of the situation.

Having come at eleven o'clock, they had been at it for an hour, and there had been raised voices and heated words, with no unanimity or anything. Take the question, did they accept the assumption that Jacobs had been killed to keep him from squealing? Knapp and Harvey said no, he might have been killed from some quite different motive; it might have been merely coincidence. Dexter and Oshin said yes, that they couldn't get from under a responsibility by laying it to coincidence. Imhof and Amy Wynn and Cora Ballard were on the fence. Wolfe ended that argument by saying that it didn't matter whether they accepted the assumption or not; the police had made it, and so had he, as a working hypothesis.

Of course that led to a hotter question. If Jacobs had been killed to keep him from telling who had written "What's Mine Is Yours" and got him to make his claim on Richard Echols, the murderer must have known about the plan to pry Jacobs open. Who had told him? That was what the cops had been after when they called on the members of the committee, and that was what Wolfe wanted, but look what they got:

Amy Wynn had told two friends, a man and a woman, with whom she had dined Monday evening. Cora Ballard had told the president and vice-president of NAAD and two members of its council. Mortimer Oshin had told his lawyer, his agent, his producer, and his wife. Gerald Knapp had told his lawyer and two members of his firm. Reuben Imhof had told three of his associates at Victory Press. Philip Harvey had told no one, he said. Thomas Dexter had told his secretary, his lawyer, and six members of the board of directors of Title House. So, counting the committee members and Wolfe and me, thirty-three people had known about it. Supposing they had passed it on to others as an interesting inside item, averaging one apiece, which wasn't hard to suppose, that would make a total of sixty-six. And supposing . . . You do it.

Hopeless.

Another question: what was the committee going to do now? In Gerald Knapp's opinion, it should do nothing. It should await events. Since the police were assuming that the murderer had been motivated by the urgent necessity to silence Jacobs, they would concentrate on the effort to learn who had written the stories and instigated the claims, and, though that would have its disagreeable aspects, it meant that the purpose for which the committee was formed was now being served by the vast resources of the New York police, and in comparison the resources of the committee were nothing. Philip Harvey agreed, possibly because for the third time in nine days he had had to be up and out before noon and he wanted to catch up on his sleep. Amy Wynn supposed it wouldn't hurt to wait and see what the police did. Cora Ballard thought there should be a special meeting of the NAAD council to consider the matter, that the council had authorized the committee to deal with plagiarism claims, not with murder.

But Thomas Dexter and Mortimer Oshin couldn't see it, and neither could Reuben Imhof. They were all emphatic that Wolfe should be told to go ahead, though for different reasons. Imhof's point was that there was no telling how long it would take the police to find the plagiarist, if they ever did, and their messing around and the publicity would be bad for both publishers and authors. Oshin's point was more personal. He had put up ten thousend dollars in cash in the hope that it would help to stop Kenneth Rennert, and he wanted Wolfe to go ahead and use it for that purpose, with or without the concurrence of the committee. Thomas Dexter's point was even more personal, as you saw from the speech he made to Harvey. He regarded himself as guilty of incitation to murder. Apparently he had an old-fashioned conscience. He went on to say that he couldn't shift his responsibility to the police, he wanted Wolfe to go ahead and spare no pains or expense, and he would contribute any sum that might be required. He didn't even say "within reason."

He ended by making a motion, and the chairman asked for hands. Three went up at once—Dexter's, Imhof's, and Oshin's. Then Amy Wynn's, not with enthusiasm. Cora Ballard remarked that she wasn't a committee member and couldn't vote. Gerald Knapp asked her to record him as voting nay.

"Even if the chairman could vote," Harvey said, "it would be four to two." He turned to Wolfe. "So you go ahead. The last time you went ahead you got a man killed. What next?"

"That's pretty raw," Oshin said. "It was my idea, and the vote was unanimous."

Harvey ignored him. He repeated to Wolfe, "What next?"

Wolfe cleared his throat. "I am twice a jackass," he said.

They stared. He nodded. "First, I should never have accepted a committee as a client. That was egregious. Second, I should not have consented to act as a mere conveyor of bait. That was fatuous. It dulled my faculties. Having become a party to a procedure which made an obvious target of a man, which put a man in imminent danger, and aware that all of you knew of it and others soon would, I was an ass not to take precautions. I should have seen to it that he was not harmed. It was even quite possible that one of you was the wretch I had engaged to expose."

"Sure," Harvey said. "Now you're getting hot."

"It could be you, Mr. Harvey. With your most successful book only in its ninth thousand, you must have been open to temptation. So while I do not have Mr. Dexter's feeling of guilt, that I incited to murder, I do strongly feel that I failed to function properly. But for my default Mr. Jacobs would be alive, and probably we would have our man. It was understood that you may terminate your engagement with me at will. I invite you to do so now."

Three of them said no—Oshin, Imhof, and Dexter. The others said nothing. Wolfe asked the chairman, "Do you want a vote on it, Mr. Harvey?"

"No," Harvey said. "It would be four to one again."

"It would be unanimous," Gerald Knapp said. "I did not suggest that we should terminate the engagement."

Wolfe grunted. "Very well. I should tell you that if you do terminate it, I shall not withdraw. I have a score to settle—with myself. I have bruised my self-esteem and I intend to heal it. I am going to expose the murderer of Simon Jacobs, anticipating the police if possible, and presumably that will also solve your problem. I shall do that in any case, but if I act as your agent it must be with a free hand. I won't tell you what I intend to do. If one of you makes a suggestion other than privately, as Mr. Oshin did, I'll reject it without reference to its merits. Since I can't rely on your discretion, you will have to rely on mine."

"That's a lot to ask," Knapp said.

"No, sir. It is asking nothing; it is merely notifying you. If I told you I intended to do something and then did something else, I would still be your agent. You must trust my probity and my judgment in any case, or dismiss me."

"What the hell," Oshin said. "You've got my ten thousand, go ahead and use it." He looked at his watch and stood up. "I'm late for an appointment."

The meeting adjourned at 12:48 p.m. without a motion. Thomas Dexter stayed for a word with Wolfe, not to make a private suggestion but to repeat that he felt a personal responsibility and would personally contribute any necessary amount. This time, however, he added "within reason." It's fine to have a conscience, but you can't just let it run wild.

When Dexter had gone, Wolfe leaned back and closed his eyes. I put the extra chairs back in place, treated myself to a good stretch, went to the kitchen and drank a glass of water, and returned. I stood and looked down at him.

"I was wondering," I said. "Am I included in that?"

"In what?" he asked without opening his eyes.

"In the lockout. I won't be much help if you refuse to tell me what you intend to do."

"Pfui."

"I'm glad to hear it. I would like to say that I have a little self-esteem too, of course not in the same class as yours, and it needs attention. Yesterday Purley Stebbins asked me, and I quote, 'Why the hell did you set the guy up like that and then come here today and expect to find him whole?' That was the first time a Homicide man has ever asked me a question I couldn't answer. If I had told him because you were a jackass and so was I, he would have wanted to include it in my signed statement."

He grunted. He hadn't opened his eyes.

"So we're to go ahead," I said. "Lunch is about ready, and business is out at the table, and you like to rest your brain during digestion, so you might give me instructions now. Where do we start?"

"I have no idea."

"It might be a good plan to get one, since you intend to anticipate the police. I suppose I could call on the committee members separately and ask for suggestions—"

"Shut up."

So we were back to normal.

When Wolfe went up to the plant rooms at four o'clock I still had no instructions, but I wasn't biting nails. During the hour and a half since lunch he had picked up his current book four times, read a paragraph, and put it down again; he had turned on the television three times and turned it off; he had counted the bottle caps in his desk drawer twice; and he had got up and walked over to the big globe and spent ten minutes studying geography. So, since he was hard at work, there was no point in needling him.

I passed the time—an hour of it in comparing the typewriting of "Opportunity Knocks," by Alice Porter, with "There Is Only Love," also by Alice Porter, and "What's Mine Is Yours," by Simon Jacobs. No two on the same machine. I reread the carbon of the statment I had given Purley Stebbins, found nothing that needed correcting, and filed it. I reread the piece in the morning *Times* about the murder, and when the *Gazette* came, around five-thirty, I read that. The *Times* had no mention of plagiarism or the NAAD or the BPA. The *Gazette* had a paragraph about the plagiarism charge Jacobs had made against Richard Echols in 1956, but there was no hint that his death had any connection with it. I was wondering why Lon Cohen hadn't called when the phone rang and there he was. He stated his case: I had phoned him nine days ago to ask him about the NAAD and the BPA. Simon Jacobs, murdered Monday night, was a member of NAAD. Tuesday evening I had arrived at Homicide West on 20th Street with Sergeant Stebbins, who was working on the Jacobs case, and had stayed four hours. Would I therefore please tell him immediately why I had inquired about the NAAD, who was Wolfe's client, and who had killed Jacobs and why, with all relevant details which the public had a right to know. I told him I would call him back as soon as I had anything fit to print, probably in a couple of months, and said I would be glad to send him a glossy of a photograph I had just had taken, which the public had a right to see.

There was another phone call, from Cora Ballard, the executive secretary. She said she had been worrying about the decision of the committee to let Nero Wolfe go ahead with a free hand. She appreciated the fact that a private detective couldn't very well tell a group of people what he was doing and going to do, but the committee had no authority to hire a detective to investigate a murder, and naturally she was worried. It wouldn't be easy to get a large attendance of the NAAD council on short notice, but she could probably set one up for Monday or Tuesday of next week, and would I ask Mr. Wolfe to take no important steps until then? She was afraid that if he went ahead and did something drastic he would be acting without authority, and she thought he ought to know that. I told her I thought so too and I would certainly tell him. There's no point in being rude when you can end a conversation quicker by being polite.

I had the radio on for the six-o'clock news when Wolfe came down from the plant rooms. He had a cluster of Phalaenopsis Aphrodite in his hand, and he got a vase from the shelf, took it to the kitchen for water, brought it back, put the stem in, and placed it on his desk. That's the only hard work he ever does around the office. When the news stopped for a commerical I turned it off and told him, "Still nothing about plagiarism or our clients or you. If the cops have made any headway they're playing it close—"

The doorbell rang, and I stepped to the hall for a look through the one-way glass panel. A glance was enough. I turned to tell Wolfe, "Cramer."

He made a face. "Alone?"

"Yes."

He took a breath. "Let him in."

10

Inspector Cramer of Homicide West had sat in the red leather chair facing the end of Wolfe's desk oftener and longer than any other three people combined. He just about filled it. How he sat depended on circumstances. I have seen him leaning back with his legs crossed, comfortable and relaxed, with a glass of beer in his hand. I have also seen him with his broad rump just catching the edge, his jaw set and his lips tight, his big red face three shades redder, his gray eyes bulging.

That day he was in between, at least at the start. He declined Wolfe's offer of beer, but he made himself comfortable. He said he'd just stopped in on his way somewhere, which meant he wanted something he knew damn well a phone call wouldn't get. Wolfe said it was pleasant to see him, which meant "What do you want?" Cramer took a cigar from his pocket, which meant that he expected it to take more than a couple of minutes to get what he was after.

"This Jacobs thing is a hash if I ever saw one," Cramer said.

Wolfe nodded. "It is indeed."

"One thing about it, I've heard something I never heard before. I've heard Sergeant Stebbins pay you and Goodwin a compliment. He says as smart as you are, you couldn't possibly have arranged that scheme to buy Jacobs, with all that gang knowing about it, without having a pretty good idea of what might happen. He even says you expected it to happen, but of course that's stretching it. I can't see you conniving at murder."

"Give Mr. Stebbins my regards," Wolfe said, "and my thanks for the compliment."

"I will. Is that all you have to say?"

Wolfe slapped a palm on the desk. "What the devil do you expect me to say? Did you come here for the pleasure of screwing from me an admission that I bungled? I'll oblige you. I bungled. Anything else?"

"You're not a bungler." Cramer waved it away with the cigar. "Okay, we'll skip that; we might as well. What's bothering me is that the theory of the case the way we're going at it is based on something you know about and we don't. I've read Goodwin's statement three times. According to him, you decided that the three stories were all written by the same person, and it wasn't Alice Porter or Simon Jacobs or Jane Ogilvy. Is that correct?"

"It is."

"And you decided that by comparing them with books two of them had written and a transcript of Jane Ogilvy's testimony in court."

"Yes."

"Then we'd like to check it. I agree with Sergeant Stebbins that you're smart, I ought to know, but the whole approach depends on that, and naturally we want to check it. I understand that you have all that stuff here—the stories and the transcript and the books—and we want them. I'm no expert on writing myself, but we know a man who is. If this theory is right they'll probably be needed as evidence sooner or later. You have them?"

Wolfe nodded. "And I intend to keep them."

Cramer stuck the cigar between his lips and clamped his teeth on it. I had seen him light one only once, years ago. The cigar had a specific function, the idea being that with his teeth closed on it he couldn't speak the words that were on his tongue, and that gave him time to swallow them and substitute others. In five seconds he removed the cigar and said, "That's not reasonable."

"Mr. Cramer," Wolfe said. "Let's avoid a squabble if possible. The books are mine; you can get other copies elsewhere. The transcript and manuscripts belong to others and are in my care. I will surrender them only upon request from the owners. You can get them by court order only by establishing that they are material evidence, and I doubt if you can do that as things now stand. You can try."

"You goddam arrog—" Cramer stuck the cigar in his mouth and set his teeth on it. In four seconds he took it out. "Listen, Wolfe. Just answer a question. Would I be a sap if I worked a homicide case on a theory that rested entirely on something you and Goodwin said, not under oath?"

A corner of Wolfe's mouth twitched. That was his smile. "Yes," he said, "I must concede that. Perhaps we can resolve the difficulty. I offer a trade. In twenty-four hours you have doubtless gathered information that I would like to have. Give it to me. Then I will lend you what you came for, provided you sign an agreement to return it to me within twenty-four hours, intact."

"It would take all night to tell you all we've gathered."

"I don't want it all. Half an hour should do it, maybe less."

Cramer eyed him. "Forty-eight hours."

Wolfe's shoulders went up an eighth of an inch and down again. "I won't haggle. Very well, forty-eight. First and most important, have you discovered anything that contravenes the theory?"

"No."

"Have you discovered anything that suggests some other theory?"

"No."

"Have you discovered anything that supports the theory?"

"Only that the members of that committee verify Goodwin's statement. That doesn't prove you were right in the conclusion you made from reading that stuff, and that's why I want it. The widow knows nothing about it. She says. She also says that Jacobs had no enemies, that there couldn't have been anybody who had a reason to kill him except maybe one person, and that was a man named Goodwin who came to see him last Thursday. Because Jacobs told her to shut the door on him if he came again. We haven't asked Goodwin where he was Monday night from nine to eleven."

"I'm sure he appreciates your forbearance. Mr. Stebbins told Mr. Goodwin the period was nine to twelve."

"That was tentative. The stomach contents squeezed it a little. Nine to eleven."

"Good. Mr. Goodwin was here with me. Of course you have learned, or tried to, how many people knew of the plan to allure Jacobs. How many?"

"So far, forty-seven."

"They have all been spoken with?"

"All but two who are out of town."

"Do any of them merit attention?"

"They all do as long as we're on this theory. None of them especially. We haven't spotted anything that looks like a lead."

Wolfe grunted. "No wonder you want to confirm my conclusion. What about the routine? Is it still assumed that the body was taken there in a motor car?"

"Yes. Or a helicopter or a wheelbarrow."

Wolfe grunted again. "I am aware, Mr. Cramer, that you are too canny to jump to conclusions. I'll lump a hundred questions into one. Have you learned anything helpful from inspection of the scene, or examination of the body and clothing, or random inquiries?"

"Yes. That the blade of the knife was an inch wide and at least five inches long, that there was probably no struggle, and that he died between nine and eleven Monday night."

"Nothing else?"

"Nothing worth mentioning. Nothing to chew on."

"You have of course inquired about the payments made to Alice Porter, Simon Jacobs, and Jane Ogilvy, in settlement of the claims. If our theory is sound, substantial portions of those payments eventually found their way to another person."

"Certainly."

"Then who?"

"There is no record. In each case the check settling the claim was deposited and then a large amount was withdrawn in cash. We're still on that, but it looks hopeless."

"A moment ago, speaking of Mrs. Jacobs, you said, 'She says.' Do you question her candor?"

"No. I think she's straight."

"And she has no idea where her husband was going, or whom he was going to see, when he went out Monday evening?"

"No."

"Did he have anything with him that was not found on his body?"

"If he did she doesn't know it."

Wolfe shut his eyes. In a moment he opened them. "It is remarkable," he remarked, "how little a large group of competent trained investigators can gather in a night and a day. I intend no offense. You can't pick plums in a desert. Archie. Type this with two carbons: 'I acknowledge receipt of (list the items) from Nero Wolfe, as a personal loan to me. I guarantee to return all of the above-named items, intact, to Nero Wolfe not later than seven p.m. Friday, May 29th, 1959.' Make a package of the items."

"One thing," Cramer said. He put the cigar in the ashtray on the stand at his elbow. "You've got a client. That committee."

"Yes, sir."

"Okay, that's your business. My business is to investigate homicides as an officer of the law. I've answered your questions because you've got something I need and we made a deal, but that doesn't mean I'm sanctioning your horning in on *my* business. I've told you this before and I'm telling you again. Watch your step. Some day you're going to lose a leg, and don't expect me to give a damn."

"I won't." Wolfe eyed him. "I promise you, Mr. Cramer, that I will never plead your sanction to justify my conduct. My engagement with my client is to catch a swindler. Apparently he is also a murderer, and if so your claim will be superior. If and when I get him I'll bear that in mind. I don't suppose you challenge my right to expose a swindler?"

The rest of it was rather personal. I was busy typing the receipt and guarantee and then collecting the items and making the package, so I missed some of it. When I was tying the string it occurred to Cramer that he wanted to check the items against the list in the receipt, so I had to unwrap it, and then it occurred to him to ask about fingerprints on the manuscripts. You mustn't judge his abilities as a police inspector by that performance; Wolfe always has that effect on him. He gets behind.

When I returned to the office after letting him out it was only half an hour till dinnertime, and Wolfe had opened a book, not by a member of the committee, and was scowling at it, so I went for a walk. His brain works better when he is sitting down and mine when I am on my feet. Not that I would dream of comparing mine with his, though I do believe that in one or two respects– Oh, well.

Back in the office after dinner, and after coffee, I said politely that if I wasn't needed I would go and do a couple of personal errands. He asked if they were urgent, and I said no but I might as well get them done if we had nothing on hand.

"That's uncalled for," he growled. "Have you a suggestion?"

"No. None that I like."

"Neither have I. We have never been in a comparable situation. We can't explore motives; we know the motive. We can't set a trap; where would we put it? We can't ask questions of people; whom would we ask, and what? The forty-seven that Mr. Cramer's men have already seen and will see again? Pfui. Five hours for each would take ten hours a day for three weeks and more. We're almost as badly off as on Monday, when I told that confounded committee that it was no longer my kind of job and then idiotically consented to proceed with the plan proposed by Mr. Oshin. I admit it might have worked if we had taken proper precautions. Now Simon Jacobs is dead. I invite suggestions."

"Yeah. When I went for a walk you knew I wanted to think. I did. When I got back you knew from the expression on my face that I was empty, and I knew you were. The best I can do is remind you that thinking is your department. I haven't pestered you, have I? I know darned well it's a beaut."

"Then *I* have a suggestion. I don't like it, but we must either act or capitulate. You told Mr. Oshin on Monday that Jane Ogilvy might grab at the bait or she might spurn it. We have his ten thousand dollars and Mr. Dexter's offer to make any necessary contribution. It may be worth trying."

"It may," I conceded. "Wait till you see her."

"I'm not going to see her. That's for you. You are adept at dealing with personable young women, and I am not. Of course you will be severely handicapped. For Simon Jacobs you were provided with agreements by Richard Echols and Title House not to prosecute or demand reimbursement. You can't offer that inducement to Jane Ogilvy. She won her case in court, and even if we could get a similar agreement from Marjorie Lippin's heirs and from Nahm and Son, her publishers, which is doubtful, again our plan would be known to a number of people."

"Then it's a hell of a suggestion."

He nodded. "But it leads to another. From Jane Ogilvy's testimony at the trial, and from your report of your encounter with her, I gather that she is daft, and therefore unpredictable. Another approach might get her. Appeal to her sensibilities. Disclose the situation to her, all of it. Explain why we know that her claim against Marjorie Lippin was instigated by some person unknown to us, X. That X, threatened by imminent exposure, killed Simon Jacobs. Describe the grief and the plight of the widow and children; you might take her to see them and talk with them. Can you get a photograph of the corpse?"

"Probably, from Lon Cohen."

"Show it to her. Get one that shows the face, if possible; the face of a dead man before it has been rearranged is much more affecting than a mere heap of clothing. If you can't stir her sympathy perhaps you can arouse her fear. She is herself in peril; X may decide that she too must be removed. It would probably be a mistake to try to get her to supply evidence and details of her association with X, of the swindling of Marjorie Lippin; that would scare her off; all you really need is his name. Once we know him he is doomed. I want your opinion."

I glanced at the clock: ten minutes past nine. "It may take a while to find Lon. After seven o'clock there's no telling where he is. And the photograph would help."

"You think it's worth trying?"

"Sure. It may work. We've got to try something."

"We have indeed. Then as early in the morning as may be."

I turned to the phone and started after Lon Cohen.

11

At a quarter to ten Thursday morning I braked the Heron sedan to a stop in front of 78 Haddon Place, Riverdale. Perhaps that wasn't "as early as may be," but I didn't want to tackle her before she had had breakfast, and besides, I hadn't been able to get the photograph until Lon got to the *Gazette* office at nine o'clock. As I was soon to learn, it didn't matter anyway, since she had already been dead about twelve hours.

If it had been a nice sunny morning I might have gone around to the side for a look at the terrace where I had found her before, but it was cloudy and cool, so I went up the walk to the entrance and pushed the button. The door was opened by a DAR type, a tall, upright female with a strong chin, in a gray dress with black buttons. Unquestionably the mother under whose devotion Jane had once been suffocating and probably still was.

"Good morning," she said.

"Good morning," I said. "My name is Archie Goodwin. Are you Mrs. Ogilvy?"

"I am."

"I would like to see your daughter, Miss Jane Ogilvy."

"Does she know you?"

"We have met. She may not recognize the name."

"She is in the cloister."

Good Lord, I thought, she has taken the veil. "Cloister?" I said.

"Yes. She may not be up yet. Go around the house to the left and from the terrace take the path through the shrubbery." She backstepped and was closing the door.

I followed directions. I had a feeling that I might have known she had a cloister—a cloister felt though not perceived. Rounding the house to the terrace, which was deserted, I took a graveled path which disappeared into bushes that gave it a roof. After winding among the bushes for some distance it left them and straightened out to pass between two big maples to the door of a small building—one story, gray stone, sloping roof, a curtained window on each side of the door. I proceeded and used the knocker, a big bronze flower with a red agate in the center. When nothing happened I knocked again, waited twenty seconds, turned the knob, found the door wasn't locked, opened it a couple of inches, and called through the crack, "Miss Ogilvy!" No response. I swung the door open and stepped in.

It was a fine well-furnished cloister and probably contained many objects that were worth a look, but my attention centered immediately on its tenant. She was on her back on the floor in front of an oversized couch, dressed in a blue garment that I would call a smock but she probably had called something else. One of her legs was bent a little, but the other one was out straight. Crossing to her, I stooped to get her hand and found that the arm was completely stiff. I got a foot, which was covered by a sock but no shoe; the leg was stiff too. She had been dead a minimum of six hours, and almost certainly more.

There was a dark red stain at heart level around a slit in the smock, not a big one. My hand started to open the zipper for a look underneath, but I drew it back. Let the medical examiner do it. I straightened up and looked around. There was no sign of a struggle or of any disturbance—no drawers open or anything scattered around. Everything was as it should be except that she was dead.

I said aloud, with feeling, "The sonofabitch."

There was a phone on a table against a wall, and I went and lifted the receiver, using my handkerchief, and put it to my ear. The dial tone came. There was a chance that it was an extension, but probably not; the number on the disk was not the same as the one listed for Ogilvy in the phone book. I dialed, and got Fritz, and asked him to buzz the plant rooms.

Wolfe's voice: "Yes?"

I apologized. "I'm sorry to disturb you so often when you're up with the orchids, but I've hit another snag. I'm in a building in the rear of the Ogilvy grounds which Jane called the cloister. Her corpse is here on the floor. Stabbed in the chest. She died at least six hours ago, probably more. At the house her mother told me she was here and might not be up yet, and I came here alone. I have touched nothing but the knocker and the doorknob. If you want me to hurry home for new instructions, okay, I knocked a few times and got no response, and left. I can stop at the house and tell Mrs. Ogilvy that."

He growled, "If you had gone last night."

"Yeah. Maybe. She was probably killed about the time I started trying to find Lon Cohen. If I leave I should leave quick."

"Why leave? How in the name of heaven could I have new instructions?"

"I thought you might want to discuss the situation."

"Pfui. Discussion wouldn't help it any."

"Then I stick."

"Yes."

He hung up. I cradled the phone, considered for half a minute, stepped to the door and on out, shut the door, wiped the knob with my handkerchief, followed the path back to the house and around to the front entrance, and pushed the button. Again the door was opened by the devoted mother.

"I'm sorry to bother you again," I said, "but I thought I ought to tell you. Miss Ogilvy doesn't seem to be there. I knocked several times, and knocked loud, and got no response."

She wasn't alarmed. "She must be there. She hasn't been in for breakfast."

"I knocked hard."

"Then she's gone somewhere. There's a lane in back of the cloister, and she keeps her car there."

"Gone without breakfast?"

"She might. She never has, but she might."

I took a chance. It was highly unlikely that X had gone off with her car. "What make is her car?"

"Jaguar."

"It's there. I looked around a little and saw it. I think you ought to come and see, Mrs. Ogilvy. She might have had a stroke or something."

"She doesn't have strokes. I never go to the cloister." She tightened her lips. "But perhaps I should– All right. You come along."

She crossed the sill and shut the door, and I moved aside to let her by. She strode like a female sergeant, around to the terrace and across it, and along the path. When she reached the door of the cloister she started her hand for the knob, but changed her mind and raised it to the knocker. She knocked three times, at intervals, turned her head to look at me, grabbed the knob and opened the door, and entered. I followed. In three steps she saw it and stopped. I said something, went on by, on to it, squatted, and touched an arm. I unzipped the smock, spread it open, and took a look.

I stood up. Mother hadn't moved, except that her mouth was working. "She's dead," I said. "Stabbed in the chest. She has been dead quite a while."

"So she did it," Mrs. Ogilvy said.

"No. Someone else did it. There's no weapon."

"It's under her. It's somewhere."

"No. If she did it and pulled the weapon out, still alive, there would be a lot of blood, and there is almost none. It was pulled out after her heart stopped."

"You know a lot about it."

"I know that much. Will you call the police or shall I?"

"She did it."

"No. She did not."

"Who are you?"

"My name is Archie Goodwin. I'm a private detective. I've had some experience with death by violence."

"Do you mean she was murdered?"

"Yes."

"Are you sure?"

"Yes."

"Thank God." She turned her head, saw a chair, went to it, and sat. She started to slump, then jerked her shoulders back. "Then you must call the police?"

"Certainly." I had moved to face her. "It might help if I could give them some information on the phone. Could you answer a few questions?"

"If I choose to."

"When did you last see your daughter?"

"When she left the house last evening to come here."

"What time was that?"

"Right after dinner. Half past eight—a little later."

"Was anyone with her?"

"No."

"Did she always sleep here?"

"Not always. Frequently. She has her room in the house."

"Were there guests at dinner?"

"No. Just my husband and I, and her."

"Was she expecting someone to call?"

"Not that I knew of, but I wouldn't. I seldom did."

"You know nothing of any letter or phone call she got yesterday?"

"No. I wouldn't."

"Did anyone come to see her after she left the house last evening, or call her on the phone?"

"No. Not at the house. Someone might have come here."

"Someone did. How? By the lane in back?"

"Yes. It's a public road. Dipper Lane. I've forgotten your name. What is it?"

"Goodwin. Archie Goodwin. Did you hear a car on the lane last evening, stopping here or starting here?"

"No." Abruptly she left the chair. "I'm going to phone my husband. He should be here when the police come. How soon will they come?"

"Ten minutes, maybe less. Have you any idea who killed your daughter? Any idea at all?"

"No." She turned and marched out, still a sergeant.

I went to the phone, used my handkerchief to lift the receiver, and dialed.

12

I ate lunch that day, two hamburgers and a glass of milk, at the office of the Bronx District Attorney, in the room of an assistant DA named Halloran whom I had never seen before. I ate dinner, if two corned-beef sandwiches and lukewarm coffee in a paper cup can be called dinner, in the office of the District Attorney of the County of New York, in the room of an assistant DA named Mandelbaum whom I knew quite well from various contacts on other occasions. When I finally got back to the old brownstone on West 35th Street it was going on ten o'clock. Fritz offered to warm up the lamb loaf and said it would be edible, but I told him I was too tired to eat and might nibble a snack later.

It was nearly eleven when I finished reporting to Wolfe. Actually I knew very little more than I had when Mrs. Ogilvy had left the cloister and I had dialed SP 7-3100, but Wolfe was now trying to find a straw to grab at. He wanted everything I had, every sight and sound of my twelve-hour day, even including the session at the Bronx DA's office, though Halloran had known nothing of the background. He had me repeat my conversation with Mrs. Ogilvy three times. He almost never asks me to repeat anything even once, but of course he was desperate. When there was nothing left to ask me he still had a question; he wanted to know what conclusions I had drawn.

I shook my head. "You draw the conclusions. I only make guesses. I guess we might as well quit. I guess this bird is too fast and too slick. I guess he hasn't left one little crumb for the cops, either with Simon Jacobs or Jane Ogilvy, and as for us, I guess he's a step ahead and intends to stay ahead. I guess we had better consider how to approach Alice Porter so we can get her a little sooner than we have the others—say when she's been dead only an hour or two."

Wolfe grunted. "I have already considered her."

"Good. Then she may still be warm."

"I have also acted. Saul and Fred and Orrie have her under surveillance. Also Miss Bonner and that operative in Miss Bonner's employ. Miss Corbett."

My brows went up. "You don't say. Since when?"

"Shortly after you called this morning. Orrie is there now. Since four o'clock he has been there in concealment with the house in view. His car is nearby, also in concealment. Miss Corbett, with a rented car, is posted near the junction of the dirt road and the surfaced road. Saul will relieve Orrie at midnight, and Miss Corbett will leave. Fred and Miss Bonner will take over at eight in the morning. Miss Corbett phoned at seven-thirty that Alice Porter was at home and had had no visitors."

My brows were still up. "I must say that when you consider, you consider. At that rate Oshin's ten grand won't last long. I don't say it's being wasted, but you may remember that when he asked me which one of the four we should go for I said that Alice Porter has just made her claim on Amy Wynn and is expecting to collect, so she probably wouldn't be open for a deal. Also you know how she reacted to my approach."

Wolfe nodded. "But that was before her manuscript had been found and we learned that it had been written by her, not by the person who wrote the others. He may or may not know about that; probably he does. In any case, even if it is likely that she would scorn any inducement we can offer her, he may not think so. He is bold and ruthless, and he is now close to panic. If he thinks her as great a menace as Jane Ogilvy he won't hesitate. Saul and Fred and Orrie, and Miss Bonner and Miss Corbett, have full instructions. Anyone who approaches Alice Porter is to be suspected. If possible he is to be stopped before he strikes, but of course he can't be challenged until it is apparent that he intends to strike."

"Yeah." I was looking at it. "It's a problem. Fred or Orrie is there, in broad daylight, and someone drives up to the house and goes in. There's no decent cover within a hundred yards of the house. He can't possibly get close enough to see if it's just a lightning-rod salesman or a friend, without being seen. All he can do is wait until the company goes and then wait for Alice Porter to show, or go to a phone and dial her number and see if she answers. If it's X, she's a goner. I admit we'll have him."

He grunted. "Can you do better?"

"No, sir. I'm not complaining. What about Kenneth Rennert? If X is in a panic he might do him next."

"That's possible, but I doubt it. Rennert may not even know who X is;

he may merely have imitated him. He wrote not a story but a play outline, and we haven't seen it."

"Okay." I glanced at the clock: 11:23. "I suppose Saul will call when he goes on at midnight, and Orrie will call after he is relieved?"

"Yes."

"I'll expect them. What else for me? Have I a program?"

"No."

"Then I have a suggestion. I don't like it, but I have it. Across the street from Rennert's address is a tailor shop with a nice clean window. For five bucks a day the owner would let me use it to look through, with a chair to sit on. After dark I could move across the street, to be closer. I am almost as good as Saul Panzer at remembering faces. When Rennert's body is discovered and they decide when he was killed, I would know who had been there. If it was someone I recognized, for instance a member of the Joint Committee on Plagiarism, I could even name him. I can start right now. I hate that kind of a job, who doesn't, but I've been sent twice now to see people who were already dead, and that's enough."

He shook his head. "Two objections. One, you need sleep. Two, Mr. Rennert is not at home. As I said, his operation may have been solely on his own and he may have had no connection with X, but I haven't ignored him. I rang his number twice this morning and twice this afternoon, and got no answer. At three o'clock Saul went there, and, getting no response to his ring, saw the building superintendent and asked when he had last seen Mr. Rennert. Early last evening Mr. Rennert told the building superintendent that he would leave today to spend the Memorial Day weekend in the country and would return on Monday. He didn't say where in the country."

"If we knew where we could ring him and warn him to keep away from poison ivy. It would be nice to hear his voice."

"I agree. But we don't."

"I could scout around in the morning and probably find out. We have a lot of names of people he has borrowed money from."

He vetoed it. He said he wanted me at hand, and a call might come at any time of the day or night from Saul Panzer or Fred Durkin or Orrie Cather or Dol Bonner or Sally Corbett that would require immediate action. Also Philip Harvey had phoned twice, and Cora Ballard once, to ask if he could be present at a meeting of the NAAD council on Monday, and they would probably phone again tomorrow, and he didn't want to listen to them. That settled, he went up to bed. At 11:42 Saul Panzer called, from a booth in Carmel, to say that he was on his way to relieve Orrie Cather. At 12:18 Orrie called, also from

Carmel, to report that the light had gone out a little before eleven in Alice Porter's house, and presumably she was safe in bed. I mounted two flights to mine.

Friday morning I was pulling my pants on when Fred Durkin phoned that he was on his way to relieve Saul, and Dol Bonner was with him, to go on post near the junction of the blacktop and the dirt road. I was in the kitchen, pouring hot maple syrup on a waffle, with the *Times* propped on the rack, when Saul phoned to say that when he left at eight o'clock Alice Porter had been hoeing in the vegetable garden. I was in the office, rereading copies of the statements I had given the two assistant DAs, when Cora Ballard phoned to ask if Wolfe would come to the NAAD council meeting, which would be held at the Clover Club on Monday at twelve-thirty. If Wolfe preferred to join them after lunch two o'clock would do, or even two-thirty. When I reminded her that he never left the house on business she said she knew that, but this was an emergency. I said it wasn't much of an emergency that set a meeting three days off, and she said that with authors and dramatists two or three weeks was the best she could usually do, and anyway it was the Memorial Day weekend, and could she speak with Mr. Wolfe. I told her he wasn't available and it wouldn't do any good even if he was, and what he would certainly say was that he would send me. If they wanted me, let me know.

I was filing the copies of the statements in the folder marked PLAGIARISM, JOINT COMMITTEE ON when Inspector Cramer phoned to say that he would drop in for a few minutes about a quarter past eleven. I told him he would probably be admitted. I was listening to the ten-o'clock news broadcast when Lon Cohen phoned to say it was high time I loosened up. They had five different pictures of me in the morgue, and they would run the best one, the one that made me look almost human, as the discoverer of Jane Ogilvy's body, if I would supply some interesting detail like why had two people who had collected damages on plagiarism charges been croaked within forty-eight hours. Any fool knew damn well it wasn't coincidence, so what was it? I told him I would ask the DA and call him back.

I was tearing yesterday's page from Wolfe's desk calendar when the president of the National Association of Authors and Dramatists phoned. His name was Jerome Tabb. I had read one of his books. Wolfe had read four of them, and all four were still on the shelves, none of them dog-eared. They had all been A's. He was a VIP even by Wolfe's standards, and Wolfe would undoubtedly have liked to speak with him, but the rule was never buzz the plant rooms for a phone call except in extreme emergency. Tabb had just had a call from Cora

Ballard, and he wanted to tell Wolfe how important it was for him to be present at the council meeting on Monday. He was leaving town for the weekend, and he would like me to give Wolfe this message, that the officers and council of the NAAD would deeply appreciate it if he would arrange to meet with them.

When Wolfe came down at eleven I reported the phone calls in chronological order, which put Tabb last. When I finished he sat and glared at me but said nothing. He was stuck. He knew that I knew he would like to speak with Jerome Tabb, but he couldn't very well jump me for obeying the rules. So he took another tack. Glaring at me, he said, "You were too emphatic with Miss Ballard and Mr. Tabb. I may decide to go to that meeting." Absolutely childish. It called for a cutting reply, and one was on its way to my tongue when the doorbell rang and I had to skip it.

It was Cramer. When I opened the door he marched by me with no greeting but an excuse for a nod, and on to the office. I followed. Wolfe told him good morning and invited him to sit, but he stood.

"I've only got a minute," he said. "So your theory was right."

Wolfe grunted. "My theory and yours."

"Yeah. It's too bad that Ogilvy girl had to die to prove it."

He stopped. Wolfe asked, "Will you sit? As you know, I like eyes at a level."

"I can't stay. The Ogilvy homicide was in the Bronx, but obviously it's tied in with Jacobs', so it's mine. You can save me a lot ot time and trouble. If we have to we can find out from about fifty people how many of them you told that you were going to put the squeeze on Jane Ogilvy, and which ones, but it's simpler to ask you. So I'm asking."

"Mr. Goodwin has already answered that question several times. To the District Attorney."

"I know he has, and I don't believe him. I think you bungled again. I think you picked certain people out of the bunch that had known you were going after Jacobs—I don't know how you picked them, but you do—you picked certain ones and let them know you were going after Jane Ogilvy. Then you sent a man or men, probably Panzer and Durkin, to cover her, and they slipped up. Maybe they didn't know about that lane in back. Maybe they didn't even know about that building she called the cloister. Cloister my ass. I want to know who you told and why. If you won't tell me I'll find out the hard way, and when we get this cleared up and we know which one killed her, and we know he killed her because he knew you were going after her, and he knew because you or Goodwin had told him, this will be the time you lose a leg. I've got just one question: are you going to tell me?"

"I'll answer it in a moment." Wolfe wiggled a finger at him. "First I remind you that you are to return that stuff to me by seven o'clock this evening—less than eight hours from now. You haven't forgotten that?"

"No. You'll have it."

"Good. As for your question, I don't resent it. I blundered so lamentably with Simon Jacobs that it's no wonder you suspect me of an even bigger blunder with Jane Ogilvy. If I had I would confess it, abandon the case, and close my office permanently. I didn't. No one knew of our intention to tackle Jane Ogilvy but Mr. Goodwin and me."

"So you're not telling."

"There's nothing to tell. Mr. Goodwin has—"

"Go to hell." He turned and marched out. I went to the hall to see that when the door banged he was outside. As I stepped back in the phone rang. It was Mortimer Oshin, wanting to know if Philip Harvey had notified Wolfe that his arrangement with the committee was terminated. I said no, apparently that was to be discussed by the NAAD council on Monday. He said that if and when it was terminated he wanted to engage Wolfe personally, and I said it was nice to know that.

Wolfe, not bothering to comment on Cramer, told me to take my notebook and dictated a letter to a guy in Chicago, declining a request to come and give a talk at the annual banquet of the Midwest Association of Private Inquiry Agents. Then one, a long one, to a woman in Nebraska who had written to ask if it was possible to fatten a capon so that its liver would make as good a pâté as that of a fattened goose. Then others. I agree in principle with his notion that no letter should go unanswered, but of course he can always hand one to me and say, "Answer that," and often does. We were on one to a man in Atlanta, saying that he couldn't undertake to find a daughter who had left for New York a month ago and had never written, when Fritz announced lunch. As we were crossing the hall the phone rang, and I went back to get it. It was Fred Durkin.

"I'm in Carmel." He had his mouth too close to the transmitter, as usual. He's a good operative, but he has his faults. "The subject left the house at twelve forty-two and got in her car and drove off. She had been wearing slacks, but she had changed to a dress. I had to wait till she was out of sight to leave cover, then I went to my car and followed, but of course she was gone. Dol Bonner's car wasn't at her post, so she picked her up. Neither of their cars is parked here in the center of town. Shall I ask around to find out which way they went?"

"No. Go back and hide your car again and take cover. Somebody might come and wait there for her."

"It's a hell of a long wait."

"Yeah, I know. The first two weeks are the hardest. Study nature. There's plenty of it around there."

I joined Wolfe in the dining room, took my seat, and relayed the news. He grunted and picked up his napkin.

An hour and ten minutes later we were back in the office, finishing with the mail, when the phone interrupted; and when a soft but businesslike voice said, "This is Dol Bonner," I motioned to Wolfe to get on.

"Yes, Miss Bonner," I said. "Where are you?"

"In a phone booth in a drugstore. At twelve forty-nine the subject's car came out of the dirt road and turned left on the blacktop. I followed. She went to the Taconic State Parkway, no stops, and headed south. At Hawthorne Circle she took the Saw Mill River. I nearly lost her twice but got her again. She left the West Side Highway at Nineteenth Street. She put her car in a parking lot on Christopher Street and walked here, five blocks. I found a space at the curb."

"Where is here?"

"This drugstore is at the corner of Arbor Street and Bailey Street. She went in the vestibule at Forty-two Arbor Street and pushed a button, and waited half a minute, and opened the door and entered. That was eight minutes ago. I can't see the entrance from the booth, so if you want—"

"Did you say Forty-two?"

"Yes."

"Hold it." I turned to Wolfe. "Amy Wynn lives at Forty-two Arbor Street."

"Indeed. This is Nero Wolfe, Miss Bonner. Can you see the entrance from where your car is parked?"

"Yes."

"Then go to your car. If she comes out, follow her. Mr. Goodwin will join you if you're still there when he arrives. Satisfactory?"

We hung up. We looked at each other. "Nonsense," Wolfe growled.

"Close to it," I agreed. "But it's possible. You told them Wednesday that it could be that one of them was it. If I had voted, Amy Wynn wouldn't have been my choice, but it's possible. Simon Jacobs was no athlete. If she had him in a car she could have sunk a knife in him. Certainly Jane Ogilvy would have been no problem. And for Alice Porter she has a double motive—not only to keep her from blabbing the Ellen Sturdevant operation but also to settle the claim Alice Porter has made against *her*. That's one way to settle a claim out of court. I wouldn't think she would pick her own apartment as the best place for it, but you said she was close to panic—only you said 'he.' Also she might have some original and nifty plan for getting rid of a body. She or he is quite a planner, you can't deny that. I could go and drop in on her and say I'm making the rounds of the committee members, to ask them not to fire you. If I was too late to save Alice Porter's life I would at least be in time to interfere with her body-disposal plan."

"Pfui."

"Cramer won't think it's phooey if Alice Porter is number three, another homicide in his jurisdiction, and he learns that you had Dol Bonner there in a car with her eye on the door. Your crack about closing your office permanently may turn out—"

The phone rang, and I got it. It was Reuben Imhof. He asked for Wolfe, and Wolfe got on.

"Something interesting," Imhof said. "I just had a phone call from Amy Wynn. Alice Porter rang her this morning and said she wanted to come and see her. If Miss Wynn had told me about it, I would probably have advised her not to see her, but she didn't. Anyway, Alice Porter is there with her now, in her apartment. She offers to settle her claim for twenty thousand dollars cash. Miss Wynn wants to know if I think she should accept the offer. I told her no. It looks to me as if the two murders have got Alice Porter scared. She suspects they were committed by the man who got her to make the claim on Ellen Sturdevant, and if he's caught he may talk, and she'll be sunk, and she wants to get what she can quick and clear out. What do you think?"

"You are probably correct. My offhand opinion."

"Yes. That's the way it looks. But after I hung up I wasn't so sure I had given Miss Wynn good advice. Alice Porter would probably take half the amount she named, even less. If Miss Wynn can get a general release for, say, five thousand dollars perhaps that's what she ought to do. If she doesn't she may eventually have to pay ten times that, or more. On the other hand, if you or the police get the man you're after and rip it open, she won't have to pay anything. So I'm asking you. Shall I call Miss Wynn and advise her to make a deal if she can get one for ten thousand or less, or not?"

Wolfe grunted. "You can't expect me to answer that. Miss Wynn is not my client, and neither are you. As a member of the committee you may ask me if I expect to expose that swindler and murderer."

"All right, I do."

"The answer is yes. Soon or late, he is doomed."

"That suits me. Then I won't call her."

Wolfe cradled the phone and gave me a look, with a corner of his mouth slanting up.

"Okay." I left my chair. "I only said it was possible. Would it be a good idea for me to help Dol Bonner tail her back to Carmel?"

"No."

"Any special instructions for Miss Bonner?"

"No. Presumably she will find Miss Corbett at her post."

I beat it.

13

Forty-two hours later, at nine o'clock Sunday morning, as I put down my empty coffee cup, thanked Fritz for the meal, and headed for the office, I told myself aloud, "What a hell of a way to spend a Memorial Day weekend." I had been invited to the country. I had been invited to a boat in the Sound. I had been invited to accompany a friend to Yankee Stadium that afternoon. And here I was. The only reason I was up and dressed was that the phone had roused me at twenty to eight, Fred calling to say that he was on his way to relieve Saul; and half an hour later Saul had reported that Alice Porter slept late on Sunday, which was the most exciting piece of news I had heard for quite a while. On Friday, tailed by Dol Bonner, she had driven from Arbor Street straight back to Carmel, done some shopping at a supermarket and a drugstore, and then home.

Entering the office, I went to my desk and started to plow through the mountain of the Sunday *Times*—my copy; Wolfe's was up in his room—for the section I looked at first. I yanked it out, scowled at it, said aloud, "Oh nuts," and tossed it on the floor. Either I had meant it when I thought to myself last night, as I sat watching a cowboy take off his boots and wiggle his toes on TV, that it would be more interesting to be in jail, or I hadn't. If I had it was up to me. I would be losing nothing if I got nabbed for a misdemeanor or even a minor felony. I went to the phone, dialed the number of Kenneth Rennert's apartment, got no answer after thirteen rings, and hung up. I went to a cabinet and unlocked a drawer, took out six boxes of assorted keys, and spent twenty minutes making selections. From another drawer I got a pair of rubber gloves. I went to the kitchen and told Fritz I was going for a walk and would be back in an hour or so, and left the house. It was only a twenty-minute stroll.

I was not actually determined to get tossed in the coop. I thought I might find something helpful in Rennert's nice big room. I knew from past experience that Wolfe would have approved, but if I had told him in advance he would have been responsible, me being his agent, and it was fair for him to share the risk of my law-breaking when it was his idea, but not when it was mine. I wasn't hoping to find evidence that Rennert was X, but there was a chance of digging up something to indicate that X had instigated his claim against Mortimer Oshin, or that he hadn't. Either one would help a little, and I might get more.

After pushing the Rennert button in the vestibule three times, with waits between, and getting no reaction, I started to work on the door. My position on locks is about the same as on fingerprints—I couldn't qualify as an expert witness, but I have picked up a lot of pointers. Of course I had noticed on my previous visit that the street-door lock and the one upstairs were both Hansens. Anywhere and everywhere you go you should always notice the kind of lock, in case it becomes necessary at some future time to get in without help.

Hansens are good locks, but I had a good assortment. I was under no pressure; if someone had appeared from either direction, I was merely using the wrong key. In three minutes, maybe less, I got it and was inside. The elevator wasn't there; I pushed the button to bring it down, entered, and pushed the "4" button. The door to the apartment took longer than the one downstairs because I was too stubborn in trying to make the same key do, but finally I had it. I swung the door gently six inches and stood with my ear cocked. At that hour Sunday morning Rennert might have ignored the phone and the doorbell. Hearing nothing except traffic sounds from the street, I swung the door farther and entered the nice big room.

He was lying on the nice big couch, on his back. One swift glance, even from a distance, was enough to show that he wasn't asleep. His face was so swollen that no one would have dreamed of calling him handsome, and the handle of a knife was protruding from his chest, which was bare because the dressing gown he had on was open in front down to the belt. I crossed over. The skin of his belly was green. I pressed a finger on the skin at a couple of spots below the ribs; it was tight and rubbery. I put on the rubber gloves and removed one of his slippers and tried the toes; they were flabby. I bent over to get my nose an inch from his open mouth and inhaled; once was enough. He had been dead at least two days, and probably three or four.

I looked around; no sign of a disturbance or search. On a stand near the head of the couch were a half-full bottle of bourbon, two tall glasses, a pack of cigarettes, a book of matches with the flap open, and an ashtray with nothing in it. Having made a guess, that a guy of Rennert's build and condition wouldn't lie quietly on his back while someone stuck a knife in him unless he had been somehow processed, which was sound, I stooped to smell the glasses, which was dumb. The best-known drug for a Mickey Finn has almost no taste or odor, and even if it had, it couldn't be detected by the naked nose after three or four days.

The knife handle was brown plastic. I made another guess, as to why the weapon had been left in place this time, and to check it I crossed to an arch through which a refrigerator could be seen, and looked in. It was a nice little kitchenette. The second drawer I opened contained, among other items, two knives with brown plastic handles, one with a three-inch blade and one with a five-inch. The blade in Rennert's chest was probably seven-inch. That supported my other guess. You don't sneak a knife from your host's kitchen drawer and take it to the living room to kill him with if his eyes are open and his muscles usable.

Having made two good guesses, I decided that would do for a Sunday morning. The idea of spending a couple of hours going over the place, even with rubber gloves, didn't appeal to me. Being found in a man's castle which you have entered illegally can be embarrassing, but if he is there with you with a knife in his chest, even if he has started to decompose, it can be really ticklish. I decided that I hadn't *really* meant it when I thought it would be more interesting to be in jail. Besides, I had told Fritz I would be back in an hour or so.

I left. I used my handkerchief to wipe the only things I had touched with my bare fingers: the knob of the apartment door, the elevator door, and the button in the elevator. Before starting the elevator down I took off the rubber gloves and stuffed them in my pocket. Everything under control. I would wipe the button on the panel downstairs.

But I didn't. When the elevator stopped at the bottom, naturally I took a look through the square of glass before I opened the door. No one was in view in the lobby, but in a tenth of a second there would be. The door to the vestibule was being pushed open from the outside by a little guy in his shirt sleeves, and towering behind him was the big square face of Sergeant Purley Stebbins. At a moment like that you don't use your head because there isn't time. You use your finger, to press the "2" button in the elevator. Which I did. Electricity is wonderful; the elevator started up. When it stopped at the second floor, I stepped out. When the door closed, the elevator started down, showing that someone had pushed the button in the lobby. Really wonderful.

I stood in the little hall. It was now a question of odds. There was one chance in a thousand trillion that Purley would get out at the second floor, but if he did all the gods in heaven obviously had it in for me and I was sunk no matter what I did. The elevator went on by, and I made for the stairs. There was one chance in a thousand that the shirt-sleeved guy, who had to be the janitor—I beg his pardon, building superintendent—had stayed in the lobby instead of going up with Purley to let him in Rennert's apartment, but if so only a couple of minor gods were against me, and I could cope with them. I descended and found the lobby empty. Now the odds were the other way. It was fifty to one that there was a police car outside with a man in it, and ten to one that if I emerged to the sidewalk he would see me. That was simple; I didn't emerge. I went to the vestibule and pressed the button by Rennert's name and took the receiver from the hook. In a moment a voice came. "Who is it?"

I told the grill, "It's Archie Goodwin, Mr. Rennert. You may remember I was here ten days ago. You didn't like the deal I offered, but I've got a new angle that makes it different. I think you ought to hear it. I'm pretty sure it will appeal to you."

"All right, come on up."

The buzz sounded, and I opened the door and entered, went to the elevator, and pushed the button to bring it down. That button wouldn't have to be wiped now. When it came I stepped in and pushed the "4" button. When I got out at the fourth floor my face was ready with a friendly grin for Rennert, but at sight of Sergeant Stebbins my mouth opened in shocked surprise and I gawked.

"Not *you,*" I said.

"This is just too goddam pat," he said. He sounded a little hoarse. He whirled to Shirt-sleeves, who was in the doorway. "Take a look at this man. Have you seen him hanging around?"

"No, Sergeant, I haven't." The building superintendent looked a little sick. "I never saw him before. Excuse me, I've got to—"

"Don't touch anything in there!"

"Then I've got to—" He dashed to the stairs and was gone.

"I wish I *had* been hanging around," I said. "I might have seen the murderer enter or leave, or both. How long has Rennert been dead?"

"How do you know he's dead?"

"Now come. Not only you here and the mood you're in, but also him looking for somewhere to puke. Was it today? Was he stabbed like the others?"

He advanced a step, to arm's length. "I want to know exactly why you came here at exactly this time." He was hoarser. "I had been at that Jacobs place five minutes, and there you came. I've been here three minutes, and here you come. You didn't come to see Rennert. You'd ring his number first to see if he was here. You knew damn well it wasn't him that asked you who is it. You knew it was me. You're good on voices. And you're good at lies, and I've had enough of 'em. *You* puke. Puke a little truth."

"You would too," I said.

"I would too what?"

"Ring his number first. And when you ring a number and get no answer, do you always assume that the ringee is dead and go to see? I should hope not. Why did *you* come here at exactly this time?"

His jaw worked. "Okay, I'll tell you. The janitor got a phone call Friday from the people where Rennert was supposed to go for the week-end, and another one yesterday. He thought Rennert had just decided to go somewhere else, and he didn't want to enter the apartment, but he phoned the Missing Persons Bureau. They thought it was just another false alarm, but this morning someone at the bureau remembered he had seen Rennert's name on a report and called us. Now it's your turn, and by God, I want it straight! And fast!"

I was frowning thoughtfully. "It's too bad," I said, "that I always seem to rub you the wrong way. As sore as you are, the best thing you could do would be to take me down and book me, but I don't know what for. It's not even a misdemeanor to ring a man's doorbell. What I would like to do is help, since I'm here. If you've only been here three minutes you haven't had time to try all the tests, and maybe he's not dead. I'd be glad to–"

"Get going!" His hands were fists, and a muscle at the side of his neck was working. "Get!"

I didn't take the elevator. Purley knew that the natural thing would be for me to find the janitor and pump him, so I took the stairs. He had made it all the way to the basement. I found him there, pale and upset. He was too sick to talk, or too scared, or he may have thought I was the murderer. I told him the best thing was strong hot tea, no sugar, found my way to the sidewalk, and headed for home. I walked, taking my time. There was no point in disturbing Wolfe in the plant rooms, since there was no emergency. Rennert's belly had already turned green, and another half an hour wouldn't matter.

I had returned the keys and rubber gloves to the drawers, and fixed myself a gin and tonic because I wanted to swallow something and the idea of milk or water didn't seem to appeal to my stomach, and was looking at the sports section of the *Times* when Wolfe came down. We exchanged good mornings, and he went to the only chair in the world he really approves of, sat, rang for beer, and said I might as well go for a walk. He has some sort of an idea that my going for a walk is good for him.

"I already have," I told him. "I found another corpse, this time in an advanced condition. Kenneth Rennert."

"I'm in no mood for flummery. Take a walk."

"No flummery." I put the paper down. "I dialed Rennert's number and got no answer. I walked to his address and rang the bell and got no answer. Happening to have keys and rubber gloves with me, and thinking I might find something interesting, I went in and up to his apartment. For three or four days he has been lying on a couch with a knife in his chest, and is still there. So is the knife. He was probably fed a dose in a drink before—"

I stopped because he was having a fit. He had closed his right hand to make a fist and was hitting the desk with it, and he was bellowing. He was roaring something in a language that was probably the one he had used as a boy in Montenegro, the one that he and Marko Vukčić had sometimes talked. He had roared like that when he heard that Marko had been killed, and on three other occasions over the years. Fritz, entering with beer, stopped and looked at me reproachfully. Wolfe quit bellowing as abruptly as he had started, glared at Fritz, and said coldly, "Take that back. I don't want it."

"But it will do—"

"Take it back. I shall drink no beer until I get my fingers around that creature's throat. And I shall eat no meat."

"But impossible! The squabs are marinating!"

"Throw them out."

"Wait a minute," I objected. "What about Fritz and Theodore and me? Okay, Fritz. We've had a shock. I shall eat no boiled cucumbers."

Fritz opened his mouth, closed it again, turned, and went. Wolfe, his fists on the desk, commanded me, "Report."

Six minutes would have been enough for it, but I thought it would be well to give him time to calm down a little, so I stretched it to ten, and when I ran out of facts I continued, "I would want full price, no discount, for my two guesses—that the knife came from his kitchen drawer, and that he was drugged, unconscious, when he was stabbed. I have another guess on which I'd allow five per cent off for cash, no more—that he had been dead eighty hours. Between eighty and eighty-five. He was killed late Wednesday night. X went straight to him after killing Jane Ogilvy. If he had put it off until after the news about Jane Ogilvy was out, Rennert would have been too much on his guard to let X put something in his drink. Rennert may or may not have suspected that X had killed Simon Jacobs, since nothing had been published connecting his death with the plagiarism charge he had made three years ago. But if Rennert had known about Jane Ogilvy too, he certainly would have suspected. Hell, he would have known. So X couldn't wait, and he didn't. He went to Rennert to discuss their claim against Mortimer Oshin, knowing that Rennert would offer him a drink. He offered me one before I had been in his place three minutes."

I stopped for breath. Wolfe opened his fists and worked his fingers.

"Three comments," I said. "First, one question is answered—whether Rennert's operation was independent or was one of X's string. X has answered that for us. I admit it doesn't help any, with Rennert dead, but it makes it neater, and you like things neat. Second, with Rennert dead, his claim against Mortimer Oshin is dead too, and Oshin may want his ten grand back, and the committee may fire you tomorrow, and the Alice Porter surveillance is costing over three hundred bucks a day. Third, your beer and meat pledge. We'll ignore it. You were temporarily off your nut. This is tough enough as it is, and with you starving and dying of thirst it would be impossible." I left my chair. "I'll bring the beer."

"No." He made fists again. "I have committed myself. Sit down."

"God help us," I said, and sat.

14

We were in conference, off and on, all the rest of the day, with time out for meals. The meals were dismal. Squab marinated in light cream, rolled in flour seasoned with salt, pepper, nutmeg, clove, thyme, and crushed juniper berries, sautéed in olive oil, and served on toast spread with red currant jelly, with Madeira cream sauce poured over it, is one of Wolfe's favorite tidbits. He ordinarily consumes three of them, though I have known him to make it four. That day I wanted to eat in the kitchen, but no. I had to sit and down my two while he grimly pecked away at his green peas and salad and cheese. The Sunday-evening snack was just as bad. He usually has something like cheese and anchovy spread or pâté de foie gras or herring in sour cream, but apparently the meat pledge included fish. He ate crackers and cheese and drank four cups of coffee. Later, in the office, he finished off a bowl of pecans, and then went to the kitchen for a brush and pan to collect the bits of shell on his desk and the rug. He sure was piling on the agony.

In the state he was in now, he would have been willing to try one or more of the routine lines, even one the cops had already covered or were covering, if it had offered any hope at all. We discussed all of them, and I made a list:

1. Combing Rennert's apartment and Jane Ogilvy's cloister.
2. Trying to pry something out of Mrs. Jacobs and Mr. and Mrs. Ogilvy.
3. Getting the names of everybody who had known of the plan to go after Jacobs, analyzing them, and seeing those who were at all possible.
4. Trying to trace Jacobs to his meeting with X Monday evening, May 25th.
5. Trying to find someone who had seen a car parked in the lane back of the cloister Wednesday evening, May 27th.
6. Trying to find someone who had seen X, any stranger, entering the 37th Street building Wednesday night, May 27th.
7. Seeing a few hundred of the friends and associates of Jacobs, Jane Ogilvy, and Rennert, to find out if all three of them had been acquainted with a certain person or persons.

8. Trying to learn how Jacobs and Jane Ogilvy had disposed of the loot they got from Richard Echols and the estate of Marjorie Lippin; and, supposing they had transferred a big share of it to X, trying to trace the transfers. Also the loot Alice Porter had got from Ellen Sturdevant.
9. Trying on Alice Porter the approach we had meant to try on Jane Ogilvy. Or trying to throw a scare into her. Or trying to get from Ellen Sturdevant and her publishers, McMurray & Co., an agreement not to prosecute or demand repayment if Alice Porter would identify X.
10. Get a membership list of the NAAD and go over it, name by name, with Cora Ballard.
11. Have a couple of hundred copies made of "There Is Only Love," "What's Mine Is Yours," and "On Earth but Not in Heaven," and send them to editors and book reviewers, with a letter citing the internal evidence that they had all been written by the same person, and asking if they knew of any published material, or, with editors, submitted material, apparently by that person.

During the discussion of this last item Wolfe had before him the manuscripts of the first two, and the copy of the third, they having been returned by Cramer Friday afternoon as agreed.

There were other suggestions that I didn't bother to put down. To each of the items listed I could have added the objections and difficulties, but they're so obvious, especially to the routine ones, the first eight, that I didn't think it was necessary.

The stymie was the motive. In ninety-nine murder investigations out of a hundred it gets narrowed down before long to just a few people who had motives, often only two or three, and you go on from there. This time the motive had been out in full view from the start; the trouble was, who had it? It could be anyone within reach who could read and write and drive a car—say five million in the metropolitan area, and except for Alice Porter there was absolutely no pointer. She was still alive at midnight Sunday. Orrie Cather, phoning from Carmel at 12:23 to report that Saul Panzer had relieved him on schedule, said that the light in the house had gone out at 10:52 and all had been quiet since. Wolfe had gone up to bed, leaving it that we would decide in the morning how to tackle Alice Porter.

In the kitchen at a quarter to nine Monday morning, as I was pouring a third cup of coffee, Fritz asked me what I was nervous about. I said I wasn't nervous. He said of course I was, I had been jerky for the last ten minutes, and I was taking a third cup of coffee. I said everybody in that house was too damned observant. He said, "See? You're very nervous"—and I took the coffee to the office.

I *was* nervous. Fred Durkin had phoned at 7:39 to say that he was on his way to relieve Saul, and Dol Bonner was with him, and Saul should have phoned by 8:20 to report, certainly not later than 8:30, and he hadn't. He still hadn't at 8:45. If it had been Fred or Orrie I would have thought it was probably some little snag like a flat tire, but Saul has never had a flat tire and never will. At nine o'clock I was sure there was some kind of hell to pay. At 9:15 I was sure that Alice Porter was dead. At 9:20 I was sure that Saul was dead too. When the phone rang at 9:25 I grabbed it and barked at it, "Well?"—which is no way to answer a phone.

"Archie?"

"Yes."

"Saul. We've got a circus up here."

I was so relieved to hear that all he had was a circus that I grinned at him. "You don't say. Did you get bit by a lion?"

"No. I got bit by a deputy sheriff and a state cop. Fred didn't show, and at eight-fifteen I went to where my car was hid. He was there, refusing to answer questions being asked by a deputy sheriff of Putnam County. Standing by was an old friend of yours, Sergeant Purley Stebbins."

"Oh. Ah."

"Yeah. Stebbins told the DS that I was another one of Nero Wolfe's operatives. That's all Stebbins said the whole time. He was leaving it to the DS, who said plenty. Evidently Fred had shown his driving license and then clammed. I thought that was a little extreme, especially with Stebbins there, and I supplied some essential details, but that didn't help any. The DS took both of us for trespassing and loitering, and then he added disturbing the peace. He used the radio in his car, and pretty soon a state cop came. On that dirt road it was a traffic jam. The state cop brought us to Carmel, and we are being held. This is my phone call to my lawyer. Apparently the DS is going to loiter near that house, and maybe Stebbins is too. On the way here we stopped for a couple of minutes on the blacktop where another state car was parked behind Dol Bonner's car at the roadside. Where she had had it behind some trees I suppose she was trespassing. She and a state cop were standing there chatting. If they have brought her on to Carmel I haven't seen her. I'm talking from a booth in the building where the sheriff's office is. The number of the sheriff's office is Carmel five-three-four-six-six."

When Saul makes a report there is nothing left to ask about. I asked, "Have you had any breakfast?"

"Not yet. I wanted to get you first. I will now."

"Eat plenty of meat. We'll try to spring you by the Fourth of July. By the way, did you see Alice Porter before you left?"

"Sure. She was mowing the lawn."

I said that was fine, hung up, sat for two minutes looking at it, went to the stairs and mounted three flights to the plant rooms, and entered. At that point there were ten thousand orchid plants between me and my goal, many of them in full bloom, and the dazzle was enough to stop anyone, even one who had seen it as often as I had, but I kept going—through the first room, the moderate, then the tropical, and then the cool—on into the potting room. Theodore was at the sink, washing pots. Wolfe was at the big bench, putting peat mixture into flasks. When he heard my step and turned, his lips tightened and his chin went up. He knew I wouldn't mount three flights and bust in there for anything trivial.

"Relax," I said. "She's still alive, or was two hours ago. Mowing the lawn. But Saul and Fred are in the hoosegow, and Dol Bonner is having an affair with a state cop."

He turned to put the flask he was holding on the bench, and turned back. "Go on."

I did so, repeating verbatim what Saul and I had said. His chin went back to normal, but his lips stayed tight. When I finished he said, "So you regard my giving up meat as a subject for jest."

"I do not. I was being bitter."

"I know you. That deputy sheriff is probably an oaf. Have you phoned Mr. Parker?"

"No."

"Do so at once. Tell him to get those absurd charges dismissed if possible; if not, arrange for bail. And phone Mr. Harvey or Miss Ballard or Mr. Tabb that I shall be at that meeting at half past two."

I stared. "What?"

"Must I repeat it?"

"No. Do you want me along?"

"Certainly."

I was thinking, as I returned down the aisles between the benches of orchids and on down the stairs, that this thing was going to set a record for smashing rules before we were through with it—if we ever got through. At my desk I rang the office of Nathaniel Parker, the lawyer Wolfe always uses when only a lawyer will do, and found him in. He didn't like the picture. He said rural communities resented having New York private detectives snooping around, especially when the snoopee was a property-owner and not a known criminal, and they weren't fond of New York lawyers either. He thought it would be better for him to relay the job to an attorney in Carmel whom he knew, instead of going up there himself, and I told him to go ahead. Another five Cs down the drain, at least.

I started to dial Philip Harvey's number but remembered in time that I had promised never to call him before noon except for an emergency, and dialed Jerome Tabb's instead. A female voice told me that Mr. Tabb was working and couldn't be disturbed until one o'clock, and would I leave a message. She seemed surprised and a little indignant that there was anyone on earth who didn't know that. I told her to tell him that Nero Wolfe would come to the council meeting at two-thirty, but, knowing that messages aren't always delivered, I got Cora Ballard at the NAAD office. She was delighted to hear that Wolfe would be present. I made two more calls, to Orrie Cather at home and to Sally Corbett at Dol Bonner's office, informing them about the circus and telling them the operation was off until further notice. Orrie, who was a free-lance, wanted to know if he was free to lance, and I told him no, to stand by. What the hell, another forty bucks was peanuts.

When I went to the kitchen to tell Fritz that lunch would be at one o'clock sharp because we were leaving at two for an appointment, he had a question. For Wolfe he was going to make a special omelet which he had just invented in his head, and would that do for me or should he broil some ham? I asked what would be in the omelet, and he said four eggs, salt, pepper, one tablespoon tarragon butter, two tablespoons cream, two tablespoons dry white wine, one-half teaspoon minced shallots, one-third cup whole almonds, and twenty fresh mushrooms. I thought that would do for two, but he said my God, no, that would be for Mr. Wolfe, and did I want one like it? I did. He warned me that he might decide at the last minute to fold some apricot jam in, and I said I would risk it.

15

At 2:35 p.m. Wolfe and I, both of us well fueled with omelet, stepped out of a wobbly old elevator on the third floor of the Clover Club, which is in the Sixties just off Fifth Avenue. The hall was spacious and high-ceilinged and looked its age, but not much the worse for it. There was no one in sight. We glanced around, heard voices beyond a closed door, crossed to it, opened it, and entered.

Some three dozen people, all but six of them men, were seated around a long rectangular table covered with a white cloth. There were coffee cups, water glasses, ashtrays, pads of paper, and pencils. We stood, Wolfe with his hat in one hand and his cane in the other. Three or four of them were talking at once, and no one paid any attention to us. At the right end of the table were three of the committee members: Amy Wynn, Philip Harvey, and Mortimer Oshin. At the other end was Cora Ballard, and next to her was the president of the NAAD, Jerome Tabb. His picture had been on the jacket of his book I had read. Next to Tabb was the vice-president, a man who, according to an article I had read recently, averaged a million dollars a year from the musicals for which he had written the books and lyrics. I had recognized some other faces—four novelists, three dramatists, and a biographer or something—by the time Harvey got up and came over to us. The talk stopped, and heads were turned our way.

"Nero Wolfe," Harvey told them. "Archie Goodwin."

He took Wolfe's hat and cane. An author or dramatist went and got two chairs and moved them near the table. If I had been the president or the executive secretary the chairs would have been in place; after all, we were expected.

As we sat, Jerome Tabb raised his voice. "You're a little early, Mr. Wolfe." He glanced at his wrist. "It's the time agreed, I know, but we haven't finished our discussion."

"A sentry in the hall could have stopped us." Wolfe was gruff. He always was when he had put his fanny on a chair seat that was too small. "If the discussion doesn't concern me you can finish it after I leave. If it does concern me, proceed."

A famous woman novelist tittered, and two men laughed. A famous dramatist said, "Let's hear what he has to say. Why not?" A man raised his hand. "Mr. President! As I said before, this is very irregular. We almost never admit outsiders to a council meeting, and I see no reason for making this an exception. The chairman of the Joint Committee on Plagiarism has reported and made a recommendation, and that should be the basis of our . . ." He finished his sentence, but I didn't catch it because five or six other voices drowned him out.

Tabb tapped on a glass with a spoon, and the voices subsided. "Having Mr. Wolfe here has been decided," he said with authority. "I told you he had been invited, and a motion was made and seconded to admit him and hear him, and it carried by a voice vote. We won't go into that again. And I don't see how we can take a position based solely on the report and recommendation of the chairman of the joint committee. One reason we had to call this special meeting was that the three NAAD members of the committee don't agree. They actively disagree. I'm going to ask Mr. Wolfe to state his case, but first he ought to know in a general way how our discussion has gone. Now there shouldn't be any interruptions. Mr. Harvey, you first. Briefly."

The committee chairman cleared his throat. He looked around. "I've told you how I feel," he said. "I was never enthusiastic about hiring a private detective, but I went along with the majority of the committee. Now this matter has gone far beyond the province of the committee, what it was set up for. Three people have been killed. Nero Wolfe told the committee last week, last Wednesday, that he was going to expose the murderer of Simon Jacobs whether we terminated our engagement with him or not. Now I suppose he's going to expose the murderer of Jane Ogilvy and Kenneth Rennert. All right, that's fine, I'm all for exposing murderers, but that's not the job of this committee. It's not only not our job, it's probably illegal and it could get us into serious trouble. We have no control over what Nero Wolfe does. He said he would have to have a free hand, that he wouldn't tell us what he was doing or was going to do. I say that's dangerous. As I said before, if the council doesn't instruct the committee to terminate the engagement with Nero Wolfe, the only thing I can do is resign from the committee. The way I feel, I'll have to."

Two or three of them started to say something, but Tabb tapped on the glass. "You'll all get a chance later. Mr. Oshin? Briefly."

Oshin squashed a cigarette in an ashtray. "I'm in a different position now," he said, "now that Kenneth Rennert's dead. Before today I could be accused of having a personal interest, and I did. I don't deny that when I kicked in ten thousand dollars it was chiefly because I thought it might save me paying Rennert ten times that. Now personally I'm out from under. My ten thousand was a contribution to the expenses of the committee, and one of the publisher members, Dexter, has said he'll contribute whatever is necessary, and I think we should tell Nero Wolfe to go ahead. If we don't we're quitters. If he wants to expose a murderer, all right, if he exposes a murderer he will also expose the man that has been back of this plagiarism racket, and that's what we hired him for. *He* hasn't been murdered, he's still alive and still loose, and are we going to back out just because we've found out that he's not only a racketeer but a killer? I don't like threats to resign, I never have, but if you instruct the committee to fire Nero Wolfe I'll *have* to resign, and I wish I could resign from the NAAD too."

There were murmurs, and Tabb tapped on the glass again. "Miss Wynn? Briefly, please."

Amy Wynn's nose had been twitching. Her clasped hands were resting on the edge of the table. She was up against it, since Reuben Imhof wasn't there for her to look at. "I really don't think," she said, "that I should take a position on this. Because I'm in the same—"

"Louder, Miss Wynn, please."

She raised her voice a little. "I'm in the same position that Mr. Oshin was. The man that made the claim against him is dead, but the woman that has made a claim against me, Alice Porter, is still alive. Nero Wolfe says that my case is different, that the story she bases her claim on wasn't written by the man who wrote the others, that Alice Porter wrote it herself, but that doesn't really matter, because he wrote the story that she used for her claim against Ellen Sturdevant, so if he's caught and it all comes out she'll be caught too, and I'll be out from under too, as Mr. Oshin put it. So I still have a personal interest, a strong personal interest, and I don't think I should take a position. Perhaps I shouldn't be on the committee. I'll resign if you think I ought to."

"Damn fine committee," someone muttered. "They're *all* going to resign." Harvey started to speak, but Tabb tapped on the glass. "We're not through," he said. "I'm going to ask our counsel to say a word about Mr. Harvey's statement that it's probably illegal for us to continue the arrangement with Mr. Wolfe and it might get us into serious trouble. Mr. Sachs?"

A compact, broad-shouldered guy about my age with sharp dark eyes passed his tongue over his lips. "It's not a very complicated situation legally," he said. "There should be a letter to Mr. Wolfe stating definitely and specifically that you have engaged him to investigate the plagiarism claims and nothing else. Then if he does something that causes him to be charged with some offense against the law, for instance withholding evidence or obstructing justice, no matter what, you wouldn't be liable legally. Of course there could be bad publicity, there might be a stigma because you had hired him, but it's not actionable to hire a man who breaks a law while he is in your employ unless his offense is committed under your direction or with your knowledge and consent. If you decide to send such a letter I'll be glad to draft it if you want me to."

Wolfe and I exchanged glances. He sounded exactly like Nathaniel Parker. Tabb spoke. "Apparently that settles that. I'm going to ask Miss Ballard what she thinks. She tried a couple of times to tell us, but we didn't let her finish. Cora? Briefly."

The executive secretary looked apologetic. She was tapping on a pad with her pencil. "I don't know," she said, "I guess the fact is I'm just afraid. I know Mr. Wolfe is a very brilliant man, I know a little bit about how he does things, I suppose you all do, and of course I'm not going to criticize him, he knows his business just as you know your business of writing, but I'd hate to have the association get involved in something sensational like a murder trial. One thing Mr. Harvey didn't say, the New York police are working on this now, and since there have been three murders I think you can be pretty sure they won't quit until they get the man they're after, and since he's the man we're after too I shouldn't think you'd have to pay a private detective to do what they're doing." She smiled apologetically. "I hope Mr. Oshin won't mind if I don't agree that you would be quitters."

"I don't agree either," Philip Harvey blurted. "I don't see how we could be expected—"

Tabb was tapping on the glass. Harvey was going on anyhow, but several of them shushed him. "I think we've covered the various viewpoints pretty well," Tabb said. "Mr. Wolfe? If you care to comment?"

Wolfe's head went from right to left and back again. Those with their backs to us twisted around on their chairs. "First," he said, "I remark that with your books two of you have given me pleasure, three of you have informed me, and one of you has stimulated my mental processes. Two or—"

"Name them," the famous woman novelist demanded.

Laughter. Tabb tapped on the glass.

Wolfe resumed. "Two or three of you have irritated or bored me, but on balance I owe you much. That's why I'm here. Having seen your names on the letterhead of your association, I wanted to prevent you from forsaking a responsibility. You are collectively responsible for the death by violence of three people."

Five or six of them spoke at once. Tabb didn't tap on the glass. Wolfe showed them a palm. "If you please. I merely stated a fact. You appointed a committee for a specific purpose. Pursuant to that purpose, the committee hired me to investigate. It provided me with the record—various documents and other material. Studying it, I formed a conclusion that should have been reached long ago: that the three first claims of plagiarism had all been instigated by a single person. I procured more material, books written by the claimants, and formed a second conclusion: that none of the three claimants had been the instigator. That changed completely the character of the investigation. It widened its scope so greatly that I told the committee it was no longer my kind of job. It was a member of the committee who suggested a plan to beguile one of the claimants, Simon Jacobs, into turning informer. At the request of the committee, reluctantly, I agreed to carry out the plan, which by its nature had to be imparted to various people. Forty-seven persons knew of it within a few hours. As a direct result of the plan Simon Jacobs was killed before Mr. Goodwin got to him; and as a further direct result, because the man we were after feared that a similar plan would be tried on Jane Ogilvy or Kenneth Rennert, they too were killed."

Wolfe's head went left and right again. "I repeat that the conclusions I formed should have been reached long ago, if a competent investigation had been made. The evidence on which they were based had been at hand, all of it, for more than a year. Because of those conclusions, formed in my pursuit of the stated purpose of the committee, and because of a plan of procedure approved by your committee and suggested by one of its members, Mr. Oshin, three people were killed. You are now considering whether or not to scuttle. That might be prudent; certainly it would not be gallant; some might think it less than honorable. I submit it to your judgment. Mr. Harvey. Do you challenge any of my facts?"

"Your facts are straight enough," Harvey conceded, "but you left one out. You told us yourself that you failed to function properly. You admitted that but for your default Jacobs would still be alive. Are we responsible for your blunder?"

"No." Wolfe was blunt. "With the plan known to so many, I should have taken precautions to safeguard Mr. Jacobs from harm. But you have shifted your ground. My default does not relieve this body of its responsibility. If you wish to dismiss me for incompetence I offer no objection, but then, to honor your obligation, you'll have to hire somebody else. Mr. Tabb. You invited my comments and I have made them." He stood up. "If that's all—"

"Wait a minute." Tabb's eyes moved. "Do you want to ask Mr. Wolfe any questions?"

"I have one," a man said. "Mr. Wolfe, you heard Mr. Sachs's suggestion, that we write you a letter saying that you are to investigate the plagiarism claims and nothing else. Would you accept such a letter?"

"Certainly. If I get the swindler, which will satisfy you, I'll also get the murderer, which will satisfy me."

"Then I make a motion. I move that we instruct the chairman of the committee to ask Mr. Sachs to draft the letter, and sign it and send it to Nero Wolfe, and tell him to go ahead with the investigation."

Two of them, a man and a woman, seconded it.

"You understand," Harvey said, "that I couldn't obey those instructions. If the motion passes you'll have to get a new chairman."

"Mortimer Oshin," someone said.

"That will come after we act on the motion," Tabb said. "Or it won't. Before we discuss it, have you any more questions for Mr. Wolfe?"

"I'd like to ask him," a woman said, "if he knows who the murderer is."

Wolfe, on his feet, grunted. "If I did I wouldn't be here."

"Any further questions?" Tabb asked. Apparently not. "Then discussion of the motion."

"You don't need us for that," Wolfe said. "I appreciate the courtesy of your invitation to be present, and if my opening remark gave you the impression that I accepted it solely to prevent you from forsaking a responsibility I wish to correct it. I also wish to earn a fee. Come, Archie."

He wheeled and headed for the door, and I circled around him to open it, detouring to get his hat and cane from a chair.

16

We got home at 3:55, just in the nick of time for Wolfe to keep his afternoon date with the orchids. On my desk were three memos from Fritz, reporting phone calls—one from Lon Cohen, one from Dexter of Title House, and one from a personal friend. I rang Dexter. He wanted to know if there was any truth in the rumor that the NAAD council was holding a special meeting for the purpose of instructing the joint committee to terminate its engagement with Wolfe. Thinking it would be unwise to tell a publisher, even one with a conscience, what authors and dramatists had done or were doing, I said we had heard the rumor but knew nothing definite, which was true, since we hadn't stayed for the vote on the motion. He said if the NAAD council didn't know that they couldn't give orders to a *joint* committee they would soon find out. I didn't bother with Lon Cohen; he could ring again. The personal friend was a personal matter, and I attended to it.

A little after five Saul Panzer called, from a booth in a Carmel drugstore. "We've been liberated," he said. "Free as crows. No charges. The lawyer is at the fountain with Miss Bonner and Fred, having a milkshake. Now what?"

"No program," I told him. "I don't suppose there's any chance of keeping on her?"

"I doubt it. I don't see how. I just got back from a little ride out that way. There's a car there in the same spot we've been using, I suppose a deputy sheriff's. He's probably covering the house. Also there's a car near the spot Miss Bonner and Miss Corbett were using, with a man in it. It looks as if Stebbins has fed Putnam County a line. About the only way would be to come in from the back, walk in about a mile from another road to a hill with trees on it, and use binoculars. Five hundred yards from the house. Of course that would be no good after dark."

I said it wouldn't be much better even before dark and told him to go home and get some sleep and stand by, and the same for Fred. Also to tell Dol Bonner she would hear from us when we had anything to say. Two minutes after I hung up the phone rang again.

"Nero Wolfe's office, Archie Goodwin speaking."

"This is the chairman of the Joint Committee on Plagiarism. You may recognize my voice."

"I do. Was it a close vote?"

"We don't reveal details of our deliberations to outsiders, but it wasn't close. The letter has been drafted and you'll have it tomorrow. I don't ask you what the next move is, since Wolfe doesn't reveal details either, but I thought he'd like to know that we're both gallant and honorable. Sometimes."

"He will, Mr. Oshin. Congratulations. Who's the new committee member?"

"Oh, Harvey's still on the committee. He only resigned as chairman. I think he wants to keep his eye on us. Let me know if you need a bat boy."

I said I would.

When Wolfe came down at six o'clock I reported the calls to him—Dexter and Saul and Oshin. As I finished, Fritz entered with a tray—a bottle of beer and a glass. Wolfe glared at him, and he stopped halfway to the desk.

"Archie put you up to this," Wolfe said coldly.

"No, sir. I thought perhaps—"

"Take it back. I am committed. Take it back!"

Fritz went. Wolfe transferred the glare to me. "Is Alice Porter still alive?"

"I don't know. Saul saw her at eight this morning, ten hours ago."

"I want to see her. Bring her."

"Now?"

"Yes."

I regarded him. "Some day," I said, "you're going to tell me to bring you the Queen of England, and I'll do my best. But I remind you that two or three times, when you have told me to bring someone and I have done so, you didn't like the method I used. Do you want to suggest one this time?"

"Yes. Tell her that I am ready to make a settlement with her for her claim against Amy Wynn."

I raised a brow. "What if she wants to know what kind of a settlement?"

"You don't know. You only know that I am ready to make one, and tomorrow may be too late."

"What if she phones Amy Wynn and learns that you haven't been told to make a settlement?"

"That's why you're going after her instead of phoning. She probably won't; but if she does you'll say that I am not making the offer on behalf of Miss Wynn. I am making it on behalf of my client, the committee. I would prefer not to have that said unless it's necessary."

"Okay." I got up. "Would it help if I had some idea of what you *are* going to say to her?"

"No. It only occurred to me as I was coming down in the elevator. It should have occurred to me long ago. I am beginning to suspect that my mind is going. It should have occurred to you. A screw to use on that woman has been staring us in the face for a full week, and neither of us had the wit to see it. Now that I've told you it's there, of course you will."

But I didn't. I had plenty of time to try to, going to the garage to get the car, and then a ninety-minute drive, but I simply couldn't see it. You probably have, and if not you will now if you spend three minutes looking for it, and of course you'll think I'm as dumb as they come, but you've had it all in one package while with me it had been dragging along for two weeks and a lot of things had been on my mind, including three murders. Anyhow, dumb or not, I didn't hit on it until just as I was turning off of Route 301 onto the blacktop. Then, suddenly seeing it, I braked the car, steered it onto the grass shoulder, stopped, and sat looking it over. No wonder Wolfe had suspected his mind was going. It was perfectly obvious. I fed gas, eased back onto the road, and went on. We had her.

But I had to get her first. If X had got there ahead of me and stuck a knife in her, I would reverse my stand on boiled cucumbers; I would eat nothing *but* boiled cucumbers until we nailed him. I had intended to take it easy along the stretch of blacktop and see if I could spot the man in the car near the place Dol Bonner and Sally Corbett had used, but now I was in a hurry. Almost too much of a hurry; I wasn't careful enough on the half-mile of narrow winding dirt road and scraped my bottom on a high center. That's no way to treat a Heron sedan. Slowing down, I turned into the lane through the gap and bumped along the ruts to the little blue house. It was ten minutes past eight, and the sun was just sinking behind the rim of a ridge.

I had seen her before I stopped the car. She was a couple of hundred yards off to the left, standing by a stone fence. The bicolored mutt was there beside her, wagging his tail, and on the other side of the fence was the upper half of a man. Her raised voice came across the meadow. I got out and headed for them, and as I approached I could hear her words: ". . . and you can tell the sheriff I don't need any protection and don't want any! You get out of here and stay out! I'm not in any danger, and if I am I can handle it! I told that state trooper this morning that I don't want—"

The man's eyes had left her to come to me, and she whirled around. "You here again?" she demanded.

I stopped at the fence and addressed the man on the other side. "Trespassing and loitering," I said sternly. "Also disturbing the peace. A peeping Tom can get up to three years. Beat it."

"You too," Alice Porter said. "Both of you beat it."

"I'm an officer of the law," the man said, raising a hand to exhibit a medal. "Deputy Sheriff Putnam County."

Everyone glared at everyone. "Tell Sergeant Stebbins," I instructed the man, "that Archie Goodwin was here. It will please him." I turned to her. "When I saw you ten days ago you said you wouldn't talk, not a word, and evidently you haven't changed your mind. But you also said you'd listen if I had come to make an offer. Okay, I have one."

"What kind of an offer?"

"It's just for you. I doubt if the deputy sheriff would be interested."

When she looked straight at you her eyes seemed even closer together, and her little nose almost wasn't there. "All right," she said, "I'll listen." She told the man, "You clear out of here and stay out." She turned and headed for the house.

It was a procession across the meadow. First her, then the dog, then me; and what made it a procession was the deputy sheriff, who climbed the wall and tagged along behind, ten paces back of me. She didn't look back until she reached the door of the house; then she saw him. He had stopped at my car and opened the door on the other side, the driver's side. "That's all right," I told her, "let him inspect it. He needs something to do." When she opened the door the dog trotted in, and I followed.

It was a bigger room than you would expect from the outside, and wasn't bad at all. She said, "Sit down if you want to," and went and deposited her 160 pounds on a long wicker bench. I pulled a chair around. "What kind of an offer?" she asked.

I sat. "I haven't actually got it, Miss Porter. Nero Wolfe has it. If you'll come with me to his house in New York he'll tell you about it. It's an offer to settle your claim against Amy Wynn."

"An offer from her?"

"I don't know all the details, but I think so."

"Then you think wrong."

"I often do. That's just the impression I got. It could be that Mr.

Wolfe wants to make an offer on behalf of his client, the Joint Committee on Plagiarism of the National Association of Authors and Dramatists and the Book Publishers of America. But I think it's from Amy Wynn."

"You're not very good at thinking. You'd better stop trying. I'm not going to go to New York to see Nero Wolfe. If he really has an offer and you don't know what it is, call him on the phone and ask him. There's the phone. Reverse the charges."

She meant it. I had crossed my legs. Now I uncrossed them. Since the method Wolfe had suggested wouldn't work, I would have to roll my own. "Look, Miss Porter. I drove all the way up here instead of phoning because I thought your line might be tapped. Why has that deputy sheriff been hiding behind that stone fence all day? Why is another one in a car hiding behind some bushes near the road a mile from here? Why did a state cop come to see you this morning? Who started all the fuss? I can tell you. A man named Purley Stebbins of the New York police. He's a sergeant on the Manhattan West Homicide Squad. He's investigating three murders that have taken place in the past two weeks that you have probably heard about. That man out there said he's here to protect you. Blah. He's here to see that you don't skip. We'll be followed when we drive to New York, see if we're not. I don't—"

"I'm not going to New York."

"You're a damn fool if you don't. I don't know what Stebbins has on you for the murders, but he must have something, or thinks he has, or he wouldn't have come up here and sicked Putnam County on you. I'm telling the truth when I say that Nero Wolfe didn't tell me exactly why he wants to see you, and see you quick, but I know this, he doesn't suspect you of murder."

"You said he wants to make me an offer."

"Maybe he does. He said to tell you that. All I know is this, if I were in any way connected with a murder, let alone three murders, and if Nero Wolfe was investigating them, and if he wanted to see me and said it was urgent, and if I was innocent, I wouldn't sit around arguing about it."

"I'm not connected with any murder." She was hooked; I could see it in her eyes.

"Good. Tell Sergeant Stebbins that." I left the chair. "He'll be glad to know it. I apologize for butting in on your talk with your protector." I turned and was going, and was halfway to the door when her voice came.

"Wait a minute."

I stood. She was biting her lip. She wasn't looking at me, but here and there. Finally she focused on me. "If I go with you, how will I get home? I could take my car, but I don't like to drive at night."

"I'll bring you home."

She arose. "I'll put on a dress. Go out and tell that damn deputy sheriff to go soak his head."

I went out, but I didn't deliver the message. The officer of the law wasn't in sight at first glance, but then I saw him, across the meadow by the stone fence, anl there were two of him. Apparently it was an around-the-clock cover, and his relief had come. To show there was no hard feeling I waved at them, but they didn't wave back. I got the car turned around, looked in the trunk to see that my emergency kit was still there, and checked the contents of the dash compartment, and pretty soon Alice Porter emerged, locked the door, patted the dog, and came and got in. The dog escorted us through the gap to the dirt road and then let us go.

I stayed under thirty on the blacktop to give anyone who might be interested time to see that she was in the car with me, and to get out to the road and fall in, and when I stopped at the junction with Route 301 I picked him up in the mirror, but I didn't call Alice Porter's attention to him until we were the other side of Carmel and I was sure it was a tail. It's fun to drop a tail, but it would help to put her in a proper mood for conversation with Wolfe if he stuck all the way, so I made no difficulties. She twisted around in the seat about every four minutes for a look back, and by the time we rolled into the garage on Tenth Avenue her neck must have needed a rest. I don't know if he got his car parked, and out of it, in time to stalk us a block to 35th Street and around the corner to the old brownstone.

I put her in the front room and showed her the door to the bathroom, and then, instead of using the connecting door to the office, went around by the hall. Wolfe, at his desk with a French magazine, looked up. "You got her?"

I nodded. "I thought I'd better report first. Her reaction seemed a little peculiar."

"How peculiar?"

I gave it to him verbatim. He took ten seconds to digest it and said, "Bring her." I went and opened the connecting door and said, "In here, Miss Porter." She had taken off her jacket, and either she didn't wear a bra or she needed a new one. Wolfe was on his feet; I have never understood why, considering how he feels about women, he bothers to stand when one enters the room. He waited until she was in the red leather chair, with her jacket draped over the arm, to resume his seat.

He eyed her. "Mr. Goodwin tells me," he said civilly, "that you and your home are well guarded."

She was forward in the chair, her elbows resting on the arms. "I don't need any guard," she said. "He got me to come here by trying to scare me about being suspected of murder. I don't scare easy. I'm not scared."

"But you came."

She nodded. "I'm here. I wanted to see what kind of a game this is. He talked about an offer, but I don't believe you've got an offer. What have you got?"

"You're wrong, Miss Porter." Wolfe leaned back, comfortable. "I do have an offer. I'm prepared to offer you easement from the threat of prosecution for an offense you have committed. Naturally I want something in return."

"Nobody's going to prosecute me. I haven't committed any offense."

"But you have." Wolfe stayed affable, not accusing, just stating a fact. "A serious one. A felony. Before I describe the offense I'm referring to, the one for which you will pay no penalty if you accept my offer, I must fill in some background. Four years ago, in nineteen fifty-five, you entered into a conspiracy with some person, to me unknown, to extort money from Ellen Sturdevant by making a false claim of plagiarism. It—"

"That's a lie."

"If so it's defamatory and you have me. The next year, nineteen fifty-six, that same person, call him X, entered into a similar conspiracy with a man named Simon Jacobs to defraud Richard Echols; and in nineteen fifty-seven he repeated the performance with a woman named Jane Ogilvy, to defraud Marjorie Lippin. All three of the conspiracies were successful; large sums were paid. Last year, nineteen fifty-eight, X tried it again, with a man named Kenneth Rennert; that time the target was a playwright, Mortimer Oshin. No settlement had been made at the time Rennert died, five days ago."

"It's probably all lies. The one about me is."

Wolfe ignored it. "I'm making this as brief as possible, including only what is essential for you to understand my offer. I learned of the existence of X by a textual study of the three stories that were the basis of the claims made by you, Simon Jacobs, and Jane Ogilvy. They were all written by the same person. That is demonstrable and beyond question. I communicated my discovery to seven people, perforce, and they passed it on. A plan was made to entice Simon Jacobs into revealing the identity of X, and it became known to some fifty persons. X learned of it, and he killed Simon Jacobs before we got to him; and, fearing that we would try some similar plan with Jane Ogilvy or Kenneth Rennert, he killed them also. I don't know why he hasn't killed you too. He or she."

"Why should he? I don't know any X. I wrote that story myself. 'There Is Only Love.'"

"If so you are X, and I have reason to believe that you are not." Wolfe shook his head. "No. Did you write that book that was published under your name? *The Moth That Ate Peanuts?*"

"Certainly I wrote it!"

"Then you didn't write that story. That too is demonstrable. And that is the background." Wolfe straightened up and flattened a palm on the desk. "Now. Here is the point. I have also studied the text of 'Opportunity Knocks,' the story on which you have based your claim against Amy Wynn. Did you write that?"

"Certainly I did!"

"I believe you. It was written by the person who wrote *The Moth That Ate Peanuts.* But in that case you did *not* write 'There Is Only Love.' I will undertake to establish that fact beyond a reasonable doubt to the satisfaction of both a learned judge and a motley jury; and if it can be demonstrated that your claim against Ellen Sturdevant was a fraud, that it was based on a story you did not write, how much credence will be given to your good faith in your claim against Amy Wynn? I am prepared to advise Miss Wynn to reject your claim out of hand."

"Go ahead." Evidently she had meant it when she said she didn't scare easy.

"You are not impressed?" Wolfe was still affable.

"I certainly am not. You're lying and you're bluffing—if I get what you're driving at. You think you can prove I didn't write that story, 'There Is Only Love,' by showing that its style is different from my book, *The Moth That Ate Peanuts.* Is that it?"

"Yes. If you include all the elements of style—vocabulary, syntax, paragraphing. Yes."

"I'd like to see you try." She was scornful. "Any writer that's any good can imitate a style. They do it all the time. Look at all the parodies."

Wolfe nodded. "Of course. There have been many masters of parody in the world's literature. But you're overlooking a vital point. As I said, the three stories that were the basis of the first three claims *were all written by the same person.* Or, if you prefer, put it that a comparison of their texts would convince any qualified student of writing, an experienced editor or writer, that they were written by the same person.

You will either have to concede that or you will have to contend that when you wrote 'There Is Only Love' you either invented a style quite different from your normal style as in your book, or you parodied the style of someone else, call him Y; that when Simon Jacobs wrote 'What's Mine Is Yours' he parodied either Y or your story; and that when Jane Ogilvy wrote 'On Earth but Not in Heaven' she parodied either Y, or your story, which had not been published, or Simon Jacobs' story, also unpublished. That is patently preposterous. If you offered that fantasy in a courtroom the jury wouldn't even leave the box. Do you still maintain that you wrote 'There Is Only Love'?"

"Yes." But her tone was different and so were her eyes. "I have never seen those stories by Simon Jacobs and Jane Ogilvy. I still say you're bluffing."

"I have them here. Archie. Get them. Including Miss Porter's."

I went and got them from the safe and handed them to her, and stood there.

"Take your time," Wolfe told her. "We have all night."

Hers was on top. She only glanced at it, the first page, and put it on the stand beside the chair. The next one was "What's Mine Is Yours," by Simon Jacobs. She read the first page and part of the second, and put it on top of hers on the stand. With "On Earth but Not in Heaven," by Jane Ogilvy, she finished the first page but didn't even glance at the second. As she put it down I circled around her chair to get them, but Wolfe told me to leave them, saying that she might want to inspect them further.

He regarded her. "So you know I'm not bluffing."

"I haven't said so."

"You have indicated it by your cursory examination of those manuscripts. Either study them as they deserve or yield the point."

"I'm not yielding anything. You said you have an offer. What is it?"

His tone sharpened. "First the threat. A double threat. There is good ground, I think, for Ellen Sturdevant to bring an action against you for libel and for recovery of the money she paid you. Legal points on the rules of evidence would be involved, and I am not a lawyer. But I am certain that Amy Wynn can successfully sue you for libel and can also have you charged with attempted extortion, a criminal offense."

"Let her try. She wouldn't dare."

"I think she would. Also I have read your letter to the Victory Press, in which you demanded payment from them as well as Amy Wynn. When I explain the situation to Mr. Imhof as I have explained it to you, I shall suggest that he take steps to have you charged with attempted extortion, either jointly with Miss Wynn or independently.

I'm sure he won't hesitate. He resents the planting of the manuscript in his office."

She was impressed at last. She opened her mouth and closed it again. She swallowed. She bit her lip. Finally she spoke. "The manuscript wasn't planted."

"Really, Miss Porter." Wolfe shook his head. "If you have any wits at all you must know that won't do. Do you wish to examine those stories further?"

"No."

"Then take them, Archie."

I went and got them, put them in the safe, and closed the door. As I returned to my desk Wolfe was resuming. "So much for the threats. Now for the offer. One: I will not advise Ellen Sturdevant to bring an action against you. It's possible she will do so of her own accord, but I won't instigate it. Two: I will prevail upon Miss Wynn and Mr. Imhof to bring no action against you, either civil or criminal. I'm sure I can. Those are the two items of my part of the bargain. Your part also has two items. One: you will renounce your claim against Amy Wynn and the Victory Press, in writing. Not a confession of wrongdoing; merely a renunciation of the claim because it was made in error. It will be drawn by a lawyer. Two: you will tell me X's name. That's all I ask; you need not—"

"I don't know any X."

"Pfui. You need not furnish any evidence or particulars; I'll get them myself. Nothing in writing; merely tell me his name and where to find him. I am not supposing that you know anything of his conspiracies with Simon Jacobs and Jane Ogilvy and Kenneth Rennert, or of his killing them; I am willing to assume your total ignorance of those events. Just tell me the name of the man or woman who wrote 'There Is Only Love.' "

"I wrote it."

"Nonsense. That won't do, Miss Porter."

"It will have to do." Her hands were in her lap, tightly clasped, and there was sweat on her forehead. "The other part, about the Victory Press and Amy Wynn, all right, I'll do that. If they'll sign a paper not to sue me or have me prosecuted or anything, I'll sign one giving up my claim because I made it in error. I still don't think you could prove what you said you could. Maybe you're not bluffing, but you can't prove anything just by showing there's something similar about the way those stories were written. If you want to think there's an X somewhere, I can't help that, but I can't tell you his name if I don't know anything about him."

I was focused on her. I wouldn't have supposed she was such a good liar. I was thinking that no matter how good you think you are at sizing people up, you can never be sure how well a certain specimen can do a certain thing until you see him try. Or her. I was also thinking that the screw we had thought would squeeze it out of her apparently wasn't going to work without more pressure, and how would Wolfe give it another turn? Evidently, since he wasn't speaking, he was asking the same question, and I moved my eyes to him.

And got a surprise. He not only wasn't speaking; he wasn't looking. He was leaning back with his eyes closed and his lips moving. He was pushing out his lips, puckered, and drawing them in—out and in, out and in. He only does that, and always does it, when he has found the crack he has been looking for, or thinks he has found it, and is trying to see through; and as I say, I was surprised. It shouldn't have been such a strain on his brain to figure out how to bear down on Alice Porter; he simply had to show her what she was in for if he made good on his threats. I looked back at her. She had got a handkerchief from her bag and was wiping her brow.

Wolfe opened his eyes, straightened up, and cocked his head. "Very well, Miss Porter," he said. "You can't tell me what you don't know, assuming that you really don't. I'll have to reexamine my conjectures and my conclusions. You'll hear from me again when I have conferred with Miss Wynn and Mr. Imhof. They will surely agree to the proposed arrangement. Mr. Goodwin will drive you home. Archie?"

So the strain on his brain had been something else, I had no idea what. Whenever that happens, when he goes off somewhere out of sight, I am not supposed to yodel at him, especially with company present, so I got to my feet and asked if there were any errands on the way, and he said no. Alice Porter was going to say something and decided not to. When I held her jacket she missed the armhole twice, and I admit it could have been partly my fault. My mind was occupied. It was starting back over the conversation, her part of it, trying to spot what had opened up a crack for Wolfe.

It was still trying three hours and twenty minutes later, at half past two in the morning, when I mounted the stoop of the old brownstone and let myself in. At one point on the way back, as I was rolling along on the parkway, I had thought I had it. Alice Porter was X. When she had written the first one, "There Is Only Love," she had used another style, as different as she could make it from her own style in her book. But there were three things wrong with that. First, if she had been slick enough to make up a style for the first one, why hadn't she made up other styles for the other two instead of copying that one? Second, why had she used her own style for "Opportunity Knocks," the one she had used on Amy Wynn? Third, what had she said that gave Wolfe so strong a suspicion that she was X that he called a halt and started on his lip routine? I had to try again, and was still at it when I got home.

There was a note on my desk for me:

AG:

Saul, Fred, Orrie, Miss Bonner, and Miss Corbett will come at eight in the morning and come to my room. I have taken $1000 from the safe to give them for expenses. You will not be needed. You will of course sleep late.

NW

Wolfe has his rules and I have mine. I absolutely refuse to permit any wear and tear on my brain after my head hits the pillow. Usually it works automatically, but that night a little discipline was needed. It took me a full three minutes to fade out.

17

In bed at three and out of it at ten Wednesday morning, I was an hour short of my regular requirement of eight hours' sleep, but with Wolfe working his lips and giving up on Alice Porter and arranging a before-breakfast session with the hired hands, all five of them, it looked as if we were getting set for a showdown, and in that case I should be willing to make a major personal sacrifice, so I rolled out at ten. Also I made it snappy showering and dressing and eating breakfast, and got to the office at 11:15, only a quarter of an hour after Wolfe got down from the plant rooms. He was at his desk with the morning mail. I went and sat and watched him slit envelopes. His hands are quick and accurate, and he would be good at manual labor provided he could do it sitting down. I asked if he wanted help and he said no. I asked if there were any instructions.

"Perhaps." He quit slitting and looked up. "After we discuss a matter."

"Good. I guess I'm awake enough to discuss if it's not too complicated. First I'll report my conversation with Alice Porter during our drive to Carmel. At one point she said, 'I never drive at night on account of my eyes. It gives me a headache.' That's the crop. Not another word. I made no advances because after the way you suddenly quit on her I had no idea where to poke. Next, it wouldn't hurt if I had some notion of what Saul and Fred and Orrie and Dol Bonner and Sally Corbett are up to. So that when they call in I'll know what they're talking about."

"They'll report to me."

"I see. Like that again. What I don't know won't hurt you."

"What you don't know will make no demands on your powers of dissimulation." He put the letter-opener down. It was a knife with a horn handle that had been thrown at him in 1954, in the cellar of an old border fort in Albania, by a man named Bua. The Marley .38 with which I had shot Bua was in a drawer of my desk. He continued, "Besides, you won't be here. I have made an assumption which was prompted by the question, why is Alice Porter alive? Why did X remove the other three so expeditiously and make no attempt to remove her? And why is she so cocksure that she is in no danger? Alone in that secluded house, with no companion but a dog that dotes on strangers, she shows no trepidation whatever, though X could be lurking at her door or behind a bush by day or by night. Why?"

I flipped a hand. "Any one of a dozen reasons. The best is the simplest. Also it's been done so often that she wouldn't have to invent it. She wrote a detailed account of how she and X put the bite on Ellen Sturdevant, probably saying it was X's idea, and put it in an envelope. She also put in the envelope things that would corroborate it, for instance something in X's handwriting, maybe a couple of letters he had written her; that would make it better. She sealed the envelope thoroughly with wax and tape, and wrote on it, 'To be opened on my death and not before,' and signed it. Then she deposited it with somebody she was sure she could trust to follow the instructions, and she told X about it, probably sending him or giving him a copy of what she had written. So X was up a stump. It was done first about three thousand B.C., and maybe a million times since, but it still works. It has saved the lives of thousands of blackmailers, and also of a lot of fine citizens like Alice Porter." I flipped a hand again. "I like that best, but of course there are others."

He grunted. "That one will do. That's the assumption I have made. I think it highly probable. So where is the envelope?"

I raised a brow. "Probably somewhere in the United States, and there are now fifty of them. I doubt if she sent it out of the country. Do you want me to find it?"

"Yes."

I got up. "Are you in a hurry?"

"Don't clown. If such an envelope exists, and I strongly suspect that it does, I want to know where it is. If we can get our hands on it, all the better, but merely to locate it would be enough. Where would you start?"

"I'd have to think it over. Her bank, her lawyer if she has one, her pastor if she goes to church, a relative or an intimate friend—"

"Much too diffuse. It would take days. You might get a hint, or even better than a hint, from that executive secretary, Cora Ballard. Alice Porter joined that association in nineteen fifty-one, was dropped for nonpayment of dues in nineteen fifty-four, and rejoined in nineteen fifty-six. I gathered that Miss Ballard is extremely well informed about the members, and presumably she will help if she can. See her."

"Okay. She may not be enthusiastic. She wanted them to fire you. But I suppose she'll—"

The doorbell rang. I stepped to the hall, took a look through the one-way glass panel, and turned to tell Wolfe, "Cramer." He made a face and growled, "I have nothing for him." I asked if I should tell him that and ask him to come back tomorrow, and he said yes, and then said, "Confound it, he'll be after me all day and you won't be here. Let him in."

I went to the front and opened the door and got a shock, or rather, a series of shocks. Cramer said, "Good morning," distinctly, as he crossed the threshold, plainly implying that I was a fellow being. Then he dropped his hat on the bench and waited while I closed the door, instead of tramping on to the office. Then he not only told Wolfe good morning but asked him how he was. Evidently it was Brotherhood Day. I had to control an impulse to slap him on the back or poke him in the ribs. To cap it, he said as he sat in the red leather chair, "I hope you won't be charging me rent for this chair." Wolfe said politely that a guest was always welcome to a seat to rest his legs, and Cramer said, "And a glass of beer?"

It was a ticklish situation. If Wolfe pushed the button, the beer signal, two shorts and a long, Fritz would get a wrong impression and there would have to be an explanation. He looked at me, and I got up and went to the kitchen, got a tray and a bottle and a glass, telling Fritz it was for a guest, and returned. As I entered Cramer was saying, ". . . but I never expected to see the day when you would cut down on your beer. What next? Thank you, Goodwin." He poured. "What I'm here for, I came to apologize. One day last week—Friday, I think it was—I accused you of using Jane Ogilvy for a decoy and bungling it. I may have been wrong. If you or Goodwin told anybody you were going after her he's not admitting it. And Kenneth Rennert was killed that same night, and you certainly wouldn't have set them both up. So I owe you an apology." He picked up the glass and drank.

"It's welcome," Wolfe told him. "All the more since you owe me a dozen other apologies that you have never made. Let this one do for all."

"You're so goddam impervious." Cramer put the glass down on the stand. "Instead of coming to apologize, I could have come to tell you to stop interfering with a homicide investigation. You sent Goodwin to Putnam County to coerce a woman into coming to see you, a woman who was under surveillance by officers of the law."

"Possibly you did."

"Did what?"

"Come for that purpose. There was no coercion."

"The hell there wasn't. She went to the sheriff's office in Carmel this morning and told him to keep his men away from her place, and she said that Goodwin had told her that Sergeant Stebbins had sicked Putnam County on her because he suspected her of murder, and she had better go with him to see you, and go quick. That's not coercion?" He looked at me. "Did you tell her that?"

"Sure I did. Why not? Have you crossed her off?"

"No." He went to Wolfe. "He admits it. I call that interfering in a murder investigation, and so would any judge. And this is once too often. I'm being fair. I have apologized for accusing you of something I can't prove. But by God, I can prove this."

Wolfe put his palms on the chair arms. "Mr. Cramer. I know, of course, what you're after. You have no intention or desire to charge me formally with obstructing justice; that would be both troublesome and futile. What you want is to learn whether I got any information that would help you in a case that has you baffled; and if I did, you want to know what it is. I'm willing to oblige you, and to the full. As you know, Mr. Goodwin has an extraordinary memory. Archie. Give Mr. Cramer our conversation with Miss Porter last evening. In toto. Omit nothing."

I shut my eyes for a moment to concentrate. Getting it straight with no fumbling would be a little tricky, with all the names and titles and dates, and the way Wolfe had steered it along to the main point. Evidently, for some reason, he wanted Cramer to have it all, and I didn't want him stopping me to insert something I was leaving out. I started slow, speeded up when I got going, and tripped only once, when I said "extortion" instead of "attempted extortion," and I caught that and corrected it. Toward the end, knowing that I had it by the tail, I leaned back and crossed my legs just to show that there was really nothing to it for a man of my caliber. Finishing, I yawned. "Sorry," I said, "but I'm a little short on sleep. Did I skip anything?"

"No," Wolfe said. "Satisfactory." His eyes went to Cramer. "So you have it, every word. There was manifestly no attempt to interfere with a homicide investigation; murder was mentioned only incidentally. You are welcome to the information I got from her."

"Yeah." Cramer didn't sound grateful. "I could put it under a fingernail. She didn't tell you a single solitary thing. And I don't believe it, and you don't expect me to. Why did you let her go? You had her. You had her backed into a corner that she couldn't possibly squirm out of, and you quit and sent her home. Why?"

Wolfe turned a hand over. "Because nothing more was to be expected of her, at the moment. She had identified X for me. More accurately, she had given me a hint, a strong one, and I wanted to confirm it. I have done so. Now that I know him, or her, the rest should be easy."

Cramer took a cigar from his pocket, stuck it in his mouth, and clamped his teeth on it. I wasn't as impressed as he was, since the second I had seen Wolfe lean back and shut his eyes and start his lips going I had known there would soon be some fireworks, though I hadn't expected anything quite so showy. Not caring to have Cramer know that this development was as new to me as to him, I yawned again.

Cramer removed the cigar. "You mean that, do you? You know who killed Simon Jacobs and Jane Ogilvy and Kenneth Rennert?"

Wolfe shook his head. "I haven't said so. I know who wrote those stories and instigated the plagiarism claims. You're investigating a series of murders; I'm investigating a series of frauds. I have my X and you have yours. True, the two Xs are the same person, but I need only expose a swindler; it will be your job to expose a murderer."

"You know who he is?"

"Yes."

"And you got it from what Alice Porter told you last night? And Goodwin has repeated all of it?"

"Yes. I have confirmed the hint she gave me."

Cramer's fingers had closed on the cigar, which was probably no longer fit for chewing, let alone smoking. "Okay. That's not your kind of lie. What was the hint?"

"You have heard it." Wolfe's fingertips met at the peak of his middle mound. "No, Mr. Cramer. Surely that's enough. I asked Mr. Goodwin to repeat that conversation, and I told you it contained a disclosure of the identity of X, only because I felt I owed you something and I don't like to be in debt. I know what it cost you to tender me an apology. Even though you did it in desperation, because you're stumped, and even though you immediately reverted to your customary manner, it took great will power and I appreciate it. So now we're even. You know everything that I know, and it will be interesting to see whether you get your murderer first, or I my swindler."

Cramer stuck the cigar in his mouth, learned too late that it was in shreds, jerked it out and threw it at my wastebasket, and missed by two feet.

A while back, when it took me nearly two hours to spot the screw Wolfe was going to use on Alice Porter, I remarked that you had probably seen it and thought me as dumb as they come, and now of course you are thinking that Cramer and I were both dumb, since you have almost certainly caught on to the hint Wolfe had got from Alice Porter and you now know who X was. But you're reading it, and Cramer and

I were in it. If you don't believe that makes a big difference, try it once. Anyhow, even though you now know X's name, you may be curious to see how Wolfe nailed him—or her. So I'll go on.

When Cramer left, some ten minutes later, he wasn't curious because there wasn't room enough in him for it. He was too damn sore. When I stepped back into the office after going to the hall to see that he didn't forget to cross the sill before he shut the door, the phone was ringing and I went and got it. It was Saul Panzer. He asked for Wolfe, and Wolfe, lifting his receiver, told me, "You might catch Miss Ballard before she goes to lunch."

I may not be much at hints, but I got that one. I departed.

18

Of all the thousands of ways of getting a credit mark from a woman, young or old, high on the list is to take her to lunch at Rusterman's, the restaurant that was owned and operated by Marko Vukčić when he died. Since Wolfe is still the trustee of the estate, there is always a table for me, and when Cora Ballard and I edged through the crowd to the green rope and Felix caught sight of me, he led us to the banquette at the left wall. As we sat and took our napkins Cora Ballard said, "If you're trying to impress me you're doing fine."

I'm all for Wolfe's rule not to discuss business at meals, but that time it couldn't be helped because she had to be back at her office by two-thirty for an appointment. So after we had taken a sip of our cocktails I said I supposed she knew a good deal about all of the NAAD members. No, she said, not all of them. Many of them lived in other parts of the country, and of those in the metropolitan area some were active in NAAD affairs and some weren't. How well did she know Alice Porter? Fairly well; she had always come to craft meetings until recently, and in 1954, when Best and Green had decided to publish her book, *The Moth That Ate Peanuts,* she had visited the NAAD office several times for advice on the contract.

Time out to get started on our ham timbales.

What I was after, I said, was a document that we had reason to believe Alice Porter had left in somebody's care. Did members deposit important documents with the NAAD for safekeeping? No, the association had no facilities for that kind of service. Did she have any idea with whom or where Alice Porter might leave something very important—for instance, an envelope to be opened if and when she died?

She had started a loaded fork to her mouth but stopped it. "I see," she said. "That might be pretty smart, if— What's in the envelope?"

"I don't know. I don't even know there is one. Detectives spend most of their time looking for things that don't exist. Mr. Wolfe thought it was possible she had left it with you."

"She didn't. If we started doing things like that for members we'd have to have a vault. But I might have some ideas. Let's see. . . . Alice Porter." She opened her mouth for the forkload.

She had six ideas:

1. Alice Porter's safe-deposit box, if she had one.

2. Mr. Arnold Green of Best and Green, who had published her book. He was one of the few publishers who liked to do favors for authors, even one whose book had been a flop.

3. Her father and mother, who lived somewhere on the West Coast, Miss Ballard thought in Oregon.

4. Her agent, if she still had one. Lyle Bascomb had taken her on after her book had been published, but he might have dropped her by now.

5. The woman who ran Collander House on West 82nd Street, the hive-home for girls and women who couldn't afford anything fancy, where Alice Porter had lived for several years. Her name was Garvin, Mrs. Something Garvin. One of the girls in the NAAD office was living there now. She was the kind of woman anybody would trust with anything.

6. The lawyer who handled her suit against Ellen Sturdevant. Cora Ballard couldn't remember his name, but I did, from the pile of paper I had waded through at the office.

Over the years I have chased a lot of wild geese, but that was about the wildest, asking a bunch of strangers about something that maybe didn't exist, and if it did maybe they had never heard of it, and if one of them had it why should he tell me? So I spent five hours at it. I tackled Lyle Bascomb, the agent, first, because his office was only a short walk from Rusterman's. He was out to lunch and would be back any minute. So I waited fifty minutes. He returned from lunch at 3:33, and his eyes were having a little trouble focusing. He had to think a minute before he could remember who Alice Porter was. Oh yes, that one. He had taken her on when she had a book published, but had dropped her when she made that plagiarism claim. I gathered from his tone that anyone who made a plagiarism claim was a louse.

At the lawyer's office I had to wait only thirty minutes, which was an improvement. He would be glad to help. When a lawyer says he will be glad to help he means that he will be glad to relieve you of any information you may have that he could ever possibly use, and at the same time will carefully refrain from burdening you with any information that you don't already have. That one wasn't even going to admit that he had ever heard of a woman named Alice Porter until I told him I had read three letters signed by him referring to her as his client. I finally pried it out of him that he hadn't seen her or communicated with her for some time. Two years? Three? He couldn't say definitely, but an extended period. As for the information he relieved me of, I will only say that I put him under no obligation.

It was after five o'clock when I arrived at the office of Best and Green, so it was a tossup whether I would catch him, but I did. The receptionist halted a lipstick operation long enough to tell me that Mr. Green was in conference, and I was asking her if she had any idea how long the conference would last, when a man appeared from within and headed for the door, and she called to him, "Mr. Green, someone to see you," and I went for him, pronouncing my name, and he said, "I'm making a train," and loped out. So, as I say, I caught him.

I had used up half of Cora Ballard's ideas. Of those left, two weren't very promising. There are about a thousand banks with safe-deposit vaults in New York, and anyway I didn't have keys to all the boxes, and besides, it was after hours. Taking a plane to the West Coast to look up Alice Porter's parents seemed a little headlong. Finding an empty taxi in midtown Manhattan at that time of day was almost as hopeless, but I finally grabbed one and gave the driver the address on West 82nd Street.

Collander House could have been worse. The girl in the neat little office had a vase of daisies on her desk, and the room across the hall, which she called the lounge, where she sent me to wait for Mrs. Garvin, had two vases of daisies, comfortable chairs, and rugs on the floor. Another thirty-minute wait. When Mrs. Garvin finally appeared, one straight look from her sharp gray eyes confirmed Cora Ballard's statement that anyone would trust her with anything. Certainly she remembered Alice Porter, who had lived there from August 1951 until May 1956. She had the dates in her head because she had looked them up at the request of a city detective last week, and had recalled them that morning because a woman had come and asked about Alice Porter. She hadn't seen Alice Porter for three years and was keeping nothing for her. Not even some little thing like an envelope? No. Which didn't mean a thing. She was a busy woman, and it was quicker to say no than to explain that it was none of my business and have me trying to persuade her that it was. A lie isn't a lie if it is in reply to a question that the questioner has no right to ask.

All in all, a hell of an afternoon. Not one little crumb. And the immediate future was as bleak as the immediate past: another meatless dinner for Wolfe, after a beerless day. More gloom. He would be there at his desk, glaring into space, wallowing in it. As I climbed out of the taxi in front of the old brownstone I had a notion to go to Bert's diner around the corner and eat hamburgers and slaw and discuss the world situation for an hour or so, but, deciding it wouldn't be fair to deprive him of an audience, I mounted the stoop and used my key on the door; and, with one foot inside and one out, stopped and stared. Wolfe was emerging from the kitchen, carrying a large tray loaded with glasses. He turned in at the office. I brought my other foot in, shut the door, and proceeded.

I stood and looked it over. One of the yellow chairs was at the end of my desk. Six of them were in two rows facing Wolfe's desk. Five more of them were grouped over by the big globe. The table at the far wall was covered with a yellow cloth, and on it was an assortment of bottles. Wolfe was there, transferring the glasses from the tray to the table.

I spoke. "Can I help?"

"No. It's done."

"A big party, apparently."

"Yes. At nine o'clock."

"Have the guests all been invited?"

"Yes."

"Am I invited?"

"I was wondering where you were."

"Working. I found no envelope. Is Fritz disabled?"

"No. He is grilling a steak."

"The hell he is. Then the party's a celebration?"

"No. I am anticipating events by a few hours. I have a job ahead of me that I prefer not to tackle on an empty stomach."

"Do I get some of the steak?"

"Yes. There are two."

"Then I'll go up and comb my hair."

I went.

19

Wolfe, at his desk, put down his coffee cup and sent his eyes to the ex-chairman of the Joint Committee on Plagiarism. "I like my way better, Mr. Harvey," he said curtly. "You may ask questions when I finish if I haven't already answered them." His head went right, and left. "I could merely name the culprit and tell you that I have enough evidence to convict her, but while that would complete my job it wouldn't satisfy your curiosity."

Mortimer Oshin had the red leather chair ex officio. The committee members and the executive secretary had the six yellow chairs in front of Wolfe's desk. In the front row were Amy Wynn, nearest me, then Philip Harvey, and then Cora Ballard. In the rear were Reuben Imhof, Thomas Dexter, and Gerald Knapp—the three publishers. Grouped over by the big globe were Dol Bonner, Sally Corbett, Saul Panzer, Fred Durkin, and Orrie Cather. In a spot by herself, at the end of my desk, was Alice Porter, who was sipping root beer from a glass that was perfectly steady in her hand. I had coffee. The others had their choices —gin and tonic, scotch and soda, scotch and water, rye and ginger ale, bourbon on the rocks, and one, Oshin, cognac. Evidently Oshin knew brandy. After he had taken a sip he had asked if he might see the bottle and had studied the label thoroughly, and after another sip he had asked, "For God's sake, how much of this have you got?" I had taken the hint and given him a dividend, and he hadn't lit a cigarette for at least five minutes.

Wolfe's head went right and left again. "I should explain," he told them, "the reason for Miss Porter's outburst. It was justified. She is here because I lied to her. I told her on the phone that I was prepared to hand her a paper signed by Mr. Imhof and Miss Wynn in exchange for one signed by her. The word 'prepared' was a misrepresentation. When this discussion is ended I am confident that Miss Porter will be in no fear of prosecution by Mr. Imhof or Miss Wynn, but I was not actually 'prepared' when I phoned her this afternoon. In fairness to her

I must say that her indignation, when she arrived and found a crowd, was warranted. She stayed because I told her I was going to demonstrate to you that she was guilty of a criminal act and I advised her to hear me."

Alice Porter blurted, "You just admitted you're a liar!"

Wolfe ignored it. "I'll give you the essentials first," he told the committee, "and the conclusions I reached, and then fill in the details. A week ago yesterday, eight days ago, Mr. Goodwin gave you a full report of the brief talks he had had with those four people—Simon Jacobs, Kenneth Rennert, Jane Ogilvy, and Alice Porter. I don't know if any of you noticed that his talk with Miss Porter was quite remarkable—that is, her part of it. He told her that a New York newspaper was considering making her a substantial offer for the first serial rights to her story, and what did she say? That she would think it over. Beyond that, not a word. Not a question. All seven of you know writers better than I do, but I know a little of men and women. Miss Porter was not a famous and successful author; her only book had been a failure; her stories were barely sufficient, in quantity and quality, to preserve her standing as a professional. But she didn't even ask Mr. Goodwin the name of the newspaper. She asked him nothing. I thought that remarkable. Did none of you?"

"I did," Cora Ballard said. "But she was on a spot. I thought she was just scared."

"Of what? If she doubted Mr. Goodwin's bona fides, if she suspected that he might not have such an offer from a newspaper, why didn't she question him? At the very least, why didn't she ask him the name of the newspaper? It seemed to me a fair surmise that she didn't doubt or suspect Mr. Goodwin; she *knew* he was lying. She knew that this committee had hired me, and that he was trying by subterfuge to get a copy of the story on which she had based her claim against Miss Wynn. At the moment—"

"How could she know?" Harvey demanded. "Who told her?"

Wolfe nodded. "Of course that was the point. At the moment the surmise was only of minor interest, but the next day, when it was learned that Simon Jacobs had been murdered, it took on weight; and more weight when Jane Ogilvy too was killed; and still more when Kenneth Rennert made it three—and Alice Porter was still alive. Attention was focused on her, but I continued to doubt that she was the target because I could not believe that she had invented a style of composition for 'There Is Only Love' for her claim against Ellen Sturdevant, and imitated it for 'What's Mine Is Yours' for the claim made by Simon Jacobs against Richard Echols, and again imitated it for 'On

Earth but Not in Heaven' for the claim made by Jane Ogilvy against Marjorie Lippin, and then abandoned it and used her natural style for 'Opportunity Knocks' for the claim made by her against Amy Wynn. But last evening—"

Mortimer Oshin cut in, "Wait a minute. What if she knew how that would look?" There was still a little cognac in his glass, and he still hadn't lit a cigarette.

"Just so, Mr. Oshin. Last evening Mr. Goodwin brought her here, and after an hour with her I asked that question myself. What if she had been shrewd enough to realize in advance, at the time she enlisted Simon Jacobs in the plot against Richard Echols, that the best shield against suspicion would be a modus operandi so fantastic that she would not even be considered? After an hour with her I thought it possible that such superlative cunning was not beyond her; at least it was worth exploring. When she had gone I spent an hour on the telephone, getting five people, highly competent detectives who help me on occasion; and when they came at eight o'clock this morning I gave them assignments. They are present and I wish to introduce them. If you will please turn your heads?"

They twisted around.

"In front at the left," Wolfe told them, "is Miss Theodolinda Bonner. Beside her is Miss Sally Corbett. In the rear at the left is Mr. Saul Panzer, next to him is Mr. Fred Durkin, and at the right is Mr. Orrie Cather. I should explain that before they went on their separate errands they were supplied with photographs of Alice Porter, procured by Mr. Panzer at a newspaper office. I'm going to ask them to report to you. Mr. Cather?"

Orrie got up and went to the corner of Wolfe's desk and stood facing the committee. "My job," he said, "was to find out if she had ever been in contact with Simon Jacobs. Of course the best place to start was with the widow. I went to the apartment on Twenty-first Street and there was no one there. I asked around among the other tenants, and I—"

"Briefly, Orrie. Just the meat."

"Yes, sir. I finally found her at a friend's house in New Jersey. She didn't want to talk, and I had a time with her. I showed her the photograph, and she recognized it. She had seen the subject twice about three years ago. The subject had come to the apartment to see her husband and had stayed quite a while both times, two hours or more. She didn't know what they had talked about. Her husband had told her it was about some stories for a magazine. I tried to get her more exact on the time, but the closest she could come was that it was in the spring of nineteen fifty-six and the two visits were about three weeks apart. Her husband hadn't told her the name of the subject.

Wolfe asked, "Was her recognition of the photograph at all doubtful?"

"No, she was positive. She recognized it right away. She said she—"

Alice Porter blurted, "You're a liar! I never went to see Simon Jacobs! I never saw him anywhere!"

"You'll get a turn, Miss Porter," Wolfe told her. "As long a turn as you want. That will do, Orrie. Miss Corbett?"

Sally Corbett was one of the two women who, a couple of years back, had made me feel that there might be some flaw in my attitude toward female dicks. The other one was Dol Bonner. Their physical characteristics, including their faces, were quite different, but were both of a description that makes a woman looked at from a personal viewpoint; and they were good operatives. Sally went and took Orrie's place at the corner of Wolfe's desk, turned her head to look at him, got a nod, and faced the audience.

"My job was the same as Mr. Cather's," she said, "except that it was with Jane Ogilvy instead of Simon Jacobs. I didn't get to see Mrs. Ogilvy, Jane's mother, until this afternoon. I showed her the photograph and asked her if she had ever seen the subject. After studying it she said she was pretty sure she had. She said that one day more than two years ago the subject had come to see her daughter, and they had gone to the cloister. If you have read the newspapers you know about the building that Jane called the cloister. In half an hour or so they returned to the house because the electric heater in the cloister was out of order. They went up to Jane's room and were there for three hours or more. Mrs. Ogilvy didn't learn the subject's name and never saw her again. By association with other matters she figured that it was in February nineteen fifty-seven that the subject had come to see her daughter. She didn't make the identification positive, but she said she could, one way or the other, if she saw the subject in person instead of a photograph."

I turned my head for a look at Alice Porter. She was on the edge of the chair, rigid, her eyes half closed, her head thrust forward, and her lips parted with the tip of her tongue showing. She was looking at Wolfe, oblivious of the eight pairs of eyes, including mine, that were aimed at her. When Sally Corbett returned to her chair and Fred Durkin took her place at the corner of Wolfe's desk, Alice Porter's gaze didn't leave Wolfe, even when Fred spoke.

"I had Kenneth Rennert," Fred said, "and the trouble was there wasn't any widow or mother or anyone like that. I saw about twenty people, other tenants in the building and the building superintendent, and friends and acquaintances, but none of them recognized the subject from the photograph. From two or three of them I got a steer to a restaurant on Fifty-second Street, the Pot-au-Feu, where Rennert often ate lunch and sometimes dinner, and that was the only place I got anything at all. One of the waiters, the one that had the table where Rennert usually sat, thought the subject had been there twice with Rennert, once for lunch and once for dinner. He was cagey. Of course he knew Rennert had been murdered. He might have opened up more if I had slipped him a twenty, but of course that was out. He thought it had been in the late winter or spring last year. He thought if he saw the subject he could tell better than from a photograph. He had liked Rennert. The only reason he talked at all was because I told him it might help to get the murderer. I think if he was sure of that and if he saw the subject in person—"

Wolfe stopped him. "That will serve, Fred. The ifs are ahead of us. Mr. Panzer?" As Fred went back to his chair and Saul came forward, Wolfe told the committee, "I should explain that Mr. Panzer's assignment was of a different nature. It was given to him because it required illegal entry to a private dwelling. Yes, Saul?"

The committee had Saul's profile because he was turned to face Alice Porter. "Yesterday evening," he said, "as instructed, I drove to Alice Porter's home near Carmel, arriving at twelve minutes past ten. I opened the door with a key, one of an assortment I had, and entered, and made a search. On a shelf in a cupboard I found some sheets of paper with typewriting, clipped together, twenty-five pages. The first page was headed 'Opportunity Knocks,' and below that it said 'By Alice Porter.' It was an original, not a carbon. I have delivered it to Mr. Wolfe."

He glanced at Wolfe, and Wolfe spoke. "It's here in a drawer of my desk. I have read it. In plot and characters and action it is identical with the story, 'Opportunity Knocks,' by Alice Porter, the manuscript of which was found in a file in the office of the Victory Press. But that one, the one found in the file, was written in Alice Porter's natural style, the style of her published book, *The Moth That Ate Peanuts,* whereas this one, the one found by Mr. Panzer in Miss Porter's house, was written in her assumed style, the one she had used for the three stories on which the previous claims had been based. Call them A and B. The obvious inference is that in writing the story that was to be the basis for her claim against Amy Wynn she had tried both styles, A and B, and had decided, for whatever reason, to use the one in style B. What else did you find, Saul?"

Saul's eyes were again on Alice Porter. "That was all in the house," he said. "But she had gone to New York with Mr. Goodwin in his car, so her car was there, and I searched it. Under the front seat, wrapped in newspaper, I found a knife, a kitchen knife with a black handle. Its blade is seven inches long and an inch wide. I have delivered it to Mr. Wolfe. If he has examined it with—"

He sprang forward. Alice Porter had bounced out of her chair and dived for Amy Wynn, her arms stretched and her fingers curved to claws. I was right there, so I had her right arm half a second before Saul got her left one, but she had moved so fast that the fingernails of her left hand got to Amy Wynn's face before we jerked her back. Philip Harvey, on Amy Wynn's right, had lunged forward to intervene, and Reuben Imhof, back of Amy Wynn, was on his feet, bending over her. Alice Porter was trying to wriggle loose, but Saul and I had her back against Wolfe's desk, and she gave it up and started yapping. She glared at Amy Wynn and yapped, "You dirty sneak, you double-crosser, you dirty sneak, you double—"

"Turn her around," Wolfe snapped. Saul and I obeyed. He eyed her. "Are you demented?" he demanded.

No answer. She was panting. "Why assault Miss Wynn?" he demanded. "She didn't corner you. I did."

She spoke. "I'm not cornered. Tell them to let go of me."

"Will you control yourself?"

"Yes."

Saul and I let go but stayed between her and Amy Wynn, and Harvey and Imhof were there too. She moved, back to her chair, and sat. She looked at Wolfe. "I don't know if you're in it with her," she said, "but if you are you'll regret it. She's a liar and a murderer and now she thinks she can frame me for it, but she can't. Neither can you. That's all lies about my seeing those people. I never saw any of them. And if that story was found in my house and that knife was found in my car she put them there. Or you did."

"Are you saying that Amy Wynn killed Simon Jacobs and Jane Ogilvy and Kenneth Rennert?"

"I am. I wish to God I had never seen her. She's a liar and a sneak and a double-crosser and a murderer, and I can prove it."

"How?"

"Don't worry, I can prove it. I've got the typewriter that she used to write that story, 'There Is Only Love,' when she got me to make that claim against Ellen Sturdevant. And I know how she planted it in a bureau drawer in Ellen Sturdevant's house. And that's all I'm going to tell you. And if you're in it with her you're going to regret it." She stood up, bumping me. "You get out of my way." Saul and I stayed put.

Wolfe's tone sharpened. "I'm not in it with her, Miss Porter. On the contrary, I'm in it with you, up to a point. I ask one question, and there's no reason why you shouldn't answer it. Did you write an account of your association with Miss Wynn, put it in an envelope, and entrust the envelope to someone with instructions that it was to be opened if and when you died?"

She stared. She sat down. "How did you know that?"

"I didn't. I surmised it. It was the simplest and best way to account for your remaining alive and not in trepidation. Where is it? You might as well tell me, now that its contents are no longer a secret. You have just revealed them, their essence. Where is it?"

"A woman named Garvin has it. Mrs. Ruth Garvin."

"Very well." Wolfe leaned back and took a breath. "It would have made things easier for both of us if you had been candid with me last evening. It would have saved me the trouble of all this hocus-pocus to force you to speak up. Miss Wynn did not put a manuscript in your house or a knife in your car. Mr. Panzer did not go there last evening. He spent the day composing and typing the kind of story he described because I thought you might demand to see it. He also bought the kind of knife he described."

Alice Porter was staring again. "Then that was all lies. Then you *were* in it."

Wolfe shook his head. "If by 'in it' you mean a conspiracy with Miss Wynn to make you pay for her crimes, no. If you mean a trap to force the truth out of you, yes. As for Mr. Cather and Miss Corbett and Mr. Durkin, they told no lies; they merely permitted you to infer that the photographs they showed to various people were of you, but they weren't. They were photographs of Amy Wynn—and by the way, we can now hear from Miss Bonner. You needn't leave your chair, Miss Bonner. Report briefly."

Dol Bonner cleared her throat. "I showed a photograph of Amy Wynn to the woman who runs Collander House on West Eighty-second Street, Mrs. Ruth Garvin. She said that Amy Wynn lived there for three months in the winter of nineteen fifty-four and fifty-five, and that Alice Porter also lived there at that time. Is that enough?"

"For the present, yes." Wolfe's eyes moved to take in his client, the committee. "That, I think, should suffice. I have established a link between Miss Wynn and each of her four accomplices. You have heard Miss Porter. If you wish, I can proceed to collect ample evidence to persuade a jury to convict Miss Wynn of her swindles, but it would be a waste of your money and my time, since she will go to trial not for extortion, but for murder, and that is not your concern. The police and the District Attorney will attend to that. As for—"

Reuben Imhof suddenly exploded. "I can't believe it!" he cried. "By God, I *can't* believe it!" He appealed to Amy Wynn. "For God's sake, Amy! Say something! Don't just sit there! Say something!"

I was back in my chair, and by stretching an arm I could have touched her. She hadn't moved a muscle since Wolfe had asked Alice Porter about the envelope. Her hands were pressed flat against her breasts, as if to hold them up, and her shoulders were pulled back, far back. Down her right cheek, from just below the eye almost to her jaw, were two red streaks where Alice Porter's nails had scraped. She paid no attention to Imhof and probably she didn't hear him. Her eyes were fixed on Wolfe. Her lips moved but there was no sound. Someone muttered something. Mortimer Oshin took his empty glass from the stand, went to the table at the far wall, poured a triple portion of brandy, took a swallow, and came back.

Amy Wynn spoke to Wolfe, her voice so low that it was just audible. "You knew that first day," she said. "The first time we came. Didn't you?"

Wolfe shook his head. "No, madam. I had no inkling. I am not clairvoyant."

"When did you know?" She might have been in a trance.

"Last evening. Alice Porter gave me the hint, unwittingly. When I showed her that her position was untenable and told her that I would advise you to prosecute, she was not concerned, she said you wouldn't dare, but when I added that I would also advise Mr. Imhof to prosecute she took alarm. That was highly suggestive. Upon consideration I sent her home, and I did something I might have done much sooner if there had been the faintest reason to suspect you. I read your book, *Knock at My Door,* or enough of it to conclude that you had written the stories on which the first three claims had been based. That was manifest from the characteristics of your style."

Her head moved, slowly, from side to side. "No," she said. "You knew before that. You knew the third time we were here. You said it was possible it was one of us."

"That was only talk. At that point anything was possible."

"I was sure you knew," she insisted. "I was sure you had read my book. That was what I'd been afraid of since the second time we came, when you told us about comparing the stories. That was when I realized how stupid I had been not to write them in a different style, but you see I didn't really know I had a style. I thought only good writers had a style. But I was stupid. That was my big mistake. Wasn't it?"

They were all staring at her, and no wonder. From her tone and her expression you might have thought Wolfe was conducting a class in the technique of writing and she was anxious to learn. "I doubt if it could properly be called a mistake," he said. "A little thoughtless, perhaps. After all, no one had ever compared the stories before I did, and I wouldn't have compared them with your book if I hadn't got that hint from Miss Porter. Indeed, Miss Wynn, I wouldn't say that you made any mistakes at all."

"Of course I did." She was quietly indignant. "You're just being polite. All my life I've been making mistakes. The biggest one was when I decided I was going to be a writer, but of course I was young then. You don't mind if I talk about it? I want to."

"Go ahead. But fourteen people are listening."

"It's you I want to talk to. I've been wanting to ever since the first time we came and I thought you knew. If I had talked to you then I wouldn't have had to—to do what I did. But I didn't think you would say I didn't make any mistakes. I shouldn't have told Alice about you. You told us when you started, I mean when you started today, that she gave it away that she knew about our hiring you when Mr. Goodwin told her he had an offer from a newspaper, and so your attention was focused on her. But I had made the worst mistake with her before that, when she claimed my book was plagiarized from a story she wrote. Of course I know that was poetic justice. I know I deserved it. But after so many years, when I actually had a book published, and the first printing sold out, and then three more printings, and it was actually third on the best-seller list, and then my publisher got that letter from Alice, I lost my head. That was an awful mistake. I should have told her I wouldn't pay her anything, not a cent. I should have dared her to try to make me. But I was so scared I gave in to her. Wasn't that a mistake?"

Wolfe grunted. "If so, not an egregious one. She had the upper hand—especially after the manuscript of her story was found in a file in your publisher's office."

"But that was part of the mistake, my putting it there. She made me. She said if I didn't she would tell everything—about the claim against Ellen Sturdevant, and of course that would bring it out about the others. And she told me—"

"My God." Reuben Imhof groaned. He had gripped her arm. "Amy, look at me. Damn it, look at me! *You* put that manuscript in that file?"

"You're hurting my arm," she said.

"Look at me! You did that?"

"I'm talking to Mr. Wolfe."

"Incredible." He groaned again. He let go of her arm. "Absolutely incredible."

Wolfe asked, "You were saying, Miss Wynn?"

"I was saying that she told me about what she had put in an envelope and left with somebody to be opened if she died. I don't see how you can say I didn't make any mistakes. I hadn't realized how dangerous it was for her to have the typewriter I used to write that story for her to use, 'There Is Only Love.' We thought it would be a good idea for her to have it because she was supposed to have written the story, but I hadn't realized that it could be traced to me because I had bought it. I had bought it secondhand, but typewriters have numbers on them somewhere. You can't say I didn't make any mistakes. You ought to say I didn't do anything right. Did I?"

"If by 'right' you mean 'well,' you did indeed."

"What? What did I do well? Tell me."

"It would take an hour, Miss Wynn. You did a thousand things well. Your conception and execution of the swindles were impeccable, providing for all details and avoiding all pitfalls. Your choice of accomplices was admirable. Your handling of the situation these past two weeks has been superb. I have had some experience with people under stress wearing masks, both men and women, and I have never seen finer performances than yours—the first time you called on me with your fellow committee members, two weeks ago today, when I questioned you at some length; the second time, when Mr. Oshin made his suggestion about Simon Jacobs and asked you to contribute ten thousand dollars; later that day at Mr. Imhof's office when Mr. Goodwin was told of the discovery of the manuscript which you had yourself put in the file; the third time you came with the committee, when the question whether to dismiss me was debated; the meeting of that council yesterday, when that question was again discussed in my presence—your performance on all of those occasions was extraordinary."

Wolfe turned a palm up. "On one occasion you showed ready and notable wit—on Friday, four days ago, when Miss Porter drove to New York to see you at your apartment. By then, of course, she was confronting you with a direr menace than exposure of your swindles; she was threatening to reveal you as a murderer. That is true?"

"Yes. That's why she came to see me. How did I show any wit?"

Wolfe shook his head. "Mr. Imhof used the right word for you, Miss Wynn. 'Incredible.' Apparently you have performed prodigies of sagacity and finesse without knowing it. Not surely by inadvertence; it must be that your singular faculties operate below the level of consciousness—or above it. Perhaps the psychologists should add a new term, superconscious. When Miss Porter came to your apartment on Friday afternoon did she tell you that she had been followed?"

"No. But I was afraid that maybe she had been."

"That makes it even better. Brilliant. So you telephoned Mr. Imhof and told him Miss Porter was there with an offer to settle her claim, and asked his advice. You don't call that brilliant?"

"Of course not." She meant it. "It was just common sense."

Wolfe shook his head again. "You are beyond me. Added to your other achievements, you committed three murders in an emergency with such resourcefulness and dexterity that a highly skilled police force is completely at sea. I offer a suggestion. I suggest that you request the District Attorney to arrange for your brain to be turned over to competent scientists. I shall myself suggest it to Mr. Cramer of the police. Will you do that?"

A sound came from Cora Ballard, half gasp and half moan. It was the first sound from any of them except Imhof since Dol Bonner had reported. No one looked at her. No one was looking at anyone but Amy Wynn.

"You're just being polite," Amy Wynn said. "If I had any brains this wouldn't be happening. It's crazy to say I didn't make any mistakes."

"You made one," Wolfe said. "Only one of any consequence. You shouldn't have allowed the committee to hire me. I don't know how you could have managed it, but I don't know how you have managed any of your miracles, and you don't either. If it had occurred to you, you would have done it somehow. I am not crowing; I merely say that it is unlikely that anyone else would have hit upon the combination of maneuvers by which you have been exposed. You wanted to talk. Have you anything else to say?"

Her nose twitched. "You have never shaken hands with me."

"I rarely shake hands with anyone. I beg you not to offer yours."

"Oh, I wouldn't expect you to now." She stood up. "No, there's nothing else. I have some things to do before I—I have some things to do." She was moving.

She *was* incredible. I was absolutely glued to my chair. I don't say that if there had been only the three of us, Wolfe and her and me, I would have sat there and let her walk out, but the fact remains that I didn't stir. She passed, in no hurry, in front of Philip Harvey and between Cora Ballard and Mortimer Oshin; and when, four paces from the door, she found her way blocked by Saul and Fred and Orrie, she turned square around and looked at Wolfe. Just looked. No more talk. Her nose twitched.

Wolfe turned his head to me. "Get Mr. Cramer, Archie."

Another sound came from Cora Ballard, louder than before, as I swiveled to get the phone.

Triple Jeopardy

Home to Roost

I

"Our nephew Arthur was the romantic type," said Mrs. Benjamin Rackell with the least possible movement of her thin tight lips. "He thought being a Communist was romantic."

Nero Wolfe, behind his desk in his outsized chair that thought nothing of his seventh of a ton, scowled at her. I, at my own desk with a notebook and pen, permitted myself a private grin, not unsympathetic. Wolfe was controlling himself under severe provocation. The appointment for Mr. Rackell to call at Wolfe's office on the ground floor of his old brownstone house on West Thirty-fifth Street, at six p.m., had been made by phone by a secretary in the office of the Rackell Importing Company, and nothing had been said about a wife coming along. And the wife, no treat as a spectacle to begin with, was an interrupter and a cliché tosser, enough to make Wolfe scowl at any man, let alone a woman.

"But," he objected, not too caustic, "you say that he was not a Communist, that, on the contrary, he was acting for the FBI when he joined the Communist party."

He would have loved to tell her to get lost. But his house had five stories, counting the basement and the plant rooms full of orchids on the roof, and there was Fritz the chef and Theodore the botanist and me, Archie Goodwin, the fairly confidential assistant, with nothing to carry the load but his income as a private detective; and the Rackell check for three thousand bucks, offered as a retainer, was under a paperweight on his desk.

"That's just it," Mrs. Rackell said impatiently. "Isn't it romantic to work for the FBI? But that wasn't why he did it; he did it to serve his country, and that's why they killed him. His being the romantic type had nothing to do with it."

Wolfe made a face and undertook to bypass her. His eyes went to Rackell. She would probably have called her husband the stubby type, with his short arms and legs, but he was no runt. His trunk was long and broad and his head long and narrow. His eyes pointed down at the corners, and so did his mouth, making him look mournful.

Wolfe asked him, "Have you spoken with the FBI, Mr. Rackell?"

But the wife answered. "No, he hasn't," she said. "I went myself yesterday, and I never heard anything to equal it. They wouldn't tell me a single thing. They wouldn't even admit Arthur was working for them as a spy for his country! They said it was a matter for the New York police and I should talk to them—as if I hadn't!"

"I told you, Pauline," Rackell said mildly but not timidly, "that the FBI won't tell people things. And the police won't either, not when it's murder, and especially when the Communists come into it. That's why I insisted on coming to Nero Wolfe to find out what's going on. If the FBI doesn't want it known that Arthur was with them, even if it means not getting his murderer, what else can you expect?"

"I expect justice!" Mrs. Rackell declared, her lips actually moving visibly.

I gave it a line to itself in the notebook.

Wolfe was frowning at Rackell. "There seems to be some confusion. I understood that you want a murder investigated. Now you say you came to me to find out what's going on. If you mean you want me to investigate the police and the FBI, that's too big a bite."

"I didn't say that," Rackell protested.

"No, but clear it up. What do you want?"

Rackell's down-pointing eyes looked even mournfuller. "We want facts," he declared. "I think the police and the FBI are quite capable of sacrificing the rights of a private citizen to what they consider the public interest. Our nephew was murdered, and my wife had a right to ask them what line they're proceeding on, and they wouldn't tell her. I don't intend to just let it go at that. Is this a democracy or isn't it? I'm not—"

"No!" the wife snapped. "It's not a democracy, it's a republic."

"I suggest," said Wolfe, exasperated, "that I recapitulate to see if I have it straight. I'll combine what I have read in the papers with what you have told me." He focused on the wife, probably figuring that she would be less apt to cut in if he held her eye. "Arthur Rackell, your husband's orphaned nephew, was a fairly efficient employee of his importing business, drawing a good salary, living at your home here in New York, on Sixty-eighth Street. Some three years ago you noted that he was taking a radically leftist position in discussions of political and social questions, and you remonstrated without effect. As time passed he became more leftist and more outspoken, until his opinions and arguments were identical with the Communist line. You, both you and your husband, argued with him and entreated him, but—"

"I did," Mrs. Rackell snapped. "My husband didn't."

"Now, Pauline," Rackell protested. "I argued with him some." He looked at Wolfe. "I didn't entreat him because I didn't think I had a right to. I don't believe in entreating people about their convictions. I was paying him a salary and I didn't want him to think he had to—" The importer fluttered a hand. "I liked Arthur, and he was my brother's son."

"In any case," Wolfe went on brusquely, still at the wife, "he did not change. He stubbornly adhered to the Communist position. He applauded the Communist attack in Korea and denounced the action of the United Nations. You finally found it insufferable and gave him an ultimatum: either he would abandon his outrageous—"

"Not an ultimatum," Mrs. Rackell corrected. "My husband refused to permit it. I merely—"

Wolfe outspoke her. "At least you made it plain that you had had enough and he was no longer welcome in your home. You must have made it fairly strong, since he was moved to disclose an extremely tight secret: that he had been persuaded by the FBI, back in nineteen forty-eight, to join the Communist party for the purpose of espionage. No easy admonition would have dragged that out of him, surely."

"I didn't say it was easy. I told him—" She stopped, and the thin lips really did tighten. She relaxed them enough to let words out. "I think he thought he would lose his job, and he was well paid. Much more than he earned, the amount of work he did."

Wolfe nodded. "Anyhow, he told you his secret, and you promised to keep it, becoming a confederate. Privately admiring him, with others you had to pretend to maintain your condemnation. You told your husband and no one else. That was about a week ago, you say?"

"Yes."

"And Saturday evening, three days ago, your nephew was murdered. Now to that. You have added little to what the papers have carried, but let's see. He left the apartment, your home, and took a taxi to Chezar's restaurant, where he had a dinner engagement. He had invited three women and two men to dine with him, and they were all there when he arrived, in the bar. When your nephew came they went with him to the table he had reserved and had cocktails. He took a small metal box from—"

"Gold."

"Gold is a metal, madam. He took it from a pocket, his side coat pocket, put it on the table, and left it there while he conferred with the waiter. There was conversation. When plates and rolls and butter were brought, the pillbox got pushed around. It was on the table altogether some ten or twelve minutes. When hors d'oeuvres were served, your nephew started to eat, remembered the pillbox, found it behind the basket of rolls, got from it a vitamin capsule, swallowed the capsule with a sip of water, and began on his hors d'oeuvres. Six or seven minutes later he suddenly cried out, sprang to his feet, overturning his chair, made convulsive gestures, became rigid, collapsed and crumpled to the floor, and died. A doctor arrived shortly, but he was already dead. It has been found that two other capsules in the metal box, similar in appearance to the one he took, contained what they were supposed to and were harmless; but your nephew had swallowed potassium cyanide. He was murdered by replacing a vitamin capsule with a capsule filled with poison."

"Certainly. That's what—"

"I'll go on, please. You were and are convinced that the substitution was made by one of his dinner companions who is a Communist and who learned that your nephew was acting for the FBI, and you so informed Inspector Cramer of the police. You were not satisfied with his acceptance of that information, especially in a subsequent talk with him yesterday morning, Monday, and went yourself to the office of the FBI, saw a Mr. Anstrey, and found him noncommittal. He took the position that a homicide in Manhattan is the business of the New York police. Exasperated, you went to Inspector Cramer's office, were unable to see him, talked with a sergeant named Stebbins, came away further exasperated, regarded with favor your husband's suggestion, made this morning, that I be consulted, and here you are. Have I left out anything important?"

"One little point." Rackell cleared his throat. "Our telling Inspector Cramer about Arthur's joining the Communist party for the FBI—that was in confidence. Of course this talk with you is confidential too, naturally, since we're your clients."

Wolfe shook his head. "Not yet. You want to hire me to investigate the death of your nephew?"

"Yes. Certainly."

"Then you should know that while no one excels me in discretion I will not work under restrictions."

"That's fair enough."

"Good. I'll let you know tomorrow, probably by noon." Wolfe reached to push the paperweight aside and pick up the check. "Shall I keep this meanwhile and return it if I can't take the job?"

Rackell frowned, perplexed. His wife snapped, "Why on earth couldn't you take it?"

"I don't know, madam. I hope to. I need the money. But I'll have to look into it a little—discreetly, of course. I'll let you know tomorrow at the latest." He extended a hand with the check. "Unless you prefer to take this and try elsewhere."

They didn't like it, especially her. She even left the red leather chair to take the check, her lips tight, but after some give-and-take with her husband they decided to let it ride, and she put the check back on the desk. They wanted to give us more details, especially about their nephew's five dinner guests, but Wolfe said that could wait, and they left, none too pleased. As I let them out at the front door Rackell gave me a polite thank-you nod, but she didn't even know I was there.

Returning to the office, I got the check and put it in the safe and then stood to regard Wolfe. His nose was twitching. He looked as if he had an oyster with horseradish on it in his mouth, a combination he detests.

"It can't be helped," I told him. "It takes all kinds to make a clientele. What are we going to look into a little?"

He sighed. "Get Mr. Wengert of the FBI. You want to see him, this evening if possible. I'll talk."

"It's nearly seven o'clock."

"Try."

I went to the phone on my desk, dialed RE 2-3500, talked to a stranger and to a man I had met a couple of times, and reported to Wolfe, "Not available. Tomorrow morning."

"Make an appointment."

I did so and hung up.

Wolfe sat scowling at me. He spoke. "I'll give you instructions after dinner. Have we got the *Gazette* of the past three days?"

"Sure."

"Let me have them, please. Confound it." He sighed again. "Saturday, and tomorrow's Wednesday. Like a warmed-over meal." He came erect and his face brightened. "I wonder how Fritz is making out with that fish."

He left his chair and headed for the hall and the kitchen.

II

Wednesday morning all the air in Manhattan was conditioned—the wrong way. It was no place for penguins. On my way to Foley Square my jacket was beside me on the seat of the taxi, but when I had paid the driver and got out I put it on. Sweat or no sweat, I had to show the world that a private detective can be tough enough to take it.

When, after some waiting, I got admitted to Wengert's big corner room I found him in his shirt sleeves with his tie and collar loosened. He got up to shake hands and invited me to sit. We exchanged remarks.

"I haven't seen you," I told him, "since you got elevated here. Congratulations."

"Thanks."

"You're welcome. I notice you've got brass in your voice, but I guess that can't be helped. Mr. Wolfe sends his regards."

"Give him mine." His voice warmed up a little, just perceptibly. "I'll never forget how he came through on that mercury thing." He glanced at the watch on his wrist. "What can I do for you, Goodwin?"

Back a few years, when we had been in G2 together, it had been Archie, but then he hadn't had a corner room with five phones on his desk. I crossed my legs to show there was no rush.

"Not a thing," I told him. "Mr. Wolfe just wants to clear. Yesterday a man and wife named Rackell came to see him. They want him to investigate the death of their nephew, Arthur Rackell. Do you know about it, or do you want to call someone in? Mrs. Rackell has talked with a Mr. Anstrey."

"I know. Go ahead."

"Then I won't have to draw pictures. Our bank says that Rackell rates seven figures west of the decimal point, and we would like to earn a fee by tagging a murderer, but our country right or wrong. We would hate to torpedo the ship of state in this bad weather. The Rackells came to Mr. Wolfe because they think the FBI and the NYPD regard the death of Arthur as a regrettable but minor incident. They say he was killed by a Commie who discovered that he was an FBI plant. Before we proceed on that theory Mr. Wolfe wants to clear with you. Of course you may not want to say, even under the rug to us, that he was yours. May you?"

"It's hotter than yesterday," Wengert stated.

"Yeah. Would you care to make any sign at all, for instance a wink?"

"No."

"Then I'll try something more general. There has been nothing in the papers about the Commie angle, not a word, so there has been no mention of the FBI. Is the FBI working on the murder, officially or otherwise?"

"Much hotter," he said.

"It sure is. How about the others, the five dinner guests? Of course they're our meat. Any suggestions, requests, or orders? Any strings you wouldn't want us to trip on?"

"The humidity, too."

"Absolutely. I realize that you would like to tell us to lay off on general principles, but you're afraid there might be a headline tomorrow, FBI WARNS NERO WOLFE TO KEEP HANDS OFF OF RACKELL MURDER. Besides, if you give us a stop sign you'll have to say why or we'll keep going. Just to clean it up, is there any question I might ask that would take your mind off the weather?"

"No." He stood up. "It was nice to see you for old time's sake, and you can still give Wolfe my regards, but tell him to go climb a tree. Some nerve. Sending you here with that bull about wanting to clear! Why didn't he ask me to send him up the files? Come again when I'm not here."

I was on my way, but before I reached the door I turned. "The radio said this morning it would hit ninety-five," I told him and went.

There are always taxis at Foley Square. I removed my jacket, climbed into one, and gave an address on West Twentieth Street. When we got there my shirt was stuck to the back of the seat. I pulled loose, paid, got out, put on the jacket, and went into a building. The headquarters of the Homicide Squad, Manhattan West, was much more familiar to me than the United States Courthouse. So were the inmates, one in particular, the one sitting at a dingy little desk in a dingy little room to which I was escorted. They have never let me roam loose in that building since the day I took a snapshot of a piece of paper they were saving, though they couldn't prove it.

Sergeant Purley Stebbins was big and strong but not handsome. His rusty old swivel chair squeaked and groaned as he leaned back.

"Oh, hell," I said, sitting, "I forgot. I meant to bring a can of oil for that chair my next trip here." I cocked my head. "What are you glaring about? Is my face dirty?"

"It don't have to be dirty." He went on glaring. "Goddam it, why did they have to pick Nero Wolfe?"

I considered a moment, maybe two seconds. "I am glad to know," I said pleasantly, "that the cops and the feds are collaborating so closely. Citizens can sleep sound. Wengert must have phoned the minute I left. What did he say?"

"He spoke to the Inspector. What do you want?"

"Maybe I should speak to the Inspector."

"He's busy. So the Rackells have hired Wolfe?"

I lifted my nose. "Mr. and Mrs. Rackell have asked Mr. Wolfe to investigate the death of their nephew. Before he starts to whiz through it like a cyclone he wants to know whether he will be cramping the style of those responsible for the national security. I've seen Wengert, and the heat has got him. He's not interested. I am now seeing you because of the Commie angle, which has not appeared in the papers. If it is against the public interest for us to take the job, tell me why. I know you and Cramer think it's against the public interest for us to eat, let alone detect, but that's not enough. We would need facts."

"Uh-huh," Purley growled. "We give 'em to you and Wolfe decides he can use 'em better than we can. Nuts. I'll tell you one fact: this one has got stingers. Lay off."

I nodded sympathetically. "That's probably good advice. I'll tell Mr. Wolfe." I arose. "We would like you to sign a statement covering the substance of this interview. Three copies, one—"

"Go somewhere," he rasped. "On out. Beat it."

I thought he was getting careless, but my escort, a paunchy old veteran with a pushed-in nose, was waiting in the hall. As I strode to the front and the entrance he waddled along behind.

It was past eleven by the time I got back to the office, so Wolfe had finished his two hours in the plant rooms and was behind his desk, with beer. It would have been impossible for anything with life in it to look less like a cyclone.

"Well?" he muttered at me.

I sat. "We deposit the check. Wengert sends his regards. Purley doesn't. They both think you sent me merely to get the dope for free and they sneer at the idea of our caring for the public welfare. Wengert phoned Cramer the minute I left. Not a peep from either one. We only know what we see in the papers."

He grunted. "Get Mr. Rackell."

So we had a case.

III

There were two open questions about the seven people gathered in the office after dinner that Wednesday evening: were any of them Commies, and was one of them a murderer? I make it seven, including our clients, not to seem prejudiced.

I had given them the eye as they arrived and gathered and now, as I sat at my desk with them all in sight, I was placing no bets. There had been a time, years back, when I had had the notion that no murderer, man or woman, could stand exposed to view and not let it show somewhere if you had good enough eyes, but now I knew better. However, I was using my eyes.

The one nearest me was a lanky middle-aged guy named Ormond Leddegard. He may have been expert at handling labor-management relations, which was how he made a living, but he was a fumbler with his fingers. Getting out a pack of cigarettes, and matches, and lighting up, he was all thumbs, and that would have put him low on the list if it hadn't been for the possibility that he was being subtle. If I could figure that thumbs wouldn't have been up to the job of sneaking a pillbox from a cluttered table, making a substitution, and returning the box without detection, so could he. Of course that little point could be easily settled by having a good man, say Saul Panzer, spend a couple of days interviewing a dozen or so of his friends and acquaintances.

Next to him, with her legs crossed just right to be photographed from any angle, was Fifi Goheen. The leg-crossing technique was automatic, from an old habit. Seven or eight years ago she had been the Deb of the Year and no magazine would have dared to go to press without a shot of her; then it became all a memory; and now she was a front-page item as a murder suspect. She hadn't married. It was said that a hundred males, lured by the attractions, opening their mouths for the big proposition, had seen the hard glint in her lovely dark eyes and lost their tongues. So she was still Miss Fifi Goheen, living with Pop and Mom on Park Avenue.

Beyond her in the arc facing Wolfe's desk was Benjamin Rackell, whose check had been deposited in our bank that afternoon, with his long narrow face more mournful even than the day before. At his right was a specimen who was a female anatomically but otherwise a what-is-it. Her name was Della Devlin, and her age was beside the point. She was a resident buyer of novelties for out-of-town stores. There are ten thousand of her in midtown New York any weekday, and they're all being imposed on. You see it in their faces. The problem is to find out who it is that's imposing on them, and some day I may tackle it. Aside from that there was nothing visibly wrong with Della Devlin, except her ears were too big.

Next to her was a celebrity—though of course they were all celebrities for the time being, you might say ex officio. Henry Jameson Heath, now crowding fifty, had inherited money in his youth, quite a pile, but very few people in his financial bracket were speaking to him. There was no telling whether he had contributed dough to the Communist party or cause, or if so how much, but there was no secret about his being one of the chief providers and collectors of bail for the Commies who had been indicted. He had recently been indicted too, for contempt of Congress, and was probably headed for a modest stretch. He wore an old seersucker suit that was too small for him, had a round pudgy face, and couldn't look at you without staring.

Beyond Heath, at the end of the arc, was Carol Berk, the only one toward whom I had a personal attitude worth mentioning. Whenever we have a flock of guests I handle the seating, and if there is one who seems worthy of study I put her in the chair nearest mine. I had done so with this Carol Berk, but while I was in the hall admitting Leddegard, who had come last, she had switched on me, and I resented it. I felt that she deserved attention. Checking on her, along with the others, that afternoon with Lon Cohen of the *Gazette,* I had learned that she was supposed to be free-lancing as a TV contact specialist but no one actually claimed her, that she had a reputation as an extremely fast mover, and that there were six different versions of why she had left Hollywood three years ago. Added to that was the question whether it was a pleasure to look at her or not. In cases where it's a quick no, the big majority, or a quick yes, the small minority, that settles it and what the hell; but the borderline numbers take application and sound judgment. I had listed Carol Berk as one when, crossing the doorsill, she had darted a sidewise glance at me with brown eyes that were dead dull from the front. Now, in the chair she had changed to, she was a good five paces away.

Mrs. Benjamin Rackell, her lips tighter than ever, was in the red leather chair at the end of Wolfe's desk.

Wolfe's gaze swept the arc. "I won't thank you for coming," he rumbled at them, "because it would be impertinent. You are here at the request of Mr. and Mrs. Rackell. Whether you came to oblige them or because you thought it unwise not to is immaterial."

Also, it seemed to me, it was close to immaterial whether they were there or not. Apparently, since he had sent me to Foley Square and Homicide to clear, Wolfe was proceeding on the Rackell theory that Arthur had got it because a Commie or Commies had discovered that he was an FBI plant. But that theory had not been published, and Wolfe couldn't blurt it out. You don't disclose the identity of FBI undercover men, even dead ones, if you make your living as a private detective and want to keep your license. And if by any chance Arthur had fed his aunt one with a worm in it, if he had actually had no more connection with the FBI than me with the DAR—no, that was one to steer clear of.

So not only could Wolfe not come to the point, he couldn't even let out a hint of what the point was. How could he talk at all?

He talked. "I don't know," he said, "whether the police have made it clear to you how you stand. They don't like it that I'm taking a hand in this. The entrance to my house has been under surveillance since this morning, when they learned that Mr. and Mrs. Rackell had consulted me. One or more of you were probably followed here this evening. But Mr. Rackell may properly hire me, I may properly work for him, and you may properly give me information if you feel like it."

"We don't know whether we do or not." Leddegard shifted in his chair, stretching his lanky legs. "At least I don't. I came as a courtesy to people in bereavement."

"It is appreciated," Wolfe assured him. "Now for how you stand. I talked with Mr. and Mrs. Rackell yesterday, and with Mrs. Rackell again this afternoon. It is characteristic of the newspapers to focus attention on you five people; it's obvious and dramatic, and, after all, you were there when Arthur Rackell swallowed poison and died. But beyond the obvious, why you? Have the police been candid?"

"That's a damn silly question," Heath declared. He had a flat but aggressive baritone. "The police are never candid."

"I knew a candid cop once," Fifi Goheen said helpfully.

"It seems to me," Carol Berk told Wolfe, "that you're being dramatic too, getting us down here. It would have taken a sleight-of-hand artist to get the pillbox from his pocket and switch a capsule and put it back, without being seen. And while the box was on the table it was right under our eyes."

Wolfe grunted. "You were all staring at it? For twelve minutes straight?"

"She didn't say we were staring at it," Leddegard blurted offensively.

"Pfui." Wolfe was disgusted. "A lummox could have managed it. Reaching for something—a roll, a cocktail glass—dropping the hand onto the box, checking glances while withdrawing the hand, changing capsules beneath the table, returning the box with another casual unnoticeable gesture. I would undertake it myself with thin inducement, and I'm not Houdini."

"Tell me something," Leddegard demanded. "I may be thick, but why did it have to be done at the restaurant? Why not before?"

Wolfe nodded. "That's not excluded, certainly. You five people were not the only ones intimate enough with Arthur Rackell to know about his pink vitamin capsules and that he took three a day, one before each meal. Nor did you have a monopoly of opportunity. However—" His glance went left. "Mrs. Rackell, will you repeat what you told me this afternoon? About Saturday evening?"

She had been keeping her eyes at Wolfe but now moved her head to take the others in. Judging from her expression as she went down the line, apparently she was convinced not that one of them was a Commie and a murderer, but that they all were—excluding her husband, of course.

She returned to Wolfe. "My husband and Arthur had spent the afternoon getting an important shipment released, and got home a little before six. They went to their rooms to take a shower and change. While Arthur was in the shower my cook and housekeeper, Mrs. Kremp, went to his room to get things out for him, shirt and socks and underwear—she's like that; she's been doing it for years. The articles he had taken from his pockets were on the bureau, and she looked in the pillbox and saw it was empty, and she got three capsules from the bottle in a drawer—it held a hundred and was half full—and put them in the box. She did that too, every day. She is a competent woman, but she's extremely sentimental."

"And she had no reason," Wolfe inquired, "for wishing your nephew dead?"

"Certainly not!"

"She has of course told the police?"

"Of course."

"Was there anyone in the apartment other than you four—you, your husband, your nephew, and Mrs. Kremp?"

"No. No one. The maid was away. My husband and I were going to the country for the weekend."

"After Mrs. Kremp put the capsules in the box, and before your nephew came from the shower to dress—did you enter your nephew's room during that period?"

"No. I didn't enter it at all."

"Did you, Mr. Rackell?"

"I did not." He sounded as mournful as he looked.

Wolfe's eyes went left to right, from Carol Berk at one end to Ledgard at the other. "Then we have Arthur Rackell bathed and dressed, the pillbox in his pocket. The police are not confiding in me, but I read newspapers. Leaving the apartment, he went down in the elevator and out to the sidewalk, and the doorman got a taxi for him. He was alone in the taxi, and it took him straight to the restaurant. The capsules left in the bottle have been examined and had not been tampered with. There we are. Are you prepared to impeach Mrs. Kremp, or Mr. or Mrs. Rackell? Can you support the assumption that one of them murdered Arthur Rackell?"

"It's not inconceivable," Della Devlin murmured.

"No," Wolfe conceded. "Nor is it inconceivable that he chose that moment and method to kill himself, nor even that a capsule of poison got into the bottle by accident. But I exclude them as too improbable for consideration, and so will everyone else, including the police. The inquiring mind is rarely blessed with a certainty; it must make shift with assumptions; and I am assuming, on the evidence, that when Arthur arrived at the restaurant the capsules in the box in his pocket were innocent. I invite you to challenge it. If you can't the substitution was made at the restaurant, and you see how you stand. The police are after you, and so am I. One of you? Or all of you? I intend to find out."

"You're scaring me stiff," Fifi Goheen said. "I'm frail and I may collaspe." She stood up. "Come on, Leddy, I'll buy you a drink."

Leddegard reached for her elbow and gave it a little shake. "Hold it, Fee," he told her gruffly. "This guy has been known to do flips. Let's see. Sit down."

"Blah. You *are* scared. You've got a reputation." She jerked her arm loose and took two quick steps to the edge of Wolfe's desk. Her voice rose a little. "I don't like the atmosphere here. You're too fat to look at. Orchids, for God's sake!" Her hand darted to the bowl of Miltonias, and with a flip of the wrist she sent it skidding along the slick surface and off to the floor.

There was some commotion. Mrs. Rackell jerked her feet back, away from the tumbling bowl. Carol Berk said something. Leddegard left his chair and started for Fifi, but she whirled away to Henry Jameson Heath, pressed her palms to his cheeks, and bent to him. She implored him, "Hank, I love you! Do you love me? Take me somewhere and buy me a drink."

Della Devlin sprang up, hauled off, and smacked Fifi on the side of the head. It was not merely a tap, and Fifi, off balance, nearly toppled. Heath came upright and was between them. Della stood, glaring and panting. They held the tableau long enough for a take, then Fifi broke it up by addressing Della past Heath's shoulder.

"That won't help any, Del. Can he help it when he's with you if he wishes it was me? Can I help it? This only makes it worse. If he'll buy a new suit and quit bailing out Commies and stay out of jail, I may make him happy." She touched Heath's cheek with her fingertips. "Say when, Hank." She swerved around him to the desk and told Wolfe, "Look, *you* buy me a drink."

I was there, retrieving the bowl. The water wouldn't hurt the rug. Taking her arm firmly, I escorted her across to the table by the big globe, which Fritz and I had outfitted, and told her to name it. She said Scotch on the rocks, and I made it ample. The others, invited, stated their preferences, and Carol Berk came to help me. Rackell, who had been between Della and Fifi, decided to move and went to Carol's chair, so when we had finished serving she took his.

Throughout the interlude two had neither moved nor spoken—Mrs. Rackell and Wolfe. Now Wolfe sent his eyes from left to right and back again.

"I trust," he said sourly, "that Miss Goheen has completed her impromptu performance. I was trying to make it clear that you five people are in a fix. I'm not going to pester you about your positions and movements at the restaurant that evening, what you saw or didn't see; if there was anything in that to point or eliminate the police would have already acted on it and I'm too far behind. I might spend a few hours digging at you, trying to find a reason why one or more of you wanted Arthur Rackell dead, but the police have had four days on that too, and I doubt if I could catch up. Since you were good enough to come here at Mrs. Rackell's request, I suppose you would be willing to answer some questions, but there doesn't seem to be any worth asking. Have you people been together at any time since Saturday evening?"

Glances were exchanged. Leddegard inquired, "Do you mean all five of us?"

"Yes."

"No, we haven't."

"Then I should think you would want to talk. Go ahead. I'll drink some beer and eavesdrop. Of course at least one of you will be on guard, but the others can speak freely. You might say something useful."

Carol Berk, now nearer me, let out a little snort. Fritz had brought a tray, and Wolfe opened a bottle, poured, waited for the foam to reach the right level, and drank. Nobody said a word.

Leddegard spoke. "It doesn't seem to work. Did you expect it to?"

"We ought to make it work," Fifi declared. "I think he's damn considerate even if he is fat, and we should help." Her head turned. "Carol, let's talk."

"Glad to," Carol agreed. "You start. Shoot."

"Well, how's this? We all knew Arthur was practically a commissar, I always called him comrade, and we knew his aunt and uncle hated it, and he was afraid he might lose his job and have to go on relief but he was so damn brave and honest he couldn't keep his mouth shut. We all knew that?"

"Of course."

"Did you know this too? He told me—a week ago today, I think it was. His aunt put it to him, reform or out on the street, and he told her he was secretly working for the FBI, spying on the Commies, but he wasn't. He thought the FBI was practically the Gestapo. I told him he shouldn't—"

"That's a lie!"

Mrs. Rackell didn't shout but she put lots of feeling in it. All eyes went to her. Her husband got up and put a hand on her shoulder. There were murmurs.

"That's an infamous lie," she said. "My nephew was a patriotic American. More than you are, all of you. All of you!" She left her chair. "I've had enough of this. I shouldn't have come. Come, Ben, we're going."

She marched out. Rackell muttered to Wolfe, "A shock for her—a real shock—I'll phone you—" and trotted after her. I went to the hall to let them out, but she had already opened the door and was on the stoop, and Rackell followed. I shut the door and went back to the office.

They were buzzing. Fifi had started them talking, all right. Wolfe was refilling his glass, watching the foam rise. I crossed to Fifi and took her glass and went to the table to replenish it, thinking she had earned a little service. She was the center of the buzzing, supplying the details of her revelation. She was sure Arthur had not been stringing her; he had told her in strict confidence, at a place and time she declined to specify, that he had told his aunt a barefaced lie—that he was working for the FBI and it must not be known. No, she hadn't told the police. She didn't like the police, especially a Lieutenant Rowcliff, who had questioned her three times and was a lout.

I looked and listened and tried to decide if Fifi was putting on an act. She was hard to tag. Was one of the others covering, and if so which one? I reached no conclusion and had no hunch. They were all interested and inquisitive, even Della Devlin, though she didn't address Fifi directly.

The only one who knew I was there was Carol Berk, who sent me a slanting glance and saw me catch it. I raised a brow at her. "What is it, a pitchout?"

"You name it." She smiled, the way she might smile at a panhandler, humane but superior. "Why, who's on base?"

I decided it right then, she was worth looking at, if for nothing else, to find out what she was keeping back. "They're loaded," I told her. "Five of you. It's against the rules. The umpire won't allow it. Mr. Wolfe is the umpire."

"He looks to me more like the backstop," she said indifferently.

I saw that it might be necessary, if events permitted, to find an opportunity to spend enough time with her to make it clear that I didn't like her.

All of a sudden Fifi Goheen let fly again. Returning from the bar with her second refill, she brought the bottle of Scotch along and poured a good three fingers in Wolfe's beer glass. She put the bottle on his desk, leaned over to stretch an arm and pat him on top of the head, straightened up, and grinned at him.

"Get high," she said urgently.

He glared at her.

"Do a flip," she commanded.

He glared.

"It's a damn shame," she declared. "The cops aren't speaking to you, and here you're buying the drinks and we're not even sociable. Why shouldn't we tell you what the cops have already found out? If they're any good they have. Take Miss Devlin here." She waved a hand. "Dozens of people will tell you that she would have got Hank Heath to make it legal long ago if Arthur hadn't told him something about her, God knows what. Any woman would kill a man for that. And—"

"Shut up, Fee!" Leddegard barked at her.

"Let her rave," Della Devlin said, white-faced.

Fifi ignored them. "And Mr. Leddegard, who is a dear friend of mine, with him it's a question of his wife—don't be a fool, Leddy. Everybody knows it." Back to Wolfe. "She went to South America with Arthur a couple of years ago and caught a disease and died there. I have no idea why Mr. Leddegard waited so long to kill him."

She drained her glass and put it on the desk. "This Arthur Rackell," she said, "was quite a guy, of his kind. Carol Berk and I discovered only a month ago that he was driving double, by a little mischance I'd rather not describe. It was quite embarrassing. I don't know how she felt about it, you can ask her, but I know about me. All I needed was the poison, and all you need is to find out how I got it. I understand that potassium cyanide is used for a lot of things and is easy to get if you really want it. Then there's Hank Heath. He thought Arthur had me taped, which was true in a way, but would a man kill another man just to get a woman, even one as pure and beautiful as me? You can ask him. No, I'll ask him."

She wheeled. "Would you, Hank?" She wheeled again to Wolfe. "As you see, that was quite a dinner party Arthur got up, but he doesn't deserve all the credit. I dared him to. I wanted a good audience, one that would appreciate—hey, that hurts!"

Heath was beside her, gripping her arm. She jerked away and bumped into Della Devlin, also out of her chair. Carol Berk said something, and so did Leddegard. Heath spoke to Wolfe. "This is a joke, and it's not funny."

Wolfe's brows went up. "It's not my joke, sir."

"You asked us to come here." His voice was soft but very sour, and his glassy eyes looked about ready to pop out of his round pudgy face. "Miss Goheen has been making a fool of you, and there—"

"I have not!" Fifi was back, at his elbow. "I wouldn't dream of it," she told Wolfe. "You know, there's something about you, fat as you are." She reached to pick up the glass of beer and Scotch. "Open your mouth and I'll—hey! Where you going?"

She got no reply. Out of his chair and headed for the door, Wolfe kept on, turning left in the hall, toward the kitchen.

That ended the party. They made remarks, especially Leddegard and Heath, and I was sympathetic as I wrangled them into the hall and on to the front. I went out and stood on the stoop as they descended to the sidewalk and headed for Tenth Avenue, just to see, but by the time they had gone fifty paces no furtive figures had sneaked out of areaways along the line, so I thought what the hell and went back in. A glance in the office showed me it was empty, and I went on to the kitchen.

Fritz was pouring something thick into a big stone jar. Wolfe stood watching him, a slice of sturgeon in one hand and a glass of beer in the other. His mouth was occupied.

I attacked head on. "I admit," I said, "that she was set to toss it at you, but I was there to help wipe it off. What good does it do to duck? There are at least eighty-six things you have to know before you can even start, and you had them there and didn't even try. My vacation starts next Monday. And what about your rule on not eating at bedtime?"

He swallowed. He drank beer, put the glass and the sturgeon on the table, reached to a shelf for a Bursatto melon, got a knife from the rack, cut the melon open, and began spooning the seeds onto a plate.

"The precise moment," he said. "Do you want some?"

"Certainly not," I said coldly. The peach-colored meat was so juicy there was a little pool in each half, and a breeze from the open window carried the smell to me. I reached for one of the halves, got a spoon, scooped out a bite—and another . . .

Wolfe never talks business during meals, but this was not a meal. In the middle of his melon he remarked, "For us the past is impossible."

I darted my tongue to catch a drop of juice. "Oh. It is?"

"Yes. It would take an army. The police and the FBI have already had four days for it. The source of the poison. Mrs. Kremp. Mrs. Rackell's surmise of the motive. Mr. Heath is presumably a Communist, but what about the others? Anyone might be a Communist, just as anyone might have a hidden carcinoma."

He scooped a bite of melon and dealt with it. "What of the motives suggested by that fantastic female buffoon? Are any of them authentic, and if so which one or ones? That alone would need a regiment. As for the police and the FBI, we have nothing to bargain with. Are they all Communists? Were they all in on it? Must we expose not one murderer but five? All those questions and others would have to be answered. How long would it take?"

"A year ought to do it."

"I doubt it. The past is hopeless. There's too much of it."

I raised my shoulders and let them drop. "Okay, you don't have to rub it in. So we cross it off. Do I draw a check to Rackell for his three grand tonight or wait till morning?"

"Have I asked you to draw a check?"

"No, sir."

He picked up the slice of sturgeon and took a bite. He never skimped on his chewing, and it took him a good four minutes to finish. Meanwhile I disposed of my melon.

"Archie," he said.

"Yes, sir."

"How does Mr. Heath feel about Miss Goheen?"

"Well." I considered. "There are different ways of putting it. I would say something like you would feel about a dish of stewed terrapin with sherry—within your sight and smell—if you thought you knew how it would taste but had never had any."

He grunted. "Don't be fanciful. It's a serious question in a field where you are qualified as an expert and I'm not. Is his appetite deeply aroused? Would he take a risk for her?"

"I don't know how he is on risks, but I saw how he looked at her and how he reacted when she touched him. Also I saw Della Devlin, and so did you. I would say he would try crossing a high shaky bridge with a wind blowing, but not unless it had rails."

"That was the impression I got. We'll have to try it."

"Try what?"

"A shove. A dig in their ribs. If their past is too much for us, their future isn't, or shouldn't be. We'll have to try it. If it doesn't work we'll try again." He was scowling. "The best I can give it is one chance in twenty. Confound it, it requires the cooperation of Mrs. Rackell, so I'll have to see her again; that can't be helped."

He scooped a bite of melon. "You'll need some instructions. I'll finish this, and we'll go to the office."

He put the bite where it belonged and concentrated on his taste buds.

IV

It didn't work out as scheduled. The program called for getting Mrs. Rackell to the office at eleven o'clock the next morning, Thursday, but when I phoned a little before nine the maid said it was too early to disturb her. At ten she hadn't called back, and I tried again and got her. I explained that Wolfe had an important confidential question to put to her, and she said she would be at the office not later than eleven-thirty. Shortly before eleven she phoned again to say that she had called her husband at his office, and it had been decided if the question was important and confidential they should both be present to consider it. Her husband would be free for an hour or so after lunch but had a four-o'clock appointment he would have to keep. We finally settled for six o'clock, and I called Rackell at his office and confirmed it.

Henry Jameson Heath was on the front page of the *Gazette* again that morning, not in connection with homicide. Once more he had refused to disclose the names of contributors to the fund for bail for the indicted Communists and apparently he was going to stick to it no matter how much contempt he rolled up. The day's installment on the Rackell murder was on page seven, and there wasn't enough meat in it to feed a cricket. As for me, after an hour at the phone, locating Saul Panzer and Fred Durkin and Orrie Cather and passing them the word, I might as well have gone to the ball game. Wolfe had given me plenty of instructions, but I couldn't act on them until and unless the clients agreed to string along.

Mrs. Rackell arrived first, at six on the dot. A minute later Wolfe came down from the plant rooms, and she started in on him. She had the idea that he was responsible for Fifi Goheen's slanderous lie about her dead nephew, since it had been uttered in his office, and what did he propose to do about it? Why didn't he have her arrested? Wolfe controlled himself fairly well, but his tone was beginning to get sharp when the doorbell rang and I beat it to the front to let Rackell in. He jogged past me to the office on his short legs, nodded at Wolfe, kissed his wife on the cheek, dropped onto a chair, wiped his long narrow face with a handkerchief, and asked wearily, "What is it? Did you get anywhere with them?"

"No." Wolfe was short. "Not to any conclusion."

"What's this important question?"

"It's blunt and simple. I need to know whether you want the truth enough to pay for it, and if so how much."

Rackell looked at his wife. "What's he talking about?"

"We haven't discussed it," Wolfe told him. "We've been considering a point your wife raised, which I regard as frivolous. This question of mine—perhaps I should call it a suggestion. I have one to offer."

"What?"

"First I'll give you the basis for it." Wolfe leaned back and half closed his eyes. "You heard me tell those five people yesterday why it is assumed that one of them substituted the capsules. On that assumption, after further talk with them, I stack another: that it is highly improbable that the substitution could have been made, under the circumstances as established, entirely unobserved. It would have required a coincidence of remarkable dexterity and uncommon luck, and I will not accept such a coincidence except on weighty evidence. So, assuming that the substitution was made in the restaurant, I also assume, for a test at least, that one of the others saw it and knows who did it. In short, that there was an eyewitness to the murder."

Rackell's mournful face did not light up with interest. His lips were puckered, making the droop at the corners more pronounced. "That may be," he conceded, "but what good does it do if he won't talk?"

"I propose to make him talk. Or her."

"How?"

Wolfe rubbed his chin with a thumb and forefinger. His eyes moved to Mrs. Rackell and back to the husband. "This sort of thing," he said, "requires delicacy, discretion, and reticence. I'll put it this way. I will not conspire to get a man punished for a crime he did not commit. It is true that all five of those people may be Communists and therefore enemies of this country, but that does not justify framing one of them for murder. My purpose is clear and innocent—to expose the real murderer and bring him to account; and I suggest a devious method only because no other seems likely to succeed. Evidently the police, after five days on it, are up a tree, and so is the FBI—if it is engaged, and you think it is. I want to earn my fee, and I wouldn't mind the kudos."

Rackell was frowning. "I still don't know exactly what you're suggesting."

"I know it; I've been long-winded. I didn't want you to misunderstand." Wolfe came forward in his chair and put his palms on the desk. "The eyewitness is obviously reluctant. I suggest that you consent to provide twenty thousand dollars, to be paid only if my method succeeds. That will cover my fee for the unusual service I will render and also any extraordinary expense I may incur. Two things must be understood: you approve the expenditure in your interest, and the express purpose is to catch the guilty person." He upturned his palms. "There it is."

"My God. Twenty thousand." Rackell shook his head. "That's a lot of money. You mean you want a check for that amount now?"

"No. To be paid if and when earned. An oral commitment will do. Mr. Goodwin hears us and has a good memory."

Rackell opened his mouth and closed it again. He looked at his wife. He looked back at Wolfe. "Look here," he said earnestly, "maybe I'm thickheaded. It sounds to me as if what this amounts to is bribing a witness. With my money."

"Don't be a fool, Ben," his wife said sharply.

"I think you misunderstand," Wolfe told him. "To bribe is to influence corruptly by some consideration. Anyone who receives any of your money through me will get it only as an inducement to tell the truth. Influence, yes. Corrupt, surely not. As for the amount, I don't wonder that you hesitate. It's quite a sum, but I wouldn't undertake it for less."

Rackell looked at his wife again. "What did you mean, Pauline, don't be a fool?"

"I meant you'd be a fool not to do it, of course." She felt so strongly about it that her lips moved. "It was you who wanted to come to Mr. Wolfe in the first place, and now when he really wants to do something you talk about bribing. If it's the money, I have plenty of my own and I'll pay—" She stopped abruptly, tightening her lips. "I'll pay half," she said. "That's fair enough; we'll each pay half." She went to Wolfe. "Who is it, that Goheen woman?"

Wolfe ignored her. He asked Rackell, "Well, sir? How about it?"

Rackell didn't like it. He avoided his wife's gaze, but he knew it was on him, and it was pressing. He even looked at me, as if my eye might somehow help, but I was deadpan. Then he returned to Wolfe.

"All right," he said.

"You accept the proposal as I made it?"

"Yes. Only I'll pay it. I'd rather not—I'd rather pay it myself. You said to be paid if and when earned. Who decides whether you've earned it or not?"

"You do. I doubt if that will be a bone to pick."

"A question my wife asked—do you know who the eyewitness is?"

"Your wife was witless to ask it. If I knew would I tell you? Or would you want me to? Now?"

Rackell shook his head. "No, I guess not. No, I can see that it's better just to let you—" He left it hanging. "Is there anything else you want to say about it?"

Wolfe said there wasn't. Rackell got up and stood there as if he would like to say something but didn't know what. I arose and moved toward the door. I didn't want to be rude to a client who had just bought a suggestion that would cost him twenty grand, but now that he had okayed it I had a job to do and I wanted to get going. I still didn't know where Wolfe thought he was headed for, but the sooner I got started on my instructions the sooner I would know. They finally came, and I went ahead and opened the front door for them. She held his elbow going down the stoop. I shut the door and rejoined Wolfe in the office.

"Well?" I demanded. "Do I proceed?"

"Yes."

"It's nearly half-past six. If I offer to buy her a meal—I doubt if that's the right approach."

"You know the approaches to women, I don't."

"Yeah." I sat at my desk and pulled the phone to me. "If you ask me this stunt you've hatched is a swell approach to a trip to the hoosegow. For both of us."

He grunted. I started dialing a number.

V

New York can have pleasant summer evenings when it wants to, and that was one of them—warm but not hot and not muggy. I paid the taxi driver when he rolled to the curb at the address on Fifty-first Street east of Lexington, got out, and took a look. In bright sunshine the old gray brick building would probably show signs of wear and tear, but now in twilight it wasn't too bad. Entering the vestibule, I scanned the tier of names on the wall panel. The one next to the top said DEVLIN–BERK. I pushed the button, shoved the door open when the click came, went in, glanced around for an elevator and saw none, and started to climb stairs. Three flights up a door stood open, and there waiting was Della Devlin.

I told her hello, friendly but not profuse. She nodded, not so friendly, hugged the wall to let me pass, shut the door, and went by me to lead the way through an arch into a living room. I sent my eyes around with an expression of comradely interest. The chairs and couch were attractive and cool in summer slips. There were shelves of books. The windows were on the street, and there were three doors besides the arch, two of them standing open and one not quite closed.

She sat and invited me to. "I can't imagine," she said in a louder voice than seemed necessary, in spite of the street noises from the open windows, "what you want to ask me that's so mysterious."

Sitting, I regarded her. Only one corner lamp was on, and in the dim light she wasn't at all bad looking. With smaller ears she would have been a worthy specimen, with no glare on her.

"It's not mysterious," I protested. "As I said on the phone, it's private and confidential, that's all. Mr. Wolfe felt it would be an imposition to ask you to come to his office again, so he sent me. Miss Berk is out, is she?"

"Yes, she went to a show with a friend. *Guys and Dolls.*"

"Fine. It's a good show. This really is confidential, Miss Devlin. So we're alone?"

"Certainly we are. What is it, anyhow?"

There were three things wrong. First, I had a hunch, and my batting average on hunches is high. Second, she was talking too loud. Third, her telling me where Carol Berk was, even naming the show, was off key.

"The reason it's so confidential," I said, "is simply that you ought to decide for yourself what you want to do. I doubt if you realize what lengths other people may go to to help you decide. You say we're alone, but it wouldn't surprise me a bit—"

I sprang up, marched across to the door that wasn't quite closed, thinking it the most likely, and jerked it open. Behind me a little smothered shriek came from Della Devlin. In front of me, backed up against closet shelves piled with cartons and miscellany, was Carol Berk. One look at her satisfied me on one point—what her eyes were like when something happened that really aroused her.

I stepped back. Della Devlin was at my elbow, jabbering. I gripped her arm hard enough to hurt a little and addressed Carol Berk as she emerged from the closet. "My God, do I look like that big a sap? Maybe your sidewise glance isn't as keen as you think—"

Della was yapping at me. "You get out! Get out!"

Carol stopped her. "Let him stay, Della." She was calm and contemptuous. "He's only a crummy little stooge, trying to slip one over for his boss. I'll be back in an hour or so."

She moved. Della, protesting, caught her arm, but she pulled loose and left through one of the open doors. There were sounds from the adjoining room, then she appeared again, with a thing on her head and a jacket and handbag, and passed through to the foyer. The outer door opened and then closed. I crossed to a window and stuck my head out and in a minute saw her emerge to the sidewalk and turn west.

I went back to my chair and sat. The open closet door was unsightly, and I got up and closed it and then sat again. "Just forget it," I said cheerfully. "The closet was a bum idea anyhow; she would have stifled in there. Sit down and relax while I try to slip one over for my boss."

She stood. "I'm not interested in anything you have to say."

"Then you shouldn't have let me in. Certainly you shouldn't have stuck Miss Berk in that closet. Let's get it over with. I merely want to find out whether you have any use for ten thousand dollars."

She gawked. "Whether I what?"

"Sit down and I'll tell you."

She went to a chair and sat, and I shifted position to be more comfortable facing her. "First I want to tell you a couple of things about murder investigations. In–"

"I've heard all I want to about murder."

"I know you have, but that's one of the things. When you get involved in one it's not a question of what or how much you want to hear. That's the one question nobody asks you. Until and unless the Rackell case is solved, with the answers all in, you'll be hearing about it the rest of your life. Face it, Miss Devlin."

She didn't say anything. She clasped her hands.

"The other thing about murder investigations. Someone gets murdered, and the cops go to work on it. Everybody that might possibly have a piece of useful information gets questioned. Say they question fifty different people. How many of the fifty answer every question truthfully. Maybe ten, maybe only four or five. Ask any experienced homicide man. They know it and they expect it, and that's why, when they think it's worth it, they go over the same questions with the same person again and again, after the truth. They often get it that way and they nearly always do with people who have cooked up a story, something they did or saw, with details. Of course you're not one of those. You haven't cooked up a detailed story. You have only answered a simple question 'No' instead of 'Yes.' They can't catch you–"

"What question? What do you mean?"

"I'm coming to it. I want–"

"Do you mean I lied? About what?"

I shook my head, not to call her a liar. "Wait till I get to it. You would of course show shocked surprise if I made the flat statement that Fifi Goheen murdered Arthur Rackell by changing his capsules at the restaurant that evening and that you saw her do it. Naturally you would, since the police have asked you if you saw anyone perform that action or any part of it, and you have answered no. Wouldn't you?"

She was frowning, concentrated. Her hands were still clasped. "But you–you haven't made any such statement."

"Right. I'd rather put it another way. Nero Wolfe has his own way of investigating and his own way of reaching conclusions. He has concluded that if he sends me to see you, to ask you to tell the police that you saw Fifi Goheen substituting the capsules, it will serve the interest of truth and justice. So he sent me, and I'm asking you. It will be embarrassing for you, but not so bad. As I explained, it won't be the first time they've had somebody suddenly remembering something. You can say you and Miss Goheen have been friends and you hated to come out with it, but now you see you have to. You can even say I came here and persuaded you to speak, if you want to, but you certainly shouldn't mention the ten thousand dollars. That—"

"What ten thousand dollars?"

"I'm telling you. Mr. Wolfe has also concluded that it would not be reasonable to expect you to undergo such embarrassment without some consideration. He has made a suggestion to Mr. and Mrs. Rackell, and they have agreed to provide a certain sum of money. Ten thousand of it will come to you, in appreciation of your cooperation in the cause of justice. It will be given you in cash, in currency, within forty-eight hours after you have done your part—and we'll have to discuss that, exactly what you'll tell the police. Speaking for Nero Wolfe, I guarantee the payment within forty-eight hours, or, if you want to, come down to his office with me now and he'll guarantee it himself. Don't ask me what it was that made him conclude that Fifi Goheen did it and that you saw her, because I don't know. Anyhow, if he's right, and he usually is, she'll only be getting what she deserves. You know that's true."

I stopped. She sat motionless, staring at me. There wasn't much light, and I couldn't tell anything from her eyes, but they looked absolutely blank. As the seconds grew to a minute and on I began to think I had literally stupefied her, and I gave her a nudge.

"Have I made it plain?"

"Yes," she mumbled, "you've made it plain."

Suddenly a shudder ran over her whole body, her head dropped forward, and her hands lifted to cover her face, her elbows on her knees. The shudder quit, and she froze like that. She held it so long that I decided another nudge was required, but before I got it out she straightened up and demanded, "What made you think I would do such a thing?"

"I don't think. Mr. Wolfe does the thinking. I'm just a crummy little stooge."

"You'd better go. Please go!"

I stood up and I hesitated. My feeling was that I had run through it smooth as silk, as instructed, but at that point I wasn't sure. Should I make a play of trying to crowd her into a yes or no, or leave it hanging? I couldn't stand there forever, debating it with her staring at me, so I told her, "I do think it's a good offer. The number's in the phone book."

She had nothing to tell my back as I walked to the foyer. I let myself out, descended the three flights, walked to Lexington, found a phone booth in a drugstore, and dialed the number I knew best. In a moment Wolfe's voice was in my ear.

"Okay," I said. "I'm in a booth. I just left her."

"In what mind?"

"I'm not sure. She had Carol Berk hid in a closet. After that had been attended to and we were alone I followed the script, and she was impressed. I'm so good at explaining things that she didn't have to ask questions. The light wasn't very good, but as far as I could tell the prospect of collecting ten grand wasn't absolutely repulsive to her, and neither was the idea of flipping Miss Goheen into the soup. She was torn. She told me to go, and I thought it wise to oblige. When I left she was in a clinch with herself."

"What is she going to do?"

"Don't quote me. But I told her we'd have to discuss exactly what she would tell the cops, so we'll hear from her if she decides to play. Do you want my guesses?"

"Yes."

"Well. On her spilling it to the cops, the one thing that would spoil it, forty to one against. That isn't how her mind will work. On her deciding to play ball with us, twenty to one against. She's not tough enough. On her just keeping it to herself, fifteen to one against. On general principles. On her telling Miss Goheen, ten to one against. She hates her too much. On her telling Carol Berk, two to one against, but I wouldn't dig deep on that one either way. On her telling Mr. H, even money, no matter who is a Commie and who isn't. It would show him how fine and big-hearted and noble she is. She could be, at that. It has been done. Is Saul there?"

"Yes. I never spent anybody's money, not even my own, on a slimmer chance."

"Especially your own. And incidentally sticking *my* neck out. You don't know the meaning of fear when it comes to sticking my neck out. Do we proceed?"

"What alternative is there?"

"None. Has Saul got his men there?"

"Yes."

"Tell him to step on it and meet me at the northeast corner of Sixty-ninth and Fifth Avenue. She could be phoning Heath right now."

"Very well. Then you'll come home?"

I said I would, hung up, and got out of the oven. Nothing would have been more appreciated right then than a large coke-and-lime with the ice brushing my lips, but it was possible that Della was already phoning him and he was at home to get the call, so I marched on by the fountain and out. A taxi got me to the corner of Sixty-ninth and Fifth in six minutes. My watch said 9:42.

I strolled east on Sixty-ninth and stopped across the street from the canopied entrance of the towering tenement of which Henry Jameson Heath was a tenant. It was no casing problem for me, since Saul Panzer had been there in the afternoon to make a survey and spot foxholes. That was elaborate but desirable, because it was to be a very fancy tail, using three shifts of three men each, with Saul in charge of one, Fred Durkin of the second, and Orrie Cather of the third. Fifteen skins an hour that setup would cost, which was quite a disbursement on what Wolfe had admitted was a one-in-twenty chance. Seeing no one but a uniformed doorman in evidence around the canopy, I moseyed back to the corner.

A taxi pulled up, and three men got out. Two of them were just men whose names I knew and with whose records I was fairly familiar, but the third was Saul Panzer, the one guy I want within hearing the day I get hung on the face of a cliff with jet eagles zooming at me. With his saggy shoulders and his face all nose, he looks one-fifth as strong and hardy, and one-tenth as smart, as he really is. I shook hands with him, not having seen him for a week or so, and nodded to the other two.

"Is there anything to say?" I asked him.

"I don't think so. Mr. Wolfe filled me in."

"Okay, take it. You know the Homicide boys may be on him too?"

"Sure. We'll try not to trip on 'em."

"You know it's a long shot and the only bet we've got? So lose him quick, what do we care."

"We'll lose him or die."

"That's the spirit. That's what puts statues of private detectives in the park. See you on the witness stand."

I left them. My immediate and urgent objective was Madison Avenue for a coke-and-lime, but I went a block north to Seventieth Street. Sixty-ninth Street now belonged to Saul and his squad.

VI

At eleven o'clock the next morning, Friday, I sat in the office listening to the clank of Wolfe's elevator as it brought him down from the plant rooms.

There had been no cheep from Della Devlin, but we hadn't wanted one anyway. What we wanted we had got, at least the first installment. At 12:42 Thursday night Saul had phoned that Heath had checked in at Sixty-ninth Street, arriving in a taxi, alone. That was all for the night. At 6:20 in the morning he had phoned that Fred Durkin and his two men had taken over and had been briefed on the terrain. And at 10:23 Fred had phoned that Heath had left his tenement and taken a taxi to 719 East Fifty-first Street and entered the building. That was the gray brick house I had visited the day before. Fred said they had seen no sign of an official tail. They were deployed. I told him he was my favorite mick and still would be if he hung on, and buzzed Wolfe in the plant rooms to inform him.

Wolfe entered, got at his desk, looked over the morning mail, signed a couple of checks, dictated a letter of inquiry about sausage to a man in Wisconsin, and settled down with the crossword puzzle in the London *Times*. I carried on my routine neatly and normally, making it perfectly plain that I could be just as placid as him, no matter how tense and ticklish it got. I had just finished typing the envelope for the letter and was twirling it out of the machine when the doorbell rang. I went to the hall to answer it, took one look through the one-way glass panel, wheeled and returned to the office, and spoke.

"I guess I'm through as a bookie. I said forty to one she wouldn't spill it. Wengert and Cramer want in. We can sneak out the back way and head for Mexico."

He finished putting in a letter, with precision, before he looked up. "Is this flummery?"

"No, sir. It's them."

"Indeed." His brows went up a trifle. "Bring them in."

I went out and to the door, turned the knob, and pulled it open. "Hello hello," I said brightly. "Mr. Wolfe was saying only a minute ago that he would like to see Mr. Cramer and Mr. Wengert, and here you are."

Bright as it was, it didn't go over so well because they stepped in with the first hello and were well along the hall by the time I finished. I shut the door and followed. Entering the office, it struck me as encouraging that Wengert and Wolfe were shaking hands, but then I remembered the District Attorney who always shook hands with the defendant before he opened up, to show there was no personal feeling. Cramer usually took the red leather chair at the end of Wolfe's desk, but this time he let Wengert have it, and I moved up one of the yellow ones for him.

"I sent you my regards the other day by Goodwin," Wengert said. "I hope he remembered."

Wolfe inclined his head. "He did. Thank you."

"I didn't know then I'd be seeing you so soon."

"Nor did I."

"No, I suppose not." Wengert crossed his legs and leaned back. "Goodwin said you had taken on a job for Mr. and Mrs. Benjamin Rackell."

"That's right." Wolfe was casual. "To investigate the death of their nephew. They said he had been working for the FBI. It would have been impolitic to wander into your line of fire, so I sent Mr. Goodwin to see you."

"Let's cut the blah. You sent him to get information you could use."

Wolfe shrugged. "Confronted with omniscience, I bow. My motives are often obscure to myself, but you know all about them. Your advantage. If that was his errand, he failed. You told him nothing."

"Right. Our files are for us, not for private operators. My coming here tells you that we've got a hand in this case, but that's not for publication. If you didn't want to get into our line of fire you certainly stumbled. But officially it's a Manhattan homicide, so I'm here to listen." He nodded at Cramer. "Go ahead, Inspector."

Cramer had been holding in with difficulty. Holding in is a chronic problem with him, and it shows in various ways, chiefly by his big red face getting redder, with the color spreading lower on his thick muscular neck. He blurted at Wolfe, "Honest to God, I'm surprised! Not at Goodwin so much, but you! Subornation of perjury. Attempting to bribe a witness to give false testimony. I've known you to take some fat risks, but holy saints, this ain't risking it, it's yelling for it!"

Wolfe was frowning. "Are you saying that Mr. Goodwin and I have suborned perjury?"

"You've tried to!"

"Good heavens, that's a serious charge. You must have warrants. Serve them, by all means."

"Just give it to him, Inspector," Wengert advised.

Cramer's head jerked to me. "Did you go last evening to the apartment of Della Devlin on Fifty-first Street?"

"It's hotter than yesterday," I stated.

"I asked you a question!"

"This is infantile," Wolfe told him. "You must know the legal procedure with suspected felons. We do."

"Just give it to him," Wengert repeated.

Cramer was glaring at Wolfe. "What you know about legal procedures. Okay. Yesterday you sent Goodwin to see Della Devlin. In your name he offered her ten thousand dollars to testify falsely that she saw Fifi Goheen take the pillbox from the table, remove a capsule and replace it with another, and put the box back on the table. He said the money would be supplied by Mr. and Mrs. Rackell and would be handed her in currency after she had so testified. I shouldn't have said subornation of perjury, I should have said attempt. Now do I ask Goodwin some questions?"

"I'd like to ask him one myself." Wolfe's eyes moved. "Archie. Is what Mr. Cramer just said true?"

"No, sir."

"Then don't answer questions. A policeman has no right to make an inaccurate statement to a citizen about his actions and then order him to answer questions about it." He went to Cramer. "We could drag this out interminably. Why not resolve it sensibly and conclusively?" He came to me. "Archie, get Miss Devlin on the phone and ask her to come down here at once."

I turned and started to dial.

"Cut it, Goodwin," Wengert snapped. I went on dialing. Cramer, who can move when he wants to, left his chair and was by me, pushing down the button. I cocked my head to look up at him. He scowled down at me. I put it back in the cradle. He returned to his chair.

"Then we'll have to change the subject," Wolfe said dryly. "Surely your position is untenable. You want to bullyrag us for what Mr. Goodwin, as my agent, said to Miss Devlin; the first thing to establish is what was actually said; and the only satisfactory way to establish it is to have them both here. Yet you not only didn't bring her with you, you are even determined that we shall not communicate with her. Obviously you don't want her to know what's going on. It's quite preposterous, but I draw no conclusion. It's hard to believe that the New York police and the FBI would conspire to bamboozle a citizen, even me."

Cramer was reddening up again.

Wengert cleared his throat. "Look, Wolfe," he said, not belligerently, "we're here to talk sense."

"Good. Why not start?"

"I am. The interest of the people and government of the United States is involved in this case. My job is to protect that interest. I know you and Goodwin can keep your mouths shut when you want to. I am now talking off the record. Is that understood?"

"Yes, sir."

"Goodwin?"

"Good here."

"See that you keep it good. Arthur Rackell told his aunt that he was working with the FBI. That was a lie. He was either a member of the Communist party or a fellow traveler, we're not sure which. We don't know who he told, besides his aunt, that he was with the FBI, but we're working on it and so are the police. He may have been killed by a Communist who heard it somehow and believed it. There were other motives, personal ones, but the Communist angle comes first until and unless it's ruled out. So you can see why we're in on it. The public interest is involved, not only of this city and state but the whole country. You see that?"

"I saw it," Wolfe muttered, "when I sent Mr. Goodwin to see you day before yesterday."

"We'll skip that." Wengert didn't want to offend. "The point is, what about you? I concede that all you're after is to catch the murderer and collect a fee. But we know you sent Goodwin to Miss Devlin yesterday to offer to pay her to say that she saw Miss Goheen in the act. We also know that you are not likely to pull such a stunt just for the hell of it. You knew exactly what you were doing and why you were doing it. You say you have regard for the public interest. All right, the inspector here represents it, and so do I, and we want you to open up for us. We confidently expect you to. What and whom are you after, and where does that stunt get you?"

Wolfe was regarding him sympathetically through half-closed eyes. "You're not a nincompoop, Mr. Wengert." The eyes moved. "Nor you, Mr. Cramer."

"That's something," Cramer growled.

"It is indeed, considering the average. But your coming here to put this to me, either peremptorily or politely, was ill considered. Shall I explain?"

"If it's not too much bother."

"I'll be as brief as possible. Let us make a complex supposition—that I got Mr. and Mrs. Rackell's permission for an extraordinary disbursement for a stated purpose; that I sent Mr. Goodwin to see Miss Devlin; that he told her I had concluded that Miss Goheen had murdered Arthur Rackell and she had seen the act; that I suggested that she should inform the police of that fact; and that, as compensation for her embarrassment and distress, I engaged to pay her a large sum of money which would be provided by Mr. and Mrs. Rackell."

Wolfe upturned a palm. "Supposing I did that, it was not an attempt to suborn perjury, since it cannot be shown that I intended her to swear falsely, but certainly I was exposing myself to a claim for damages from Miss Goheen. That was a calculated risk I had to take, and whether the calculation was sound depended on the event. There was also a risk of being charged with obstruction of justice, and that too depended on the event. Should it prove to serve justice instead of obstructing it, and should Miss Goheen suffer no unmerited damage, I would be fully justified. I hope to be. I expect to be."

"Then you can—"

"If you please. But suppose, having done all that, I now admit it to you and tell you my calculations and intentions. Then you'll either have to try to head me off or be in it with me. It would be jackassery for you to head me off—take my word for it; it would be unthinkable. But it would also be unthinkable for you to be in it, either actively or passively. Whatever the outcome may be, you cannot afford to be associated with an offer to pay a large sum of money to a person involved in a murder case for disclosing a fact, even an authentic one. Your positions forbid it. I'm a private citizen and can stand it; you can't. What the devil did you come here for? If I'm headed for defeat, opprobrium, and punishment, then I am. Why dash up here only to get yourselves confronted with unthinkable alternatives?"

Wolfe fluttered a hand. "Luckily, this is just talk. I was merely discussing a complex supposition. To return to reality, I will be glad to give you gentlemen any information that you may properly require—and Mr. Goodwin too, of course. So?"

They looked at each other. Cramer let out a snort. Wengert pulled at his ear and gazed at me, and I returned the gaze, open-faced and perfectly innocent. He found that not helpful and transferred to Wolfe.

"You called the turn," he said, "when you told Goodwin to phone Miss Devlin. I should have foreseen that. That was dumb."

The phone rang, and I swiveled and got it. "Nero Wolfe's office, Archie Goodwin speaking."

"This is Rattner."

"Oh, hello. Keep it down, my ears are sensitive."

"Durkin sent me to phone so he could stay on the subject. The subject came out of the house at seven nineteen East Fifty-first Street at eleven forty-one. He was alone. He walked to Lexington and around the corner to a drugstore and is in there now in a phone booth. I'm across the street in a restaurant. Any instructions?"

"Not a thing, thank you. Give my love to the family."

"Right."

It clicked off, and I hung up and swiveled back to rejoin the party, but apparently it was over. They were on their feet, and Wengert was turning to go. Cramer was saying, ". . . but it's not *all* off the record. I just want that understood."

He turned and followed Wengert out. I saw no point in dashing past them out to the door, since two grown men should be up to turning a knob and pulling, but I stepped to the hall to observe. When they were outside and the door closed I went back in and remarked to Wolfe, "Very neat. But what if they had let me phone her?"

He made a face. "Pfui. If they had got it from her they wouldn't have called on me. They would have sent for you, possibly with a warrant. That was one of the contingencies."

"They might have let me phone her anyway."

"Unlikely, since that would have disclosed their knowledge—to her and therefore to anyone—and betrayed their informant. But if they had, while she was on her way I would have proceeded with them, and they would have left before she arrived."

I put the yellow chair back in place. "All the same I'm glad they didn't and so are you. That was Rattner on the phone, reporting for Fred. Heath was with Miss Devlin an hour and four minutes. He left at eleven forty-one and was in a phone booth in a drugstore when Rattner called."

"Satisfactory." He picked up his pencil and bent over the crossword puzzle with a little sigh.

VII

June twenty-first is supposed to be the longest day, but this year it was August third. It went on for weeks after Cramer and Wengert left. I spent it all in the office, and it was no fun. There was only one thing that could keep us floating, but there were a dozen that could sink us. They might lose him. Or he might handle it by phone—most unlikely, but not impossible. Or Wolfe might have it figured entirely wrong; he himself gave it one in twenty. Or Heath might meet him or her some place where they couldn't be nailed. Or a city or federal employee might horn in and ruin it. Or and or and or.

Five bucks an hour had been added to the outgo. If and when the call came that would start me moving, I didn't want to waste any precious minutes or even seconds finding transportation, so Herb Aronson had his taxi parked at the filling station at the corner of Eleventh Avenue, on us. Also he came to us for lunch and again, at seven in the evening, for dinner.

Every time the phone rang and I grabbed it, I wanted it and I didn't. It might be the starting gun, but on the other hand it might be the awful news that they had lost him. Keeping a tail on a guy in New York, especially if he has an important reason for wanting privacy, needs not only great skill but also plenty of luck. We were buying the skill, in Saul and Fred and Orrie, but you can't buy luck.

The luck held, and so did they. There were two more calls from Fred, via Rattner, before two o'clock, when he was relieved by Orrie Cather. One was to report that Heath, after calls at an optician's and a bookstore, had entered a restaurant on Forty-fifth Street and was lunching with two men, not known to me as described, and the other was to tell where Orrie could find him. There was still no sign of an official tail. During the afternoon and early evening there was a series of reports from Orrie. Heath and his companions left the restaurant at 2:52, taxied to the apartment house on Sixty-ninth Street where Heath lived, and entered. At 5:35 the two men emerged and walked off. At 7:03 Heath came out and took a taxi to Chezar's restaurant, where he met Della Devlin and they dined. At 9:14 they left and taxied to the gray brick house on Fifty-first Street and went in. Heath was still in there at ten o'clock, the hour for Orrie to be relieved by Saul Panzer, and it was at the corner of Fifty-first and Lexington that Orrie and Saul connected.

By that time I would have been chewing on a railroad spike if I had had one, and Wolfe was working hard trying to be serene. Between nine-thirty and ten-thirty he made four trips to the bookshelves, trying different ones, setting a record.

I snarled at him, "What's the matter, restless?"

"Yes," he said placidly. "Are you?"

"Yes."

It came a little before eleven. The phone rang, and I got it. It was Bill Doyle.

He seemed to be panting. "I'm out of breath," he said, wasting some of it. "When he left there he got smart and started tricks. We let him spot Al and ditch him, you know how Saul works it, but even then we damn near lost him. He came to Eighty-sixth and Fifth and went in the park on foot. A woman was sitting on a bench with a collie on a leash, and he stopped and started talking to her. Saul thinks you'd better come."

"So do I. Describe the woman."

"I can't. I was keeping back and didn't get close enough."

"Where is Saul?"

"On the ground under a bush."

"Where are you?"

"Drugstore. Eighty-sixth and Madison."

"Be at the Eighty-sixth-Street park entrance. I'm coming."

I whirled and told Wolfe, "In Central Park. He met a woman with a dog. So long."

"Are you armed?"

"Certainly." I was at the door.

"They will be desperate."

"I already am."

I let myself out, ran down the stoop and to the corner. Herb was in his hack, listening to the radio. At sight of me on the lope he switched it off, and by the time I was in he had the engine started. I told him, "Eighty-sixth and Fifth," and we rolled.

We went up Eleventh Avenue instead of Tenth because with the staggered lights on Tenth you can't average better than twenty-five. On Eleventh you can make twelve or more blocks on a light if you sprint, and we sprinted. At Fifty-sixth we turned east, had fair luck crosstown, and turned left on Fifth Avenue. I told Herb to quit crawling, and he told me to get out and walk. When we reached Eighty-sixth Street I had the door open before the wheels stopped, hopped out, and crossed the avenue to the park side.

Bill Doyle was there. He was the pale gaunt type, from reading too much about horses and believing it. I asked him, "Anything new?"

"No. I been here waiting."

"Can you show me Saul's bush without rousing the dog?"

"I can if he's still there. It's quite a ways."

"Within a hundred yards of them take to the grass. They mustn't hear our footsteps stopping. Let's go."

He entered the park by the paved path, and I trailed. The first thirty paces it was upgrade, curving right. Under a park light two young couples had stopped to have an argument, and we detoured around them. The path leveled and straightened under overhanging branches of trees. We passed another light. A man swinging a cane came striding from the opposite direction and on by. The path turned left, crossed an open space, and entered shrubbery. A little further on there was a fork, and Doyle stopped.

"They're down there a couple of hundred feet," he whispered, pointing to the left branch of the fork. "Or they were. Saul's over that way."

"Okay, I'll lead. Steer me by touch."

I stepped onto the grass and started alongside the right branch of the fork. It was uphill a little, and I had to duck under branches. I hadn't gone far when Doyle tugged at my sleeve, and when I turned he pointed to the left. "That bunch of bushes there," he whispered. "The big one in the middle. That's where he went, but I can't see him."

My sight is twenty-twenty, and my eyes had got adjusted to the night, but for a minute I couldn't pick him up. When I did the huddled hump under the bush was perfectly plain. A ripple ran up my spine. Since Saul was still there, Heath was still there too, under his eye, and almost certainly the woman with the dog was there also. Of course I couldn't see them, on account of the bushes. I considered what to do. I wanted to confront them together, before they separated, but if Saul was close enough to hear their words I didn't want to bust it up. The most attractive idea was to sneak across to Saul's bush and join him, but I might be heard, if not by them by the dog. Standing there, peering toward Saul's bush, concentrated, with Doyle beside me, I became aware of footsteps behind me, approaching along the path, but supposed it was just a late park stroller and didn't turn—until the footsteps stopped and a voice came.

"Looking for tigers?"

I wheeled. It was a flatfoot on park patrol. "Good evening, officer," I said respectfully. "Nope, just getting air."

"The air's the same if you stay on the path." He approached on the grass, looking not at us but past us, in the direction we had been gazing. Suddenly he grunted, quickened his step, and headed straight for Saul's bush. Apparently he had good eyes too. There was no time to consider. I muttered fast at Doyle's ear, "Grab his cap and run—jump, damn it!"

He did. I will always love him for it, especially for not hesitating a tenth of a second. Four leaps got him to the cop, a swoop of his hand got the cap, and away he scooted, swerving right to double back to the path. I stood in my tracks. The cop acted by reflex. Instead of ignoring the playful prank and proceeding to inspect the object under the bush, or making for me, he bounded after Doyle and his cap, calling a command to halt. Doyle, reaching the path and streaking along it, had a good lead, but the cop was no snail. They disappeared.

All that commotion changed the situation entirely. I made it double quick to the left across the grass until I reached the other fork of the path, and kept going. Around a bend, there they were—Heath seated on a bench with a woman, a big collie lying at their feet. When I stopped in front of them the collie rose to its haunches and made a noise, asking a question. I had a hand in a coat pocket.

"Tell the dog it's okay," I suggested. "I hate to shoot a dog."

"Why should you—" Heath started, and stopped. He stood up.

"Yeah, it's me," I said. "Representing Nero Wolfe. It won't help if you scream, there's two of us. Come on out, Saul. Watch the dog, it may not wait for orders."

There was a sound from the direction of the bushes, and in a moment Saul appeared, circling around to join me on the right. The dog made a noise that was more of a whine than a growl, but it didn't move. The woman put a hand on its head. I asked Saul, "Could you hear what they said?"

"Most of it. I heard enough."

"Was it interesting?"

"Yes."

"This is illegal," Heath stated. He was half choked with indignation or something. "This is an invasion—"

"Nuts. Save it; you may need it. I have a cab parked at the Eighty-sixth-Street entrance. Four of us with the dog will just fill it comfortably. Mr. Wolfe is expecting us. Let's go."

"You're armed," Heath said. "This is assault with a deadly weapon."

"I'm going home," the woman said, speaking for the first time. "I'll telephone Mr. Wolfe, or my husband will, and we'll see about this. I brought my dog to the park, and this gentleman and I happened to get into conversation. This is outrageous. You won't dare to harm my dog."

She got up, and the collie was instantly erect by her, against her knee.

"Well," I conceded, "I admit I hate to shoot a dog. I also admit that Mr. Wolfe likes himself so well that he'll steal the throne on the Day of Judgment if they don't watch him. So you go on home with Towser, and Saul and I will call on the police and the FBI, and I'll tell them what I saw, and Saul will tell them what he saw and heard. But don't make the mistake of thinking you can talk them out of believing us. We have our reputations just as you have yours."

They looked at each other. They looked at me and back at each other.

"We'll see Mr. Wolfe," the woman said.

Heath looked right and then left, as if hoping there might be someone else around to see, and then nodded at her.

"That's sensible," I told them. "You lead the way, Saul. Eighty-sixth-Street entrance."

VIII

We left the collie in Herb's taxi, parked at the curb in front of Wolfe's place. There has never been a dog in that house, and I saw no point in breaking the precedent for one who was on such strained terms with me. Herb, on advice, closed the glass panels.

I went ahead up the stoop to open the door and let them in, put them in the front room with Saul, and went through to the office.

"Okay," I told Wolfe, "it's your turn. They're here."

Behind his desk, he closed the book he had been reading and put it down. He asked, "Mrs. Rackell?"

"Yes. They were there on a bench, with dog, and Saul was behind a bush and could hear, but I don't know what. I gave them their choice of the law or you, and they preferred you. She probably thinks she can buy out. You want Saul first?"

"No. Bring them in."

"But Saul can tell you—"

"I don't need it. Or if I do—we'll see."

"You want him in too?"

"Yes."

I went and opened the connecting door and invited them, and they entered. As Mrs. Rackell crossed to the red leather chair and sat her lips were so tight there were none. Heath's face had no expression at all, but it must be hard to display feeling with that kind of round pudgy frontispiece even if you try. Saul took a chair against the far wall, but Wolfe told him to move up, and he transferred to one at the end of my desk.

Mrs. Rackell grabbed the ball. She said it was absolutely contemptible, spying on her and threatening her with the police. It was infamous and treacherous. She wouldn't tolerate it.

Wolfe let her get it out and then said dryly, "You astonish me, madam." He shook his head. "You chatter about proprieties when you are under the menace of a mortal peril. Don't you realize what I've done? Don't you know where we stand?"

"You're chattering yourself," Heath said harshly. "We were brought here under a threat. By what right?"

"I'll tell you." Wolfe leaned back. "This is no pleasure for me, so I'll hurry it—my part of it. But you need to know exactly what the situation is, for you have a vital decision to make. First let me introduce

Mr. Saul Panzer." His eyes moved. "Saul, you followed Mr. Heath to a clandestine meeting with Mrs. Rackell?"

"Yes, sir."

"Then I'll risk an assumption. I assume that his purpose was to protest against her supplying funds to inculpate Miss Goheen, and to demand that the attempt be abandoned. You heard much of what they said?"

"Yes, sir."

"Did it impeach my assumption?"

"No, sir."

"Did it support it?"

"Yes, sir. Plenty."

Wolfe went to Heath. "Mr. Panzer's quality is known, though not to you until now. I think a jury will believe him, and I'm sure the police and the FBI will. My advice, sir, is to cut the loss."

"Loss?" Heath was trying to sneer but with that face he couldn't make it. "I haven't lost anything."

"You're about to. You can't help it." Wolfe wiggled a finger at him. "Must I spell it out for you? Wednesday evening, day before yesterday, when you and six others were here, I was nonplused. I had my choice of giving up or of attempting simultaneously a dozen elaborate lines of inquiry, any one of which would have strained my resources. Neither was tolerable. Since I was helpless with what had already happened, I had to try to make something happen under my eye, and I devised a stratagem—a clumsy one, but the best I could do. I made a proposal to Mr. and Mrs. Rackell. I phrased it with care, but in effect I asked for money to bribe a witness and solve the case by chicanery."

Wolfe's eyes darted to Mrs. Rackell. "And you idiotically exposed yourself."

"I did?" She was contemptuous. "How?"

"You grabbed at it. Your husband, in his innocence, was dubious, but not you. You thought that, having decided the job was beyond me, I was trying to earn a fee by knavery, and you eagerly acquiesced. Why? It was out of character and indeed preposterous. What you had said you wanted was the murderer of your nephew caught and punished, but apparently you were willing to spend a large sum of money, your own money, on a frame-up. Either that or you were excessively naive, and at least it justified speculation."

His gaze was straight at her, and she was meeting it. He went on, "So I speculated. What if you had yourself killed your nephew? As for getting the poison, that was as feasible for you as for the others. As for opportunity, you said you had not entered your nephew's room after

Mrs. Kremp had been there and put the capsules in the pillbox, but could you prove it? There was nothing to my knowledge that excluded you. Your harassment of the FBI and the police could have been for assurance that you were safe. It was your husband who insisted on coming to me, and naturally you would have wanted to be present. As for motive, that would have to be explored, but for speculation there was material at hand, furnished by you. You were positive, with no real evidence for it, that your nephew had been killed by a Communist who had discovered that he was betraying the cause; you got that in first thing when you called here Tuesday with your husband. Might it not be true and you yourself the Communist?"

"Rot!" She snorted.

Wolfe shook his head. "Not necessarily. I deplore the current tendency to accuse people of pro-communism irresponsibly and unjustly, but anybody could be one secretly, no matter what façade he presented. There was the question, if you were in fact a Communist or a sympathizer, why did you so badger your nephew that he had to pacify you by telling the lie that he was working for the FBI? Why didn't you confide in him your own devotion to the cause? Of course you didn't dare. There would have been the danger that he might recant; he might have become an ex-Communist and told all he knew, as so many have done the past year or two; and to preserve your façade for your husband and friends you had to keep after him. It must have been a severe shock when you learned, or thought you did, that he was an agent of communism's implacable enemy. It made him an imminent threat, there in your own household."

Wolfe came forward in his chair. "That was all speculation two days ago, but not now. Your meeting with Mr. Heath has made it a confident assumption. Why would you make a secret rendezvous with him? What could give him the right to demand that you withdraw the offer of money for Miss Devlin? Well. If you are secretly a Communist, almost certainly you have contributed substantial sums of money—to the party of course, but also to the bail fund; and Mr. Heath is the trustee of the bail fund and is inviting a term in jail rather than disclose the names of the contributors. So, madam, my stratagem worked—with, I confess, a full share of luck. Mr. Goodwin and I have been under some strain. Until a few minutes ago, when he entered and told me you two were here, I wouldn't have wagered a nickel on it. Now it's over, thank heaven. My assumptions are on rock. You're cooked."

"You're a conceited fool," Mrs. Rackell said flatly. For the first time I thought she was really impressive. He hadn't made a dent in her. She was still dead sure of herself. "With your crazy assumptions," she said.

"I was resting on a park bench, and this Mr. Heath came along and spoke." She darted a contemptuous glance at Saul. "Whatever lies that man tells about what he heard."

Wolfe nodded. "That of course is your best position, and no doubt you're capable of defending it against all assault, so I won't try butting it." He looked at Heath. "But yours is much weaker, and I don't see how you can hold it."

"I have withstood better men than you," Heath declared. "Men in positions of great power. Men who head the imperialist conspiracy to dominate the world."

"No doubt," Wolfe conceded. "But even if you appraise them correctly, which I question, right now you have to appraise me. I head no conspiracy to dominate anything, but I've got you in a hole you can't scramble out of. Must I spell it out for you? You're a trustee of that Communist bail fund, amounting to nearly a million dollars, and at great personal risk you are determined to keep the names of the contributors secret. Court orders haven't budged you. Obviously you prefer any alternative to disclosure of the names. But you're going to disclose one of them to me now: Mrs. Benjamin Rackell. And the amounts and dates of her contributions. Well?"

"No comment."

"Pfui. I say you can't hold it. Consider what's going to happen. I am convinced that Mrs. Rackell murdered her nephew because she thought he was spying on Communists for the FBI, and therefore, of course, her own secret was in danger. The FBI and the police will now share that conviction. Whether it takes a day or a year, do you think there's any chance we won't get her? Knowing she had the poison, do you think we won't discover where and how she got it?"

Wolfe shook his head. "No. You'll have to ditch her. She's too hot to hold. The police will put it to you—have you any knowledge or evidence that she has been in sympathy with the Communist cause? You say no or refuse to answer. Subsequently they get such evidence, with proof that you were aware of it; it is easily possible that, through some process which you cannot avert, they will get the whole list of contributors. And instead of a brief commitment for contempt of court you'll get a considerable term for withholding vital evidence in a murder case. Besides, what of the cause you're devoted to? You know the opinion of communism held by most Americans, including me. To the odium already attached to it would you add the stigma of shielding a murderer?"

Wolfe raised his brows. "Really, Mr. Heath. There are plenty of precedents to guide you. This will be by no means the first time that an act of misguided zeal by a Communist has come home to roost. In the countries they rule the jails are full—let alone the graves—of former comrades who were indiscreet. In America, where you don't rule and I hope you never will, can you afford the luxury of shielding a murderer? No. She's too much for you. How much has she contributed and when?"

Heath's face was really something. If he hadn't inherited money he could have piled it up playing poker. From looking at him no one could have got the faintest notion how to bet.

He stood up. "I'll let you know tomorrow," he said.

Wolfe grunted. "Oh no. I want to phone the police to come for her. They'll want a statement from you. Archie?"

I got up and moved and was between the company and the door. Heath moved too. "I'm going," he said, and came. When I stood pat he swerved to circle around me. It would have been a pleasure to plug him, but I refrained and merely got his shoulder, whirled him, and propelled him a little. He stumbled but stayed upright.

"This is assault," he told Wolfe, not me. "And illegal restraint. You'll regret this."

"Bosh." Wolfe suddenly blew up. "Confound it, do you think I'm going to let you walk out to call a meeting of your Politburo? Do you think I don't know when I've got you hooked? You can't possibly hang onto her. Talk sense! Can you?"

"No," he said.

"Are you ready to disclose the facts?"

"Not to you. To the police, yes."

Mrs. Rackell snapped at him, "Have you gone mad, you fool?"

He stared at her. I've heard a lot of phony cracks in that office, of all kinds and shapes, but that one by Henry Jameson Heath took the cake. Staring at her, he said calmly, "I must do my duty as a citizen, Mrs. Rackell."

Wolfe spoke. "Archie, get Mr. Cramer."

I stepped to my desk and dialed.

IX

Saturday noon, the next day, Wengert and Cramer stood there in the office, at the end of Wolfe's desk. They were standing because, having been there nearly an hour and covered all the points, they were ready to leave. They had not admitted in so many words that Wolfe had done the American people, including them, a favor, but on the whole they had been sociable.

As they were turning to go I said, "Excuse me, one little thing."

They looked at me. I spoke to Wengert. "I thought Mr. Wolfe might mention it, but he didn't, and neither did you. I only bring it up to offer a constructive criticism. An FBI undercover girl, even one disguised as a Commie, shouldn't get in the habit of hurting people's feelings just for the hell of it. It didn't do a particle of good for Carol Berk to call me a crummy little stooge before a witness. Of course she was sore because I found her in the closet, but even so. I think you ought to speak to her about it."

Wengert was frowning at me. "Carol Berk? What kind of a gag is this?"

"Oh, come off it." I was disgusted. "How thick could I get? It was so obvious Mr. Wolfe didn't even bother to comment on it. Who else could have told you about my talk with Della Devlin? She trusted Miss Berk enough to let her hide in the closet, so of course she told her about it. Do you want to debate it with me on TV?"

"No. Nor with anybody else. You talk too damn much."

"Only with the right people. Say please, and I'll promise not to tell. I just wanted to make a helpful suggestion. I may be crummy and I may be a stooge, but I'm not little."

Cramer snorted. "If you ask me there's too much of you. About a hundred and eighty pounds too much. Come on, Wengert, I'm late."

They went. I supposed that was the last of that, but a couple of days later, Monday afternoon, while Wolfe was dictating a letter, the phone rang and a voice said it was Carol Berk. I said hello, showing no enthusiasm, and asked her, "How are your manners?"

"Rotten when required," she said cheerfully. "Privately like this, from a phone booth, I can be charming. I thought it was only fair for me to apologize for calling you little."

"Okay, go ahead."

"I thought you might prefer it face to face. I'm willing to take the trouble if you insist."

"Well, I'll tell you. I had an idea last week, Wednesday I think it was, that I ought to find time some day to tell you why I don't like you. We could meet and clean it up. I'll tell you why I don't like you, and you'll apologize. The Churchill bar at four-thirty? Can you be seen with me in public?"

"Certainly, I'm supposed to be seen in public."

"Fine. I'll have a hammer and sickle in my buttonhole."

As I hung up and swiveled I told Wolfe, "That was Carol Berk. I'm going to buy her a drink and possibly food. Since she was connected with the case we've just finished, of course I'll put it on the expense account."

"You will not," he asserted and resumed the dictation.

The Cop-Killer

I

There were several reasons why I had no complaints as I walked along West Thirty-fifth Street that morning, approaching the stoop of Nero Wolfe's old brownstone house. The day was sunny and sparkling, my new shoes felt fine after the two-mile walk, a complicated infringement case had been polished off for a big client, and I had just deposited a check in five figures to Wolfe's account in the bank.

Five paces short of the stoop I became aware that two people, a man and a woman, were standing on the sidewalk across the street, staring either at the stoop or at me, or maybe both. That lifted me a notch higher, with the thought that while two rubbernecks might not put us in a class with the White House still it was nothing to sneeze at, until a second glance made me realize that I had seen them before. But where? Instead of turning up the steps I faced them, just as they stepped off the curb and started to me.

"Mr. Goodwin," the woman said in a sort of gasping whisper that barely reached me.

She was fair-skinned and blue-eyed, young enough, kind of nice-looking and neat in a dark blue assembly-line coat. He was as dark as she was fair, not much bigger than her, with his nose slanting slightly to the left and a full wide mouth. My delay in recognizing him was because I had never seen him with a hat on before. He was the hat-and-coat-and-tie custodian at the barber shop I went to.

"Oh, it's you, Carl—"

"Can we go in with you?" the woman asked in the same gasping whisper, and then I knew her too. She was also from the barber shop, a manicure. I had never hired her, since I do my own nails, but had seen her around and had heard her called Tina.

I looked down at her smooth white little face with its pointed chin and didn't care for the expression on it. I glanced at Carl, and he looked even worse.

"What's the matter?" I guess I was gruff. "Trouble?"

"Please not out here," Tina pleaded. Her eyes darted left and right and back up at me. "We just got enough brave to go to the door when you came. We were thinking which door, the one down below or up the steps. Please let us in?"

It did not suit my plans. I had counted on getting a few little chores done before Wolfe came down from the plant rooms at eleven o'clock. There could be no profit in this.

"You told me once," Carl practically whined, "that people in danger only have to mention your name."

"Nuts. A pleasantry. I talk too much." But I was stuck. "Okay, come in and tell me about it."

I led the way up the steps and let us in with my key. Inside, the first door on the left of the long wide hall was to what we called the front room, not much used, and I opened it, thinking to get it over with in there, but Fritz was there, dusting, so I took them along to the next door and on into the office. After moving a couple of chairs so they would be facing me I sat at my desk and nodded at them impatiently. Tina had looked around swiftly before she sat.

"Such a nice safe room," she said, "for you and Mr. Wolfe, two such great men."

"He's the great one," I corrected her. "I just caddy. What's this about danger?"

"We love this country," Carl said emphatically. All of a sudden he started trembling, first his hands, then his arms and shoulders, then all over. Tina darted to him and grabbed his elbows and shook him, not gently, and said things to him in some language I wasn't up on. He mumbled back at her and then got more vocal, and after a little the trembling stopped, and she returned to her chair.

"We do love this country," she declared.

I nodded. "Wait till you see Chillicothe, Ohio, where I was born. Then you *will* love it. How far west have you been, Tenth Avenue?"

"I don't think so." Tina was doubtful. "I think Eighth Avenue. But that's what we want to do, go west." She decided it would help to let me have a smile, but it didn't work too well. "We can't go east, can we, into the ocean?" She opened her blue leather handbag and, with no fingering or digging, took something from it. "But you see, we don't know where to go. This Ohio, maybe? I have fifty dollars here."

"That would get you there," I allowed.

She shook her head. "Oh, no. The fifty dollars is for you. You know our name, Vardas? You know we are married? So there is no question of morals, we are very high in morals, only all we want is to do our work and live in private, Carl and me, and we think—"

Having heard the clatter of Wolfe's elevator descending from the plant rooms on the roof, I had known an interruption was coming but had let her proceed. Now she stopped as Wolfe's steps sounded and he appeared at the door. Carl and Tina both bounced to their feet. Two paces in, after a quick glance at them, Wolfe stopped short and glowered at me.

"I didn't tell you we had callers," I said cheerfully, "because I knew you would be down soon. You know Carl, at the barber shop? And Tina, you've seen her there too. It's all right, they're married. They just dropped in to buy fifty bucks' worth of—"

Without a word or even a nod, Wolfe turned all of his seventh of a ton and beat it out and toward the door to the kitchen at the rear. The Vardas family stared at the doorway a moment and then turned to me.

"Sit down," I invited them. "As you said, he's a great man. He's sore because I didn't notify him we had company, and he was expecting to sit there behind his desk"—I waved a hand—"and ring for beer and enjoy himself. He wouldn't wiggle a finger for fifty dollars. Maybe I won't either, but let's see." I looked at Tina, who was back on the edge of her chair. "You were saying . . ."

"We don't want Mr. Wolfe mad at us," she said in distress.

"Forget it. He's only mad at me, which is chronic. What do you want to go to Ohio for?"

"Maybe not Ohio." She tried to smile again. "It's what I said, we love this country and we want to go more into it—far in. We would like to be in the middle of it. We want you to tell us where to go, to help us—"

"No, no." I was brusque. "Start from here. Look at you, you're both scared stiff. What's the danger Carl mentioned?"

"I don't think," she protested, "it makes any difference—"

"That's no good," Carl said harshly. His hands started trembling again, but he gripped the sides of his chair seat, and they stopped. His dark eyes fastened on me. "I met Tina," he said in a low level voice, trying to keep feeling out of it, "three years ago in a concentration camp in Russia. If you want me to I will tell you why it was that they would never have let us get out of there alive, not in one hundred years, but I would rather not talk so much about it. It makes me start to tremble, and I am trying to learn to act and talk of a manner so I can quit trembling."

I concurred. "Save it for some day after you stop trembling. But you did get out alive?"

"Plainly. We are here." There was an edge of triumph to the level voice. "I will not tell you about that either. But they think we are dead.

Of course Vardas was not our name then, neither of us. We took that name later, when we got married in Istanbul. Then we so managed—"

"You shouldn't tell any places," Tina scolded him. "No places at all and no people at all."

"You are most right," Carl admitted. He informed me, "It was not Istanbul."

I nodded. "Istanbul is out. You would have had to swim. You got married, that's the point."

"Yes. Then, later, we nearly got caught again. We did get caught, but—"

"No!" Tina said positively.

"Very well, Tina. You are most right. We went many other places, and at a certain time in a certain way we crossed the ocean. We had tried very hard to come to this country according to your rules, but it was in no way possible. When we did get into New York it was more by an accident—no, I did not say that. I will not say that much. Only I will say we got into New York. For a while it was so difficult, but it has been nearly a year now, since we got the jobs at the barber shop, that life has been so fine and sweet that we are almost healthy again. What we eat! We have even got some money saved! We have got—"

"Fifty dollars," Tina said hastily.

"Most right," Carl agreed. "Fifty American dollars. I can say as a fact that we would be healthy and happy beyond our utmost dreams three years ago, except for the danger. The danger is that we did not follow your rules. I will not deny that they are good rules, but for us they were impossible. We cannot expect ourselves to be happy when we don't know what minute someone may come and ask us how we got here. The minute that just went by, that was all right, no one asked, but here is the next minute. Every day is full of those minutes, so many. We have found a way to learn what would happen, and we know where we would be sent back to. We know exactly what would happen to us. I would not be surprised if you felt a deep contempt when you saw me trembling the way I do, but to understand a situation like this I believe you have to be somewhat close to it. As I am. As Tina is. I am not saying you would tremble like me—after all, Tina never does—but I think you might have your own way of showing that you were not really happy."

"Yeah, I might," I agreed. I glanced at Tina, but the expression on her face could have made me uncomfortable, so I looked back at Carl. "But if I tried to figure a way out I doubt if I would pick on spilling it to a guy named Archie Goodwin just because he came to the barber shop where I worked. He might be crazy about the rules you couldn't follow, and anyhow there are just as many minutes in Ohio as there are in New York."

"There is that fifty dollars." Carl extended his hands, not trembling, toward me.

Tina gestured impatiently. "That's nothing to you," she said, letting bitterness into it for the first time. "We know that, it's nothing. But the danger has come, and we had to have someone tell us where to go. This morning a man came to the barber shop and asked us questions. An official! A policeman!"

"Oh." I glanced from one to the other. "That's different. A policeman in uniform?"

"No, in regular clothes, but he showed us a card in a case, New York Police Department. His name was on it, Jacob Wallen."

"What time this morning?"

"A little after nine o'clock, soon after the shop was open. He talked first with Mr. Fickler, the owner, and Mr. Fickler brought him around behind the partition to my booth, where I do customers when they're through in the chair or when they only want a manicure, and I was there, getting things together, and he sat down and took out a notebook and asked me questions. Then he—"

"What kind of questions?"

"All about me. My name, where I lived, where I came from, how long I've been working there, all that kind, and then about last night, where I was and what I was doing last night."

"Did he say why he was curious about last night?"

"No. He just asked questions."

"What part of last night did he ask about? All of it?"

"Yes, from the time the shop closes, half-past six, from then on."

"Where did you tell him you came from?"

"I said Carl and I are DPs from Italy. That's what we had decided to say. We have to say something when people are just curious."

"I suppose you do. Did he ask to see your papers?"

"No. That will come next." She set her jaw. "We can't go back there. We have to leave New York today—now."

"What else did he ask?"

"That's all. It was mostly about last night."

"Then what? Did he question Carl too?"

"Yes, but not right after me. He sent me away, and Mr. Fickler sent Philip to him in the booth, and when Philip came out he sent Carl in, and when Carl came out he sent Jimmie in. Jimmie was still in the booth with him when I went to Carl, up front by the rack, and we knew we had to get out. We waited until Mr. Fickler had gone to the back of the shop for something, and then we just walked out. We went to our room down on the East Side and packed our stuff and started for Grand Central with it, and then we realized we didn't know anything about where to go and might make some terrible mistake, so there in Grand Central we talked it over. We decided that since the police were after us already it couldn't be any worse, but we weren't sure enough about any of the people we have met in New York, so the best thing would be to come to you and pay you to help us. You're a professional detective, and anyway Carl likes you about the best of all the customers. You only tip him a dime, so it's not that. I have noticed you myself, the way you look. You look like a man who would break rules too—if you had to."

I gave her a sharp look, suspicious, but if she was trying to butter me she was very good. All that showed in her blue eyes was the scare that had put them on the run and the hope of me they were hanging on to for dear life. I looked at Carl. The scare was there too, but I couldn't see the hope. Still he sat solid on the chair, with no sign of trembling, as I thought to myself that it would have been no surprise to him if I had picked up the phone and called the cops. Either he had his full share of guts or he had run out entirely.

I was irritated. "Damn it," I protested, "you bring it here already broke. What did you beat it for? That alone fixes you. He was questioning the others too and he was concentrating on last night. What about last night? What were you doing, breaking some more rules?"

They both started to answer, but she let him take it. He said no, they weren't. They had gone straight home from work and eaten in their room as usual. Tina had washed some clothes, and Carl had read a book. Around nine they had gone for a walk, and had been back in their room and in bed before ten-thirty.

I was disgusted. "You sure did it up," I declared. "If you're clean for last night, why didn't you stay put? You must have something in your heads or you wouldn't have stayed alive and got this far. Why didn't you use it?"

Carl smiled at me. He really did smile, but it didn't make me want to smile back. "A policeman asking questions," he said in the level tone he had used before, "has a different effect on different people. If you have a country like this one and you are innocent of crime, all the people of your country are saying it with you when you answer the questions. That is true even when you are away from home—especially when you are away from home. But Tina and I have no country at all. The country we had once, it is no longer a country, it is just a place to wait to die, only if we are sent back there we will not have to wait. Two people alone cannot answer a policeman's questions anywhere in the world. It takes a whole country to speak to a policeman, and Tina and I—we do not have one."

"You see," Tina said. "Here, take it." She got up and came to me, extending a hand with the money in it. "Take it, Mr. Goodwin! Just tell us where to go, all the little facts that will help us—"

"Or we thought," Carl suggested, not hopefully, "that you might give us a letter to some friend, in this Ohio perhaps—not that we should expect too much for fifty dollars."

I looked at them, with my lips pressed together. The morning was shot now anyway, with Wolfe sore and my chores not done. I swiveled to my desk and picked up the phone. Any one of three or four city employees would probably find out for me what kind of errand had taken a dick named Wallen to the Goldenrod Barber Shop, unless it was something very special. But with my finger in the dial hole I hesitated and then replaced the phone. If it was something hot I would be starting PD cars for our address, and Wolfe and I both have a prejudice against cops yanking people out of his office, no matter who they are, unless we ourselves have got them ready for delivery. So I swiveled again. Carl was frowning at me, his head moving from side to side. Tina was standing tense, the money clutched in her fist.

"This is silly," I said. "If they're really after you, you'd be throwing your money away on carfare to Ohio or anywhere else. Save it for a lawyer. I'll have to go up there and see what it's all about." I got up, crossed to the soundproof door to the front room, and opened it. "You can wait here. In here, please."

"We'll go," Tina said, back to her gasping whisper again. "We won't bother you any more. Come, Carl—"

"Skip it," I said curtly. "If this amounts to anything more than petty larceny you'd be nabbed sure as hell. This is my day for breaking a rule, and I'll be back soon. Come on, I'll put you in here, and I advise you to stay put."

They looked at each other.

"I like him," Carl said.

Tina moved. She came and passed through into the front room, and Carl was right behind her.

I told them to sit down and relax and not get restless, shut the door, went to the kitchen, where Wolfe was seated at the far end of the long table, drinking beer, and told him, "The check from Pendexter came and has been deposited. That pair of foreigners have got themselves in a mess. I put them in the front room and told them to say there until I get back."

"Where are you going?" he demanded.

"A little detective work, not in your class. I won't be gone long. You can dock me."

I left.

II

The Goldenrod Barber Shop was in the basement of an office building on Lexington Avenue in the upper Thirties. I had been patronizing one of the staff, named Ed, for several years. Formerly, from away back, Wolfe had gone to an artist in a shop on Twenty-eighth Street, named Fletcher. When Fletcher had retired a couple of years ago Wolfe had switched to Goldenrod and tried my man, Ed, hadn't liked him, had experimented with the rest of the Goldenrod staff, and had settled on Jimmie. His position now, after two years, was that Jimmie was no Fletcher, especially with a shampoo, but that he was some better than tolerable.

Goldenrod, with only six chairs and usually only four of them manned, and two manicures, was no Framinelli's, but it was well equipped and clean, and anyhow it had Ed, who was a little rough at tilting a head maybe but knew exactly how to handle my hair and had a razor so sharp and slick you never knew it was on you.

I hadn't shaved that morning and as, at noon, I paid the taxi driver, entered the building, and descended the stairs to the basement, my plan of campaign was simple. I would get in Ed's chair, waiting if necessary, and ask him to give me a once-over, and the rest would be easy.

But it was neither simple nor easy. A medium-sized mob of white-collar workers, buzzing and chattering, was ranged three deep along the wall of the corridor facing the door of the shop. Others, passing by in both directions, were stopping to try to look in, and a flatfoot, posted in the doorway, was telling them to keep moving. That did not look promising, or else it did, if that's how you like things. I swerved aside and halted for a survey through the open door and the glass. Joel Fickler, the boss, was at the rack where Carl usually presided, taking a man's coat to put on a hanger. A man with his hat on was backed up to the cashier's counter, with his elbows on it, facing the whole shop. Two other men with their hats on were seated near the middle of the row of chairs for waiting customers, one of them next to the little table for magazines. They were discussing something without much enthusiasm. Two of the barbers' chairs, Ed's and Tom's, were occupied. The other two barbers, Jimmie and Philip, were on their stools against the wall. Janet, the other manicure, was not in sight.

I stepped to the doorway and was going on in. The flatfoot blocked me.

I lifted my brows at him. "What's all the excitement?"

"Accident in here. No one allowed in."

"How did the customers in the chairs get in? I'm a customer."

"Only customers with appointments. You got one?"

"Certainly." I stuck my head through the doorway and yelled, "Ed! How soon?"

The man leaning on the counter straightened up and turned for a look. At sight of me he grunted. "I'll be damned. Who whistled for you?"

The presence of my old friend and enemy Sergeant Purley Stebbins of Manhattan Homicide gave the thing an entirely different flavor. Up to then I had just been mildly curious, floating along. Now all my nerves and muscles snapped to attention. Sergeant Stebbins is not interested in petty larceny. I didn't care for the possibility of having shown a pair of murderers to chairs in our front room.

"Good God," Purley grumbled, "is this going to turn into one of them Nero Wolfe babies?"

"Not unless you turn it." I grinned at him. "Whatever it is, I dropped in for a shave, that's all, and here you boys are, to my surprise." The flatfoot had given me leeway, and I had crossed the sill. "I'm a regular customer here." I turned to Fickler, who had trotted over to us. "How long have I been leaving my hair here, Joel?"

None of Fickler's bones were anywhere near the surface except on his bald head. He was six inches shorter than me, which may have been one reason why I had never got a straight look into his narrow black eyes. He had never liked me much since the day he had forgotten to list an appointment with Ed I had made on the phone, and I, under provocation, had made a few pointed remarks. Now he looked as if he had been annoyed by something much worse than remarks.

"Over six years, Mr. Goodwin," he said. "This," he told Purley, "is the famous detective, Mr. Archie Goodwin. Mr. Nero Wolfe comes here too."

"The hell he does." Purley, scowling at me, said in a certain tone, "Famous."

I shrugged. "Just a burden. A damn nuisance."

"Yeah. Don't let it get you down. You just dropped in for a shave?"

"Yes, sir. Write it down, and I'll sign it."

"Who's your barber?"

"Ed."

"That's Graboff. He's busy."

"So I see. I'm not pressed. I'll chat with you or read a magazine or get a manicure."

"I don't feel like chatting." Purley had not relaxed the scowl. "You know a guy that works here named Carl Vardas? And his wife, Tina, a manicure?"

"I know Carl well enough to pay him a dime for my hat and coat and tie. I can't say I know Tina, but of course I've seen her here. Why?"

"I'm just asking. There's no law against your coming here for a shave, since you need one and this is where you come, but the sight of either you or Wolfe makes me want to scratch. No wonder, huh? So to have it on the record in case it's needed, have you seen Vardas or his wife this morning?"

"Sure I have." I stretched my neck to get closer to his ear and whispered, "I put them in our front room and told them to wait, and beat it up here to tell you, and if you'll step on it—"

"I don't care for gags," he growled. "Not right now. They killed a cop, or one of them did. You know how much we like that."

I did indeed and adjusted my face accordingly. "The hell they did. One of yours? Did I know him?"

"No. A dick from the Twentieth Precinct, Jake Wallen."

"Where and when?"

"This morning, right here. The other side of that partition, in her manicure booth. Stuck a long pair of scissors in his back and got his pump. Apparently he never made a sound, but them massage things are going here off and on. By the time he was found they had gone. It took us an hour to find out where they lived, and when we got there they had been and got their stuff and beat it."

I grunted sympathetically. "Is it tied up? Prints on the scissors or something?"

"We'll do all right without prints," Purley said grimly. "Didn't I say they lammed?"

"Yes, but," I objected, not aggressively, "some people can get awful scared at sight of a man with scissors sticking in his back. I wasn't intimate with Carl, but he didn't strike me as a man who would stab a cop just on principle. Was Wallen here to take him?"

Purley's reply was stopped before it got started. Tom had finished with his customer, and the two men with hats on in the row of chairs ranged along the partition were keeping their eyes on the customer as he went to the rack for his tie. Tom, having brushed himself off, had walked to the front and up to us. Usually Tom bounced around like a high-school kid—from his chair to the wall cabinet and back again, or over to the steamer behind the partition for a hot towel—in spite of his white-haired sixty-some years, but today his feet dragged. Nor did he tell me hello, though he gave me a sort of a glance before he spoke to Purley.

"It's my lunchtime, Sergeant. I just go to the cafeteria at the end of the hall."

Purley called a name that sounded like Joffe, and one of the dicks on a chair by the partition got up and came.

"Yerkes is going to lunch," Purley told him. "Go along and stay with him."

"I want to phone my wife," Tom said resolutely.

"Why not? Stay with him, Joffe."

"Yes, sir."

They went, with Tom in front. Purley and I moved out of the way as the customer approached to pay his check and Fickler sidled around behind the cash register.

"I thought," I said politely, "you had settled for Carl and Tina. Why does Tom have to have company at lunch?"

"We haven't got Carl and Tina."

"But you soon will have, the way the personnel feels about cop-killers. Why pester these innocent barbers? If one of them gets nervous and slices a customer, then what?"

Purley merely snarled.

I stiffened. "Excuse me. I'm not so partial to cop-killers either. It seemed only natural to show some interest. Luckily I can read, so I'll catch it in the evening paper."

"Don't bust a gut." Purley's eyes were following the customer as he walked to the door and on out past the flatfoot. "Sure we'll get Carl and Tina, but if you don't mind we'll just watch these guys' appetites. You asked what Jake Wallen was here for."

"I asked if he came to take Carl."

"Yeah. I think he did but I can't prove it yet. Last night around midnight a couple of pedestrians, two women, were hit by a car at Eighty-first and Broadway. Both killed. The car kept going. It was found later parked at Ninety-sixth and Broadway, just across from the subway entrance. We haven't found anyone who saw the driver, either at the scene of the accident or where the car was parked. The car was hot. It had been parked by its owner at eight o'clock on Forty-eighth Street between Ninth and Tenth, and was gone when he went for it at eleven-thirty."

Purley paused to watch a customer enter. The customer got past the flatfoot with Joel Fickler's help, left things at the rack, and went and got on Jimmie's chair. Purley returned to me. "When the car was spotted by a squad car at Ninety-sixth and Broadway with a dented fender and blood and other items that tagged it, the Twentieth Precinct sent Jake Wallen to it. He was the first one to give it a look. Later, of course, there was a gang from all over, including the laboratory, before they moved it. Wallen was supposed to go home and to bed at eight in the morning when his trick ended, but he didn't. He phoned his wife that he had a hot lead on a hit-and-run killer and was going to handle it himself and grab a promotion. Not only that, he phoned the owner of the car at his home in Yonkers, and asked him if he had any connection with the Goldenrod Barber Shop or knew anyone who had, or if he had ever been there. The owner had never heard of it. Of course we've collected all this since we were called here at ten-fifteen and found Wallen DOA with scissors in his back."

I was frowning. "But what gave him the lead to this shop?"

"We'd like to know. It had to be something he found in the car, we don't know what. The goddam fool kept it to himself and came here and got killed."

"Didn't he show it or mention it to anyone here?"

"They say not. All he had with him was a newspaper. We've got it—today's *News,* the early, out last night. We can't spot anything in it. There was nothing in his pockets, nothing on him, that helps any."

I humphed. "Fool is right. Even if he had cleaned it up he wouldn't have grabbed a promotion. He would have been more apt to grab a uniform and a beat."

"Yeah, he was that kind. There's too many of that kind. Not to mention names, but these precinct men—"

A phone rang. Fickler, by the cash register, looked at Purley, who stepped to the counter where the phone was and answered the call. It was for him. When, after a minute, it seemed to be going on, I moved away and had gone a few paces when a voice came.

"Hello, Mr. Goodwin."

It was Jimmie, Wolfe's man, using comb and scissors above his customer's right ear. He was the youngest of the staff, about my age, and by far the handsomest, with curly lips and white teeth and dancing dark eyes. I had never understood why he wasn't at Framinelli's. I told him hello.

"Mr. Wolfe ought to be here," he said.

Under the circumstances I thought that a little tactless, and was even prepared to tell him so when Ed called to me from two chairs down. "Fifteen minutes, Mr. Goodwin? All right?"

I told him okay, I would wait, went to the rack and undressed to my shirt, and crossed to one of the chairs over by the partition, next to the table with magazines. I thought it would be fitting to pick up a magazine, but I had already read the one on top, the latest *New Yorker*, and the one on top on the shelf below was the *Time* of two weeks ago. So I leaned back and let my eyes go, slow motion, from left to right and back again. Though I had been coming there for six years I didn't really know those people, in spite of the reputation barbers have as conversationalists. I knew that Fickler, the boss, had once been attacked bodily there in the shop by his ex-wife; that Philip had had two sons killed in World War II; that Tom had once been accused by Fickler of swiping lotions and other supplies and had slapped Fickler's face; that Ed played the horses and was always in debt; that Jimmie had to be watched or he would take magazines from the shop while they were still current; and that Janet, who had only been there a year, was suspected of having a sideline, maybe dope peddling. Aside from such items as those, they were strangers.

Suddenly Janet was there in front of me. She had come from around the end of the partition, and not alone. The man with her was a broad-shouldered husky, gray-haired and gray-eyed, with an unlit cigar slanting up from a corner of his mouth. His eyes swept the whole shop, and since he started at the far right he ended up at me.

He stared. "For God's sake," he muttered. "You? Now what?"

I was surprised for a second to see Inspector Cramer himself, head of Manhattan Homicide, there on the job. But even an inspector likes to be well thought of by the rank and file, and here it was no mere citizen who had met his end but one of them. The whole force would appreciate it. Besides, I have to admit he's a good cop.

"Just waiting for a shave," I told him. "I'm an old customer here. Ask Purley."

Purley came over and verified me, but Cramer checked with Ed himself. Then he drew Purley aside, and they mumbled back and forth a while, after which Cramer summoned Philip and escorted him around the end of the partition.

Janet seated herself in the chair next to mine. She looked even better in profile than head on, with her nice chin and straight little nose and long home-grown lashes. I felt a little in debt to her for the mild pleasure I had got occasionally as I sat in Ed's chair and glanced at her while she worked on the customer in the next chair.

"I was wondering where you were," I remarked.

She turned to me. She wasn't old enough to have wrinkles or seams but she looked old enough then. She was putting a strain on every muscle in her face, and it certainly showed.

"Did you say something?" she asked.

"Nothing vital. My name's Goodwin. Call me Archie."

"I know. You're a detective. How can I keep them from having my picture in the paper?"

"You can't if they've already got it. Have they?"

"I think so. I wish I was dead."

"I don't." I made it not loud but emphatic.

"Why should you? I do. My folks in Michigan think I'm acting or modeling. I leave it vague. And here—oh, my God."

Her chin worked, but she controlled it.

"Work is work," I said. "My parents wanted me to be a college president, and I wanted to be a second baseman, and look at me. Anyhow, if your picture gets printed and it's a good likeness, who knows what will happen?"

"This is my Gethsemane," she said.

That made me suspicious, naturally. She had mentioned acting. "Come off it," I advised her. "Think of someone else. Think of the guy that got stabbed—no, he's out of it—think of his wife, how do you suppose she feels? Or Inspector Cramer, with the job he's got. What was he asking you just now?"

She didn't hear me. She said through clamped teeth, "I only wish I had some guts."

"Why? What would you do?"

"I'd tell all about it."

"All about what?"

"About what happened."

"You mean last night? Why not try it out on me and see how it goes? That doesn't take guts, just go ahead and let it come, keep your voice down and let it flow."

She didn't hear a word. Her ears were disconnected. She kept her brown eyes, under the long lashes, straight at me.

"How it happened this morning. How I was going back to my booth after I finished Mr. Levinson in Philip's chair, and he called me into Tina's booth and he seized me, with one hand on my throat so I couldn't scream, and there was no doubt at all what he intended, so I grabbed the scissors from the shelf and, without realizing what I was doing, plunged them into him with all my strength, and his grip on me loosened, and he collapsed onto the chair. That's what I would do if I had any guts and if I really want a successful career the way I say I do. I would have to be arrested and have a trial, and then—"

"Hold it. Your pronouns. Mr. Levinson called you into Tina's booth?"

"Certainly not. That man that got killed." She tilted her head back. "See the marks on my throat?"

There was no mark whatever on her smooth pretty throat.

"Good Lord," I said. "That would get you top billing anywhere."

"That's what I was saying."

"Then go ahead and tell it."

"I can't! I simply can't! It would be so darned vulgar."

Her full face was there, only sixteen inches away, with the muscles no longer under strain, the closest I had ever been to it, and there was no question about how lovely it was. Under different circumstances my reaction would have been merely normal and healthy, but at the moment I could have slapped it with pleasure. I had felt a familiar tingle at the base of my spine when I thought she was going to open up about a midnight ride up Broadway, probably with one of her co-workers, possibly with the boss himself, and then she had danced off into this folderol.

She needed a lesson. "I understand your position," I said, "a girl as sweet and fine and strong as you, but it's bound to come out in the end, and I want to help. Incidentally, I am not married. I'll go to Inspector Cramer right now and tell him about it. He'll want to take photographs of your throat. I know the warden down at the jail and I'll see that you get good treatment, no rough stuff. Do you know any lawyers?"

She shook her head, answering, I thought, my question about lawyers, but no. She didn't believe in answering questions. "About your being married," she said, "I hadn't even thought. There was an article in the *American* magazine last month about career girls getting married. Did you read it?"

"No. I may be able to persuade the district attorney to make it a manslaughter charge instead of murder, which would please your folks in Michigan." I drew my feet back and slid forward on the chair, ready to rise. "Okay, I'll go tell Cramer."

"That article was silly," she said. "I think a girl must get her career established *first*. That's why when I see an attractive man I never wonder if he's married; by the time I'm ready for one these will be too old. That's why I wouldn't ask you if you know anyone in show business, because I wouldn't take help from a man. I think a girl—"

If Ed hadn't signaled to me just then, his customer having left the chair, there's no telling how it would have ended. It would have been vulgar to slap her, and no words would have been any good since she was deaf, but surely I might have thought of something that would have taken effect. As it was, I didn't want to keep Ed waiting so I got up and crossed to his chair and climbed in.

"Just scrape the face," I told him.

He got a bib on me and tilted me back. "Did you phone?" he asked. "Did that fathead forget again?"

I told him no, that I had been caught midtown with a stubble and an unforeseen errand for which I should be presentable and added, "You seem to have had some excitement."

He went to the cabinet for a tube of prefabricated lather, got some on me, and started rubbing. "We sure did," he said with feeling. "Carl, you know Carl, he killed a man in Tina's booth. Then they both ran. I'm sorry for Tina, she was all right, but Carl, I don't know." He moved to my left cheek.

I couldn't articulate with him rubbing. He finished, went to wipe his fingers, and came with the razor. I rolled my head into position, to the left, and remarked, "I'd sort of watch it, Ed. It's a little risky to go blabbing that Carl killed him unless you can prove it."

"Well, he had fits." The razor was as sharp and slick as usual. "What did he run for?"

"I couldn't say. But the cops are still poking around here, even an inspector."

"Sure they are, they're after evidence. You gotta have evidence." Ed pulled the skin tight over the jawbone. "For instance, they ask me did he show me anything or ask me anything about some article from the shop. I say he didn't. That would be evidence, see?"

"Yes, I get it." I could only mumble. "What did he ask you?"

"Oh, all about me, name, married or single—you know, insurance men, income tax, they all ask the same things. But when he asked about last night I told him where to get off, but then I thought what the hell and told him. Why not? That's my philosophy, Mr. Goodwin—why not? It saves trouble."

He was prying my chin up, doing the throat. That clean, I rolled my head to the right to turn the other cheek.

"Of course," he said, "the police have to get it straight, but they can't expect us to remember everything. When he came in first he talked with Fickler, maybe five minutes. Then Fickler took him to Tina's booth, and he talked with Tina. After that Fickler sent Philip in, and then Carl and then Jimmie and then Tom and then me and then Janet. I think it's pretty good to remember that."

I mumbled agreement. He was at the corner of my mouth.

"But I can't remember everything, and they can't make me. I don't know how long it was after Janet came back out before Fickler went to Tina's booth and found him dead. They ask me was it nearer ten minutes or nearer fifteen, but I say I had a customer at the time, we all did but Philip, and I don't know. They ask me how many of us went behind the partition after Janet came out, to the steamer or the vat or to get the lamp or something, but I say again I had a customer at the time, and I don't know, except I know I didn't go because I was trimming Mr. Howell at the time. I was working the top when Fickler yelled and came running out. They can ask Mr. Howell."

"They probably have," I said, but to no one, because Ed had gone for a hot towel.

He returned and used the towel and got the lilac water. Patting it on, he resumed, "They ask me exactly when Carl and Tina went, they ask me that twenty times, but I can't say and I won't say. Carl did it all right, but they can't prove it by me. They've gotta have evidence, but I don't. Cold towel today?"

"No, I'll keep the smell."

He patted me dry, levered me upright, and brought a comb and brush. "Can I remember what I don't know?" he demanded.

"I know I can't."

"And I'm no great detective like you." Ed was a little rough with a brush. "And now I go for lunch but I've got to have a cop along. We can't even go to the can alone. They searched all of us down to the skin, and they even brought a woman to search Janet. They took our fingerprints. I admit they've gotta have evidence." He flipped the bib off. "How was the razor, all right?"

I told him it was fine as usual, stepped down, fished for a quarter, and exchanged it for my check. Purley Stebbins, nearby, was watching both of us. There had been times when I had seen fit to kid Purley at the scene of a murder, but not now. A cop had been killed.

He spoke, not belligerently. "The inspector don't like your being here."

"Neither do I," I declared. "Thank God this didn't happen to be Mr. Wolfe's day for a haircut, you would never have believed it. I'm just a minor coincidence. Nice to see you."

I went and paid my check to Fickler, got my things on, and departed.

III

As I emerged into Lexington Avenue there were several things on my mind. The most immediate was this: if Cramer's suspicion had been aroused enough to spend a man on me, and if I were seen going directly home from the shop, there might be too much curiosity as to why I had chosen to spend six bits for a shave at that time of day. So instead of taking a taxi, which would have had to crawl crosstown anyhow, I walked, and when I got to Altman's I used their aisles and exits to make sure I had no tail. That left my mind free for other things the rest of the way home.

One leading question was whether Carl and Tina would still be where I had left them, in the front room. That was what took me up the seven steps of the stoop two at a time, and on in quick. The answer to the question was no. The front room was empty.

I strode down the hall to the office but stopped there because I heard Wolfe's voice. It was coming through the open door to the dining room, across the hall, and it was saying, "No, Mr. Vardas, I cannot agree that mountain climbing is merely one manifestation of man's spiritual aspirations. I think instead it is an hysterical paroxysm of his infantile vanity. One of the prime ambitions of a jackass is to bray louder than any other jackass, and man is not . . ."

I crossed the hall and the dining-room sill. Wolfe was at his end of the table, and Fritz, standing at his elbow, had just removed the lid from a steaming platter. At his left was Tina, and Carl was at his right, my place when there was no company. Wolfe saw me but finished his paragraph on mountain climbing before attending to me.

"In time, Archie. You like veal and mushrooms."

Talk about infantile. His not being willing to sit to his lunch with unfed people in the house was all well enough, but why not send trays in to them? That was easy—he was sore at me, and I had called them foreigners.

I stepped to the end of the table and said, "I know you have a paroxysm if I try to bring up business during meals, but eighteen thousand cops would give a month's pay to get their hands on Carl and Tina, your guests."

"Indeed." Wolfe was serving the veal and accessories. "Why?"

"Have you talked with them?"

"No. I merely invited them to lunch."

"Then don't until I've reported. I ran into Cramer and Stebbins at the barber shop."

"Confound it." The serving spoon stopped en route.

"Yeah. It's quite interesting. But first lunch, of course. I'll go put the chain bolt on. Please dish me some veal?"

Carl and Tina were speechless.

That lunch was one of Wolfe's best performances; I admit it. He didn't know a damn thing about Carl and Tina except that they were in a jam, he knew that Cramer and Stebbins dealt only with homicide, and he had a strong prejudice against entertaining murderers at his table. Some years back a female prospective client had dined with us in an emergency, on roast Watertown goose. It turned out that she was a husband-poisoner, and roast goose had been off our menu for a solid year, though Wolfe was very fond of it. His only hope now was his knowledge that I was aware of his prejudice and even shared it, and I took my seat at the end of the table and disposed of a big helping of the veal and mushrooms, followed by pumpkin puffs, without batting an eye. He must have been fairly tight inside, but he stayed the polite host clear to the end, with no sign of hurry even with the coffee. Then, however, the tension began to tell. Ordinarily his return to the office after a meal was leisurely and lazy, but this time he went right along, followed by his guests and me. He marched across to his chair behind the desk, got his bulk deposited, and snapped at me, "What have you got us into now?"

I was pulling chairs around so the Vardas family would be facing him, but stopped to give him an eye.

"Us?" I inquired.

"Yes."

"Okay," I said courteously, "if that's how it is. I did not invite them to come here, let alone to lunch. They came on their own, and I let them in, which is one of my functions. Having started it, I'll finish it. May I use the front room, please? I'll have them out of here in ten minutes."

"Pfui." He was supercilious. "I am now responsible for their presence, since they were my guests at lunch. Sit down, sir. Sit down, Mrs. Vardas, please."

Carl and Tina didn't know what from which. I had to push the chairs up behind their knees. Then I went to my own chair and swiveled to face Wolfe.

"I have a question to ask them," I told him, "but first you need a couple of facts. They're in this country without papers. They were in a concentration camp in Russia and they're not telling how they got here if they can help it. They could be spies, but I doubt it after hearing them talk. Naturally they jump a mile if they hear someone say boo, and when a man came to the barber shop this morning and showed a police card and asked who they were and where they came from and what they were doing last night they scooted the first chance they got. But they didn't know where to go so they came here to buy fifty bucks' worth of advice and information. I got bighearted and went to the shop disguised as a Boy Scout."

"You went?" Tina gasped.

I turned to them. "Sure I went. It's a complicated situation, and you made it worse by beating it, but you did and here we are. I think I can handle it if you two can be kept out of the way. It would be dangerous for you to stay here. I know a safe place up in the Bronx for you to lay low for a few days. You shouldn't take a chance on a taxi or the subway, so we'll go around the corner to the garage and get Mr. Wolfe's car, and you can drive it up there. Then I'll—"

"Excuse me," Carl said urgently. "You would drive us up there?"

"No, I'll be busy. Then I'll—"

"But I can't drive a car! I don't know how!"

"Then your wife will drive. You can leave—"

"She can't! She don't know either!"

I sprang from my chair and stood over them. "Look," I said savagely, "save that for the cops. Can't drive a car? Certainly you can! Everybody can!"

They were looking up at me, Carl bewildered, Tina frowning. "In America, yes," she said. "But we are not Americans, not yet. We have never had a chance to learn."

"You have never driven a car?"

"No. Never."

"And Carl?"

"Never."

"What the devil is this?" Wolfe demanded.

I returned to my chair. "That," I said, "was the question I wanted to ask. It has a bearing, as you'll soon see." I regarded Carl and Tina. "If you're lying about this, not knowing how to drive a car, you won't be sent back home to die, you'll die right here. It will be a cinch to find out if you're lying."

"Why should we?" Carl demanded. "What is so important in it?"

"Once more," I insisted. "Can you drive a car?"

"No."

"Can you, Tina?"

"No!"

"Okay." I turned to Wolfe. "The caller at the barber shop this morning was a precinct dick named Wallen. Fickler took him to Tina's booth, and he questioned Tina first. Then the others had sessions with him in the booth, in this order: Philip, Carl, Jimmie, Tom, Ed, and Janet. You may not know that the manicure booths are around behind the long partition. After Janet came out there was a period of ten or fifteen minutes when Wallen was in the booth alone. Then Fickler went to see, and what he saw was Wallen's body with scissors buried in his back. Someone had stabbed him to death. Since Carl and Tina had lammed—"

Tina's cry was more of a gasp, a last gasp, an awful sound. With one leap she was out of her chair and at Carl, grasping him and begging wildly, "Carl, no! No, no! Oh, Carl—"

"Make her stop," Wolfe snapped.

I had to try, because Wolfe would rather be in a room with a hungry tiger than with a woman out of hand. I went and got a grip on her shoulder but released it at sight of the expression on Carl's face as he pushed to his feet against her pressure. It looked as if he could and would handle it. He did. He straightened her up, standing against her, his face nearly touching hers, and told her, "No! Do you understand? No!"

He eased her back to her chair and down onto it, and turned to me. "That man was killed there in Tina's booth?"

"Yes."

Carl smiled as he had once before, and I wished he would stop trying it. "Then of course," he said as if he were conceding a point in a tight argument, "this is the end for us. But please I must ask you not to blame my wife. Because we have been through many things together she is ready to credit me with many deeds that are far beyond me. She has a big idea of me, and I have a big idea of her. But I did not kill that man. I did not touch him." He frowned. "I don't understand why you suggested riding in a car to the Bronx. Of course you will give us to the police."

"Forget the Bronx." I was frowning back. "Every cop in town has his eye peeled for you. Sit down."

He stood. He looked at Tina, at Wolfe, and back down at me. "Sit down, damn it!"

He went to his chair and sat.

"About driving a car," Wolfe muttered. "Was that flummery?"

"No, sir, that comes next. Last night around midnight a hit-and-run driver in a stolen car killed two women up on Broadway. The car was found parked at Broadway and Ninety-sixth Street. Wallen, from the Twentieth Precinct, was the first dick to look it over. In it he apparently found something that led him to the Goldenrod Barber Shop—anyhow he phoned his wife that he was on a hot one that would lead to glory and a raise and then he showed up at the shop and called the roll, as described. With the result also as described. Cramer has bought it that the hit-and-run driver found himself cornered and used the scissors, and Cramer, don't quote me, is not a dope. To qualify as a hit-and-run driver you must meet certain specifications, and one of them is knowing how to drive a car. So the best plan would be for Carl and Tina to go back to the shop and report for duty and for the official quiz, if it wasn't for two things. First, the fact that they lammed will make it very tough, and second, even though it is settled that they didn't kill a cop, their lack of documents will fix them anyhow."

I waved a hand. "So actually what's the difference? If they're sent back where they came from they're doomed there, that's all they have to pick from. One interesting angle is that you are harboring fugitives from justice, and I am not. I told Purley they're here. So you're—"

"You what?" Wolfe bellowed.

"What I said. That's the advantage of having a reputation for gags, you can say practically anything if you handle your face right. I told him they were here in our front room, and he sailed right over it. So I'm clean, but you're not. You can't even just show them out. If you don't want to call Cramer yourself, which I admit would be a little thick since they were your luncheon guests, I could get Purley at the shop and tell him they're still here and why hasn't he sent for them."

"It might be better," Tina said, not with hope, "just a little better, if you would let us go ourselves? No?"

She got no answer. Wolfe was glaring at me. It wasn't that he needed my description of the situation to realize what a pickle he was in; I have never tried to deny that the interior decorator did a snappier job inside his skull than in mine. What had him boiling was my little stunt of getting it down that neither Carl nor Tina could drive a car. But for that it would still have been possible to let them meet the law and take what they got, and more or less shrug it off; now that was out of the question. Also, naturally, he resented my putting the burden on him. If I had taken a stand as a champion of humanity he could have blamed me for any trouble he was put to—and didn't I know he would.

"There is," he said, glaring, "another alternative to consider."

"Yes, sir. What?"

"Let us just go ourselves," Tina said.

"Pfui." He moved the glare to her. "You would try to skedaddle and be caught within an hour." Back to me. "You have told Mr. Stebbins they are here. We can simply keep them here and await developments. Since Mr. Cramer and Mr. Stebbins are still there at work, they may at any moment disclose the murderer."

"Sure they may," I agreed, "but I doubt it. They're just being thorough; they've really settled for Carl and Tina, and what they're looking for is evidence, especially what it was that led Wallen to the barber shop—though I suppose they haven't much hope of that, since Carl and Tina could have taken it along. Anyway, you know how it is when they've got their minds aimed in one direction."

Wolfe's eyes went to Carl. "Did you and your wife leave the shop together?"

Carl shook his head. "That might have been noticed, so she went first. There is no place for ladies to go in the shop, so Tina and the other girl, Janet, go to a place down the hall when they need to, and she could leave with no attention. When she was gone I waited until they were all busy and Mr. Fickler was walking behind the partition, then I went quick out the door and ran upstairs to meet her there."

"When was that?" I asked. "Who was in Tina's booth with Wallen?"

"I don't think anybody was. Janet had come out a while before. She was at Jimmie's chair with a customer."

"Good God." I turned my palms up. "You left that place less than a minute, maybe only a few seconds, before Fickler found Wallen dead!"

"I don't know." Carl wasn't fazed. "I only know I went and I didn't touch that man."

"This," I told Wolfe, "makes it even nicer. There was a slim chance we could get it that they left sooner."

"Yes." He regarded me. "It must be assumed that Wallen was alive when Ed left the booth, since that young woman—what's her name?"

"Janet."

"I call few men, and no women, by their first names. What's her name?"

"That's all I know, Janet. It won't bite you."

"Stahl," Tina said. "Janet Stahl."

"Thank you. Wallen was presumably alive when Ed left the booth, since Miss Stahl followed him. So Miss Stahl, who saw Wallen last, and Mr. Fickler, who reported him dead—manifestly they had opportunity. What about the others?"

"You must remember," I told him, "that I had just dropped in for a shave. I had to show the right amount of intellectual curiosity but I had to be damn careful not to carry it too far. From what Ed said, I gathered that opportunity is fairly wide open, except he excludes himself. As you know, they all keep darting behind that partition for one thing or another. Ed can't remember who did and who didn't during that ten or fifteen minutes, and it's a safe bet that the others can't remember either. The fact that the cops were interested enough to ask shows that Carl and Tina haven't got a complete monopoly on it. As Ed remarked, they've gotta have evidence, and they're still looking."

Wolfe grunted in disgust.

"It also shows," I went on, "that they haven't got any real stopper to cork it, like prints from the car or localizing the scissors or anything they found on the corpse. They sure want Carl and Tina, and you know what happens when they get them, but they're still short on exhibits. If you like your suggestion to keep our guests here until Cramer and Stebbins get their paws on the right guy it might work fine as a long-term policy, but you're against the idea of women living here, or even a woman, and after a few months it might get on your nerves."

"It is no good," Tina said, back to her gasping whisper again. "Just let us go! I beg you, do that! We'll find our way to the country, we know how. You are wonderful detectives, but it is no good!"

Wolfe ignored her. He leaned back, closed his eyes, and heaved a deep sigh, and from the way his nose began to twitch I knew he was coercing himself into facing the hard fact that he would have to go to work—either that or tell me to call Purley, and that was ruled out of bounds by both his self-respect and his professional vanity. The Vardas family sat gazing at him, not in hope, but not in utter despair either. I guess they had run out of despair long ago and had none left to call on. I watched Wolfe too, his twitching nose until it stopped, and then his lips in their familiar movement, pushed out and then pulled in, out and in again, which meant he had accepted the inevitable and was getting the machinery going. I had seen him like that for an hour at a stretch, but this time it was only minutes.

He sighed again, opened his eyes, and rasped at Tina, "Except for Mr. Fickler, that man questioned you first. Is that right?"

"Yes, sir."

"Tell me what he said. What he asked. I want every word."

I thought Tina did pretty well under the circumstances. Convinced that her goose was cooked and that therefore what Wallen had asked couldn't affect her fate one way or the other, she tried to play ball anyway. She wrinkled her brow and concentrated, and it looked as if Wolfe got it all out of her. But she couldn't give him what she didn't have.

He kept after it. "You are certain he produced no object, showed you no object whatever?"

"Yes, I'm sure he didn't."

"He asked about no object, anything, in the shop?"

"No."

"He mentioned no object at all?"

"No."

"He took nothing from his pocket?"

"No."

"The newspaper he had. Didn't he take that from his pocket?"

"No, like I said, he had it in his hand when he came in the booth."

"In his hand or under his arm?"

"In his hand. I think—yes, I'm sure."

"Was it folded up?"

"Well, of course newspapers are folded."

"Yes, Mrs. Vardas. Just remember the newspaper as you saw it in his hand. I'm making a point of it because there is nothing else to make a point of, and we must have a point if we can find one. Was the newspaper folded up as if he had had it in his pocket?"

"No, it wasn't." She was trying hard. "It wasn't folded that much. Like I said, it was a *News*. When he sat down he put it on the table, at the end by his right hand—yes, that's right, my left hand; I moved some of my things to make room—and it was the way it is on the newsstand, so that's all it was folded."

"But he didn't mention it?"

"No."

"And you noticed nothing unusual about it? I mean the newspaper?"

She shook her head. "It was just a newspaper."

Wolfe repeated the performance with Carl and got more of the same. No object produced or mentioned, no hint of any. The only one on exhibit, the newspaper, had been there on the end of the table when Carl, sent by Fickler, had entered and sat, and Wallen had made no reference to it. Carl was more practical than Tina. He didn't work as hard as she had trying to remember Wallen's exact words, and I must say I couldn't blame him.

Wolfe gave up trying to get what they didn't have. He leaned back, compressed his lips, closed his eyes, and tapped with his forefingers on the ends of his chair arms. Carl and Tina looked at each other a while, then she got up and went to him, started combing his hair with her fingers, saw I was looking, began to blush, God knows why, and went back to her chair.

Finally Wolfe opened his eyes. "Confound it," he said peevishly, "it's impossible. Even if I had a move to make I couldn't make it. If I so much as stir a finger Mr. Cramer will start yelping, and I have no muzzle for him. Any effort to—"

The doorbell rang. During lunch Fritz had been told to leave it to me, so I arose, crossed to the hall, and went front. But not all the way. Four paces short of the door I saw, through the one-way glass panel, the red rugged face and the heavy broad shoulders. I wheeled and returned to the office, not dawdling, and told Wolfe, "The man to fix the chair."

"Indeed." His head jerked up. "The front room."

"I could tell him—"

"No."

Carl and Tina, warned by our tone and tempo, were on their feet. The bell rang again. I moved fast to the door to the front room and pulled it open, telling them, "In here quick. Step on it." They obeyed without a word, as if they had known me and trusted me for years, but what choice did they have? When they had passed through I said, "Relax and keep quiet," shut the door, glanced at Wolfe and got a nod, went to the hall and to the door, opened it, and said morosely, "Hello. What now?"

"It took you long enough," Inspector Cramer growled, crossing the threshold.

IV

Wolfe can move when he wants to. I have seen him prove it more than once, as he did then. By the time I was back in the office, following Cramer, he had scattered in front of him on his desk pads of paper, pencils, and a dozen folders of plant germination records for which he had had to go to the filing cabinet. One of the folders was spread open, and he was scowling at us above it. He grunted a greeting but not a welcome. Cramer grunted back, moved to the red leather chair, and planted himself in it.

I got myself at my desk. I was wishing I wasn't involved so I could just enjoy it. If Wolfe succeeded in keeping Cramer's claws off of the Vardas family and at the same time kept himself out of jail I would show my appreciation by not hitting him for a raise for at least a month.

Fritz entered with a tray, so Wolfe had found time to push a button too. It was the fixed allotment, three bottles of beer. Wolfe, getting the opener from his drawer, told Fritz to bring another glass, but Cramer said no thanks.

Suddenly Cramer looked at me and demanded, "Where did you go when you left the barber shop?"

My brows went up. "Just like that?"

"Yes."

"Well, then. If you really cared you could have put a tail on me. If you didn't care enough to put a tail on me you're just being nosy, and I resent it. Next question."

"Why not answer that one?"

"Because some of the errands I get sent on are confidential, and I don't want to start a bad habit."

Cramer turned abruptly to Wolfe. "You know a police officer was killed this morning there in that shop."

"Yes." Wolfe halted a foaming glass on its way to his mouth. "Archie told me about it."

"Maybe he did."

"Not maybe. He did."

"Okay." Cramer cocked his head and watched Wolfe empty the glass and use his handkerchief on his lips. Then he said, "Look. This is what brought me here. I have learned over a stretch of years that when I find you within a mile of a murder, and Goodwin is a part of you, something fancy can be expected. I don't need to itemize that; your memory is as good as mine. Wait a second, let me finish. I don't say there's no such thing as a coincidence. I know you've been going to that shop for two years, and Goodwin for six years. It wouldn't be so remarkable if he happened in there this particular day, two hours after a murder, if it wasn't for certain features. He told Graboff, his barber, that he needed an emergency shave to go to an appointment. Incidentally, it couldn't have been much of an emergency, since he waited nearly half an hour while Graboff finished with a customer, but I might concede that. The point is that Graboff and Fickler both say that in the six years Goodwin has been going there he has never gone just for a shave. Not once. He goes only for the works, haircut, scalp massage, shampoo, *and* shave. That makes it too remarkable. Just one day in six years an emergency sends him there for a shave, and this is the day. I don't believe it."

Wolfe shrugged. "Then you don't. I'm not responsible for your credulity quotient, Mr. Cramer. Neither is Mr. Goodwin. I don't see how we can help you."

"Nobody would believe it," Cramer said stubbornly, refusing to get riled. "That's why I'm here. I do believe that Goodwin went to that shop because he knew a man had been murdered there."

"Then you believe wrong," I told him. "Your credulity quotient needs an overhaul. Until I got there I hadn't the slightest idea or suspicion that a man had been murdered, there or anywhere else."

"You have been known to lie, Goodwin."

"Only within limits, and I know what they are. I will state that in an affidavit. Write it out, and there's a notary at the corner drugstore. That would be perjury, which I'm allergic to."

"Your going there had nothing whatever to do with the murder?"

"Put it that way if you prefer it. It did not."

Wolfe was pouring beer. "How," he inquired, not belligerently, "was Mr. Goodwin supposed to have learned of the murder? Had you fitted that in?"

"I don't know." Cramer gestured impatiently. "I didn't come here with a diagram. I only know what it means, what it always has meant, when I'm on a homicide, which is what I work at, and suddenly there you are, or Goodwin. And there Goodwin was, two hours after it happened, and I asked some questions and I can take only so much coincidence. Frankly I have no idea where you come in. You work only for big money. That hit-and-run driver could be a man with money, but if so it couldn't be someone who works in that shop. No one there has the kind of dough that hires Nero Wolfe. So I don't see how it could be money that pulled you in, and I frankly admit I have no idea what else could. I guess I'll have a little beer after all, if you don't mind. I'm tired."

Wolfe leaned forward to push the button.

"What was on my mind," Cramer said, "was two things. First, I did not believe that Goodwin just happened to drop in at the scene of a murder. I admit he's not quite brazen enough to commit perjury." He looked at me. "I want that affidavit. Today. Word it yourself, but say it right."

"You'll get it," I assured him.

"Today."

"Yep."

"Don't forget it."

Fritz entered with another tray, put it down on the little table at Cramer's elbow, and uncapped the bottle. "Shall I pour, sir?"

"Thanks, I will." Cramer took the glass in his left hand, tilted it, and poured with his right. Unlike Wolfe, he didn't care for a lot of foam. "Second," he said, "I thought that what took Goodwin there might be something you would be ready to tell me about, but he wouldn't because you're the boss and he's such a goddam clam unless you say the word. I don't pretend to have anything to pry it out of you with. You know the law about withholding evidence as well as I do, you ought to by this time, the stunts you've pulled—"

The foam was down to where he liked it, and he stopped to take a swig.

"You thought," Wolfe asked, "that I had sent Archie to the shop on business?"

Cramer ran his tongue over his lips. "Yes. For the reason given. I still think so."

"You're wrong. I didn't. Since you're to get an affidavit from Archie, you might as well have one from me too and get it settled. In it I will say that I did not send him to the barber shop, that I did not know he was going there, and that I heard and knew nothing of the murder until he returned and told me."

"You'll swear to that?"

"As a favor to you, yes. You've wasted your time coming here, and you might as well get a little something out of it." Wolfe reached for his second bottle. "By the way, I still don't know why you came. According to Archie, the murderer is known and all you have to do is find him—that man at the clothes rack—uh, Carl. And his wife, you said, Archie?"

"Yes, sir. Tina, one of the manicures. Purley told me straight they had done it and scooted."

Wolfe frowned at Cramer. "Then what could you expect to get from me? How could I help?"

"What I said, that's all," Cramer insisted doggedly, pouring the rest of his beer. "When I see Goodwin poking around I want to know why."

"I don't believe it," Wolfe said rudely. He turned to me. "Archie. I think you're responsible for this. You're brash and you talk too much. I think it was something you did or said. What was it?"

"Sure, it's always me." I was hurt. "What I did, I got a shave, and Ed had a customer and I had to wait, so I talked with Purley and looked at a magazine—no, I started to but didn't—and with Inspector Cramer and then with Janet, Miss Stahl to you, and with Ed while I was in the chair—that is, he talked—"

"What did you say to Mr. Cramer?"

"Practically nothing. Just answered a civil question."

"What did you say to Mr. Stebbins?"

I thought I knew now where he was headed and hoped to God I was right. "Oh, just asked what was going on, and he told me. I've told you about it."

"Not verbatim. What did you say?"

"Nothing, damn it! Of course Purley wanted to know what brought me there, and I told him I—say, wait a minute! Maybe you're right at that! He asked me if I had seen Carl or Tina this morning, and I said sure, I had put them here in the front room and told them to wait, and if he would step on it—"

"Ha!" Wolfe snorted. "I knew it! Your confounded tongue. So that's it." He looked at Cramer. "Why have you waited to pounce?" he asked, trying not to sound too contemptuous, for after all Cramer was drinking his beer. "Since Archie has rashly disclosed our little secret, it would be useless for me to try to keep it. That's what we use the front room for mainly, to keep murderers in. You're armed, I suppose? Go in and get them. Archie, open the door for him."

I went to the door to the front room and pulled it open, not too wide. "I'm scared of murderers myself," I said courteously, "or I'd be glad to help."

Cramer had a glass half full of beer in his hand, and it may well be that that took the trick. Bullheaded as he was, he might have been capable of getting up and walking over for a look into the room, even though our build-up had convinced him it was empty, not caring how much we would enjoy it or how silly he would look coming out. But the glass of beer complicated it. He would either have to take it with him or reach first to put it down on the little table—or throw it at Wolfe.

"Nuts," he said and lifted the glass to drink.

I swung the door to carelessly, without bothering to see that it latched, and yawned on the way back to my chair.

"At least," Wolfe said, rubbing it in, "I can't be jailed for harboring a fugitive—one of your favorite threats. But I really don't know what you're after. If it was those two you'll get them, of course. What else is there?"

"Nothing but a little more evidence." Cramer glanced at his wrist-watch. "I'll get down to my office. That's where I started for, and this was on the way so I thought I'd stop to see what you had to say. We'll get 'em all right. It don't pay to kill a cop in this town." He stood up. "It wouldn't pay for anyone to hide a cop-killer in their front room, either. Thanks for the beer. I'll be expecting those affidavits, and in case—"

The phone rang. I swiveled and got it. "Nero Wolfe's office, Archie Goodwin speaking."

"Inspector Cramer there?"

I said yes, hold it. "For you," I told him and moved aside, and he came and took it. He spoke not more than twenty words altogether, between spells of listening. He dropped the phone onto the cradle, growled something about more trouble, and headed for the door.

"Have they found 'em?" I asked his back.

"No." He didn't turn. "Someone's hurt—the Stahl girl."

I marched after him, thinking the least I could do was cooperate by opening another door for him, but he was there and on out before I caught up, so I about-faced and returned to the office.

Wolfe was standing up, and I wondered why all the exertion, but a glance at the wall clock showed me 3:55, nearly time for his afternoon visit to the plant rooms.

"He said Janet got hurt," I stated.

Wolfe, finishing the last of his beer, grunted.

"I owe Janet something. Besides, it could mean that Carl and Tina are out of it. We ought to know, and they would like to know. I don't usually get shaved twice a day, but there's no law against it. I can be there in ten minutes. Why not?"

"No." He put the glass down. "We'll see."

"I don't feel like we'll seeing. I need to do something. I lost ten pounds in ten seconds, standing there holding that doorknob, trying to look as if it would be fun to watch him coming to look in. If it wasn't for our guests I almost wish he had, just to see what you would do, not to mention me. I've got to do something now."

"There's nothing to do." He looked at the clock and moved. "Put those folders back, please?" Halfway to the door he turned. "Disturb me only if it is unavoidable. And admit no more displaced persons to the house. Two at a time is enough."

"It was you who fed—" I began with feeling, but he was gone. In a moment I heard the sound of his elevator.

I put the folders away and took the beer remains to the kitchen and then went to the front room. Tina, who was lying on the couch, sat up as I entered and saw to her skirt hem. She had nice legs, but my mind was occupied. Carl, on a chair near the foot of the couch, stood up and asked a string of questions with his eyes.

"As you were," I told them gruffly. I heartily agreed with Wolfe that two was enough. "I hope you didn't go near the windows?"

"We have learned so long ago to stay away from windows," Carl said. "But we want to go. We will pay the fifty dollars gladly."

"You can't go." I was irritated and emphatic. "That was Inspector Cramer, a very important policeman. We told him you were in here, and so—"

"You told him—" Tina gasped.

"Yes. It's the Hitler-Stalin technique in reverse. They tell barefaced lies to have them taken for the truth, and we told the barefaced truth to have it taken for a lie. It worked. You were within a hair's breadth of getting flushed, and I'll never be the same again, but it worked. So now we're stuck, and you are too. You stay here. We've told the cops you're in this room, and you're not going to leave it, at least not until bedtime. I'm locking you in." I pointed to a door. "That's a bathroom, and there's a glass if you want a drink. It has another door into the office, but I'll lock it. The windows have bars."

I crossed to the door to the hall and locked it with my master key. I went through to the office, entered the bathroom in the corner, turned the bolt flange on the door to the front room, opened the door an inch, returned to the office, locked that door with my key, and went back to the front room. Carl and Tina, speaking in low tones, fell silent as I entered.

"All set," I told them. "Make yourselves comfortable. If you need anything don't yell, this room is soundproofed; push this button." I put my finger on it, under the edge of the table. "I'll give you the news as soon as there is any." I was going.

"But this is hanging in the air on a thread," Carl protested.

"You're damn right it is," I agreed grimly. "Your only hope is that Mr. Wolfe has now put his foot in it, and it's up to him to get both you and him loose, not to mention me. He can't possibly do it, which is an advantage, because the only things he ever really strains himself on are those that can't be done. The next two hours are time out. He doesn't let anything interfere with his afternoon session, from four to six, with his orchids up on the roof. By the way, there is a small gleam. Inspector Cramer beat it back to the shop because he got a phone call that Janet had been hurt. If she got hurt with scissors with you not there, it may be a real break."

"Janet?" Tina was distressed. "Was she hurt much?"

I looked at her suspiciously. Surely that was phony. But she looked as if she really meant it. Maybe with some people who have been hurt plenty and often themselves, that's the way they react when someone else gets it, someone they know.

"I don't know," I said, "and I'm not going to try to find out. Curiosity can be justified only up to a point, and this is no time to stretch it. We'll have to sit it out, at least until six o'clock." I glanced at my wrist. "That's only an hour and twenty minutes. Then we'll see if Mr. Wolfe has cooked up a charade. If not, he may at least invite you to dinner. See you later."

As I turned to go Carl sprang and broke my neck.

I have had enough unpleasant surprises over the years so that I am never completely off guard, but I admit I was careless that time because I underestimated him. He was a full three inches and thirty pounds under me, but I should have known that a guy who had managed a getaway from a concentration camp, and also from a continent, must have learned some good tricks. He had. The one he tried on me took him off the floor and through the air at my back, got his knees in my spine and his arm hooked under my chin. I was careless, but not quite careless enough. I heard and felt his rush too late to wheel or step, but in time to arch my back and drop my chin. He fastened onto me piggy-back, and his muscles were a real surprise.

If he was that quick on the spring he might be just as quick with his left hand getting out a knife, so I didn't try to get subtle. I bent my knees, called on my legs for all they had, jumped straight up as high as I could with him on me, jerked backwards in the air to horizontal, and hit the floor—or he did, with me on top. It squashed air out of him and jolted his arm loose. I bounced off to the right, got my feet under me, and came up, facing Tina in case she was prepared to help.

She wasn't. She was just standing there, frozen, with no blood left in her, anyway not in her face. I moved my head a little from left to right and then slowly in a circle. "I thought he broke my neck," I told her, "but he didn't. He only tried to."

She had no comment. Carl was on the floor, pulling air in for replacement. I stepped to him, reached down for his arm, yanked him upright, and went over him good. The only tool he had was a pocket knife with two little blades.

I backed up a step and remarked, "You act on impulse, don't you?"

"I couldn't break your neck," he said, as if his feelings were hurt. "You're too strong."

"You sure could try."

"No. I only wanted to go. If we stay here there is no hope. It would have made you numb, that was all."

"Yeah. Napoleon's been numb for over a century. I hope your ribs hurt. If so, think of me."

I went to the door to the office, passed through, closed the door, and locked it. There in privacy I took a survey, physical and mental. It was no pleasure to move my head, especially backward, but it did move. My back was sore where his knees had hit it, but some assorted twisting and bending proved that all the joints worked without cracking. I sat at my desk for the mental part. Getting my neck broke, or damn near it, had cleared my brain. Being smart enough to get it in that neither Carl nor Tina could drive a car was all right as far as it went, but it proved nothing at all about the scissors in Jake Wallen's back; it merely showed that there are motives and motives. The cops thought Wallen had been killed by a cornered hit-and-run driver, but what did I think? And even more important, what did Wolfe think? Was he up ahead of me as usual, or was he being too offhand, since no fee was involved, and maybe letting us in for a bloody nose?

I sat and surveyed and got so dissatisfied that I rang the plant rooms, told Wolfe about Carl's attempt to numb me, and tried to go on from there, but he brushed me off and said it could wait until six o'clock. I sat some more, practiced moving my head in various directions, and then got up to do back exercises. I was bending to touch the floor with my fingers when the phone rang.

It was Sergeant Purley Stebbins. "Archie? Purley. I'm at the barber shop. We want you here quick."

Two things told me it was no hostile mandate: his tone and the "Archie." The nature of my encounters with him usually had him calling me Goodwin, but occasionally it was Archie.

I responded in kind. "I'm busy but I guess so. If you really want me. Do you care to specify?"

"When you get here. You're needed, that's all. Grab a cab."

I buzzed Wolfe on the house phone and reported the development. Then I got a gun from the drawer, went to the kitchen and gave it to Fritz, described the status of the guests, and told him to keep his eyes and ears open. Then I hopped.

V

The crowd of spectators ganged up in the corridor outside the Goldenrod Barber Shop was twice as big as it had been before, for two reasons. It was just past five o'clock, and home-goers were flocking through for the subway; and inside the shop there was a fine assortment of cops and dicks to look at. The corridor sported not one flatfoot, but three, keeping people away from the entrance and moving. I told one of them my name and errand and was ordered to wait, and in a minute Purley came and escorted me in.

I darted a glance around. The barber chairs were all empty. Fickler and three of the barbers, Jimmie, Ed, and Philip, were seated along the row of waiting chairs, in their white jackets, each with a dick beside him. Tom was not in view. Other city employees were scattered around.

Purley had guided me to the corner by the cash register. "How long have you known that Janet Stahl?" he demanded.

I shook my head reproachfully. "Not that way. You said I was needed, and I came on the run. If you merely want my biography, call at the office any time during hours. If you call me Archie, even after hours."

"Cut the comedy. How long have you known her?"

"No, sir. I know a lawyer. Lay a foundation."

Purley's right shoulder twitched. It was only a reflex of his impulse to sock me, beyond his control and therefore nothing to resent. "Some day," he said, setting his jaw and then releasing it. "She was found on the floor of her booth, out from a blow on her head. We brought her to, and she can talk but she won't. She won't tell us anything. She says she don't know us. She says she won't talk to anybody except her friend Archie Goodwin. How long have you known her?"

"I'm touched," I said with emotion. "Until today I've merely leered at her, with no conversation or bodily contact of any kind. The only chat I've ever had with her was here today under your eye, but look what it did to her. Is it any wonder my opinion of myself is what it is?"

"Listen, Goodwin, we're after a murderer."

"I know you are. I'm all for it."

"You've never seen her outside this shop?"

"No."

"That can be checked maybe. Right now we want you to get her to talk. Goddam her, she's stopped us dead. Come on." He moved.

I caught his elbow. "Hold it. If she sticks to it that she'll only talk with me I'll have to think up questions. I ought to know what happened."

"Yeah." Purley wanted no more delay, but obviously I had a point. "There were only three of us left, me here at the front, and Joffe and Sullivan there on chairs. The barbers were all working on customers. Fickler was moving around. I was on the phone half the time. We had squeezed out everything we could here, for the present anyhow, and it was a letdown, you know how that is."

"Where was Janet?"

"I'm telling you. Toracco, that's Philip, finished with a customer, and a new one got in his chair—we were letting regular customers in. The new one wanted a manicure, and Toracco called Janet, but she didn't come. Fickler was helping the outgoing customer on with his coat. Toracco went behind the partition to get Janet, and there she was on the floor of her booth, cold. She had gone there fifteen minutes before, possibly twenty. I think all of them had gone behind the partition at least once during that time."

"You think?"

"Yes, I think."

"It must have been quite a letdown."

"I said I was on the phone a lot. Joffe and Sullivan will not be jumped up, and don't they know it. You know damn well how much we like it, her getting bopped with three of us right here."

"How bad is she hurt?"

"Not enough for the hospital. Doc let us keep her here. She was hit above the right ear with a bottle taken from the supply shelf against the partition, six feet from the entrance to her booth. The bottle was big and heavy, full of oil. It was there by her on the floor."

"Prints?"

"For God's sake, start a school. He had a towel in his hand or something. Come on."

"One second. What did the doctor say when you asked him if she could have been just testing her skull?"

"He said it was possible but he doubted it. Come and ask her."

Feeling that I had enough for a basis for conversation, I followed him. As we went toward the partition all the barbers and dicks along the row of chairs gave us looks, none of them cheerful. Fickler was absolutely forlorn.

I had never been behind the partition before. The space ran about half the length of the shop. Against the partition were steamers, vats, lamps, and other paraphernalia, and then a series of cupboards and shelves. Across a wide aisle were the manicure booths, four of them, though I had never seen more than two operators in the shop. As we passed the entrance to the first booth in the line a glance showed me Inspector Cramer seated at a little table across from Tom, the barber with white hair. Cramer saw me and arose. I followed Purley to the third booth, and on in. Then steps came behind me, and Cramer was there.

It was a big booth, eight by eight, but was now crowded. In addition to us three and the furniture, a city employee was standing in a corner, and, on a row of chairs lined up against the right wall, Janet Stahl was lying on her back, her head resting on a stack of towels. She had moved her eyes, but not her head, to take in us visitors. She looked beautiful.

"Here's your friend Goodwin," Purley told her, trying to sound sympathetic.

"Hello there," I said professionally. "What does this mean?"

The long home-grown lashes fluttered at me. "You," she said.

"Yep. Your friend Archie Goodwin." There was a chair there, the only one she wasn't using, and I squeezed past Purley and sat, facing her and close. "How do you feel, terrible?"

"No, I don't feel at all. I am past feeling."

I reached for her wrist, got my fingers on the spot, and looked at my watch. In thirty seconds I said, "Your pump isn't bad. May I inspect your head?"

"If you're careful."

"Groan if it hurts." I used all fingers to part the fine brown hair, and gently but thoroughly investigated the scalp. She closed her eyes and flinched once, but there was no groan. "A lump to write home about," I announced. "Doing your hair will be a problem. I'd like to give the guy that did it a piece of my mind before plugging him. Who was it?"

"Send them away, and I'll tell you."

I turned to the kibitzers. "Get out," I said sternly. "If I had been here this would never have happened. Leave us."

They went without a word. I sat listening to the sound of their retreating footsteps outside in the aisle, then thought I had better provide sound to cover in case they were careless tiptoeing back. They had their choice of posts, just outside the open entrance or in the adjoining booths. The partitions were only six feet high. "It was dastardly," I said. "He might have killed you or disfigured you for life, and either one would have ruined your career. Thank God you've got a good strong thick skull."

"I started to scream," she said, "but it was too late."

"What started you to scream? Seeing him, or hearing him?"

"It was both. I wasn't in my chair, I was in the customer's chair, with my back to the door—I was just sitting trying to think—and there was a little noise behind me, like a stealthy step, and I looked up and saw him reflected in the glass, right behind me with his arm raised, and I started to scream, but before I could get it out he struck—"

"Wait a minute." I got up and moved my chair to the outer side of the little table and sat in it. "These details are important. You were like this?"

"That's it. I was sitting thinking."

I felt that the opinion I had formed of her previously had not done her justice. The crinkly glass of the partition wall could reflect no object whatever, no matter how the light was. Her contempt for mental processes was absolutely spectacular. I moved my chair back beside her. From that angle, as she lay there flat on her back, not only was her face lovely to see, but the rest of her was good for the eyes too.

I asked, "But you saw his reflection before he struck?"

"Oh, yes."

"Did you recognize him?"

"Of course I did. That's why I wouldn't speak to them. That's why I had to see you. It was that big one with the big ears and gold tooth, the one they call Stebbins, or they call him Sergeant."

I wasn't surprised. I knew her quality now. "You mean it was him that hit you with the bottle?"

"I can't say it was him that hit me. I think people should be careful what they accuse other people of. I only know it was him I saw standing behind me with his arm raised, and then something hit me. From that anyone can only draw conclusions, but there are other reasons too. He was rude to me this morning, asking me questions, and all day he has been looking at me in a rude way, not the way a girl is willing for a man to look at her because she has to expect that. And then you can just be logical. Would Ed want to kill me, or Philip or Jimmie or Tom or Mr. Fickler? Why would they? So it must have been him even if I hadn't seen him."

"It does sound logical," I conceded. "But I've known Stebbins for years and have never known him to strike a woman without cause. What did he have against you?"

"I don't know." She frowned a little. "When they ask me that I'll just have to say I don't know. That's one of the first things you must tell me, how to answer things to the reporters. I shouldn't think I can keep on saying I don't know, or why would they print it? What hit you I don't know, who hit you I don't know, why did he hit you I don't know, my Lord, who would want to read that? What shall I say when they ask why he hit me?"

"We'll come back to that. First we—"

"We ought to settle it now." She was pouting fit for a *Life* cover, but determined. "That's how you'll earn your ten per cent."

"My ten per cent of what?"

"Of everything I get. As my manager." She extended a hand, her eyes straight at mine. "Shake on it."

To avoid a contractual shake without offending, I grasped the back of her hand with my left, turning her palm up, and ran the fingers of my right from her wrist to her fingertips. "It's a darned good idea," I said appreciatively, "but we'll have to postpone it. I'm going through bankruptcy just now, and it would be illegal for me to make a contract. About—"

"I can tell the reporters to ask you about things I don't know. It's called referring them to my manager."

"I know it is. Later on it will—"

"I don't need you later on. I need you right now."

"Here I am, you've got me, but not under contract yet." I released her hand, which I had kept as something to hold onto, and got emphatic. "If you tell reporters I'm your manager I'll give you a lump that will make that one seem as flat as a pool table. If they ask why he hit you don't say you don't know, say it's a mystery. People love a mystery. Now—"

"That's it!" She was delighted. "That's the kind of thing!"

"Sure. Tell 'em that. Now we've got to consider the cops. Stebbins is a cop, and they won't want it hung on him. They've had one cop killed here today already. They'll try to tie this up with that. I know how they work, I know them only too well. They'll try to make it that somebody here killed Wallen, and he found out that you knew something about it so he tried to kill you. They may even think they have some kind of evidence—for instance, something you were heard to say. So we have to be prepared. We have to go back over it. Are you listening?"

"Certainly. What do I say when the reporters ask me if I'm going to go on working here? Couldn't I say I don't want to desert Mr. Fickler in a time of trouble?"

It took control to stay in that chair. I would have given a good deal to be able to get up and walk out, go to Purley and Cramer at their eavesdropping posts, tell them she was all theirs and they were welcome to her, and go on home. But at home there were the guests locked in the front room, and sometime, somehow, we had to get rid of them. I looked at her charming enchanting comely face, with its nice chin and straight little nose and the eyelashes, and realized that the matter would be approached from her angle or not at all.

"That's the ticket," I said warmly. "Say you've got to be loyal to Mr. Fickler. That's the main thing to work on, how to handle the reporters. Have you ever been interviewed before?"

"No, this will be the first, and I want to start right."

"Good for you. What they like best of all is to get the jump on the police. If you can tell them something the cops don't know they'll love you forever. For instance, the fact that Stebbins crowned you doesn't prove that he's the only one involved. He must have an accomplice here in the shop, or why did Wallen come here in the first place? We'll call the accomplice X. Now listen. Sometime today, some time or other after Wallen's body was found, you saw something or heard something, and X knew you did. He knew it, and he knew that if you told about it—if you told me, for example—it would put him and Stebbins on the spot. Naturally both of them would want to kill you. It could have been X that tried to, but since you say you saw Stebbins reflected in the glass we'll let it go at that for now. Here's the point: if you can remember what it was you saw or heard that scared X, and if you tell the reporters before the cops get wise to it, they'll be your friends for life. Now for God's sake don't miss this chance. Concentrate. Remember everything you saw and heard here today, and everything you did and said too. Even if this takes us all night we've got to work it out."

She was frowning. "I don't remember anything that would scare anybody."

"Don't go at it like that. It was probably some little thing that didn't seem important to you at all. We may have to start at the beginning and go over every—"

I stopped on account of her face. The frown had left it, and she was looking past me, not seeing me, with an expression that told me plainly, if I knew her half as well as I thought I did, what was going on inside. I snapped at her, "Do you want the reporters hating you? Off of you for good?"

She was startled. "Of course not! That would be awful!"

"Then watch your step. This has got to be all wool. A girl with a fine mind like you, so much imagination, it would be a cinch for you to be creative, but don't. They'll double-check everything you say, and if they find it's not completely straight you're ruined. They'll never forgive you. You'll never need a manager."

"But I can't remember anything like that!"

"Not right off the bat, who could? Sometimes a thing like this takes days, let alone hours." Her hand was right there, and I patted it. "I guess we'd better go over it together, right straight through. That's the way Nero Wolfe would do it. What time did you get to work this morning?"

"When I always do, a quarter to nine. I'm punctual."

"Were the others already here?"

"Some were and some weren't."

"Who was and who wasn't?"

"My Lord, I don't know. I didn't notice." She was resentful. "If you're going to expect me to remember things like that we might as well quit, and you wouldn't be a good manager. When I came to work I was thinking of something else. A lot of the time I am thinking of something else, so how would I notice?"

I had to be patient. "Okay, we'll start at another point. You remember when Wallen came in and spoke with Fickler and went to Tina's booth and talked with her, and when Tina came out Fickler sent Philip in to him. You remember that?"

She nodded. "I guess so."

"Guesses won't get us anywhere. Just recall the situation, where you all were when Philip came back after talking with Wallen. Where were you?"

"I didn't notice."

"I'm not saying you noticed, but look back. There's Philip, coming around the end of the partition after talking with Wallen. Did you hear him say anything? Did you say anything to him?"

"I don't think Philip was this X," she declared. "He is married, with children. I think it was Jimmie Kirk. He tried to make passes at me when I first came, and he drinks, you can ask Ed about that, and he thinks he's superior. A barber being superior!" She looked pleased. "That's a good idea about Jimmie being X, because I don't have to say he really tried to kill me. I'll try to remember something he said. Would it matter exactly when he said it?"

I had had enough, but a man can't hit a woman when she's down, so I ended it without violence.

"Not at all," I told her, "but I've got an idea. I'll go and see if I can get something out of Jimmie. Meanwhile I'll send a reporter in to break the ice with you, from the *Gazette* probably. I know a lot of them." I was on my feet. "Just use your common sense and stick to facts. See you later."

"But Mr. Goodwin! I want—"

I was gone. Three steps got me out of the booth, and I strode down the aisle and around the end of the partition. There I halted, and it wasn't long before I was joined by Cramer and Purley. Their faces were expressive. I didn't have to ask if they had got it all.

"If you shoot her," I suggested, "send her brain to Johns Hopkins, if you can find it."

"Jesus," Purley said. That was all he said.

Cramer grunted. "Did she do it herself?"

"I doubt it. It was a pretty solid blow to raise that lump, and you didn't find her prints on the bottle. Bothering about prints is beneath her. I had to come up for air, but I left you an in. Better pick a strong character to play the role of reporter from the *Gazette*."

"Send for Biatti," Cramer snapped at Purley.

"Yeah," I agreed, "he can take it. Now I go home?"

"No. She might insist on seeing her manager again."

"I wouldn't pass that around," I warned them. "How would you like a broadcast of her line on Sergeant Stebbins? I'd like to be home for dinner. We're having fresh pork tenderloin."

"We would all like to be home for dinner." Cramer's look and tone were both sour. They didn't change when he shifted to Purley. "What about it? Is the Vardas pair still all you want?"

"They're what I want most," Purley said doggedly, "in spite of her getting it when they weren't here, but I guess we've got to spread out more. You can finish with them here and go home to dinner, and I suppose we've got to take 'em all downtown. I'm not sold that the Stahl girl is unfurnished inside her head, and we know she's capable of using her hands, since only three months ago she pushed a full-grown man out of his own car into a ditch and drove off. No matter how hard he was playing her, that's quite a stunt. I still want to be shown she couldn't have used that bottle on herself and I don't have to be shown that she could have used the scissors on Wallen if she felt like it. Or if she performed with the bottle to have something to tell reporters about, the Vardases are still what I want most. But I admit the other if is the biggest one. If someone here conked her, finding out who and why comes first until we get the Vardases."

Cramer stayed sour. "You haven't even started."

"Maybe that's a little too strong, Inspector."

"I don't think so."

"We were on the Vardases, but we didn't clear out of here, we kept close. Then when we found the Stahl girl and brought her to she shut the valve and had to see Goodwin. Even so, I wouldn't say we haven't made a start with the others. Ed Graboff plays the horses and owes a bookie nine hundred dollars, and he had to sell his car. Philip Toracco went off the rails in 1945 and spent a year in a booby hatch. Joel Fickler has been seen in public places with Horny Gallagher, and while that don't prove—"

Cramer cut in to shoot at me, "Is Fickler a racket boy?"

I shook my head. "Sorry. Blank. I've never been anything but a customer."

"If he is we'll get it." Purley was riled and didn't care who knew it. "Jimmie Kirk apparently only goes back three years, and he has expensive habits for a barber. Tom Yerkes did a turn in nineteen thirty-nine for assault, beat up a guy who took his young granddaughter for a fast weekend, and he is known for having a quick take-off. So I don't think you can say we haven't even started. We've got to take 'em all downtown and get thorough, especially about last night, sure we do. But I still want the Vardases."

"Are all alibis for last night being checked?" Cramer demanded.

"They have been."

"Do them over, and good. Get it going. Use as many men as you need. And not only alibis, records too. I want the Vardas pair as much as you do, but if the Stahl girl didn't use that bottle on herself, I also want someone else. Get Biatti here. Let him have a try at her before you take her down."

"He's not on duty, Inspector."

"Tell them to find him. Get him here."

"Yes, sir."

Purley moved. He went to the phone at the cashier's counter. I went to the one in the booth at the end of the clothes rack and dialed the number I knew best. Fritz answered, and I asked him to buzz the extension in the plant rooms, since it was still a few minutes short of six o'clock.

"Where are you?" Wolfe demanded. He was always testy when interrupted up there.

"At the barber shop." I was none too genial myself. "Janet was sitting in her booth and got hit on the head with a bottle of oil. They have gone through the routine and are still at the starting line. Her condition is no more critical than it was before she got hit. She insisted on seeing me, and I have had a long intimate talk with her. I can't say I made no progress, because she asked me to be her manager, and I am now giving you notice, quitting at the end of this week. Aside from that I got nowhere. She's one in a million. I would love to see you take her on. I have been requested to stick around. I'm willing, but I advise you to tell Fritz to increase the grocery orders until further notice."

Silence. Then, "Who is there?"

"Everybody. Cramer, Purley, squad men, the staff. They quit letting customers in after Janet got rapped. The whole party will be moved downtown in an hour or so, including Janet. Everyone is glum, including me."

"No progress whatever has been made?"

"Not as far as I know, except what I told you, I am now Janet's manag—"

"Pfui." Silence. In a moment, "Stay there."

The connection went.

I left the booth. Neither Purley nor Cramer was in sight. Only one flatfoot was at the door, and the throng outside in the corridor was no longer a throng, merely a knot, and a small one. I moseyed toward the rear, with the line of empty barber chairs on my left and the row of waiting chairs against the partition on my right. Fickler was there, and three of the barbers—Ed being the missing one now—with dicks in between. They weren't interested in me at all, and I made no effort to try to change their attitude.

The chair on the left of the magazine table was empty, and I dropped into it. Apparently no one had felt like reading today, since the same *New Yorker* was on top and the two-weeks-old *Time* was still on the shelf below. I would have been glad to employ my mind analyzing the situation if there had been anything to analyze, but there was no place to start, and after sitting a few minutes I became aware that I was trying to analyze Janet. Of course that was even more hopeless, and I mention it only to show you the condition I was in. But it did look as if Janet was the key, and in that case the thing to do was to figure some way of handling her. I sat and worked on that problem. There must be some practical method of digging up from her memory the fact or facts that we had to have. Hypnotize her, maybe? That might work. I was considering suggesting it to Cramer when I became aware of movement over at the door and lifted my eyes.

The flatfoot was blocking the entrance to keep a man fully twice his weight from entering, and was explaining the situation.

The man let him finish and then spoke. "I know, I know." His eyes came at me over the flatfoot's shoulder, and he bellowed, "Archie! Where's Mr. Cramer?"

VI

I got up and made for the door in no haste or jubilation. There have been times when the sight and sound of Wolfe have given me a lift, but that wasn't one of them. I had told him on the phone that I would love to see him take Janet on, but that had been rhetorical. One would get him ten he couldn't make a dent in her.

"Do you want in?" I asked.

"What the devil," he roared, "do you suppose I came for?"

"Okay, take it easy. I'll go see—"

But I didn't have to go. His first bellow had carried within, and Cramer's voice came from right behind me. "Well! Dynamite?"

"I'll be damned," Purley, there too, growled.

The flatfoot had moved aside, leaving it to the brass, and Wolfe had crossed the sill. "I came to get a haircut," he stated and marched past the sergeant and inspector to the rack, took off his hat, coat, vest, and tie, hung them up, crossed to Jimmie's chair, the second in the line, and got his bulk up onto the seat. In the mirrored wall fronting him he had a panorama of the row of barbers and dicks in his rear, and without turning his head he called, "Jimmie! If you please?"

Jimmie's dancing dark eyes came to Cramer and Purley, there by me. So did others. Cramer stood scowling at Wolfe. We all held our poses while Cramer slowly lifted his right hand and carefully and thoroughly scratched the side of his nose with his forefinger. That attended to, he decided to sit down. He went, not in a hurry, to the first chair in the line, the one Fickler himself used occasionally when there was a rush, turned it to face Wolfe, and mounted. He spoke.

"You want a haircut, huh?"

"Yes, sir. As you can see, I need one."

"Yeah." Cramer turned his head. "All right, Kirk. Come and cut his hair."

Jimmie got up and went past the chair to the cabinet for an apron. Everybody stirred, as if a climax had been reached and passed. Purley strode to the third chair in the line, Philip's, and got on it. That way he and Cramer had Wolfe surrounded, and it seemed only fair for me to be handy, so I detoured around Cramer, pulled Jimmie's stool to one side, and perched on it.

Jimmie had Wolfe aproned, and his scissors were singing above the right ear. Wolfe barred clippers.

"You just dropped in," Cramer rasped. "Like Goodwin this morning."

"Certainly not." Wolfe was curt but not pugnacious. There was no meeting of eyes, since Cramer had Wolfe's profile straight and Wolfe had Cramer's profile in the mirror. "You summoned Mr. Goodwin. He told me on the phone of his fruitless talk with Miss Stahl, and I thought it well to come."

Cramer grunted. "Okay, you're here. You won't leave your place on business for anybody or any fee, but you're here. And you're not going to leave until I know why, without any such crap as murderers in your front room."

"Not as short behind as last time," Wolfe commanded.

"Yes, sir." Jimmie had never had as big or attentive an audience and he was giving a good show. The comb and scissors flitted and sang.

"Naturally," Wolfe said tolerantly, "I expected that. You can badger me if that's what you're after, and get nowhere, but I offer a suggestion. Why not work first? Why don't we see if we can settle this business, and then, if you still insist, go after me? Or would you rather harass me than catch a murderer?"

"I'm working now. I want the murderer. What about you?"

"Forget me for the moment. You can hound me any time. I would like to propose certain assumptions about what happened here today. Do you care to hear them?"

"I'll listen, but don't drag it out."

"I won't. Please don't waste time challenging the assumptions; I don't intend to defend them, much less validate them. They are merely a basis of exploration, to be tested. The first is this, that Wallen found something in the car, the car that had killed two women—no, I don't like it this way. I want a direct view, not reflections. Jimmie, turn me around, please."

Jimmie whirled the chair a half-turn, so that Wolfe's back was to the mirrored wall, also to me, and he was facing those seated in the chairs against the partition, with Cramer on his right and Purley on his left.

"That right, sir?"

"Yes. Thank you."

I spoke up. "Ed isn't here."

"I left him in the booth," Purley rumbled.

"Get him," Wolfe instructed. "And Miss Stahl, where is she?"

"In her booth, lying down. With her head."

"We want her. She can sit up, can't she?"

"I don't know. God only knows."

"Archie. Bring Miss Stahl."

He had a nerve picking on me, with an inspector and a sergeant and three dicks there, but I postponed telling him so and went, as Purley went for Ed. In the booth Janet was still on her back on the chairs, her eyes wide open. At sight of me she fired immediately.

"You said you were going to send a reporter, but I've been thinking—"

I raised my voice to top her. "Listen to me, girlie. You're getting a break. Nero Wolfe is here with a suggestion and wants your opinion of it. Can you sit up a while?"

"Certainly I can, but—"

"No buts. He's waiting for you. Shall I carry you?"

"Certainly not!" She started up.

"Take it easy." I put an arm behind her shoulders and got her upright and then onto her feet. "Are you dizzy?"

"I'm never dizzy," she said scornfully and moved. I kept hold of her arm. She was a little unsteady on the way down the aisle to the end of the partition, but when we came in view of the audience she shook me off and went on solo. She wasn't taking help from a man, and of course I wasn't her manager yet. She took the chair I had vacated when Wolfe appeared, next to the magazine table. Ed had been brought by Purley, who was back in Philip's chair, flanking Wolfe. I returned to the stool.

Jimmie had finished above the ears and was doing the back, so Wolfe's head was tilted forward.

"Your assumptions?" Cramer asked impatiently.

"Yes. I was saying, the first is that Wallen found something in the car that led him to this shop. It couldn't have been something he was told, for there was no one to tell him anything. It was some object. I asked you not to challenge me, but I didn't mean to exclude contradictions. If there are facts that repudiate this assumption, or any other, I want them by all means."

"We made that one without any help."

"And it still holds?"

"Yes."

"Good. That's fortunate, since all of my assumptions concern that object. The second is that Wallen had it with him when he came here. I can support that with sound—"

"You don't need to. We made it and we hold it."

"Very well. That saves time. Not too short back there, Jimmie."

"No, sir."

"The third is that he had the object inside the newspaper he was carrying. This is slenderer, but it must be tested. He had not bought the paper shortly before coming here, for it was an early edition of the *News*, on sale last evening, not on sale this morning. It was not merely stuffed in his pocket, not merely not discarded; he had it in his hand, not folded up, as it is stacked on the newsstand. It is—"

"You know a lot about it," Cramer growled.

"Do me later," Wolfe snapped. "I know nothing you don't know. It is difficult to account for his carrying a stale newspaper in that manner except on the assumption that it was a container for some object—at least, the assumption is good enough to work on. The fourth is that, whatever the object was, the murderer got it and disposed of it. More than an assumption, that is. No object that could have led him to this shop was found on Wallen's person or in the booth, so if he had it the murderer got it. The fifth assumption is that the murderer was neither Carl nor Tina. I shall—"

"What the hell!" Purley blurted.

"Ah," Cramer said. "Tell us why."

"No. I shall not support that assumption; I merely make it and submit it to our test. Don't waste time clawing at me. Since Carl and Tina are not involved and therefore didn't take the object away with them, it is still here in the shop. That is the sixth assumption, and it is good only if your surveillance of these people here all these hours has been constant and alert. What about it? Could any of them have removed such an object from the shop?"

"I want to know," Cramer demanded, "why you're excluding Carl and Tina."

"No. Not now." Wolfe and Cramer couldn't see each other because Jimmie was in between, starting on the top. "First we'll complete this test. We must know whether the object has been removed, *not* by Carl or Tina."

"No," Purley said.

"How good a no?"

"Good enough for me. No man has stepped outside this shop alone. Something could have been slipped to a customer, but that's stretching it, and we've had them under our eyes."

"Not, apparently, the one who assaulted Miss Stahl."

"That was in the shop. Is that a point?"

"I suppose not. Then we assume that the object is still here. The seventh and last assumption is this, that no proper search for such an object has been made. I hasten to add, Mr. Stebbins, that that is not a point either. You and your men are unquestionably capable of making a proper search, but I assume that you haven't done so here on account of Carl and Tina. Thinking them guilty, naturally you thought they wouldn't leave an incriminating object behind them. However, I can just ask you. Have you searched thoroughly?"

"We've looked."

"Yes. But granting all my assumptions, which of course you don't, has there been a proper search?"

"No."

"Then it's about time. Mr. Fickler!"

Fickler nearly jumped out of his skin. He, like all the others, had been buried, intent on Wolfe's buildup, and the sudden pop and crackle of his own name startled him. He jerked his head up, and I had never seen his pudgy face look so bloated.

"Me?" he squeaked.

"You run this place and can help us. However, I address all of you who work here. Put your minds on this. You too, Jimmie. Stop a moment and listen."

"I can work and listen too."

"No. I want full attention."

Jimmie backed off a step and stood.

"This," Wolfe said, "could take a few minutes or it could take all night. What we're after is an object with something on it that identifies it as coming from this shop. Ideally it should be the name and address or phone number, but we'll take less if we have to. Since we're proceeding on my assumptions, we are supposing that it was inside the newspaper as Wallen was carrying it, so it is not a business card or match folder or bottle or comb or brush. It should be flat and of considerable dimensions. Another point, it should be easily recognizable. All of you went to the booth and were questioned by Wallen, but he showed you no such object and mentioned none. Is that correct?"

They nodded and mumbled affirmatives. Ed said "Yes!" in a loud voice.

"Then only the murderer saw it or was told of it. Wallen must for some reason have shown it to him or asked him about it, and not the rest of you; or its edge may have been protruding from the newspaper, unnoticed by the others; or the murderer may merely have suspected that Wallen had it. In any case, when opportunity offered later for him to dive into the booth and kill Wallen he got the object and disposed of it. If Mr. Stebbins is right about the surveillance that has been maintained, it is still here in the shop. I put it to you, and especially to you, Mr. Fickler: what is it and where is it?"

They looked at one another and back at Wolfe. Philip said in his thin tenor, "Maybe it was the newspaper itself."

"Possibly. I doubt it. Where is it, Mr. Cramer?"

"At the laboratory. There's nothing on it or in it that could have brought Wallen here."

"What else has been taken from here to the laboratory?"

"Nothing but the scissors and the bottle that was used on Miss Stahl."

"Then it's here. All right, Jimmie, finish."

Jimmie moved to the left of him and carried on.

"It looks to me," Purley objected in his bass rumble, "like a turkey. Even with your assumptions. Say we find something like what you want, how do we know it's it? Even if we think it's it, where does that get us?"

"We'll see when we find it." Wolfe was curt. "For one thing, fingerprints."

"Nuts. If it belongs here of course it will have their prints."

"Not *their* prints, Mr. Stebbins. Wallen's prints. If he picked it up in the car he touched it. If he touched it he left prints. As I understand it, he didn't go around touching things here. He entered, spoke to Mr. Fickler, was taken to the booth, and never left it alive. If we find anything with his prints on it we've got it. Have you equipment here? If not, I advise you to send for it at once, and also for Wallen's prints from your file. Will you do that?"

Purley grunted. He didn't move.

"Go ahead," Cramer told him. "Phone. Give him what he wants. Get it over. Then he'll give us what we want, what he's here for, or else."

Purley descended from the chair and headed for the phone at the cashier's counter.

"The search," Wolfe said, "must be thorough and will take time. First I ask all of you to search your minds. What object is here, belongs here, that meets the specifications as I have described them? Surely you can tell us. Mr. Fickler?"

"I've been thinking." Fickler shook his head. "I've been thinking hard. I don't know unless it's a towel, and why would he carry a towel like that?"

"He wouldn't. Anyway a towel wouldn't help us any, so I reject it. Philip?"

"No, sir. I don't know what."

"Tom?"

Tom just shook his head gloomily.

"Ed?"

"You've got me. Pass."

"Miss Stahl?"

"I think he might have been keeping the paper because there was something in it he wanted to read. I know I often do that, say it's in an evening paper and I don't have time—"

"Yes. We'll consider that. Jimmie?"

"I don't know a thing like that in the shop, Mr. Wolfe. Not a thing."

"Pfui." Wolfe was disgusted. "Either you have no brains at all, or they're temporarily paralyzed, or you're all in a conspiracy. I'm looking straight at such an object right now."

From behind I couldn't see where his gaze was directed, but I didn't have to. The others could, and I saw them. Eleven pairs of eyes, including Purley's—he had finished at the phone and rejoined us—were aimed at the magazine table next to Janet's chair from eleven different angles. Up to that moment my brain may have been as paralyzed as the others', but it could still react to a stimulus. I left the stool and stood right behind Wolfe, ready if and when needed.

"You mean the magazines?" Cramer demanded.

"Yes. You subscribe to them, Mr. Fickler? They come through the mail? Then the name and address is on them."

"Not on this one," said the dick on the other side of the magazine table, picking up the *New Yorker* on top.

"Drop it!" Cramer barked. "Don't touch it!"

"No," Wolfe conceded, "that comes in a wrapper. But others don't. For instance that *Time,* there on the shelf below—the addressee is on the cover. Surely it deserves examination, and others too. What if he took it from here and had it in his pocket when he stole the car and drove up Broadway? And in the excitement of his misadventure he failed to notice that it had dropped from his pocket and was on the seat of the car? And Wallen found it there, took it, and saw the name and address on it? You have sent for the equipment and Wallen's prints, Mr. Stebbins? Then we—"

"Oh! I remember!" Janet cried. She was pointing a finger. "You remember, Jimmie? This morning I was standing here, and you came by with a hot towel and you had that magazine and you tossed it under there, and I asked if you had been steaming it, and you said—"

Jimmie leaped. I thought his prey was Janet and in spite of everything I was willing to save her life, but Wolfe and the chair were in my way and cost me a fifth of a second. And it wasn't Janet he was after, it was the magazine. He went for it in a hurtling dive and got his hands on it, but then the three dicks, not to mention Cramer and

Purley, were on his neck and various other parts of him. It was a handsome pile-up. Janet, except for pulling her feet back under her chair out of harm's way, did not move, nor did she make a sound. I suppose she was considering what to say to the reporters.

"Confound it," Wolfe grumbled savagely behind me. "*My* barber."

Anyhow that haircut was practically done.

VII

As stubborn as Cramer was, he never did learn why Wolfe went to get a haircut that day. Eventually he stopped trying.

He learned plenty about Jimmie Kirk. Kirk was wanted as a bail-jumper, under another name, in Wheeling, West Virginia, on an old charge as a car stealer, with various fancy complications such as slugging a respected citizen who had surprised him in the act. Apparently he had gone straight in New York for a couple of years and had then resumed his former avocation. Unquestionably he had been fortified with liquids that Monday evening. Driving a stolen car while drunk is a risky operation, especially with a stolen magazine in your pocket.

As for Carl and Tina, I took a strong position on them Tuesday evening in the office after they had been sent up to the south room to bed.

"You know damn well what will happen," I told Wolfe. "They won't go to Ohio or anywhere else, they'll stay here. Some day, maybe next week, maybe next year, they'll be confronted and they'll be in trouble. Being in trouble, they will come to me, because Carl likes me and because I rescued them this time—"

Wolfe snorted. "*You* did!"

"Yes, sir. I had already noticed that magazine there several times, and it just happened to catch your eye. Anyhow, I am secretly infatuated with Tina so I'll try to help them and will get my finger caught, and you'll have to butt in again because you can't get along without me. It will go on like that year after year. Why not take care of it now and live in peace? There are people in Washington who owe you something, for instance Carpenter. Start him working on it. Do you want them hanging in the air on a thread over your head the rest of your life? I don't. It will cost a measly buck for a phone call, and I can get that from the fifty they have earmarked for us. I have Carpenter's home number, and I might as well get him right now."

No comment.

I put my hand on the phone. "Person to person, huh?"

Wolfe grunted. "I got my naturalization papers twenty-four years ago."

"I wasn't discussing you. You've caught it from Janet," I said coldly and lifted the phone and dialed.

The Squirt and the Monkey

I

I was doing two things at once. With my hands I was getting my armpit holster and the Marley .32 from a drawer of my desk, and with my tongue I was giving Nero Wolfe a lecture on economics.

"The most you can hope to soak him," I stated, "is five hundred bucks. Deduct a C for twenty per cent for overhead and another C for expenses incurred, that leaves three hundred. Eighty-five per cent for income tax will leave you with forty-five bucks clear for the wear and tear on your brain and my legs, not to mention the risk. That wouldn't buy—"

"Risk of what?" He muttered that only to be courteous, to show that he had heard what I said, though actually he wasn't listening. Seated behind his desk, he was scowling, not at me but at the crossword puzzle in the London *Times*.

"Complications," I said darkly. "You heard him explain it. Playing games with a gun is sappy." I was contorted, buckling the strap of the holster. That done, I picked up my coat. "Since you're listed in the red book as a detective, and since I draw pay, such as it is, as your licensed assistant, I'm all for detecting for people on request. But this bozo wants to do it himself, using our firearm as a prop." I felt my tie to see if it was straight. I didn't cross to the large mirror on the far wall of the office for a look, because whenever I did so in Wolfe's presence he snorted. "We might just as well," I declared, "send it up to him by messenger."

"Pfui," Wolfe muttered. "It is a thoroughly conventional proceeding. You are merely out of humor because you don't like Dazzle Dan. If it were Pleistocene Polly you would be zealous."

"Nuts. I look at the comics occasionally just to be cultured. It wouldn't hurt any if you did."

I went to the hall for my things, let myself out, descended the stoop, and headed toward Tenth Avenue for a taxi. A cold gusty wind came at my back from across the Hudson, and I made it brisk, swinging my arms, to get my blood going.

It was true that I did not care for Dazzle Dan, the hero of the comic strip that was syndicated to two thousand newspapers—or was it two million?—throughout the land. Also I did not care for his creator, Harry Koven, who had called at the office Saturday evening, forty hours ago. He had kept chewing his upper lip with jagged yellow teeth, and it had seemed to me that he might at least have chewed the lower lip instead of the upper, which doesn't show teeth. Moreover, I had not cared for his job as he outlined it. Not that I was getting snooty about the renown of Nero Wolfe—a guy who has had a gun lifted has got as much right to buy good detective work as a rich duchess accused of murder—but the way this Harry Koven had programmed it he was going to do the detecting himself, so the only difference between me and a messenger boy was that I was taking a taxi instead of the subway.

Anyhow Wolfe had taken the job and there I was. I pulled a slip of paper from my pocket, typed on by me from notes taken of the talk with Harry Koven, and gave it a look.

MARCELLE KOVEN, wife
ADRIAN GETZ, friend or camp follower, maybe both
PATRICIA LOWELL, agent (manager?), promoter
PETE JORDAN, artist, draws Dazzle Dan
BYRAM HILDEBRAND, artist, also draws D.D.

One of those five, according to Harry Koven, had stolen his gun, a Marley .32, and he wanted to know which one. As he had told it, that was all there was to it, but it was a cinch that if the missing object had been an electric shaver or a pair of cufflinks it would not have called for all that lip-chewing, not to mention other signs of strain. He had gone out of his way, not once but twice, to declare that he had no reason to suspect any of the five of wanting to do any shooting. The second time he had made it so emphatic that Wolfe had grunted and I had lifted a brow.

Since a Marley .32 is by no means a collector's item, it was no great coincidence that there was one in our arsenal and that therefore we were equipped to furnish Koven with the prop he wanted for his performance. As for the performance itself, the judicious thing to do was wait and see, but there was no point in being judicious about something I didn't like, so I had already checked it off as a dud.

I dismissed the taxi at the address on Seventy-sixth Street, east of Lexington Avenue. The house had had its front done over for the current century, unlike Nero Wolfe's old brownstone on West Thirty-fifth Street, which still sported the same front stoop it had started with. To enter this one you went down four steps instead of up seven, and I did so, after noting the pink shutters at the windows of all four floors and the tubs of evergreens flanking the entrance.

I was let in by a maid in uniform, with a pug nose and lipstick about as thick as Wolfe spreads Camembert on a wafer. I told her I had an appointment with Mr. Koven. She said Mr. Koven was not yet available and seemed to think that settled it, making me no offer for my hat and coat.

I said, "Our old brownstone, run by men only, is run better. When Fritz or I admit someone with an appointment we take his things."

"What's your name?" she demanded in a tone indicating that she doubted if I had one.

A loud male voice came from somewhere within. "Is that the man from Furnari's?"

A loud female voice came from up above. "Cora, is that my dress?"

I called out, "It's Archie Goodwin, expected by Mr. Koven at noon! It is now two minutes past twelve!"

That got action. The female voice, not quite so loud, told me to come up. The maid, looking frustrated, beat it. I took off my coat and put it on a chair, and my hat. A man came through a doorway at the rear of the hall and approached, speaking.

"More noise. Noisiest goddam place. Up this way." He started up the stairs. "When you have an appointment with Sir Harry, always add an hour."

I followed him. At the top of the flight there was a large square hall with wide archways to rooms at right and left. He led me through the one at the left.

There are few rooms I can't take in at a glance, but that was one of them. Two huge TV cabinets, a monkey in a cage in a corner, chairs of all sizes and colors, rugs overlapping, a fireplace blazing away, the temperature around eighty—I gave it up and focused on the inhabitant. That was not only simpler but pleasanter. She was smaller than I would specify by choice, but otherwise acceptable, especially the wide smooth brow above the serious gray eyes, and the cheekbones. She must have been part salamander, to look so cool and silky in that oven.

"Dearest Pete," she said, "you are going to stop calling my husband Sir Harry."

I admired that as a time-saver. Instead of the usual pronouncement of names, she let me know that she was Marcelle, Mrs. Harry Koven, and that the young man was Pete Jordan, and at the same time told him something.

Pete Jordan walked across to her as for a purpose. He might have been going to take her in his arms or slap her or anything in between. But a pace short of her he stopped.

"You're wrong," he told her in his aggressive baritone. "It's according to plan. It's the only way I can prove I'm not a louse. No one but a louse would stick at this, doing this crap month after month, and here look at me just because I like to eat. I haven't got the guts to quit and starve a while, so I call him Sir Harry to make you sore, working myself up to calling him something that will make him sore, and eventually I'll come to a boil and figure out a way to make Getz sore, and then I'll get bounced and I can start starving and be an artist. It's a plan."

He turned and glared at me. "I'm more apt to go through with it if I announce it in front of a witness. You're the witness. My name's Jordan, Pete Jordan."

He shouldn't have tried glaring because he wasn't built for it. He wasn't much bigger than Mrs. Koven, and he had narrow shoulders and broad hips. An aggressive baritone and a defiant glare coming from that make-up just couldn't have the effect he was after. He needed coaching.

"You have already made me sore," she told his back in a nice low voice, but not a weak one. "You act like a brat and you're too old to be a brat. Why not grow up?"

He wheeled and snapped at her, "I look on you as a mother!"

That was a foul. They were both younger than me, and she couldn't have had more than three or four years on him.

I spoke. "Excuse me," I said, "but I am not a professional witness. I came to see Mr. Koven at his request. Shall I go hunt for him?"

A thin squeak came from behind me. "Good morning, Mrs. Koven. Am I early?"

As she answered I turned for a look at the owner of the squeak, who was advancing from the archway. He should have traded voices with Pete Jordan. He had both the size and presence for a deep baritone, with a well-made head topped by a healthy mat of gray hair nearly white. Everything about him was impressive and masterful, including the way he carried himself, but the squeak spoiled it completely. It continued as he joined us.

"I heard Mr. Goodwin, and Pete left, so I thought—"

Mrs. Koven and Pete were both talking too, and it didn't seem worth the effort to sort it out, especially when the monkey decided to join in and started chattering. Also I could feel sweat coming on my forehead and neck, overdressed as I was with a coat and vest, since Pete and the newcomer were in shirt sleeves. I couldn't follow their example without displaying my holster. They kept it up, including the monkey, ignoring me completely but informing me incidentally that the squeaker was not Adrian Getz as I had first supposed, but Byram Hildebrand, Pete's co-worker in the grind of drawing Dazzle Dan.

It was all very informal and homey, but I was starting to sizzle and I crossed to the far side of the room and opened a window wide. I expected an immediate reaction but got none. Disappointed at that but relieved by the rush of fresh air, I filled my chest, used my handkerchief on the brow and neck, and, turning, saw that we had company. Coming through the archway was a pink-cheeked creature in a mink coat with a dark green slab of cork or something perched on her brown hair at a cocky slant. With no one bothering to glance at her except me, she moved across toward the fireplace, slid the coat off onto a couch, displaying a tricky plaid suit with an assortment of restrained colors, and said in a throaty voice that carried without being raised, "Rookaloo will be dead in an hour."

They were all shocked into silence except the monkey. Mrs. Koven looked at her, looked around, saw the open window, and demanded, "Who did that?"

"I did," I said manfully.

Byram Hildebrand strode to the window like a general in front of troops and pulled it shut. The monkey stopped talking and started to cough.

"Listen to him," Pete Jordan said. His baritone mellowed when he was pleased. "Pneumonia already! That's an idea! That's what I'll do when I work up to making Getz sore."

Three of them went to the cage to take a look at Rookaloo, not bothering to greet or thank her who had come just in time to save the monkey's life. She stepped to me, asking cordially, "You're Archie Goodwin? I'm Pat Lowell." She put out a hand, and I took it. She had talent as a handclasper and backed it up with a good straight look out of clear brown eyes. "I was going to phone you this morning to warn you that Mr. Koven is never ready on time for an appointment, but he arranged this himself so I didn't."

"Never again," I told her, "pass up an excuse for phoning me."

"I won't." She took her hand back and glanced at her wrist. "You're early anyway. He told us the conference would be at twelve-thirty."

"I was to come at twelve."

"Oh." She was taking me in—nothing offensive, but she sure was rating me. "To talk with him first?"

I shrugged. "I guess so."

She nodded, frowning a little. "This is a new one on me. I've been his agent and manager for three years now, handling all his business, everything from endorsements of cough drops to putting Dazzle Dan on scooters, and this is the first time a thing like this has happened, him getting someone in for a conference without consulting me—and Nero Wolfe, no less! I understand it's about a tie-up of Nero Wolfe and Dazzle Dan, having Dan start a detective agency?"

I put that question mark there, though her inflection left it to me whether to call it a question or merely a statement. I was caught off guard, so it probably showed on my face—my glee at the prospect of telling Wolfe about a tie-up between him and Dazzle Dan, with full details. I tried to erase it.

"We'd better wait," I said discreetly, "and let Mr. Koven tell it. As I understand it, I'm only here as a technical adviser, representing Mr. Wolfe because he never goes out on business. Of course you would handle the business end, and if that means you and I will have to have a lot of talks—"

I stopped because I had lost her. Her eyes were aimed past my left shoulder toward the archway, and their expression had suddenly and completely changed. They weren't exactly more alive or alert, but more concentrated. I turned, and there was Harry Koven crossing to us. His mop of black hair hadn't been combed, and he hadn't shaved. His big frame was enclosed in a red silk robe embroidered with yellow Dazzle Dans. A little guy in a dark blue suit was with him, at his elbow.

"Good morning, my little dazzlers!" Koven boomed.

"It seems cool in here," the little guy said in a gentle worried voice.

In some mysterious way the gentle little voice seemed to make more noise than the big boom. Certainly it was the gentle little voice that chopped off the return greetings from the dazzlers, but it could have been the combination of the two, the big man and the small one, that had so abruptly changed the atmosphere of the room. Before they had all been screwy perhaps, but all free and easy; now they were all tightened up. They even seemed to be tongue-tied, so I spoke.

"I opened a window," I said.

"Good heavens," the little guy mildly reproached me and trotted over to the monkey's cage. Mrs. Koven and Pete Jordan were in his path, and they hastily moved out of it, as if afraid of getting trampled, though he didn't look up to trampling anything bigger than a cricket.

Not only was he too little and too old, but also he was vaguely deformed and trotted with a jerk.

Koven boomed at me, "So you got here! Don't mind the Squirt and his damn monkey. He loves that damn monkey. I call this the steam room." He let out a laugh. "How is it, Squirt, okay?"

"I think so, Harry. I hope so." The low gentle voice filled the room again.

"I hope so too, or God help Goodwin." Koven turned on Byram Hildebrand. "Has seven-twenty-eight come, By?"

"No," Hildebrand squeaked. "I phoned Furnari, and he said it would be right over."

"Late again. We may have to change. When it comes, do a revise on the third frame. Where Dan says, 'Not tonight, my dear,' make it, 'Not today, my dear.' Got it?"

"But we discussed that—"

"I know, but change it. We'll change seven-twenty-nine to fit. Have you finished seven-thirty-three?"

"No. It's only—"

"Then what are you doing up here?"

"Why, Goodwin came, and you said you wanted us at twelve-thirty—"

"I'll let you know when we're ready—sometime after lunch. Show me the revise on seven-twenty-eight." Koven glanced around masterfully. "How is everybody? Blooming? See you all later. Come along, Goodwin, sorry you had to wait. Come with me."

He headed for the archway, and I followed, across the hall and up the next flight of stairs. There the arrangement was different; instead of a big square hall there was a narrow corridor with four doors, all closed. He turned left, to the door at that end, opened it, held it for me to pass through, and shut it again. This room was an improvement in several ways: it was ten degrees cooler, it had no monkey, and the furniture left more room to move around. The most prominent item was a big old scarred desk over by a window. After inviting me to sit, Koven went and sat at the desk and removed covers from dishes that were there on a tray.

"Breakfast," he said. "You had yours."

It wasn't a question, but I said yes to be sociable. He needed all the sociability he could get, from the looks of the tray. There was one dejected poached egg, one wavy thin piece of toast, three undersized prunes with about a teaspoonful of juice, a split of tonic water, and a glass. It was an awful sight. He waded into the prunes. When they were gone he poured the tonic water into the glass, took a sip, and demanded, "Did you bring it?"

"The gun? Sure."

"Let me see it."

"It's the one we showed you at the office." I moved to another chair, closer to him. "I'm supposed to check with you before we proceed. Is that the desk you kept your gun in?"

He nodded and swallowed a nibble of toast. "Here in this left-hand drawer, in the back."

"Loaded."

"Yes. I told you so."

"So you did. You also told us that you bought it two years ago in Montana, when you were there at a dude ranch, and brought it home with you and never bothered to get a license for it, and it's been there in the drawer right along. You saw it there a week or ten days ago, and last Friday you saw it was gone. You didn't want to call the cops for two reasons, because you have no license for it, and because you think it was taken by one of the five people whose names you gave—"

"I think it *may* have been."

"You didn't put it like that. However, skip it. You gave us the five names. By the way, was that Adrian Getz, the one you called Squirt?"

"Yes."

"Then they're all five here, and we can go ahead and get it over with. As I understand it, I am to put my gun there in the drawer where yours was, and you get them up here for a conference, with me present. You were to cook up something to account for me. Have you done that?"

He swallowed another nibble of toast and egg. Wolfe would have had that meal down in five seconds flat—or rather, he would have had it out the window. "I thought this might do," Koven said. "I can say that I'm considering a new stunt for Dan, have him start a detective agency, and I've called Nero Wolfe in for consultation, and he sent you up for a conference. We can discuss it a little, and I ask you to show us how a detective searches a room to give us an idea of the picture potential. You shouldn't start with the desk; start maybe with the shelves back of me. When you come to do the desk I'll push my chair back to be out of your way, and I'll have them right in front of me. When you open the drawer and take the gun out and they see it—"

"I thought you were going to do that."

"I know, that's what I said, but this is better because this way they'll be looking at the gun and you, and I'll be watching their faces. I'll have my eye right on them, and the one that took my gun, if one of them did it—when he or she suddenly sees you pull a gun out of the drawer that's exactly like it, it's going to show on his face, and I'm going to see it. We'll do it that way."

I admit it sounded better there on the spot than it had in Wolfe's office—and besides, he had revised it. This way he might really get what he wanted. I considered it, watching him finish the tonic water. The toast and egg were gone.

"It sounds all right," I conceded, "except for one thing. You'll be expecting a look of surprise, but what if there are five looks of surprise? At seeing me take a gun out of your desk—those who don't know you had a gun there."

"But they do know."

"All of them?"

"Certainly. I thought I told you that. Anyhow, they all know. Everybody knows everything around this place. They thought I ought to get rid of it, and now I wish I had. You understand, Goodwin, all there is to this—I just want to know where the damn thing is, I want to know who took it, and I'll handle it myself from there. I told Wolfe that."

"I know you did." I got up and went to his side of the desk, at his left, and pulled a drawer open. "In here?"

"Yes."

"The rear compartment?"

"Yes."

I reached to my holster for the Marley, broke it, removed the cartridges and dropped them into my vest pocket, put the gun in the drawer, shut the drawer, and returned to my chair.

"Okay," I said, "get them up here. We can ad lib it all right without any rehearsing."

He looked at me. He opened the drawer for a peek at the gun, not touching it, and pushed the drawer to. He shoved the tray away, leaned back, and began working on his upper lip with the jagged yellow teeth.

"I'm going to have to get my nerve up," he said, as if appealing to me. "I'm never much good until late afternoon."

I grunted. "What the hell. You told me to be here at noon and called the conference for twelve-thirty."

"I know I did. I do things like that." He chewed the lip some more. "And I've got to dress." Suddenly his voice went high in protest. "Don't try to rush me, understand?"

I was fed up, but had already invested a lot of time and a dollar for a taxi on the case, so kept calm. "I know," I told him, "artists are temperamental. But I'll explain how Mr. Wolfe charges. He sets a fee, depending on the job, and if it takes more of my time than he thinks reasonable he adds an extra hundred dollars an hour. Keeping me here until late afternoon would be expensive. I could go and come back."

He didn't like that and said so, explaining why, the idea being that with me there in the house it would be easier for him to get his nerve up and it might only take an hour or so. He got up and walked to the door and opened it, then turned and demanded, "Do you know how much I make an hour? The time I spend on my work? Over a thousand dollars. More than a thousand an hour! I'll go get some clothes on."

He went, shutting the door.

My wristwatch said 1:17. My stomach agreed. I sat maybe ten minutes, then went to the phone on the desk, dialed, got Wolfe, and told him how it was. He told me to go out and get some lunch, naturally, and I said I would, but after hanging up I went back to my chair. If I went out, sure as hell Koven would get his nerve up in my absence, and by the time I got back he would have lost it again and have to start over. I explained the situation to my stomach, and it made a polite sound of protest, but I was the boss. I was glancing at my watch again and seeing 1:42 when the door opened and Mrs. Koven was with me.

When I stood, her serious gray eyes beneath the wide smooth brow were level with the knot in my four-in-hand. She said her husband had told her that I was staying for a conference at a later hour. I confirmed it. She said I ought to have something to eat. I agreed that it was not a bad notion.

"Won't you," she invited, "come down and have a sandwich with us? We don't do any cooking, we even have our breakfast sent in, but there are some sandwiches."

"I don't want to be rude," I told her, "but are they in the room with the monkey?"

"Oh, no." She stayed serious. "Wouldn't that be awful? Downstairs in the workroom." She touched my arm. "Come on, do."

I went downstairs with her.

II

In a large room at the rear on the ground floor the other four suspects were seated around a plain wooden table, dealing with the sandwiches. The room was a mess—drawing tables under fluorescent lights, open shelves crammed with papers, cans of all sizes, and miscellaneous objects, chairs scattered around, other shelves with books and portfolios, and tables with more stacks of papers. Messy as it was to the eye, it was even messier to the ear, for two radios were going full blast.

Marcelle Koven and I joined them at the lunch table, and I perked up at once. There was a basket of French bread and pumpernickel, paper platters piled with slices of ham, smoked turkey, sturgeon, and hot corned beef, a big slab of butter, mustard and other accessories, bottles of milk, a pot of steaming coffee, and a one-pound jar of fresh caviar. Seeing Pete Jordan spooning caviar onto a piece of bread crust, I got what he meant about liking to eat.

"Help yourself!" Pat Lowell yelled into my ear.

I reached for the bread with one hand and the corned beef with the other and yelled back, "Why doesn't someone turn them down or even off?"

She took a sip of coffee from a paper cup and shook her head. "One's By Hildebrand's and one's Pete Jordan's! They like different programs when they're working! They have to go for volume!"

It was a hell of a din, but the corned beef was wonderful and the bread must have been from Rusterman's, nor was there anything wrong with the turkey and sturgeon. Since the radio duel precluded table talk, I used my eyes for diversion and was impressed by Adrian Getz, whom Koven called the Squirt. He would break off a rectangle of bread crust, place a rectangle of sturgeon on it, arrange a mound of caviar on top, and pop it in. When it was down he would take three sips of coffee and then start over. He was doing that when Mrs. Koven and I arrived and he was still doing it when I was full and reaching for another paper napkin.

Eventually, though, he stopped. He pushed back his chair, left it, went over to a sink at the wall, held his fingers under the faucet, and dried them with his handkerchief. Then he trotted over to a radio and turned it off, and to the other one and turned that off. Then he trotted back to us and spoke apologetically.

"That was uncivil, I know."

No one contradicted him.

"It was only," he went on, "that I wanted to ask Mr. Goodwin something before going up for my nap." His eyes settled on me. "Did you know when you opened that window that sudden cold drafts are dangerous for tropical monkeys?"

His tone was more than mild, it was wistful. But something about him—I didn't know what and didn't ask for time out to go into it—got my goat.

"Sure," I said cheerfully. "I was trying it out."

"That was thoughtless," he said, not complaining, just giving his modest opinion, and turned and trotted out of the room.

There was a strained silence. Pat Lowell reached for the pot to pour some coffee.

"Goodwin, God help you," Pete Jordan muttered.

"Why? Does he sting?"

"Don't ask me why, but watch your step. I think he's a kobold." He tossed his paper napkin onto the table. "Want to see an artist create? Come and look." He marched to one of the radios and turned it on, then to a drawing table and sat.

"I'll clean up," Pat Lowell offered.

Byram Hildebrand, who had not squeaked once that I heard, went and turned on the other radio before he took his place at another drawing table.

Mrs. Koven left us. I helped Pat Lowell clear up the lunch table, but all that did was pass time, since both radios were going and I rely mostly on talk to develop an acquaintance in the early stages. Then she left, and I strolled over to watch the artists. So far nothing had occurred to change my opinion of Dazzle Dan, but I had to admire the way they did him. Working from rough sketches which all looked alike to me, they turned out the finished product in three colors so fast I could barely keep up, walking back and forth. The only interruptions for a long stretch were when Hildebrand jumped up to go and turned his radio louder, and a minute later Pete Jordan did likewise. I sat down and concentrated on the experiment of listening to two stations at once, but after a while my brain started to curdle and I got out of there.

A door toward the front of the lower hall was standing open, and I looked in and stepped inside when I saw Pat Lowell at a desk, working with papers. She looked up to nod and went on working.

"Listen a minute," I said. "We're here on a desert island, and for months you have been holding me at arm's length, and I'm desperate. It is not mere propinquity. In rags and tatters as you are, without make-up, I have come to look upon you—"

"I'm busy," she said emphatically. "Go play with a coconut."

"You'll regret this," I said savagely and went to the hall and looked through the glass of the front door at the outside world. The view was nothing to brag about, and the radios were still at my eardrums, so I went upstairs. Looking through the archway into the room at the left, and seeing no one but the monkey in its cage, I crossed to the other room and entered. It was full of furniture, but there was no sign of life. As I went up the second flight of stairs it seemed that the sound of the radios was getting louder instead of softer, and at the top I knew why. A radio was going the other side of one of the closed doors. I went and opened the door to the room where I had talked with Koven; not there. I tried another door and was faced by shelves stacked with linen. I knocked on another, got no response, opened it, and stepped in. It was a large bedroom, very fancy, with an oversized bed. The furniture and fittings showed that it was co-ed. A radio on a stand was giving with a soap opera, and stretched out on a couch was Mrs. Koven, sound asleep. She looked softer and not so serious, with her lips parted a little and relaxed fingers curled on the cushion, in spite of the yapping radio on the bedside table. I damn well intended to find Koven, and took a couple of steps with a vague notion of looking under the bed for him, when a glance through an open door at the right into the next room discovered him. He was standing at a window with his back to me. Thinking it might seem a little familiar on short acquaintance for me to enter from the bedroom where his wife was snoozing, I backed out to the hall, pulling the door to, moved to the next door, and knocked. Getting no reaction, I turned the knob and entered.

The radio had drowned out my noise. He remained at the window. I banged the door shut. He jerked around. He said something, but I didn't get it on account of the radio. I went and closed the door to the bedroom, and that helped some.

"Well?" he demanded, as if he couldn't imagine who I was or what I wanted.

He had shaved and combed and had on a well-made brown homespun suit, with a tan shirt and red tie.

"It's going on four o'clock," I said, "and I'll be going soon and taking my gun with me."

He took his hands from his pockets and dropped into a chair. Evidently this was the Koven personal living room, from the way it was furnished, and it looked fairly livable.

He spoke. "I was standing at the window thinking."

"Yeah. Any luck?"

He sighed and stretched his legs out. "Fame and fortune," he said, "are not all a man needs for happiness."

I sat down. Obviously the only alternatives were to wrangle him into it or call it off.

"What else would you suggest?" I asked brightly.

He undertook to tell me. He went on and on, but I won't report it verbatim because I doubt if it contained any helpful hints for you—I know it didn't for me. I grunted from time to time to be polite. I listened to him for a while and then got a little relief by listening to the soap opera on the radio, which was muffled some by the closed door but by no means inaudible. Eventually, of course, he got around to his wife, first briefing me by explaining that she was his third and they had been married only two years. To my surprise he didn't tear her apart. He said she was wonderful. His point was that even when you added to fame and fortune the companionship of a beloved and loving wife who was fourteen years younger than you, that still wasn't all you needed for happiness.

There was one interruption—a knock on the door and the appearance of Byram Hildebrand. He had come to show the revise on the third frame of Number 728. They discussed art some, and Koven okayed the revise, and Hildebrand departed. I hoped that the intermission had sidetracked Koven, but no; he took up again where he had left off.

I can take a lot when I'm working on a case, even a kindergarten problem like that one, but finally, after the twentieth sidewise glance at my wrist, I called a halt.

"Look," I said, "this has given me a new slant on life entirely, and don't think I don't appreciate it, but it's a quarter past four and it's getting dark. I would call it late afternoon. What do you say we go ahead with our act?"

He closed his trap and frowned at me. He started chewing his lip. After some of that he suddenly arose, went to a cabinet, and got out a bottle.

"Will you join me?" He produced two glasses. "I'm not supposed to drink until five o'clock, but I'll make this an exception." He came to me. "Bourbon all right? Say when."

I would have liked to plug him. He had known from the beginning that he would have to drink himself up to it but had sucked me in with a noon appointment. Anything I felt like saying would have been justified, but I held in. I accepted mine and raised it with him, to encourage him, and took a swallow. He took a dainty sip, raised his eyes to the ceiling, and then emptied the glass at a gulp. He picked up the bottle and poured a refill.

"Why don't we go in there with the refreshment," I suggested, "and go over it a little?"

"Don't rush me," he said gloomily. He took a deep breath, swelling his chest, and suddenly grinned at me, showing the teeth. He lifted the glass and drained it, reached for the bottle and tilted it to pour, and changed his mind.

"Come on," he said, heading for the door. I stepped around him to open the door, since both his hands were occupied, closed it behind us, and followed him down the hall. At the farther end we entered the room where we were to stage it. He went to the desk and sat, poured himself a drink, and put the bottle down. I went to the desk too, but not to sit. I had taken the precaution of removing the cartridges from my gun, but even so a glance at it wouldn't hurt any. I pulled the drawer open and was relieved to see that it was still there. I shut the drawer.

"I'll go get them," I offered.

"I said don't rush me," Koven protested, but no longer gloomy.

Thinking that two more drinks would surely do it, I moved to a chair. But I didn't sit. Something wasn't right, and it came to me what it was: I had placed the gun with the muzzle pointing to the right, and it wasn't that way now. I returned to the desk, took the gun out, and gave it a look.

It was a Marley .32 all right, but not mine.

III

I put my eye on Koven. The gun was in my left hand, and my right hand was a fist. If I had hit him that first second, which I nearly did, mad as I was, I would have cracked some knuckles.

"What's the matter?" he demanded.

My eyes were on him and through him. I kept them there for five pulse beats. It wasn't possible, I decided, that he was that good. Nobody could be.

I backed up a pace. "We've found your gun."

He gawked at me. "What?"

I broke it, saw that the cylinder was empty, and held it out. "Take a look."

He took it. "It looks the same—no, it doesn't."

"Certainly it doesn't. Mine was clean and bright. Is it yours?"

"I don't know. It looks like it. But how in the name of God—"

I reached and took it from him. "How do you think?" I was so damn mad I nearly stuttered. "Someone with hands took mine out and put yours in. It could have been you. Was it?"

"No. Me?" Suddenly he got indignant. "How the hell could it have been me when I didn't know where mine was?"

"You said you didn't. I ought to stretch you out and tamp you down. Keeping me here the whole goddam day, and now this! If you ever talk straight and to the point, now is the time. Did you touch my gun?"

"No. But you're—"

"Do you know who did?"

"No. But you're—"

"Shut up!" I went around the desk to the phone, lifted it, and dialed. At that hour Wolfe would be up in the plant rooms for his afternoon shift with the orchids, where he was not to be disturbed except in emergency, but this was one. When Fritz answered I asked him to buzz the extension, and in a moment I had Wolfe.

"Yes, Archie?" Naturally he was peevish.

"Sorry to bother you, but. I'm at Koven's. I put my gun in his desk, and we were all set for his stunt, but he kept putting it off until now. His will power sticks and has to be primed with alcohol. I roamed around. We just came in here where his desk is, and I opened the drawer for a look. Someone has taken my gun and substituted his—his that was stolen, you know? It's back where it belongs, but mine is gone."

"You shouldn't have left it there."

"Okay, you can have that, and you sure will, but I need instructions for now. Three choices: I can call a cop, or I can bring the whole bunch down there to you, don't think I can't the way I feel, or I can handle it myself. Which?"

"Confound it, not the police. They would enjoy it too much. And why bring them here? The gun's there, not here."

"Then that leaves me. I go ahead?"

"Certainly—with due discretion. It's a prank." He chuckled. "I would like to see your face. Try to get home for dinner." He hung up.

"My God, don't call a cop!" Koven protested.

"I don't intend to," I said grimly. I slipped his gun into my armpit holster. "Not if I can help it. It depends partly on you. You stay put, right here. I'm going down and get them. Your wife's asleep in the bedroom. If I find when I get back that you've gone and started chatting with her I'll either slap you down with your own gun or phone the police, I don't know which, maybe both. Stay put."

"This is my house, Goodwin, and—"

"Goddam it, don't you know a raving maniac when you see one?" I tapped my chest with a forefinger. "Me. When I'm as sore as I am now the safest thing would be for *you* to call a cop. I want my gun."

As I made for the door he was reaching for the bottle. By the time I got down to the ground floor I had myself well enough in hand to speak to them without betraying any special urgency, telling them that Koven was ready for them upstairs, for the conference. I found Pat Lowell still at the desk in the room in front and Hildebrand and Jordan still at their drawing tables in the workroom. I even replied appropriately when Pat Lowell asked how I had made out with the coconut. As Hildebrand and Jordan left their tables and turned off their radios

I had a keener eye on them than before; someone here had swiped my gun. As we ascended the first flight of stairs, with me in the rear, I asked their backs where I would find Adrian Getz.

Pat Lowell answered. "He may be in his room on the top floor." They halted at the landing, the edge of the big square hall, and I joined them. We could hear the radio going upstairs. She indicated the room to the left. "He takes his afternoon nap in there with Rookaloo, but not this late usually."

I thought I might as well glance in, and moved to the archway. A draft of cold air hit me, and I went on in. A window was wide open! I marched over and closed it, then went to take a look at the monkey. It was huddled on the floor in a corner of the cage, making angry little noises, with something clutched in its fingers against its chest. The light was dim, but I have good eyes, and not only was the something unmistakably a gun, but it was my Marley on a bet. Needing light, and looking for a wall switch, I was passing the large couch which faced the fireplace when suddenly I stopped and froze. Adrian Getz, the Squirt, was lying on the couch but he wasn't taking a nap.

I bent over him for a close-up and saw a hole in his skull northeast of his right ear, and some red juice. I stuck a hand inside the V of his vest and flattened it against him and held my breath for eight seconds. He was through taking naps.

I straightened up and called, "Come in here, all three of you, and switch on a light as you come!"

They appeared through the archway, and one of them put a hand to the wall. Lights shone. The back of the couch hid Getz from their view as they approached.

"It's cold in here," Pat Lowell was saying. "Did you open another—"

Seeing Getz stopped her, and the others too. They goggled.

"Don't touch him," I warned them. "He's dead, so you can't help him any. Don't touch anything. You three stay here together, right here in this room, while I—"

"Christ Almighty," Pete Jordan blurted. Hildebrand squeaked something. Pat Lowell put out a hand, found the couch back, and gripped it. She asked something, but I wasn't listening. I was at the cage, with my back to them, peering at the monkey. It was my Marley the monkey was clutching. I had to curl my fingers until the nails sank in to keep from opening the cage door and grabbing that gun.

I whirled. "Stick here together. Understand?" I was on my way. "I'm going up and phone."

Ignoring their noises, I left them. I mounted the stairs in no hurry, because if I had been a raving maniac before, I was now stiff with fury and I needed a few seconds to get under control. In the room upstairs Harry Koven was still seated at the desk, staring at the open drawer. He looked up and fired a question at me but got no answer. I went to the phone, lifted it, and dialed a number. When I got Wolfe he started to sputter at being disturbed again.

"I'm sorry," I told him, "but I wish to report that I have found my gun. It's in the cage with the monkey, who is—"

"What monkey?"

"Its name is Rookaloo, but please don't interrupt. It is holding my gun to its breast, I suspect because it is cold and the gun is warm, having recently been fired. Lying there on a couch is the body of a man, Adrian Getz, with a bullet hole in the head. It is no longer a question whether I call a cop, I merely wanted to report the situation to you before I do so. A thousand to one Getz was shot and killed with my gun. I will not be—hold it—"

I dropped the phone and jumped. Koven had made a dive for the door. I caught him before he reached it, got an arm and his chin, and heaved. There was a lot of feeling in it, and big as he was he sailed to a wall, bounced off, and went to the floor.

"I would love to do it again," I said, meaning it, and returned to the phone and told Wolfe, "Excuse me, Koven tried to interrupt. I was only going to say I will not be home to dinner."

"The man is dead."

"Yes, sir."

"Have you anything satisfactory for the police?"

"Sure. My apologies for bringing my gun here to oblige a murderer. That's all."

"We haven't answered today's mail."

"I know. It's a damn shame. I'll get away as soon as I can."

"Very well."

The connection went. I held the button down a moment, with an eye on Koven, who was upright again but not asking for an encore, then released it and dialed RE 7-5260.

IV

I haven't kept anything like an accurate score, but I would say that over the years I haven't told the cops more than a couple of dozen barefaced lies, maybe not that many. They are seldom practical. On the other hand, I can't recall any murder case Wolfe and I were in on and I've had my story gone into at length where I have simply opened the bag and given them all I had, with no dodging and no withholding, except one, and this is it. On the murder of Adrian Getz I didn't have a single thing on my mind that I wasn't willing and eager to shovel out, so I let them have it.

It worked fine. They called me a liar.

Not right away, of course. At first even Inspector Cramer appreciated my cooperation, knowing as he did that there wasn't a man in his army who could shade me at seeing and hearing, remembering, and reporting. It was generously conceded that upon finding the body I had performed properly and promptly, herding the trio into the room and keeping the Kovens from holding a family council until the law arrived. From there on, of course, everyone had been under surveillance, including me.

At six-thirty, when the scientists were still monopolizing the room where Getz had got it, and city employees were wandering all over the place, and the various inmates were still in various rooms conversing privately with Homicide men, and I had typed and signed my own frank and full statement, I was confidently expecting that I would soon be out on the sidewalk unattended, flagging a taxi. I was in the front room on the ground floor, seated at Pat Lowell's desk, having used her typewriter, and Sergeant Purley Stebbins was sitting across from me, looking over my statement.

He lifted his head and regarded me, perfectly friendly. A perfectly friendly look from Stebbins would, from almost anyone else, cause you to get your guard up and be ready to either duck or counter, but Purley wasn't responsible for the design of his big bony face and his pig-bristle eyebrows.

"I guess you got it all in," he admitted. "As you told it."

"I suggest," I said modestly, "that when this case is put away you send that to the school to be used as a model report."

"Yeah." He stood up. "You're a good typist." He turned to go.

I arose too, saying casually, "I can run along now?"

The door opened, and Inspector Cramer entered. I didn't like his expression as he darted a glance at me. Knowing him well in all his moods, I didn't like the way his broad shoulders were hunched, or his clamped jaw, or the glint in his eye.

"Here's Goodwin's statement," Purley said. "Okay."

"As he told it?"

"Yes."

"Send him downtown and hold him."

It caught me completely off balance. "Hold *me?*" I demanded, squeaking almost like Hildebrand.

"Yes, sir." Nothing could catch Purley off balance. "On your order?"

"No, charge him. Sullivan Act. He has no license for the gun we found on him."

"Ha, ha," I said. "Ha, ha, and ha, ha. There, you got your laugh. A very fine gag. Ha."

"You're going down, Goodwin. I'll be down to see you later."

As I said, I knew him well. He meant it. I had his eyes. "This," I said, "is way out of my reach. I've told you where and how and why I got that gun." I pointed to the paper in Purley's hand. "Read it. It's all down, punctuated."

"You had the gun in your holster and you have no license for it."

"Nuts. But I get it. You've been hoping for years to hang something on Nero Wolfe, and to you I'm just a part of him, and you think here's your chance. Of course it won't stick. Wouldn't you rather have something that will? Like resisting arrest and assaulting an officer? Glad to oblige. Watch it—"

Tipping forward, I started a left hook for his jaw, fast and vicious, then jerked it down and went back on my heels. It didn't create a panic, but I had the satisfaction of seeing Cramer take a quick step back and Stebbins one forward. They bumped.

"There," I said. "With both of you to swear to it, that ought to be good for at least two years. I'll throw the typewriter at you if you'll promise to catch it."

"Cut the clowning," Purley growled.

"You lied about that gun," Cramer snapped. "If you don't want to get taken down to think it over, think now. Tell me what you came here for and what happened."

"I've told you."

"A string of lies."

"No, sir."

"You can have 'em back. I'm not trying to hang something on Wolfe, or you either. I want to know why you came here and what happened."

"Oh, for God's sake." I moved my eyes. "Okay, Purley, where's my escort?"

Cramer strode four paces to the door, opened it, and called, "Bring Mr. Koven in here!"

Harry Koven entered with a dick at his elbow. He looked as if he was even farther away from happiness than before.

"We'll sit down," Cramer said.

He left me behind the desk. Purley and the dick took chairs in the background. Cramer stationed himself across the desk from me, where Purley had been, with Koven on a chair at his left. He opened up.

"I told you, Mr. Koven, that I would ask you to repeat your story in Goodwin's presence, and you said you would."

Koven nodded. "That's right." He was hoarse.

"We won't need all the details. Just answer me briefly. When you called on Nero Wolfe last Saturday evening, what did you ask him to do?"

"I told him I was going to have Dazzle Dan start a detective agency in a new series." The hoarseness bothered Koven, and he cleared his throat explosively. "I told him I needed technical assistance, and possibly a tie-up, if we could arrange—"

There was a pad of ruled paper on the desk. I reached for it, and a pencil, and started doing shorthand. Cramer leaned over, stretched an arm, grabbed a corner of the pad, and jerked it away. I could feel the blood coming to my head, which was silly of it with an inspector, a sergeant, and a private all in the room.

"We need your full attention," Cramer growled. He went to Koven. "Did you say anything to Wolfe about your gun being taken from your desk?"

"Certainly not. It hadn't been taken. I did mention that I had a gun in my desk for which I had no license, but that I never carried it, and I asked if that was risky. I told them what make it was, a Marley thirty-two. I asked how much trouble it would be to get a license, and if—"

"We'll keep it brief. Just cover the points. What arrangement did you make with Wolfe?"

"He agreed to send Goodwin to my place on Monday for a conference with my staff and me."

"About what?"

"About the technical problems of having Dazzle Dan do detective work, and possibly a tie-up."

"And Goodwin came?"

"Yes, today around noon." Koven's hoarseness kept interfering with him, and he kept clearing his throat. My eyes were at his face, but he hadn't met them. Of course he was talking to Cramer and had to be polite. He went on, "The conference was for twelve-thirty, but I had a little talk with Goodwin and asked him to wait. I have to be careful what I do with Dan and I wanted to think it over some more. Anyway I'm like that, I put things off. It was after four o'clock when he—"

"Was your talk with Goodwin about your gun being gone?"

"Certainly not. We might have mentioned the gun, about my not having a license for it, I don't remember—no, wait a minute, we must have, because I pulled the drawer open and we glanced in at it. Except for that, we only talked—"

"Did you or Goodwin take your gun out of the drawer?"

"No. Absolutely not."

"Did he put his gun in the drawer?"

"Absolutely not."

I slid in, "When I took my gun from my holster to show it to you, did you—"

"Nothing doing," Cramer snapped at me. "You're listening. Just the high spots for now." He returned to Koven. "Did you have another talk with Goodwin later?"

Koven nodded. "Yes, around half-past three he came up to my room —the living room. We talked until after four, there and in my office, and then—"

"In your office did Goodwin open the drawer of the desk and take the gun out and say it had been changed?"

"Certainly not!"

"What did he do?"

"Nothing, only we talked, and then he left to go down and get the others to come up for the conference. After a while he came back alone, and without saying anything he came to the desk and took my gun from the drawer and put it under his coat. Then he went to the phone and called Nero Wolfe. When I heard him tell Wolfe that Adrian Getz had been shot, that he was on a couch downstairs dead, I got up to go down there, and Goodwin jumped me from behind and knocked me out. When I came to he was still talking to Wolfe, I don't know what he was telling him, and then he called the police. He wouldn't let me—"

"Hold it," Cramer said curtly. "That covers that. One more point. Do you know of any motive for Goodwin's wanting to murder Adrian Getz?"

"No, I don't. I told—"

"Then if Getz was shot with Goodwin's gun how would you account for it? You're not obliged to account for it, but if you don't mind just repeat what you told me."

"Well—" Koven hesitated. He cleared his throat for the twentieth time. "I told you about the monkey. Goodwin opened a window, and that's enough to kill that kind of a monkey, and Getz was very fond of it. He didn't show how upset he was but Getz was very quiet and didn't show things much. I understand Goodwin likes to kid people. Of course I don't know what happened, but if Goodwin went in there later when Getz was there, and started to open a window, you can't tell. When Getz once got aroused he was apt to do anything. He couldn't have hurt Goodwin any, but Goodwin might have got out his gun just for a gag, and Getz tried to take it away, and it went off accidentally. That wouldn't be murder, would it?"

"No," Cramer said, "that would only be a regrettable accident. That's all for now, Mr. Koven. Take him out, Sol, and bring Hildebrand."

As Koven arose and the dick came forward I reached for the phone on Pat Lowell's desk. My hand got there, but so did Cramer's, hard on top of mine.

"The lines here are busy," he stated. "There'll be a phone you can use downtown. Do you want to hear Hildebrand before you comment?"

"I'm crazy to hear Hildebrand," I assured him. "No doubt he'll explain that I tossed the gun in the monkey's cage to frame the monkey. Let's just wait for Hildebrand."

It wasn't much of a wait; the Homicide boys are snappy. Byram Hildebrand, ushered in by Sol, stood and gave me a long straight look before he took the chair Koven had vacated. He still had good presence, with his fine mat of nearly white hair, but his extremities were nervous. When he sat he couldn't find comfortable spots for either his hands or his feet.

"This will only take a minute," Cramer told him. "I just want to check on Sunday morning. Yesterday. You were here working?"

Hildebrand nodded, and the squeak came. "I was putting on some touches. I often work Sundays."

"You were in there in the workroom?"

"Yes. Mr. Getz was there, making some suggestions. I was doubtful about one of his suggestions and went upstairs to consult Mr. Koven, but Mrs. Koven was there in the hall and—"

"You mean the big hall one flight up?"

"Yes. She said Mr. Koven wasn't up yet and Miss Lowell was in his office waiting to see him. Miss Lowell has extremely good judgment, and I went up to consult her. She disapproved of Mr. Getz's suggestion, and we discussed various matters, and mention was made of the gun Mr. Koven kept in his desk drawer. I pulled the drawer open just to look at it, with no special purpose, merely to look at it, and closed the drawer again. Shortly afterward I returned downstairs."

"Was the gun there in the drawer?"

"Yes."

"Did you take it out?"

"No. Neither did Miss Lowell. We didn't touch it."

"But you recognized it as the same gun?"

"I can't say that I did, no. I had never examined the gun, never had it in my hand. I can only say that it looked the same as before. It was my opinion that our concern about the gun being kept there was quite childish, but I see now that I was wrong. After what happened today—"

"Yeah." Cramer cut him off. "Concern about a loaded gun is never childish. That's all I'm after now. Sunday morning, in Miss Lowell's presence, you opened the drawer of Koven's desk and saw the gun which you took to be the gun you had seen there before. Is that correct?"

"That's correct," Hildebrand squeaked.

"Okay, that's all." Cramer nodded at Sol. "Take him back to Rowcliff."

I treated myself to a good deep breath. Purley was squinting at me, not gloating, just concentrating. Cramer turned his head to see that the door was closed after the dick and the artist and then turned back to me.

"Your turn," he growled.

I shook my head. "Lost my voice," I whispered, hissing.

"You're not funny, Goodwin. You're never as funny as you think you are. This time you're not funny at all. You can have five minutes to go over it and realize how complicated it is. When you phoned Wolfe *before* you phoned us, you couldn't possibly have arranged all the details. I've got you. I'll be leaving here before long to join you downtown, and on my way I'll stop in at Wolfe's place for a talk. He won't clam up on this one. At the very least I've got you good on the Sullivan Act. Want five minutes?"

"No, sir." I was calm but emphatic. "I want five days and I would advise you to take a full week. Complicated doesn't begin to describe it. Before I leave for downtown, if you're actually going to crawl out on that one, I wish to remind you of something, and don't forget it. When I voluntarily took Koven's gun from my holster and turned it over—it wasn't 'found on me,' as you put it—I also turned over six nice clean cartridges which I had in my vest pocket, having previously removed them from my gun. I hope none of your heroes gets careless and mixes them up with the cartridges found in my gun, if any, when you retrieved it from the monkey. That would be a mistake. The point is, if I removed the cartridges from my gun in order to insert one or more from Koven's gun, when and why did I do it? There's a day's work for you right there. And if I did do it, then Koven's friendly effort to fix me up for justifiable manslaughter is wasted, much as I appreciate it, because I must have been premeditating something, and you know what. Why fiddle around with the Sullivan Act? Make it the big one, and I can't get bail. Now I button up."

I set my jaw.

Cramer eyed me. "Even a suspended sentence," he said, "you lose your license."

I grinned at him.

"You goddam mule," Purley rumbled.

I included him in the grin.

"Send him down," Cramer rasped and got up and left.

V

Even when a man is caught smack in the middle of a felony, as I had been, there is a certain amount of red tape to getting him behind bars, and in my case not only red tape but also other activities postponed my attainment of privacy. First I had a long conversation with an assistant district attorney, who was the suave and subtle type and even ate sandwiches with me. When it was over, a little after nine o'clock, both of us were only slightly more confused than when we started. He left me in a room with a specimen in uniform with slick brown hair and a wart on his cheek. I told him how to get rid of the wart, recommending Doc Vollmer.

I was expecting the promised visit by Inspector Cramer any minute. Naturally I was nursing an assorted collection of resentments, but the one on top was at not being there to see and hear the talk between Cramer and Wolfe. Any chat those two had was always worth listening to, and that one must have been outstanding, with Wolfe learning not only that his client was lying five ways from Sunday, which was bad enough, but also that I had been tossed in the can and the day's mail would have to go unanswered.

When the door finally opened and a visitor entered it wasn't Inspector Cramer. It was Lieutenant Rowcliff, whose murder I will not have to premeditate when I get around to it because I have already done the premeditating. There are not many murderers so vicious and inhuman that I would enjoy seeing them caught by Rowcliff. He jerked a chair around to sit facing me and said with oily satisfaction, "At last we've got you, by God."

That set the tone of the interview.

I would enjoy recording in full that two-hour session with Rowcliff, but it would sound like bragging, and therefore I don't suppose you would enjoy it too. His biggest handicap is that when he gets irritated to a certain point he can't help stuttering, and I'm onto him enough to tell when he's just about there, and then I start stuttering before he does. Even with a close watch and careful timing it takes luck to do it right, and that evening I was lucky. He came closer than ever before to plugging me, but didn't, because he wants to be a captain so bad he can taste it and he's not absolutely sure that Wolfe hasn't got a solid in with the Commissioner or the Mayor or possibly Grover Whalen himself.

Cramer never showed up, and that added another resentment to my healthy pile. I knew he had been to see Wolfe, because when they had finally let me make my phone call, around eight o'clock, and I had got Wolfe and started to tell him about it, he had interrupted me in a voice as cold as an Eskimo's nose.

"I know where you are and how you got there. Mr. Cramer is here. I have phoned Mr. Parker, but it's too late to do anything tonight. Have you had anything to eat?"

"No, sir. I'm afraid of poison and I'm on a hunger strike."

"You should eat something. Mr. Cramer is worse than a jackass, he's demented. I intend to persuade him, if possible, of the desirability of releasing you at once."

He hung up.

When, shortly after eleven, Rowcliff called it off and I was shown to my room, there had been no sign of Cramer. The room was in no way remarkable, merely what was to be expected in a structure of that type, but it was fairly clean, strongly scented with disinfectant, and was in a favorable location since the nearest corridor light was six paces away and therefore did not glare through the bars of my door. Also it was a single, which I appreciated. Alone at last, away from telephones and other interruptions, I undressed and arranged my gray pinstripe on the chair, draped my shirt over the end of the blankets, got in, stretched, and settled down for a complete survey of the complications. But my brain and nerves had other plans, and in twenty seconds I was asleep.

In the morning there was a certain amount of activity, with the check-off and a trip to the lavatory and breakfast, but after that I had more privacy than I really cared for. My watch had slowed down. I tested the second hand by counting, with no decisive result. By noon I would almost have welcomed a visit from Rowcliff and was beginning to suspect that someone had lost a paper and there was no record of me anywhere and everyone was too busy to stop and think. Lunch, which I will not describe, broke the monotony some, but then, back in my room, I was alone with my wristwatch. For the tenth time I decided to spread all the pieces out, sort them, and have a look at the picture as it had been drawn to date, and for the tenth time it got so damn jumbled that I couldn't make first base, let alone on around.

At 1:09 my door swung open and the floorwalker, a chunky short guy with only half an ear on the right side, told me to come along. I went willingly, on out of the block to an elevator, and along a ground-floor corridor to an office. There I was pleased to see the tall lanky figure and long pale face of Henry George Parker, the only lawyer Wolfe would admit to the bar if he had the say. He came to shake my hand and said he'd have me out of there in a minute now.

"No rush," I said stiffly. "Don't let it interfere with anything important."

He laughed, haw-haw, and took me inside the gate. All the formalities but one which required my presence had already been attended to, and he made good on his minute. On the way up in the taxi he explained why I had been left to rot until past noon. Getting bail on the Sullivan Act charge had been simple, but I had also been tagged with a material witness warrant, and the DA had asked the judge to put it at fifty grand! He had been stubborn about it, and the best Parker could do was talk it down to twenty, and he had had to report back to Wolfe before closing the deal. I was not to leave the jurisdiction. As the taxi crossed Thirty-fourth Street I looked west across the river. I had never cared much for New Jersey, but now the idea of driving through the tunnel and on among the billboards seemed attractive.

I preceded Parker up the stoop at the old brownstone on West Thirty-fifth, used my key but found that the chain bolt was on, which was normal but not invariable when I was out of the house, and had to push the button. Fritz Brenner, chef and house manager, let us in and stood while we disposed of our coats and hats.

"Are you all right, Archie?" he inquired.

"No," I said frankly. "Don't you smell me?"

As we went down the hall Wolfe appeared, coming from the door to the dining room. He stopped and regarded me. I returned his gaze with my chin up.

"I'll go up and rinse off," I said, "while you're finishing lunch."

"I've finished," he said grimly. "Have you eaten?"

"Enough to hold me."

"Then we'll get started."

He marched into the office, across the hall from the dining room, went to his oversized chair behind his desk, sat, and got himself adjusted for comfort. Parker took the red leather chair. As I crossed to my desk I started talking, to get the jump on him.

"It will help," I said, not aggressively but pointedly, "if we first get it settled about my leaving that room with my gun there in the drawer. I do not—"

"Shut up!" Wolfe snapped.

"In that case," I demanded, "why didn't you leave me in the coop? I'll go back and—"

"Sit down!"

I sat.

"I deny," he said, "that you were in the slightest degree imprudent. Even if you were, this has transcended such petty considerations." He picked up a sheet of paper from his desk. "This is a letter which came yesterday from a Mrs. E. R. Baumgarten. She wants me to investigate the activities of a nephew who is employed by the business she owns. I wish to reply. Your notebook."

He was using what I call his conclusive tone, leaving no room for questions, let alone argument. I got my notebook and pen.

"Dear Mrs. Baumgarten." He went at it as if he had already composed it in his mind. "Thank you very much for your letter of the thirteenth, requesting me to undertake an investigation for you. Paragraph. I am sorry that I cannot be of service to you. I am compelled to decline because I have been informed by an official of the New York Police Department that my license to operate a private detective agency is about to be taken away from me. Sincerely yours."

Parker ejaculated something and got ignored. I stayed deadpan, but among my emotions was renewed regret that I had missed Wolfe's and Cramer's talk.

Wolfe was saying, "Type it at once and send Fritz to mail it. If any requests for appointments come by telephone refuse them, giving the reason and keeping a record."

"The reason given in the letter?"

"Yes."

I swiveled the typewriter to me, got paper and carbon in, and hit the keys. I had to concentrate. This was Cramer's farthest north. Parker was asking questions, and Wolfe was grunting at him. I finished the letter and envelope, had Wolfe sign it, went to the kitchen and told Fritz to take it to Eighth Avenue immediately, and returned to the office.

"Now," Wolfe said, "I want all of it. Go ahead."

Ordinarily when I start giving Wolfe a full report of an event, no matter how extended and involved, I just glide in and keep going with no effort at all, thanks to my long and hard training. That time, having just got a severe jolt, I wasn't so hot at the beginning, since I was supposed to include every word and movement, but by the time I had got to where I opened the window it was coming smooth and easy. As usual, Wolfe soaked it all in without making any interruptions.

It took all of an hour and a half, and then came questions, but not many. I rate a report by the number of questions he has when I'm through, and by that test this was up toward the top. Wolfe leaned back and closed his eyes.

Parker spoke. "It could have been any of them, but it must have been Koven. Or why his string of lies, knowing that you and Goodwin would both contradict him?" The lawyer haw-hawed. "That is, if they're lies—considering your settled policy of telling your counselor only what you think he should know."

"Pfui." Wolfe's eyes came open. "This is extraordinarily intricate, Archie. Have you examined it any?"

"I've started. When I pick at it, it gets worse instead of better."

"Yes. I'm afraid you'll have to type it out. By eleven tomorrow morning?"

"I guess so, but I need a bath first. Anyway, what for? What can we do with it without a license? I suppose it's suspended?"

He ignored it. "What the devil is that smell?" he demanded.

"Disinfectant. It's for the bloodhounds in case you escape." I arose. "I'll go scrub."

"No." He glanced at the wall clock, which said 3:45—fifteen minutes to go until he was due to join Theodore and the orchids up on the roof. "An errand first. I believe it's the *Gazette* that carries the Dazzle Dan comic strip?"

"Yes, sir."

"Daily and Sunday?"

"Yes, sir."

"I want all of them for the past three years. Can you get them?"

"I can try."

"Do so."

"Now?"

"Yes. Wait a minute—confound it, don't be a cyclone! You should hear my instructions for Mr. Parker, but first one for you. Mail Mr. Koven a bill for recovery of his gun, five hundred dollars. It should go today."

"Any extras, under the circumstances?"

"No. Five hundred flat." Wolfe turned to the lawyer. "Mr. Parker, how long will it take to enter a suit for damages and serve a summons on the defendant?"

"That depends." Parker sounded like a lawyer. "If it's rushed all possible and there are no unforeseen obstacles and the defendant is accessible for service, it could be merely a matter of hours."

"By noon tomorrow?"

"Quite possibly, yes."

"Then proceed, please. Mr. Koven has destroyed, by slander, my means of livelihood. I wish to bring an action demanding payment by him of the sum of one million dollars."

"M-m-m-m," Parker said. He was frowning.

I addressed Wolfe. "I want to apologize," I told him, "for jumping to a conclusion. I was supposing you had lost control for once and buried it too deep in Cramer. Whereas you did it purposely, getting set for this. I'll be damned."

Wolfe grunted.

"In this sort of thing," Parker said, "it is usual, and desirable, to first send a written request for recompense, by your attorney if you prefer. It looks better."

"I don't care how it looks. I want immediate action."

"Then we'll act." That was one of the reasons Wolfe stuck to Parker; he was no dilly-dallier. "But I must ask, isn't the sum a little flamboyant? A full million?"

"It is not flamboyant. At a hundred thousand a year, a modest expectation, my income would be a million in ten years. A detective license once lost in this fashion is not easily regained."

"All right. A million. I'll need all the facts for drafting a complaint."

"You have them. You've just heard Archie recount them. Must you stickle for more?"

"No. I'll manage." Parker got to his feet. "One thing, though, service of process may be a problem. Policemen may still be around, and even if they aren't I doubt if strangers will be getting into that house tomorrow."

"Archie will send Saul Panzer to you. Saul can get in anywhere and do anything." Wolfe wiggled a finger. "I want Mr. Koven to get that. I want to see him in this room. Five times this morning I tried to get him on the phone, without success. If that doesn't get him I'll devise something that will."

"He'll give it to his attorney."

"Then the attorney will come, and if he's not an imbecile I'll give myself thirty minutes to make him send for his client or go and get him. Well?"

Parker turned and left, not loitering. I got at the typewriter to make out a bill for half a grand, which seemed like a waste of paper after what I had just heard.

VI

At midnight that Tuesday the office was a sight. It has often been a mess, one way and another, including the time the strangled Cynthia Brown was lying on the floor with her tongue protruding, but this was something new. Dazzle Dan, both black-and-white and color, was all over the place. On account of our shortage in manpower, with me tied up on my typing job, Fritz and Theodore had been drafted for the chore of tearing out the pages and stacking them chronologically, ready for Wolfe to study. With Wolfe's permission, I had bribed Lon Cohen of the *Gazette* to have three years of Dazzle Dan assembled and delivered to us, by offering him an exclusive. Naturally he demanded specifications.

"Nothing much," I told him on the phone. "Only that Nero Wolfe is out of the detective business because Inspector Cramer is taking away his license."

"Quite a gag," Lon conceded.

"No gag. Straight."

"You mean it?"

"We're offering it for publication. Exclusive, unless Cramer's office spills it, and I don't think they will."

"The Getz murder?"

"Yes. Only a couple of paragraphs, because details are not yet available, even to you. I'm out on bail."

"I know you are. This is pie. We'll raid the files and get it over there as soon as we can."

He hung up without pressing for details. Of course that meant he would send Dazzle Dan COD, with a reporter. When the reporter arrived a couple of hours later, shortly after Wolfe had come down from the plant rooms at six o'clock, it wasn't just a man with a notebook, it was Lon Cohen himself. He came to the office with me, dumped a big heavy carton on the floor by my desk, removed his coat and dropped it on the carton to show that Dazzle Dan was his property until paid for, and demanded, "I want the works. What Wolfe said and what Cramer said. A picture of Wolfe studying Dazzle Dan—"

I pushed him into a chair, courteously, and gave him all we were ready to turn loose of. Naturally that wasn't enough; it never is. I let him fire questions up to a dozen or so, even answering one or two, and then made it clear that that was all for now and I had work to do. He admitted it was a bargain, stuck his notebook in his pocket, and got up and picked up his coat.

"If you're not in a hurry, Mr. Cohen," muttered Wolfe, who had left the interview to me.

Lon dropped the coat and sat down. "I have nineteen years, Mr. Wolfe. Before I retire."

"I won't detain you that long." Wolfe sighed. "I am no longer a detective, but I'm a primate and therefore curious. The function of a newspaperman is to satisfy curiosity. Who killed Mr. Getz?"

Lon's brows went up. "Archie Goodwin? It was his gun."

"Nonsense. I'm quite serious. Also I'm discreet. I am excluded from the customary sources of information by the jackassery of Mr. Cramer. I—"

"May I print that?"

"No. None of this. Nor shall I quote you. This is a private conversation. I would like to know what your colleagues are saying but not printing. Who killed Mr. Getz? Miss Lowell? If so, why?"

Lon pulled his lower lip down and let it up again. "You mean we're just talking."

"Yes."

"This might possibly lead to another talk that could be printed."

"It might. I make no commitment." Wolfe wasn't eager.

"You wouldn't. As for Miss Lowell, she has not been scratched. It is said that Getz learned she was chiseling on royalties from makers of Dazzle Dan products and intended to hang it on her. That could have been big money."

"Any names or dates?"

"None that are repeatable. By me. Yet."

"Any evidence?"

"I haven't seen any."

Wolfe grunted. "Mr. Hildebrand. If so, why?"

"That's shorter and sadder. He has told friends about it. He has been with Koven for eight years and was told last week he could leave at the end of the month, and he blamed it on Getz. He might or might not get another job at his age."

Wolfe nodded. "Mr. Jordan?"

Lon hesitated. "This I don't like, but others are talking, so why not us? They say Jordan has painted some pictures, modern stuff, and twice he has tried to get a gallery to show them, two different galleries, and both times Getz has somehow kiboshed it. This has names and dates, but whether because Getz was born a louse or whether he wanted to keep Jordan—"

"I'll do my own speculating, thank you. Mr. Getz may not have liked the pictures. Mr. Koven?"

Lon turned a hand over. "Well? What better could you ask? Getz had him buffaloed, no doubt about it. Getz ruled the roost, plenty of evidence on that, and nobody knows why, so the only question is what he had on Koven. It must have been good, but what was it? You say this is a private conversation?"

"Yes."

"Then here's something we got started on just this afternoon. It has to be checked before we print it. That house on Seventy-sixth Street is in Getz's name."

"Indeed." Wolfe shut his eyes and opened them again. "And Mrs. Koven?"

Lon turned his other hand over. "Husband and wife are one, aren't they?"

"Yes. Man and wife make one fool."

Lon's chin jerked up. "I want to print that. Why not?"

"It was printed more than three hundred years ago. Ben Jonson wrote it." Wolfe sighed. "Confound it, what can I do with only a few scraps?" He pointed at the carton. "You want that stuff back, I suppose?"

Lon said he did. He also said he would be glad to go on with the private conversation in the interest of justice and the public welfare, but apparently Wolfe had all the scraps he could use at the moment. After ushering Lon to the door I went up to my room to spend an hour attending to purely personal matters, a detail that had been too long postponed. I was out of the shower, selecting a shirt, when a call came from Saul Panzer in response to the message I had left. I gave him all the features of the picture that would help and told him to report to Parker's law office in the morning.

After dinner that evening we were all hard at it in the office. Fritz and Theodore were unfolding *Gazettes,* finding the right page and tearing it out, and carrying off the leavings. I was banging away at my machine, three pages an hour. Wolfe was at his desk, concentrating on a methodical and exhaustive study of three years of Dazzle Dan. It was well after midnight when he pushed back his chair, arose, stretched, rubbed his eyes, and told us, "It's bedtime. This morass of fatuity has given me indigestion. Good night."

Wednesday morning he tried to put one over. His routine was breakfast in his room, with the morning paper, at eight; then shaving and dressing; then, from nine to eleven, his morning shift up in the plant rooms. He never went to the office before eleven, and the detective business was never allowed to mingle with the orchids. But that Wednesday he fudged. While I was in the kitchen with Fritz, enjoying griddle cakes, Darst's sausage, honey, and plenty of coffee, and going through the morning papers, with two readings for the *Gazette's* account of Wolfe's enforced retirement, Wolfe sneaked downstairs into the office and made off with a stack of Dazzle Dan. The way I knew, before breakfast I had gone in there to straighten up a little, and I am trained to observe. Returning after breakfast, and glancing around before starting at my typewriter, I saw that half of a pile of Dan was gone. I don't think I had ever seen him quite so hot under the collar. I admit I fully approved. Not only did I not make an excuse for a trip up to the roof to catch him at it, but I even took the trouble to be out of the office when he came down at eleven o'clock, to give him a chance to get Dan back unseen.

My first job after breakfast had been to carry out some instructions Wolfe had given me the evening before. Manhattan office hours being what they are, I got no answer at the number of Levay Recorders, Inc., until 9:35. Then it took some talking to get a promise of immediate action, and if it hadn't been for the name of Nero Wolfe I wouldn't have made it. But I got both the promise and the action. A little after ten two men arrived with cartons of equipment and tool kits, and in less than an hour they were through and gone, and it was a neat and nifty job. It would have taken an expert search to reveal anything suspicious in the office, and the wire to the kitchen, running around the baseboard and on through, wouldn't be suspicious even if seen.

It was hard going at the typewriter on account of the phone ringing, chiefly reporters wanting to talk to Wolfe, or at least me, and finally I had to ask Fritz in to answer the damn thing and give everybody a brush-off. A call he switched to me was one from the DA's office. They had the nerve to ask me to come down there so they could ask me something. I told them I was busy answering Help Wanted ads and couldn't spare the time. Half an hour later Fritz switched another one to me. It was Sergeant Purley Stebbins. He was good and sore, beefing about Wolfe having no authority to break the news about losing his license, and it wasn't official yet, and where did I think it would get me refusing to cooperate with the DA on a murder when I had discovered the body, and I could have my choice of coming down quick or having a PD car come and get me. I let him use up his breath.

"Listen, brother," I told him, "I hadn't heard that the name of this city has been changed to Moscow. If Mr. Wolfe wants to publish it that he's out of business, hoping that someone will pass the hat or offer him a job as doorman, that's his affair. As for my cooperating, nuts.

You have already got me sewed up on two charges, and on advice of counsel *and* my doctor I am staying home, taking aspirin and gargling with prune juice and gin. If you come here, no matter who, you won't get in without a search warrant. If you come with another warrant for me, say for cruelty to animals because I opened that window, you can either wait on the stoop until I emerge or shoot the door down, whichever you prefer. I am now hanging up."

"If you'll listen a minute, damn it."

"Good-by, you double-breasted nitwit."

I cradled the phone, sat thirty seconds to calm down, and resumed at the typewriter. The next interruption came not from the outside but from Wolfe, a little before noon. He was back at his desk, analyzing Dazzle Dan. Suddenly he pronounced my name, and I swiveled.

"Yes, sir."

"Look at this."

He slid a sheet of the *Gazette* across his desk, and I got up and took it. It was a Sunday half-page, in color, from four months back. In the first frame Dazzle Dan was scooting along a country road on a motorcycle, passing a roadside sign that read:

PEACHES RIGHT FROM THE TREE!
AGGIE GHOOL AND HAGGIE KROOL

Frame two, D.D. had stopped his bike alongside a peach tree full of red and yellow fruit. Standing there were two females, presumably Aggie Ghool and Haggie Krool. One was old and bent, dressed in burlap as near as I could tell; the other was young and pink-cheeked, wearing a mink coat. If you say surely not a mink coat, I say I'm telling what I saw. D.D. was saying, in his balloon, "Gimme a dozen."

Frame three, the young female was handing D.D. the peaches, and the old one was extending her hand for payment. Frame four, the old one was giving D.D. his change from a bill. Frame five, the old one was handing the young one a coin and saying, "Here's your ten per cent, Haggie," and the young one was saying, "Thank you very much, Aggie." Frame six, D.D. was asking Aggie, "Why don't you split it even?" and Aggie was telling him, "Because it's my tree." Frame seven, D.D. was off again on the bike, but I felt I had had enough and looked at Wolfe inquiringly.

"Am I supposed to comment?"

"If it would help, yes."

"I pass. If it's a feed from the National Industrialists' League it's the wrong angle. If you mean the mink coat, Pat Lowell's may not be paid for."

He grunted. "There have been two similar episodes, one each year, with the same characters."

"Then it may be paid for."

"Is that all?"

"It's all for now. I'm not a brain, I'm a typist. I've got to finish this damn report."

I tossed the art back to him and returned to work.

At 12:28 I handed him the finished report, and he dropped D.D. and started on it. I went to the kitchen to tell Fritz I would take on the phone again, and as I re-entered the office it was ringing. I crossed to my desk and got it. My daytime formula was, "Nero Wolfe's office, Archie Goodwin speaking," but with our license gone it was presumably illegal to have an office, so I said, "Nero Wolfe's residence, Archie Goodwin speaking," and heard Saul Panzer's husky voice.

"Reporting in, Archie. No trouble at all. Koven is served. Put it in his hand five minutes ago."

"In the house?"

"Yes. I'll call Parker—"

"How did you get in?"

"Oh, simple. The man that delivers stuff from that Furnari's you told me about has got the itch bad, and it only took ten bucks. Of course after I got inside I had to use my head and legs both, but with your sketch of the layout it was a cinch."

"For you, yes. Mr. Wolfe says satisfactory, which as you know is as far as he ever goes. I say you show promise. You'll call Parker?"

"Yes. I have to go there to sign a paper."

"Okay. Be seeing you."

I hung up and told Wolfe. He lifted his eyes, said, "Ah!" and returned to the report.

After lunch there was an important chore, involving Wolfe, me, our memory of the talk Saturday evening with Koven, and the equipment that had been installed by Levay Recorders, Inc. We spent nearly an hour at it, with three separate tries, before we got it done to Wolfe's satisfaction.

After that it dragged along, at least for me. The phone calls had fallen off. Wolfe, at his desk, finished with the report, put it in a drawer, leaned back, and closed his eyes. I would just as soon have opened a conversation, but pretty soon his lips started working—pushing out, drawing back, and pushing out again—and I knew his brain was busy so I went to the cabinet for a batch of the germination records and settled down to making entries. He didn't need a license to go on growing orchids, though the question would soon arise of how to pay the bills. At four o'clock he left to go up to the plant rooms, and I went on with the records. During the next two hours there were a few phone calls, but none from Koven or his lawyer or Parker. At two minutes past six I was telling myself that Koven was probably drinking himself up to something, no telling what, when two things happened at once: the sound came from the hall of Wolfe's elevator jerking to a stop, and the doorbell rang.

I went to the hall, switched on the stoop light, and took a look through the panel of one-way glass in the front door. It was a mink coat all right, but the hat was different. I went closer, passing Wolfe on his way to the office, got a view of the face, and saw that she was alone. I marched to the office door and announced, "Miss Patricia Lowell. Will she do?"

He made a face. He seldom welcomes a man crossing his threshold; he never welcomes a woman. "Let her in," he muttered.

I stepped to the front, slid the bolt off, and opened up. "This is the kind of surprise I like," I said heartily. She entered, and I shut the door and bolted it. "Couldn't you find a coconut?"

"I want to see Nero Wolfe," she said in a voice so hard that it was out of character, considering her pink cheeks.

"Sure. This way." I ushered her down the hall and on in. Once in a while Wolfe rises when a woman enters his office, but this time he kept not only his chair but also his tongue. He inclined his head a quarter of an inch when I pronounced her name, but said nothing. I gave her the red leather chair, helped her throw her coat back, and went to my desk.

"So you're Nero Wolfe," she said.

That called for no comment and got none.

"I'm scared to death," she said.

"You don't look it," Wolfe growled.

"I hope I don't; I'm trying not to." She started to put her bag on the little table at her elbow, changed her mind, and kept it in her lap. She took off a glove. "I was sent here by Mr. Koven."

No comment. We were looking at her. She looked at me, then back at Wolfe, and protested, "My God, don't you ever say anything?"

"Only on occasion." Wolfe leaned back. "Give me one. You say something."

She compressed her lips. She was sitting forward and erect in the big roomy chair, with no contact with the upholstered back. "Mr. Koven sent me," she said, clipping it, "about the ridiculous suit for damages you have brought. He intends to enter a counterclaim for damage to his reputation through actions of your acknowledged agent,

Archie Goodwin. Of course he denies that there is any basis for your suit."

She stopped. Wolfe met her gaze and kept his trap shut.

"That's the situation," she said belligerently.

"Thank you for coming to tell me," Wolfe murmured. "If you'll show Miss Lowell the way out, please, Archie?"

I stood up. She looked at me as if I had offered her a deadly insult, and looked back at Wolfe. "I don't think," she said, "that your attitude is very sensible. I think you and Mr. Koven should come to an agreement on this. Why wouldn't this be the way to do it—say the claims cancel each other, and you abandon yours and he abandons his?"

"Because," Wolfe said dryly, "my claim is valid and his isn't. If you're a member of the bar, Miss Lowell, you should know that this is a little improper, or anyway unconventional. You should be talking with my attorney, not with me."

"I'm not a lawyer, Mr. Wolfe. I'm Mr. Koven's agent and business manager. He thinks lawyers would just make this more of a mess than it is, and I agree with him. He thinks you and he should settle it between you. Isn't that possible?"

"I don't know. We can try. There's a phone. Get him down here."

She shook her head. "He's not—he's too upset. I'm sure you'll find it more practical to deal with me, and if we come to an understanding he'll approve, I guarantee that. Why don't we go into it—the two claims?"

"I doubt if it will get us anywhere." Wolfe sounded perfectly willing to come halfway. "For one thing, a factor in both claims is the question who killed Adrian Getz and why? If it was Mr. Goodwin, Mr. Koven's claim has a footing, and I freely concede it; if it was someone else I concede nothing. If I discussed it with you I would have to begin by considering that aspect; I would have to ask you some pointed questions; and I doubt if you would dare to risk answering them."

"I can always button up. What kind of questions?"

"Well—" Wolfe pursed his lips. "For example, how's the monkey?"

"I can risk answering that. It's sick. It's at the Speyer Hospital. They don't expect it to live."

"Exposure from the open window?"

"Yes. They're very delicate, that kind."

Wolfe nodded. "That table over there by the globe—that pile of stuff on it is Dazzle Dan for the past three years. I've been looking through it. Last August and September a monkey had a prominent role. It was drawn by two different persons, or at least with two different conceptions. In its first seventeen appearances it was depicted maliciously—

on a conjecture, by someone with a distaste for monkeys. Thereafter it was drawn sympathetically and humorously. The change was abrupt and noticeable. Why? On instructions from Mr. Koven?"

Pat Lowell was frowning. Her lips parted and went together again.

"You have four choices," Wolfe said bluntly. "The truth, a lie, evasion, or refusal to answer. Either of the last two would make me curious, and I would get my curiosity satisfied somehow. If you try a lie it may work, but I'm an expert on lies and liars."

"There's nothing to lie about. I was thinking back. Mr. Getz objected to the way the monkey was drawn, and Mr. Koven had Mr. Jordan do it instead of Mr. Hildebrand."

"Mr. Jordan likes monkeys?"

"He likes animals. He said the monkey looked like Napoleon."

"Mr. Hildebrand does not like monkeys?"

"He didn't like that one. Rookaloo knew it, of course, and bit him once. Isn't this pretty silly, Mr. Wolfe? Are you going on with this?"

"Unless you walk out, yes. I'm investigating Mr. Koven's counterclaim, and this is how I do it. With any question you have your four choices—and a fifth too, of course: get up and go. How did you feel about the monkey?"

"I thought it was an awful nuisance, but it had its points as a diversion. It was my fault it was there, since I gave it to Mr. Getz."

"Indeed. When?"

"About a year ago. A friend returning from South America gave it to me, and I couldn't take care of it so I gave it to him."

"Mr. Getz lives at the Koven house?"

"Yes."

"Then actually you were dumping it onto Mrs. Koven. Did she appreciate it?"

"She has never said so. I didn't—I know I should have considered that. I apologized to her, and she was nice about it."

"Did Mr. Koven like the monkey?"

"He liked to tease it. But he didn't dislike it; he teased it just to annoy Mr. Getz."

Wolfe leaned back and clasped his hands behind his head. "You know, Miss Lowell, I did not find the Dazzle Dan saga hopelessly inane. There is a sustained sardonic tone, some fertility of invention, and even an occasional touch of imagination. Monday evening, while Mr. Goodwin was in jail, I telephoned a couple of people who are supposed to know things and was referred by them to others. I was told that it is generally believed, though not published, that the conception of Dazzle Dan was originally supplied to Mr. Koven by Mr.

Getz, that Mr. Getz was the continuing source of inspiration for the story and pictures, and that without him Mr. Koven will be up a stump. What about it?"

Pat Lowell had stiffened. "Talk." She was scornful. "Just cheap talk."

"You should know." Wolfe sounded relieved. "If that belief could be validated I admit I would be up a stump myself. To support my claim against Mr. Koven, and to discredit his against me, I need to demonstrate that Mr. Goodwin did not kill Mr. Getz, either accidentally or otherwise. If he didn't, then who did? One of you five. But all of you had a direct personal interest in the continued success of Dazzle Dan, sharing as you did in the prodigious proceeds; and if Mr. Getz was responsible for the success, why kill him?" Wolfe chuckled. "So you see I'm not silly at all. We've been at it only twenty minutes, and already you've helped me enormously. Give us another four or five hours, and we'll see. By the way."

He leaned forward to press a button at the edge of his desk, and in a moment Fritz appeared.

"There'll be a guest for dinner, Fritz."

"Yes, sir." Fritz went.

"Four or five hours?" Pat Lowell demanded.

"At least that. With a recess for dinner; I banish business from the table. Half for me and half for you. This affair is extremely complicated, and if you came here to get an agreement we'll have to cover it all. Let's see, where were we?"

She regarded him. "About Getz, I didn't say he had nothing to do with the success of Dazzle Dan. After all, so do I. I didn't say he won't be a loss. Everyone knows he was Mr. Koven's oldest and closest friend. We were all quite aware that Mr. Koven relied on him—"

Wolfe showed her a palm. "Please, Miss Lowell, don't spoil it for me. Don't give me a point and then try to snatch it back. Next you'll be saying that Koven called Getz 'the Squirt' to show his affection, as a man will call his dearest friend an old bastard, whereas I prefer to regard it as an inferiority complex, deeply resentful, showing its biceps. Or telling me that all of you, without exception, were inordinately fond of Mr. Getz and submissively grateful to him. Don't forget that Mr. Goodwin spent hours in that house among you and has fully reported to me; also you should know that I had a talk with Inspector Cramer Monday evening and learned from him some of the plain facts, such as the pillow lying on the floor, scorched and pierced, showing that it had been used to muffle the sound of the shot, and the failure of all of you to prove lack of opportunity."

Wolfe kept going. "But if you insist on minimizing Koven's dependence as a fact, let me assume it as a hypothesis in order to put a question. Say, just for my question, that Koven felt strongly about his debt to Getz and his reliance on him, that he proposed to do something about it, and that he found it necessary to confide in one of you people, to get help or advice. Which of you would he have come to? We must of course put his wife first, ex officio and to sustain convention—and anyway, out of courtesy I must suppose you incapable of revealing your employer's conjugal privities. Which of you three would he have come to—Mr. Hildebrand, Mr. Jordan, or you?"

Miss Lowell was wary. "On your hypothesis, you mean."

"Yes."

"None of us."

"But if he felt he had to?"

"Not with anything as intimate as that. He wouldn't have let himself have to. None of us three has ever got within miles of him on anything really personal."

"Surely he confides in you, his agent and manager?"

"On business matters, yes. Not on personal things, except superficialities."

"Why were all of you so concerned about the gun in his desk?"

"We weren't concerned, not *really* concerned—at least I wasn't. I just didn't like it's being there, loaded, so easy to get at, and I knew he didn't have a license for it."

Wolfe kept on about the gun for a good ten minutes—how often had she seen it, had she ever picked it up, and so forth, with special emphasis on Sunday morning, when she and Hildebrand had opened the drawer and looked at it. On that detail she corroborated Hildebrand as I had heard him tell it to Cramer. Finally she balked. She said they weren't getting anywhere, and she certainly wasn't going to stay for dinner if afterward it was only going to be more of the same.

Wolfe nodded in agreement. "You're quite right," he told her. "We've gone as far as we can, you and I. We need all of them. It's time for you to call Mr. Koven and tell him so. Tell him to be here at eight-thirty with Mrs. Koven, Mr. Jordan, and Mr. Hildebrand."

She was staring at him. "Are you trying to be funny?" she demanded.

He skipped it. "I don't know," he said, "whether you can handle it properly; if not, I'll talk to him. The validity of my claim, and of his, depends primarily on who killed Mr. Getz. I now know who killed him. I'll have to tell the police but first I want to settle the matter of my claim with Mr. Koven. Tell him that. Tell him that if I have to inform the police before I have a talk with him and the others there will be no compromise on my claim, and I'll collect it."

"This is a bluff."

"Then call it."

"I'm going to." She left the chair and got the coat around her. Her eyes blazed at him. "I'm not such a sap!" She started for the door.

"Get Inspector Cramer, Archie!" Wolfe snapped. He called, "They'll be there by the time you are!"

I lifted the phone and dialed. She was out in the hall, but I heard neither footsteps nor the door opening.

"Hello," I told the transmitter, loud enough. "Manhattan Homicide West? Inspector Cramer, please. This is—"

A hand darted past me, and a finger pressed the button down, and a mink coat dropped to the floor. "Damn you!" she said, hard and cold, but the hand was shaking so that the finger slipped off the button. I cradled the phone.

"Get Mr. Koven's number for her, Archie," Wolfe purred.

VII

At twenty minutes to nine Wolfe's eyes moved slowly from left to right, to take in the faces of our assembled visitors. He was in a nasty humor. He hated to work right after dinner, and from the way he kept his chin down and a slight twitch of a muscle in his cheek I knew it was going to be real work. Whether he had got them there with a bluff or not, and my guess was that he had, it would take more than a bluff to rake in the pot he was after now.

Pat Lowell had not dined with us. Not only had she declined to come along to the dining room; she had also left untouched the tray which Fritz had taken to her in the office. Of course that got Wolfe's goat and probably got some pointed remarks from him, but I wasn't there to hear them because I had gone to the kitchen to check with Fritz on the operation of the installation that had been made by Levay Recorders, Inc. That was the one part of the program that I clearly understood. I was still in the kitchen, rehearsing with Fritz, when the doorbell rang and I went to the front and found them there in a body. They got better hall service than I had got at their place, and also better chair service in the office.

When they were seated Wolfe took them in from left to right—Harry Koven in the red leather chair, then his wife, then Pat Lowell, and, after a gap, Pete Jordan and Byram Hildebrand over toward me.

I don't know what impression Wolfe got from his survey, but from where I sat it looked as if he was up against a united front.

"This time," Koven blurted, "you can't cook up a fancy lie with Goodwin. There are witnesses."

He was keyed up. I would have said he had had six drinks, but it might have been more.

"We won't get anywhere that way, Mr. Koven," Wolfe objected. "We're all tangled up, and it will take more than blather to get us loose. You don't want to pay me a million dollars. I don't want to lose my license. The police don't want to add another unsolved murder to the long list. The central and dominant factor is the violent death of Mr. Getz, and I propose to deal with that at length. If we can get that settled—"

"You told Miss Lowell you know who killed him. If so, why don't you tell the police? That ought to settle it."

Wolfe's eyes narrowed. "You don't mean that, Mr. Koven—"

"You're damn right I mean it!"

"Then there's a misunderstanding. I heard Miss Lowell's talk with you on the phone, both ends of it. I got the impression that my threat to inform the police about Mr. Getz's death was what brought you down here. Now you seem—"

"It wasn't any threat that brought me here! It's that blackmailing suit you started! I want to make you eat it and I'm going to!"

"Indeed. Then I gather that you don't care who gets my information first, you or the police. But I do. For one thing, when I talk to the police I like to be able—"

The doorbell rang. When visitors were present Fritz usually answered the door, but he had orders to stick to his post in the kitchen, so I got up and went to the hall, circling behind the arc of the chairs. I switched on the stoop light for a look through the one-way glass. One glance was enough. Stepping back into the office, I stood until Wolfe caught my eye.

"The man about the chair," I told him.

He frowned. "Tell him I'm—" He stopped, and the frown cleared. "No. I'll see him. If you'll excuse me a moment?" He pushed his chair back, made it to his feet, and came, detouring around Koven. I let him precede me into the hall and closed that door before joining him. He strode to the front, peered through the glass, and opened the door. The chain bolt stopped it at a crack of two inches.

Wolfe spoke through the crack. "Well, sir?"

Inspector Cramer's voice was anything but friendly. "I'm coming in."

"I doubt it. What for?"

"Patricia Lowell entered here at six o'clock and is still here. The other four entered fifteen minutes ago. I told you Monday evening to lay off. I told you your license was suspended, and here you are with your office full. I'm coming in."

"I still doubt it. I have no client. My job for Mr. Koven, which you know about, has been finished, and I have sent him a bill. These people are here to discuss an action for damages which I have brought against Mr. Koven. I don't need a license for that. I'm shutting the door."

He tried to, but it didn't budge. I could see the tip of Cramer's toe at the bottom of the crack.

"By God, this does it," Cramer said savagely. "You're through."

"I thought I was already through. But this—"

"I can't hear you! The wind."

"This is preposterous, talking through a crack. Descend to the sidewalk, and I'll come out. Did you hear that?"

"Yes."

"Very well. To the sidewalk."

Wolfe marched to the big old walnut rack and reached for his overcoat. After I had held it for him and handed him his hat I got my coat and slipped into it and then took a look through the glass. The stoop was empty. A burly figure was at the bottom of the steps. I unbolted the door and opened it, followed Wolfe over the sill, pulled the door shut, and made sure it was locked. A gust of wind pounced on us, slashing at us with sleet. I wanted to take Wolfe's elbow as we went down the steps, thinking where it would leave me if he fell and cracked his skull, but knew I hadn't better.

He made it safely, got his back to the sleety wind, which meant that Cramer had to face it, and raised his voice. "I don't like fighting a blizzard, so let's get to the point. You don't want these people talking with me, but there's nothing you can do about it. You have blundered and you know it. You arrested Mr. Goodwin on a trumpery charge. You came and blustered me and went too far. Now you're afraid I'm going to explode Mr. Koven's lies. More, you're afraid I'm going to catch a murderer and toss him to the district attorney. So you—"

"I'm not afraid of a goddam thing." Cramer was squinting to protect his eyes from the cutting sleet. "I told you to lay off, and by God you're going to. Your suit against Koven is a phony."

"It isn't, but let's stick to the point. I'm uncomfortable. I am not an outdoors man. You want to enter my house. You may, under a condition. The five callers are in my office. There is a hole in the wall, concealed from view in the office by what is apparently a picture. Standing, or on a stool, in a nook at the end of the hall, you can see and hear us in the office. The condition is that you enter quietly—confound it!"

The wind had taken his hat. I made a quick dive and stab but missed, and away it went. He had only had it fourteen years.

"The condition," he repeated, "is that you enter quietly, take your post in the nook, oversee us from there, and give me half an hour. Thereafter you will be free to join us if you think you should. I warn you not to be impetuous. Up to a certain point your presence would make it harder for me, if not impossible, and I doubt if you'll know when that point is reached. I'm after a murderer, and there's one chance in five, I should say, that I'll get him. I want—"

"I thought you said you were discussing an action for damages."

"We are. I'll get either the murderer or the damages. Do you want to harp on that?"

"No."

"You've cooled off, and no wonder, in this hurricane. My hair will go next. I'm going in. If you come along it must be under the condition as stated. Are you coming?"

"Yes."

"You accept the condition?"

"Yes."

Wolfe headed for the steps. I passed him to go ahead and unlock the door. When they were inside I closed it and put the bolt back on. They hung up their coats, and Wolfe took Cramer down the hall and around the corner to the nook. I brought a stool from the kitchen, but Cramer shook his head. Wolfe slid the panel aside, making no sound, looked through, and nodded to Cramer. Cramer took a look and nodded back, and we left him. At the door to the office Wolfe muttered about his hair, and I let him use my pocket comb.

From the way they looked at us as we entered you might have thought they suspected we had been in the cellar fusing a bomb, but one more suspicion wouldn't make it any harder. I circled to my desk and sat. Wolfe got himself back in place, took a deep breath, and passed his eyes over them.

"I'm sorry," he said politely, "but that was unavoidable. Suppose we start over"—he looked at Koven—"say with your surmise to the police that Getz was shot by Mr. Goodwin accidentally in a scuffle. That's absurd. Getz was shot with a cartridge that had been taken from your gun and put into Goodwin's gun. Manifestly Goodwin couldn't have done that, since when he first saw your gun Getz was already dead. Therefore—"

"That's not true!" Koven cut in. "He had seen it before, when he came to my office. He could have gone back later and got the cartridges."

Wolfe glared at him in astonishment. "Do you really dare, sir, in front of me, to my face, to cling to that fantastic tale you told the police? That rigmarole?"

"You're damn right I do!"

"Pfui." Wolfe was disgusted. "I had hoped, here together, we were prepared to get down to reality. It would have been better to adopt your suggestion to take my information to the police. Perhaps—"

"I made no such suggestion!"

"In this room, Mr. Koven, some fifteen minutes ago?"

"No!"

Wolfe made a face. "I see," he said quietly. "It's impossible to get on solid ground with a man like you, but I still have to try. Archie, bring the tape from the kitchen, please?"

I went. I didn't like it. I thought he was rushing it. Granting that he had been jostled off his stride by Cramer's arrival, I felt that it was far from one of his best performances, and this looked like a situation where nothing less than his best would do. So I went to the kitchen, passing Cramer in his nook without a glance, told Fritz to stop the machine and wind, and stood and scowled at it turning. When it stopped I removed the wheel and slipped it into a carton and, carton in hand, returned to the office.

"We're waiting," Wolfe said curtly.

That hurried me. There was a stack of similar cartons on my desk, and in my haste I knocked them over as I was putting down the one I had brought. It was embarrassing with all eyes on me, and I gave them a cold look as I crossed to the cabinet to get the player. It needed a whole corner of my desk, and I had to shove the tumbled cartons aside to make room. Finally I had the player in position and connected, and the wheel of tape, taken from the carton, in place.

"All right?" I asked Wolfe.

"Go ahead."

I flipped the switch. There was a crackle and a little spitting, and then Wolfe's voice came:

"It's not that, Mr. Koven, not at all. I only doubt if it's worth it to you, considering the size of my minimum fee, to hire me for anything so trivial as finding a stolen gun, or even discovering the thief. I should think—"

"No!" Wolfe bellowed.

I switched it off. I was flustered. "Excuse it," I said. "The wrong one."

"Must I do it myself?" Wolfe asked sarcastically.

I muttered something, turning the wheel to rewind. I removed it, pawed among the cartons, picked one, took out the wheel, put it on, and turned the switch. This time the voice that came on was not Wolfe's but Koven's—loud and clear.

"This time you can't cook up a fancy lie with Goodwin. There are witnesses."

Then Wolfe's: *"We won't get anywhere that way, Mr. Koven. We're all tangled up, and it will take more than blather to get us loose. You don't want to pay me a million dollars. I don't want to lose my license. The police don't want to add another unsolved murder to the long list. The central and dominant factor is the violent death of Mr. Getz, and I propose to deal with that at length. If we can get that settled—"*

Koven's: *"You told Miss Lowell you know who killed him. If so, why don't you tell the police? That ought to settle it."*

Wolfe: *"You don't mean that, Mr. Koven—"*

Koven: *"You're damn right I mean it!"*

Wolfe: *"Then there's a misunderstanding. I heard Miss Lowell's talk with you on the phone, both ends of it. I got the impression that my threat to inform the police—"*

"That's enough!" Wolfe called. I turned it off. Wolfe looked at Koven. "I would call that," he said dryly, "a suggestion that I take my information to the police. Wouldn't you?"

Koven wasn't saying. Wolfe's eyes moved. "Wouldn't you, Miss Lowell?"

She shook her head. "I'm not an expert on suggestions."

Wolfe left her. "We won't quarrel over terms, Mr. Koven. You heard it. Incidentally, about the other tape you heard the start of through Mr. Goodwin's clumsiness, you may wonder why I haven't given it to the police to refute you. Monday evening, when Inspector Cramer came to see me, I still considered you as my client and I didn't want to discomfit you until I heard what you had to say. Before Mr. Cramer left he had made himself so offensive that I was disinclined to tell him anything whatever. Now you are no longer my client. We'll discuss this matter realistically or not at all. I don't care to badger you into an explicit statement that you lied to the police; I'll leave that to you and them; I merely insist that we proceed on the basis of what we both know to be the truth. With that understood—"

"Wait a minute," Pat Lowell put in. "The gun was in the drawer Sunday morning. I saw it."

"I know you did. That's one of the knots in the tangle, and we'll come to it." His eyes swept the arc. "We want to know who killed

Adrian Getz. Let's get at it. What do we know about him or her? We know a lot.

"First, he took Koven's gun from the drawer sometime previous to last Friday and kept it somewhere. For that gun was put back in the drawer when Goodwin's was removed shortly before Getz was killed, and cartridges from it were placed in Goodwin's gun.

"Second, the thought of Getz continuing to live was for some reason so repugnant to him as to be intolerable.

"Third, he knew the purpose of Koven's visit here Saturday evening, and of Goodwin's errand at the Koven house on Monday, and he knew the details of the procedure planned by Koven and Goodwin. Only with—"

"I don't know them even yet," Hildebrand squeaked.

"Neither do I," Pete Jordan declared.

"The innocent can afford ignorance," Wolfe told them. "Enjoy it if you have it. Only with that knowledge could he have devised his intricate scheme and carried it out.

"Fourth, his mental processes are devious but defective. His deliberate and spectacular plan to make it appear that Goodwin had killed Getz, while ingenious in some respects, was in others witless. Going to Koven's office to get Goodwin's gun from the drawer and placing Koven's gun there, transferring the cartridges from Koven's gun to Goodwin's, proceeding to the room below to find Getz asleep, shooting him in the head, using a pillow to muffle the sound—all that was well enough, competently conceived and daringly executed, but then what? Wanting to make sure that the gun would be quickly found on the spot, a quite unnecessary precaution, he slipped it into the monkey's cage. That was probably improvisation and utterly brainless. Mr. Goodwin couldn't possibly be such a vapid fool.

"Fifth, he hated the monkey deeply and bitterly, either on its own account or because of its association with Getz. Having just killed a man, and needing to leave the spot with all possible speed, he went and opened a window, from only one conceivable motive. That took a peculiar, indeed an unexampled, malevolence. I admit it was effective. Miss Lowell tells me the monkey is dying.

"Sixth, he placed Koven's gun in the drawer Sunday morning and, after it had been seen there, took it out again. That was the most remarkable stratagem of all. Since there was no point in putting it there unless it was to be seen, he arranged that it should be seen. Why? It could only have been that he already knew what was to happen on Monday when Mr. Goodwin came, he had already conceived his scheme for framing Goodwin for the homicide, and he thought he was arranging in advance to discredit Goodwin's story. So he not only put the gun in the drawer Sunday morning, he also made sure its presence would be noted—and not, of course, by Mr. Koven."

Wolfe focused on one of them. "You saw the gun in the drawer Sunday morning, Mr. Hildebrand?"

"Yes." The squeak was off pitch. "But I didn't put it there!"

"I didn't say you did. Your claim to innocence has not yet been challenged. You were in the workroom, went up to consult Mr. Koven, encountered Mrs. Koven one flight up, were told by her that Mr. Koven was still in bed, ascended to the office, found Miss Lowell there, and you pulled the drawer open and both of you saw the gun there. Is that correct?"

"I didn't go up there to look in that drawer. We just—"

"Stop meeting accusations that haven't been made. It's a bad habit. Had you been upstairs earlier that morning?"

"No!"

"Had he, Miss Lowell?"

"Not that I know of." She spoke slowly, with a drag, as if she had only so many words and had to count them. "Our looking into the drawer was only incidental."

"Had he, Mrs. Koven?"

The wife jerked her head up. "Had what?" she demanded.

"Had Mr. Hildebrand been upstairs earlier that morning?"

She looked bewildered. "Earlier than what?"

"You met him in the second-floor hall and told him that your husband was still in bed and that Miss Lowell was up in the office. Had he been upstairs before that? That morning?"

"I haven't the slightest idea."

"Then you don't say that he had been?"

"I know nothing about it."

"There's nothing as safe as ignorance—or as dangerous." Wolfe spread his gaze again. "To complete the list of what we know about the murderer. Seventh and last, his repugnance to Getz was so extreme that he even scorned the risk that by killing Getz he might be killing Dazzle Dan. How essential Getz was to Dazzle Dan—"

"*I* make Dazzle Dan!" Harry Koven roared. "Dazzle Dan is mine!" He was glaring at everybody. "*I* am Dazzle Dan!"

"For God's sake shut up, Harry!" Pat Lowell said sharply.

Koven's chin was quivering. He needed three drinks.

"I was saying," Wolfe went on, "that I do not know how essential Getz was to Dazzle Dan. The testimony conflicts. In any case the murderer wanted him dead. I've identified the murderer for you by now, surely?"

"You have not," Pat Lowell said aggressively.

"Then I'll specify." Wolfe leaned forward at them. "But first let me say a word for the police, particularly Mr. Cramer. He is quite capable of unraveling a tangle like this, with its superficial complexities. What flummoxed him was Mr. Koven's elaborate lie, apparently corroborated by Miss Lowell and Mr. Hildebrand. If he had had the gumption to proceed on the assumption that Mr. Goodwin and I were telling the truth and all of it, he would have found it simple. This should be a lesson to him."

Wolfe considered a moment. "It might be better to specify by elimination. If you recall my list of seven facts about the murderer, that is child's play. Mr. Jordan, for instance, is eliminated by Number Six; he wasn't there Sunday morning. Mr. Hildebrand is eliminated by three or four of them, especially Number Six again; he had made no earlier trip upstairs. Miss Lowell is eliminated, for me, by Numbers Four and Five; and I am convinced that none of the three I have named can meet the requirements of Number Three. I do not believe that Mr. Koven would have confided in any of them so intimately. Nor do I—"

"Hold it!" The gruff voice came from the doorway.

Heads jerked around. Cramer advanced and stopped at Koven's left, between him and his wife. There was dead silence. Koven had his neck twisted to stare up at Cramer, then suddenly he fell apart and buried his face in his hands.

Cramer, scowling at Wolfe, boiling with rage, spoke. "Damn you, if you had given it to us! You and your numbers game!"

"I can't give you what you won't take," Wolfe said bitingly. "You can have her now. Do you want more help? Mr. Koven was still in bed Sunday morning when two of them saw the gun in the drawer. More? Spend the night with Mr. Hildebrand. I'll stake my license against your badge that he'll remember that when he spoke with Mrs. Koven in the hall she said something that caused him to open the drawer and look at the gun. Still more? Take all the contents of her room to your laboratory. She must have hid the gun among her intimate things, and you should find evidence. You can't put him on the stand and ask him if and when he told her what he was doing; he can't testify against his wife; but surely—"

Mrs. Koven stood up. She was pale but under control, perfectly steady. She looked down at the back of her husband's bent head.

"Take me home, Harry," she said.

Cramer, in one short step, was at her elbow.

"Harry!" she said, softly insistent. "Take me home."

His head lifted and turned to look at her. I couldn't see his face. "Sit down, Marcy," he said. "I'll handle this." He looked at Wolfe. "If you've got a record of what I said here Saturday, all right. I lied to the cops. So what? I didn't want—"

"Be quiet, Harry," Pat Lowell blurted at him. "Get a lawyer and let him talk. Don't say anything."

Wolfe nodded. "That's good advice. Especially, Mr. Koven, since I hadn't quite finished. It is a matter of record that Mr. Getz not only owned the house you live in but also that he owned Dazzle Dan and permitted you to take only ten per cent of the proceeds."

Mrs. Koven dropped back into the chair and froze, staring at him. Wolfe spoke to her. "I suppose, madam, that after you killed him you went to his room to look for documents and possibly found some and destroyed them. That must have been part of your plan last week when you first took the gun from the drawer—to destroy all evidence of his ownership of Dazzle Dan after killing him. That was foolish, since a man like Mr. Getz would surely not leave invaluable papers in so accessible a spot, and they will certainly be found; we can leave that to Mr. Cramer. When I said it is a matter of record I meant a record that I have inspected and have in my possession."

Wolfe pointed. "That stack of stuff on that table is Dazzle Dan for the past three years. In one episode, repeated annually with variations, he buys peaches from two characters named Aggie Ghool and Haggie Krool, and Aggie Ghool, saying that she owns the tree, gives Haggie Krool ten per cent of the amount received and pockets the rest. A.G. are the initials of Adrian Getz; H.K. are the initials of Harry Koven. It is not credible that that is coincidence or merely a prank, especially since the episode was repeated annually. Mr. Getz must have had a singularly contorted psyche, taking delight as he did in hiding the fact of his ownership and control of that monster, but compelling the nominal owner to publish it each year in a childish allegory. For a meager ten per cent—"

"Not of the net," Koven objected. "Ten per cent of the gross. Over four hundred a week clear, and I—"

He stopped. His wife had said, "You worm." Leaving her chair, she stood looking down at him, stiff and towering, overwhelming, small as she was.

"You worm!" she said in bitter contempt. "Not even a worm. Worms have guts, don't they?"

She whirled to face Wolfe. "All right, you've got him. The one time he ever acted like a man, and he didn't have the guts to see it through.

Getz owned Dazzle Dan, that's right. When he got the idea and sold it, years ago, and took Harry in to draw it and front it, Harry should have insisted on an even split right then and didn't. He never had it in him to insist on anything, and never would, and Getz knew it. When Dazzle Dan caught on, and the years went by and it kept getting bigger and bigger, Getz didn't mind Harry having the name and the fame as long as he owned it and got the money. You said he had a contorted psyche, maybe that was it, only that's not what I'd call it. Getz was a vampire."

"I'll accept that," Wolfe murmured.

"That's the way it was when I met Harry, but I didn't know it until we were married, two years ago. I admit Getz might not have got killed if it hadn't been for me. When I found out how it was I tried to talk sense into Harry. I told him his name had been connected with Dazzle Dan so long that Getz would have to give him a bigger share, at least half, if he demanded it. He claimed he tried, but he just wasn't man enough. I told him his name was so well known that he could cut loose and start another one on his own, but he wasn't man enough for that either. He's not a man, he's a worm. I didn't let up. I kept after him, I admit that. I'll admit it on the witness stand if I have to. And I admit I didn't know him as well as I thought I did. I didn't know there was any danger of making him desperate enough to commit murder. I didn't know he had it in him. Of course he'll break down, but if he says I knew that he had decided to kill Getz I'll have to deny it because it's not true. I didn't."

Her husband was staring up at the back of her head, his mouth hanging open.

"I see." Wolfe's voice was hard and cold. "First you plan to put it on a stranger, Mr. Goodwin—indeed, two strangers, for I am in it too. That failing, you put it on your husband." He shook his head. "No, madam. Your silliest mistake was opening the window to kill the monkey, but there were others. Mr. Cramer?"

Cramer had to take only one step to get her arm.

"Good God!" Koven groaned.

Pat Lowell said to Wolfe in a thin sharp voice, "So this is what you worked me for."

She was a tough baby too, that girl.